BLOOD READ

A MADS & LYNDSEY MYSTERY

D S FLOYD

Dave Floyd

**BLACK
SHEEP**

First Published 2019 by Black Sheep Design

ISBN 978-1-898735-03-8

Black Sheep Design
info@bsdpub.com

Dedicated to Corin

Who gives me belief in myself when my inner demons tell me otherwise.

Acknowledgements

Thanks to Sue Horlock and Corin Floyd, who read early versions of this novel and provided me with useful feedback. If they missed any glaring errors or typos, the blame clearly lies with them.

Thanks to Jackie Spencer for answering my questions on how hospitals operate in the current day NHS. Any errors present in the hospital visit section are consequently hers.

Not really, very many thanks for your help, ladies. It is much appreciated.

Thanks to everyone who bought the first book and are now looking forward to this one ... and those who have got this far and are now thinking, 'Damn, there's a first book?'

And a very special thank you to those heroes who accompany me on the annual Mads & Lyndsey pub crawl when we visit every pub mentioned in the books. It wouldn't be the same without you all.
Email me on dave@dsfloyd.com if you'd like to join us.

Thadadup. Thadadup. Thadadup.

Lyndsey tidied the books on her market stall as the hypnotic sound of the rain thudded against the canvas roof. Content, she sat and watched other traders scurrying about, covering their stock with plastic sheeting. In the alcove where hers and Mads' stalls were situated, only they and Ranjit on the diagonally opposite corner kept permanent roofs erected all weekend. As autumn acquiesced to winter, most would erect temporary tarpaulins, but the forecast for this unseasonably mild October weekend had been fine. Relishing in its opportunity to humiliate the meteorologists, rain splattered on the concrete, collecting in rivulets running to the drain at the alcove entrance.

She closed her eyes and took a deep breath, absorbing the wet concrete smell and wondering if a word existed to describe the phenomenon. She was reluctant to use petrichor, associating that more with damp earth and leaves and felt its urban cousin should be given a distinct word of its own. Breathing out and back in again, she married the smell with the sound of the rain.

Thadadup. Thadadup. Thadadup.

Urbichor has a certain charm.

'Here you go, get your laughing gear around that.'

She opened her eyes at the sound of Mads' voice and smiled at the sight of her holding out a cardboard cup of black tea.

'Thanks. I didn't realise how tired my legs were until I sat down.'

'I'm not surprised. You haven't stopped since eight this morning. The article in yesterday's local paper captured peoples' imaginations and inspired them to come and check out the stalls.'

Lyndsey laughed. 'Yes, everyone wanted to nose at the two amateur sleuths who caught the market murderer. We were lucky with the rain as well, that made them desperate to shelter from the wet. Your idea to install the roof was brilliant. Did you sell any paintings while they huddled about?'

'A couple of small ones. I handed out plenty of cards though, so I hope people will follow through and order something from the website. I'm pleased the people who use these pitches during the week were happy to use the roof too. Dismantling it every week would be a nightmare.'

Lyndsey shuddered. 'You're not kidding. What says we drink this tea and pack up? It's one o'clock and the weather isn't likely to improve judging by the clouds and gloomy light.'

'Sounds like a plan.' Mads sidled back towards her corner stall.

Half an hour ago, the market had been bustling with customers, but since the weather had turned they had either gone home or were herding their way around the indoor stalls at the back end of the market.

She watched as Bill slowly backed up his pantechnicon so he and Rhonda could start loading furniture from their stall across the end of the alcove. They had had enough for the day. Rhonda saw her looking and gave her a smile and a wave, which Lyndsey returned.

The mirror stall was showing no signs of life, and Lyndsey assumed that Jools was sheltering from the elements in the van. Jools' husband, Bob, was chatting to Grandad on the stall directly opposite them. Bob and Jools had made a point of coming across right before opening time that morning and insisted on being her first customers, both of them carrying a small pile of books away with them. She'd known them years, and they had been like surrogate parents to her since her real parents had died in a car accident fifteen years earlier.

She put the cup down and removed the lid to allow the tea to cool, before standing up and walking across to Mads.

'Do you want a hand packing the paintings? My books are boxed so can go straight into the van once all these are loaded.'

'Please, if you don't mind. Start with the large ones, I put the foam wrap I used on the way here below each piece, so everything should fit perfectly. It's like stuffing large envelopes.'

Lyndsey set about packing, and as Mads had predicted, matching each painting to its accompanying wrapper was childs' play.

'When are you going to start selling your own artwork?'

'I've been putting together some watercolours of local pubs and I hope I'll be brave enough in a week or so to display them here and risk receiving third party opinion. Until then, Pete and Jen's work will keep me busy on the stall. How's your writing going? Plotted any best sellers yet?'

'I'm still mulling ideas around. I've accumulated a bulging notebook but nothing's grabbing me.'

'Do you want to brainstorm some of them later? That might be fun, fleshing out some plots together and populating the worlds with characters. What do you think?'

'That could be interesting, are you sure you don't need to be doing anything else? You spend all your time with me lately. I'm not complaining, but I don't want to be monopolising your life. Nigel will forget who you are. I appreciate you letting me move into your house and all that, but I'm happy to go out and give you both a night in when he's not away and you said he'd be back this morning.'

'Don't you worry about him. His business trip's been extended and when he finally deigns to return, he'll be off again before we even realise he's in our way. We can throw together some grazing food this evening and set about hammering some order into your ideas.'

'Why not? I need to work on something and, as I start that temp job Monday, I need to stop procrastinating. Every spare moment will be precious when a job is eating into my time.'

'I can't believe you found a job in a library. I couldn't think of anything more perfect for you. Hey, you could treat your job as research, write a book about a murder in the library.'

'Haha, right? I'm not sure university libraries are a likely place for murder, do you? And I'm only doing a boring admin job, for a few weeks at that. Hardly a match made in heaven, Mads.'

'At least you'll bring some money in, and once they

Faruq shook her hand in the same way as Francis and Cordelia had. This was getting weird.

'Pleased to meet you, Lyndsey. If Francis or any of the others aren't about and you need to know something, you only have to ask.'

'Thanks, I will.'

'Yes, Faruq knows more about the library than I do regarding the technicalities ... and in the corner is Morgan, she's one of the supervisors.'

Morgan was on the phone but glanced up to wave and smile before scribbling a note on her pad and speaking into the handset.

They left the office and had a brief tour of all three floors of the library proper during which she introduced herself to a million people, none of whom she would remember. Finally, they arrived back at the office on the fourth floor.

'In theory, we are open twenty-four seven during term times, but in reality, only the first and second floors are fully functional. Students can access the books on the third and fourth floors, should they wish, but when no movement is detected, the lights turn off, so they are impractical for studying. Normally, students will take the books downstairs rather than sit and wave their arms every few minutes, though we place small study tables at the end of each row in case. This floor is where we file the oversized books and music manuscripts, so used far less than the other three.'

Lyndsey nodded, prompting him to continue.

'We lock these offices and those on the ground floor when staff go home. That reminds me, I couldn't introduce you to the librarians as they are in a meeting, but once they've finished, I'll take you to the third floor again so you can all meet. Did HR sort you out with a computer log-in?'

Lyndsey pulled a piece of paper from her back pocket. 'Yes, I have it written down on here.'

'If you can log in to the system, I'll give you a quick walk through.'

Lyndsey sat down and turned the computer on, waiting for the log-in screen to appear. Francis standing over her watching every move was off-putting, and as she logged in her fingers felt like fat sausages. She breathed a sigh of relief as the computer accepted her credentials and sat taking a few notes as Francis went through the basics of which folders housed specific types of files. He turned his attention to the pile of paper lying on the in-tray, explaining what needed doing with each. Despite everything being obvious, she dutifully made notes until he had finished and returned to his office. Within a minute he was back out again.

'We lunch at one until two, so if you could take your break at a different time to cover us?'

'Could I split mine and take half at twelve-thirty with the rest at two o'clock?'

'I don't see why not, as long as the others are happy with the arrangement. Make sure you check with them.'

'Thanks,' she said to Francis's back as he disappeared back into his office.

Her phone beeped softly and she slid it out of her jacket pocket. It was a text message from Mads.

'How's your first day?'

'Fine, what are you up to?'

'Nothing much, sitting at home with a cup of tea and my feet up. Talk to you later.'

Lyndsey replaced the phone and started working her way through the in-tray.

Mads had been anything but relaxing, truth be told. While she loved having Lyndsey stay with her, living in each other's pockets made it difficult to investigate her surreptitiously.

Barry had been murdered a few weeks earlier and Lyndsey had been the police's chief suspect until Mads had stumbled upon the real killer. As thrilling as that had been, she was sure there was something strange about Barry as well as being a few, as yet, unexplained other odd occurrences.

A suspicious man had given Lyndsey some photos of her parents looking far healthier than people who had been dead for fifteen years deserved to. And who was the other man who'd come to her stall a day later asking about photographs? Lyndsey had brushed aside suggestions that both events might be related, but what if they were? And what had Barry been up to? Had he been spying on her or was their getting together a coincidence?

Regardless of the answers, she couldn't involve Lyndsey at this stage. She'd only just stopped having nightmares over seeing Barry fall out of her wardrobe with a knife in his chest, and the thought her parents might be alive after all this time wouldn't help her recover.

Where were they? Why hadn't they contacted her?

Questions were flying around Mads' head like midges on the river path in summer and, for her own sanity, she needed to find some answers.

She dug out Barry's old contacts book from its hiding place in the attic. They had found it while searching Barry's flat. Inspector Savage had found evidence suggesting that Lyndsey had been in the flat while it was taped shut as a crime scene, so Mads had squirrelled away everything relating to that digression in case the police had wanted to take the issue further. In the end, Mads' lawyer had suggested a plausible alternative to the timeline Inspector Savage had pieced together and he'd decided not to pursue the matter.

Barry's book used a code system that Lyndsey had explained to her. It comprised initials for names or descriptions, with a series of numbers resembling phone numbers but often meant something else. The difficulty lay in finding which were which. The code to the padlock securing his lock-up had been obscured as a phone number and Mads was sure other secrets lurked inside those pages. Such as the password to the zip file they had found on his hard disk.

She'd worked her way through the book twice now, but anything that appeared interesting hadn't worked. She put it down and went to make a cup of tea, texting Lyndsey while the kettle boiled. She drank her tea in the conservatory watching a family of foxes in the back garden lounging about and eating something beneath a bush before they disappeared into their den, wherever that was.

Refreshed, she made her way back to the computer and book and steeled herself for the long haul.

'OK, Barry. Attrition it is.'

She worked her way through the book trying each entry one by one. The time was almost two o'clock before she found the correct password for the file and slumped back into the chair with relief. Inside the zip file were dozens of folders, all titled with a name. Figuring unpacking them all could take ages, she created a folder titled Barry, dragged the contents across and went to make more tea.

When she returned with a mug of tea and a celebratory slice of carrot cake the process was complete and she scrolled down the names until, to her surprise, she reached a folder with Lyndsey's name.

What was inside made Mads gasp. Records and recordings of phone calls, texts, social media messages, geographic tracking of all her movements ... this was nothing less than a detailed dossier of every aspect of Lyndsey's life over the last two years.

Mads was in two minds whether to be appalled on Lyndsey's behalf at the intrusion or impressed at its extent, and grudgingly settled on a combination of both in the end. Barry had either been a sick and obsessive individual or his priority hadn't been romance.

Or both.

Questions were raised again in Mads' mind. What was the fascination amongst shady characters with her friend, who until the last few weeks had appeared so ordinary? The photo guy, the man looking for the photos he'd given her and now this all pointed towards something far more outlandish than Lyndsey warranted. Mads needed to find out more before she said anything, that was for sure.

But where to start?

Lyndsey was making solid progress on the work pile by eleven o'clock when a woman in her forties wearing a grey suit and a white blouse came bowling out of the lift and marched towards Lyndsey's desk.

'Hello, you must be the temp. I'm Gloria, one of the library managers.'

Her accent was slight, so Lyndsey had difficulty guessing where she was from, though coupled with her features would guess either South America or one of the Mediterranean countries. Gloria held out her hand and smiled, so Lyndsey stood to shake hands with her. This time she encountered a more solid grip. So the handshake wasn't a secret code, or perhaps Gloria had just been left out of the loop.

'Hello, I'm Lyndsey.'

'I've been in a meeting this morning, I hope someone was here to show you around?'

'Yes, Francis gave me the tour.'

'Did he show you where the break room was?'

Lyndsey shook her head. 'Not that I remember.'

'Well, isn't that typical? Let me drop my bag and I'll take you.'

Lyndsey smiled. 'That's OK, I'm not thirsty.'

'Don't think I'm being altruistic. If you can't find the break room, you won't be making me coffee, and that will never do.'

She gave a laugh and went into the office. A couple of minutes later she was back.

'Come on, take a break from that and drink a coffee with me. I insist.'

Lyndsey followed her to a small room a few metres behind her desk that contained a hot water dispenser and a wide selection of instant coffees and teas.

'Grab a cup from here,' said Gloria, helping herself to a mug that read, "World's Best Manager", 'and make whatever you like. Milk's in the water machine and sugar's the other side of the tea.'

After perusing the choices, Lyndsey picked a "Brentford FC Promotion 2014" mug and made herself a tea.

'No milk?'

'No, I'm vegan.'

Gloria raised her eyebrows.

'That must be difficult to maintain. My son's girlfriend's a vegan. She won't touch meat or dairy and only eats fish when we go out.'

Lyndsey debated with herself whether to say anything. Things were always awkward with a new boss, even as a temp, and she didn't want to appear like a know-all. After a couple of seconds of silence that dragged like minutes, she took the plunge.

'So she's a pescatarian?'

'A what?'

'A pescatarian avoids meat except for fish.'

'Well, I don't know about that. She calls herself vegan. She doesn't buy fish to eat at home, only when she goes out with us.'

'Yes, but ....'

The defensive tone in Gloria's voice made Lyndsey reconsider continuing. Sometimes one was better being quietly correct, and one of those times, she reasoned, is within two hours of starting a new job when you're talking to one of your managers.

'Have you worked here long?'

'Over twenty years. I stumbled into the job by accident. Started doing a science degree but landed a library job and enjoyed the atmosphere so much I switched courses after my first year. Once I graduated, a vacancy for the sciences librarian came up and I applied. The library only had one manager in those days, and things worked a lot better than they do now. Once she retired, they split the responsibilities, so I became head librarian and Margaret, who retired herself a couple of years ago, became head of acquisitions. Joe replaced her around the time of ...', Gloria lifted her hands to make quote signs, '... "the great reorganisation," when the University decided, in its infinite wisdom, that we also needed a head of customer services and another manager to rule over the three of us, so Francis and Elliot both appeared. If you're aware of the phrase, "Too many chiefs and not enough indians", you'll find the concept embodied here. Have you met Elliot and Joe yet?'

'Not yet, no.'

'You won't see Elliot much. On the whole, he keeps himself to himself in his office thinking of ways he can trim our budgets to justify his huge salary. And I think Joe had a meeting at the other campus this morning so he should be here by lunchtime. He can be a little abrupt, try to ignore him. I don't think he intends to be, he isn't much of a people person. Did Francis sort out lunchtimes with you?'

'Yes, he asked me to make sure I was here to cover between one and two so I'll split my lunch into two parts. Twelve-thirty and two o'clock, if that's OK with you and Joe.'

'No problem.' Gloria finished her coffee and rinsed out her cup. 'I don't suppose you've met the librarians yet?'

'No, they were in a meeting.'

'I'll take you down and introduce you once you've finished your tea. They're a lovely bunch, I'm sure you'll like them.'

Lyndsey picked up her mug but her tea was still hot so blew on the top and watched the steam billow away from her.

'No rush, love. I wasn't meaning that you should rush, take your time. Do you need to ask anything else?'

'I don't think so, but if I think of anything I will do.'

'You do that, and if the other two give you any trouble, tell me and I'll sort them out for you. I don't want you walking out due to any unreasonableness on their parts.'

'Francis came across as an amiable sort.'

'Yes, he'll always be nice to your face. Worry about what he's like behind your back. Joe's the opposite, he can be blunt and borderline obnoxious, but at least you can be sure where you stand with him. If he isn't happy he'll tell you straight. As will I, but there's no reason to be rude about such things, don't you agree?'

'Yes, I try to rub along with everyone.'

'Best way, if you ask me. Are you done?'

Lyndsey drank the rest of her tea and rinsed the mug

before following Gloria out of the break room and towards the stairs. They walked down a floor and made their way to the librarian's room. They totalled eight in all, and were a friendly bunch, but appeared nervous around Gloria.

Twelve-thirty didn't take long to arrive, and Lyndsey went to the third floor for the first part of her lunch. She sat at a table by the window where she ate a sandwich she'd brought in with her while playing around with a few story ideas on her laptop that she had run through with Mads in the pub the night before. Things were starting to gel together when, to her disappointment, it was time to return to work. She put the computer into her bag and trudged upstairs to her desk. As she arrived, Francis was hovering in the vicinity.

'Ah, you're back. I've emailed you the details of a report. Could you knock it into shape for me, please? Everything should all be self-explanatory. If it could be finished by the time I return from lunch, that would be wonderful.'

'I'll try, do you need it sent anywhere?'

'No, just email it to back me so I can check everything before it gets emailed out. Thanks.'

He stood still for a moment with his hands hanging limply over his belly and a smug smile on his face before turning and leaving as Gloria and a man Lyndsey hadn't seen before walked out of the office.

'Lyndsey, this is Joe, your third boss, so to speak,' said Gloria.

'Hello,' she said and smiled.

'I have a project for you after lunch.' He said without returning her greeting. 'I'll brief you when I get back.'

'No problem. When do you need it done for?'

'By the end of the day,' he said, turning and heading for

the lifts.

'Don't mind him, love. I told you he could be abrupt, it's just his way. I'm going to the High Street, do you need anything?'

'No, thanks.'

Gloria followed Joe towards the lifts and Lyndsey put her bag into the bottom drawer of her desk. Only when she sat down, did she find a brown, A4 envelope placed over her keyboard with a printed label stating, "For the attention of the library managers".

She opened it and found a sheet of paper, laser printed with an elaborate gothic design and two lines of text in the centre.

WHAT TRICKS WHAT CRASS CHICANERY
SPEW MANAGERS OF THE LIBRARY

She dropped the sheet not wanting to contaminate it with her fingerprints any more than she already had. After a few moments, she used another sheet of paper folded in half to pick it up again and made some photocopies. Back at her desk, she put the original back in the envelope and tucked it away in her drawer. One copy went into her bag and the others she put to one side to show the managers when they returned from lunch. She was adding the finishing touches to Francis's report when Joe arrived back and strode past her desk. She picked up the note and followed him into the office.

'Sorry, I know you're at lunch, but someone left this on my desk while I was away.'

She handed a copy across to him and he perused it for a few moments.

'I wouldn't worry. It's October so probably a student

Halloween prank.'

'Do you think?' Lyndsey hadn't even considered the possibility that the letter might be a student prank.

'Throw it in the bin and forget about it. While you're here, could you make me a cup of tea?' He pointed towards the bookcase behind his chair. 'You'll find my tea bags in the caddy on the top shelf. I can't bear the ordinary stuff. No milk or sugar, they're a herbal mix I have specially made.'

He handed the note back and continued to read his newspaper as if Lyndsey wasn't standing there. She took a tea bag from a tin on the shelf marked "TEA" and after making and delivering what turned out to be a most foul-smelling brew, returned to her desk. Gloria was next back and smiled at her as she passed and at 1.59 Francis reappeared.

'I'll take my second break now, Francis. Your report is in your inbox.'

'Thank you.'

Following her break, Lyndsey had just put her bag into the drawer when Joe appeared.

'Where were you? I told you I had an urgent project.'

'I was at lunch.'

A confused expression crossed his face.

'I thought you'd already taken your lunch.'

She explained what she had agreed with the other two.

'Humph. No one told me. Here's what I need doing. I've explained everything as best I can on the top sheet, but if you have any problems come through and ask.'

She smiled at him. 'I'm sure I'll manage.'

Joe returned to the office and Lyndsey breathed a sigh of relief.

This was gearing up to be a very long few weeks.

Mads's alarm chirped at five o'clock reminding her that Lyndsey would soon leave work. She saved everything and hid the memory stick and contact book in the attic again before heading to the kitchen to decide what to make for dinner.

Her opinion of Barry, never what one might term high, had been on a downward trajectory the longer she read through the folders. None of the other records contained the same level of detail as those he had accumulated on Lyndsey, but the information he had led her to believe that he had been a blackmailer. She hadn't yet discovered where the money was going but was certain she would find out somehow.

But then what? She couldn't tell the police without also saying where the information had come from and if she told them that, they might arrest her and Lyndsey for disturbing a crime scene.

As she put a vegetable pie into the oven, the doorbell rang and she went to open the door.

'Hi, are you Mads? I'm Viran, I spoke to you on the

phone earlier.'

'Yes, come in. Can I make you a cup of tea?'

'No thanks. You wanted me to check through a mobile?'

'Yes, please come through.' Mads led him into the front room and indicated that he should sit in the armchair which he did. 'It's my friend's phone that needs checking and she isn't home from work yet. Are you sure I can't get you anything?'

'No, honestly. So you think the phone is infected with spyware? Any idea which package?'

'Not a clue. I think her ex installed the package and we can't contact him, I'm afraid. Is that a problem?'

'No, that scenario isn't as rare as you might think. It just takes longer as I have to find what the package is before disabling and removing it.'

'It seems silly now, her ex is dead so he won't be monitoring her any more, but I don't like the thought that the information's out there, do you know what I mean?'

'Of course, not to mention how much it could be eating up her data plan and slowing the phone down. It's never a waste of time to give your phones and computer equipment a health check every so often.'

Lyndsey's key slid into the lock and turned.

'Here she is now. Can you pretend to be doing something with mine, please? I'd rather she wasn't aware of the spyware, not yet, anyway.'

She handed him her phone and left the room to meet Lyndsey at the door.

'Hi, how was your day?'

'A little strange, not what I expected, that's for sure.'

'Aww, come through to the kitchen and tell me everything over a cup of tea. I've got a vegetable pie in the oven. I've also got a man in the front room giving my phone an annual check-up. Where's your phone, he can do yours as well while he's here. You'll think you have a new phone when he's finished.'

'Really?' Lyndsey shrugged. 'How the other half live, eh? I don't suppose it will do any harm, here you go.'

Mads took it from her and went through to the front room with Lyndsey trailing behind her.

'Here you go, Viran. Can you do this one too, please?'

'Of course, do you have a code to bypass the home screen?'

'Yes,' said Lyndsey. Let me write it down for you.'

He handed Lyndsey a pen and a small pad and she wrote down the code.

'Thanks, Viran,' said Mads. 'Tell us when you're done, we'll be in the kitchen. If you change your mind about refreshments, please shout.'

She led Lyndsey to the kitchen and put the kettle on.

'Come on, sit down and tell me all about your day. What could possibly be that bad about working in a library?'

Lyndsey sighed as she sat at the table.

'I have three bosses. One of them appears to be very nice, but I'm not sure. She's in charge of the librarians, and their attitudes towards her suggest she isn't the person she appears to be. They seemed scared of Gloria when she introduced me to them. As for the other two, one's a wet fish and the other is abrupt to the point of rudeness.'

'Oh Sweetie, don't let them rattle you. Once a few more days pass by and you've all got used to each other, everything will be fine.'

The kettle boiled and Mads set about making the tea.

'How about everyone else? I can't believe the whole library is full of idiots.'

'I didn't have much of an opportunity to mingle. The only times I came across any of the other staff was during official introductions. Something weird happened while I was at lunch, though.'

Mads brought the mugs of tea to the table.

'Here you go, a cup of tea will brighten your outlook a little. So what happened?'

'Well.' Lyndsey opened her bag and took out her copy of the note. 'Someone left this on my desk in an envelope addressed to the Library Managers.'

Mads read it and raised her eyebrows.

'So what did you do?'

'What could I do? I took some copies, stashed the original in my desk just in case, and passed one on to Joe, but he wasn't interested. Said it looked like a student prank leading up to Halloween.'

'That is strange,' said Mads giving the sheet back. 'I can understand how he might make the student link with the graphic style but the content doesn't come across as much of a Halloween joke to me. What did the others say?'

'Nothing to me, if Joe even told them.'

'And you've no clue who left it? Don't they have CCTV?'

'I'm sure they have, but I doubt a temp could gain access to the recordings. If any more messages show up, I'll think about taking them to security and hope they can solve the mystery.'

'That sounds sensible, this kind of thing is what they're paid for. What do you fancy with the pie?'

'I'm not sure, how about some mash and gravy with a couple of thick slices of that bloomer we picked up yesterday. I'll knock those together now, unless you'd rather have something different?'

'You don't have to.'

'Yes, but as I'm living here rent free, the least I can do is help out once in a while.' She stood and headed towards the freezer. 'What did you do with yourself today?'

'Nothing much. I went to the studio for a while and splashed around with a few ideas then came home again.'

'Keep trying, your mojo will come back. Creativity's a habit as much as anything, at least that's the theory I'm working on with my writing.'

'Did you write anything at lunchtime?'

'A little, I could do with talking it through and fleshing the bones out a bit more if you don't mind.'

'Sounds like a plan, let's eat dinner, crack open some refreshments and disappear down the rabbit hole of Lyndsey's mind.'

'Haha, that would be enough to drive anyone crazy. No one needs to know what goes on in here.'

As they were finishing dinner, Viran poked his head around the kitchen door and held out their phones.

'All done, I'll email you the invoice, Mads.'

'Please do, let me see you out.' She took the phones from him and followed him to the door. 'Did you find any spyware?'

'Yes, and removed it. The phone will be more responsive and no one will be looking over your friend's shoulder.'

'Thanks for that. I'll pay you as soon as the invoice arrives.'

'Any more phone or computer problems don't hesitate to call me.'

'Bye.' She closed the door and walked back towards the kitchen. At least that was one thing ticked off the to-do list.

As soon as Lyndsey left for work the next day, Mads dashed upstairs and found her husband's back up phone book in his desk. He always kept a hard copy of all his contacts in case disaster struck and both his phone and laptop were out of commission. Mads had teased him about his obsession in the past, given that he also had online backups of all his data, but now she was pleased he had a safety-first attitude. She found the number she wanted and dialled.

After a few rings, a man answered with a gruff, 'Hello?'

'Hi Saint, it's Mads, Nigel's wife.'

Saint said nothing. Mads sat patiently, assuming he was trying to remember who she was. They had met once before at a party, and Nigel had mentioned that should she need anything rather less than legal, he was the man to contact. She realised at this moment, there was a possibility Nigel had been joking and she was about to make herself appear stupid, but too late now.

'Mads, blonde lady, yes? How is Nigel? I haven't seen hide or hair of him in a while.'

'He's fine, overworking, as ever.'

'Cool, so what can I do for you?'

'I need a phone.'

'What sort of phone?'

'I'm not worried about make or anything. I don't need internet, only calls, and I need credit and untraceability, if that's even a word.'

'It is now, I know what you mean sweet enough. How much credit?'

'Say a hundred?'

'No problem, I've got an old Nokia here. It'll run you a monkey, that OK?'

'That will be fine. When can get it from you?'

'You're in West London aren't you?'

'Yes, Chiswick.'

'I've got to meet someone in Brentford about eleven so could meet you a bit before that, if you like. How about Jenny's for ten-thirty?'

'Perfect. See you later.'

She hung up and Googled "monkey" to check they were on the same page and got herself ready to go to the bank. By ten-fifteen she was sitting outside Jenny's with a mug of black tea watching the world make its merry way along Brentford High Street, not a little surprised that even halfway through October the weather was still warm enough to sit outside. Saint cut her musings short by sitting at the table.

'Morning darlin'. How are you? Here you go.'

He placed a package in front of her wrapped in aluminium foil.

'Thanks,' said Mads delving into her bag. She slid an envelope containing £500 across the table which he pocketed without so much as checking what was in it.

'The phone's fully charged and the charger's in with

it. Common sense, but make sure you turn it off and wrap it in foil before going home. If you're really paranoid, you can also remove the SIM but you shouldn't need to unless you're attracting Carl's attention. There is a card you can use to top up with, but bear in mind, if you top up using a bank card you'll be traceable and anywhere you can top up with cash will have CCTV. Those problems aren't insurmountable, but for the moment you'll be able to use the phone anonymously until the credit runs out. Any questions?'

'Carl?'

Saint laughed a deep belly laugh. 'Carl Orff … auths … slang abbreviation for the authorities. Pigs, spooks, CIA, I don't care what you need it for and whose cages you might be rattling. I'm just saying, is all.'

'Gotcha. Will you buy the phone back when I'm done?'

He sucked air through his teeth like a plumber about to quote on a blocked drain. 'I can, but couldn't give you more than a pony. You might be better off keeping it as a spare. Or if you are really worried someone might trace it to you, remove the SIM and lob them off a bridge into the river.'

Sound ecological advice there, Saint.

'Fair enough, thanks.'

'Same to you. Regards to Nigel.'

He stood and slunk off down the road with his hands in his pockets. Mads put the silver package into her bag and used her proper phone to check how much a pony was, just in case. After a couple of minutes mulling over why you couldn't have sums of money called armadillos or warthogs, out came the phone again and she found the slang terms monkey and pony referred to the pictures on the 500 and 25 rupee notes from the days of the British Raj in India. Animal slang curiosity sated, she finished her tea and pondered where to go. Given the unseasonal mildness of the day, she decided to head somewhere pretty.

Kew Gardens was as splendid as ever and she made her way around the edge until she reached the wild area, named because they left that part of the Gardens to its own devices for the benefit of local flora and fauna. Even in the summer, she had noticed that this part of the gardens didn't attract as many visitors as the other areas so figured she would remain undisturbed and unobserved while making her calls.

She sat on a bench and took Barry's notebook from her bag along with one she had bought to transfer the numbers across with meaningful descriptions, once she had them. She began to work her way through, but only at the fourth entry did someone answer.

'Hello?'

'Hi, I'm trying to find Barry Williams and I believe you're a friend of his.'

The line went dead. She ran a few alternative approaches through her head before calling again. This time the phone went straight to voicemail.

'Hello, I'm a private detective. Nothing to do with the police and you're not in trouble, but I need some information on Barry Williams. Could you please call me back on ...'

She fumbled for the card with the number printed on and reeled it off before hanging up. She had as much success over the next couple of hours and, realising she was hungry, she strolled to the Botanical Restaurant for lunch. A vegan burger and sorbet later, she returned to the same bench with renewed vigour and enthusiasm. The mood didn't last, and as the light began to fade she had about had enough but pushed herself to complete the Cs. The second last number rang like many of the others had. Unlike many of the others, however, a woman answered.

'Hello?'

'Hi, I'm a private detective and I got your number from Barry Williams.' Well, nearly true.

'I'll tell you what I told him. I've no idea where they are. Is that clear?'

The woman's voice was slurred, as if she been drinking.

'Sorry? Who are you referring to?'

'Don't be coy.'

'I'm not intending to be, who do you think I'm calling about?'

The woman at the other end sighed in exasperation.

'My daughter and her bloody husband, or Sue and Carl as you'll know them. Susan and Carl Marshall.'

Mads was speechless for a moment.

'So ... so you're Lyndsey's grandmother?'

'Who did you think I was?'

'Well, I knew she lived with her grandfather but assumed you were, um ...'

'Dead? I might as bloody well be for all the thought they give me. Not seen or heard a thing from either of them since the divorce ten years ago, and don't start me off about my daughter, disappearing like she did.'

'Didn't she die with Carl in a car crash?'

The woman snorted.

'If you believe that, you're soft in the head. I've never known a faster cremation, all arranged while hepatitis confined me to my sickbed. I took some to a lab but they said they couldn't do anything with ashes. I've still got some and given the way science has come along I might try again sometime. They have no problem testing ashes on the telly nowadays, do they?'

'No, you're right, they don't seem to,' said Mads, not convinced that television shows were the best way of gauging scientific advancement. Testing had improved though, so perhaps sending the remains for testing would be worth a shot. 'I don't suppose you'd let me do that for you? I'll pay for the tests and send you a copy of the report after the lab have completed their testing.'

When the second note appeared on Tuesday, Lyndsey opened the envelope wearing a pair of gloves from the first aid box before making copies. She took one through to show Gloria when she returned, but she was as dismissive as Joe had been so when the third one appeared after her first lunch break on Wednesday she made some copies and filed them away. She had meant to give a copy to security after her second break, but she'd no sooner returned at two-thirty when Francis came out of the office brandishing a clipboard and she forgot.

'Lyndsey, here's a list of missing books. Could you check the shelves and see if you can find them, please?'

She laughed. 'Isn't there a clue in the word, missing?'

Francis remained by her desk, his hands in their standard pose. Lyndsey decided it was less begging dog and more meerkat.

'Just because the system thinks they're missing, doesn't mean they are. Sometimes books are returned to the shelves without being checked back in.'

'Fair enough, leave the list with me.'

He placed the clipboard on the corner of the desk and grimaced a smile that for a split second gave Lyndsey the impression he had wind, before returning to the office. Lyndsey took a deep breath, picked up the clipboard and headed for the first floor where the smallest reference numbers of the Dewey decimal system began.

This task wasn't as straightforward as it seemed. Not difficult, but awkward when she found multiple copies of a title. Then she needed to check inside each one for the unique identifier given to each individual book to see whether any of the shelved items were the 'missing' copies. She was partway through the second sheet when she noticed two library assistants approaching. They were easy to spot due to their bright red polo shirts that served as uniforms. The uniforms were also why they referred to themselves as elves. She recognised their faces from Monday when they had been introduced.

'Hi, you're Lyndsey, right?' said one of them. She was a black girl, about Lyndsey's height with anarchistic hair adorned with a flash of red on one side. Her associate was a little taller with bottle-blonde hair and brown roots showing. They were both smiling.

'Hi. Sorry, I don't remember your names.'

'I'm Dani and this is Astrid. How are you finding the place?'

'Not so bad, the work's varied enough.'

'Getting on OK with FC?'

'You mean Francis?'

They both sniggered. 'Yes, though we usually call him The Fat Controller when he's not in earshot.'

Lyndsey couldn't help laughing. As a nickname, The Fat Controller fitted him rather well.

'So what's this we hear about threatening letters?'

Like in any workplace, rumours spread quickly through the library. Lyndsey assumed the leak must have been Gloria, as Joe didn't come across as a man who would gossip at the water cooler.

'They're nothing much, the managers aren't worried. They think some student's having a Halloween joke.'

'What about you? Aren't you the person who found them?'

'Yes, someone left them on my desk, but they aren't threatening. More derogatory towards the library managers than anything else. At a guess, they're from someone who doesn't think too highly of them.'

'That doesn't cut down the list of suspects much,' said Astrid. 'Nobody here has a complimentary word to say about the manager in control of their department. I don't envy you, that's for sure. Working for the three of them must be hell.'

'I don't know, they're all challenging in their own way, but nothing that would scare the horses too much. I'm only here for a month or two, I'm sure I can handle their quirks.'

'So do they all hate each other?' asked Dani.

'Hate each other?' Lyndsey laughed. 'Why would you think they hate each other?'

Astrid and Dani shared a brief glance. 'Hate might be too strong a word, but I get the impression that each of them would be thrilled if the other two left. None of them will leave though, because if they did, they would feel the others had won the war.'

Lyndsey laughed again. 'I can't imagine where your ideas come from, but I'll keep an eye out for anything like you're describing as it would be hilarious if true. My problem would be not bursting into laughter, as explaining what I was laughing at could prove tricky.'

They laughed with her. 'Don't get into trouble on our account. Astrid's birthday is on Friday and some of us elves are going for pizza at lunchtime. Do you fancy joining us?'

'I'd love to, but it might be difficult to fit in with you all. I hope you have a wonderful birthday, Astrid.'

'Thanks, I'm sure I will. If you change your mind, we'll be going at one o'clock to the independent next to Oxfam as you near the High Street.'

'Like I said, I'd love to, but I have to cover the office from one until two while the managers are at lunch.'

Judging by Astrid's facial expression, she was genuinely disappointed, something that amused Lyndsey bearing in mind that they'd only known each other for five minutes.

'Crap,' said Dani looking over Lyndsey's shoulder through the bookshelf. 'Faruq's here. We'd better make like we're busy. Chat to you later, Lyndsey.'

They scurried off towards a trolley full of books, leaving Lyndsey pondering the conversation. It was interesting that they said everyone hated the managers. Did that mean the notes might be from a member of staff rather than the student body? Could they even be from one of the managers themselves?

Having run into Astrid and wished her a happy birthday, Lyndsey arrived back from her first lunch a minute past one o'clock on Friday. Gloria met her at the lift.

'Lyndsey, I've put some reports on your desk with a few changes to make. Do you think you could have them ready for me by two, please?'

'I can only try but I'll do my best.'

'Thanks, love. I won't be long.'

Gloria grabbed the lift before the doors closed and went to lunch. Lyndsey got back to her desk and put her bag underneath as Joe walked out of his office.

'I'm delivering a presentation this afternoon at the other campus so I've forwarded my calls to your phone. If you could take any messages and leave them on my desk I'll deal with them on Monday morning.'

'No problem, Joe. I hope the presentation goes well.'

For a moment, Lyndsey thought Joe was about to say something, but if he was he thought better of it and left. As he did, Francis strutted past and gave her a brief nod en route to the lift.

She sat down and picked up Gloria's report to find out what needed changing. Beneath the report was another envelope. She sighed and put on the gloves before opening the envelope and removing the note. As she read the letter she gasped in surprise, this was far more intense than the other four. She went to the photocopier to make copies and decided to escalate the issue above the heads of the managers. They may not be worried but she was. She put her copy into her bag, filed the original with the envelope, took the week's backup copies out of the drawer, added the latest note and rang the security manager.

Ten minutes later he was standing at her desk, looking as if he was about to explode.

'You mean you've received one of these every day this week and haven't contacted me? What were you thinking?'

'I told Joe on Monday, but he said to throw them away because he thought the first one was a student prank. Gloria said much the same on Tuesday but I didn't think it would do any harm to keep them in my drawer, just in case. I planned to call you Wednesday and Thursday, but I was busy and forgot,' she said in a voice that sounded wimpier than intended. 'Can't you search the CCTV recordings to find who keeps putting them on my desk?'

He stared at her for a moment, put his arms out and stared up at the ceiling, mock searching for something.

'Would you care to point out the cameras facing your desk?'

'Aren't there any monitoring people's movements?'

'Not so much, the entry gates at all the entrances and exits record comings and goings, so we know who is on campus at any given time. Cameras were only placed to watch things of value. Upper management decided in their infinite wisdom that as your computer is secured to the desk it would be a waste of money using cameras too. On top of that, the one facing the lifts is fake as it would only duplicate the work carried out by the cameras in the lifts themselves. The only working cameras on this floor are the ones pointing along the aisles of books.' He pointed behind him. 'I can check the lift recordings but if our phantom note writer used the stairs and kept to the wall beneath the aisle cameras, we'll be none the wiser. If you'd told me earlier in the week, I could have rigged something up, but given the tone of this letter, I don't expect any more to follow.'

He held the folder up and Lyndsey read the latest note again.

WHEN HALLOWEEN DOTH REAR ITS HEAD
THE LIBRARY MANAGERS WILL BE DEAD

She had to admit he had a point but didn't think she should take all the blame.

'I reported it to two managers. If you want to shout at anyone, you should shout at them. It was my first day when Joe told me to ignore them so I wasn't in much of a position to argue.'

'I will be having words with them, don't you worry. Are you sure these are the times they appeared so I can check the videos from the lifts?' He held up the sticky note containing the times and stuck it to the front of the file containing the notes.

'Yes, they appeared while I was at lunch so I'm certain of the times. Always my first break, too, from twelve-thirty to one o'clock, as if they wanted me to find them during the lunch period when I'd be alone.'

'Tell me immediately if another one appears and I'll sort

some monitoring out. I would ask one of the guys to come up and keep watch from twelve-thirty to one o'clock on Monday, but the presence of a guard is more likely to scare our phantom letter writer away so we'd be none the wiser even if he appeared.' He shook his head once more, turned and left, leaving Lyndsey simmering with indignation. She went to make a cup of tea to calm herself and set about Gloria's report edits with a fury she hadn't felt for a while, stabbing at the keyboard as if each key was one of the security manager's eyes. She'd just finished when Gloria returned from lunch a few minutes early.

'Hello, love. Did you get the reports done?'

'They're printing as we speak. I would have had everything finished but another note arrived so I called security.'

'Why? I thought we agreed they were just some student's idea of a joke?'

'Today's was more threatening so I figured it was best to involve security, just in case. He wasn't happy, said I should have phoned him Monday.'

'Silly man. Did he upset you? You seem on edge.'

'I'll be fine, I've calmed down now.'

'If you get any more trouble from him let me know and I'll sort him out for you.'

'Thanks, I'll bring the reports through with a coffee if you'd like one.'

'That would be lovely, thank you. I have another little job that needs doing later, but it shouldn't take long.'

'OK, but Francis needs this done,' she said pointing at a pile of papers.

Gloria scanned the top sheet. 'That isn't too urgent, keep at it until three-thirty or so, then switch to mine so you can finish it before home time. You'll only need to find some books and attach labels to the spines. That will be more interesting than computerising the data from those dusty old papers, that's for sure.'

Lyndsey nodded. 'I suppose so, though Francis gave me the impression this was urgent.'

'I'm sure he did, love. I'll deal with him for you, don't worry. You'll find out soon enough that everything to do with Francis is important. In his own little world, at least.'

'If you say so, let me make you that coffee.'

Lyndsey retrieved Gloria's mug from her desk and walked to the break room. By the time she returned, Gloria was talking into the phone.

'Thanks, John. If you could email me copies by three o'clock or so, that will be perfect. Speak again soon.'

She hung up and smiled as Lyndsey placed the mug on her desk.

'Thanks, Lyndsey. I'd never manage to last the day without coffee. Here you go, this is the job I need doing.'

Lyndsey took a few sheets of paper and some labels from her and returned to her desk where she reacquainted herself with Francis's task. As she started entering data into the spreadsheet, Francis appeared.

'How are you finding that job, Lyndsey? Any problems?'

She smiled at him. 'None at all, I'll tell you when I'm finished, though it may not be today. Gloria has a more urgent task she wants done later.'

He stood there for a few seconds as if he wasn't sure what to say next.

'Glad it's self-explanatory. You know where I am if you aren't sure on anything.'

He made his way into the office and sat down. Through the doorway, she saw him clench his desk with both hands and pull himself into position.

'Ouch!' He studied his finger and stuck it in his mouth.

'What's the matter, Francis?' asked Gloria.

'I've cut my finger, there must be something sharp under the desk.' He pushed his chair back with his legs.

'Oh, let me look. Lyndsey, could you bring the first aid box through from the shelf next to your desk, love?' She rushed around her desk to Francis as Lyndsey grabbed the box and entered the office. 'It doesn't look that bad. The shock's probably the worst part.'

Lyndsey put the first aid box on the desk, and Gloria rifled through, removing some cotton wool, a bottle of antiseptic and a sticking plaster.

'Here Lyndsey, Francis is the official first aider for the office so you can deputise on this occasion. As blood's involved, put on a pair of gloves and clean the wound for him while I try to find what caused the damage.'

'No, no, I'm fine,' said Francis holding his finger in the air like a schoolboy desperately needing the toilet. 'It's only a scratch.'

Lyndsey stopped herself laughing just in time.

'Don't argue, you could go down with tetanus. Don't listen to him, love.'

Listen? I'm too busy internally reciting Monty Python's Holy Grail to listen.

As Gloria ducked beneath the desk, Lyndsey donned some gloves, opened the antiseptic, soaked a lump of cotton wool and tended to Francis's finger. The cut was about a centimetre long but didn't look too deep, though it was hard to tell with the blood. By the time Gloria reappeared, the blood flow had almost stopped, and Lyndsey applied a plaster to his finger.

'Well, I can't find anything under the desk. A loose splinter of wood or something, perhaps. Run and make

Francis a cup of sweet tea for the shock, Lyndsey. I'll put the first aid box away and write a note in the injury book.'

As Lyndsey left the office, Francis was peering beneath his desk trying to find whatever had cut him. By the time she got back with his tea, they were both sitting behind their desks again.

'Here you go, Francis. Is your finger bearable?'

'Yes, thanks. I don't know what you used but I can't feel anything now.'

'Glad to hear, though I'm not sure that's how antiseptic works. Maybe your nervous system has blanked out the pain.'

The rest of the afternoon passed without incident. The task Gloria had given her was a welcome relief from data entry, as she had predicted. Gloria had found her around four o'clock and said goodnight as she was leaving early to attend a dentist appointment.

A few minutes before five, she'd returned to the office and thought it unusual that the managers' door was closed and the lights out, but they flickered on when she opened it to place the list on Gloria's desk. Francis was still sat concentrating on his computer screen.

'Sitting in the dark, Francis? Whatever you're working on must be engrossing.'

He didn't reply, and she walked out to her desk, shut down her computer and grabbed her coat.

'Goodnight, Francis, see you Monday. Do you want the door closed again?'

Francis didn't acknowledge her and after a few seconds, Lyndsey shrugged, closed the office door and left.

What a miserable git he is.

Francis felt strange. His hand had been the first to lose feeling, but the numbness had coursed up his arm and through the rest of his body. He tried to push himself back from his desk to stand, but couldn't move. He tried to speak, but his tongue refused to cooperate. He concentrated all his efforts into making a noise. Any noise. As much as he tried he could not move a muscle. He started to panic and began to struggle for breath.

What is going on?

Eventually, he regained some composure and concentrated on breathing. Over his monitor, he saw Lyndsey leave her desk carrying Gloria's sheets of paper and some labels.

Will no one notice me? Does no one think it strange that I haven't moved or spoken for ages?

At 16.03, according to his computer task bar, Gloria stood and retrieved her coat from the coat rack behind the door.

'I have a dentist appointment so need to run off now, see you Monday, Francis.'

Look at me. Ask yourself why I am not responding? Come back!

She walked out and closed the door behind her. He was alone. At 16.18, the movement sensors turned the lights off leaving the room murky as the heavy clouds outside blocked most of the light from the weak autumn sun.

At 16:57, lights flickered back on as the door opened again and Lyndsey entered.

'Sitting in the dark, Francis? Whatever you're working on must be engrossing.'

She strolled across to Gloria's desk and put the list down, glanced at her watch and went back to her own desk to turn off her computer. While it was shutting down, she put her coat on.

'Goodnight, Francis, see you Monday. Do you want the door closed again?'

Please, come and check on me. Please.

Lyndsey closed the office door and left. At 17.15, the movement sensors turned the lights off again, leaving only the glow from his computer screen. It wasn't until 19:17 that he heard the office door open.

At last, it must be security or a cleaner.

The lights clicked back on, momentarily blinding him. All he could make out was a shape heading towards his desk.

'Well, well. Are you still here FC? How unusual for you to work late. Let me help you drag yourself away from the computer screen.'

Thank goodness! Help me!

Francis' chair wheeled backwards away from his desk. He expected to tip forwards, but when he didn't, figured that his shoulder was being held to steady him.

'What's wrong, Francis? Cat got your tongue?'

What are you doing? Phone for an ambulance. Why are you wearing a ski mask and hoodie?

He felt himself being wheeled towards the door. As they left the office, he noticed the fourth floor of the library was mostly in darkness, only the dim night lights illuminating the main walkway that separated the office from the shelves. He tried once again to scream, but nothing came out.

They turned into a bay between two shelves and as they did, the lights flickered on above their heads. Francis saw a small stepladder and a few books strewn across the floor. At the end of the bay was a low table and seat, as was standard in the library to allow students to sit and browse through a book close to where it lived, not that such a convenience helped many of them put the books back where they found them.

'You shouldn't have climbed that stepladder, Francis. You're not built for that kind of thing, are you?'

For what seemed like the thousandth time, Francis tried to move or make any sound at all, but to no avail. The library remained as quiet as a ... well, there was a clue in the name.

The chair stopped moving and as the full horror of what was about to happen to him became clear, he prayed to a god that he didn't believe in to come to his rescue. His belated prayer was for nothing.

The last thing Francis saw was the corner of the reading table racing towards his face as his body was propelled from his chair.

10

Mads was questioning her decisions. Phoning everyone in Barry's book had seemed a solid plan in the light of Monday morning, driven by enthusiasm, but by Thursday evening she had reached the end of the Ts and been pleased she could take a break from it to visit Lyndsey's grandmother and collect the ashes next day.

Even that hadn't been easy. Despite her drink-fuelled willingness to talk, things getting real with Mads' offer to pay for testing had seemed to sober her up no end. Convincing her she was Lyndsey's friend who wouldn't do anything with the results that might put her in danger had been a struggle in itself. Mads also wondered if there wasn't a little fear involved, with her wanting to hang onto her conspiracy theory without the uncertainty of testing its veracity one way or another.

Eventually, she had agreed and Mads drove to Clacton-on-Sea as soon as Lyndsey left for work with the form downloaded and completed ready for sending with the sample. She'd already paid the, not insubstantial, fee online and received a booking number, so could post it straight from Clacton. Thanks to the traffic on the North Circular, she hadn't long thrown her bag on the sofa in the front room and collapsed into an armchair when Lyndsey came through the front door.

'Hi, Lynds, how was your day?'

'Grr, let me change and I'll fill you in.'

'Uh oh, I don't like the sound of that. Do you want a drink?'

'Do I ever.'

'OK, I'll fix you one then we can head out to wash the dust of the week off ourselves.'

Lyndsey sighed. 'Really? Can't I just sit here and drink?'

'Don't be silly. Listen to your Aunty Mads, she always knows best. Go change and freshen up so we can grab another seitan burger at The Railway.'

Lyndsey trudged upstairs, wanting to do nothing of the kind, but started to feel a little better once she'd leapt in the shower and changed her clothes. By the time she came back downstairs, Mads had made her what appeared to be a very large gin and tonic.

'I bet you're feeling better already. Sorry, we're all out of beer.'

Lyndsey took a large mouthful of the cold drink and crunched an ice cube between her teeth.

'Don't worry, you would stand a chance at tempting me with turps at the moment. I'm hungry now you've mentioned food. Get your shoes on.'

'Will do, but don't you want to tell me what got your goat today first?'

'No, plenty of time down the pub.'

'Fair enough, anything else happening you want to do tonight while we're out?'

Lyndsey thought for a moment. 'After The Railway,

let's have a couple of quiet beers at The Forest in Isleworth then scamper through the alley to the Green Tiger. The Wessex Pistols are playing tonight, they're always fun.'

'Wow, a shower and a mouthful of gin and you're back to life. That sounds like a plan, I'll ready myself while you finish your drink.'

About seven-thirty they walked into The Forest. Regulars stood along the bar either reading newspapers or chatting with each other. Mads and Lyndsey stared at the beer on offer, then at each other and curled their top lips in silent comment.

'London Pride, I suppose,' said Lyndsey.

'My thinking exactly, though is a choice between Pride and Doom Bar any kind of choice at all? Shall we go straight to the Tiger?'

'It'll be too noisy to talk. Close your eyes and be thankful they don't serve John Smith's.'

Once the barmaid had served them, they sat at a table by the door and both let out a sigh as they sat down. Realising what they'd done they both burst out laughing.

'We sound like we're in our sixties,' said Mads. 'So tell me, what went wrong with your day? It's not like you to stress over little things like temp jobs. And why couldn't we talk in the Railway?'

'The Railway was too busy to chat without everyone knowing our business. With my luck, we'd be talking in earshot of someone who knows my managers, who were more of a pain than usual today. And on top of that I got chewed out by the head of security.'

'Oh no, what did you do? Didn't I warn you not to steal office pens and paper clips?'

Lyndsey sighed and reached for her bag.

'Weird things are happening. Someone keeps leaving

notes on my desk while I'm at lunch.'

'Cool, a stalker? How exciting. Did you want the security guy to hunt him down?'

'Trust you to think of something like that. Speaking of which, I've lived at your house a few weeks now and not seen any sign of Nigel. Are you two OK?'

Mads displayed a sheepish expression for a moment. 'Don't change the subject. What about these notes?'

Lyndsey raised an eyebrow but continued. 'These notes are more sinister than fan mail from a secret admirer. Remember the one I showed you Monday? Welcome to the lunatic series.'

She took them from her bag and handed them over.

'One arrived each day, regular as anything during my first lunch break. If you remember, I showed a copy of the first one to Joe but he told me to throw it away as it was a student prank.'

'Mads laughed. 'Which, of course, you did.'

'Yeah, well. I didn't want to be hung out to dry if something happened. The next day I approached Gloria, but she was as dismissive as Joe had been. I'd had every intention of contacting security on Wednesday and Thursday but got distracted by work and clean forgot.'

Mads studied the first note again.

'They might have a point. Doggerel and gothic style imagery are classic student markers.'

She moved on to the second note.

WHEN COMES THE STROKE OF HALLOWEEN
THE LIBRARY MANAGERS WON'T BE SEEN

'That's a fair bet, from what you tell me there isn't much proof they exist after five o'clock strikes.'

'Francis, for sure. The others aren't as prompt in getting out of the door, though they're no slouches. Having said that, it means I can shoot off on the dot too without being guilted into doing a few more minutes here and there, so don't think for a moment I'm complaining. Which reminds me, another weird event in a week full of them, Francis was still at his computer when I left this evening.'

'Mr Four Fifty-Nine? Was he watching porn?'

Mads moved on to the third and fourth notes.

THEY WHINE AND WHINGE AND CATERWAUL
THE LIBRARY MANAGERS WILL FALL

WHILE LIBRARIANS HAVE PURPOSE
THE MANAGERS ARE MERE SURPLUS

She turned to Lyndsey. 'These read like they were written by someone with a grudge. Are you sure the writer isn't a librarian?'

'I'm not sure of anything. Today's upped the ante, though.'

Mads moved on and raised her eyebrows.

'I see what you mean, it's definitely more threatening than the others.'

'I thought that, so I called security and he was angry I hadn't phoned on Monday.'

'But if your managers told you to ignore them that isn't your fault. Can't they check the CCTV recordings?'

'Don't get me started. Upper management figured CCTV was a waste of money where nothing's worth stealing. They took the trouble to stick a fake up facing the lifts, mind.'

Mads laughed. 'Top bosses are the same everywhere. The only place they won't scrimp is in their pay packets and bonus packages. So what are they going to do?'

'He said he'll check what recordings there are, but not to hold out much hope. Now I feel like an idiot. If I'd done what my instincts told me in the first place, we might have cleared everything up by Tuesday afternoon.'

'Don't beat yourself up, your managers are to blame and the security guy shouldn't have been hard on you. Not only that, I bet nothing else happens. Halloween is a week and a half away. By then, the culprit will pull some showy stunt and everything will be over.'

'Yes, I suppose you're right. So tell me about you and Nigel.'

Mads sighed. 'If I do, you mustn't tell anyone, not even Nigel. He mustn't know that you know.'

'Of course I won't, not that I can if I never see him. So what's the story? You're intriguing me now.'

Mads leant in towards Lyndsey and started whispering.

'I'm not immensely proud of this, but we only got married to split a trust fund set up by his grandfather. He inherits after five years of marriage.'

Lyndsey gasped. 'You're kidding me. Why would you do something like that?'

'I'd like to say that I selflessly acted as Nigel's friend, but that would be a lie. Money is the easy answer. If I learnt one thing from growing up in rural poverty, it was that I never wanted to live like that again.'

'But still, why would he need ... unless ... don't tell me I was right when I teased you for dating a gay guy?'

'Yes, but initially he wasn't aware himself, or so he says. We concocted this scheme once he admitted his sexuality to me over a long drunken evening. Letting the money go to waste seemed nothing but an empty gesture. I figured I could pretend for five years easily enough, like doing a job you hate because you appreciate the rewards. One thing I hadn't anticipated was the loneliness, so I was delighted when you reappeared.'

'So what would happen to the trust if he hadn't married?'

'I've no idea, his grandfather has somewhat old-fashioned ideas of the world so it's fair to assume he wouldn't approve of Nigel's lifestyle. I think he must have suspected, hence setting up the trust fund in the first place. I nearly pulled out of the arrangement a couple of times during the engagement, but as time went on the lie got bigger and bigger until I couldn't back out. Don't judge me Lynds, it's done now and will be over in a year or two.'

'Of course I won't, but I'm shocked. I poked fun at you about the relationship sometimes, but I never thought for a moment that you were Nigel's beard. Wow, what a pair we are. I get involved with a cheating hound and you marry a gay guy.'

'Yes but don't say a word to anyone.'

'I won't.' Lyndsey drank the remains of her beer. 'Another pint here or head for the Green Tiger and hope to grab a table? The pub always gets stupid packed when the Wessex Pistols play.'

Mads handed back Lyndsey's notes and shrugged.

'Might as well make a move, the beer must be more adventurous over there.'

As Lyndsey had predicted the Green Tiger was heaving, but after getting served they squeezed themselves into the room containing the stage and propped themselves against the area of the bar used for collecting empty glasses. The band was energetic and full of enthusiasm and after the show, Mads & Lyndsey made their way back and both collapsed into an exhausted sleep.

It had been a very bleary-eyed pair who got out of bed next morning and set off for the market, but once they had their stalls ready and grabbed some breakfast from Madge's catering truck, they both started to feel human again.

'I'm glad you decided to exhibit your paintings this week, alongside the others.'

'I thought I would. It seems silly to go to the trouble of painting if I'm too worried about getting a negative comment to show the results to anyone.'

'I think they're brilliant. With the sun behind the Droop, it's as if someone's exploded a nuclear bomb where the market is and you were lucky enough to capture the moment.'

'Haha, I'll take that as a compliment, and brilliant call last night, Lynds. That band was amazing.'

'I thought you'd like them. We deserve an early night tonight, though. These late nights and early mornings will catch up on us. By the time we reach thirty, we'll be looking more like fifty if we keep this up.'

'Don't worry about that. Spas were invented to ease away the cares and wrinkles. Speaking of which, isn't your birthday in a month or two? What mischief can we get up to? What do you want to do, any thoughts?'

'I've not given my birthday a moment's thought. A few quiet days away somewhere might be welcome.'

'Now you're talking.'

Lyndsey paused for a moment and raised an eyebrow. 'Somewhere warm, preferably. A hotel in Hackney and a week getting ratted at the Pig's Ear Festival isn't what I have in mind.'

'I can do warm. Let me have your passport details and I'll conjure something up. I think we both deserve some time away with nothing to worry about except where the waiter's disappeared to.'

The market eased itself into life and they were both busy with browsers and customers for the next couple of hours. A woman was admiring some of Mads' paintings.

'I like those two,' she said pointing at pictures of the Droop and the Phoenix. 'They remind me of my late husband. If he wasn't in one, I could usually find him in the other.'

Mads laughed. 'If you want both, I'm sure we could hammer out a deal.'

'Thank you, dear. I appreciate the offer, but they'd still be a little much for me, I'm afraid. They are very evocative, though. Did you paint them or are you selling them for someone else?'

'Those are mine. I've not painted anything for a few years, so figured local pubs would be as good a place to retrain myself as any.'

'There are no lack of local pubs, so you're not going to run short of material. Best of luck, and if I have a good night at the bingo, I might be back to see if they're still available.'

'I sell limited edition prints too, if price is the sticking point. You'll find them on my website at madsart.uk. Hang on, let me find a card.' She found the box of business cards and handed one across. 'You can always order online and collect from me here, to save spending on postage, if you prefer.'

'How thoughtful, I'll give that some consideration,' she said as she put the card into her handbag. 'Have a lovely day, dear, and best of luck with your painting.'

'Thanks, and thank you for liking them.'

As the woman strolled off, Mads realised she had a small window of opportunity to buy refreshments and turned to Lyndsey.

'Cup of tea?'

'Love one, please.'

'OK, keep an eye on the stall for me.'

Mads grabbed her bag and headed for the catering truck. As she was queuing, she could hear a phone, but it wasn't until after a few rings that she realised the sound was coming from her bag. She scrabbled around before pulling out the Nokia and peered at the small screen. She must have forgotten to turn it off on Thursday.

Who would call me on this? If it's those damned road traffic accident ambulance chasers, I'll give them a piece of my mind.

She decided the best way of finding out who was calling, was to answer.

'Hello?'

The line was quiet for a few moments before a throaty voice broke the silence.

'Who is this?'

'Sorry? You rang me, remember?'

'No, love, you rang me last week and left a message about Barry so who are you and how did you get this number?'

'Oh.' She thought for a few seconds then took a chance. 'Barry's away for a few weeks and left me in charge, but I'm struggling to reconcile everything. Could tell me your details and where you make your payments so I can check and mark you as paid. I wouldn't like to make any mistakes.'

The line went quiet again and Mads was wondering whether they'd been cut off when the man started talking again.

'You're lying.'

'What makes you think so?'

He laughed, a gravelly, rasping sound that spoke of too many cigarettes and dark alleyways if the noir films Mads had watched were anything to go by.

'If you knew how this worked, you'd have the answer to that, love.'

She took a deep breath and collected her nerves, which were in danger of turning her into a gibbering wreck. What if he could trace the phone and hunt her down? She cursed herself for not remembering to turn it off.

'OK, you're right. I don't know how this works, but we both have information the other needs. Can we meet somewhere? I'm not comfortable talking on the phone.'

'Finally, a bit of sense. When and where? Somewhere public, with no cameras.'

Mads thought for a moment. 'How about Gunnersbury Triangle, early Monday morning? Eight o'clock?'

'Make it seven, I start work at eight.'

'No problem. Do you know the Triangle well? There's a grass area near the back with a bench.'

'Works for me. I'll see you then, and you'd better

make it worth my while, you hear?'

'I will.'

He disconnected. Mads made sure she turned the phone off and wrapped it in the silver foil this time, before burying the shiny package deep in her bag. She had no clue whether or not that had gone well. It was either a welcome breakthrough or crass stupidity on her part, and she couldn't decide which. Only after she had paid for the teas and went to pick them up did she realise she was shaking.

'Sorry, can I have a tray for the teas, please? Not feeling myself this morning.'

'You can, my darling. Heavy night?' Madge cackled with laughter as she found a cardboard tray big enough for two cups. 'We've all had nights like that, I'm sure. Here you go.'

She placed the tray on the counter and inserted the cups into the sockets.

'Thanks,' said Mads, picking up the tray and slowly making her way back.

Lyndsey rubbed her hands together as Mads disappeared to buy the teas. Having a cup to warm them up with sounded as welcoming as drinking the tea itself. And a holiday, that sounded like a marvellous idea. She began to imagine warm beaches and cold beers on the sand while sunbathing, not that she much enjoyed sunbathing but Mads would be all over the idea given half a chance. They'd need some kind of compromise between slobbing out and doing things.

She became so lost in reverie that she was surprised when a voice ripped her out of it and back to reality.

'Where are my photos?'

She spun her head to face the direction of the voice and saw the man who had asked her about some photos a few weeks earlier when she'd been working her grandad's stall.

'Try asking at the stall over there,' she said, pointing at her grandad's pitch. 'No one will offer me photos here, will they?'

'Don't try to be smart, it doesn't become you. Someone

gave you a box of photographs when you were on the stall across the way, the day the kid running the record stall got stabbed. Where are they?'

Lyndsey paused for a moment. 'I've no idea what you mean. I don't have any photographs. I told you that the other week.'

'But you do. Maybe a photo might work as a prompt.'

He pulled a picture from his coat pocket and thrust it in front of Lyndsey's face. She glanced at it for a moment, then spun her head away, repulsed.

'Do you recognise him?'

She looked again. There was no telling. The face in the photo was covered in blood and had been beaten so badly, she doubted his own mother would be able to ID him with any confidence. She averted her eyes again but the image had already burnt its way into her mind.

'No, why who is it?'

'This is the man who gave my photos to you. As you can see, he met with a small accident afterwards.'

'I don't have any photographs, leave me alone.'

'You're pushing your luck, Lyndsey, not something you want to do, believe me. I've been patient so far, hoping you'd ring and sell them to me, but your time limit on that offer will soon be expiring.'

'How do you know my name?'

He smiled a cold smile. 'Merely the tip of the iceberg where it comes to what I know about you, Lyndsey. You still have my number, I assume. If not, here it is again.'

He held out a piece of paper containing the word PHOTOS and a phone number.

'Not that you deserve it, but I'm going to be generous. I'll give you £1500 for the photos up to and including 1st November. After that, every day that passes without me hearing your dulcet tones on the phone the price drops by £25. Once the total reaches zero, I stop playing Mr Nice Guy. Do I make myself clear?'

Lyndsey took the paper from his gloved hand. 'But I don't ...'

Before she could finish what she was saying, his hand shot out and grabbed her by the throat. He pulled her face towards him, forcing her to lean across the stall flap. He bent down too, so their noses were almost touching and stared into her eyes. The stench of garlic and stale beer on his breath was nauseous.

'Stop lying, Lyndsey, to yourself as much as me. I've told you the deal, and I'd rather be civil about it, but I'm prepared to go about this any way necessary. Come to your senses before the end of the year and make some money. Otherwise ... let's just say it would be a shame for you and your pretty little friend to get hurt.'

His grip was so tight, Lyndsey was struggling to breathe, let alone reply. She tried to yell to attract someone's attention but couldn't utter a sound louder than a gurgle. She became lightheaded and the sound of blood rushing through her ears began to drown everything else out. Suddenly, he let go and her face was splashed by hot liquid.

'Oi, leave my mate alone.'

As she gasped for breath, Lyndsey turned to see Mads about ten metres away threatening to throw a second cup at the man. He glanced down at his soaked coat and wiped some liquid from his face with his glove, just as Bob yelled from across the alcove and started across.

'Don't forget, end of December,' he said before turning and running off, vanishing into the crowd of people that was forming to watch the spectacle.

Bob arrived a few seconds before Mads and seemed in

two minds whether to try to catch the man, but instead, ducked under the stall flap so he could see how Lyndsey was.

'What was all that about, Lynds? Sorry, I wasn't paying attention else I'd have come across earlier.'

'Nothing, Barry owed him money. He figured that as I was his ex, I should cough up.'

'Who is he? I'll make sure he doesn't bother you again.'

Lyndsey slipped the piece of paper containing the phone number into her back pocket and wiped a splattering of tea from her face.

'I don't know, and I doubt he'll return, but if he crosses my path again the first thing I'll do is shout for you, OK?'

'You'd better. Are you sure you're all right?'

'Shaken, but I'll be fine, Bob. Thanks. Mads will look after me now she's back.'

'Mads needs another cup of tea,' said Mads.

'You stay here with Lynds and I'll buy you one. Black with no sugar? Impressive shot, by the way.'

Mads walked round the counter through her stall rather than duck underneath and placed the remaining cup of tea in front of Lyndsey.

'Lucky more than anything. I didn't expect to hit him but was hoping I'd at least attract someone's attention. I couldn't think what else to do.'

'You done great, love,' said Bob, giving her a quick squeeze around the shoulders. 'Stay here and I'll grab you that tea.'

He ducked under the flap and headed for the catering truck.

'What was that about, Lynds? And don't give me that BS about Barry owing him money. What was he after?'

Lyndsey sighed. 'Remember those photos? It seems

they're important to him.'

'How important?'

'Enough that he's offered me £1500 for their return, or potential violence against the two of us if money doesn't do the trick.'

Mads opened her mouth wide. 'You're kidding. What are you going to do?'

Lyndsey shook her head. 'I don't know. He scares me, and I've no idea why he wants them. What if my parents are still alive and he needs the photos to find them? I'd hate to discover they're alive and help him kill them before we've had a chance to talk.'

'But what if he doesn't want to kill them. He might want to keep your parents hidden and needs the photos back in case someone else goes hunting for them. If they are alive.'

'Yes,' she said, slumping to the concrete and staring at the ground for a few seconds. 'But I'd say that was least likely, wouldn't you? If he told me they were in hiding but could be in serious danger if the photos got into the wrong hands, I might hand them over, or at least destroy them. But he wants the photos, and to me at least, that says he doesn't know where they are.'

Mads nodded. She considered telling Lyndsey about the cremains she'd sent off for DNA testing but decided to wait until she had something more concrete to report.

'Yes, you might have a point. Did he give you a time limit?'

'Until the end of December, but the money he's offering drops every day. Not that the money's important, I'm more invested in hoping no one gets hurt. And when I say anyone, my priority is us, if I'm honest.'

Mads saw something on the floor behind Lyndsey and bent down to pick it up.

'What's this?'

Lyndsey glanced at the photo Mads had found, then looked away just as quickly.

'If he was telling the truth, that's the poor guy who gave me the photos. I guess he tracked him down, or had someone else do it for him.'

'Jesus! Don't worry yet, you have plenty of time before we reach that stage. We'll come up with a plan over a few beers one night, I'm sure.'

Lyndsey smiled. 'Not sure the best time to be making life or death decisions is after a few beers, Mads, but thanks anyway. I'll sleep on it for a couple of days. Maybe I should stop putting myself on show here and concentrate on the library. Nothing out of the ordinary ever happens in libraries.'

'Aside from the notes, you mean?'

'Well yes, but I'm coming round to the idea that those are a poor student joke. At least whoever's leaving them isn't throttling me and threatening worse.'

'There is that, still, I doubt he'll be back, and I'm sure Bob will keep a very close eye out so he's unlikely to get near enough to try that again.'

'I hope you're right.'

13

The rest of the weekend at the market passed without drama, at least none involving Mads and Lyndsey, but Lyndsey had been jumpy for the duration so Mads dragged her to the Dachshund after they had dropped everything back home Sunday afternoon. She'd been much more relaxed when they rolled home at closing time, and Mads no less so, culminating in her finding it very hard to get out of bed when the alarm went off at five o'clock.

Having snoozed twice, she finally bit the bullet and dragged herself from beneath the cosy quilt and into the bathroom. Following a quick shower, she dragged some clothes on and set off for Gunnersbury Triangle.

She arrived a little after six and went into the café across the road from the entrance for some breakfast. It hadn't long been open and as the first customer she had no problem bagging the table by the window and settled down to wait.

She'd cross referenced the phone number against her decoded list of Barry's contacts on Saturday night, so she knew she was meeting someone with the initials

JP. She had also read his file which had caused her pause over whether to go through with the meeting. He was a most unsavoury character with a penchant for underage boys and, as far as she was concerned, if anyone deserved blackmailing, he was a contender. She decided against cancelling, though, and figured she'd decide later whether to give Barry's dossier to the police. In the meantime, he was her only lead regarding how the blackmail scheme worked.

At 6.50, she saw a man leave the tube station next to the café and scurry across the road where he entered Gunnersbury Triangle. She waited five minutes in case any other suspicious-looking characters appeared, and when they didn't she paid for breakfast and followed him into the nature reserve. Once she was out of sight of the road, she whipped her phone out and selected the flashlight app to light her way along the dark paths. When she reached the bench, JP was nowhere to be seen so she sat down to wait, assuming he hadn't known the best route to take.

There was a brief rustling behind her in the bushes, but before she could turn around, an arm was around her neck and a knife was in front of her eyes. She sat rigid, looking with terror at the light from a distant streetlight glinting on the hard metal blade.

'Who are you and how are you linked to Barry?'

'I'm not ... if you relax your grip on my throat I'll be able to speak a little easier.'

Nothing happened for a moment, then he withdrew his arm from around her neck, instead grabbing her hair from behind. He moved the knife from eye level and rested it against her neck.

'Is that better? Now, answer the question.'

'Before I do,' Mads gulped , 'you need to know three

things. And move the knife back a smidge, please. It's making me nervous.'

He moved it a few millimetres so the metal no longer touched her skin, but she was under no illusions that it was no less dangerous.

'OK, let's play it your way. What are these three things?'

'First, I'm only a PI and know nothing about you except your initials, JP, and your phone number. I only know that much because I stumbled on Barry's phone book while investigating something else.'

'OK, continue.'

'Second, I'm not dumb enough to come here alone. Where the Triangle's surrounded by tube lines, there's only one way in or out. If you leave before me, you won't live long enough to reach the tube station.'

She paused, wondering if he might remove the knife from the vicinity of her throat but he didn't. She continued, hoping he didn't question the likelihood of her second point too hard.

'Third, we both have information the other needs. If you answer my questions, I'll tell you what you need to know. If not, we may as well go our separate ways now.'

'How do I know you're not lying, or an undercover copper?'

'Mate, if I was a cop this nature reserve would be teeming with police who would have taken you down not long after you arrived and we'd be having this conversation at the station. As for the information I have for you, it will mean you can stop making the monthly payments. How does that sound?'

She tried to keep her breathing level while he mulled this over. The silence couldn't have lasted longer than a few seconds but seemed like minutes from where she sat.

'OK, but if you try to screw me over, I'll take my chances with whoever's waiting outside. If there even is anyone.'

'There is, trust me. I'm not stupid, but also didn't want to scare you off by bringing him in with me. So, do we have a deal? You answer my questions, I'll tell you what you want to know, and we both walk out one at a time, all the better for what we've learnt.'

She felt him relax his grip on her hair a little, allowing her to hold her head naturally. She let out a sigh of relief.

'Ask your questions,' he said.

'How does the blackmail scheme work? How did you know I was lying on the phone?'

'That's an easy one. There's never any doubt who makes a payment. Barry forced me to open a bank account in my name. He took the bank card and the login details to access it online. I assume he changed the PIN and password. I also had to give him my personal details, such as date and place of birth, mother's maiden name, secret word, you know the kind of thing. The information the bank ask you when you phone them. I've since transferred £250 a month into that account and I imagine he's been withdrawing from various cashpoints. I knew I couldn't be the only one he was shaking down. Everything was too practiced for it to be a one-off. He also stressed that he was part of a larger organisation, so should anything happen to him, the blackmail would not only continue but the price would go up as an admin fee for finding me a new minder.'

Mads couldn't help smiling at that titbit. The age-old chestnut of a larger organisation being involved to keep the fish on the hook. She'd lost count how many times that had cropped up in crime films.

'OK, I can't think of anything else I need. Thanks.'

'What about you? What do I need to know?'

'Barry's dead, and there is no organisation. It was only Barry all along. You can stop paying as of now.'

There was a long pause and Mads could swear JP had stopped breathing.

'Are you serious? What about the photos?'

'I've no idea where they are or anything else he might have on you or his other victims. I only came across his phone book by accident. That's as much as I know and I don't care to learn any more, to be frank, so I think we're even?'

'If you're a PI, could I employ you to find where he kept all his incriminating evidence on people? To ensure it gets destroyed, nothing else.'

'Not my line, JP. I work solely for women who think their partner is cheating on them. Barry wasn't as pure as snow where it came to innocence in that department.'

'So what should I do now?'

'Stop paying, stop looking over your shoulder, and hope he didn't keep detailed records, or at least didn't pass them to someone else who might see any value in them. To all intents and purposes, you've dodged a bullet. Keep your nose clean in future and don't get caught again, whatever you did.'

He paused again, then slowly removed the knife from her neck.

'Fair enough, give me a minute to move back into these bushes so you don't put a face to the initials. Once I'm hidden, you make your way out and call your partner off.'

'Will do, thanks for the information.'

'What did you want it for, if you don't mind me asking? What does it matter to you what he was doing if he's dead?'

She shrugged. 'Because now I know what he was up to, there are plenty more initials who need to be contacted to tell them to stop paying. It's not something I have to do as such, but I'd feel like an accomplice if I didn't at least try.'

He went quiet again, and she heard the rustle of leaves once more.

'OK, off you go. And thanks.'

She took out her phone, turned the flashlight back on and walked away, far more calmly than her churning insides felt like doing. When out of view and sure JP wasn't following, she took a deep breath and calmed herself a little.

I must be missing something. I need to do a systematic check through Barry's stuff.

14

When Lyndsey arrived at work on Monday morning, she ws surprised to find all the library staff milling around near the front desk. Seeing Dani talking with another elf she made a beeline for her.

'What's happened?'

'Hi, Lyndsey. We're not sure, but someone said FC had an accident. Was he still here when you left on Friday or did he come in over the weekend?'

'He was still here staring at something on his computer when I left. I thought it was strange, but he didn't even acknowledge me so I figured something must be important. Oh wow, you don't think he was sitting there already dead, do you?'

'No, according to the cleaner who found him this morning, he fell off a ladder.'

Lyndsey couldn't help but laugh and raised her hand to her mouth to stifle the sound so as not to attract attention.

'Francis? Climbing a ladder? Why would he do that? I've not so much as seen him touch a book in the week I've been here.'

Dani and her friend covered up laughs.

'Oh, this is Adi. Adi, this is Lyndsey. She has the unenviable job of being assistant to the managers.'

'Hello, Lyndsey. Your job just got twenty-five percent easier,' she smiled.

'Ouch, way too soon,' said Dani.

'And it also remains to be seen,' replied Lyndsey. 'So why are we all out here? Couldn't we at least congregate in the office?'

'The police have commandeered the downstairs office as an operations centre for the moment,' said Dani. 'Your floor is a potential crime scene and they've closed the rest of the library while they investigate what might have happened.'

'I can't believe no one found him over the weekend. You'd think someone would have gone upstairs, or at least seen him on the cameras. I'm sure the security manager said they have cameras facing the book aisles.'

Adi shrugged. 'No idea, but with any luck we'll find out something now,' she said, nodding towards the doors to the office that Inspector Savage was walking through. He cast his eyes around the group and waited for them to stop talking amongst themselves. Once everyone was quiet, he started speaking.

'Thank you for waiting, everybody. Unfortunately, you won't be able to open the library today, but we can allow you access to the ground floor office. We will set up our operations centre on the first floor out of the way. I've briefed your managers, so if you make your way into the ground floor office they will fill you in. We will need to talk to everyone so please wait until we've done so before you disappear off home.'

He scanned the huddled faces once more, turned and

headed for the lifts. Immediately he had gone, a low-level hubbub began as people started gossiping and speculating as they slowly made their way to the office. It was a tight squeeze with all the librarians and the allocations team, but everyone found a spot and they all stared at Faruq and the other managers in expectation.

'I'm sure most of you have heard the sad news,' said Faruq, 'but to ensure we're all up to speed, one of the cleaning staff found Francis Collins dead this morning on the fourth floor. While it appears to have been an accident, the police are keen to eliminate all doubt before they sign it off as such, so they would appreciate our help towards that end.'

He took a breath and waited for any comments or questions, but when no one said anything he continued.

'They will need to talk to everyone who works in the library, but don't worry yourselves as it's only routine. Once they have interviewed you, you can go home and return when your next shift starts.'

'Will we still be paid for today?' asked someone near the front.

'The university has agreed to pay you all four hours for today and we will rearrange any scheduled hours above that across the next few weeks. The librarians and allocations staff can work from this office until the police allow them access to their own offices. It will be cosy, but we'll manage somehow. As for the rest of you, I suggest you sit in the refectory and wait. I'll check how the police want to conduct the interviews and come and get you in the order they suggest. Unless there's anything else?'

No one said anything and as the elves filed out of the room, Lyndsey approached Joe and Gloria.

'What about me?'

'I don't know,' said Gloria. 'I doubt we'll be able to do much today and as everything upstairs is out of bounds, I suppose you might as well take the day off too. Is that OK with you, Joe?' She bent forward and whispered. 'Don't worry, we'll pay you for the full day, but make sure you don't tell the others.'

Joe threw Gloria an annoyed glance as if he didn't appreciate her making decisions on his behalf, but nodded brusquely. 'I don't have a problem with that. Faruq, could you include Lyndsey on your police interview list, please?'

'Yes, of course. Join the others in the refectory and I'll call you when it's your turn.'

'You poor dear,' said Gloria. 'It must be a shock for you. Only been here a week and there's a dead body. I don't suppose you've known many people who have died at your age.'

Aside from most of my grandparents, my parents and ex-boyfriend, fewer than one springs to mind.

'Not really, no,' she said, not wishing to make her intimate acquaintance with death common knowledge.

She joined the elves in the refectory and sat chatting to Dani until, one by one, they were all called and she was on her own. She whipped out her laptop to continue her writing and when Faruq disturbed her ten minutes later felt a wave of disappointment.

'Lyndsey, they're ready for you upstairs. Head for the first-floor office.'

'OK, thanks,' she said, slipping the computer into her bag. When she arrived upstairs the office door was open, and she entered to find an exasperated Inspector Savage sitting at a desk.

'Well well, Miss Marshall. Please, take a seat. Imagine

my delight when I discovered you were close to another dead body. Have you ever considered having a health warning tattooed on your forehead?'

Lyndsey sat down and stayed quiet.

'So, what was your relationship with the deceased?'

'I worked for him and the other two library managers. I'm temping and only started a week ago.'

'So I gather, yet your name comes up more than anyone else's in the other interviews. What are these threatening letters I've heard so much about, and why did you not consider contacting the police when they arrived?'

'They started appearing last Monday, my first day. I took the first one to Joe, and he told me to throw it away. When the second one arrived, Gloria also said to ignore them.'

'And did you?'

'No, I didn't. I contacted security on Friday when they became more threatening.'

'Yes, we've already spoken to the security manager who, for some reason, also thought we wouldn't be interested. It would have been more useful, Miss Marshall, had you contacted us at the outset and given us the notes before half the university handled them.'

'I filed the originals out of harm's way, if you want them.'

Savage sat up in his chair. Lyndsey could see she had piqued his interest.

'You have the originals? And no one has manhandled them?'

'Only me, and after Monday I was careful not to touch them with my hands. I used a folded piece of paper or gloves to remove them from the envelope and photocopied the letters so they wouldn't become tainted.'

'Even though your managers instructed you to ignore them?'

'Yes, I was covering my back in case anything happened, as I suppose it may have done. Do you think it wasn't an accident?'

'It's too early to say, but something doesn't sit right to me.' He paused. 'Off the record, of course. Please don't tell anyone I said that.'

'Your secret's safe with me, Inspector.'

'Whether it's treated as a murder is a decision taken above my pay grade, and given the latest tranche of cutbacks from central government, I suspect my bosses will sway towards the accident theory unless I can unearth something compelling to tempt them in.'

He paused for a moment and looked Lyndsey square in the eyes.

'Please don't take that as an invitation to run your own investigation, Miss Marshall. However much your enthusiastic friend might fancy herself as a young Miss Marple, she was very lucky to escape with nothing worse than a bump on the head last time, and I don't want to be investigating her death next week. If you hear or suspect anything, please call my number. In case you can't find it, please have one of my cards.' Savage handed a business card across the desk with a flourish. 'Do I make myself clear?'

Lyndsey nodded and smiled at him. If Mads got it into her head to do something, there was little Lyndsey could do to dissuade her, she knew that well enough.

'So tell me about Francis Collins. What were your impressions of him and was he out of sorts on Friday?'

Lyndsey told the Inspector how it was unusual for Francis to stay late and how she thought it strange that he would shelve books at all, especially after working hours.

'So you would think this out of character?'

'Yes, I've only been here a week, but I could set my watch by the time he arrived in the morning and left at night. And to be honest, he seemed more like a person who was better at appearing busy than actively doing anything. The thought he'd be up a ladder shelving books is laughable. Unless he had something stashed away that he didn't want anyone to know about.'

She laughed, but stopped as she realised Savage wasn't laughing with her.

'Ignore me, it was only a throwaway comment.'

'Jesters do oft prove prophets, Miss Marshall, if you'll forgive a brief quote from the bard. Is there anything else you can think of? If not, we might as well get those original notes and you can go home. Are you still at the same address if we need to contact you?'

'No, I've moved in with Mads, but my phone number's the same. I don't suppose it's relevant, but Francis had a small accident after lunch on Friday. He cut his finger on his desk somehow, but we patched him up and he seemed fine afterwards if a little quiet.'

'What did you use to tend to him?'

'Some antiseptic from the first aid box and a plaster, I can show you when we go upstairs.'

'Yes, please do. One never knows what might prove useful at this stage. Let's go up, shall we?'

Savage stood and Lyndsey led the way to the lifts. She retrieved the envelope containing the original letters from her desk and showed the Inspector the first aid box she'd used.

'And where did Mr Collins sit?'

'That one there,' she said pointing to the farthest desk

in the office. 'Will the library be open again tomorrow?'

'I think so, but this office and some of this floor will be out of bounds until further notice. I'm sure the managers will sort something out by morning and if the CSIs have finished, you might be able to work at your desk.'

'I thought you called them SOCOs over here?'

'Yes, oldies like me would still like to, but stopping Americanisms from making their way across the Atlantic is as futile as Cnut trying to stop the tide itself. I shudder internally every time I hear someone use the phrase "train station", but under instructions from my doctor I'm learning to accept that keeping my blood pressure down is more important than fighting losing battles.'

Savage stood still, looking into the managers' office.

'What are those track marks in the carpet, Miss Marshall? Move this way a little, they're highlighted by the light from the window. It appears as if someone wheeled something heavy across the office recently. To your knowledge, has anybody moved something that caused that? A new desk or cupboard, perhaps?'

'No, nothing. Not while I've been here.'

Savage nodded his head slowly.

'Thank you, Miss Marshall. You may go. I'm sure we will bump into each other again before this investigation is over.'

Lyndsey made her way downstairs and found Gloria to tell her she was going home and would be back in the morning. As she left for the bus stop, she had a sickly feeling in her stomach. She hoped Francis had died in an accident. Being involved, even peripherally, in another murder investigation was not something she was looking forward to.

'Amazing, what's the plan?'

Lyndsey sat and stared at Mads.

'What do you mean? There is no plan. Did you miss the part where Inspector Savage said we're not to get involved?'

'He has to say that. What's wrong with giving him a helping hand. I can use my alumni card to access the campus. Worst-case scenario is I refresh my art knowledge and find some inspiration from reading through the art books while I sit around keeping my eyes and ears open.'

'Grr, I wish I'd said nothing now. I knew you wouldn't listen.'

'Oh, don't overreact. I'm like a ninja, you'll never notice me unless I choose to reveal myself. If you'd asked for my help last week to keep an eye out while you went to lunch, you'd know who was responsible for the notes by now.'

'Perhaps, but neither of us thought of it. However, especially after being warned not to dabble, I can't think of any reason for you to poke your big nose into a police investigation.'

'I won't be poking my perfectly formed nose anywhere, just keeping my eyes and ears open for discoveries that neither you nor the police are likely to have access to. What could be wrong with that?'

Lyndsey sighed. 'Says the woman who got abducted by a murderer while innocently going to see her friends' artwork. Mads, trouble finds you, you don't need to hunt it down.'

Mads shrugged and smiled. 'So I might as well do what I want. My dad says you're more likely to be injured shying away from tackles rather than throwing yourself full into them.'

'Which may be fine advice when playing rugby or hurling, but has what relevance to a murder investigation?'

'For god's sake, you and your details. It's an analogy and a design for life, Lynds. You're meant to be the wordsmith, aren't you?'

'Yes, and I can recognise out of context BS when I hear it.' She stopped to take a breath. 'I don't want to argue, the day's been stressful enough already. Whatever I say, you'll do what you want to do and that's fine. All I ask is be careful and don't invite trouble to my desk. Remember, I'm working there and don't want to be let go any earlier than needs be.'

'Don't you worry, I won't be getting either of us into trouble. But don't deny you're intrigued as well. Why else did you keep copies of the letters, and not only a copy so you wouldn't handle the originals but another one for yourself?'

'The difference is that I'm scared and would love to be sitting in an office doing tedious work to earn a living for a while. You, on the other hand, don't need to involve yourself, but your instinct is to run into the burning building because it's more exciting than watching from afar. I don't get it.'

'Not sure about running into burning buildings, my hair might get singed. Libraries are another matter. You have no need to worry, Lynds, I'll be looking out for you.'

Lyndsey sighed inwardly as she stood to make a cup of tea. Yes, Mads would be, but whether that was cause to worry was a matter for debate.

Lyndsey was delighted to be told she could work at her normal desk next morning, though Inspector Savage gave her a long and tedious monologue about not entering the managers' office. He made it clear, without putting it in so many words, that he knew she had breached a crime scene once and would not hesitate to act to the full extent of the law should she do so again.

As she sat down after taking her first break, Mads stepped out from between the bookshelves.

'Hi, no one went near your desk while you were away.'

'Goodness, Mads. You gave me a fright.'

'I told you, Mads the ninja.' She took on a quick martial arts stance. 'If the office is free, can't we hunt for clues?'

Lyndsey laughed. 'Not for a moment, the police have gone over the entire office with a fine-tooth comb. And Savage made a big deal about locking it this morning after lecturing me about not going in, so don't even think about it, even if you could think of a way through the locked door.'

'Fair enough. How's your day been? Nothing suspicious?'

'Nothing at all, unless you count my two remaining managers being able to last a few hours without my help. Strange how not having me in view increases their abilities like that.'

'I imagine they're too lazy to make the journey up when it's almost as quick for them to do whatever they would ask you to do.'

'You might be right, much of the time they want me to make coffee or that herbal tea Joe drinks. Once one of them has a long, tedious task to do they will appear as if by magic.'

'Ooh, like the shopkeeper from the television series, Mr Benn. Do you remember that? I used to love that show when I was a kid.'

Before Lyndsey could answer, a lift pinged and Mads withdrew back to the bookshelves before she was seen. As the doors slid open, Gloria marched out and headed straight for the office door. When she found it locked, she let out an exasperated grunt and turned to Lyndsey.

'Do you have the key, Lyndsey? I need something.'

'No, sorry. Inspector Savage has the key and told me that no one is to enter as they haven't finished yet. I could phone him if you like and he could get you something specific, if you need it. '

Gloria's face darkened and Lyndsey expected her to yell. She glared at Lyndsey, then for no apparent reason, relaxed and smiled as if nothing had happened.

'Not to worry, I'll make do until later. You must be lonely up here, what a shame there's no room downstairs.'

'Oh, don't mind me. It's giving me an opportunity to work through the backlog with no distractions.'

'I'm on my way out to lunch, but while I'm here, I have a project for you. The university has decided to hold a remembrance service for Francis on Thursday. Would you mind organising a few basics like drinks and nibbles, please? I've made a rough list here, but feel free to change anything you think might need adjusting. I'm not very knowledgeable as to what vegans and vegetarians eat nowadays. It was so much easier when food was food and everyone ate anything, wasn't it?' She handed Lyndsey a scribbled list.

'Well, I'm not sure about that, but leave everything with me. Any idea how many will attend? Who do you suggest I order from? Wouldn't the catering department be the best people to approach?'

Gloria sighed. 'They might have been before the Dean privatised everything. Now, they would be expensive and more hassle than they're worth. We have a departmental account with the local supermarket. The login details are at the bottom of the sheet. I think our credit limit is somewhere around £1000 but try to keep within £500 or thereabouts. The university will reimburse us so the cost won't impact our budget. If they can deliver on Thursday morning, everything will be ready for the service. As for attendees, I've emailed announcements to departmental heads asking for approximate numbers from each of them so we'll have to play that by ear until I get some replies.'

'No worries, if I have any problems, I'll tell you.'

'Thanks, Lyndsey.' She stopped and sniffed. 'It would be too upsetting for me to do this on my own, so this is very much appreciated.'

She smiled and turned for the lifts. When she had gone, Mads reappeared.

'So that's the famous Gloria? I doubt she'll win any prizes for acting. Too upsetting, my arse. More like below her perceived station. And what was with that palaver about the door being locked? I thought she was going to go off on one at first, then she talks to you as if butter wouldn't melt.'

Lyndsey smiled. 'She's not the first. Joe was up here not long after the Inspector left, freaking out as if I'd personally declared the office a crime scene. I told him to contact the Inspector, and he glared at me as if I was speaking in tongues. In the end, I phoned Savage and asked him to liberate Joe's disgusting tea, which he did after taking some samples from the caddy. This is the nonsense I have to put up with. They are like spoilt children at times, though don't forget, poor old Gloria might have managed the catering if it wasn't for us awful vegans making things so difficult.'

They both laughed.

'Ooh, maybe Gloria killed FC and is annoyed she can't return to the scene of the crime?' said Mads.

'Don't start with that, I'm sure she'd have picked a time I wasn't here if that was the case.'

'I'm not so sure. I don't know why you're so quick to shoot down my theories.' She put on a hurt expression. 'Despite your cynicism, I'll hang out around the art books on this floor until you've had your second break. Assuming no one leaves anything suspicious, I'll slope off downstairs afterwards and earwig about a bit. Do you need anything? A cup of tea, perhaps?'

'No thanks, Mads. Walking to the break room gives me a welcome, albeit short, escape from the humdrum. Enjoy the art books.'

'I will, I'd forgotten how many interesting books they have, particularly here in the oversized section. Just as well FC didn't die in the art book aisle. I'd have been beside myself wanting to break through the tape.'

Lyndsey's lunch passed by note-free and Mads made her way downstairs with two books under her arm. She headed for the group study room where students could chat quietly and sat at a table in a corner. She was disappointed to discover that most talk in the room was study based, and the conversations that weren't, invariably involved planning nights out. After an hour she moved on and, after putting the books from upstairs on a trolley, sauntered around each floor of the library pretending to browse shelves.

On the third floor, she could hear a raised voice through a closed office door marked Librarians and positioned herself at a shelf where she had a clear view. A few minutes later, Gloria came strutting out leaving the door open behind her.

Mads moved closer to the doorway and perused a display shelf containing the latest journals and magazines the university subscribed to. Above the shelf was a poster advertising a forthcoming student play, "Death at Dinner". She hoped it was better than some of the student productions she remembered from her days as an undergraduate. She picked up an arts magazine and started thumbing through the pages.

'Don't let her upset you.'

'Easy for you to say.' Whoever was speaking sniffed. Mads listened to the sounds of a paper hanky being taken from a box and sneezed into.

'It's nothing personal. She talks to us all like that at times, and I've never worked out any rhyme or reason to her outbursts. Next time she sees you she'll act as if nothing happened.'

'That makes matters worse. If there was any kind of justification to her outbursts they might be avoidable, but there never is. I'm sick and tired of treading on eggshells. If I don't land that job I applied for I'm tempted to just leave.'

'Don't do anything rash. She's stressed from Francis dying over the weekend. You know the rumours about the notes the same as I do. Having threats hanging over your head would be enough to send anyone a bit crazy.'

'Stop making excuses. She's been unstable since her husband walked out on her, and I can't imagine how he put up with her for as long as he did. That she's been ten times worse since, makes me think he was her whipping boy until he finally saw sense and decided he'd had enough.'

'You might be right, but you need to give her some leeway. Just keep your head down and let her work her way through whatever's stressing her out.'

'Humph. Work her way through? I hope whoever's sending those notes isn't joking, and she's next on his list.'

'You don't mean that. If something was to happen to Gloria now, you'd be horrified that you said it out loud. Blow your nose again and I'll make you a cup of tea. Things will work themselves out, don't you worry.'

Mads moved away from the door to the other end of the display shelf to appear as if she wasn't intentionally listening to the conversation and waited for the librarian to come out. She was about 5 feet 8 inches tall and had mouse-brown hair to her shoulders fashioned into a side parting. She wore a brown dress, something that seemed a popular choice amongst the librarians along with grey or black. Mads mused over librarian attire. Was there a dress code or was it just the case that those drawn to librarianship were inclined to dress in a conservative fashion? As the woman walked past her, Mads decided to take a closer look at whoever Gloria had upset. She replaced the magazine in the rack and entered the office. Contrary to Mads' expectations, the librarian was wearing a bright red dress which, unfortunately, accentuated her red eyes.

Aha, the red sheep of the librarian family.

'Hello, sorry, I'm not sure who I need to ask, but I was wondering about post-grad arts courses the university offers. Could you help me, or point me towards someone who could?'

'Sorry, arts isn't my department, and you'd be better off asking at the art department office rather than here. They'll have all the information you want. Hold on, I'll find out where they are.'

She stood and walked across to a filing cabinet. She opened the drawer and rifled through some papers before pulling one out. She had dark brown hair, once again in a side parting but cut into a bob.

'Here you are,' she said as she sat down again and picked up a pink highlighter pen. 'We're here and you'll find the art department office here, across campus in the admin building,' she said as she dabbed both locations with a pink blob. 'I think they're on the first floor, but don't take my word for it. You'll find a list of departments on the wall as you go in, and failing that, I'm sure you'll find someone to ask.' She managed a smile as she handed the map to Mads.

'Thanks very much.'

She took the map and left the office. That was interesting, Lyndsey had been right about Gloria. She wasn't as nice as she thought she was, or at least wanted to appear.

But even taking into account the note that mentioned librarians, Mads couldn't imagine either of the women she'd just seen sending threatening notes, let alone killing anyone.

Then again, what if one of them had a friend or family member who also worked here and decided they had had enough of their loved one being bullied. Perhaps, one had a child who was a student at the uni, tying into the previous theory that it would be a student? Although neither of the librarians she had seen so far seemed old enough to have university-aged children, Lyndsey had said there were eight in all, perhaps some of the others were older.

Or what if they were all guilty? Not finding the backbone individually to confront the bullying management, they had concocted a scheme together in which they were all complicit. Hunting down and doing for the managers like a feral pack of wolves.

She liked this idea. All she needed now was some evidence to bring the principal players in this rendition of "Murder on the Library Express" to book.

Mads went to the second floor where she found a couple more art books, then returned to the third and sat in view of the librarians' office, staking them out.

Lyndsey stared across the kitchen table at Mads.

'So let me get this straight. You think the librarians are murdering the managers?' Lyndsey couldn't help but laugh at the thought.

'I'm just saying we shouldn't discount the idea. Given the way Gloria talks to them, I wouldn't be surprised if one of them snapped.'

Lyndsey fell into another spasm of laughter before wiping her eyes with her hands.

'Mads, you've seen the librarians? They wouldn't say boo to a pigeon, let alone dare to approach geese. And, just in case one minuscule detail didn't occur to you, Gloria's still alive. Francis is dead, and I don't think he ever shouted at anyone. He may have patronised a few people to within an inch of their lives, but I doubt that'd be enough to turn a librarian into a killing machine, let alone a pack of librarians slavering for blood.'

'What if one of their friends or family is acting on their behalf? The librarians may have no idea what horrors are being planned in their names.'

'Once again, why Francis?'

'Well ...'. Mads screwed up her face in concentration for a moment. 'They are trying to cover their tracks by making the deaths a series. That way the police will find it harder to make the connection.'

Lyndsey bent over the table and buried her head in her arms, laughing so hard that her sides hurt by the time she gained some sense of normality.

'Mads, no more theories, please, not tonight. Let my aching ribs rest a little. What you're suggesting makes no sense. You're saying, that instead of finding a job at a different university, a librarian, or someone working on their behalf, or an entire pack of rabid librarians—and I don't think that last one can possibly be overstated—concocted a plan to murder the library managers because none of them have much in the way of interpersonal skills? Listen to yourself. And stop giving me your death stare.'

Mads continued glaring. 'They may sound a little outlandish, but they are partly formed ideas and stranger things have happened. The only other suspect I have is Gloria. She comes across as dangerously unstable, and would have access to your desk and the office without raising suspicion.'

'Gloria is odd, I'll grant you, but I'm not sure that makes her a killer. I think her a thousand times more likely than the librarians, though. I'll keep an eye and an ear open for anything she says or does that appears suspicious, but I wouldn't hold your breath.'

'Fair enough, but just for laughing at me you can cook dinner. You have no appreciation for what hard work it is playing Nancy Drew.'

Lyndsey laughed again. 'No problem, what do you fancy? Or shall I just cobble together what I find?'

'Whatever you come up with will be great. I'm going to take a shower ... I expect dinner on the table by the time I'm back, else there will be big trouble, woman.'

She wagged her finger at Lyndsey.

'Yeah? If that's the case you'll want to delay the shower as you'll be wearing your dinner, Bucko.'

They both glared at each other, then burst out laughing.

'Goodness, what was that from? Was it a film?' asked Lyndsey.

'No, that god-awful play my ex, Chris, wrote and acted in at uni. Don't you remember, we both struggled to keep straight faces when we told him how much we'd enjoyed the show and how good he'd been?'

'That's right, "A Tube Train Named Desire".'

They both collapsed into laughter again.

'Spot on, and somehow the name was the best part of the entire production.'

'Never have I gone to anything with such low expectations and had them so savagely dashed.'

'I'm sure you won't ever again. As a boyfriend his days were already numbered by forcing me to audition then giving the part to that trollope, Katie Bradshaw. One of those glorious events you look back on and pinpoint as the exact moment a relationship was doomed to failure. I wonder if he stuck with theatre.'

'I hope not for the sake of audiences everywhere. I'd forgotten you did a bit of acting. You ought to take it up again, if only on an amateur basis. I'm sure there must be plenty of Amateur Dramatics groups in Chiswick and surrounding areas.'

'Maybe I will, though I haven't had much spare time of late. That's the kind of advice I needed three years ago.'

'Better late than never, as they say. Go and hop in the

shower, I'm starving

'OK, I still think the librarians and Gloria are in the frame, but make the most of your laughter now. I won't miss a chance to say "I told you so!" if I turn out to be right.'

When lunchtime arrived, Lyndsey felt she had already done a day's work. She saw Mads sitting at a table in the refectory and plonked herself down with a cup of tea.

Mads glanced across at her. 'You all right?'

'Grr, if Gloria keeps on like she's been this morning, I'll kill her myself. Three times I've calculated what we need to order for tomorrow's service, only for Gloria to tell me to rework everything. So much for her £500 limit, she's got me spending more than that on wine alone. It's just as well the supermarket offers free wine glass loans else I don't know what I'd have done.'

'This event sounds more interesting by the day. Can anyone attend?' Mads smiled.

'Yes, which is why Gloria's freaking out so much. We only have a vague idea of how many are coming and she doesn't want to order too little. At the same time, she worries about appearing profligate. Be warned, the wine isn't the same quality that you buy.'

'I'll bear that in mind, though I've reluctantly become accustomed to the sad fact that to find wine of the same or better quality than mine, I'd have to search out an old mate.'

'Anyone I know?'

'I don't think so, but Chappo's nose for wine is legendary. He used to go on mega tasting tours in France and order the best ones by the case. I swear, if he could have lived on nothing but cheese and wine, he'd have done so. Best thing is, he falls asleep after two glasses so everyone else drinks more of the wine than he does. I'll find his number and get us an invitation for an evening of Dionysian delights.'

'I can't wait.'

'You'll like them, him and his wife are two of the loveliest people you could wish to meet. What time does the service start?'

'Three o'clock, after all, we wouldn't want management types to have to encroach on their lunch breaks for something like a memorial service, would we?'

'I'm sure everything will go fine. Just point me towards the vegan nibbles and I'll occupy myself happily. Are you having to lay everything out as well?'

'Yes, with the aid of some elves, and to make matters worse the supermarket has no delivery slots at this late stage, either. I'll have to collect everything. May I borrow the van?'

'Of course, I'll even drive and help with the loading and unloading. How does that sound?'

'Thanks, I was hoping you had nothing else to do. At least they'll pick the order tonight and have it waiting for us. The person I spoke to wasn't keen at first, but when I mentioned it was all for a funeral service she became ever so helpful. What have you been up to this morning?'

'Not much, mooching around keeping ears and eyes

open. You would be surprised how few people in real life lurk in corners, rubbing their hands together while muttering "Mwahaha" to themselves.'

Lyndsey laughed. 'Would it astound you if I guessed right first time?'

'All the students act just like we remember students behaving, though they do more studying than we used to.'

'That's because the ones in the library are taking academic courses rather than arts degrees. I've always had a certain admiration for anyone willing to submerge themselves in the sheer amount of work it takes to gain a degree in psychology or similar. Every day the entire group are in the library studying together. I don't mind spending time and effort learning things, but I could never sign up for a course knowing there was that much work to do. I'd feel defeated before I began.'

'On the plus side, at least you'd know why you felt like that,' said Mads with a smile.

When she got back to her desk, Lyndsey was pleased to find a note from Gloria approving the last shopping list she had compiled. She navigated to the supermarket website to confirm the provisional order that she had saved. With that task done, she went to make herself a celebratory cup of tea.

Meanwhile, Mads had found a couple of interesting books on van Gogh and sat at the small table at the end of the row parallel to the group chat section on the third floor to browse and make a few notes while keeping an ear open for any interesting conversations that sprung up. She hadn't been sitting more than ten minutes when a student approached her.

'Sorry to bother you, are you using that book?' She pointed towards the one Mads wasn't reading. 'I only need it for a few minutes.'

'Help yourself,' said Mads, sliding the book across the table towards her.

'Thanks.'

'Sit there if you like,' said Mads, pointing to the chair across the table.

'If no one's here I will, thanks.'

She flicked through the book finding the section she needed and started scribbling a few notes down. Twenty minutes later, she slid the book back to Mads.

'Thanks for that, you can only get so far with the internet and I have to hand the assignment in tomorrow.'

'No problem, are you second year?'

'Yes, I was nervous coming in here, what with the death and everything. How about you? Are you in a different group?'

'No, I graduated a few years ago. I'm just doing some research as alumni for inspiration. How are you finding the course?'

'Loving it, but there's so much to do. I don't find time to paint any more, except for assignments. Once I graduate, I'll have time to create what I want.'

Mads smiled, remembering back to the time when she held such unrealistic ideas.

'It'll surprise you how much time life takes once you leave uni. One of the most frequent complaints people have after finishing an arts course is that they stressed too much about unimportant details and didn't realise how much time they had. Make sure you free up time to pursue what interests you, alongside everything you need to complete for the course.'

Mads stopped a moment and reflected that she was sounding like her mother.

'Still, enough of my unasked-for advice. Why does the death make you nervous?'

'I don't know, it's strange that someone who I only spoke to a couple of weeks ago is dead. I don't think I've known anyone who's died before. Sheltered life, I suppose. Don't you find it spooky?'

'Not sure about that. At night when it's quiet it might be, but during the day when students are milling about it's more like evidence that life goes on regardless, wouldn't you say?'

She shrugged. 'I guess that I haven't had the same experience of death that someone your age has.'

Mads watched as the young woman's face reacted in shock to the words she heard herself say and the expression on Mads' face.

'Oh god, I'm sorry. I didn't mean you're old, just older than me.'

'Don't worry about it. I must resemble a blonde dinosaur to someone your age.'

Mads reset her face, though her reaction hadn't been to the comment on her perceived age. It had been to the semi-whispered words she had heard from the other side of the bookshelf, "So how should we kill the second one?".

20

'What do you mean, you didn't see who said it? Whoever it was was a bookshelf away.'

'I know, but by the time I'd convinced the girl that her age comment hadn't offended me, they were leaving. Of course, if I'm honest, I was mortified, but I couldn't let it show. Do I really look that old?'

'To a nineteen-year-old, I'm sure you do. I bet you're older than some of her tutors, given the rush by universities to employ ever younger and cheaper. Enough of your vanity, what did you see?'

'The backs of two guys as they walked out to the lift lobby. By the time I got there the lift had come and gone. I'll recognise one of the student's jackets if I see it again. He had an elaborate dragon embroidered on the back and they are sure to go to the library again, don't you think?'

Lyndsey sighed. 'If not, the refectory before lectures start at ten and two might make for fertile hunting ground.'

'Excellent idea, I hadn't thought of that. Let's hope he wears the same jacket every day.' Mads parked the van as close to the supermarket doors as she could. 'Shall we use the sack barrow or trollies?'

'The sack barrow would be best. Imagine the mess a wobbly trolley full of wine and glasses would make if it tipped over? If we have to make a few journeys, so be it.'

'OK, let's do this.'

They approached the customer services counter, where an employee was very pleased to see them as the boxes they were collecting were taking up more space than was usual for collections and getting in his way. After asking them both to provide proof of age, something that cheered Mads up no end, they loaded the sack trolley and took some wine to the van first. As Mads transferred it into the van, Lyndsey went back in to collect more.

Before long, everything was loaded and they drove back at the university where Lyndsey commandeered a large platform trolley so they only needed to make a single trip to the hall where the service was being held. By the time they had set everything up and labelled it all for dietary requirements, it was almost lunchtime. Lyndsey put some sheets over the food and turned to Mads.

'Fancy grabbing some lunch?'

'I thought we were nibbling as we went? I'm stuffed.'

'Mads!'

Mads laughed. 'Oh, stop it, your face is a picture. There's plenty of food left, don't you worry. And I approve of your selections, I could do with a cup of tea to wash everything down, mind. I guess you'd disapprove of me sampling the wine before everything starts?'

Lyndsey gave her a glare and scanned the tables to check everything was covered.

'You go and find a table in the refectory, I'll contact Security to lock up the room while we're gone, just in case there are any other people who fancy grazing. I should have thought to ask him for the key when he opened the room for us, it didn't occur to me.'

'Not to worry, I'll buy you a tea. And I'd recommend those vegan sausage rolls while you're waiting.'

Mads winked at her and left the room.

21

'Wow, everything looks lovely,' said Gloria as she swept into the room at 2.30. 'You've put together a wonderful spread, Lyndsey, and written little cards with dietary information. Splendid stuff. Is everything else ready?'

Lyndsey nodded. 'Yes, the sound system is set up and Faruq is sending five library elves across to serve wine to act as waiters in a few minutes. Anything else you can think of that needs doing? Oh, this is my friend Mads who gave me a hand with collecting everything and the setting up.'

'Hello, Mads,' said Gloria, 'thanks for helping.'

'No problem, I send the invoice to you, yes?'

Gloria's eyebrows rose and her mouth opened wide before Mads laughed.

'Don't worry, I'm only joking.'

'Oh, right.' She took a few seconds to breathe deeply and relax her facial muscles back into a tight smile. 'Funny one. I'll go and check the sound man has everything under control. Well done, Lyndsey.'

She walked across the hall and Lyndsey slapped Mads

on the arm.

'What are you doing, I have to work for that woman?' she hissed into her ear.

'Oh relax, she's just nervous about the service.'

'No, I'd bet good money she's wound that tight after a massage. She can be unpredictable, as I've told you. What do you have planned for this afternoon? I can't imagine you'll be staying just for the speeches.'

'I want to study the crowd. My guy in the jacket might turn up for one, and if not I want to keep an eye out for anything or anyone suspicious.'

'Ah, your fictional theory about criminals turning up to the scene of the crime or anything related to it?'

'Don't knock it, you can only imagine how many books and films it took to gain me this much knowledge. I've no idea why anyone bothers with criminology degrees, to be honest.'

'Ha, I'm sure there would be more to the degree than you think. Excellent, here come the elves. I'll leave you to your own devices while I organise them. Don't, I repeat don't, talk to Gloria unless she approaches you. And if she does, no more of your "jokes", OK?'

'You're no fun, but I'll manage. If the elves want to test their skills, I'll have a glass of the white, please.' She smiled sweetly at Lyndsey as if butter wouldn't melt in her mouth.

Lyndsey shook her head and strolled across to the small gang of elves.

'Hi, I'm thinking one of you pour glasses of wine at the drinks table, three walk around with wine on trays and the other can be in charge of the food tables? So, who wants to do what?'

The elves glanced at each other, then all at once the two more stationary jobs got snapped up by the quickest thinkers.

'Thanks, guys, I'll leave you to it. All muck in to fill the table with pre-poured glasses first so people don't have to wait as they come in, and if you need anything I'll be floating around by the door greeting people.'

The elves took their places at the tables and organised themselves into a wine pouring machine. Lyndsey smiled and walked away, but after a couple of steps turned back again and retrieved two glasses of white wine, one of which she offered to Mads.

'I hope this all goes well, I'm under no illusions it will turn out to be my fault if it doesn't.'

'Don't worry about it, you're a temp. Management always blame their underlings, which is why they have them. Football club directors used to pick the teams each week until they realised they would receive far less grief from the fans if they employed a scapegoat to take the flak for poor results. Thus was born the football manager who, in turn, employs coaches, and so on.'

'Really? Football, Mads? I've never known you mention the game, how did you become so knowledgeable?'

'Don't get excited, I've exhausted my football knowledge with that snippet, and I got it from a newspaper article that used it as an analogy for the class system.'

'And another first, Mads the socialist. Who are you and what have you done to my friend?'

'Yeah, yeah. Hey, the crowd is starting to filter in. I'll leave you to point them to the food and drink and ready myself for a tough afternoon mingling and observing.'

'Don't wear yourself out, I'll catch you later. And stay away from my bosses!'

Mads sauntered off and spent the next twenty minutes looking out for the student from the library and listening to random conversations as she moved about. An elf passed within arm's length and she placed her empty glass on the drinks tray while picking up a fresh one.

'Well, well. If it isn't Ms Walsh. Not poking your nose anywhere it has no business, I hope?'

Mads turned around to face the speaker with a beaming smile on her face.

'Inspector Savage, how lovely to meet you again. No innocent civilians for you to arrest elsewhere?'

'Not something I'm in the habit of doing, Ms Walsh. Your friend was helping me with my enquiries. So what are you doing here?'

'I helped Lyndsey with the setting up and thought I'd make sure she didn't finish the day murdered. After all, the police don't appear to be much of a deterrent in that respect, do they?'

He raised his eyebrow. 'I told Miss Marshall and I'll tell you. Do not involve yourself with trying to solve this case. If you come across anything suspicious, tell me immediately. Is that clear?'

'Of course, Inspector. Not that I'm likely to, am I? I come in to use the library occasionally as alumni, but aside from that I mind my own business.'

'Yet here you are. I don't believe in coincidences, Ms Walsh. Please don't test my patience.'

'I shan't, Inspector. Well, as lovely as it's been catching up with you, I'm going to find somewhere to watch the speeches. I have no doubt we'll meet again.'

'Goodbye, Ms Walsh. And remember what I said. Don't go poking the bear.'

She smiled and strolled off across the room and stood against the wall where she could view the room and gauge as many reactions from the audience as possible. After forty-five minutes of speeches about what a wonderful person Francis had been, she wandered across towards the drinks table and joined Lyndsey.

'Thrilling stuff, eh?' she whispered.

'I can't recognise the Francis I knew from these platitudes, I really can't.'

'The usual after death whitewash. I think they should hold memorial services while people are alive so you could secretly watch on video and pretend that everyone loves you.'

Lyndsey stifled a laugh. 'I'm not sure that would work, but an interesting idea. I hope they stop yakking soon, we'll run out of wine before the mingling and chatting part if they don't.'

'Speaking of which,' said Mads, turning towards the wine table where she put down her empty glass and picked up two white wines before turning back. Lyndsey reached out to take one.

'Oh, sorry. Did you want one? I was stocking up because I heard tell of an impending shortage. Here you go.' She handed her a glass and moved back to pick up a replacement. 'Go easy, Lynds, I'll need a designated driver for the trip home.'

'You're terrible, people like you create the shortages, and the designated driver horse bolted a couple of glasses ago so we'll have to catch the bus and pick the van up in the morning,' said Lyndsey, just as the Vice-Chancellor finished his speech and invited everyone to observe a minute's silence to remember Francis.

As the silence neared its end, there was a crash, and Lyndsey spun around to see Gloria fall into a heap on the floor. Some of the food table's contents lay scattered on the floor where she had dragged the tablecloth on her way down.

'Oh no, do you think she's drunk?' she asked Mads.

Mads put her arm around Lyndsey to whisper quietly in her ear. 'I'm no expert, Lynds, but given the grey pallor to her face, I think it more likely she's dead.'

22

Within seconds, Inspector Savage squatted by Gloria and took her pulse. He whipped out his phone and speed dialled a number.

'This is Savage. Get an ambulance to the university memorial service immediately along with as many officers as we can spare to interview the witnesses. I'd guess there are about two hundred present, so it could take some time ... a woman has collapsed, she's still breathing and has a faint pulse.'

He hung up and laid his jacket beneath Gloria's head before he stood.

'Ladies and gentlemen,' he said to the crowd who were closing in to peer at Gloria's body. 'Could you all move back to allow the lady some air, please. No one may leave this room until you have given a statement to one of my officers who will be here shortly. Sorry for any inconvenience, but you are all potential witnesses and may have seen something relevant. We will try to be as quick as we can. Thank you for your cooperation.'

His assistant, whom Lyndsey had never met before,

stood by the doors to reinforce the point that no one should leave. Within five minutes, an ambulance crew appeared. After checking Gloria and having a brief conversation with Inspector Savage, they secured her to a stretcher and wheeled her out. Inspector Savage turned to the elves behind the food and drink tables who had all clustered together in a group.

'I'll interview you all myself as you're most likely to have seen something relevant. Bear with me. Who organised the food and drink? Do you know?'

As five heads turned to face Mads and Lyndsey, Inspector Savage followed their eyes and sighed.

'Would you ladies mind coming with me, please? Let's find somewhere quiet for a chat.' He moved towards the doors and they both followed. 'John, no one else is to leave until the team have their statements, please. They'll be here soon. Once they arrive, get them interviewing people from the main audience. I'll do the workers myself.'

'Will do, sir.'

They walked through the doors and Inspector Savage signalled that they should follow him towards the lifts. When they reached the fourth floor, he walked past Lyndsey's desk and sat in the break room, inviting Mads and Lyndsey to do the same with a wave of his hand. He sighed again and took his notebook from his pocket before looking at them both.

'Why is it that every time someone dies around here, you two aren't far away? And before you jump to conclusions, I don't think you're guilty of killing anyone. I'm just intrigued at your uncanny ability for sensing impending death, like a pair of mascaraed vultures.'

Mads and Lyndsey gave each other a look, but said nothing in reply.

'OK, so walk me through your day.'

Lyndsey gave him a summary of everything they'd done while he took some notes.

'So the food and drink was unsupervised for about an hour and a half during lunch?'

She nodded. 'Yes, but I called security and they locked the door so nobody could have tampered with it.'

'I assume there are other keys?'

'I expect so, you'll have to ask security. We left here just before one and got back about quarter past two. Nothing had been disturbed, at least, nothing we noticed.'

'Fair enough, so did you see any suspicious characters around the food or drink tables? Did anyone take anything to give to Gloria, for instance?'

'I didn't,' said Lyndsey, 'but I was more interested in checking whether we ran out of anything or how the elves were doing rather than people helping themselves to food and drink. Did anything leap out at you, Mads?'

Mads shook her head. 'No, sorry. I was mingling until the speeches started. When I joined Lyndsey, we stood facing the stage with our backs to the tables.'

'The elves?' asked the Inspector with a raised eyebrow.

Lyndsey laughed. 'It's just a general nickname for the library assistants. I'm not sure who started it, but they refer to themselves as elves, so they don't consider it an offensive term.'

'Thank you, ladies. I assume your details haven't changed in the last few weeks?'

'I've moved to Mads's house, as I think I told you the other day, but aside from that we have the same phone numbers as before.'

Savage made another note. 'I'll let you both go. We will be interviewing for the next couple of hours, so I suggest you go home and return to tidy up in the morning, though we will take the food and any opened, unconsumed wine with us for testing. Is there anything else?'

'How is Gloria? I assume she was alive when the paramedics wheeled her off?'

'She was, yes, but obviously, I've heard nothing since. I'm hoping she'll pull through and be able to help us with our enquiries. Well, I have a very busy afternoon ahead of me, so I won't detain you any longer. Here is my card should anything occur to you.'

They both nodded as they took a card from him and left the room. Once they were in the lift, Mads turned to Lyndsey.

'I guess I can scratch Gloria off the suspect list? We're down to the librarians, the elves, or the student with the jacket.'

Lyndsey raised an eyebrow. 'Or two hundred others present at the memorial service. And the elves? You're adding the elves?'

'They were working the food and drink stalls, no one would have been better placed to tamper with something Gloria consumed.'

'Yes, but they would also realise they would be prime suspects if something happened.'

'They could have underestimated the time it would take for the poison to take effect. And while I take your point about the other attendees, I find it unlikely that someone randomly poisoned something in the hope Gloria would pick it up. It would have to have been somebody who delivered it to her, and if anyone took some wine or food to Gloria, I'm sure Savage will be all over them like a rash.'

The lift opened, and they both stepped out.

'Let me drop the keys to the room off to Security and

tell them I'll tidy up in the morning when the police have finished.'

'No problem, home, change and down the pub. I think you need another drink before any shock takes hold. We need to check out that refurbished pub in Brentford, The Dachshund. It's only been open a couple of days and from what I've heard, they have a great beer selection.'

By the time they'd got home, changed and caught a bus to Brentford, they didn't arrive at the Dachshund until about seven-thirty and were both surprised when they opened the door and walked into the warm and welcoming atmosphere of a full pub.

'Wow, hard to believe this is the same pub as the old one,' said Lyndsey. She pointed to the table just inside the door. 'Shall we sit here, I don't see any other tables free?'

'Yes, grab it now before someone else does. Let's peruse the menu and choose what to eat before we order drinks.'

They removed their jackets and sat on the bench seat with their backs to the wall, both still marvelling at the place. There was chatter from all the tables and, although Lyndsey saw an album cover displayed behind the bar above a lighted sign stating "NOW PLAYING", no music was audible over the myriad conversations.

'Real vinyl, just like the Railway. This is what I call a renovation. Do you remember the old place? I think we only came here once then pretended it didn't exist.'

'Something like that. Wasn't this one of the Brentford pubs where there was a stabbing?' asked Mads, picking up the menu.

'Yes, ages ago. It didn't have much going for it before, and that didn't help. It stayed closed for years, I hate to think what a nightmare it was to clean after all that time.'

'They've done a stunning job, and they have a vegan

option on the menu. Saffron, tomato, aubergine, and chickpea stew with lemon barley and couscous. I assume we're both hungry, not just me?' She grinned across the menu at Lyndsey.

'I'm starving. Those snacks filled a gap, but I need something more substantial now. Let's give it a go. What do you want to drink?'

'Don't you worry, It's my round.'

'Mads, you're always buying, give a girl a chance.'

'I can afford it, you buy the next round. Do you want whatever I'm having or do you want to check them out first? It looks a decent choice up there.'

'Whatever you like the look of. After today I'm not minded to be fussy.'

'Back in a mo.'

Mads went to the bar, ordered the food and sampled a couple of beers before making her mind up. She walked back to the table and placed one in front of Lyndsey.

'If you don't like it, I'll have them both and buy you something else.'

'Why wouldn't I like it? What is it?'

'Tiny Rebel brew, Pump Up the Jam. Think liquid jam doughnut in a glass. Try it.'

Lyndsey raised her eyebrow and gave Mads a stare. 'You're kidding me, right?'

Mads said nothing, just picked up her glass and took a mouthful. Lyndsey picked hers up and did the same.

'Oh wow, this is gorgeous.' She took a larger mouthful and let it roll down her throat, savouring the flavours as they went down. 'At this rate, my body will think it's full before the food arrives.'

'How decadent are we, drinking our pudding before dinner's delivered?'

Just after nine o'clock next morning, Mads and Lyndsey collected the keys from the security office and headed to the room where the service had been, not having a clue what state they would find it in and expecting the worst. Lyndsey unlocked the door and paused for a moment before pushing it open and looking around, finding everything neat and tidy with wine boxes neatly stacked against the wall next to the boxes full of glasses.

'Oh, I wasn't expecting that.'

Mads followed her in and smiled. 'I guess the elves or the police did most of the heavy lifting for us. All we have to do is recycle the rubbish and give the keys back. Are the boxes full of empties or are we the proud owners of a veritable wine lake?'

Lyndsey walked across and checked some boxes on top of the pile.

'I think they're all empty. I'm sure someone on a higher pay grade than mine organised the removal of any remaining wine.'

'Typical. Never mind, at least this is easy. We just

have to take them to a recycling bin and everything will be done. I assume the university has a recycling facility somewhere?'

'There are loads of small bins all over the place, but if I contact Cleaning Services, I'm sure they'll take these to some giant glass and cardboard bins for us, or at least point me in the right direction. Thanks for coming, I was expecting everything to be in a right old state.'

'Me too. Come on, let's ring the cleaners. If I'm not needed for anything else, I'll drop the glasses back on the way home and press on with a few bits I need to do.'

Mads stacked the glasses onto the sack barrow and carefully wheeled it out. Lyndsey locked the door behind them and they headed for the lifts. One was waiting, and they entered the car to come face to face with Joe. Seeing it was her, he pressed doors open button.

'Ah, Lyndsey. I was just coming up to your desk. No point in travelling all the way to the fourth floor now. Could you sort out a card and some flowers or something for Gloria, please? I rang the hospital when I got in and they said she's stable and allowed visitors. If everyone who's in can sign the card, I'll drop it over to her this afternoon. I was planning to leave about three o'clock.'

'Sure, shall I ask Faruq for some petty cash?'

'Yes, that makes sense. And while you're in his office, make sure you grab one of the leftover boxes of wine as a thank you for all your hard work in putting the memorial service together. There are three piled up in the corner, you can't miss them. I think both red and white are left, so take your pick.'

'Really? Thanks very much.'

'You're welcome. I'll hunt you down at three to collect the card and everything.' He walked out of the lift, leaving the doors to glide shut behind him.

'Who was that?' asked Mads.

'That was Joe, the miserable, rude boss I've moaned about countless times.'

'Really? I wouldn't have recognised him from your description.'

'Too right, I think aliens have replaced him overnight. There wasn't a fleet of lorries loaded with giant pods in the car park, was there?'

'I can't say I saw any. He doesn't seem miserable to me, you don't think he's the killer, do you? Overjoyed that the others are out of the way?'

Lyndsey thought for a moment. 'I didn't, but he's acting strangely. I swear that's the first time I've heard him use the words please and thank you, let alone giving me a box full of wine. I think he deserves to move up the suspect league table.'

Once they reached her desk, she rang Cleaning Services who told her not to worry as they'd sort out the recycling, then went to ask for some petty cash and grab a box of wine from Faruq, via security where they dropped the room keys back. Faruq's office was empty so they selected a box of white and carried it out to the van.

'That was a forward thinking move, getting them in boxes of twelve,' said Mads. 'You couldn't have planned it better.'

'I have no idea if Joe's aware how many are in a box or not, but I'm not bothering to check. He might have reverted to his normal mood by now.'

'Definitely, gift horses, mouths and all that gubbins.'

Lyndsey laughed. 'I couldn't put it better myself. Now, what should I buy for Gloria? Is it considered poor form to buy chocolates or fudge for a poison victim?'

'I'd buy vegan fudge. If she doesn't want it, anyone who visits her can tuck in.'

'You sound as if you're planning a visit yourself. OK, card, a box of fudge and a bunch of flowers should do it.'

'I can't imagine she'll complain with a selection like that,' said Mads, strapping the wine and glasses into the back of the van to stop them moving around. 'Do you want a lift anywhere?'

'No thanks, I'll just pop to the High Street. If I go too far, I'll have farther to walk back.'

'Fair enough. I'll catch you back at the house later.'

'You will. And Mads, try to leave a bottle of wine for me, won't you?'

'Haha, I'll try.'

24

Mads drove off, pleased to get away from the university and have a little time to herself. Over the past few days she'd had plenty of time to think as she lurked around the library, and now it was time to enact the next stage of her investigative plan.

On arriving home, she found her notebook containing all Barry's numbers with notes and proper names where she had discovered them. She flicked through until she found the one she wanted and called the number.

'Hello?'

'Hello, is that Mr Chowdhury?'

'Yes, who is this?'

'I'm interested in renting a flat and believe you have one free on Addams Avenue.'

There was a pause.

'No, I have none available at the moment. I'm not allowed to rent that flat out yet, I have to wait on lawyers and the Government to give me the OK.'

'Why's that, it must be costing you a fortune?'

'Tell me about it. They say I can't throw the ex-tenant's

property out until they have found a relative to claim it or three months have passed, so the flat's full of all his stuff.'

'What if I paid you a lower rent for three months and in return, put his stuff into storage so when they come looking for it they can take it from there?'

Mads heard Mr Chowdhury suck his breath through teeth at the other end, like a plumber about to give a high quote on a prospective job.

'I'm not sure, if something goes wrong it would be my responsibility.'

'I'll write up a contract taking responsibility for the property and offer you £400 a month for the flat for the next three months as well as paying to move and store all the goods. That way at least you're getting some money in. After the three months, we can negotiate a higher rent, if you like. I'll even pay you up front for the first three.'

'What about a security deposit?'

Mads smiled.

Got him.

'As I'm paying in advance, I don't think a deposit's appropriate, do you? Of course, once we negotiate a higher rent I'll be only too happy to treat it like a normal lease.'

'The rent will be £800 from February, and I'll need a security deposit of £1500.'

'With the deposit also paid in February?'

'Can we agree £500 a month for the flat now, so £1500 today and £2300 by February 1st to continue renting.'

Mads paused for a moment to make it appear as if she was thinking it over.

'Fair enough, Mr Chowdhury, you have a deal. Can I meet you at the flat this morning so we can complete the deal and exchange cash for keys? I'll type out a couple of quick contracts to put this arrangement on a businesslike footing and we can sign a proper lease in January. How does that sound?'

'I'm busy this morning, but can be there for midday. Is that convenient?'

'Yes, midday will be fine. My name's Mads, and thanks.'

Excellent, she thought. That gives me time to rent a storage unit and pop to the bank. But first, a cup of tea.

She drank it at the computer while knocking together a couple of pages, one describing the deal they had agreed and the other taking full responsibility for storing Barry's property. Once happy with the wording, she printed them out twice and set off to the bank to withdraw the money.

At the storage facility, she approached a young man behind the counter who appeared to be no more than fifteen years old and seemed woefully out of place in a suit and tie. She explained that she needed to store the contents of her flat for two or three months while she redecorated and asked if there was anything suitable near the 2100s as her friend had a unit somewhere around there and they'd like to be close if possible. He tapped at the computer, stopping every few seconds to move his floppy fringe from his eyes while he studied the screen.

'You're in luck, madam. Units 2127 and 2128 became available yesterday. Would you like to check they will be suitable?'

'Yes please,' replied Mads, and followed him to the lift and through the maze of units until they reached 2121-2140.

'Here they are, just along here,' said Floppy Fringe, stopping by the unit that read 2127 and raising the roller door.

Mads peered in while he opened 2128, and checked in there too, though as they were identical in size and design it seemed superfluous to do so.

'They're perfect, but I'm not sure how much space I'll need,' she said, smiling at him. 'Could I take one of them now and ask you to hold the other until later? I'll have a better idea once I've finished boxing everything up.'

'I suppose so, but I won't be able to hold it past 4.30.'

'That would be lovely, thank you so much.'

She gave him a beaming grin, and he closed the roller doors once more and led her back to the office where she filled out enough paperwork to have laid waste to a small forest and handed him her ID to copy. Once the legalities were complete, she got back in the van and headed for Hounslow.

She couldn't imagine she would need the second unit, but if the furniture was Barry's it might be necessary. There was a space outside the house, and she parked up and sat there for ten minutes waiting for the time to inch its way to midday. A couple of minutes before, a man who she assumed to be Mr Chowdhury walked along the road before turning into the front garden of the house where the flat was. Mads got out the van and followed him up the path.

'Mr Chowdhury? Hello, I'm Mads.'

She held out her hand as he turned and he shook it.

'You're early, please come in.'

She followed him through the front door and into the flat. It was no different to the last time they had been in there, except the pile of mail had grown.

'This is it, sorry about the mess. They told me not to throw anything out, so I just left it as it was.'

'No problem, I'll soon sort everything into boxes and into a storage unit where it will be safe. Is the furniture yours, or did it belong to the previous tenant?'

'The furniture's mine, so don't take that. Unless you wanted to move it out temporarily to decorate, of course?' he said with a hopeful smile.

'Not straight away, but once Christmas is out of the way I'll give it serious consideration.'

She scanned the rest of the flat as if it was the first time she'd seen it, opening and closing the cupboards and checking behind anything free-standing. All this would easily fit into one unit so she wouldn't need the second one.

'This will be ideal,' she said, reaching into her bag. 'I drew up these two agreements so we can sign them, that way there will be no questions about everything we discussed earlier.'

Mr Chowdhury took the sheets from her and read them. 'I'm happy with what you've written here. Do you have a pen?'

Mads produced one from her bag and handed it to him so he could sign the agreements while she took the money from her purse and counted it out. She handed it to him to check and signed the agreements herself.

'Thanks for finding me a solution to my problem, Mads. Here are the keys and I'll post a proper lease agreement through the door in January so you can have everything ready for the end of the month.'

'Wonderful, thanks very much.'

'May I ask how you knew the flat was empty?'

'I'm a friend of the last tenant's ex-girlfriend. I saw her yesterday and mentioned I was looking for somewhere to live and she told me this place might be available and gave me your number. Lucky meeting, really. I hate flat hunting.'

'Why did you leave your last place?'

Mads sighed. 'I broke up with my boyfriend,' she said. 'I've been sleeping on a friend's couch for a few weeks, but that can't last forever.'

'Fair enough, let me take the gas and electricity readings while we're here and we can both verify them. Then I'll leave you to settle in, or move out, I suppose would be a better description. Did you hire a storage unit?'

'I already had one for my stuff, so I can simultaneously move all this in as my things come out.'

He took the readings and wrote them on the bottom of both copies of the rent agreement and added his phone number to Mads' copy.

'I know you have it, but it doesn't hurt to write it here too. Could you add your number to my copy, please?'

Mads did so annd thankd Mr Chowdhury again as she saw him to the door, then flopped onto the sofa and breathed a sigh of relief. That had gone pretty well. She picked up the pile of unopened mail and flicked through the envelopes. Most were bills and advertising until she came across a letter with the storage company's logo printed on it. She put the rest back on the coffee table and sat there staring at the envelope in her hands.

Come on, Mads. Yes, it's illegal, but he's dead.

She threw caution to the wind and opened the letter. It was a reminder for Barry, stating he needed to make another payment by the end of the month for his lock-up. She laughed to herself.

Oh well, both units needed after all. Best ring Floppy Fringe and buy two padlocks from the hardware store on my way back.

Mads arrived home at 4.30, took a pie she had made a few weeks ago out of the freezer and popped it into the oven to bake along with two large potatoes. She set the oven timer for 45 minutes and poured herself a generous measure of Sipsmith's VSOP, mixed it with a bottle of Mediterranean tonic and sat in the armchair in the front room with her eyes shut, trying to ooze the achiness from her body. She must have dozed off, as the next thing she heard was Lyndsey's key in the door.

'Hi, Lynds, I'm in the front room.' She picked up her G&T from the arm of the chair and took a sip.

Lovely, we must book a tour, being as the distillery's only down the road.

'Hey, Mads. What are you making? It smells delicious?'

'Do you remember that soya chunk and mushroom pie I threw together the other week? This is its sister.'

'Yummy, let me freshen up and I'll give you a hand.'

By the time Lyndsey came back downstairs, Mads was ready to serve.

'What do you fancy doing tonight?' asked Mads.

'I don't mind, but I'd rather not have a serious session anywhere. Staggering home in the early hours of the morning when we need to leave for the market at five is getting old and I'm not getting any younger.'

Mads laughed. 'Oh, you poor old thing. I'll search the market tomorrow, try to pick you up a nice walking stick, dear.'

'Laugh all you like, but with this job, I'm not getting time to recharge my batteries. Having said that, I wouldn't mind a couple down the Cow's Tail or something.'

'Sounds like a fair compromise, though we'd best not leave too late. The Tail fills quickly when the weather's too cold to sit outside by the river.'

'We'll need to wrap up warm, the wind out there is bitter, swirling every which way.'

They were both refreshed for getting some food inside themselves and prepared to face the elements.

'I hope it doesn't rain,' said Mads as they walked out the door. 'An umbrella will be next to useless in this.'

'As long as it stops before the weekend, it can do what it likes. I'd rather it rained now than when we're working the stalls.'

'True enough, but I don't think weather works like that.'

'Conveniently?'

'Not in my experience. Wind and rain only exist so they can mess up my hair at the worst possible moments.'

'It's all part of a conspiracy. I hear the BBC weather presenter has changed her name to Carol "Scourge of Mads" Kirkwood by deed poll.'

'This is what I'm saying? They're not even bothering to hide it now. I'd become accustomed to the Tory bias on BBC news, but messing with a girl's hair is beyond the pale.'

'Not beyond the blonde?'

'I like that. Rhyming and alliteration in a simple phrase. I think I'll start using it.'

'As long as you don't mind people thinking you're bonkers, you carry on.'

'Are you saying there might be people who don't?'

'How would I know? Aside from work I pretty much only talk to you and I'm used to your ways by now.'

They turned into the small road that led to the river and Mads thrust her hands deep into her coat pockets in reaction to the wind that whipped past them along the narrow channel. She was thankful to reach the pub and shut out the cold behind them. They both ordered a pint of Wimbledon Hop Harvest and sat at a table by the window in an alcove.

'This is better,' said Mads. 'Lovely and warm, a real fire burning and a beer in hand, while looking through the window knowing how horrible it is outside.'

'I used to love wet lunchtimes at school when I was ten or eleven and they wouldn't let us out. We'd sit in the hut our classroom was in, listening to the rain pounding against the roof and windows and feel all the cosier for it. No real fire or beer more's the pity, but you could cause yourself a nasty burn if you rested your hand on the radiator too long.'

'We had radiators like that at my primary school. The boys used to spit on them to watch their saliva bubble as it evaporated but us young ladies were too demure for the likes of that.'

'You know, Mads. For all your sweet little smiles and the "butter wouldn't melt" innocent looks you pull, I can't imagine you were ever demure.'

Mads laughed. 'Fair enough, busted. So how was your day? Did you sort the card?'

'Humph. Joe appeared at three, took the flowers, card, and box of fudge and swanned off to the hospital. I bet he'll take the credit for them, too.'

'Was he still acting weird?'

'Yes, he still seemed very pleased with himself. The more I think about it, the likelihood he's the killer goes up and up. He could have left the notes when I was at lunch without causing any suspicion.'

'And he was the one who told you to ignore them.'

'Do you think I should mention anything to Savage?'

Mads pondered the question for a moment. 'I wouldn't go that far. Were there any witnesses when he collected the card and presents from you?'

'No, I was upstairs on my own. Why?'

'Well ... it's a bit of a leap ...'

'No, not you Mads? Taking a bit of a leap?'

'Yeah, yeah, but hear me out. If he is the killer, fudge might have been a bad idea. What if he injected a piece before he handed it to Gloria?'

'You don't think he would, do you? It would be traceable to him as he was the one who delivered it.'

'But would it? You bought everything, and when you got the card signed you would have told people what else you'd bought. There were no witnesses to Joe taking the fudge, so the trail ends with you?'

'Don't even think about it. The last thing I need is for Savage to interrogate me again. The only thing that kept me together last time was the knowledge that your solicitor would soon be down to rescue me.'

'And she would be again, don't you worry. I was just following the thought through. If he poisoned a piece of fudge, she may not eat it for a few days, concealing where the poison came from.' Mads' phone rang, and she furrowed her brow as she studied the screen. 'This is an international call, I'd better take it in case it's Nigel. Sorry.'

Lyndsey waved her hand to say don't worry about it and took a mouthful of beer.

'Hello?'

'Is that Ms Madeleine Walsh?' The voice at the other end was female and sounded American.

'Speaking.'

'This is River from Private DNA in San Jose, California. You sent us some cremains for possible identification?'

'Yes, is there a problem?' She glanced across the table wondering whether she should take the call elsewhere, but Lyndsey was browsing something on her phone and appeared to be paying no attention.

'Could I ask you a couple of questions to verify your identity, please?'

Mads agreed and answered the questions, all related to the information she'd filled out on the form that had accompanied the cremains.

'Thanks for that, Ms Walsh. We've run some preliminary tests on the sample you sent, and the good news is that there was a large enough piece of bone or tooth to run a successful test. You are aware we can only read DNA from parts of cremains protected by the hard coating of either teeth or bone.'

'I read that on your website.'

'I mention it so you will be confident in our findings. The primary reason I'm phoning is to check whether you sent the correct sample.'

'Certain, I only had one to send.' She wondered whether Lyndsey's grandmother might have made a mistake, but she'd not mentioned having any other remains lying around and had kept these locked away, so it seemed unlikely. 'Why, what's the problem?'

There was a brief silence on the line.

'Well, the thing is, these cremains aren't human.'

'What?'

'The cremains you sent us are of canine origin.'

'A dog? Are you certain? Don't answer that, of course you are. Oh my god, I'm lost for words.'

'Obviously, there would be no point in us completing the full tests and comparison checks, and I'm sorry but our terms and conditions preclude giving any refunds except in the rare case where we have erred.'

'Yes, don't worry about the money. Can you send me the results you have, please? The ones that show the source of the cremains.'

'Certainly, I'll email you a copy now and drop a report in the mail along with the return of what's left of your sample. Sorry to break the news to you like this, but we felt it was important to check that you had not made a mistake, rather than send you a report as if nothing was out of the ordinary.'

'No problem, thank you for phoning.'

'You're very welcome, Ms Walsh, and please keep us in mind for all your future DNA testing requirements.'

'I will, thanks.'

Mads hung up and stared out of the window at the rain that was now splattering against the window.

Lyndsey took a drink and waited for Mads to speak, but she just stared out of the window. After a few seconds, she decided to give her a verbal prod.

'What's up, Mads? I only heard half of that and it sounded weird. Dog? Results? You don't have a dog.'

Mads sighed. 'Promise you won't be angry, Lynds. I should have told you, but I didn't want to raise your hopes or upset you, what with it being so soon after Barry.'

Lyndsey raised her eyebrows. This sounded ominous. 'I won't be angry, I promise. What have you done?'

'Well, I've been doing a bit of investigating into Barry's dodgy dealings.'

For goodness sake, Mads! Why can't you leave anything alone? The guy is dead and good riddance.

'Why would you do that?'

'Because I want to find out what he was up to. We need to learn things, and some of them are odd. Who is that man who wants the photos? Why does he want them? I've also uncovered strong evidence that Barry was investigating you while pretending it was a proper relationship.'

Lyndsey sat back in her chair. 'I don't believe ...'

'Hey, bear with me. You promised you wouldn't be angry.'

Lyndsey rolled her eyes and gazed up at the ceiling. After a couple of deep breaths, she looked back at Mads and sarcastically signalled with her hand that Mads should carry on.

'So, I was working my way through his coded phone book and one number turned out to be your grandmother's.'

'I don't have a grandmother.'

'Well, it turns out you do, hon. On your mother's side. She lives in Clacton in Essex.'

Lyndsey's jaw dropped. Mads continued talking and she could hear words but could no longer process any meaning in them. Gran was alive? Why had Grandad told her otherwise, and more to the point, whose funeral had they attended that day when she had thought it was Gran in the coffin? And what did Mads mean, Barry was investigating her? Investigating her for what? None of this made sense. She had the urge to run away but that would solve nothing. She did need to move though, to calm down a little and settle her head down.

She grabbed her glass, downed the remaining beer in one and stood.

'Same again?'

Without waiting for a reply she headed to the bar and stood there for a few seconds before realising the barman was talking to her.

'Sorry, I was miles away. Two pints of Hop Harvest, please.'

He went to the other bar to pour the drinks, and she retreated back into her own world, blotting everything else out.

This couldn't be happening. Until a month ago, she had lived an unexceptional and seemingly normal life. She wanted to move back in time, back to the halcyon days of September before it had all started to unravel. Losing her parents had been traumatic, but that was nothing compared to facing the fact that they might be alive.

And Barry was something other than she'd thought.

Gran was alive.

It seemed as if her whole life had been a lie, and complicit throughout must have been Grandad. Apart from Barry, or was he involved too? Was it possible Grandad had paid Barry to monitor her, to make sure she discovered nothing regarding the truth?

That sounded far-fetched now she thought it "out loud" in her head, but wasn't the rest? A month ago, it would all have sounded barmy. She became aware the barman had returned and was talking again.

'Sorry?'

'Are you OK, love? Sure, I'm a dish and all, but it isn't usual for customers to cry just because I go to the other bar for two minutes.'

Lyndsey wiped her eyes clumsily with her arm. 'Sorry, I've just had some bad news.'

'I'm sorry to hear that.' He reached down below the bar and produced a couple of tissues he handed to her. 'Here you go and have the beers on me.'

Lyndsey dried her eyes and blew her nose. 'Don't be silly, how much do I owe you?' She put her hand in her pocket before realising that she had left her cards in her coat at the table.

'I mean it, you owe me nothing. I hope whatever the bad news was improves, or at least becomes bearable.'

She smiled. 'Thanks, I'll be OK.'

She picked up the beer and returned to the table where Mads was looking across at the bar towards her with an anxious look on her face. She put the glasses on the table.

'Just popping to the loo. Won't be a minute.'

She lowered the seat cover and sat for a moment, staring at the back of the cubicle door through bleary, tearful eyes.

Come on, Lynds, pull it together.

She grabbed a wad of toilet paper and blew her nose again, harder this time, before grabbing another wad and drying her eyes. She took a few deep breaths, flushed the toilet paper and went to the sink to wash her face. In the absence of any paper towels, she dried her face on the front of her sweatshirt, took another deep breath, gave herself a look of determination in the mirror, and returned to the table.

'Sorry, Mads. I was overwhelmed there for a moment.'

'Are you all right?'

Lyndsey nodded. 'I'll be fine. What were you saying about Gran?'

'She's very much alive in Clacton-on-Sea. I drove across and met her.'

'Grandad said she died years ago. Not only that, we went to her funeral. Whose bloody funeral did we go to?'

'That might be a question best aimed at your grandad. I spoke to your grandmother on the phone and she doesn't believe your parents are dead. She mentioned she had some of their ashes and had been meaning to test them for DNA, so I offered to pay to test them for her. I took a few hairs from your hairbrush for comparison, I didn't think you'd mind.'

'Mads, compared with everything else you're saying, trust me, a few hairs are among the least of my worries. Carry on.'

'The phone call was from the testing laboratory. It turns out the cremains your grandmother has aren't those of your parents. Come to that, they aren't even human.'

'They're the ashes of a dog?'

'So they said. This means that coupled with the photos, the evidence is pointing towards your parents being alive. Oh, and as a bonus, you have a grandmother.'

Lyndsey shook her head and took a long drink.

'This is a positive thing, Lynds. If we find your parents we can find out why they are hiding and maybe neutralise the photo guy, somehow.'

Lyndsey stared at Mads and drank another mouthful. The beer went down, but she didn't taste a thing as it did. 'Wait until I talk to Grandad tomorrow, I'll rip him a new one. How dare he lie to me about something like this?'

'I'm sure he had his reasons, and if he didn't, do you really want him to know that you know?'

'I can't think of any reason to tell me all my relatives except him are dead, can you? Perhaps we ought to test his DNA against mine to check we're related at all.'

Lyndsey's voice was getting louder and a couple on a nearby table glanced over with concerned expressions on their faces. Or they may just be annoyed that their quiet drink was being disturbed. Mads didn't care to analyse it. She reached across to hold Lyndsey's hands.

'Come on, Lynds. Let's not go crazy. You were fifteen when your parents died, or disappeared, so not even I imagine he abducted you.'

Lyndsey stared across the table, wide-eyed. 'I was joking, I hadn't considered that. What if the people I thought were my parents aren't? What if they're in prison for abducting me and Grandad staged their death to hide that?'

'That theory would be fanciful even by my standards.'

'Maybe, but something's wrong, like you said, and if we're honest, neither of us have the faintest idea what.'

28

A chilly Saturday morning at the market matched the bleak despondency in Lyndsey's heart. She finished setting up and glared across at Grandad.

'Cup of tea, Mads?'

'Love one,' she said, still busy displaying the artwork on her stall.

'I'll grab two toasties as well. Won't be long.'

She cut through Mads' space rather than duck under the flap, but rather than head for the catering truck she walked straight across the alcove.

'Hello, love,' said Grandad when she reached his stall. 'We never seem to talk any more since you moved out.'

Lyndsey fought to stay calm.

'Do you remember Gran's funeral?'

'Yes, I do. It was a charming service, I thought. The celebrant put a lot of work into his speeches. Why are you bringing that up now, it's been years?'

Lyndsey paused, hunting for the words she wanted. She needed to keep a lid on her emotions else she'd be in danger of launching herself at his throat, like a rabid, B movie zombie.

'Who was in the box? Because while some might consider Clacton-on-Sea to be a fate worse than death, I've been told Gran's living there. She'll be disappointed to find she missed her funeral service.'

Grandad stared at her for a moment.

'What makes you think that, love?'

'Who was in the coffin, Grandad?'

He shuffled his feet and glowered down as if scared his feet might run off on their own if unsupervised. After a pause that seemed like an age to Lyndsey, he made eye contact with her again.

'You have to understand, it was a difficult time. Your gran was out of her mind. She was unstable before Sue's death, but that pushed her over the edge into a long and painful tailspin. She was bitter after the divorce, saying plenty of upsetting things that you didn't need to hear. I thought it was best for everyone if there was a clean break.'

'A clean break? Killing her off isn't what I'd call clean, Grandad. I was in my first year at university. Don't you think I was old enough to make up my own mind?'

'You say that, but how did you find out? Did she contact you?'

'No she didn't, and it doesn't matter how I found out. I did. What else are you hiding from me? How many other family members should I expect to appear from the grave?'

He paused for a few seconds. 'None, love. Honest.'

Lyndsey was minded of Grandad's sales patter - "Yes, mate, this knife's from the Boer War. Honest." - and as on those occasions, felt the addition of the word "honest" highlighted the lie to anyone who had listened to him week after week. Until now she had thought her parents being alive was a mirage thrown up by strange events. Now she was not only convinced they were alive, but convinced Grandad knew they were.

'Is Gran aware she's dead or is it just our little secret?'

'There was only one person outside my tight circle of friends who knew, and he didn't tell you.'

'What makes you think that?'

'Because that person was Barry and he's dead. He's also, ironically, one of the reasons I question your judgement when it comes to people you can trust.'

'Barry knew?' It shocked Lyndsey to hear this and thought back to what Mads had said the night before. 'Did you pay him to keep tabs on me?'

'Ha, what? Are you kidding? I wouldn't deal with lowlifes like Barry. And what makes you think he was keeping tabs on you?'

Lyndsey paused a moment, she didn't want to involve Mads.

'Just odd things he said or did that occur to me now he's dead. I'm probably overthinking things.'

'He tried to blackmail me, forgetting the first rules of blackmail. Never try to scam someone who knows where you live, especially one who has better contacts.'

'Blackmail you about what? Gran's death?'

'Yes, no idea how he discovered she was alive, but he did and expected me to pay him a monthly fee to keep it secret.'

'So what happened?'

'One day when I knew you were busy so not with him, and purely by chance, of course, he ran into two friends of mine who happen to be keen baseball players. He decided it was better left as a secret.'

'So he knew and didn't tell me?'

'He was far too scared to tell you, love. But the question remains. Who isn't afraid?'

'Is Gran aware you've killed her? At least fictionally?'

'Not in so many words, but she knows better than to make contact. That was very clear in the divorce settlement, in exchange for our seaside cottage and half the value of the Brentford house. How did you find out?'

Lyndsey panicked for a moment, she hoped she wasn't getting Gran into trouble somewhere along the way.

'She didn't contact me, I haven't even spoken to her. In fact, I expected you to deny everything and leave me wondering whether I'd been lied to, but your secret clearly isn't as private as you thought. If Barry knew, there must be others. I ran into someone yesterday who told me she was alive and I have no intention of telling you who it was. Does this mean I might meet your baseball-loving friends, Grandad?'

He smiled and shook his head. 'Of course not, love. You might not see it now, but all I said and did was to protect you and I'll carry on protecting you as best I can. Don't think for a moment I'd threaten you with violence.'

'So whose funeral did we attend?'

Grandad tried to fashion a shamefaced, hangdog expression, but Lyndsey noticed a small smirk as if he was proud at how well he'd pulled it off.

'An old mate of mine on the market. His mother had died and owned nothing. Not two pennies to rub together, but a few hundred in debts here and there. Tabs at the local shops and some pubs to last her between pension days. Well, my mate didn't want to claim the body as he'd have had to pay for the funeral, and probably the debts as well. He planned to let the Council give her a pauper's funeral.'

'You know some charming people, don't you?'

'Different times, love. You didn't have your middle classes selling £4 loaves of bread at the market in those days, and no one would have been daft enough to buy them if they'd tried. But this guy's mum had the same first name as your gran, Sara, and that gave me the idea to do a deal with him. He'd claim the body, and I'd cover the cost of her funeral and debts as long as I could pretend it was my Sara. He attended, as it happens. Sat at the back and scarpered at the end. I told the celebrant a few stories about your gran's life that I knew you'd remember, and said to him that there had been a lot of scandal regarding her numerous marriages, so not to mention her surname. That way, any of her many families could attend without feeling awkward or excluded. All I needed to add were a few old pictures of my Sara and an audience.'

Lyndsey was speechless. Why would he expend so much time, money, and effort just to make sure there was no contact between her and Gran? A sentence formed in her mind that she had never dreamt she would think.

I really must visit Clacton-on-Sea.

'So am I forgiven, Lynds? Are we good?'

'I don't believe your front. Trust me, you are not forgiven in the slightest. I can't believe you did this, I really can't. No, we are not good.'

She turned and stormed off towards the catering stall. As she left the alcove, she glanced back over her shoulder and saw Grandad in conversation with Bob.

Oh please, no. Don't tell me Bob's involved in this too. If it wasn't for Mads, I'd have absolutely no one.

Mads watched Lyndsey argue with her grandad and stride off towards the catering truck.

So much for taking my advice, Lynds.

Ten minutes later she came back with the teas and baked bean toasties.

'How did that go, I'm guessing not well?'

'Grrr, he's unbelievable. Keeps secrets from me and gets the hump that I found out, as if it was my fault all along.

'So how did you say you found out?'

'I didn't. I wouldn't put you in the firing line and, apparently, Gran had to sign an agreement stipulating no contact with me when they got divorced so don't want to get her into trouble, either. I guess I should be pleased Grandad's on my side, he doesn't seem a good person to cross.'

'Really? Bert has always come across as charming to me.'

'You would think that, he's always joke flirting with you. I've always thought so too, but I saw a whole different side to him today. I knew he had some dodgy friends, but assumed that was the kind of person you ran into when you'd worked a market stall for a while.'

'At least he's got your back, it could come in handy if the photo guy comes by again.'

'I hope he doesn't. Do you fancy coming to Clacton with me? I need to find out what's going on and I'm not going to learn anything from Grandad.'

Mads furrowed her brow. 'Are you sure that's wise? If she's not meant to have any contact with you, she won't thank you for appearing out of nowhere.'

Lyndsey shrugged. 'Yes, I guess you're right. I don't want to put Gran in an awkward position. It would probably be best if I phoned, anyway. Or would it? She'd find it easier to hang up the phone. I don't know, I'm confused. I need to sort out what I want in my head first.'

'Leave it a week or two, there might be other ways to dig the information out. Which reminds me, what are you doing after the market shuts?

'As you know, Mads, my life is one long social whirl, but you've managed to catch me on a day I'm doing nothing special. What did you have in mind?'

'Do you fancy helping me clear and tidy a flat?'

Lyndsey smirked. 'A flat? Is this your way of saying the time for me to move has arrived?'

'Haha, don't be silly. You can stay as long as you like, it got lonely in that big house on my own.'

'So what flat do you need cleaning, and why?'

'Well, don't laugh, but I've rented out the flat you and Barry lived in. I can't help thinking there has to be more to find if I can go through his stuff a little more scientifically. I talked the landlord into a cheap rent on condition I store all Barry's gear for him. I've rented two storage units, one for Barry's flat contents and another for his unit's contents, as he needs to pay again by the end of the month.'

Lyndsey gaped at Mads as if she was crazy. 'You've rented our old flat and also want to move the contents of a storage unit into a storage unit. What makes you think it needs paying, or don't I want to know?'

'I might have accidentally opened a letter from the storage company. It's done now, I just need to move everything into my storage units, then I can hunt through everything at my leisure.'

Lyndsey shook her head. 'You never cease to amaze me, Mads. I don't think you'll find anything of use to us, but I'll help. Please tell me your units are close to Barry's?'

'Almost next door. His is 2130, mine are 2127 and 2128.'

'Thank goodness for that. For a moment I had visions of having to manoeuvre everything from one side of the building to the other.'

'I asked for something in the 2100s, pretending I had a friend who rented one in that area. 2127 and 2128 had become vacant yesterday morning, so I took them both.'

'Brilliant,' said Lyndsey, though her weak smile and downbeat demeanour didn't convince Mads she meant it.

The day passed without further drama, though from where Mads stood, the glares being passed between Lyndsey and her grandad told their own story. They packed up about one-thirty and made their way back home.

'Quick cup of tea and a bite to eat then head to Hounslow?' asked Mads.

'Sounds as good a plan as any. I still don't have a Scoobie what you expect to find in Barry's things, though.'

'We're missing something. I met with one of his victims last week ...'

'You did what? When? Where?'

Mads parked the van in the drive and clambered out.

'Let's unpack the van first, I'll fill you in over a cup of tea.'

Twenty minutes later they were sitting at the kitchen table with steaming mugs of tea and the rest of yesterday's pie warmed up with baked potatoes.

'So, come on, the suspense is killing me. Who did you meet?'

'Remember I told you I was working my way through Barry's phone book? Well, one of them phoned me back. JP are his initials. I tried bluffing to find out how Barry's scam worked but he knew I was lying, so the only way to discover anything was to agree to meet.'

'Don't tell me you met him on your own?'

'Yes, kind of. I told him I wasn't and he chose to believe me.'

Lyndsey shook her head. 'Mads, you need to be careful. I doubt the people Barry blackmailed are very principled people, aside from Grandad, and he has spiky edges I wasn't aware of.'

'Barry blackmailed your grandad?'

'He tried.' Lyndsey related the story Grandad had told her.

Once she had finished, Mads filled her in on the rest of the events from last Monday morning, Lyndsey's face becoming more horrified with every part.

'How can you be so calm? He pulled a knife on you. I'm almost scared to go to sleep at night for fear you'll enact a madcap stunt that will have us murdered in our beds.'

'Don't mind me, I survived. It was exciting after the event, but I'll admit I was scared when he first grabbed me. But look at what we're missing? Barry would have taken the money from all these accounts regularly, so where are all the cards and account details? Where is the money, because it isn't in his day-to-day bank account? I'm sure he would have laundered some through his stall and wrote it down as sales, but there is more floating around somewhere.'

'How do you know it isn't in his bank account?'

'I might have also peeked at a bank statement after reading the letter from the storage company.'

Lyndsey sighed once more. 'Why does it matter where the money went?'

'This is a loose end, Lynds. I don't like loose ends. I feel as if I should tell these people that they no longer have to pay. Although many of them are undesirable characters and deserve some kind of comeback, there will be others whose digressions were relatively minor. I was hoping to sort them into two piles and pass on the evidence for the worst of them to the police. If I can find the money, I'll take back what the rent and storage unit cost and give the rest to The Blue Cross or something.'

'Mads, judge, jury, and virtual executioner. How do you work out which are which, Mads? Do you think for a moment they'll tell you?'

'No, but I have Barry's records. They were password protected in that zip file we found when we searched his computer. They are very detailed, far more than I wanted to know about JP, for instance.'

'Yet still you met him in a secluded spot at dawn?'

'Yes, OK Mum. It wasn't the smartest thing I'll ever do, but it worked out. Give me a break. In a nutshell, I need access to Barry's stuff in a place where I can work my way through it. I need to finish what I've started.'

They'd both finished eating so Mads walked across and placed the washing up into the machine.

'Are you fit? I figured we'd clear the flat this afternoon

and wait to transfer Barry's unit to mine when the storage unit office is closed. The camera will record us, but as no one has any reason to watch through the videos, they won't know. If they come across us emptying Barry's unit while they're there, they might be suspicious and ask what we're doing.'

'That might be the first sensible thing you've said since we got back. A glowing oasis of common sense in a vast desert of Mads fantasy.'

'Get away with you. I've got the sack barrow, loads of boxes and packing tape in the garage, so let's throw it all in the van and clear out my new flat. The quicker we empty the place, the sooner I can buy you dinner for helping.'

They were soon heading for Hounslow and found a parking space not too far from the flat. At first, the thought of boxing everything was overwhelming, but they soon got themselves into a system and ensured they wrote on each box with a marker pen so they could find what was in each one, should they need to. It took nearly three hours, but finally, the sum total of Barry's life was a pile of boxes stacked in the middle of the front room.

'Fancy a cup of tea before we take it away, or have we packed everything?'

'Sorry, I didn't think. The kettle's in that box there, along with the mugs.' Lyndsey pointed to a box marked KITCHEN halfway down the pile. 'The only things I didn't pack from the kitchen were the cleaning and food items, so we still have tea bags to hand.'

Mads scanned the flat, taking in the grubby paintwork, dusty surfaces and unvacuumed carpet. 'Barry had cleaning items?'

'Yes, I remember buying them and as you can imagine there are plenty left,' laughed Lyndsey. 'Come on, let's find that kettle and have a drink before we go. I'm thirsty now you've mentioned it.'

They had a cup of tea before trundling all the boxes to the van and driving to the storage unit. By the time they arrived, the office was already closed.

'That's handy,' said Mads. 'If you're up for doing it all today, we won't have to come back tomorrow.'

'Yes, do it now. However little I feel like it, dreading the prospect overnight won't improve matters.'

They fitted everything on two trolleys and took the boxes up in the lift before stacking them into unit 2127, then they moved Barry's stored stuff from 2130 to 2128. She snapped the padlock shut and glanced at her phone.

'Goodness, nearly seven-thirty. We'll sleep well tonight. Let's dump the van home and I'll treat you to dinner. What do you fancy?'

'Let's try The Barn by Kew Bridge. They do a huge range of ciders along with vegan pies and pizzas. I've been wanting to try it for ages.'

'Where's that? I can't place it.'

'Next to that newish pub, The Nine.'

'Oh, I know the one. Sounds interesting and I'm starving. Let's go.'

30

After market on Sunday, Lyndsey had tried enjoying a lazy afternoon, but her mind had other ideas. It insisted on scampering off in all directions, trying to make sense of what they knew about her parents, grandmother and everything else. She hadn't been able to relax at all. Having then tossed and turned for what seemed like half the night, she was exhausted as she sat at her desk on Monday morning.

All the weird occurrences were making her stressed, and coming back to work had only made matters worse. New thoughts about Francis, Gloria and the threatening notes started swirling around, adding themselves to the mental cacophony. She sauntered to the break room and sat silently for a few minutes while trying some breathing exercises. They helped a little, and when the voices had been quelled, she returned to her desk.

As long as no one mistook her for a library manager she should be safe enough here, she figured. It occurred to her that she should ask Joe how Gloria was, but not wanting to encourage him to think of some urgent task she could do, quietly got on with the work in her tray and made a mental note to go and ask before she went to lunch. She had just got back from a tea break when the lift doors swished open and two librarians that Lyndsey vaguely remembered being introduced to walked towards her.

'Hi there,' said the taller woman with brown hair held back in a ponytail. 'We're planning to visit Gloria at midday and as you were the one who organised the card and everything, we wondered if you'd like to come along.'

'Oh,' said Lyndsey. 'Yes, it will be nice to get away from the university for an hour or so. Shall I come down to the Librarians' office just before?'

'That would be perfect. Oh, in case you don't remember, and don't worry because there's no reason you should, my name's Paula, and this is Anne,' she said, indicating a redheaded woman with a bob.

Lyndsey smiled at them both. 'I remember you both from my first day introductions, but I must admit, there were so many names thrown at me I don't remember most of them. Just the faces.'

'Don't worry about it, introduction overload on starting work at a new place is something everyone can empathise with.'

They disappeared the way they'd come and Lyndsey carried on with what she was doing until a quarter to twelve when she walked down to the office Joe was sharing.

'Morning, Joe, how was Gloria?'

He looked up as if he didn't recognise her for a moment.

'She seemed fine, though was tired so I only stayed a few minutes. I gave her the card and gifts.'

'Good, I hope she liked them. Is it OK if I take lunch from twelve until one today, please?'

'Sure, could you make me a mug of tea first, though? The bags are on the bookshelf behind me.'

Lyndsey took a tea bag from his caddy and picked up his mug from the desk.

'No problem, back in a minute.'

There was no reply as she walked out of the office.

She made the tea, screwing her nose up at the stench, and took it back to him. He was on the phone and just pointed at a placemat for her to put the mug on, which she did before escaping without saying a word.

Hmm, his pleasant mood didn't last long.

She went back upstairs to grab her jacket and made her way to the Librarians' office.

'Hey Lyndsey, you're early,' said Anne, as Lyndsey walked through the door.

'Sorry, I can go away again if you like.'

Anne laughed. 'No, I meant it as a positive. Paula's just popped to the loo, we'll head off as soon as she's back.'

'I reached a natural finishing point in what I was doing and it made no sense to start something else for five minutes.'

'Do you have much to do, what with there only being one manager in?'

'Most of my days have been spent trying to work my way through the backlog. I think the three of them stacked paperwork into my inbox long before they had anyone to do it, to clear their desks as much as anything else.'

'That wouldn't surprise me in the slightest. Are you going to apply for the job if they make it permanent?'

'I'm not sure, I need the job but I'm not sure whether this wouldn't drive me crazy in a very short space of time.'

Anne smiled. 'Because of the mindless grind of admin or the ever-increasing stack of bodies?'

Before Lyndsey had a chance to reply, Paula bowled through the door.

'What am I like, keeping you both waiting? We'd best make tracks, the roads around here are usually chocka during the day.'

Despite the traffic, it only took them fifteen minutes to reach the hospital, and they found Gloria sitting up in her bed reading.

'Hello, you three. Thanks for coming to visit, such an unexpected surprise.'

Lyndsey gazed at Gloria's bedside table where the flowers sat in a vase next to the card and the box of fudge.

'The flowers are pretty,' said Anne.

'Yes, Joe brought them in on Friday. Who bought them, I don't believe for one moment that it was him?'

'I think you'll find Lyndsey here bought your goodies,' said Paula. 'Are you saying Joe wanted you to believe he did it all?'

'Of course he did. I would have asked him directly but was feeling a little weak.'

'So when are they letting you out? You're looking like you're on the way to recovery,' asked Anne.

'The doctor will run some tests later, but he thinks I might be able to leave as early as tomorrow morning, as long as I promise to stay home and rest for a few days.'

'Have they discovered what it was?' asked Paula.

'If they have, no one's sharing the information with me. Whatever it was, it knocked me for six. What does it say on my chart?'

Paula went to the end of the bed and picked it up.

'It says you ingested an unknown substance and Toxicology are running tests.'

As she replaced the chart, a nurse appeared at the end

of the bed.

'Sorry, only two visitors allowed at one time.'

'Oh, we didn't know,' said Lyndsey. 'Shall I go out and wait by the car?'

'No need for that,' said Gloria. 'They're from work, Nurse, and they'll only be here for a few more minutes. Couldn't you turn a blind eye, just this once?'

'You'll be getting me into trouble, you will, Gloria. OK, but no longer than five more minutes, and if Sister appears, I didn't see you, OK?'

'Thanks, Nurse,' said Gloria. 'So, Lyndsey. How are you coping with Joe?'

'Fine, he's in the downstairs office and I'm upstairs so our paths don't cross unless he has something urgent for me to do.'

'They still have our office sealed as a crime scene? How much longer will they take? There are things in there I need.'

'No idea. I'm sure they'll tell us when they've finished. It can't take much longer. I've not seen any police in there since Inspector Savage locked the door last Tuesday so unless he wants to preserve something specific, he's probably been too busy to release the key. He asked about some track marks in the carpet but I couldn't help. Was something heavy delivered the week before I started? A desk or a filing cabinet, perhaps?'

'Nothing I can think of. Maybe Francis wheeled himself across the room on his chair rather than walk one day when he was feeling lazy.'

Lyndsey laughed, 'Yes, that might be it, though I've always thought it harder work to do that than walk.'

'Men's brains work differently to ours, love. I think it comes with the never growing up thing. And I'm sure you're right about the police and the room, I'll have to learn to be patient.'

'No pun intended?'

'Very good, as sharp as a porcupine's quill. Given that you were so thoughtful with buying everything, please take the fudge with you. I can't stand the stuff, even when my body doesn't want to reject everything as soon as I can force it down. I do appreciate the effort you went to, though. It was a lovely thought.'

'Thanks,' said Lyndsey, picking up the unopened box and giving it a suspicious glare.

31

After dropping Lyndsey at work, Mads continued on to the storage units. Figuring the most likely place to find anything interesting was the stuff Barry had kept in his lock-up space, she opened up 2128 and sighed as she cast her eyes across the boxes. She knew she could discount the ten boxes in the back corner as she had rummaged through them with Lyndsey a few weeks back. Figuring it made little difference where she started as long as she did, Mads went through the t-shirt boxes first hoping the shirts were hiding something interesting.

They weren't.

Next, she tried the CD boxes. As most were solidly packed, there was very little scope for hiding anything in the boxes themselves. She ignored any sealed CDs and painstakingly opened the unsealed cases as she went through, in case anything was hidden in one of them.

There wasn't.

Mads checked the time and deciding that 11.45 was close enough to lunchtime, pondered where to go. Shuddering at the thought of eating in Hounslow, she drove to Isleworth and parked the van at the library while she walked around the corner to a small noodle restaurant she'd stumbled across a while back. Having eaten, she drove back, reopened the lock-up unit and sighed once more.

There was nothing for it, she had to go through the vinyl. Much as she wanted to give up, Mads knew she needed to finish the job now, else coming back to it would be worse than ever. Halfway through the fifth box, she pulled the LP out of a Gary Glitter gatefold sleeve and a brown B5 envelope plopped to the floor with a dull clinking sound.

Mads felt a jolt of excitement as she replaced the record and picked the envelope up. It was unsealed, and she lifted the flap to peer inside, finding a rental agreement from a different storage company along with a key she hoped would fit either a door or padlock attached to the unit listed in the paperwork. She skim-read the agreement, noting the address and entry number for the outside gate and, figuring there was no time to waste, locked her unit and headed off in the van towards Feltham.

It was with some trepidation that she leant out of the van window and typed the entry code when she arrived, but the gate ground its way open to allow her through to park. Following signs to the third floor where the smaller units were, she wandered through deserted corridors passing door after door until she reached the one she was looking for.

It resembled a safe more than a normal storage unit, slightly taller than she was, with a large metal handle on the outside and a heavy-duty padlock. Mads pulled the key from the envelope, slid it into the lock and turned. Only when the padlock clicked open, did she realise she had been holding her breath and took a couple of gulps of air before lifting the padlock from its mooring.

'OK, here goes nothing,' she muttered before grabbing the handle firmly, turning it and pulling the door open. Inside were four of the largest backpacks she had ever seen, with a sizeable metal cash box sat on top.

She glanced around to check no one was there before picking up the cashbox. It was unlocked, and she opened its lid to peer in. As she expected, there were a couple of hundred bank cards, the names on which would almost certainly match the initials in the book she had at home, and a Filofax organiser containing a page for each cardholder along with security questions and answers. She put the cashbox down again and opened the flap of one of the backpacks.

Mads stared at the contents for a few moments before dropping the flap and raising her hands to her open mouth.

32

Back at the library, Lyndsey said goodbye to the librarians at their floor and stayed in the lift until it reached hers. On alighting the lift it surprised her to find Inspector Savage sitting at her desk.

'Ah, Miss Marshall. When you're fixed, may I have a word, please?'

'Sure,' replied Lyndsey. 'I was going to make a quick cup of tea, would you like one?'

'Thank you, I'll have a white coffee with two sugars if I may.'

'No problem,' said Lyndsey, placing her bag in the top drawer of her desk. 'We only have creamer, is that OK?'

'I'm sure it can't be worse than the muck they expect us to drink at the station. I'll be in the office, CSI have finished with it now.'

Lyndsey went to the break room to prepare the drinks and took the two mugs to the office where Inspector Savage was sitting behind FC's desk. She placed them both on the desk and pulled up a chair for herself.

'How's the investigation going? Do your bosses think

murder is afoot or has the library just been party to a couple of unfortunate accidents?'

'Interestingly, had you asked me that question this morning, I wouldn't have been sure.'

Lyndsey paused. 'So you're sure now? What's happened?'

Savage ignored her question. 'How has your morning been, Miss Marshall?'

She tried to work out where he was going with the conversation but his face remained expressionless.

'Fine, I suppose. Same old same old, as the saying goes. Boring admin from the never-ending To-Do tray.'

'Nothing else occurred of any note?'

Lyndsey shook her head. 'Nothing I can think of. A couple of the librarians took me to the hospital to visit Gloria, we've just got back.'

'Is she well? I spoke to her Saturday and she seemed to be recovering.'

'She was still in bed, but thinks the doctors might release her tomorrow.'

'So you just did some admin work before you went to the hospital with the librarians? That is the extent of your morning?'

'Yes, why?'

'Faruq thought he saw you take Joe a mug of tea.'

'Oh, yes, I did. I needed to tell him when I'd be at lunch and he asked me to make him a cup before I left.'

'Was there anything unusual about the tea you made him?'

Lyndsey shook her head. 'Not that I can think of, at least not in the context of Joe's teas. He has his own brew that he keeps in a caddy on the shelf behind his desk. Do you remember last week, I phoned you to open this office purely to get his caddy out? It smells awful, I can only imagine how disgusting it must taste. I took a tea bag from his caddy and his mug, added hot water and steeped it for a couple of minutes before delivering it back. He'll be at lunch now, but if you ask him at two, I'm sure he can give you more information about what's in it.'

Savage nodded. 'He may struggle, Miss Marshall. A short while after drinking the tea you prepared, Joe had a violent reaction to something and died.'

Lyndsey's mouth gaped open. 'Oh no, you don't think I ...'

Savage raised his hand. 'Before you run off on flights of fancy and demand to phone your lawyer, Miss Marshall, may I say you are not a suspect in any of the events that have occurred over the last week or so. What I find interesting, is the fact that when these things happen, you appear to be the obvious choice. It's almost as if somebody is trying to guide suspicion towards you.'

'But why? I mean, aside from deflecting from themselves. Why me?'

'That I don't know. If you'd worked here some time, I might explore the possibility that someone harboured a grudge against you, but I think it unlikely in your case. You've not been here long enough to invite that kind of reaction. I can only imagine that you've been unfortunate and in the wrong place at the wrong time. A suspect of convenience, if you will.'

'Ooh, sorry but can I write that down?' said Lyndsey grabbing a pen from the desk and a scrap of paper. 'It sounds like an interesting title for a novel.'

Savage smiled. 'Yes, I'm sure it does. It's also possible that the guilty party believes you'll be top of the suspect list because you've not been here long, but that raises the problem of motive. I'm sure you would have crossed my path before now if you were the kind of person who poisoned coworkers or bosses whenever you started a new job.'

Lyndsey raised her hand to cover a smile that she couldn't stop her mouth forming.

Do people like that really exist?

'So tell me, who were the librarians who took you to the hospital?'

Lyndsey opened her eyes wide. Surely Mads' bonkers theory about the librarians couldn't be true?'

'Paula and Anne, but I can't imagine they would have anything to do with something like this.'

'I'm sure you're right, but one thing I've learnt over the years is that murderers rarely appear like murderers. Not those with a plan, at least, which this killer has. If I can work out the motive, it should lead to the killer as clearly as muddy footprints from a burglary.'

Inspector Savage wrote the names in his notebook before continuing.

'Paula and Anne may have noticed something that won't seem suspicious to them until I speak to them. Similarly, you only become a person of interest due to your proximity to the crimes. All I can do is follow the trail, Miss Marshall. Where it leads is not for me to presuppose. Could you show me where you made the tea and what you did with the tea bag, please? I'll need it tested so we can determine if it was the murder instrument.'

'Of course, it was the ground floor break room. I'll take you there.'

'Thank you, and here's the key to this office,' he said pushing it across the desk towards her. 'Your boss from upstairs asked me to hand it to you and also requests the pleasure of your company in his office after lunch.'

Lyndsey nodded and picked up the key and empty mugs. She locked the door behind them, left the mugs on her desk and took Inspector Savage to the ground floor break room where he took the entire rubbish sack from the bin and knotted it at the top.

'Thank you for your help, Miss Marshall. I'm sure we both hope this will be the last we see of each other.'

Lyndsey watched as he walked towards the office where Joe must have died. She would love to think that was the last she'd see of the Inspector, but doubted it very much.

Mads parked the van and hunted out the ID card from her bag before entering the university security gates. Once through, she scurried towards the lifts and pressed the call button. Before it arrived, she heard a familiar voice from behind her.

'Hey Mads, what are you doing here?'

She turned to face Lyndsey, wanting nothing more than to usher her into a lift and up to her desk so she could tell her what she'd found in Barry's secret lock-up, but Lyndsey's face made her pause.

'Oh my god, what's up? You look like you're ready to burst into tears.'

Lyndsey gave a weak smile. 'No, I'm not, but you won't believe what's happened.'

Mads walked away from the lift doors, ignoring the ping as they slid open, and opened the door to the stairwell so they could talk somewhere a little more private than the lift lobby.

'Tell me.'

'Two of the librarians gave me a lift to the hospital to

visit Gloria. Before I left, Joe asked me to make him some tea, which I did. Now he's dead.'

'You're kidding? From the tea?'

'Inspector Savage thinks so.'

'And he thinks you killed him?'

Lyndsey grunted a small laugh. 'No, not this time, thank goodness. But now I have to go upstairs for a meeting with Elliot. With no managers to work for, I'm not sure this job will last past the end of the day.'

'Hey, don't be such a pessimist. He might want to offer you a library manager job. I understand he has vacancies.' Mads laughed. 'Sorry, too soon?'

'You could say that, but I doubt that will happen, and given the rate the managers are dropping I'm not sure it would be sensible to accept if he did.'

'I'm sorry, hon. I'll take you out for something to eat tonight to cheer you up.'

Lyndsey raised her eyebrows. 'Mads, you take me out for dinner virtually every night of the week. As if you need an excuse.'

'Fair point, though as it's pizza BOGOF night at the Railway and I have some melty vegan mozzarella to take with us, we'd be crazy to miss it.'

'Yeah yeah. Well, I have to go upstairs to find out what Elliot wants. Do you want to hang around by my desk and we can have a cup of tea afterwards?'

'Sounds a fine plan,' replied Mads, pushing the door open so they could catch a lift.

The doors were just closing to one of them and Mads squeaked as she caught a glimpse inside. She rushed across and pressed the button to stop it leaving but was too late.

'Oh wow, in the lift. I'm certain it was the dragon jacket. Do you remember? The guy I heard the other day talking about killing someone.'

She stared up at the display and saw the lift stop at the second floor.

'Sorry, Lynds. I have to find him, he may be the piece of the puzzle we're missing. Good luck with your meeting and if not before, I'll catch you at home. OK?'

Moments later, Mads was through the door to the stairwell, taking the stairs two at a time. By the time she reached the second floor, she was out of breath.

Damn you, woman. Take your lazy arse down that gym.

She rushed through the doors into the library and seeing the startled faces of a few students, forced herself to take a deep breath and slow down to a brisk walk. She made her way towards the back, checking the shelves and tables, but there was no sign of him. Just as Mads thought she must have been mistaken, there he was, pulling some books from the second last shelf on the floor. She walked up behind him, before realising she didn't have a clue what to say. Her breathing must have alerted him to her presence, as he turned and looked her up and down.

'Wow, you're perfect.'

Had Mads compiled a possible list of lines she expected him to open with, that would have been fairly low down. She took a step back and, feeling her face redden, ran her hand through her hair to compose herself.

'Get away with you, now.'

Geez, Madeleine. Could you sound any more Irish?

'No, I'm serious. Please tell me you're not doing anything Thursday evening?'

'Er, I'm not sure. I'll have to check. Why?'

She examined him closely. He had to be six or seven years younger than her - but he was attractive, in a pretty boy kind of way - and it wasn't as if her marriage was exactly traditional.

'Sorry, I'm getting ahead of myself. I'm directing a student play on Thursday and one of the cast members pulled out over the weekend. When I saw you I felt you would be perfect for the role. You wouldn't have many lines to learn.'

Way to let a girl down, buddy.

'This wouldn't be some kind of murder mystery, would it?'

'Yes, yes it is. Of course, you must have seen the posters. Please say you'll do it. I'm sure the costume will only need minimal adjustment if any, and you resemble the vision I had of the character far better than the previous girl.'

So, a murder mystery. That explains the comment I heard.

Mads scrabbled in her bag pretending to search for her phone, hoping her face wasn't as red as it felt from the inside. After what seemed an age, she had little choice but produce it and check the total lack of plans she knew she had for Thursday.

'Well?'

'You're in luck.'

'Wonderful, if you're free now could I take you to Cathy? She's in charge of the costumes and a total whizz with a sewing machine. If you try on the costume now, she'll have it ready by Wednesday for the final dress rehearsal.'

'Wait, Wednesday too?'

'Oh, is that a problem? Sorry, I'm getting carried away again, forgetting to bring you up to speed. The doctor prescribes me meds for my nervous condition, but at moments of stress and high excitement my body overrides them. My name's Jordan, by the way.'

'Hi Jordan, I'm Mads.'

She went through the motions of checking her phone again, not sure she was happy admitting her complete lack of social engagements to anyone.

'OK, I'm free then too. You're in luck, a friend of mine rang and cancelled on me yesterday.'

'Excellent, thank you so much. Follow me, I'll introduce you to Cathy and find you a script. What's your full name? I'm so pleased I ran into you when I did, I can make the final adjustments to the programmes before I print them out.'

'Mads Walsh.'

Jordan scribbled it down in a pad he produced from his pocket and made to lead the way before stopping again.

'Sorry Mads, grab whatever books you came for first. I can't believe how self-obsessed I must seem.'

' The books will wait, let's try on this costume.'

Jordan's estimation of Mads' size had been a little optimistic, and she was feeling self-conscious as she squeezed herself into the dress and tried not to breathe as she presented herself. At least it was black, and the fringes that were layered all the way down to just above her knees would help disguise any unsightly bulges. Once she added the black, feathered headband and the matching boa, she looked quite the flapper about town.

Sensing her discomfort, Cathy made a point of commenting how unfeasibly skinny the other actress had been and told her not to worry as pretty much all she'd have to do is reverse the adaptions she had made before. She assured Mads that it would fit perfectly by Wednesday.

After Cathy had finished taking her measurements, Mads checked the time. Four-fifteen, too late for a cuppa with Lyndsey and a little early to sit around waiting for her leaving time. She decided to return to Feltham and move the contents of Barry's lock-up to the house. At least that way it wasn't in danger of being discovered due to Barry missing a payment.

Once again, no one was around and she manhandled the huge backpacks on to a flat trolley after ensuring the flaps were secure. With the money box buried beneath them, she took everything down in the lift, then had the more difficult job of moving them into the van. She settled for standing in the van and dragging them across as there was no way she could lift them. When she arrived back, she parked in the garage rather than the driveway and, after checking the garage door was locked, entered the house through the kitchen.

As she walked in, Lyndsey was studying something under the light.

'What on earth are you doing?'

'Hi, Mads. Gloria doesn't like fudge so gave it to me. The trouble is, you've got me paranoid with your talk of it being poisoned, so I'm checking there are no puncture marks in the cellophane. Just as well I found vegan fudge as I wouldn't have wanted to risk giving poisoned fudge to the librarians or something.'

Mads burst out laughing. 'I think that theory has bolted, Lynds. I can't imagine Joe poisoned the fudge, only to be killed by someone else. The odds of that happening would be astronomical.'

'Maybe,' she said, still angling the box beneath the light to find any imperfections or holes. 'Who's to say that someone didn't poison it while visiting Gloria over the weekend, though? It doesn't have to have been Joe.'

'What have I done? I've made you crazier than I am. Give the box here, I'll be your guinea pig.'

'No need, I'm pretty sure there are no punctures in the

packaging,' said Lyndsey, ripping open the plastic. 'You don't think we'll spoil our appetite, do you?'

'I have just the solution for that. Let's each have a mouthful, and once you've changed out of your work things, you can rebuild your appetite by giving me a hand upstairs with a few bags. How does that sound?'

Lyndsey raised an eyebrow at her.

'It sounds like I'm being press-ganged into something I don't want to do, but OK.'

Mads smiled and shoved a couple of lumps of fudge into her mouth. 'Dem we oh do de bub.'

Lyndsey hopped in the shower and changed. By the time she came back, Mads had covered the kitchen floor with black plastic sacks tied at the top.

'These need to go into the loft,' said Mads. 'They shouldn't be too heavy now I've repackaged everything.'

'Mads, you said a few, there must be twenty bags here.'

'Twenty-eight, but who's counting? Aside from me, of course. We'd never have lifted the giant bags upstairs even with both of us. Come on, the quicker we start, the quicker we'll be done.'

After seven journeys to the loft, Lyndsey collapsed into the armchair in the front room and closed her eyes, waiting for Mads to reappear after closing the loft hatch. She heard her flop into the other chair.

'Phew, that was a workout and a half.'

Lyndsey opened her eyes. 'You're not kidding, what on earth was in those bags?'

'Barry's extortion money.'

'Are you crazy? Why did you bring it back here? Doesn't that make us accomplices?'

'Only on a technicality, and I didn't want his lease to run out and have the storage company find it.'

'What are you going to do with it all?'

'Not sure yet. I'll count it first and make a list of a few good causes to share it between. The Blue Cross, Mama Cat Trust, things like that.'

'Do you have any idea how much there is?'

'Not really, but it will be in the tens of thousands, if not hundreds. I've never seen so much cash in my life.'

Lyndsey sat there with her mouth open for a moment. 'That much? I can't even imagine that much cash, even having helped you carry it up all those stairs. What was it bagged in originally?'

'Come on, I'll show you on the way out to the Railway. You won't believe the size of these backpacks, I think they once belonged to elephants.'

Neither of them felt like chatting as they trudged their way through the spitting rain towards the Railway. Having bought two pints of Join the Kew and ordered pizzas, they sat down in a corner where no one would overhear them.

'So, where did you find those huge bags? I feel as if I've missed something, somewhere along the way. And what happened with the jacket guy you raced off after?'

'Hmm, yes he was a false alarm. He's directing a murder mystery play at the university this Thursday, hence the conversation I overheard. I saw a poster for it next to the librarians' office last week but didn't give it much thought. On the plus side, I now have the part of Lady Buckingham.'

'Really? How are you going to learn your lines in time?'

'I only have a few, then I drop dead right before the break. I'll have it down before dress rehearsal on Wednesday. You will come, I hope?'

'I wouldn't miss it for the world. What time does it start?'

'Doors open six-thirty for seven o'clock, I think. I'll sort you out a ticket.'

'I'll finish work and grab something to eat there. It won't be worth coming home to head straight back again.'

'So you'll still have a job? How did your meeting go?'

'As well as expected. I have to clear out the managers' office by the end of the week. Box everything up and label the boxes so Elliot can organise delivery to the relevant families. He said to do Gloria's too, so I assume she'll move to another office. Maybe he's having a complete reshuffle now the opportunity has presented itself.'

'At least you're in for a few more days. It gives us a chance to solve the crimes before you leave.'

'You never give up, do you? I think we should leave it to Inspector Savage, he is paid to do this kind of thing, after all. Despite the poor first impression we formed of him, he's not as bad as we thought.'

'Yes, but with all the cutbacks they've been complaining about, I'm sure they could do with as much help as they can get.'

'Whatever you say, Mads. Where did you find those elephant backpacks?'

'Ah, well I was going through all the bits from Barry's lock-up that we hadn't bothered with before. The t-shirts and music stuff. When an envelope slipped out of one of the album covers, I felt the need to investigate further.'

'This envelope fell out with no help from you? As if it sprouted wings and was part of an animated feature?'

'OK, so I was systematically looking through all the covers.'

'That must have taken ages.'

'Yes, but my determination paid off, Lynds. Don't forget that part. Inside the envelope was a lock-up rental agreement and a key, so I scooted off to a different storage facility and found all four bags and a cash box containing loads of bank cards and all the details for the accounts Barry's victims used to pay him.'

'So now what?'

'The money isn't that important to me. I want to find out how much there is to make it easier to share out. As for the bank accounts I will try to contact the owners, if I can, or failing that close the accounts. That way, any more payments will be rejected, and those being blackmailed will be off the hook.'

'And what about the information you have on them?'

Mads sighed. 'That's more of a conundrum. Some of those people deserve locking up for what they've done, but others have only committed minor indiscretions. Not that I'm agreeing with cheating on your other half, but ultimately it's a personal matter, not a criminal one. I will have to sit down and sort them out, won't I?'

Lyndsey nodded. 'And before you close accounts too, I'd say. If you pass any information on to the police, you don't want it to appear as if you've been poking your nose in and spoiling any evidence they might need to collect.'

'I hadn't thought of that. I'm thinking I have a late night ahead of me.'

'You don't mean to say we might arrive home before ten so I can have a proper night's sleep?'

Mads furrowed her brow as she pondered the question. 'Don't hold your breath on that. This beer is tasty and we'll need a couple more to wash down the pizzas. Let's both play it by ear, eh?'

She winked and Lyndsey couldn't help but smile. She knew how this ended up, and it wasn't with an early night.

The next afternoon, Mads walked out of the lift and saw Lyndsey in the office labelling a pile of boxes. She poked her head through the open door.

'I've got an hour before rehearsal. Fancy a cup of tea or something to eat?'

Lyndsey shrugged. 'Might as well, Elliot hasn't any idea what breaks I've had.'

Lyndsey locked the office door and they walked downstairs to the refectory and bought a cup of tea and a slice of carrot cake each before finding a table.

'Did you finish sorting through your rogue's gallery last night?' asked Lyndsey.

'Around four o'clock. I'll start contacting the "good list" tomorrow, and check for any balances. After that, I might have to start closing accounts if I can't get in touch with people, but at least this time I know their names, having cross referenced the bank cards with the initials..'

'Can you do that?'

'All the accounts are at the same bank and they allow accounts to be closed by phone, else it would be tricky. On the downside, this means I'm limited to closing one or two a day. Closing too many accounts in succession is likely to raise some red flags, even with the relative anonymity of talking to call centres.'

'Make sure it can't be traced to you. We don't want the police on the doorstep.'

'Yes, I've thought about that. I have an untraceable phone for the calls and can check the balances online through an anonymous wifi somewhere. If I can avoid cameras or personal logins, I should be fine.'

'How will you avoid the bank's security checks? And closing men's accounts with a woman's voice might be a challenge.'

'I'll say one thing for Barry, he kept very detailed records. He wrote every possible security answer down. I might ask Nigel to do the male accounts next time he's in the country. How's your office tidying going?'

'I've done Francis' and Joe's desks. In the interests of looking busy for as long as possible this week, I'll leave Gloria's desk until tomorrow.'

'Exciting stuff.'

'You know it. Have you counted the money yet?'

'I haven't had time. I slept most of the morning then spent the next couple of hours playing with inflections for my five lines of dialogue. What are you going to do with yourself once you're unemployed again?'

'Writing, I suppose. At least being here every day helped focus my mind. Having less time to write took away the luxury of procrastination, so during my breaks I've started putting words together rather than umming and arring over storylines and minor details.'

'Have you got anything I can read yet?'

Lyndsey frowned. 'No chance, not before the first edit

at very least.'

'Well, hurry up, I can't wait to find out what you've done with the results from those drunken brainstorming sessions.'

'Be patient, I haven't found my ideal routine yet. Once I do, everything will fall into place a lot easier.'

Mads nodded. 'Fair enough. Another thing we need to do when you have some free time is to find out about your canine parents. We need to work out where those photos are from.'

'I suppose. Do I even want to find out. If it wasn't for that guy at the market threatening us I'd let sleeping dogs lie.'

'Haha, very good.'

Lyndsey looked blank for a moment. 'Mads! That pun was truly unintended. Far too soon for me to be able to crack dog jokes at my parents' expense. I'm not sure the time I can do that will ever arrive, to be perfectly honest with you.'

'Regardless, we need to find out everything we can before his deadline runs out. Just think, a couple of months ago I had no life. Now you've brought a bottomless pit of mystery and intrigue to my door. It's all very exciting.'

'I'm glad you think so. Life isn't quite as rosy being at the pointy end of the stick.'

'We'll sort it all out, don't you worry.' Mads checked the time. 'I'd better run to rehearsal, I shouldn't be long. Shall I meet you at the office afterwards and we can catch the bus back together?'

'If you like. Will you finish by five?'

'I'm the first dead body, keeling over just as the first half draws to a close, so I can't imagine they'll mind me slipping off assuming everything goes OK.'

'Which it will?'

'Darling, I'm a professional,' Mads gushed, along with a hand flourish. 'What could possibly go wrong?'

Lyndsey hadn't even made herself a cup of tea next morning when Paula appeared.

'Hi, sorry to bother you. If you're busy just tell me to go away again, but Anne and I have a presentation to give this afternoon and need a few bits of information. Could I ask you to hunt them down for us?'

Lyndsey nodded. 'No problem at all. What do you need?'

'Here you go,' said Paula, handing her three sheets of paper. 'Most of it you'll find online, though if we have the books mentioned on the web pages to back things up, that would be perfect. Don't worry if not, though, we don't want you to be in trouble if you have other work you should be doing.'

'Don't worry about that, this is my last week and my enthusiasm for emptying the To-Do tray has waned, somewhat. Those who wanted the work done have gone, and it would surprise me if their replacements care too much.'

'Oh no, Elliot's letting you go?'

'I'm only a temp and that's the nature of the beast. Temps are expendable by nature. Given the events of the last couple of weeks, I'm in two minds whether I'm disappointed or relieved.'

'It must be terrible for you, I've worked here for four years and find it shocking enough. I can only imagine what it must be like to be in the storm's eye.'

'Unusual and scary would begin to cover it. Leave this with me and I'll bring it down to you when I'm done. Do you want the books if we have them, or just copies of the relevant pages?'

'Copies of the pages, please, if you have time. And could you highlight the passages on the copies, then we can slot them straight in. Thanks for your help, we'd planned to do it ourselves but Elliot has come up with something else for this morning that can't possibly wait.' She rolled her eyes.

'I know how that goes, I'll bring it all down to you.'

Paula thanked her and headed for the lift, leaving Lyndsey to skim over the sheets. It seemed straightforward enough, and she welcomed having something to do that was more interesting than clearing out desks or copy typing. By the time she'd found all the information and copied any relevant book pages it was getting close to lunchtime so she took everything down to Paula on her way to the refectory.

37

Mads turned up at university about ten-thirty and made a point of pretending to tap in at the barrier. When the barrier refused to open, she smiled at the security guard sitting at the desk on the other side.

'Sorry, it doesn't want to work. Could you let me in, please, and I'll go to Card Services and have them check it?'

The security guard looked her over as she waved the ID card in the air. He flicked a switch, and the barrier opened to allow her through. She walked to his desk so he could check the card was valid, then headed towards Card Services. As she reached their section, Mads gave a quick glance over her shoulder to check the guard wasn't watching, walked straight past and onwards towards the library.

She headed for the second floor, and having found herself a corner where no one was likely to overlook or disturb her, took her laptop from her bag and logged into the wifi using the university's generic alumni password. She took out a small notebook and logged into everyone's bank accounts one at a time, making a note of any balances as she went.

Once she reached the end of her list, Mads was feeling hungry so went downstairs to the refectory. She settled for a bowl of vegetable soup with a slice of crusty bloomer to dip in. After a bit of haggling, she also talked the server into letting her have an extra slice of bread instead of the butter she didn't want.

The refectory wasn't especially busy, and she chose a table where she would be alone with her thoughts while watching the world go by as students milled around between the library and their classes. Her costume hadn't quite fitted right yesterday, so she had to collect it from Cathy by four o'clock. That left her an hour or so to kill, so she decided she would hunt Lyndsey down once she'd finished eating.

Most of the bank accounts list were men so there was little she could do regarding closing their accounts, though planned to contact those on the "nice list" again to tell them they could stop paying. Half the accounts had money in too, and she wanted to take that out before closing the accounts to make it easier. It was a shame it wasn't sunny, as sunglasses would be a believable disguise when withdrawing from ATMs, if so. Still, she reasoned, one withdrawal per bank, there should be no reason anyone will question it or search out the security footage.

Still, that was a plan for another day. There was no point in getting ahead of herself. She had the final dress rehearsal of the play to run through this evening, not that she expected anything to go amiss with it, having managed a fine performance yesterday. In fact, she'd enjoyed every moment, and was considering signing up for acting courses at Questors Theatre in Ealing once the next academic year began. She hoped her life would be a little less hectic by then.

She finished her soup, took the tray and bowl to the collection area and made her way to the lift. There was no sign of Lyndsey upstairs near her desk, so Mads figured she might as well find Cathy earlier than arranged.

Lyndsey dropped the research back to Paula and Anne at ten to twelve.

'Oh, lovely. Thanks so much. I feel we ought to take you to lunch for getting us out of a spot, there,' said Paula.

'No, don't be silly, it wasn't as if I was busy doing anything else interesting.'

'Less of that,' said Anne. 'Go and grab your coat, you're coming for pizza. We have to eat something before our presentation and neither of us will take no for an answer. Don't make us kidnap you.'

Lyndsey went back upstairs for her coat and rejoined the librarians. They went to lunch at a small independent pizza shop down the road.

'How can you eat pizza without cheese?' asked Paula. 'It seems alien to me.'

'The plus side is it isn't so heavy. When I go to the pub with my mate for pizza, we take our own vegan mozzarella with us, but eating it without is perfect for lunch.'

'I'll take your word for it,' said Anne. 'I like me a bit of cheese, I do. So what will you be doing after this week?

Have you got anything lined up?'

'Not really, I'll concentrate on my writing.'

'That's interesting. Fiction or non-fiction?'

'Fiction, I used to work for the local paper but got remaindered in the last wave of cutbacks.'

'That's a shame. What kind of fiction?' asked Paula.

'I have ideas for all sorts but I'm currently drawn towards children's stories. Maybe my mind sees it as an escape from the horrors of the world.'

'Could be. If you anything published, make sure you come back and sell us copies. We all either have kids or relatives who do..'

'You bet I will. Do you guys have any idea who's behind the murders? You see a different part of the library to me.'

They both shook their heads as Lyndsey continued.

'Well, I say murders. After Gloria and now Joe, it's easy to assume Francis didn't have an accident.'

'The whole affair is very unsettling,' said Anne. 'I don't like to think I might know anyone who would do something like that.'

'I hope we don't,' said Paula. 'but I guess you can never be sure. I can't understand why anyone would target library managers. I don't think I've ever known anyone involved with a library to inspire the hatred that would lead to them being murdered. Library work is something of a sedentary occupation, when it comes to it.'

'Not even Gloria could antagonise me that much,' added Anne. 'It would be far easier to find another job than to risk being caught.'

'Anne, really? The possibility of getting caught is the only reason you wouldn't kill Gloria?'

'No, but it has to be taken into consideration, and you're not telling me you haven't fantasised about killing her at least once or twice. How about you, Lyndsey? Do you have any ideas?'

Lyndsey shook her head. 'None. My mate's the one for the crazy theories, but none of hers have panned out. A big part of me is eager to leave, not because of the job but because of the stress.'

'It must be terrible for you, seeing all your managers drop one by one. If I was a suspicious person, I might have thought it was you,' said Paula.

Lyndsey laughed. 'Not even Inspector Savage has me down as a suspect, or so he says. I don't know how he has the patience to do what he does, much of the time he's treading water, waiting for forensic results to appear. It would drive me up the wall.'

'It must be frustrating to have a job where you're constantly waiting on others,' said Anne. 'Cool, here's the pizza.'

They ate in silence before making their way back. Lyndsey headed upstairs and began to box up everything from Gloria's bookshelves. Once the shelves and the top of her desk were empty, she sat down with a cup of tea, then seeing the time was nearing three o'clock, figured she'd best empty Gloria's drawers so everything relating to the office would be finished.

She pulled one drawer, then another, but they were locked.

Ugh, just my luck.

Lyndsey locked the office door behind her and set off to the ground floor and the security office.

'Yes, Miss. How can I help you?' asked a youngish-looking guard sat behind the counter in the office.

'Hi, I'm clearing out the library managers' office on the fourth floor, but one of the desks is locked. I don't suppose you have spare sets of keys for the desks, do you?'

'I'm not sure, wait here, I'll find out for you.'

He disappeared into a back room. Lyndsey saw the security manager poke his head around the doorway to check who she was, and dive out of view again. After a few more minutes the original guard reappeared.

'Here you go, Miss, we hold a key to each of the desks in the office, plus the desk outside. Could you sign here please, to acknowledge receipt?'

He slid a book across the counter and pointed to the place she needed to sign and print her name. She did so and passed the book back.

'Thank you, don't forget to bring them back when you've finished,' he said, handing her a small key ring containing four keys.

'I won't, you'll have them back before I leave tonight.'

She made her way to the lift. Walking down eight flights was one thing, walking back up, quite another. The lift was on the fourth floor when she pressed the button, prompting her to wonder who was on her floor. It stopped at three on the way down and she assumed it had been one of the librarians or a student searching through the oversized books.

Back upstairs she unlocked the office again, leaving the key in the inside lock so she wouldn't lose it, and tried the desk keys on Gloria's desk, finding the correct one at the second attempt. She grabbed a box and placed everything from the left-hand drawers into it. There was nothing much of any importance. Notepads, a tube of cough sweets and numerous pens and pencils. Nothing that would warrant the hissy fit Gloria had thrown last week when she couldn't gain access.

She moved on to the top right-hand drawer. Once

again there were lots of odd pieces of stationery that she threw into the box. Finally, she opened the large bottom drawer where there was a box of tissues and a tote bag. She placed the tissues in the box and lifted the bag out of the drawer to see what it contained.

'Hi, Cathy. Sorry, I'm early, no rush if you're not ready.'

'Hey, Mads. No, the dress is all done. There it is on the hanger. Try it on and I can make any final adjustments if needed.'

Mads lifted the dress from the rail went behind a screen at the back of the room. It fitted like a glove, and she sashayed out from behind the screen to admire herself in the mirror.

'Oh Mads, it looks beautiful on you. How does it feel?'

'Fantastic, as comfortable as a second skin, almost like you made it especially for me. How is it from the back? Does it hang properly?'

Cathy came up behind her and peered over Mads' shoulder into the mirror, patting down the shoulders.

'Perfect, I'd say. As clothes horses go, you can come again. How did yesterday's rehearsal go? Did you remember your lines?'

'No problem, though there are only five of them. Wait until I screw them up at the dress rehearsal later.'

'I'm sure you'll be brilliant. I'll be there tonight to attend to any last-minute costume emergencies. I'm looking forward to seeing how it all comes together. Do you fancy a cup of tea? I'm due a break.'

'Definitely, let me take this off and hang it up again else I know I'll spill something over it.'

Mads got changed again and followed Cathy to a small break room a few doors away from the workshop and sat at a small table.

'I assume you're a student, Cathy? What are you studying?'

'Fashion and design. Working with the drama class gives me hands-on experience without the pressure of doing a job. Though, on the flip side, it means I don't earn any money for my toils.'

'Is that good or bad? I understand you have more time, but aren't contacts invaluable in your line? When I did my arts degree, some of the people I met when out on work experience proved useful, or they would have if I'd pursued it as a career.'

'You gave up? What do you do instead?'

'I'm just starting up again,' said Mads, avoiding the question. 'I still have all my contacts, though, and I've kept in touch with many of them, just in case.'

'This is my second year. I'll be on work experience for the whole of the third year, then graduate after the fourth. I think they do it like that so that the work experience proves useful for us as well as the company or designer we are assigned to. There would be little point if we just got in the way and were reduced to dogsbodies.'

'With the art course, it was very hit and miss. Some of us had worthwhile experiences, others not so much. The university was very good with those who had problems, though, and tried to reassign them if things weren't working out.'

'Here's hoping it will be the same for us. Our tutors are hyped for us to go out into the big wide world and gain some real experience. I'm sure they wouldn't be so eager if it was a waste of time.'

'I hope it goes well for you. You did a great job with that costume of mine.'

Cathy blushed as she handed Mads a mug of tea.

'Thanks, there really wasn't that much to do. Do you take milk or sugar?'

'No thanks. I'll add a drop of cold water, though, to take the edge off the searing heat.'

Mads stood and topped up the mug from the tap before sitting down again.

'How many people do you think will come to the play? It seems silly, but I'm getting nervous already.'

'You'd have to ask Jordan, but don't be nervous. They do three or four a year, and the audience is always supportive. You'll enjoy it, just relax. Have you done anything like this in the past?'

'Not really, though I did once have a boyfriend who fancied himself as a playwright and actor.'

Mads regaled the Tube Train Named Desire story. By the time she had finished, Cathy was in tears of laughter.

'And after that, the opportunity to act in his future plays wasn't tempting?'

'God, no. In fact, we split up not long afterwards. I've never regretted that decision.'

'You could have been a famous actress by now.'

'Or an infamous husband killer. Take your pick.'

'I'm sure you'd have been nothing of the sort. You don't strike me as the type.'

Mads shrugged. 'Who does?'

Lyndsey stood open-mouthed as she stared into the bag. Her first instinct was to put her hand in and hunt through, but she stopped herself. She grabbed a pencil from Gloria's box and walked across to FC's old desk at the back of the room where she emptied everything on top of it, taking care nothing was broken or fell onto the floor.

She moved the contents of the bag around with the pencil to look at it better. There was an antiseptic bottle. Was it the one she had used to treat FC's cut? She wondered whether it contained antiseptic at all. Hadn't Francis mentioned strange side effects, like his arm going numb? A used swab of cotton wool was with it, maybe the one she'd tended him with. There was also a small travel iron and a box of empty tea bags along with a plastic container holding something resembling tea, but Lyndsey would be willing to bet that it was something altogether different.

She heard the door close behind her and spun round to find Gloria locking it behind her and putting the key into her pocket.

'Oh, Lyndsey. I wish you hadn't found that bag. I was

beginning to like you.'

'What do you mean?'

'Come along, are you trying to tell me you haven't pieced it together yet? That if I let you go, you'll have no idea who the killer is? Because if you are, I'm not believing you.'

'But why? It makes no sense.'

Lyndsey felt her jeans pocket before realising that her phone was in her jacket on the stand behind the door. Gloria took two steps towards her.

'You have no idea what this place is like. I should have become the sole manager of the library when the old manager retired. There was no need to give Margaret half the job. To add insult to injury, when Margaret retired, instead of leaving me to it, they added a third post at my level and Elliot's job above, without even considering me for the higher post. This library is like a boys' club, all they do is back each other up. They don't give a second thought to me and my requirements, but are very inventive when it comes to reasons for needing some of my annual budget. Temporarily, they always say, but it never comes back. Just gives them more reason to claim that I don't need the full budget the next year, and the one after that. They needed a wake-up call.'

Lyndsey noticed she had been creeping nearer as she spoke, and edged herself towards Gloria's desk to put it between them both.

'But you killed your colleagues. Regardless of the provocation, wouldn't it have been easier to find another job?'

'Ha,' said Gloria, moving still closer. 'Finding another managerial position in this economy isn't easy, and why should I give the others the satisfaction of winning? Far better to clear the way. I can cash in on the sympathy over me nearly dying to take the top job.'

'Wasn't that a risk? Weren't you worried you'd die?'

'Not really, I took a small enough dose so it was in my system but I was never in any real danger. A little exaggeration added the finishing touches. Just because I changed degrees back in the day didn't mean I stopped studying chemistry. It always fascinated me. Who knew it would turn out to be as useful as it has been?'

'But there could have been complications? It seems reckless to endanger yourself like that?'

'Being a victim diverted attention. What many people don't understand about poison is that the dose is more important than the substance. Anything can kill you given the right dosage. Hiding that tea bag in Joe's caddy low enough so I'd be in hospital when he died was a masterstroke, I thought. No thanks to Inspector Savage, mind. I had to improvise and buy new empty bags and another travel iron where my things were locked away in here.'

'I understand that, but you haven't cleared a way. You've just created vacancies alongside yours. The new managers could be as bad as the old ones, maybe worse?'

Lyndsey reached Gloria's desk and slipped behind it, relieved there was now a barrier between them.

'Assuming Elliot drinks the coffee I took him, it will just be me. Gloria the hero. And to add to my legend, I got here just in time to catch the psychopathic temp destroying the evidence of her crimes. Sadly, I wasn't quick enough to stop her from taking her own life, nor from getting revenge on Elliot for finishing her contract early. The saddest thing is, had I been 100% I may have been able to save her life, but I'm still weak from my hospital stay.'

Lyndsey was panicking. She was younger but Gloria had at least six inches on her in height and a much longer reach. Trying to fight her could end up like one of those comedy movie bouts from the silent era, where the large man holds the small one at arms length, making it impossible for his punches to connect. She was a solid unit, too. Not fat, but heavier than Lyndsey and she clearly visited the gym on a regular basis. With the maniacal glint in her eye, she was quite terrifying. Lyndsey looked around for something she could use as a weapon, but even the boxes she had filled were the other side of the desk. Unarmed, fighting her way out could only be a last resort, and probably a futile one at that. The only chance she had was to ring the police.

'No one will believe I killed myself.'

'Don't be so sure. Desperate people make desperate decisions.'

Lyndsey grabbed the phone from Gloria's desk and started to press 999. In response, Gloria grabbed its cable and wrenched it from the wall.

'Sorry, we are experiencing difficulties with the telephone lines. Please try again later.'

Lyndsey threw the phone at her face, but Gloria batted it away with her forearm without missing a beat.

'How are you planning on killing me? You realise that claiming I committed suicide by strangulation only works in American prisons, right?'

'Well dear,' said Gloria, reaching the desk and patting her left-hand jacket pocket. 'You didn't use all the poison in Elliot's coffee.'

Lyndsey almost laughed. 'So now you'll tell me you were only joking, no hard feelings and offer to make a cup of tea?'

'No need for tea,' said Gloria. 'You have no way of escaping, I just need to force feed it to you.'

She lunged forward and Lyndsey barely managed to pull back in time to evade her grasping hand. Taking advantage of Gloria being off balance, Lyndsey darted around the desk trying to reach the phone in her jacket pocket. Her foot landed on a pencil that must have fallen on the floor when she was emptying the drawers. It rolled underneath her shoe as she tried to gain traction and was enough to make her stumble and lose momentum.

Having regained her balance, Gloria swung her arm out straight, catching Lyndsey on the throat with a clothesline worthy of a professional wrestler. Lyndsey fell backwards, grabbing her throat in pain and gasping for breath because of a combination of the hit and being winded from landing flat on her back. Gloria straddled her, placing her feet over Lyndsey's shins to stop her kicking. She grabbed both her wrists and held them above Lyndsey's head.

'Now what are you going to do, my pretty?'

Lyndsey tried to scream but could only manage a dry sound, not dissimilar to a cat coughing up a hairball. She squirmed and fought to free her hands, but Gloria was too heavy to dislodge.

'If you stop struggling it will be over quickly. Wouldn't you rather die in peace than in pain?'

'I don't intend to die. Not today,' croaked Lyndsey, fighting to free her hands.

'Sorry, my dear. You have little say in the matter.'

41

Mads finished her tea.

'Thanks for that, Cathy. I'll be back about six for the dress rehearsal.' She stood and made for the sink.

'Don't worry about washing it up, I'll do that. Find somewhere quiet to read through your lines and relax. You'll be fine.'

'I'm sure I will. I'm just feeling nervous.'

Cathy got up and gave her a quick hug. 'Everyone gets bouts of nerves, use it to focus on giving the best performance you can.'

Mads smiled. 'I'll bear that in mind.'

She left the break room and debated whether to pop upstairs to find Lyndsey. Instead, she decided she fancied a cold drink, so caught the lift down to the ground floor and bought a fresh orange juice. She sipped at it, enjoying the cold feeling on her lips and the citrus flavours on her tongue, then strolled back to the lifts and pressed the call button. After a few seconds, a lift arrived, and she stepped in and pressed the button for the fourth floor. Just as the doors were sliding shut, she heard someone shout, "Wait," and pressed the door open button. When they opened again, a student barrelled in, huffing and puffing.

'Thanks,' he said, before pressing button one. 'Oh, wait. Which floor are the philosophy books on?' He scanned the sign on the lift wall and also pressed button two. 'I'll never get used to the new layout, I really won't,' he said.

'I'm sure you will,' said Mads. 'No problem, I'm in no hurry.'

They stopped at the first floor, then the student got out at the second. Mads patiently waited for the doors to close again, which they did. At the fourth floor, she poked her head out and looked across towards Lyndsey's desk, seeing it empty and the office door closed.

I wonder where she is?

She got back in the lift again and pressed Ground, figuring she would check with the office. Just as the doors were closing, she thrust her arm between them, forcing them open again. In case she didn't find her, it made sense to leave a note on Lyndsey's desk to remind her she'd be late because of the rehearsal. She got out of the lift and strolled across. When she reached the desk, she sat down and opened the drawer, finding a pen and a pad of Post-it notes. She scribbled out a message and stuck it to the centre of Lyndsey's computer monitor, figuring that it would be the most obvious place for it to be unmissable.

As she stood, a movement in the office caught her eye and she walked to the window to investigate.

'Lyndsey,' she yelled and rushed towards the door. She tried to open it but it was locked. Mads ran back to the window and banged on it with both fists. 'Lyndsey!'

Lyndsey lay on the floor, struggling with Gloria. She seemed to be saying something but Mads couldn't hear anything through the glass. She felt so helpless. Mads stared up at the polystyrene ceiling tiles then back towards the two struggling women. Gloria glanced up at Mads with a deranged smile on her face, then said something to Lyndsey.

Mads ran back to the desk, wheeled the chair around and tried to throw it at the window, but it was too heavy. It briefly left the floor before thudding against the wall below the glass and rolling back towards her. She saw the phone and considered ringing either security or the police, but they would take too long to arrive. There must be something she could do.

She scanned the office one last time, then went racing off towards the back stairs, tearing through the police tape like an athlete reaching a finishing line.

Lyndsey was fast tiring but knew she couldn't give up. She thought she heard someone shout, but the words were too muffled to understand. She heard the door handle being wiggled up and down as someone tried to open the door. For a moment, Gloria became distracted and Lyndsey freed one of her hands and swung at Gloria's face, but Gloria grabbed her arm before she could connect, then gripped her wrists even harder.

'Now you've gone and made matters worse, Lyndsey. If you'd resigned yourself to the inevitable, your friend wouldn't have to die as well, would she?'

Lyndsey saw Mads banging on the window and watched as she shouted something. Gloria leered up at Mads.

'You're crazy, you'll never get away with this.'

'We'll see about that, my dear. The only certainty is if you and your friend live, there are witnesses. I've killed three people, the sentence can't be any worse for making it five.'

Lyndsey heard a thump against the wall. She guessed

Mads was trying to break the window.

'Mads, call for help. Anyone. Hurry!' she croaked, knowing the chances of Mads hearing her were non-existent.

She could feel Gloria trying to manipulate her wrists together and realised she wanted them positioned so she could secure them with one hand. Lyndsey took a deep breath and put all her energies into forcing them apart as far as she could. Once Gloria had a free hand, it would only take her seconds to take the poison from her pocket and force-feed it to her. She turned her head towards the window again but could see nothing.

'It seems your friend's run off towards the stairs, Lyndsey. She'll never get back in time, you might as well give up.'

43

Mads threw off the strands of police tape and scanned the crime scene where FC had died.

Thank god they kept this as it was.

She ran along the shelf and picked up the stepladder, folding it closed to make it easier to carry, then raced back round to the office window. She erected the stepladder and clambered up as quickly as she dared. She punched the polystyrene ceiling tile loose and climbed higher on the ladder so she could stick her head through the hole.

She sneezed as the dust she'd disturbed billowed into her nose. It was filthy up here.

She climbed to the top step and stood on tiptoes, then holding on to the firm part of the ceiling above the window, dragged herself up. Tentatively, she squatted and checked for any electric wires using her phone as a torch but there were none in this part of the ceiling. Figuring Gloria and Lyndsey were about two tiles away, she edged her hands along the metal grid that held the tiles in place and moved along until her head was over the third tile in. She turned off the torch and managed to keep balance as she put the phone back into her pocket.

Then she pulled up her knees and placed her whole body weight on the second tile.

44

Lyndsey was still struggling with Gloria but beginning to think it was a lost cause when some dust fell from the ceiling above them. She screwed up her eyes and turned her head so the dust wouldn't blind her. With no further warning, a much larger cloud of dust, pieces of polystyrene and Mads came crashing down on top of Gloria, crushing Lyndsey, but at least freeing her hands as Gloria flailed around trying to right herself and fight off the new arrival.

Mads grabbed Gloria in a choke hold and dragged her off Lyndsey before sitting on her. Lyndsey rolled away and lay by the wall, wheezing loudly.

'Are you OK, Lynds? Where's the key?'

Lyndsey held her side in pain. 'In her right-hand pocket.'

Gloria tried to throw Mads off her like a bucking bronco and Lyndsey couldn't help a wry grin as she watched Mads punch her full in the face three times until Gloria lay still.

'You keep her at bay, Mads, I'll grab the key.'

Lyndsey crawled across and pulled the key from Gloria's pocket.

'Got it, arrange her hands behind her back, I have some

packing tape on Joe's desk.'

Grimacing, Lyndsey stood and retrieved the tape. She secured Gloria's wrists and ankles together more roughly than was needed. When she was confident that Gloria wasn't escaping, she unlocked the door, got her phone and called Inspector Savage.

Mads watched Lyndsey slump to the floor again and lean against the wall.

'Are you OK, Lynds?'

'Just about. I might have a broken rib or two. I never imagined I'd be pleased to say something like that.' She grimaced and changed her position. 'Savage is downstairs so won't be long. Thanks for the superhero act, I don't think I could have held her off much longer.'

'You need to call an ambulance.'

Lyndsey winced. 'I'll be fine, I just need to rest.'

'No, you need medical treatment. You can barely talk, for one, and if I have broken your ribs, you need them checked out. What's the point in me playing the hero if you drop dead with a punctured lung? Either you call them or I do. I'll come to the hospital with you, don't worry.'

Lyndsey frowned then figured Mads was right.

'OK, ring for an ambulance, but you have your rehearsal to go to. The play will give me something to look forward to tomorrow.'

'OK, deal,' smiled Mads. She took her phone from her

pocket and rang emergency services. 'So tell me, what was she thinking? Did she say?'

'I think she lost it a while back. Delusions of grandeur combined with a persecution complex. The librarians told me her husband left her a few months ago and that might have been the catalyst, or what do they call it on TV? The inciting incident, that's it. Since then she could have been planning everything.'

'So she was killing her way to the top, as if the university is a Mafia organisation?'

Inspector Savage walked through the door.

'Well well, ladies. If this is what you call keeping your noses out of police business, I'd hate to know what happens when you go at something full-on.'

'We didn't mean to, Gloria was trying to kill Lyndsey so I had to do something. She's down there by the desk. We've tied her up.'

'Are you OK, Lyndsey?'

'I'll be fine, Mads has called an ambulance.'

'I'm pleased to hear it,' he said, making his way over to Gloria. He checked her pulse and gave her a cursory once over. 'Do I really want to know what happened to her?'

'I may have hit her two or three times. It was the only way to stop her fighting us,' said Mads. 'I won't get into trouble, will I?'

'I wouldn't think so, but I will have to take statements from the pair of you. Is there any evidence lying around, in case she denies everything and wants to press charges?'

'On the back desk,' croaked Lyndsey. 'I didn't touch any of it with my hands, so unless she wore gloves everything's bound to have her prints on. Though if the cotton wool swab is the one I used, it might have my DNA all over it along with Francis's. I wore gloves when I treated him, but I can't remember whether I touched the swab before putting them on.'

'I'll bear that in mind. I'm sure we'll be able to find a paper trail for the drugs once we're certain what we're dealing with. While I officially disapprove of your shenanigans, well done both of you. Just don't expect me to say that in front of witnesses.'

'Thanks,' said Mads and Lyndsey together.

Inspector Savage took out his phone and rang for backup and a medic, then the emergency team arrived for Lyndsey. After asking her for details of what had happened and checking her vitals, they lifted her onto a stretcher. One of them looked across at Gloria.

'Is she OK?'

'She'll be fine,' said Savage. 'She's conscious and I've arranged for a medic to meet us at the station. You concentrate on Lyndsey. I can't have her dying on me, I suspect her statement will be most interesting.'

He nodded and turned to Mads. 'Are you a friend of the patient?'

'Yes.'

'Will you be able to follow us to the hospital? It's unusual they keep patients overnight for injuries like this and the painkillers will mean she shouldn't be catching buses on her own. Assuming you have a car.'

'I can't literally follow you, but could get there for eight or nine o'clock. Will that be all right?'

He nodded. 'Should be fine, I'll tell A&E to expect you. As you're turning up after eight, I'd suggest parking in one of the side streets nearby, rather than pay the extortionate parking charges. All the local restrictions end at eight o'clock so you'll be fine.'

'Thanks for the tip.' Mads walked across and held

Lyndsey's hand. 'Are you sure you'll be OK?'

'You go rehearse, I'll survive.'

'If you say so, I'll collect you when we've finished.'

'I'll ring if there are any complications.'

'OK, and before I forget - I told you so.'

'I was waiting for that. See you later.'

The stretcher was halfway out of the room when Lyndsey tried to sit up but found her movements restricted by the straps. She signalled for the medics to stop. 'Mads.'

Mads poked her head around the door. 'What?'

'She poisoned Elliot's coffee. He's in the office upstairs.'

Mads pushed the medic and the trolley out of the door in her haste and made for the stairs, when a barked command stopped her in her tracks.

'Ms Walsh, don't you dare go one step farther.'

She turned to face Inspector Savage.

'But, Elliot. Upstairs. Coffee.'

'Yes, and while I realise you think of yourself as a fully paid up deputy, I think that's more a job for the police, don't you? Keep an eye on Gloria while I check, and try not to assault her again if at all possible.'

He raced past her and pushed through the door to the stairs. Mads trudged back to the office.

'Feel better Lynds, I'll collect you later,' she shouted towards the stretcher waiting by the lift.

As Mads entered the room, Gloria glared up at her while struggling to free herself from the tape.

'Try all you like, I don't think you'll manage,' said Mads.

Gloria stared up at her. 'You bitch, I'll get you for this.'

Mads laughed. 'Is that all you've got? I'm sure you can do better. What about, "Damn you two, I'd have got away with it if it wasn't for you pesky kids!"?'

EPILOGUE

'I thought you were great,' said Lyndsey sipping at her post-play glass of wine.

'Thanks,' said Mads. 'I enjoyed the feeling of being on stage again. I'm going to see if I can find other local groups to join like you suggested, as well as applying for the classes at Ealing.'

'You should, the play wasn't bad either, considering it was a student affair.'

'That was a pleasant surprise.' Mads looked across the student bar. 'Isn't that Inspector Savage? What's he doing here?'

Lyndsey looked round. 'Yes, it is. Shall we go across and find out what happened with Gloria?'

'We might as well try, though I doubt he'll tell us much.'

They walked across the room. As they approached, Savage peeled away from the person he'd been talking to and smiled at them.

'Good evening, ladies. May I say, Ms Walsh, that was an enthusiastic, if brief, performance you put in there. I must admit, I had an awful feeling you would resurrect yourself and solve the crimes at the last minute. I was relieved to find that it was just my cynical outlook.'

Mads laughed. 'Thank you, Inspector. I'm surprised to see you here tonight, a murder mystery play must be something of a busman's holiday, surely? What happened with Elliot in the end? And did you discover what poisons Gloria used?'

'Sadly it was too late to save Elliot. Cyanide can be fast acting given the right quantities, and she told him the coffee was a new blend with almond flavouring so he drank it without thinking. The drug she prepared for Francis was more unusual. It was based on plant sap the Amazonians used on the tips of their spears and arrows when hunting prey. It acts on the muscles, so the Amazonians would just stroll after the animal once they had hit it, knowing it would collapse and be waiting for them further along the trail, unable to move.'

'That's horrible,' said Lyndsey. 'So Francis was conscious but unable to move when I left work that night?'

'Yes, but don't blame yourself. You had no way of knowing. She also tricked you into administering the drug by hiding it in the antiseptic bottle. It seems she wanted to make Francis look like an accident in order to give her time to set the rest of her plan into action. Her chemistry knowledge made it possible.'

Lyndsey was horrified to find she had unwittingly dosed Francis with the drug. She felt a little sick and raised her hand to her mouth instinctively.

Mads put her arm around her. 'Are you OK? You look as pale as a cannellini.'

Lyndsey nodded. 'Yes, it's just a shock to know that I was party to Francis's death, even though I had no way of knowing.'

'As I said, Miss Marshall. Don't worry yourself, it wasn't your fault.'

'What about Joe?' asked Mads.

'Some form of aconite. She mixed it with the tea from one of his bags and sealed the resulting mixture in a new bag. From what I hear about his herbal tea, I doubt he noticed much difference from his normal brew.'

'Aconite? Isn't that wolfsbane?' asked Lyndsey.

'It has various names. We're running tests on all the plants and herbs in her greenhouse. She has a veritable killing harvest in there. She had clearly been planning this for some time. Aconite was well chosen for Joe, he had a weak heart and it killed him in minutes.'

'That's terrible,' said Mads. 'Still, thanks for telling us, and for coming to see the play.'

'I must admit, I have an ulterior motive for being here, but I arrived just before it began and didn't want to spoil your night on the boards. Could we have a quiet word in the corner, Ms Walsh?'

'Sure, just me or both of us?'

'That's entirely up to you.'

He walked off and sat in a chair at a corner table where they would have some privacy. Mads turned to Lyndsey and whispered in her ear.

'What do you think this is about?'

'No idea, do you want me to come with you?'

'Please. If you feel up to it.'

'I'll be fine. Sitting down is probably a good idea, anyway. Let's go.'

They walked to the corner and sat across the table from Inspector Savage.

'Ms Walsh, do you have any idea where your husband is at this moment?'

'None at all, why? He's abroad somewhere, but I don't know where.'

Savage took his notebook out of his pocket.

'His name is Arthur Wilson, correct?'

Lyndsey snorted. 'I thought your husband was Nigel.'

Mads looked at her. 'His real name was Arthur, but he hated it so much he used his middle name.'

'Goodness, I can't imagine hating a name so much that Nigel seems a better alternative.'

'I know, right? Arthur was a family name passed down to the first born. Anyway, Inspector. Yes, Arthur Wilson, but he always went by Nigel. I didn't change my name when we married, hence the difference in surnames. How can I help you?'

'Mr Arthur Wilson, Nigel, was reported missing by his line manager today. They haven't heard from him in over a week, though as he worked remotely that wasn't especially unusual. What they find more concerning, is the multi-million dollar hole in their accounts. Do you know anything about that, Ms Walsh?'

Note from the author

Thank you for reading Blood Read and I hope you enjoyed it. If so, I would very much appreciate a review at Amazon, GoodReads or wherever your preferred book review platform may be.

If you would like to be kept up to date with anything else I am writing, please visit http://www.dsfloyd.com and sign up for my free newsletter.

This book has been checked for errors, but should you find any then please tell me via dave@dsfloyd.com so they can be rectified.

About the Author

 D S Floyd has been employed in various roles throughout his life. Most of these jobs have been done grudgingly, and to no one's surprise were relatively short lived. Having attained a masters degree in creative writing and remembering his time as a DTP designer (mainly creating record and CD covers) as being very enjoyable, when the opportunity arose to flex his writing and DTP skills on a full time basis, he leapt straight in. He also writes serial killer fiction under the name David S Floyd and poems/songs as Dave Floyd. He's pictured here with a pint outside the Cow's Tail* by the River Thames.

http://dsfloyd.com
http://davidsfloyd.com
http://madsart.uk

*The pub's book name, obviously. Can't go spoiling the magic.

Also available:

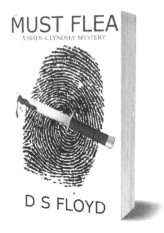

Having been laid off from work, Lyndsey grudgingly agrees to work her grandad's market stall at weekends until she finds something better. On her first morning, her ex-boyfriend tumbles out of a wardrobe on a nearby furniture stall with a knife in his ribs.

A knife from her grandad's stall.

With the local police suspecting that she is the killer, Lyndsey and her old mate, Mads, set about finding who was responsible for the murder. Can they discover who the killer is before the police arrest Lyndsey ... or before the killer finds them?

Must Flea is a light-hearted murder mystery based in Brentford, West London.

ISBN: 978-1-898735-02-1

Coming soon:

Mads' husband is missing, along with millions of dollars of his company's money. Where is he, and where is the money?

With the police looking in Mads' direction for a suspect or an accomplice, her and Lyndsey are on a race against time to find the money and a missing husband.

And things get no better for our intrepid heroines when Nigel shows up ... dead.

Missing Art is a light-hearted murder mystery based in Brentford, West London.

ISBN: 978-1-898735-04-5

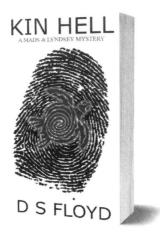

Mads & Lyndsey get to take the holiday they've been promising themselves, but there's no time for relaxation. The hunt is on for Lyndsey's parents, and our dynamic duo are right in the thick of the action.

Kin Hell is a light-hearted murder mystery (not entirely) based in Brentford, West London.

ISBN: 978-1-898735-05-2

47760845R00146

Printed in Poland
by Amazon Fulfillment
Poland Sp. z o.o., Wrocław

Far and  the best
for touring Europe

Explanation of a Campsite Entry
Touring Spain & Portugal 2015

The town under which the campsite is listed, as shown on the relevant Sites Location Map at the end of each country's site entry pages

Distance and direction of the site from the centre of the town the site is listed under in kilometres (or metres), together with site's aspect

Site Location Map grid reference

Site open all year

GPS co-ordinates – latitude and longitude

Campsite name

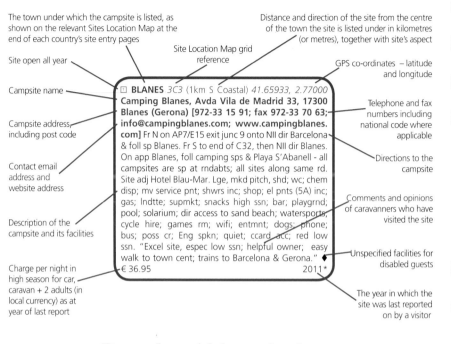

☐ **BLANES** *3C3* (1km S Coastal) *41.65933, 2.77000* **Camping Blanes, Avda Vila de Madrid 33, 17300 Blanes (Gerona) [972-33 15 91; fax 972-33 70 63; info@campingblanes.com; www.campingblanes. com]** Fr N on AP7/E15 exit junc 9 onto NII dir Barcelona & foll sp Blanes. Fr S to end of C32, then NII dir Blanes. On app Blanes, foll camping sps & Playa S'Abanell - all campsites are sp at rndabts; all sites along same rd. Site adj Hotel Blau-Mar. Lge, mkd pitch, shd; wc; chem disp; mv service pnt; shwrs inc; shop; el pnts (5A) inc; gas; lndtte; supmkt; snacks high ssn; bar; playgrnd; pool; solarium; dir access to sand beach; watersports; cycle hire; games rm; wifi; entmnt; dogs; phone; bus; poss cr; Eng spkn; quiet; ccard acc; red low ssn. "Excel site, espec low ssn; helpful owner; easy walk to town cent; trains to Barcelona & Gerona." ◆ € 36.95   2011*

Campsite address, including post code

Contact email address and website address

Description of the campsite and its facilities

Telephone and fax numbers including national code where applicable

Directions to the campsite

Comments and opinions of caravanners who have visited the site

Unspecified facilities for disabled guests

Charge per night in high season for car, caravan + 2 adults (in local currency) as at year of last report

The year in which the site was last reported on by a visitor

Popular Abbreviations
(for a full list of abbreviations please see page 10).

Site Description

sm: max 50 pitches   **med**: 51–150 pitches   **lge**: 151–500 pitches   **v lge**: 501+ pitches   **hdg**: hedged
mkd: marked   **sl**: sloping site   **pt sl**: sloping in parts   **terr**: terraced site   **shd**: plenty of shade
pt shd: part shaded   **unshd**: no shade   **hdstg**: some hard standing or gravel pitches

Popular Abbreviations for Site Facilities

Adv bkg:	advanced booking accepted
CCI or CCS:	Camping Card International or Camping Card Scandinavia accepted
chem disp:	dedicated chemical toilet disposal facilities
chem disp (wc):	no dedicated point; disposal via wc only
CL-type:	very small, privately-owned, informal and usually basic, farm or country site
El pnts:	mains electric hook-ups
Eng spkn:	English spoken
entmnt:	entertainment (facilities or organised)

lndtte:	washing machine(s) with or without tumble dryers
NH:	suitable as a night halt;
quiet:	peaceful, tranquil site
rest:	restaurant
shwrs:	hot showers available at a fee
shwrs inc:	cost included in the site fee quoted
tradsmn:	tradesmen call at the site, e.g. baker
SBS	Site Booking Reference - Ref No. for a site included in the Caravan Club's network i.e. bookable through the Club
ssn	season

Popular Generic Abbreviations

Adj: adjacent, nearby;   **app**: approach, on approaching;   **arr**: arrival, arriving   **bef**: before   **bet**: between   **c'van**: caravan; **ccard acc**: Credit and/or debit cards accepted;   **CChq acc**: Camping cheques accepted;   **clsd**: closed   **E**: East;   **ent**: entrance/ entry to   **excel**: excellent;   **facs**: facilities;   **foll**: follow;   **fr**: from;   **gd**: good;   **inc**: included/inclusive;   **L**: left;   **M'van**: motorhome / motor caravan;   **narr**: narrow   **N**: North;   **o'fits**: outfits;   **R**: right;   **rec**: recommend/ed;   **red**: reduced/reduction;   **rte**: route **S**: South;   **sp**: sign post/signposted;   **strt**: straight, straight ahead   **sw**: swimming   **vg**: very good;   **W**: West

Touring Spain & Portugal

Also available:

© The Caravan Club Limited 2015
Published by The Caravan Club Limited
East Grinstead House, East Grinstead
West Sussex RH19 1UA

General Enquiries: 01342 326944
Travel Service Reservations: 01342 316101
Red Pennant Overseas Holiday Insurance:
01342 336633
Website: www.caravanclub.co.uk
Email: enquiries@caravanclub.co.uk

Editor: Kate Walters
Email: kate.walters@caravanclub.co.uk

Printed by Stephens & George Ltd
Merthyr Tydfil

ISBN 978-0-9569510-7-6

Maps and distance charts generated from Collins
Bartholomew Digital Database

Maps © Collins Bartholomew Ltd 2014, reproduced by
permission of HarperCollins Publishers.

Cover: Seville ©Shutterstock/AdrianNunez

Travel money with the exchange experts

Enjoy our best rates online

We work with Moneycorp to offer some of the most competitive rates available in the market, consistently beating many of the leading high street and online providers.

Home Delivery

Order your travel money online with optional home delivery.

Key benefits:

- FREE next day delivery on orders of £500 or more*
- 0% commission on all currency orders
- Online track and trace and signature on delivery
- Guaranteed pre-9am and Saturday delivery options available
- Full insurance against the loss of currency

Prepaid Explorer Card

Security, flexibility and convenience

Avoid bank charges associated with overseas debit/credit card usage and secure your travel money on a multi-currency Explorer card.

Load up to £10,000 per day and don't worry about carrying around excess cash while abroad.

Prepaid Explorer Card benefits

- Apply in minutes and manage your account online
- No fees on ATM withdrawals or card transactions outside the UK†

Welcome

to Touring Spain & Portugal 2015

The Caravan Club has been producing the **Caravan Europe** guides for over 50 years, and in that time there have been a lot of changes in the way people tour on the continent. We know that those who use this guide travel in a wide range of outfits – not just caravans, but motorhomes, trailer tents and tents as well. This, above all else, is the reason for the change in the name of this guide to **Touring Spain & Portugal.**

The way that people research their trip has also changed considerably. The availability of information, especially online, means that there is far more content accessible than we are able to provide within these books. With this in mind, you will see a change to the introductory chapters - giving you the essential information you need when touring, while directing you to further good sources if you need to delve deeper.

One thing that hasn't changed over the years is our reliance on you, the users of the sites and these guides, to collate the information. The fact that all the entries are from those who stay on these sites makes the guide unique, and we very much appreciate the time and effort you continue to give in contributing to the guides. You can visit www.caravanclub.co.uk/europereport to fill in reports online, or find site report forms at the back of the guide.

I hope the changes will make the guides much easier to use, but we always welcome feedback on the changes or what you would like to see in future editions. Happy touring!

Kate Walters

Kate Walters, Editor

Contents

Continental Campsites

Site Listings

Site Report Forms   Back of Guide

See also alphabetical index at the back of the guide

How to use this guide

The information contained within *Touring Spain & Portugal* is presented in the following categories:

The Handbook

This includes general information about touring in Europe, such as legal requirements, advice and regulations. The Handbook chapters are at the front of the guide and are separated as follows:

Purple section	Planning your trip - information you'll need before you travel including information on the documents and insurance you'll need, advice on money, customs regulations and planning your channel crossings.
Green section	Motoring advice - advice on motoring overseas, essential equipment and roads in Europe including mountain passes and tunnels.
Turquoise section	During your stay - information for while you're away including telephone, internet and TV advice, medical information and advice on staying safe.
Blue section	Continental Campsites - advice on choosing your site and the differences you might find overseas.

Country Introduction

Following on from the Handbook chapters you will find the Country Introductions containing information, regulations and advice specific to each country. You should read the Country Introduction in conjunction with the Handbook chapters before you set off on your holiday.

Campsite Entries

After the Country Introduction you will find the campsite entries listed alphabetically under their nearest town or village. Where several campsites are shown in and around the same town they will be listed in clockwise order from the north.

To find a campsite all you need to do is look for the town or village of where you would like to stay, or use the maps at the back of each site section to find a town where sites are listed. Where there are no sites listed in a relatively large or popular town you may find a cross reference, directing you to closest town which does have sites.

In order to provide you with the details of as many site as possible in *Touring Spain & Portugal* we use abbreviations in the site entries.

For a full and detailed list of these abbreviations please see the following pages of this section.

We have also included some of the most regularly used abbreviations, as well as an explanation of a campsite entry, on the tear-out bookmark page.

Campsite Fees

Campsite entries show high season fees per night for an outfit plus two adults, as at the year of the last report. Prices given may not include electricity or showers, unless indicated. Outside of the main holiday season many sites offer discounts on the prices shown and some sites may also offer a reduction for longer stays.

Campsite fees may vary to the prices stated in the site entries, especially if the site has not been reported on for a few years. You are advised to always check fees when booking, or at least before pitching, as those shown in site entries should be used as a guide only.

Site Maps

Each town and village listed alphabetically in the site entry pages has a map grid reference

number, e.g. 3B4. The map grid reference number is shown on each site entry. The maps can be found at the end of each country's site entry pages. The reference number will show you where each town or village is located, and the site entry will tell you how far the site is from that town. Place names are shown on the maps in two colours:

Red where we list a site which is open all year (or for at least eleven months of the year)

Black where we only list seasonal sites which close in winter.

These maps are intended for general campsite location purposes only; a detailed road map or atlas is essential for route planning and touring.

Town names in capital letters (**RED**, **BLACK** or in *ITALICS*) correspond with towns listed on the Distance Chart.

The scale used for the map means that it is not possible to pinpoint every town or village where a campsite exists, so some sites in small villages may be listed under a nearby larger town instead.

Satellite Navigation

Most campsite entries now show a GPS (sat nav) reference. There are several different formats of writing co-ordinates, and in this guide we use decimal degrees, for example 48.85661 (latitude north) and 2.35222 (longitude east).

Minus readings, shown as -1.23456, indicate that the longitude is west of the Greenwich meridian. This will only apply to sites in the west of France, most of Spain and all of Portugal as the majority of Europe (including all countries covered in this edition of the guide) are east of the Greenwich meridian.

Manufacturers of Sat Navs all use different formats of co-ordinates so you may need to convert the co-ordinates before using them with your device. There are plenty of online conversion tools which enable you to do this quickly and easily - just type 'co-ordinate converter' into your search engine.

Please be aware if you are using a sat nav device some routes may take you on roads that are narrow and/or are not suitable for caravans or large outfits.

The GPS co-ordinates given in this guide are provided by members and checked wherever possible, however we cannot guarantee their accuracy due to the rural nature of most of the sites. The Caravan Club cannot accept responsibility for any inaccuracies, errors or omissions or for their effects.

Site Report Forms

With the exception of campsites in The Club's Overseas Site Booking Service (SBS) network, The Caravan Club does not inspect sites listed in this guide. Virtually all of the sites listed in *Touring Spain & Portugal* are from site reports submitted by users of these guides. You can tell us about great sites you have found or update the details of sites already within the books.

We rely on you, the users of this guide, to tell us about campsites you have visited

Sites which are not reported on for five years are deleted from the guide, so even if you visit a site and find nothing different from the site listing we'd appreciate a update to tell us as much.

You will find site report forms towards the back of this guide which we hope you will complete and return to us by freepost (please post when you are back in the UK). Use the abbreviated site report form if you are reporting no changes, or only minor changes, to a site entry. The full report form should be used for new sites or sites which have changed a lot since the last report.

You can complete both the full and abbreviated versions of the site report forms by visiting www.caravanclub.co.uk/europereport

Please submit reports as soon as possible. Information received by **mid August 2015** will be used wherever possible in the next edition of *Touring Spain & Portugal*. Reports received after that date are still very welcome and will appear in the following edition. The editor is unable to respond individually to site reports submitted due to the large quantity that we receive.

Tips for Completing Site Reports

- If possible fill in a site report form while at the campsite. Once back at home it can be difficult to remember details of individual sites, especially if you visited several during your trip.
- When giving directions to a site, remember to include the direction of travel, e.g. 'from north on D137, turn left onto D794 signposted Combourg' or 'on N83 from Poligny turn right at petrol station in village'. Wherever possible give road numbers, junction numbers and/or kilometre post numbers, where you exit from motorways or main roads. It is also helpful to mention useful landmarks such as bridges, roundabouts, traffic lights or prominent buildings.

We very much appreciates the time and trouble you take submitting reports on campsites that you have visited; without your valuable contributions it would be impossible to update this guide.

Acknowledgements

The Caravan Club's thanks go to the AIT/ FIA Information Centre (OTA), the Alliance Internationale de Tourisme (AIT), the Fédération International de Camping et de Caravaning (FICC) and to the national clubs and tourist offices of those countries who have assisted with this publication.

Every effort is made to ensure that information contained in this publication is accurate and that the details given in good faith in the site report forms are accurately reproduced or summarised. The Caravan Club Ltd has not checked these details by inspection or other investigation and cannot accept responsibility for the accuracy of these reports as provided by members and non-members, or for errors, omissions or their effects. In addition The Caravan Club Ltd cannot be held accountable for the quality, safety or operation of the sites concerned, or for the fact that conditions, facilities, management or prices may have changed since the last recorded visit. Any recommendations, additional comments or opinions have been contributed by caravanners and people staying on the site and are not generally those of The Caravan Club.

The inclusion of advertisements or other inserted material does not imply any form of approval or recognition, nor can The Caravan Club Ltd undertake any responsibility for checking the accuracy of advertising material.

Explanation of a
Campsite Entry

The town under which the campsite is listed, as shown on the relevant Sites Location Map at the end of each country's site entry pages

Distance and direction of the site from the centre of the town the site is listed under in kilometres (or metres), together with site's aspect

Site Location Map grid reference

Indicates that the site is open all year

Campsite name

Telephone and fax numbers including national code where applicable

Description of the campsite and its facilities

Contact email and website address

Directions to the campsite

⊞ **BLANES** *3C3* (1km S Coastal) *41.65933, 2.77000*
Camping Blanes, Avda Vila de Madrid 33, 17300 Blanes (Gerona) [972-33 15 91; fax 972-33 70 63; **info@campingblanes.com;www.campingblanes. com**] Fr N on AP7/E15 exit junc 9 onto NII dir Barcelona & foll sp Blanes. Fr S to end of C32, then NII dir Blanes. On app Blanes, foll camping sps & Playa S'Abanell - all campsites are sp at rndabts; all sites along same rd. Site adj Hotel Blau-Mar. Lge, mkd pitch, shd; wc; chem disp; mv service pnt, shwrs inc; shop; el pnts (5A) inc; gas; lndtte; supmkt; snacks high ssn; bar; playgrnd; pool; solarium; dir access to sand beach; watersports; cycle hire; games rm; wifi; entmnt; dogs; phone; bus; poss cr; Eng spkn; quiet; ccard acc; red low ssn. "Excel site, espec low ssn; helpful owner; easy walk to town cent; trains to Barcelona & Gerona." ♦
€ 36.95   2011*

Unspecified facilities for disabled guests. If followed by 'ltd' this indicates that the facilities are limited.

The year in which the site was last reported on by a visitor

Campsite address

Charge per night in high season for car, caravan + 2 adults as at year of last report

Opening dates

NOJA *1A4* (700m N Coastal) *43.49011, -3.53636*
Camping Playa Joyel, Playa del Ris, 39180 Noja (Cantabria) [942-63 00 81; fax 942-63 12 94; **playajoyel@telefonica.net; www. playajoyel.com**] Fr Santander or Bilbao foll sp A8/E70 (toll-free). Approx 15km E of Solares exit m'way junc 185 at Beranga onto CA147 N twd Noja & coast. On o'skirts of Noja turn L sp Playa del Ris, (sm brown sp) foll rd approx 1.5km to rndabt, site sp to L, 500m fr rndabt. Fr Santander take S10 for approx 8km, then join A8/E70. V lge, mkd pitch, pt sl, pt shd; wc; chem disp; mv service pnt; baby facs; shwrs inc; el pnts (6A) inc; gas; lndtte (inc dryer); supmkt; tradsmn; rest; snacks; bar; BBQ (gas/charcoal); playgrnd; pool; paddling pool; jacuzzi; direct access to sand beach adj; windsurfing; sailing; tennis; hairdresser; car wash; cash dispenser; wifi; entmnt; games/TV rm; 15% statics; no dogs; no c'vans/m'vans over 8m high ssn; phone; recep 0800-2200; poss v cr w/end & high ssn; Eng spkn; adv bkg; ccard acc; quiet at night; red low ssn/snr citizens; CCI. "Well-organised site on sheltered bay; v busy high ssn; pleasant staff; gd, clean facs; superb pool & beach; some narr site rds with kerbs; midnight silence enforced; Wed mkt outside site; highly rec." ♦
15 Apr-1 Oct. € 47.40 SBS - E05   2011*

GPS co-ordinates – latitude and longitude in decimal degrees. Minus figures indicate that the site is west of the Greenwich meridian

Comments and opinion of caravanners who ha visited the site (within inverted commas)

The site accepts Camping Cheque see the **Continental Campsite** chapter for details

Booking reference for a site the Club's Overseas Travel Service work with, i.e. bookable via The Club.

Site Description Abbreviations

Each site entry assumes the following unless stated otherwise:

Level ground, open grass pitches, drinking water on site, clean wc unless otherwise stated (own sanitation required if wc not listed), site is suitable for any length of stay within the dates shown.

aspect
urban – within a city or town, or on its outskirts
rural – within or on edge of a village or in open countryside
coastal – within one kilometre of the coast

size of site
sm – max 50 pitches
med – 51 to 150 pitches
lge – 151 to 500 pitches
v lge – 501+ pitches

pitches
hdg pitch – hedged pitches
mkd pitch – marked or numbered pitches
hdstg – some hard standing or gravel

levels
sl – sloping site
pt sl – sloping in parts
terr – terraced site

shade
shd – plenty of shade
pt shd – part shaded
unshd – no shade

Site Facilities

adv bkg
Advance booking accepted;
adv bkg rec – advance booking recommended

baby facs
Nursing room/bathroom for babies/children

beach
Beach for swimming nearby;
1km – distance to beach
sand beach – sandy beach
shgl beach – shingle beach

bus/metro/tram
Public transport within an easy walk of the site

chem disp
Dedicated chemical toilet disposal facilities;
chem disp (wc) – no dedicated point; disposal via wc only

CKE/CCI
Camping Key Europe and/or Camping Card International accepted

CL-type
Very small, privately-owned, informal and usually basic, farm or country site similar to those in the Caravan Club's network of Certificated Locations

dogs
Dogs allowed on site with appropriate certification (a daily fee may be quoted and conditions may apply)

el pnts
Mains electric hook-ups available for a fee;
inc – cost included in site fee quoted
10A – amperage provided
conn fee – one-off charge for connection to metered electricity supply
rev pol – reversed polarity may be present

(see *Electricity and Gas* in the section *DURING YOUR STAY*)

Eng spkn
English spoken by campsite reception staff

entmnt
Entertainment facilities or organised entertainment for adults and/or children

fam bthrm
Bathroom for use by families with small children

gas
Supplies of bottled gas available on site or nearby

internet
Internet point for use by visitors to site;
wifi – wireless local area network available

lndtte
Washing machine(s) with or without tumble dryers, sometimes other equipment available, eg ironing boards;
lndtte (inc dryer) – washing machine(s) and tumble dryer(s)
lndry rm – laundry room with only basic clothes-washing facilities

Mairie
Town hall (France); will usually make municipal campsite reservations

mv service pnt
Special low level waste discharge point for motor caravans; fresh water tap and rinse facilities should also be available

NH
Suitable as a night halt

noisy
Noisy site with reasons given;
quiet – peaceful, tranquil site

open 1 Apr-15 Oct
Where no specific dates are given, opening
dates are assumed to be inclusive, ie Apr-Oct –
beginning April to end October
(NB: opening dates may vary from those shown;
check before travelling, particularly when
travelling out of the main holiday season)

phone
Public payphone on or adjacent to site

playgrnd
Children's playground

pool
Swimming pool (may be open high season only);
htd – heated pool
covrd – indoor pool or one with retractable
cover

poss cr
During high season site may be crowded or
overcrowded and pitches cramped

red CCI/CCS
Reduction in fees on production of a Camping
Card International or Camping Card Scandinavia

rest
Restaurant;
bar – bar
BBQ – barbecues allowed (may be restricted to a
separate, designated area)
cooking facs – communal kitchen area
snacks – snack bar, cafeteria or takeaway

SBS
Site Booking Service (pitch reservation can be
made through the Caravan Club's Travel Service)

serviced pitch
Electric hook-ups and mains water inlet and grey
water waste outlet to pitch;
all – to all pitches
50% – percentage of pitches

shop(s)
Shop on site;
adj – shops next to site
500m – nearest shops
supmkt – supermarket
hypmkt – hypermarket
tradsmn – tradesmen call at the site, eg baker

shwrs
Hot showers available for a fee;
inc – cost included in site fee quoted

ssn
Season;
high ssn – peak holiday season
low ssn – out of peak season

50% statics
Percentage of static caravans/mobile homes/
chalets/fixed tents/cabins or long term seasonal
pitches on site, including those run by tour
operators

sw
Swimming nearby;
1km – nearest swimming
lake – in lake
rv – in river

TV
TV available for viewing by visitors (often in
the bar);
TV rm – separate TV room (often also a games
room)
cab/sat – cable or satellite connections to pitches

wc
Clean flushing toilets on site;
(cont) – continental type with floor-level hole
htd – sanitary block centrally heated in winter
own san – use of own sanitation facilities
recommended

Other Abbreviations

AIT	Alliance Internationale de Tourisme
a'bahn	Autobahn
a'pista	Autopista
a'route	Autoroute
a'strada	Autostrada
adj	Adjacent, nearby
alt	Alternative
app	Approach, on approaching
arr	Arrival, arriving
avail	Available
Ave	Avenue
bdge	Bridge
bef	Before
bet	Between
Blvd	Boulevard
C	Century, eg 16thC
c'van	Caravan
CC	Caravan Club
ccard acc	Credit and/or debit cards accepted (check with site for specific details)
CChq acc	Camping Cheques accepted

cent	Centre or central
clsd	Closed
conn	Connection
cont	Continue or continental (wc)
conv	Convenient
covrd	Covered
dep	Departure
diff	Difficult, with difficulty
dir	Direction
dist	Distance
dual c'way	Dual carriageway
E	East
ent	Entrance/entry to
espec	Especially
ess	Essential
excel	Excellent
facs	Facilities
FIA	Fédération Internationale de l'Automobile
FICC	Fédération Internationale de Camping & de Caravaning
FFCC	Fédération Française de Camping et de Caravaning
FKK/FNF	Naturist federation, ie naturist site
foll	Follow
fr	From
g'ge	Garage
gd	Good
grnd(s)	Ground(s)
hr(s)	Hour(s)
immac	Immaculate
immed	Immediate(ly)
inc	Included/inclusive
indus est	Industrial estate
INF	Naturist federation, ie naturist site
int'l	International
irreg	Irregular
junc	Junction
km	Kilometre
L	Left
LH	Left-hand
LS	Low season
ltd	Limited
mkd	Marked
mkt	Market
mob	Mobile (phone)
m'van	Motor caravan
m'way	Motorway
N	North
narr	Narrow
nr, nrby	Near, nearby
opp	Opposite
o'fits	Outfits

o'look(ing)	Overlook(ing)
o'night	Overnight
o'skts	Outskirts
PO	Post office
poss	Possible, possibly
pt	Part
R	Right
rd	Road or street
rec	Recommend/ed
recep	Reception
red	Reduced, reduction (for)
reg	Regular
req	Required
RH	Right-hand
rlwy	Railway line
rm	Room
rndabt	Roundabout
rte	Route
RV	Recreational vehicle, ie large motor caravan
rv/rvside	River/riverside
S	South
san facs	Sanitary facilities ie wc, showers, etc
snr citizens	Senior citizens
sep	Separate
sh	Short
sp	Sign post, signposted
sq	Square
ssn	Season
stn	Station
strt	Straight, straight ahead
sw	Swimming
thro	Through
TO	Tourist Office
tour ops	Tour operators
traff lts	Traffic lights
twd	Toward(s)
unrel	Unreliable
vg	Very good
vill	Village
W	West
w/end	Weekend
x-ing	Crossing
x-rds	Cross roads

Symbols Used

◆   Unspecified facilities for disabled guests check before arrival

⊞   Open all year

*   Last year site report received (see Campsite Entries in Introduction)

Documents

Camping Card Schemes

Camping Key Europe (CKE) is a useful companion for touring in Europe. Not only does it serve as a valid ID at campsites, meaning that you don't have to leave you passport with the site reception, it also entitles you to discounts at over 2200 sites.

CKE also offers Third Party Liability Insurance for up to 6 people travelling in one party, and Personal Accident Cover while on site. Full Terms and Conditions and details of the levels of cover of this insurance are provided with the card.

CKE is available to purchase from The Caravan Club by calling 01342 336633, or is provided free for all members taking out the 'Motoring' level of cover of The Club's Red Pennant Overseas Holiday Insurance.

An alternative scheme is Camping Card International (CCI) which offers similar benefits as CKE.

If you are using a CKE or CCI card as a method of ID at a site, make sure that you retrieve your card on leaving the site. Also check that you have been given your own card instead of someone else's.

See www.campingkey.com or www.campingcardinternational.com for full details of the schemes.

Driving Licence

A full, valid driving licence should be carried at all times when driving abroad as you must produce it when asked to do so by the police and other authorities. Failure to do so may result in an immediate fine and confiscation of your vehicle(s). If your driving licence is due to expire while you are away it can normally be renewed up to three months before the expiry date - contact the DVLA if you need to renew more than three months ahead.

All European Union countries recognise the pink EU-format driving licence introduced in the UK in 1990, subject to the minimum age requirements (normally 18 years for a vehicle with a maximum weight of 3,500 kg carrying no more than 8 people). However, there are exceptions in some European Countries and the Country Introductions contain specific details. Holders of an old-style green UK paper licence or a licence issued in Northern Ireland prior to 1991, which are not to EU format, should update it to a photocard licence before

travelling in order to avoid any difficulties with local authorities. A photocard driving licence is also useful as a means of identification in other situations, e.g. when using a credit card. Remember to carry both the plastic card and its paper counterpart.

Allow enough time for your application to be processed and do not apply if you will need to use your licence in the near future, e.g. to hire a car. Selected post offices and DVLA local offices offer a premium checking service for photocard applications but the service is not available for online applications.

MOT Certificate

You are advised to carry your vehicle's MOT certificate (if applicable) when driving on the Continent as you may need to show it to the authorities if your vehicle is involved in an accident, or in the event of random vehicle checks. If your MOT certificate is due to expire while you are away you should have the vehicle tested before you leave home.

Passport

Many countries require you to carry your passport at all times. Enter next-of-kin details in the back of your passport and keep a separate photocopy or record of your passport details. It's also a good idea to leave a photocopy of it with a relative or friend at home.

The following information applies to British passport holders only. For people who's passports are issued by other countries you should contact the local embassy for more information.

Applying for a Passport

Each person travelling out of the UK (including babies) must hold a valid passport. It is no longer possible to add or include children on a parent's British passport. A standard British passport is valid for ten years, or 5 years for children under 16.

All new UK passports are now biometric passports, also known as e-passports, which contain a microchip with information which can be used to authenticate the holder's identity. When your passport expires and you apply for a new one it will be replaced with a biometric passport.

Full information and application forms are available from main post offices or from the Identity & Passport Service's website, www.

gov.uk where you can complete an online application. Allow at least six weeks for first-time passport applications, for which you may need to attend an interview at your nearest Identity and Passport Service (IPS) regional office. Allow three weeks for a renewal application and the replacement of a lost, stolen or damaged passport.

Main post offices offer a 'Check & Send' service for passport applications. To find your nearest 'Check & Send' post office call 0845 611 2970 or see www.postoffice.co.uk

Passport Validity
Most countries in the EU only require your passport to be valid for the duration of your stay. However, in case your return home is delayed for any reason it is a good idea to renew your passport before you travel if there is less than 6 month's validity remaining. Any time left on a passport (up to a maximum of 9 months) will be added to the validity of your new passport.

Schengen Agreement
The Schengen Agreement allows people and vehicles to pass freely without border checks from country to country within the Schengen area (a total of 26 countries) . Where there are no longer any border checks you should still not attempt to cross land borders without a full, valid passport. It is likely that random identity checks will continue to be made for the foreseeable future in areas surrounding land borders.

The United Kingdom and Republic of Ireland do not fully participate in the Schengen Agreement.

Pet Travel Scheme (PETS)

The Pet Travel Scheme (PETS) allows owners of dogs, cats and ferrets from qualifying European countries, to bring their pets into the UK (up to a limit of five per person) without quarantine. The animal must have an EU pet passport, be microchipped and be vaccinated against rabies. Dogs must also have been treated for

tapeworm. It also allows pets to travel from the UK to other EU qualifying countries. Some countries may not allow entry to certain types or breeds of dogs and may have rules relating to matters such as muzzling and transporting dogs in cars – check the Country Introductions for any specific details or see www.caravanclub.co.uk/pets for more details. Pets normally resident in the Channel Islands, Isle of Man and the Republic of Ireland can also enter the UK under the PETS scheme if they comply with the rules. Pets resident anywhere in the British Isles (including the Republic of Ireland) are able to travel freely within the British Isles and are not subject to PETS rules.

Travelling with Children

Some countries require evidence of parental responsibility from single parents travelling alone with children before allowing them to enter the country or, in some cases, before permitting children to leave the country. The authorities may want to see a birth certificate, a letter of consent from the other parent and some evidence as to your responsibility for the child.

If you are travelling with a minor under the age of 18 who is not your own, you must carry a letter of authorisation, naming the adult in charge of the child, from the child's parent or legal guardian.

For further information on exactly what will be required at immigration contact the Embassy or Consulate of the countries you intend to visit before your visit.

Vehicle Excise Licence

While driving abroad you still need to have current UK vehicle excise licence. If your vehicle's tax is due to expire while you are abroad you may apply to re-license the vehicle at a post office, by post, or in person at a DVLA local office, up to two months in advance.

Vehicle Registration Certificate (V5C)

You must always carry your Vehicle Registration Certificate (V5C) when taking your vehicle abroad. If yours has been lost, stolen or destroyed you should apply to a DVLA local office on form V62. Call DVLA Customer Enquiries on 0300 790 6802 for more information.

Caravan – Proof of Ownership (CRIS)

In Britain and Ireland, unlike most other European countries, caravans are not formally registered in the same way as cars. This may not be fully understood by police and other authorities on the Continent. You are strongly advised, therefore, to carry a copy of your Caravan Registration Identification Scheme (CRIS) document.

Hired or Borrowed Vehicles

If using a borrowed vehicle you must obtain a letter of authority to use the vehicle from the registered owner. You should also carry the Vehicle Registration Certificate (V5C).

In the case of hired or leased vehicles, including company cars, when the user does not normally possess the V5C, ask the company which owns the vehicle to supply a Vehicle On Hire Certificate, form VE103, which is the only legal substitute for a V5C. The BVRLA, the trade body for the vehicle rental and leasing sector, provide advice on hired or leased vehicles - see www.bvrla.co.uk or call them on 01494 434747 for more information.

If you are caught driving a hired vehicle abroad without this certificate you may be fined and/or the vehicle impounded.

Visas

British citizens holding a full UK passport do not require a visa for entry into any countries covered by this guide. EU countries may require a permit for stays of more than three months and you should contact the relevant country's UK embassy before you travel for information.

British subjects, British overseas citizens, British dependent territories citizens and citizens of other countries may need visas that are not required by British citizens. Again check with the authorities of the country you are due to visit at their UK embassy or consulate. Citizens of other countries should apply to their own embassy, consulate or High Commission for information.

Insurance

Car, Motorhome and Caravan Insurance

Insurance cover for your outfit whilst travelling abroad is an absolute essential. Your car or motorhome insurance should cover you for driving in the EU or associated countries, but you should check what you are covered for before you travel. If you are travelling outside the EU or associated countries you'll need to inform your insurer and may have to pay an additional premium.

Make sure your Caravan insurance covers travel outside of the UK, speak to your insurer – most will require the dates of your holiday and it is possible there will be an extra premium to pay.

The Caravan Club's Car, Caravan and Motorhome Insurance schemes extend to provide policy cover for travel within the EU free of charge, provided the total period of foreign travel in any one year does not exceed 270 days for Car Insurance, 182 for Caravan Insurance and 270 days for Motorhome Insurance. It may be possible to extend this period, although a charge may apply.

Should you be delayed beyond these limits speak to your broker or insurer immediately in order to maintain your cover until you can return to the UK.

If your outfit is damaged during loading, unloading or travel on a ferry it must be reported to the carrier at the time the damage occurred. Most insurance policies will cover short sea crossings (up to 65 hours) but check with your insurer before travelling.

For full details of The Caravan Club's Caravan Insurance telephone 01342 336610 or for Car Insurance and Motorhome insurance, telephone 0800 0284809 or visit our website, www.caravanclub.co.uk/insurance.

European Accident Statement
Your car or motorhome insurer may provide you with a European Accident Statement form (EAS), or you may be given one if you are involved in an accident abroad. The EAS is a standard form, available in different languages, which gives all parties involved in an accident the opportunity to agree on the facts. Signing the form doesn't mean that you are accepting liability, just that you agree with what has been stated on the form. Only sign an EAS if you are completely sure that you understand what has been written and always make sure that you take a copy of the completed EAS.

Legal Costs Abroad

If an accident abroad leads to you being taken to court you may find yourself liable for legal costs – even if you are not found to be at fault. Most UK vehicle insurance policies include cover for legal costs or have the option to add cover for a small additional cost – check if you are covered before you travel.

Holiday Travel Insurance

Having insured your vehicles, there are other risks to consider and it is essential to take out adequate travel insurance. Your vehicle insurance policy won't cover you for all eventualities, such as vehicle breakdown, medical expenses or accommodation. Make sure that the holiday insurance you take out is suitable for a caravan or motorhome holiday.

The Caravan Club's Red Pennant Overseas Holiday Insurance is designed specifically for touring holidays and can cover both motoring and personal use. Depending on the level of cover chosen the policy will cover you for vehicle recovery and repair, holiday continuation, medical expenses and accommodation.

For full details visit www.caravanclub.co.uk/redpennant or call 01342 336633.

Look carefully at the exemptions to your insurance policy, including those relating to preexisting medical conditions or the use of alcohol. Be sure to declare any preexisting medical conditions to your insurer.

Holiday Insurance for Pets
Make sure that your pet is also covered if you take them on holiday with you. Some holiday insurance policies, including The Club's Red Pennant, can be extended to cover pet expenses relating to an incident normally covered under the policy – such as pet repatriation in the event that your vehicle is written off.

However in order to provide cover for pet injury or illness you will need a separate pet insurance policy which covers your pet while out of the UK. For details of The Club's Pet Insurance scheme visit www.caravanclub.co.uk/petins or call 0800 015 1396.

Home Insurance

Your home insurer may require advance notification if you are leaving your home unoccupied for 30 days or more. You may be required to turn off mains services (except electricity), drain water down and have somebody visit the home once a week. Check your policy documents or speak to your insurer or broker.

The Caravan Club's Home Insurance policy provides full cover for up to 90 days when you are away from home (for instance when touring) and requires only common sense precautions for longer periods of unoccupancy. See www.caravanclub.co.uk/homeins or call 0800 028 4815 for details.

Personal Belongings

The majority of travellers are able to cover their valuables such as jewellery, watches, cameras, laptops, and bikes under a Home insurance Policy. This includes The Caravan Club's Home Insurance scheme.

Vehicles Left Behind Abroad

If you are involved in an accident or breakdown abroad which prevents you taking your vehicle home, you must ensure that your normal insurance will cover your vehicle if left overseas while you return home. Also check if you are covered for the cost of recovering it to your home address.

You should remove all items of baggage and personal belongings from your vehicles before leaving them unattended. If this is not possible you should check with your insurer/broker to establish whether extended cover can be provided. In all circumstances, you must remove any valuables and items liable for customs duty, including wine, beer, spirits and cigarettes.

Customs Regulations

Caravans and Vehicles

You can temporarily import a caravan, trailer or vehicle from one EU country to another without any Customs formalities. Vehicles and caravans may be temporarily imported into non-EU countries generally for a maximum of six months in any twelve month period, provided they are not hired, sold or otherwise disposed of in that country.

If you intend to stay longer than six months, dispose of a vehicle while in another country or leave your vehicle there in storage you should seek advice well before your departure from the UK.

Borrowed vehicles
If you are borrowing a vehicle from a friend or relative, or loaning yours to someone, you should be aware of the following:

- The total time the vehicle spends abroad must not exceed the limit for temporary importation (generally six months).
- The owner of the caravan must provide the other person with a letter of authority.
- The owner cannot accept a hire fee or reward.
- The number plate on the caravan must match the number plate on the tow car.

- Both drivers' insurers must be informed if a caravan is being towed and any additional premium must be paid.

Currency

Any person entering or leaving the EU will have to declare the money that they are carrying if this amounts to €10,000 (or equivalent in other currencies) or more. This includes cheques, travellers' cheques, bankers' drafts and any cash - notes and coins. This ruling does not apply to anyone travelling within the EU.

For further information contact HMRC Excise & Customs Helpline on 0845 010 9000.

Customs Allowances

Travelling within the European Union
If you are travelling to the UK from within the EU you can bring an unlimited amount of most goods without being liable for any duty or tax, but certain rules apply. The goods must be for your own personal use, which can include use as a gift (if the person you are gifting the goods to reimburses you in any way this is not classed as a gift), and you must have paid duty and

tax in the country where you purchased the goods. If a customs official suspects that any goods are not for your own personal use they can question you, make further checks and ultimately seize both the goods and the vehicle used to transport them. Although no limits are in place, customs officials are less likely to question you regarding your goods if they are under the following limits:

- 800 cigarettes
- 400 cigarillos
- 200 cigars
- 1kg tobacco
- 10 litres of spirits
- 20 litres of fortified wine (e.g. port or sherry)
- 90 litres of wine
- 110 litres of beer

The same rules and guidance limits apply for travel between other EU countries.

Travelling outside the EU
There are set limits to the amount of goods you can buy in countries outside of the EU to bring back into the UK. Even within these limits goods must still be for your own personal use. Each person aged 17 and over is entitled to the following allowance:

- 200 cigarettes, or 100 cigarillos, or 50 cigars, or 250g tobacco
- 1 litre of spirits or strong liqueurs over 22 per cent volume, or 2 litres of fortified wine, sparkling wine or any other alcoholic drink that's less than 22 per cent volume
- 4 litres of still wine
- 16 litres of beer
- £390 worth of all other goods including perfume, gifts and souvenirs without having to pay tax and/or duty
- For further information contact HMRC National Advice Service on 0845 010 9000 (+44 2920 501 261 from outside the UK).

Medicines

There is no limit to the amount of medicines you can take abroad if they are obtained without prescription (i.e. over the counter medicines), but medicines prescribed by your doctor may contain controlled drugs (e.g. those containing morphine). You must obtain a licence if you are leaving the UK for 3 months or more with medication containing a controlled drug. Visit www.gov.uk/travelling-controlled-drugs or tel. 020 7035 0771 for a list of controlled drugs and to apply for a licence.

You don't need a licence if you carry supplies for less than 3 months or if your medication doesn't contain controlled drugs, but you should carry a letter from your doctor stating your name, a list of your prescribed drugs and dosages for each drug. You may have to show this letter when going through customs.

Personal Possessions

Visitors to countries within the EU are free to carry reasonable quantities of any personal possessions such as jewellery, cameras, and electrical equipment required for the duration of their stay. It is sensible to carry sales receipts for new items in case you need to prove that tax has already been paid.

Prohibited and Restricted Goods
Regardless of where you are travelling from the importation of some goods into the UK is restricted or banned, mainly to protect health and the environment. These include:

- Endangered animals or plants including live animals, birds and plants, ivory, skins, coral, hides, shells and goods made from them such as jewellery, shoes, bags and belts.
- Controlled, unlicensed or dangerous drugs.
- Counterfeit or pirated goods such as watches, CDs and clothes; goods bearing a false indication of their place of manufacture or in breach of UK copyright.

- Offensive weapons such as firearms, flick knives, knuckledusters, push daggers or knives disguised as everyday objects.

- Pornographic material depicting extreme violence or featuring children such as DVDs, magazines, videos, books and software.

This list is not exhaustive; if in doubt contact HMRC National Advice Service on 0845 010 9000 or +44 2920 501 261 from outside the UK for more information or, when returning to the UK, go through the red Customs channel or use the telephone at the Red Point and ask a Customs officer. It is your responsibility to make sure that you are not breaking the law. Never attempt to mislead or hide anything from Customs officers; penalties are severe.

Plants and Food

Travellers from within the EU may bring into the UK any fruit, vegetable or plant products without restriction as long as they are grown in the EU, are free from pests or disease and are for your own consumption. For food products Andorra, the Channel Islands, the Isle of Man, San Marino and Switzerland are treated as part of the EU.

From most countries outside the EU you are not allowed to bring into the UK any meat or dairy products. Other animal products may be severely restricted or banned and it is important that you declare any such products on entering the UK.

For up to date information please contact the Food and Environment Research Agency (Fera) on 0844 248 0071. If you are unsure about any item you are bringing in, or are simply unsure of the rules, you must go to the red Customs channel or use the phone provided at the Red Point to speak to a Customs officer.

Money

Being able to safely access your money while you're away is a necessity for you to enjoy your break. It isn't a good idea to rely on one method of payment, so always have a backup plan. A mixture of a small amount of cash plus one or two electronic means of payment are a good idea.

Travellers' cheques have become less popular in recent years as fewer banks and hotels are willing or able to cash them. There are alternative options which offer the same level of security but are easier to use, such as pre-paid credit cards.

Local Currency

It is a good idea to take enough foreign currency for your journey and immediate needs on arrival, don't forget you may need change for tolls or parking on your journey. Currency exchange facilities will be available at ports & on ferries but rates offered may not be as good as you would find elsewhere. The Post Office, many high -street banks, exchange offices and travel agents offer commission free foreign

exchange, some will charge a flat fee and some offer a 'buy back' service. All should stock Euros but during peak holiday times they may be running low so it can be a good idea to pre-order your currency. You should also pre-order any less common currencies. Shop around and compare commission and exchange rates, together with minimum charges.

Banks and money exchanges may not accept Scottish and Northern Irish bank notes and may be reluctant to change any sterling which has been written on or is creased or worn

Foreign Currency Bank Accounts

Frequent travellers or those who spend long periods abroad may find a Euro bank account useful. Most such accounts impose no currency conversion charges for debit or credit card use and allow fee-free cash withdrawals at ATMs. Some banks may also allow you to spread your account across different currencies, depending on your circumstances. Speak to your bank about the services they offer.

Travel Money Cards

Travel money cards are issued by various providers including the Post Office, Travelex, Lloyds Bank and American Express. For a comparison table see www.which-prepaid-card.co.uk.

They are increasingly popular as the PIN protected travel money card offers the security of Travellers Cheques, with the convenience of paying by card. You load the card with the amount you need before leaving home, and then use cash machines to make withdrawals or use the card to pay for goods and services as you would a credit or debit card. You can top the card up over the telephone or online while you are abroad. Please note that pre-paid cards cannot be used when you are not required to enter a PIN, so cannot be used on the French toll system.

These cards can be cheaper to use than credit or debit cards for both cash withdrawals and purchases as there are usually no loading or transaction fees to pay. In addition, because they are separate from your bank account, if the card is lost or stolen there is less risk of identity theft.

The Caravan Club have partnered with Moneycorp to offer the Explorer prepaid card to members. For more information visit www.caravanclub.co.uk/travelmoney.

Credit and Debit Cards

Credit and debit cards offer a convenient way of spending abroad. For the use of cards abroad most banks impose a foreign currency conversion charge (typically 2.75% per transaction) which is usually the same for both credit and debit cards. If you use your card to withdraw cash there will be a further commission charge of up to 3% and you will be charged interest (possibly at a higher rate than normal) as soon as you withdraw the money.

If you have several cards, take at least two in case you encounter problems. Credit and debit 'chip and PIN' cards issued by UK banks may not be universally accepted abroad so check before incurring expenditure.

Contact your credit or debit card issuer before you leave home to let them know that you will be travelling abroad. In the battle against card fraud, card issuers are frequently likely to query transactions which they regard as unusual or suspicious, causing your card to be declined or temporarily stopped. You should always carry your card issuer's helpline number with you so that you can contact them if this happens. You will also need this number should you need to report the loss or theft of your card.

Dynamic Currency Conversion
When you pay with a credit or debit card, retailers may offer you the choice of currency for payment, e.g. a euro amount will be converted into sterling and then charged to your card account. You may be asked to sign an agreement to accept the conversion rate used and final amount charged and, having done so, there is no opportunity to change your mind or obtain a refund. This is known as a 'dynamic currency conversion' but the exchange rate used is likely to be worse than the rate offered by your card issuer.

Emergency Cash

If an emergency or theft means that you need cash in a hurry, then friends or relatives at home can send you emergency cash via money transfer services.

The Post Office, MoneyGram and Western Union all offer services which, allows the transfer of money to over 233,000 money transfer agents around the world. Transfers take approximately ten minutes and charges are levied on a sliding scale.

Ferries & the Channel Tunnel

Booking Your Ferry

If travelling in July or August, or peak weekends, such as Easter and half-term, make your reservation as early as possible. Space for caravans and large vehicles is usually limited and cheaper off-peak crossings can fill up quickly. If you need any special assistance or arrangements make sure you request this at the time of booking.

When booking any ferry crossing, make sure you give the correct measurements for your outfit including bikes, roof boxes or anything else which may add to the length or height of your vehicle. If your vehicle is larger than your booking states you may be turned away at boarding.

The Caravan Club is an agent for most major ferry companies operating services. Call The Club's Travel Service on 01342 316 101 or see www.caravanclub.co.uk/ferries to book and for details of special offers, some of which are exclusive to Caravan Club members.

The tables on the following page show current ferry routes from the UK to the Continent and Ireland. Some ferry routes may not be operational all year, and during peak holiday periods the transportation of caravans or

motorhomes may be restricted. For the most up-to-date information on ferry routes and prices visit www.caravanclub.co.uk/ferries or speak to The Club's Travel Services team.

Channel Tunnel

The Channel Tunnel operator, Eurotunnel, accepts cars, caravans and motorhomes (except those running on LPG) on their service between Folkestone and Calais. You can just turn up and see if there is availability on the day, however prices increase as the crossing gets fuller so if you know your plans in advance it is best to book as early as possible.

You will be asked to open your roof vents prior to travel and you will also need to apply the caravan brake once you have parked your vehicle on the train. You will not be able to use your caravan until arrival.

On the Journey

Arrive at the port with plenty of time before your boarding time. Motorhomes and car/caravan outfits will usually either be the first or last vehicles boarded onto the ferry. Almost all ferries are now 'drive on – drive off' so

you won't be required to do any complicated manoeuvres. You may be required to show ferry staff that your gas is switched off before boarding the ferry.

Be careful using the ferry access ramps, as they are often very steep which mean there is a risk of grounding the tow bar or caravan hitch. Drive slowly and, if your ground clearance is low, consider whether removing your stabiliser and/or jockey wheel would help.

Vehicles are often parked close together on ferries, meaning that if you have towing extension mirrors they could get knocked or damaged by people trying to get past your vehicle. If you leave them attached during the ferry crossing then make sure you check their position on returning to your vehicle.

Pets on Ferries and Eurotunnel

It is possible to transport your pet on a number of ferry routes to the Continent and Ireland, as well as on Eurotunnel services from Folkestone to Calais. Advance booking is essential as restrictions apply to the number of animals allowed on any one crossing. Make sure you understand the carrier's terms and conditions for transporting pets.

Once on board pets are normally required to remain in their owner's vehicle or in kennels on the car deck and you won't be able to access your vehicle to check on your pet while the ferry is at sea. On longer crossings you should make arrangements at the on-board information desk for permission to visit your pet in order to check its well-being. You should always make sure that ferry staff know your vehicle has a pet on board.

Information and advice on the welfare of animals before and during a journey is available on the website of the Department for Environment, Food and Rural Affairs (Defra), www.gov.uk/defra.

Gas on Ferries and Eurotunnel

UK based ferry companies usually allow up to three gas cylinders per caravan, including the cylinder currently in use, however some may restrict this to a maximum of two cylinders. Some operators may ask you to hand over your gas cylinders to a member of the crew so that they can be safely stored during the crossing. Check that you know the rules of your ferry operator before you travel.

Cylinder valves should be fully closed and covered with a cap, if provided, and should remain closed during the crossing. Cylinders should be fixed securely in or on the caravan in the position specified by the manufacturer.

Gas cylinders must be declared at check-in and the crew may ask to inspect each cylinder for leakage before travel.

Eurotunnel will allow vehicles fitted with LPG tanks for the purposes of heating, lighting, cooking or refrigeration to use their service, but regulations stipulate that a total of no more than 47 kg of gas can be carried through the Channel Tunnel. Tanks must be switched off before boarding and must be less than 80% full; you will be asked to demonstrate this before you travel. Vehicles powered by LPG cannot be carried through the Channel Tunnel.

Most ferry companies will accept LPG-powered vehicles but you must let them know at the time of booking. During the crossing the tank must be no more than 75% full and it must be turned off. In the case of vehicles converted to use LPG, some ferry companies also require a certificate showing that the conversion

has been carried out to the manufacturer's specification.

The carriage of spare petrol cans, whether full or empty, is not permitted on ferries or through the Channel Tunnel. Caravan Club Sites Near Ports.

Caravan Club Sites Near Ports

If you've got a long drive to the ferry port, or want to catch an early ferry then an overnight stop near to the port gives you a relaxing start to your holiday. The following table lists Caravan Club sites which are close to ports.

Members can book online at www.caravanclub.co.uk or call 01342 327490. If you aren't a Club member you will need to contact the sites directly when they are open.

Please note that Commons Wood, Daleacres, Fairlight Wood, Hunter's Moon, Mildenhall, Old Hartley and Rookesbury Park are open to Caravan Club members only. Non-members are welcome at all the other Caravan Club sites listed below.

Port	Nearest Club Site and Town	Tel No.
Cairnryan, Stranraer	New England Bay (Drummore)	01776 860275
Dover, Folkestone, Channel Tunnel	Bearsted (Maidstone)	01622 730018
	Black Horse Farm* (Folkestone)	01303 892665
	Daleacres (Hythe)	01303 267679
	Fairlight Wood (Hastings)	01424 812333
Fishguard, Pembroke	Freshwater East (Pembroke)	01646 672341
Harwich	Cambridge Cherry Hinton*	01223 244088
	Commons Wood* (Welwyn Garden City)	01707 260786
	Mildenhall	01638 713089
Holyhead	Penrhos (Benllech)	01248 852617
Hull	York Beechwood Grange	01904 424637
	York Rowntree Park	01904 658997
Newcastle upon Tyne	Old Hartley (Whitley Bay)	0191 237 0256
Newhaven	Brighton*	01273 626546
Plymouth	Plymouth Sound	01752 862325
Poole	Hunter's Moon*, Wareham	01929 556605
Portsmouth	Rookesbury Park, Fareham	01329 834085
Rosslare	River Valley, Wicklow	00353 (0)404 41647
Weymouth	Crossways, Dorchester	01305 852032

* Site open all year

Ferry routes and Operators

Route	Operator	Approximate Crossing Time	Maximum Frequency
Belgium			
Hull – Zeebrugge	P & O Ferries	12½ hrs	1 daily
Denmark			
Harwich – Esbjerg	DFDS Seaways	18¼ hrs	3 per week
France			
Dover – Calais	P & O Ferries	1½ hrs	22 daily
Dover – Dunkerque	DFDS Seaways	2 hrs	12 daily
Folkestone – Calais	Eurotunnel	35 mins	3 per hour
Newhaven – Dieppe	Transmanche Ferries	4 hrs	2 daily
Plymouth – Roscoff	Brittany Ferries	6 hrs	2 daily
Poole – Cherbourg	Brittany Ferries	4½ hrs	1 daily
Poole – St Malo (via Channel Islands)	Condor Ferries	5 hrs	1 daily (May to Sep)
Portsmouth – Caen	Brittany Ferries	3¾ / 7½ hrs	4 daily
Portsmouth – Cherbourg	Brittany Ferries	3 / 4½ hrs	3 daily
Portsmouth – Cherbourg	Condor Ferries	5½ hrs	1 weekly (May to Sep)
Portsmouth – Le Havre	LD Lines	3¼ / 8 hrs	2 daily
Portsmouth – St Malo	Brittany Ferries	9 hrs	1 daily
Weymouth – St Malo (via Channel Islands)	Condor Ferries	9½ hrs	1 daily
Ireland – Northern			
Cairnryan/Troon – Larne	P & O Irish Sea	1 / 2 hrs	11 daily
Liverpool (Birkenhead) – Belfast	Stena Line	8 hrs	2 daily
Cairnryan – Belfast	Stena Line	2 / 3 hrs	7 daily
Ireland – Republic			
Cork – Roscoff†	Brittany Ferries	14 hrs	1 per week
Fishguard – Rosslare	Stena Line	2 / 3½ hrs	3 daily
Holyhead – Dublin	Irish Ferries	1¾ / 3¼ hrs	4 daily
Holyhead – Dublin	Stena Line	3¼ hrs	4 daily
Holyhead – Dun Loaghaire	Stena Line	2 hrs	2 daily
Liverpool – Dublin	P & O Irish Sea	8 hrs	2 daily
Liverpool (Birkenhead) – Dublin	Stena Line	7 hrs	2 daily
Pembroke – Rosslare	Irish Ferries	4 hrs	2 daily
Rosslare – Cherbourg†	Irish Ferries	19½ hrs	3 per week
Rosslare – Cherbourg†	Celtic Link Ferries	17 hrs	3 per week
Rosslare – Roscoff†	Irish Ferries	19½ hrs	4 per week
Netherlands			
Harwich – Hook of Holland	Stena Line	6½ hrs	2 daily
Hull – Rotterdam	P & O Ferries	10¼ hrs	1 daily
Newcastle – Ijmuiden (Amsterdam)	DFDS Seaways	15½ hrs	1 daily
Spain			
Portsmouth – Bilbao	Brittany Ferries	24 hrs	2 per week
Portsmouth or Plymouth – Santander	Brittany Ferries	24 / 20 hrs	4 per week

† *Not bookable through the Club's Travel Service.*
Note: Services and routes correct at time of publication but subject to change.

Motoring Advice

Preparing for Your Journey

The first priority in preparing for your outfit for your journey should be to make sure it has a full service. Make sure that you have a fully equipped spares kit, and a spare wheel and tyre for your caravan – it is easier to get hold of them from your local dealer than to have to spend time searching for spares where you don't know the local area.

If you're a member of The Caravan Club then carry your UK Sites Directory & Handbook with you, as it contains a section of technical advice which may be useful when travelling. If you have any queries you can also contact The Club's free advice service who have information on all things caravanning – you can download free information leaflets at www.caravanclub. co.uk/advice or contact the team by calling 01342 336611 or emailing technical@caravanclub.co.uk.

For advice on issues specific to countries other than the UK, Club members should contact the Travel Service Information Officer, email: travelserviceinfo@caravanclub.co.uk or call 01342 336766.

Weight Limits

From both a legal and a safety point of view, it is essential not to exceed vehicle weight limits. It is advisable to carry documentation confirming your vehicle's maximum permitted laden weight - if your Vehicle Registration Certificate (V5C) does not clearly state this, you will need to produce alternative certification, e.g. from a weighbridge.

If you are pulled over by the police and don't have certification you will be taken to a weighbridge. If your vehicle(s) are then found to be overweight you will be liable to a fine and may have to discard items to lower the weight before you can continue on your journey.

Some Final Checks

Before you start any journey make sure you complete the following checks:

- All car and caravan or motorhome lights are working and sets of spare bulbs are packed

- The coupling is correctly seated on the towball and the breakaway cable is attached

- All windows, vents, hatches and doors are shut

- All on-board water systems are drained

- All mirrors are adjusted for maximum visibility

- Corner steadies are fully wound up and the brace is handy for your arrival on site

- Any fires or flames are extinguished and the gas cylinder tap is turned off. Fire extinguishers are fully charged and close at hand

- The over-run brake is working correctly

- The jockey wheel is raised and secured, the handbrake is released.

Driving in Europe

Driving abroad for the first time can be a daunting prospect, especially when towing a caravan. Here are a few tips to make the transition easier:

Remember that Sat Navs may take you on unsuitable roads, so have a map or atlas to hand to help you find an alternative route.

- It can be tempting to try and get to your destination as quickly as possible but we recommend travelling a maximum of 250 miles a day when towing. Share the driving if possible, and if you're going a long way then plan in an overnight stop.

- Remember that if you need to overtake a slow moving vehicle or pull out around an obstruction you will not be able to see clearly from the driver's seat. If possible, always have a responsible adult in the passenger seat who can advise you when it is clear to pull out. If that is not possible then stay well back to get a better view and pull out slowly.

- If traffic builds up behind you, pull over safely and let it pass.

- Driving on the right should become second nature after a while, but pay particular attention when turning left, leaving a rest area, petrol station or site, or after a one-way system.

- Stop at least every two hours to stretch your legs and take a break.

Fuel

Grades of petrol sold on the Continent are comparable to those sold in the UK; 95 octane is frequently known as 'Essence' and 98 octane as 'Super'. Diesel may be called 'Gasoil' and is widely available across Europe.

E10 petrol (containing 10% Ethanol) can be found in certain countries in Europe. Most modern cars are E10 compatible, but those which aren't could be damaged by filling up with E10. Check your vehicle handbook or visit www.acea.be and search for 'E10' to find the publication 'Vehicle compatibility with new fuel standards'.

Members of The Caravan Club can check current average fuel prices by country at www.caravanclub.co.uk/overseasadvice.

Away from major roads and towns it is a good idea not to let your fuel tank run too low as you may have difficulty finding a petrol station, especially at night or on Sundays. Petrol stations offering a 24-hour service may involve an automated process, in some cases only accepting credit cards issued in France.

Automotive Liquified Petroleum Gas (LPG)
The increasing popularity of dual-fuelled vehicles means that the availability of LPG – also known as 'autogas' or GPL – has become an important issue for more drivers.

There are different tank-filling openings in use in different countries. Currently there is no common European filling system, and you might find a variety of systems. Most Continental motorway services will have adaptors but these should be used with care – see www.autogas.ltd.uk for more information.

Low Emission Zones

Many cities in countries around Europe have introduced 'Low Emission Zones' (LEZ's) in order to regulate vehicle pollution levels. Some schemes require you to buy a windscreen sticker, pay a fee or register your vehicle before entering the zone. You may also need to provide proof that your vehicle's emissions meet the required standard. Before you travel visit www.lowemissionzones.eu for maps and details of LEZ's across Europe. Also see the Country Introductions later in this guide for country specific information.

Motorhomes Towing Cars

A motorhome towing a small A-frame or towing dolly is illegal in most European countries. Motorhome users towing a small car should transport it on a braked trailer so that all four of the car's wheels are off the ground.

Priority and Roundabouts

When driving on the Continent it can be difficult to work out which vehicles have priority in different situations. Watch out for road signs which indicate priority and read the Country Introductions later in this guide for country specific information.

Take care at intersections – you should never rely on being given right of way, even if you have priority; especially in small towns and villages where local traffic may take right of way. Always give way to public service and military vehicles and to buses and trams.

In some countries in Europe priority at roundabouts is given to vehicles entering the roundabout (i.e. on the right) unless the road signs say otherwise.

Public Transport

In general in built-up areas be prepared to stop to allow a bus to pull out from a bus stop when the driver is signalling his intention to do so.

Take particular care when school buses have stopped and passengers are getting on and off.

Overtaking trams in motion is normally only allowed on the right, unless on a one way street where you can overtake on the left if there is not enough space on the right. Do not overtake a tram near a tram stop. These may be in the centre of the road. When a tram or bus stops to allow passengers on and off, you should stop to allow them to cross to the pavement. Give way to trams which are turning across your carriageway. Don't park or stop across tram lines; trams cannot steer round obstructions!

Pedestrian Crossings

Stopping to allow pedestrians to cross at zebra crossings is not always common practice on the Continent as it is in the UK. Pedestrians expect to wait until the road is clear before crossing, while motorists behind may be taken by surprise by your stopping. The result may be a rear-end shunt or vehicles overtaking you at the crossing and putting pedestrians at risk.

Traffic Lights

Traffic lights may not be as easily visible as they are in the UK, for instance they may be smaller or suspended across the road with a smaller set on a post at the roadside. You may find that lights change directly from red to green, bypassing amber completely. Flashing amber lights generally indicate that you may proceed with caution if it is safe to do so but you must give way to pedestrians and other vehicles.

A green filter light should be treated with caution as you may still have to give way to pedestrians who have a green light to cross the road. If a light turns red as approached, continental drivers will often speed up to get through the light instead of stopping. Be aware that if you brake sharply because a traffic light has turned red as you approached, the driver behind might not be expecting it.

Motoring Equipment

Essential Equipment

The equipment that you legally have to carry differs by country. For a full list see the Essential Equipment table at the end of this chapter, or see the Country Introductions of this book for country specific information. Please note equipment requirements and regulations can change frequently. To keep up to date with the latest equipment information please visit www.caravanclub.co.uk/overseasadvice.

Fire Extinguisher

As a safety precaution, an approved fire extinguisher should be carried in all vehicles. This is a legal requirement in several countries in Europe.

Glasses

In some countries it is a legal requirement for residents to carry a spare pair of glasses if they are needed for driving, and it is recommended that visitors also comply. Elsewhere, if you do not have a spare pair, you may find it helpful to carry a copy of your prescription.

Lights

When driving on the Continent headlights need to be adjusted to deflect to the right if they are likely to dazzle other road users. You can do this by applying beam deflectors, or some newer vehicles have a built-in adjustment system. Some modern high-density discharge (HID), xenon or halogen-type lights, may need to be taken to a dealer to make the necessary adjustment. Remember also to adjust headlights according to the load being carried and to compensate for the weight of the caravan on the back of your car. Even if you do not intend to drive at night, it is important to ensure that your headlights are correctly adjusted as you may need to use them in heavy rain, fog or in tunnels. If using tape or a pre-cut adhesive mask remember to remove it on your return home.

Dipped headlights should be used in poor weather conditions and in a tunnel even if it is well lit. You may find police waiting at the end of a tunnel to check vehicles. In some countries the use of dipped headlights is compulsory at all times and in others they must be used in built-up areas, on motorways or at certain times of the year.

Headlight-Flashing

On the Continent headlight-flashing is used as a warning of approach or as an overtaking signal at night, and not, as is commonly the case in the UK, an indication that you are giving way. Be more cautious with both flashing your headlights and when another driver flashes you.

Hazard Warning Lights

Hazard warning lights should not be used in place of a warning triangle, but they may be used in addition to it.

Nationality Plate (GB/IRL)

A nationality plate must be fixed to the rear of both your car or motorhome and caravan. Checks are made and a fine may be imposed for failure to display a nationality plate correctly. If your number plates have the Euro-Symbol on them there is no requirement to display an additional GB sticker within the EU and Switzerland. If your number plate doesn't have the EU symbol or you are planning to travel outside of the EU you will need a GB sticker.

GB is the only national identification code allowed for cars registered in the UK.

Registration plates displaying the GB Euro-Symbol must comply with the appropriate British Standard.

Reflective Jackets/Waistcoats

If you break down outside of a built-up area it is normally a legal requirement that anyone leaving the vehicle must be wearing a reflective jacket or waistcoat. Make sure that you jacket is accessible from inside the car as you will need to put it on before exiting the vehicle. Carry one for each passenger as well as the driver.

Route Planning

It is always a good idea to carry a road atlas or map of the countries you plan to visit, even if you have Satellite Navigation. You can find information on UK roads from Keep Moving – www.keepmoving.co.uk or call 09003 401100. Websites offering a European route mapping service include www.google.co.uk/maps, www.mappy.com or www.viamichelin.com.

Satellite Navigation/GPS

Continental postcodes don't cover just one street or part of a street in the same way as

UK postcodes. A French five-digit postcode, for example, can cover a very large area.

GPS co-ordinates and full addresses are given for most site entries in this guide wherever possible, so that you can programme your sat nav as accurately as possible.

It is important to remember that sat nav devices don't usually allow for towing or driving a large motorhome and may try to send you down unsuitable roads. Always use your common sense, and if a road looks unsuitable find an alternative route.

Use your sat nav in conjunction with the directions given in the site entries, which have been provided by members who have actually visited. Please note that the directions given in site entries have not been checked by The Caravan Club.

In nearly all European countries it is illegal to use car navigation systems which actively search for mobile speed cameras or interfere with police equipment (laser or radar detection). Car navigation systems which give a warning of fixed speed camera locations are legal in most countries with the exception of

France, Germany, and Switzerland where this function must be de-activated.

Seat Belts

The wearing of seat belts is compulsory throughout Europe and beyond. On-the-spot fines will be incurred for failure to wear them and, in the event of an accident failure to wear a seat belt may reduce any claim for injury. See the country introductions for specific regulations on both seat belts and car seats.

Spares

Caravan Spares

It will generally be much harder to get hold of spare parts for caravans on the continent, especially for UK manufactured caravans. It is advisable to carry any commonly required spares (such as light bulbs) with you.

Take the contact details of your UK dealer or manufacturer with you, as they may be able to assist in getting spares delivered to you.

Car Spares Kits

Some car manufacturers produce spares kits; contact your dealer for details. The choice of

spares will depend on the vehicle and how long you are away, but the following is a list of basic items which should cover the most common causes of breakdown:

- Radiator top hose
- Fan belt
- Fuses and bulbs
- Windscreen wiper blade
- Length of 12V electrical cable
- Tools, torch and WD40 or equivalent water repellent/ dispersant spray

Spare Wheel

Your local caravan dealer should be able to supply an appropriate spare wheel. If you have any difficulty in obtaining one, The Caravan Club's Technical Department can provide Club members with a list of suppliers on request.

Tyre legislation across Europe is more or less consistent and, while the Club has no specific knowledge of laws on the Continent regarding the use of space-saver spare wheels, there should be no problems in using such a wheel provided its use is in accordance with the manufacturer's instructions. Space-saver spare wheels are designed for short journeys to get your vehicle to a place where it can be repaired and there will usually be restrictions on the distance and speed at which the vehicle should be driven.

Towbar

The vast majority of cars registered after 1 August 1998 are legally required to have a European Type approved towbar (complying with European Directive 94/20) carrying a plate giving its approval number and various technical details, including the maximum noseweight. Your car dealer or specialist towbar fitter will be able to give further advice.

From 2011 for brand new motorhome designs (launched on or after that date) and 2012 for existing designs (those already being built before 29 April 2011), all new motorhomes will need some form of type approval before they can be registered in the UK and as such can only be fitted with a type approved towbar. This change will not affect older vehicles, which can continue to be fitted with non-approved towing brackets.

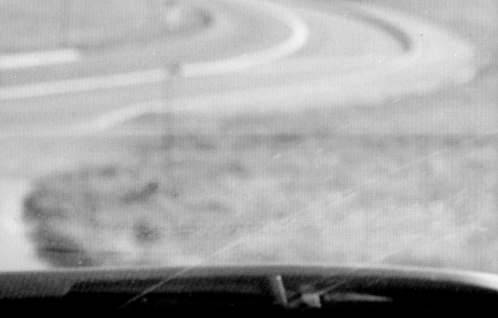

Tyres

Tyre condition has a major effect on the safe handling of your outfit. Caravan tyres must be suitable for the highest speed at which you can legally tow, even if you choose to drive slower.

Most countries require a minimum tread depth of 1.6mm but motoring organisations recommend at least 3mm. If you are planning a long journey, consider if they will still be above the legal minimum by the end of your journey.

Tyre Pressure

Tyre pressure should be checked and adjusted when the tyres are cold; checking warm tyres will result in a higher pressure reading. The correct pressures will be found in your car handbook, but unless it states otherwise to add an extra 4 - 6 pounds per square inch to the rear tyres of a car when towing to improve handling. Make sure you know what pressure your caravan tyres should be. Some require a pressure much higher than that normally used for cars. Check your caravan handbook for details.

Tyre Sizes

It is worth noting that some sizes of radial tyre to fit the 13" wheels commonly used on older UK caravans are virtually impossible to find in stock at retailers abroad, e.g. 175R13C.

After a Puncture

A lot of new cars now have a liquid sealant puncture repair kit instead of a spare wheel. These sealants should not be used to achieve a permanent repair and in some cases have been known to make repair of the tyre impossible. If you need to use a liquid sealant you should get the tyre repaired or replaced as soon as possible.

Following a caravan tyre puncture, especially on a single-axle caravan, it is advisable to have the opposite side (non-punctured) tyre removed from its wheel and checked inside and out for signs of damage resulting from overloading during the deflation of the punctured tyre.

Winter driving

Winter tyres should be in severe winter climates and in some countries it is a legal requirement. Winter tyres are designed to minimise the hardening effect of low temperatures which can lead to less traction on the road, and to provide extra grip on snow, ice or wet conditions.

Snow chains may be necessary on some roads in winter. They are compulsory in some countries, indicated by a road sign. They are not difficult to fit but it's a good idea to carry sturdy gloves to protect your hands when handling the chains in freezing conditions. Polar Automotive Ltd sells and hires out snow chains (10% discount for Caravan Club members), tel 01892 519933 www.snowchains.com, email: polar@snowchains.com.

Warning Triangles

In almost all European countries it is a legal requirement to use a warning triangle (sometimes two) in the event of a breakdown or accident.

A warning triangle should be placed on the road approximately 30 metres (100 metres on motorways) behind the broken down vehicle on the same side of the road. Always assemble the triangle before leaving your vehicle and walk with it so that the red, reflective surface is facing oncoming traffic. If a breakdown occurs round a blind corner, place the triangle in advance of the corner. Hazard warning lights may be used in conjunction with the triangle but they do not replace it.

Essential Equipment Table

The table on the following page shows the essential equipment required for each country. The Country Introduction chapters also include details of specific rules for each country. Please note that this information was correct at the time of going to print but is subject to change. For up to date equipment requirements visit www.caravanclub.co.uk/overseasadvice.

Country	Warning Triangle	Spare Bulbs	First Aid Kit	Reflective Jacket	Additional Equipment to be Carried/Used
Andorra	Yes (2)	Yes	Rec	Yes	Dipped headlights in poor daytime visibility. Winter tyres recommended; snow chains when road conditions or signs dictate.
Austria	Yes	Rec	Yes	Yes	Winter tyres from 1 Nov to 15 April.*
Belgium	Yes	Rec	Rec	Yes	Dipped headlights in poor daytime visibility.
Croatia	Yes (2 for vehicle with trailer)	Yes	Yes	Yes	Dipped headlights at all times from last Sunday in Oct - last Sunday in Mar. Spare bulbs compulsory if lights are xenon, neon or LED. Snow chains compulsory in winter in certain regions.*
Czech Rep	Yes	Yes	Yes	Yes	Dipped headlights at all times. Replacement fuses. Winter tyres or snow chains from 1 Nov - 31st March.*
Denmark	Yes	Rec	Rec	Rec	Dipped headlights at all times. On motorways use hazard warning lights when queues or danger ahead.
Finland	Yes	Rec	Rec	Yes	Dipped headlights at all times. Winter tyres Dec - Feb.*
France	Yes	Rec	Rec	Yes	Dipped headlights recommended at all times. Legal requirement to carry a breathalyser, but no penalty for non-compliance.
Germany	Rec	Rec	Rec	Rec	Dipped headlights recommended at all times. Winter tyres to be used in winter weather conditions.*
Greece	Yes	Rec	Yes	Rec	Fire extinguisher compulsory. Dipped headlights in towns at night and in poor daytime visibility.
Hungary	Yes	Rec	Yes	Yes	Dipped headlights at all times outside built-up areas and in built-up areas at night. Snow chains compulsory on some roads in winter conditions.*
Italy	Yes	Rec	Rec	Yes	Dipped headlights at all times outside built-up areas and in poor visibility. Snow chains from 15 Oct - 15 April.*
Luxembourg	Yes	Rec	Rec	Yes	Dipped headlights at night and daytime in bad weather.
Netherlands	Yes	Rec	Rec	Rec	Dipped headlights at night and in bad weather and recommended during the day.
Norway	Yes	Rec	Rec	Rec	Dipped headlights at all times. Winter tyres compulsory when snow or ice on the roads.*
Poland	Yes	Rec	Rec	Rec	Dipped headlights at all times. Fire extinguisher compulsory.
Portugal	Yes	Rec	Rec	Rec	Dipped headlights in poor daytime visibility, in tunnels and in lanes where traffic flow is reversible.
Slovakia	Yes	Rec	Yes	Yes	Dipped headlights at all times. Winter tyres compulsory when compact snow or ice on the road.*
Slovenia	Yes (2 for vehicle with trailer)	Yes	Rec	Yes	Dipped headlights at all times. Hazard warning lights when reversing. Use winter tyres or carry snow chains 15 Nov - 15 Mar.
Spain	Yes (2 Rec)	Rec	Rec	Yes	Dipped headlights at night, in tunnels and on 'special' roads (roadworks).
Sweden	Yes	Rec	Rec	Rec	Dipped headlights at all times. Winter tyres 1 Dec to 31 March.
Switzerland (inc Liechtenstein)	Yes	Rec	Rec	Rec	Dipped headlights recommended at all times, compulsory in tunnels. Snow chains where indicated by signs.

NOTES:
1) All countries: seat belts (if fitted) must be worn by all passengers.
2) Rec: not compulsory for foreign-registered vehicles, but strongly recommended
3) Headlamp converters, spare bulbs, fire extinguisher, first aid kit and reflective waistcoat are strongly recommended for all countries.
4) In some countries drivers who wear prescription glasses must carry a spare pair.
5) Please check information for any country before you travel. This information is to be used as a guide only and it is your responsibility to make sure you have the correct equipment.

* For more information and regulations on winter driving please see the Country Introductions.

Route planning

ATLANTIC
OCEAN

Motorways
Major roads
Main roads
Ferry routes
⊕ **Major airports**

N
W E
S

Bay
of
Biscay

English Cha

Cardiff
Bristol
UNITED KINGDO
Plymouth Weymouth Poole Ports
Newh

Guernsey
Jersey
Roscoff
Brest
St Malo
Rennes
Nantes
La Rochelle
Cherbourg-O
Le Hav
C
Lir
Bordeaux

Ferrol
Santiago de
Compostela
Vigo
Ourense
Braga
Porto
Aveiro
Viseu
PORTUGAL
Coimbra
Leiria
LISBOA
Setúbal
Évora

Gijón
Oviedo
León
Santander
Bilbao
Vitoria-Gasteiz
Irun
Pamplona
Logroño
Valladolid
Salamanca
Zaragoza
Lleida
Reus
ANDORI
Mai
S

SPAIN
MADRID
Alcalá de Henares
Talavera
de la Reina
Toledo
Badajoz
Puertollano
Albacete
Torrent Valencia
Sagunto
Palma de
Eivissa
Alcoy-Alcoi
Elda
Elche-Elx
Murcia
Lorca
Cartagena
Linares
Córdoba
Sevilla
Granada
Almería
Faro
El Puerto de Santa María Jerez
de la Frontera
Cádiz
Marbella
Málaga
Algeciras GIBRALTAR

Mountain Passes & Tunnels

Advice for Drivers

Mountain Passes

Mountain passes can create difficult driving conditions, especially when towing or driving a large vehicle. You should only use them if you have a good power to weight ratio and in good driving conditions. If in any doubt as to your outfit's suitability or the weather then stick to motorway routes across maintain ranges if possible.

The tables on the following pages show which passes are not suitable for caravans, and those where caravans are not permitted. Motorhomes aren't usually included in these restrictions, but relatively low powered or very large vehicles should find an alternative route. Road signs at the foot of a pass may restrict access or offer advice, especially for heavy vehicles. Warning notices are usually posted at the foot of a pass if it is closed, or if chains or winter tyres must be used.

Caravanners are particularly sensitive to gradients and traffic/road conditions on passes. The maximum gradient is usually on the inside of bends but exercise caution if it is necessary to pull out. Always engage a lower gear before taking a hairpin bend and give priority to vehicles ascending. On mountain roads it is not the gradient which puts strain on your car but the duration of the climb and the loss of power at high altitudes: approximately 10% at 915 metres (3,000 feet) and even more as you get higher. To minimise the risk of the engine overheating, take high passes in the cool part of the day, don't climb any faster than necessary and keep the engine pulling steadily. To prevent a radiator boiling, pull off the road safely, turn the heater and blower full on and switch off air conditioning. Keep an eye on water and oil levels. Never put cold water into a boiling radiator or it may crack. Check that the radiator is not obstructed by debris sucked up during the journey.

A long descent may result in overheating brakes; select the correct gear for the gradient and avoid excessive use of brakes. Even if you are using engine braking to control speed, caravan brakes may activate due to the overrun mechanism, which may cause them to overheat.

Travelling at altitude can cause a pressure build up in tanks and water pipes. You can prevent this by slightly opening the blade valve of your portable toilet and opening a tap a fraction.

Tunnels

Long tunnels are a much more commonly seen feature in Europe than in the UK, especially in mountainous regions. Tolls are usually charged for the use of major tunnels.

Dipped headlights are usually required by law even in well-lit tunnels, so switch them on before you enter. Snow chains, if used, must be removed before entering a tunnel in lay-bys provided for this purpose.

'No overtaking' signs must be strictly observed. Never cross central single or double lines. If overtaking is permitted in twin-tube tunnels, bear in mind that it is very easy to underestimate distances and speed once inside. In order to minimise the effects of exhaust fumes close all car windows and set the ventilator to circulate air, or operate the air conditioning system coupled with the recycled air option.

If you break down, try to reach the next lay-by and call for help from an emergency phone. If you cannot reach a lay-by, place your warning triangle at least 100 metres behind your vehicle. Modern tunnels have video surveillance systems to ensure prompt assistance in an emergency. Some tunnels can extend for miles and a high number of breakdowns are due to running out of fuel so make sure you have enough before entering the tunnel.

Mountain Pass Information

The dates of opening and closing given in the following tables are approximate. Before attempting late afternoon or early morning journeys across borders, check their opening times as some borders close at night.

Gradients listed are the maximum which may be encountered on the pass and may be steeper at the inside of curves, particularly on older roads.

Gravel surfaces (such as dirt and stone chips) vary considerably; they can be dusty when dry and slippery when wet. Where known to exist, this type of surface has been noted.

In fine weather winter tyres or snow chains will only be required on very high passes, or for short periods in early or late summer. In winter conditions you will probably need to use them at altitudes exceeding 600 metres (approximately 2,000 feet).

Converting Gradients

20% = 1 in 5	11% = 1 in 9
16% = 1 in 6	10% = 1 in 8
14% = 1 in 7	8% = 1 in 12
12% = 1 in 8	6% = 1 in 16

Tables and maps

Much of the information contained in the following tables was originally supplied by The Automobile Association and other motoring and tourist organisations. The Caravan Club haven't checked this information and cannot accept responsibility for the accuracy or for errors or omissions to these tables.

The mountain passes, rail and road tunnels listed in the tables are shown on the following maps. Numbers and letters against each pass or tunnel in the tables, correspond with the numbers and letters on the maps.

Abbreviations

MHV	Maximum height of vehicle
MLV	Maximum length of vehicle
MWV	Maximum width of vehicle
MWR	Minimum width of road
OC	Occasionally closed between dates
UC	Usually closed between dates
UO	Usually open between dates, although a fall of snow may obstruct the road for 24-48 hours.

Club Insurance built on firsthand experience

We've looked closely at our insurances to make sure they meet your needs

Why choose Club insurance?

- Club know-how ensures great cover
- Created with your touring needs in mind
- Superb value for money
- The aftercare you expect from The Club

I'm delighted with the service, the premium is very competitive and the online quote system was so easy

Sara Reynolds, member, Cheshire

Get peace of mind, get your quote at
www.caravanclub.co.uk or call

 Caravan Insurance 01342 488209

 Motorhome & Car Insurance 0808 223 4145*

 Overseas Holiday Insurance 01342 488363

 Home Insurance 0800 028 481

 Pet Insurance 0800 015 139

 Mayday UK Breakdown & Recovery 0800 731 011

THE CARAVAN CLUB

Major Mountain Passes – Pyrenees and Northern Spain

Before using any of these passes, PLEASE READ CAREFULLY THE ADVICE AT THE BEGINNING OF THIS CHAPTER

	Pass / Height In Metres (Feet)	From / To	Max Gradient	Conditions and Comments
1	**Aubisque** (France) 1710 (5610)	Eaux Bonnes / Argelés-Gazost	10%	UC mid Oct-Jun. MWR 3.5m (11'6") Very winding; continuous on D918 but easy ascent; descent including Col-d'Aubisque 1709m (5607 feet) and Col-du-Soulor 1450m (4757 feet); 8km (5 miles) of very narrow, rough, unguarded road with steep drop. **Not recommended for caravans**.
2	**Bonaigua** (Spain) 2072 (6797)	Viella (Vielha) / Esterri-d'Aneu	8.5%	UC Nov-Apr. MWR 4.3m (14'1") Twisting, narrow road (C28) with many hairpins and some precipitous drops. **Not recommended for caravans**. Alternative route to Lerida (Lleida) through Viella (Vielha) Tunnel is open all year. See *Pyrenean Road Tunnels* in this section.
3	**Cabrejas** (Spain) 1167 (3829)	Tarancon / Cuenca	14%	UO. On N400/A40. Sometimes blocked by snow for 24 hours. MWR 5m (16')
4	**Col-d'Haltza and Col-de-Burdincurutcheta** (France) 782 (2565) and 1135 (3724)	St Jean-Pied-de-Port / Larrau	11%	UO. A narrow road (D18/D19) leading to Iraty skiing area. Narrow with some tight hairpin bends; rarely has central white line and stretches are unguarded. Not for the faint-hearted. **Not recommended for caravans**.
5	**Envalira** (France – Andorra) 2407 (7897)	Pas-de-la-Casa / Andorra	12.5%	OC Nov-Apr. MWR 6m (19'8") Good road (N22/CG2) with wide bends on ascent and descent; fine views. MHV 3.5m (11'6") on N approach near l'Hospitalet. Early start rec in summer to avoid border delays. Envalira Tunnel (toll) reduces congestion and avoids highest part of pass. See *Pyrenean Road Tunnels* in this section.
6	**Escudo** (Spain) 1011 (3317)	Santander / Burgos	17%	UO. MWR probably 5m (16'5") Asphalt surface but many bends and steep gradients. **Not recommended in winter**. On N632; A67/N611 easier route.
7	**Guadarrama** (Spain) 1511 (4957)	Guadarrama / San Rafael	14%	UO. MWR 6m (19'8") On NVI to the NW of Madrid but may be avoided by using AP6 motorway from Villalba to San Rafael or Villacastin (toll).
8	**Ibañeta (Roncevalles)** (France – Spain) 1057 (3468)	St Jean-Pied-de-Port / Pamplona	10%	UO. MWR 4m (13'1") Slow and winding, scenic route on N135.
9	**Manzanal** (Spain) 1221 (4005)	Madrid / La Coruña	7%	UO. Sometimes blocked by snow for 24 hours. On A6.
10	**Navacerrada** (Spain) 1860 (6102)	Madrid / Segovia	17%	OC Nov-Mar. On M601/CL601. Sharp hairpins. Possible but **not recommended for caravans**.

Before using any of these passes, PLEASE READ CAREFULLY THE ADVICE AT THE BEGINNING OF THIS CHAPTER

	Pass Height In Metres (Feet)	From To	Max Gradient	Conditions and Comments
11	**Orduna** (Spain) 900 (2953)	Bilbao *Burgos*	15%	UO. On A625/BU556; sometimes blocked by snow for 24 hours. Avoid by using AP68 motorway.
12	**Pajares** (Spain) 1270 (4167)	Oviedo *Léon*	16%	UO. On N630; sometimes blocked by snow for 24 hours. **Not recommended for caravans.** Avoid by using AP66 motorway.
13	**Paramo-de-Masa** 1050 (3445)	Santander *Burgos*	8%	UO. On N623; sometimes blocked by snow for 24 hours.
14	**Peyresourde** (France) 1563 (5128)	Arreau *Bagnères-de-Luchon*	10%	UO. MWR 4m (13'1") D618 somewhat narrow with several hairpin bends, though not difficult. **Not recommended for caravans.**
15	**Picos-de-Europa: Puerto-de-San Glorio, Puerto-de-Pontón, Puerto-de-Pandetrave** (Spain), 1609 (5279)	Unquera *Riaño*	12%	UO. MWR probably 4m (13'1") Desfiladero de la Hermida on N621 good condition. Puerto-de-San-Glorio steep with many hairpin bends. For confident drivers only.
		Riaño *Cangas-de-Onis*		Puerto-de-Ponton on N625, height 1280 metres (4200 feet). Best approach fr S as from N is very long uphill pull with many tight turns.
		Portilla-la-Reina *Santa Marina-de-Valdeón*		Puerto-de-Pandetrave, height 1562 metres (5124 feet) on LE245 not rec when towing as main street of Santa Marina steep & narrow.
16	**Piqueras** (Spain) 1710 (5610)	Logroño *Soria*	7%	UO. On N111; sometimes blocked by snow for 24 hours.
17	**Port** (France) 1249 (4098)	Tarascon-sur-Ariège *Massat*	10%	OC Nov-Mar. MWR 4m (13'1") A fairly easy, scenic road (D618), but narrow on some bends.
18	**Portet-d'Aspet** (France) 1069 (3507)	Audressein *Fronsac*	14%	UO. MWR 3.5m (11'6") Approached from W by the easy Col-des-Ares and Col-de-Buret; well-engineered but narrow road (D618); care needed on hairpin bends. **Not recommended for caravans.**
19	**Pourtalet** (France – Spain) 1792 (5879)	Laruns *Biescas*	10%	UC late Oct-early Jun. MWR 3.5m (11'6") A fairly easy, unguarded road, but narrow in places. Easier from Spain (A136), steeper in France (D934). **Not recommended for caravans.**
20	**Puymorens** (France) 1915 (6283)	Ax-les-Thermes *Bourg-Madame*	10%	OC Nov-Apr. MWR 5.5m (18') MHV 3.5m (11'6") A generally easy, modern tarmac road (N20). Parallel toll road tunnel available. See *Pyrenean Road Tunnels* in this section.

Before using any of these passes, PLEASE READ CAREFULLY THE ADVICE AT THE BEGINNING OF THIS CHAPTER

Pass / Height In Metres (Feet)	From / To	Max Gradient	Conditions and Comments
21 **Quillane** (France) 1714 (5623)	Axat / Mont-Louis	8.5%	OC Nov-Mar. MWR 5m (16'5") An easy, straightforward ascent and descent on D118.
22 **Somosierra** (Spain) 1444 (4738)	Madrid / Burgos	10%	OC Mar-Dec. MWR 7m (23') On A1/E5; may be blocked following snowfalls. Snow-plough swept during winter months but wheel chains compulsory after snowfalls. Well-surfaced dual carriageway, tunnel at summit.
23 **Somport** (France – Spain) 1632 (5354)	Accous / Jaca	10%	UO. MWR 3.5m (11'6") A favoured, old-established route; not particularly easy and narrow in places with many unguarded bends on French side (N134); excellent road on Spanish side (N330). Use of road tunnel advised – see *Pyrenean Road Tunnels* in this section. NB Visitors advise re-fuelling no later than Sabiñánigo when travelling south to north.
24 **Toses (Tosas)** (Spain) 1800 (5906)	Puigcerda / Ribes-de-Freser	10%	UO MWR 5m (16'5") A fairly straightforward, but continuously winding, two-lane road (N152) with with a good surface but many sharp bends; some unguarded edges. Difficult in winter.
25 ● **Tourmalet** (France) 2114 (6936)	Ste Marie-de-Campan / Luz-St Sauveur	12.5%	UC Oct-mid Jun. MWR 4m (13'1") The highest French Pyrenean route (D918); approaches good, though winding, narrow in places and exacting over summit; sufficiently guarded. Rough surface & uneven edges on west side. Not recommended for caravans.
26 ● **Urquiola** (Spain) 713 (2340)	Durango (Bilbao) / Vitoria/Gasteiz	16%	UO. Sometimes closed by snow for 24 hours. On BI623/A623. Not recommended for caravans.

Major Alpine Mountain Passes & Tunnels - Pyrenees and Northern Spain   **47**

Keeping in Touch

Telephones and Calling

Most people need to use a telephone at some point while they're away, whether to keep in touch with family and friends back home or call ahead to sites. Even if you don't plan to use a phone while you're away, it is best to make sure you have access to one in case of emergencies.

International Direct Dial Calls

International access codes are given in the relevant Country Introduction - first dial the international access code then the local number. If the area code starts with a zero this should be omitted (except in Italy where the full number should be dialled).

The international access code to dial the UK from anywhere in the world is 0044.

Ringing Tones

Ringing tones vary from country to country, so may sound very different to UK tones. Some ringing tones sound similar to error or engaged tones that you would hear on a UK line.

Phone cards

You can buy pre-paid international phone cards which offer much lower rates for international calls than most mobile phone providers. You load the card with your chosen amount (which you can top up at any time) and then dial an access code from any mobile or landline to make your call. See www.planetphonecards. com or www.thephonecardsite.com for more details.

Using Mobile Phones Abroad

Mobile phones have an international calling option called 'roaming' which will automatically search for a local network when you switch your phone on. You should contact your service provider to ask about their roaming charges as these are partly set by the foreign networks you use and fluctuate with exchange rates. Most network providers offer added extras or 'bolt-ons' to your tariff to make the cost of calling to/from abroad cheaper.

Storing telephone numbers in your phone's contact list in international format (i.e. use the prefix of +44 and omit the initial '0') will mean that your contacts will automatically work abroad as well as in the UK.

Global SIM Cards

If you're planning on travelling to more than one country consider buying a global SIM card. This will mean mobile phone can operate on foreign mobile networks, which will be more cost effective than your service provider's

roaming charges. For details of SIM cards available, speak to your service provider or visit www.0044.co.uk or www.globalsimcard.co.uk.

You may find it simpler to buy a SIM card or cheap 'pay-as-you-go' phone abroad if you plan to use a mobile phone a lot for local calls, e.g. to book campsites or restaurants. Buying a local SIM or pay-as-you-go mobile may mean that you still have higher call charges for international calls (such as calling the UK). Before buying a different SIM card, check with you provider whether your phone is locked against use on other networks.

Hands-Free
Legislation in Europe forbids the use of mobile or car phones while driving except when using hands-free equipment. If you are involved in an accident whilst driving and, at the same time, you were using a hand-held mobile phone, your insurance company may refuse to honour the claim.

Accessing the Internet

Mobile Internet Costs - Data Roaming
Accessing the internet overseas via your mobile can be very expensive. It is recommended that you disable your internet access by switching 'data roaming' to off, in order to avoid a large mobile phone bill on your return.

Internet Access
Wi-Fi is available on lots of campsites in Europe, sometimes the cost in included in your pitch fee and other sites charge extra for access. Most larger towns may have internet cafés or libraries where you can access the internet, however lots of fast food restaurants and coffee chains now offer free Wi-Fi for customers and visiting them for a cup of coffee or bite to eat is often the most economical way if you only need access for a short time.

Many people now use their smartphones for internet access or have a dongle – a device which, when connected to your laptop or tablet, allows you to access the internet using a mobile phone network. While these methods are economical in the UK, if you do the same abroad you will be charged data roaming charges which can run into hundreds or thousands of pounds depending on how much data you use. If you plan on using your smartphone or a dongle abroad speak to your service provider before you leave the UK to make sure you understand the costs. There may even be an overseas package that you can add to your plan to make data roaming cheaper.

Making Calls from your Laptop

If you download Skype to your laptop you can make free calls to other Skype users anywhere in the world using a Wi-Fi connection. Rates for calls to non-Skype users (landline or mobile phone) are also very competitively-priced. You will need a computer with a microphone and speakers, and a webcam is handy too. It is also possible to download Skype to an internet-enabled mobile phone to take advantage of the same low-cost calls – see www.skype.com.

Club Together

If you want to chat to other members either at home or while you're away, you can do so on The Club's online community Club Together. You can ask questions and gather opinions on the forums, as well as asking for expert advice on a number of caravanning topics. Just visit www.caravanclub.co.uk/together.

Radio and Television

Radio

The BBC World Service broadcasts radio programmes 24 hours a day worldwide and you can listen on a number of platforms: online, via satellite or cable, DRM digital radio, internet radio or mobile phone. You can find detailed information and programme schedules at www.bbc.co.uk/worldservice.

Listeners in northern France can currently listen to BBC Radio 5 Live on either 693 or 909 kHz medium wave or BBC Radio 4 on 198 kHz long wave. Whereas analogue television signals were switched off in the UK during 2012, no date has yet been fixed for the switch off of analogue radio signals.

Digital Terrestrial Television

As in the UK, television transmissions in most of Europe have been converted to digital. The

UK's high definition transmission technology may be more advanced than any currently implemented or planned in Europe. This means that digital televisions intended for use in the UK might not be able to receive HD terrestrial signals in some countries.

Satellite Television

For English-language TV programmes the only realistic option is satellite, and satellite dishes are a common sight on campsites all over Europe. A satellite dish mounted on the caravan roof or clamped to a pole fixed to the drawbar, or one mounted on a foldable free-standing tripod, will provide good reception and minimal interference. Remember however that obstructions to the south east (such as tall trees or even mountains) or heavy rain, can interrupt the signals. A specialist dealer will be able to advise you on the best way of mounting your dish. You will also need a satellite receiver and ideally a satellite-finding meter.

The main entertainment channels such as BBC1, ITV1 and Channel 4 can be difficult to pick up in mainland Europe as they are now being transmitted by new narrow-beam satellites. A 60cm dish should pick up these channels in most of France, Belgium and the Netherlands but as you travel further afield, you'll need a progressively larger dish. See the website www.satelliteforcaravans. co.uk (created and operated by a Caravan Club member) for the latest changes and developments, and for information on how to set up your equipment.

Medical Matters

You can find country specific medical advice, including details of any vaccinations you may need from the NHS choices website, www.nhs.uk/healthcare abroad. Your GP surgery should also be able to give you advice on vaccinations and precautions. For general enquiries about medical care abroad you can contact NHS England on 0300 311 22 33 or email england.contactus@nhs.uk.

If you have any pre-existing medical conditions you should check with your GP that you are fit to travel. Ask your doctor for a written summary of any medical problems and a list of medications currently used. This is particularly important for travellers whose medical conditions require them to use controlled drugs or hypodermic syringes, in case customs officers question why you are carrying them.

Always make sure that you have enough of your medication to last the duration of your holiday and some extra in case you are delayed in returning to the UK. Ask your doctor for the generic name of any drugs you use, as brand names may be different abroad. If possible carry a card giving your blood group and details of any allergies or dietary restrictions (translations may be useful for restaurants).

If you have any doubts about your teeth or plan to be away a long time, have a dental check-up before departure. An emergency dental kit is available from High Street chemists which will allow you temporarily to restore a crown, bridge or filling or to dress a broken tooth until you can get to a dentist.

A good website to check before you travel is www.nathnac.org/travel. This website gives general health and safety advice and reports of disease outbreaks, as well as highlighting potential health risks by country.

European Heath Insurance Card (EHIC)

Before leaving home apply for a European Health Insurance Card (EHIC). British residents temporarily visiting another EU country, as well Norway and Switzerland, are entitled to receive state-provided emergency treatment during their stay on the same terms as residents of those countries, but you must have a valid EHIC to claim these services.

As well as treatment in the event of an emergency, this includes on-going medical care

for a chronic disease or pre-existing illness, i.e. medication, blood tests and injections. Apply online for your EHIC on www.ehic.org.uk, call 0845 6062030 or pick up an application form from a post office. An EHIC is required by each individual family member - children under 16 must be included in a parent or guardian's application.

The EHIC is free of charge, is valid for up to five years and can be renewed up to six months before its expiry date. Before you travel remember to check that your EHIC is still valid.

Private treatment is generally not covered by your EHIC, and state-provided treatment may not cover everything that you would expect to receive free of charge from the NHS. If charges are made, these cannot be refunded by the British authorities but may be refundable under the terms of your travel insurance policy.

An EHIC is not a substitute for travel insurance and it is strongly recommended that you arrange full travel insurance before leaving home regardless of the cover provided by your EHIC. Some insurance companies require you to have an EHIC and some will waive the policy excess if an EHIC has been used.

If your EHIC is stolen or lost while you are abroad contact 0044 191 2127500 for help. If you experience difficulties in getting your EHIC accepted, telephone the Department for Work & Pensions for assistance on the overseas healthcare team line 0044 (0)191 218 1999 between 8am to 5pm Monday to Friday. Residents of the Republic of Ireland, the Isle of Man and Channel Islands, should check with their own health authorities about reciprocal arrangements with other countries.

Holiday Travel Insurance

Despite the fact that you have an EHIC you may incur thousands of pounds of medical costs if you fall ill or have an accident. The cost of bringing a person back to the UK, in the event of illness or death, is never covered by the EHIC. You may also find that you end up with a bill for treatment as not all countries offer free healthcare.

Separate additional travel insurance adequate for your destination is essential, such as The Caravan Club's Red Pennant Overseas Holiday Insurance, available to Club members – see www.caravanclub.co.uk/redpennant.

First Aid

A first aid kit containing at least the basic requirements is an essential item, and in some countries it is compulsory to carry one in your vehicle (see the Essential Equipment Table in the chapter Motoring – Equipment). Kits should contain items such as sterile pads, assorted dressings, bandages and plasters, antiseptic wipes or cream, cotton wool, scissors, eye bath and tweezers. Also make sure you carry something for upset stomachs, painkillers and an antihistamine in case of hay fever or mild allergic reactions.

If you're travelling to remote areas then you may find it useful to carry a good first aid manual. The British Red Cross publishes a comprehensive First Aid Manual in conjunction with St John Ambulance and St Andrew's Ambulance Association.

Vaccinations

Your GP surgery can advise you if any vaccinations are required.

Accidents and Emergencies

If you are involved in or witness a road accident the police may want to question you about it. If possible take photographs or make sketches of the scene, and write a few notes about what happened as it may be more difficult to remember the details at a later date.

The telephone numbers for police, fire brigade and ambulance services are given in each Country Introduction, however all EU member states the number 112 can be used from landlines or mobile phones to call any of the emergency services.

Sun Protection

Never under-estimate how ill exposure to the sun can make you. If you are not used to the heat it is very easy to fall victim to heat exhaustion or heat stroke. Avoid sitting in the sun between 11am and 3pm and cover your head if sitting or walking in the sun. Use a good quality sun-cream with high sun protection factor (SPF) and re-apply frequently. Make sure you drink plenty of fluids.

Tick-Borne Encephalitis (TBE) and Lyme Disease

Hikers and outdoor sports enthusiasts planning trips to forested, rural areas should be aware of tick-borne encephalitis, which is transmitted by the bite of an infected tick. If you think you may be at risk, seek medical advice on prevention and immunisation before you leave the UK.

There is no vaccine against Lyme disease, an equally serious tick-borne infection, which, if left untreated, can attack the nervous system and joints.

You can minimise the risk by using an insect repellent containing DEET, wearing long sleeves and long trousers, and checking for ticks after outdoor activity. Avoid unpasteurised dairy products in risk areas. See www.tickalert. org or telephone 01943 468010 for more information.

Water and Food

Water from mains supplies throughout Europe is generally safe, but may be treated with chemicals which make it taste different to tap water in the UK. If in any doubt, always drink bottled water or boil it before drinking. Food poisoning is potential anywhere, and a complete change of diet may upset your stomach as well. In hot conditions avoid any food that hasn't been refrigerated or hot food that has been left to cool. Be sensible about the food that you eat – don't eat unpasteurised or undercooked food and if you aren't sure about the freshness of meat or seafood then it is best avoided.

Returning Home

If you become ill on your return home tell your doctor that you have been abroad and which countries you have visited. Even if you have received medical treatment in another country, always consult your doctor if you have been bitten or scratched by an animal while on holiday.

If you were given any medicines in another country, it may be illegal to bring them back into the UK. If in doubt, declare them at customs when you return.

Electricity and Gas

Electricity – General Advice

The voltage for mains electricity is 230V across the EU, but varying degrees of 'acceptable tolerance' mean you may find variations in the actual voltage. Most appliances sold in the UK are 220-240V so should work correctly. However, some high-powered equipment, such as microwave ovens, may not function well – check your instruction manual for any specific instructions. Appliances marked with 'CE' have been designed to meet the requirements of relevant European directives.

The table below gives an approximate idea of which appliances can be used based on the amperage which is being supplied (although not all appliances should be used at the same time). You can work it out more accurately by making a note of the wattage of each appliance in your caravan. The wattages given are based on appliances designed for use in caravans and motorhomes. Household kettles, for example, have at least a 2000W element. Each caravan circuit will also have a maximum amp rating which should not be exceeded.

Electrical Connections – EN60309-2 (CEE17)

EN60309-2 (formerly known as CEE17) is the European Standard for all newly fitted connectors. However there is no requirement

Amps	Wattage (Approx)	Fridge	Battery Charger	Air Conditioning	LCD TV	Water Heater	Kettle (750W)	Heater (1kW)
2	400	✓	✓					
4	900	✓	✓		✓	✓		
6	1300	✓	✓	*	✓	✓	✓	
8	1800	✓	✓	✓**	✓	✓	✓	✓**
10	2300	✓	✓	✓**	✓	✓	✓	✓**
16	3600	✓	✓	✓	✓	✓	✓	✓**

*   Usage possible, depending on wattage of appliance in question
** Not to be used at the same time as other high-wattage equipment

for sites to replace connectors which were installed before this was standardised so you may still find some sites where your UK 3 pin connector doesn't fit. For this reason it is a good idea to carry a 2-pin adapter. If you are already on site and find your connector doesn't fit, ask campsite staff to borrow or hire an adaptor. You may still encounter a poor electrical supply on site even with an EN60309-2 connection.

Other Connections
French – 2-pin, plus earth socket. Adaptors available from UK caravan accessory shops.

German – 2-pin, plus 2 earth strips, found in Norway and Sweden and possibly still Germany.

Switzerland - 3-pin, but not the same shape as UK 3-pin. Adapters available to purchase in Switzerland. Most campsites using the Swiss 3-pin will have adaptors available for hire or to borrow.

If the campsite does not have a modern EN60309-2 (CEE17) supply, ask to see the electrical protection for the socket outlet. If there is a device marked with IDn = 30mA, then the risk is minimised.

Hooking Up to the Mains

Connection
Connection should always be made in the following order:

- Check your outfit isolating switch is at 'off'.

- Uncoil the connecting cable from the drum. A coiled cable with current flowing through it may overheat. Take your cable and insert the connector (female end) into your outfit inlet.

- Insert the plug (male end) into the site outlet socket.

- Switch outfit isolating switch to 'on'.

- Use a polarity tester in one of the 13A sockets in the outfit to check all connections are correctly wired. Never leave it in the socket. Some caravans have these devices built in as standard.

It is recommended that the supply is not used if the polarity is incorrect (see Reversed Polarity overleaf).

Warnings:
If you are in any doubt of the safety of the system, if you don't receive electricity once connected or if the supply stops then contact the site staff.

If the fault is found to be with your outfit then call a qualified electrician rather than trying to fix the problem yourself.

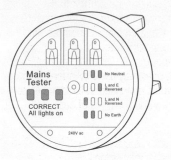

To ensure your safety you should never use an electrical system which you can't confirm to be safe. Use a mains tester such as the one shown above to test the electrical supply. Always check that a proper earth connection exists before using the electrics. Please note that these testers may not pick up all earth faults so if there is any doubt as to the integrity of the earth system do not use the electrical supply.

Disconnection

- Switch your outfit isolating switch to 'off'.
- At the site supply socket withdraw the plug.
- Disconnect the cable from your outfit.

Motorhomes – if leaving your pitch during the day, don't leave your mains cable plugged into the site supply, as this creates a hazard if the exposed live connections in the plug are touched or if the cable is not seen during grass-cutting.

Reversed Polarity

Even if the site connector meets European Standard EN60309-2 (CEE17), British caravanners are still likely to encounter the problem known as reversed polarity. This is where the site supply 'live' line connects to the outfit's 'neutral' and vice versa. You should always check the polarity immediately on connection, using a polarity tester available from caravan accessory shops. If polarity is reversed the caravan mains electricity should not be used. Try using another nearby socket instead. Frequent travellers to the Continent can make up an adaptor themselves, or ask an electrician to make one for you, with the live and neutral wires reversed. Using a reversed polarity socket will probably not affect how an electrical appliance works, however your protection is greatly reduced. For example, a lamp socket may still be live as you touch it while replacing a blown bulb, even if the light switch is turned off.

Shaver Sockets

Most campsites provide shaver sockets with a voltage of 220V or 110V. Using an incorrect voltage may cause the shaver to become

Site Hooking Up Adaptor
ADAPTATEUR DE PRISE AU SITE (SECTEUR)
CAMPINGPLATZ-ANSCHLUSS (NETZ)

EXTENSION LEAD TO CARAVAN
Câble de rallonge à la caravane
Verläëngerungskabel zum wohnwagen

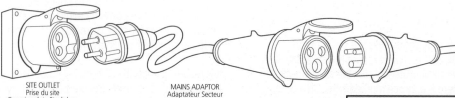

SITE OUTLET
Prise du site
Campingplatz-Steckdose

MAINS ADAPTOR
Adaptateur Secteur
Netzanschlußstacker

16A 230V AC

hot or break. The 2-pin adaptor available in the UK may not fit Continental sockets so it is advisable to buy 2-pin adaptors on the Continent. Many modern shavers will work on a range of voltages which make them suitable for travelling abroad. Check you instruction manual to see if this is the case.

Gas – General Advice

Gas usage can be difficult to predict as so many factors, such as temperature and how often you eat out, can affect the amount you need. As a rough guide allow 0.45kg of gas a day for normal summer usage.

With the exception of Campingaz, LPG cylinders normally available in the UK cannot be exchanged abroad. If possible, take enough gas with you and bring back the empty cylinders. Always check how many you can take with you as ferry and tunnel operators may restrict the number of cylinders you are permitted to carry for safety reasons.

The wide availability of Campingaz across Europe means it is worth considering using it while touring overseas. However, prices can vary from country to country, and maximum cylinder sizes are quite limited (2.75kg of gas in a 907 cylinder), making it less practical for routine use in larger vehicles with several gas appliances. A Campingaz adapter is relatively inexpensive, though, and is widely available in the UK.

If you are touring in cold weather conditions use propane gas instead of butane. Many other brands of gas are available in different countries and, as long as you have the correct regulator, adaptor and hose and the cylinders fit in your gas locker these local brands can also be used.

Gas cylinders are now standardised with a pressure of 30mbar for both butane and propane within the EU. On UK-specification caravans and motorhomes (2004 models and later) a 30mbar regulator suited to both propane and butane use is fitted to the bulkhead of the gas locker. This is connected to the cylinder with a connecting hose (and sometimes an adaptor) to suit different brands or types of gas. Older outfits and some foreign-built ones may use a cylinder-mounted regulator, which may need to be changed to suit different brands or types of gas.

Warnings:

- Refilling gas cylinders intended to be exchanged is against the law in most countries, however you may still find that some sites and dealers will offer to refill cylinders for you. Never take them up on this service as it can be dangerous; the cylinders haven't been designed for user-refilling and it is possible to overfill them with catastrophic consequences.

- Regular servicing of gas appliances is important as a faulty appliance can emit carbon monoxide, which could prove fatal. Check your vehicle or appliance handbook for service recommendations.

- Never use a hob or oven as a space heater.

The Caravan Club publishes a range of technical leaflets for its members including detailed advice on the use of electricity and gas – you can request copies or see www.caravanclub.co.uk/advice-and-training.

Safety and Security

EU countries have good legislation in place to protect your safety wherever possible. However accidents and crime will still occur and taking sensible precautions can help to minimise your risk of being involved.

Beaches, Lakes and Rivers

Check for any warning signs or flags before you swim and ensure that you know what they mean. Check the depth of water before diving and avoid diving or jumping into murky water as submerged objects may not be visible. Familiarise yourself with the location of safety apparatus and/or lifeguards.

Use only the designated areas for swimming, watersports and boating and always use life jackets where appropriate. Watch out for tides, undertows, currents and wind strength and direction before you or your children swim in the sea. This applies in particular when using inflatables, windsurfing equipment, body boards, kayaks or sailing boats. Sudden changes of wave and weather conditions combined with fast tides and currents are particularly dangerous.

Campsite Safety

Once you've settled in, take a walk around the site to familiarise yourself with its layout and locate the nearest safety equipment. Ensure that children know their way around and where your pitch is.

Natural disasters are rare, but always think about what could happen. A combination of heavy rain and a riverside pitch could lead to flash flooding, for example, so make yourself aware of site evacuation procedures.

Be aware of sources of electricity and cabling on and around your pitch – electrical safety might not be up to the same standards as in the UK.

Poison for rodent control is sometimes used on sites or surrounding farmland. Warning notices are not always posted and you are strongly advised to check if staying on a rural site with dogs or children.

Incidents of theft on campsites are rare but when leaving your caravan unattended make sure you lock all doors and shut windows. Conceal valuables from sight and lock bicycles to a tree or to your caravan.

Hintersee – Bavaria, Germany

Children

Watch out for children as you drive around the site and don't exceed walking pace.

Children's play areas are generally unsupervised. Check which are suitable for your children's ages and abilities and agree with them which ones they may use. Read and respect the displayed rules. Remember it is your responsibility to know where your children are at all times.

Be aware of any campsite rules concerning ball games or use of play equipment, such as roller blades and skateboards. When your children attend organised activities, arrange when and where to meet afterwards.

Make sure that children are aware of any places where they should not go and never leave children alone inside a caravan.

Fire

Fire prevention is important on sites, as fire can spread quickly between outfits. The following fire safety measures should be followed:

- Don't use portable paraffin or gas heaters inside your caravan. Gas heaters should only be fitted when air is taken from outside the caravan.

- Don't change your gas cylinder inside the caravan. If you smell gas (or in the event of a fire starting), turn off the cylinder immediately, extinguish all naked flames and seek professional help.

- Know where the fire points and telephones are on site and know the site fire drill. Establish a family fire drill. Make sure everyone knows how to call the emergency services.

- Where site rules permit the use of barbecues, take the following precautions to prevent fire:

- Never locate a barbecue near trees or hedges. Have a bucket of water to hand in case of sparks.

- Only use recommended fire-lighting materials.

- Do not leave a barbecue unattended when lit and dispose of hot ash safely.

- Never take a barbeque into an enclosed area or awning – even when cooling they continue to release carbon monoxide which can lead to fatal poisoning.

Swimming Pools

Familiarize yourself with the pool area before you venture in for a swim, especially if you're travelling with children. Check the pool layout – identify shallow and deep ends and the location of safety equipment. Check the gradient of the pool bottom as pools which shelve off sharply can catch weak or non-swimmers unawares.

Never dive or jump into a pool without knowing the depth – if there is a no diving rule it usually means the pool isn't deep enough for safe diving.

For pools with a supervisor or lifeguard, note any times or dates when the pool is not supervised, e.g. lunch breaks or in low season. Read safety notices and rules posted around the pool.

On the Road

Do not leave valuables on car seats or on view in caravans, even if they are locked. Ensure that items on roof racks or cycle carriers are locked securely.

Beware of a 'snatch' through open car windows at traffic lights, filling stations or in traffic jams. When driving through towns and cities keep your doors locked. Keep handbags valuables and documents out of sight at all times.

Stowaways in vehicles can be a problem on ferries and Eurotunnel, so check that your outfit is free from unexpected guests at the last practical opportunity before boarding.

If flagged down by another motorist for whatever reason, take care that your own car is locked and windows closed while you check outside, even if someone is left inside.

Be particularly careful on long, empty stretches of motorway and when you stop for fuel. Even if the people flagging you down appear to be officials (e.g. wearing yellow reflective jackets or dark, 'uniform-type' clothing) show presence of mind and lock yourselves in immediately. They may appear to be friendly and helpful, but could be opportunistic thieves. Have a mobile phone to hand and, if necessary, be seen to use it.

Road accidents are a significant risk in some countries where traffic laws may be inadequately enforced, roads may be poorly maintained, road signs and lighting inadequate, and driving standards poor. It's a good idea to keep a fully-charged mobile phone with you in your car with the number of your breakdown organisation saved into it.

Overnight Stops

Overnight stops should always be at campsites and not at motorway service areas, ferry terminal car parks, petrol station forecourts or isolated 'aires de services' or 'aires de repos' on motorways where robberies and muggings are occasionally reported. If you decide to use these areas for a rest then take appropriate precautions, for example, shutting all windows, securing locks and making a thorough external check of your vehicle(s) before departing. Safeguard your property, e.g. handbags, while out of the caravan and beware of approaches by strangers.

For a safer place to take a break, there is a wide network of 'Stellplätze', 'Aires de Services', 'Aree di Sosta' and 'Áreas de Servicio' in cities, towns and villages across Europe, many specifically for motorhomes with good security and overnight facilities. It is rare that you will be the only vehicle staying on such areas, but avoid any that are isolated, take sensible precautions and trust your instincts. For example, if the area appears run down and there are groups of people hanging around who seem intimidating, then you are probably wise to move on.

Personal Security

Petty crime happens all over the world; however as a tourist you are more vulnerable to it. This shouldn't stop you from exploring new horizons, but there are a few sensible precautions you can take to minimise the risk.

- Leave valuables and jewellery at home. If you do take them, fit a small safe in your caravan or lock them in the boot of your car. Don't leave money or valuables in a car glovebox or on view. Don't leave bags in full view when sitting outside at cafés or restaurants, or leave valuables unattended on the beach.

- When walking be security-conscious. Avoid unlit streets at night, walk away from the kerb edge and carry handbags or shoulder bags on the side away from the kerb. The less of a tourist you appear, the less of a target you are.

- Keep a separate note of your holiday insurance details and emergency telephone numbers.

- Beware of pickpockets in crowded areas, at tourist attractions and in cities, and be cautious of bogus plain-clothes policemen who may ask to see your foreign currency or credit cards and passport. If approached, decline to show your money or to hand over your passport but ask for credentials and offer instead to go to the nearest police station.

- Laws and punishment vary from country to country so make yourself aware of anything which may affect you before you travel. Be especially careful on laws involving alcohol consumption (such as drinking in public areas), and never buy or use illegal drugs abroad.

- Respect Customs regulations - smuggling is a serious offence and can carry heavy penalties. Do not carry parcels or luggage through Customs for other people and do not cross borders with people you do not know in your vehicle, such as hitchhikers.

The Foreign & Commonwealth Office produces a range of material to advise and inform British citizens travelling abroad about issues affecting their safety - www.gov.uk/foreign-travel-advice has country specific guides.

Money Security

We would rarely walk around at home carrying large amounts of cash, but as you may not have the usual access to bank accounts and credit cards you are more likely to do so on holiday. You are also less likely to have the same degree of security when online banking as you would in your own home. The following precautions are sensible to keep your money safe:

- Carry only the minimum amount of cash and don't rely on one person to carry everything. Never carry a wallet in your back pocket. Moneybelts are the most secure way to carry cash and passports.

- Keep a separate note of bank account and credit/debit card numbers. Carry your credit card issuer/bank's 24-hour UK contact number with you.

- Be careful when using cash machines (ATMs) – try to use a machine in an area with high footfall and don't allow yourself to be distracted. Put your cash away before moving away from the cash machine.

- Always guard your PIN number, both at cash machines and when using your card pay in shops and restaurants. Never let your card out of your sight while paying.

- If using internet banking do not leave the PC or mobile device unattended and make sure you log out fully at the end of the session.

British Consular Services Abroad

British Embassy and Consular staff offer practical advice, assistance and support to British travellers abroad. They can, for example, issue replacement passports, help Britons who have been the victims of crime, contact relatives and friends in the event of an accident, illness or death, provide information about transferring funds and provide details of local lawyers, doctors and interpreters. But there are limits to their powers and a British Consul cannot, for example, give legal advice, intervene in court proceedings, put up bail, pay for legal or medical bills, or for funerals or the repatriation of bodies, or undertake work more properly done by banks, motoring organisations and travel insurers.

If you are charged with a serious offence, insist on the British Consul being informed. You will be contacted as soon as possible by a Consular Officer who can advise on local procedures, provide access to lawyers and insist that you are treated as well as nationals of the country which is holding you. However, they cannot get you released as a matter of course. British and Irish embassy contact details can be found in the Country Introduction chapters.

Continental Campsites

The quantity and variety of sites across Spain and Portugal means you're sure to find one that suits your needs – from full facilities and entertainment to quiet rural retreats. If you haven't previously toured outside of the UK you may notice some differences, such as pitches being smaller or closer together. During summer hard ground may make putting up awnings difficult.

Facilities will vary from site to site – in this guide the site listings will give you a good idea of what you can expect to find on each site. In the high season all campsite facilities are usually open, however bear in mind that toilet and shower facilities may be busy. Out of season some facilities such as shops and swimming pools may be closed and office opening hours may be reduced. If the site has very low occupancy the sanitary facilities may be reduced to a few unisex toilet and shower cubicles.

Booking a Campsite

To save the hassle of arriving to find a site full it is best to book in advance, especially in high season. If you don't book ahead arrive no later than 4pm (earlier at popular resorts) to secure a pitch, after this time sites fill up quickly.

You also need to allow time to find another campsite if your first choice is fully booked.

You can usually book directly via a campsite's website using a credit or debit card to pay a deposit if required. Please be aware that some sites regard the deposit as a booking or admin fee and will not deduct the amount from your final bill.

Overseas Travel Service

The Caravan Club's Travel Service offers Club members an overseas site booking service to over 200 campsites in Europe, with over 30 of those in Spain and Portugal. Full details plus information on Ferry special offers and Red Pennant Overseas Holiday Insurance can be found in the Club's Continental Caravanning brochure – call 01342 327410 to request a copy or visit www.caravanclub.co.uk/overseas.

Overseas Site Booking Service sites are marked 'SBS' in the site listings. The Caravan Club cannot make advance reservations for any other campsites listed in this guide. Only those sites marked SBS have been inspected by Caravan Club staff.

Camping Cheques

The Caravan Club operates a low season scheme in association with Camping Cheques, offering flexible holidays. The scheme covers approximately 635 sites in 29 countries.

Camping Cheques are supplied as part of a package which includes return ferry fare and a minimum of seven Camping Cheques. Those sites which feature in the Camping Cheques scheme and which are listed in this guide are marked 'CChq' in their site entries. For full details of the Camping Cheque scheme visit www.caravanclub.co.uk/campingcheques.

Caravan Storage Abroad

Storing your caravan on a site in Europe can be a great way to avoid a long tow and to save on ferry and fuel costs. Even sites which don't offer a specific long-term storage facility may be willing to negotiate a price to store your caravan for you.

Before you leave your caravan in storage abroad always check whether your insurance covers this, as many policies don't. If you aren't covered then look for a specialist policy - Towergate Bakers (tel: 0800 4961516 or www.towergatebakers.co.uk) or K Drewe Insurance (tel: 0845 408 5929 or www. lookinsuranceservices.co.uk) both offer policies.

Facilities and Site Description

All of the site facilities shown in the site listings of this guide have been taken from member reports, as have the comments at the end of each site entry. Please remember that opinions and expectations can differ significantly from one person to the next.

The year of report is indicated at the end of each site listing – sites which haven't been reported on for a few years may have had significant changes to their prices, facilities, opening dates and standards. It is always best to check any specific details you need to know before travelling by contacting the site or looking at their website.

Sanitary Facilities

Facilities normally include toilet and shower blocks with shower cubicles, wash basins and razor sockets. In site listings the abbreviation 'wc' indicates that the site has the kind of toilets we are used to in the UK (pedestal style). Some sites have footplate 'squat' toilets and, where this is known, you will see the abbreviation 'cont', i.e. continental. European sites do not always provide sink plugs, toilet paper or soap so take them with you.

Waste Disposal

Site entries show (when known) where a campsite has a chemical disposal and/or a motorhome service point, which is assumed to include a waste (grey) water dump station and toilet cassette-emptying point. Use of the site facilities is very common on continental sites, meaning you may find fewer waste water disposal facilities.

Chemical disposal points may be fixed at a high level requiring lifting of cassettes in order to empty them. Disposal may simply be down a toilet. Wastemaster-style emptying points are not very common in Europe. Formaldehyde chemical cleaning products are banned in many countries.

Finding a Campsite

Directions are given for all campsites listed in this guide and most listings also include GPS co-ordinates. Where known full street addresses are also given. The directions have been supplied by member reports and haven't been checked in detail by The Club.

For information about using sat nav to find a site see the Motoring Equipment section.

Overnight Stops

Towns and villages across Europe may provide dedicated overnight or short stay areas specifically for motorhomes, usually with security, electricity, water and waste facilities. These are known as 'Aires de Services', 'Stellplatz' or 'Aree di Sosta' and are usually well signposted with a motorhome icon.

Many campsites in popular tourist areas will also have separate overnight areas of hardstanding with facilities often just outside the main campsite area. There are guidebooks available which list just these overnight stops, Vicarious books publish an English guide to the Aires including directions, GPS co-ordinates and photographs. Please contact 0131 208 333 or visit their website www.vicariousbooks.co.uk.

For security reasons you shouldn't spend the night on petrol station service areas, ferry terminal car parks or isolated 'aires de repos' or 'aires de services' along motorways.

Municipal Campsites

Municipal sites are found in towns and villages all over Europe. Once very basic, many have improved in standard in recent years – although you may still find some which are outdated. You can book through the local town halls or tourism office. When approaching a town you may find that municipal sites are not always named and signposts may simply state 'Camping' or show a tent or caravan symbol.

You may sometimes find that these sites are used by seasonal workers, market traders and travellers in low season – where sites try to discourage these visitors you may find that twin-axle or very large caravans aren't accepted or are charged at a much higher rate. If you may be affected check for any restrictions when you book.

Naturist Campsites

Some naturist sites are included in this guide and are shown with the word 'naturist' after their site name. Those marked 'part naturist' have separate areas for naturists. Visitors to naturist sites aged 16 and over usually require an INF card or Naturist Licence - covered by membership of British Naturism (tel 01604 620361 or www.british-naturism.org.uk).

Alternatively, holiday membership is available on arrival at any recognised naturist site (a passport-size photograph is required). When looking for a site you will find that naturist campsites generally display the initials FNF, INF or FKK on their signs.

Opening Dates and times

Opening dates (where known) are given for campsites in this guide. However sites may close without notice due to refurbishment work, a lack of visitors or bad weather. Outside the high season it is always best to contact campsites in advance, even if the site advertises itself as open all year.

Most sites will close their gates or barriers overnight – if you are planning to arrive late or are delayed on your journey you should call ahead to make sure you will be able to gain access to the site. There may be a late arrivals area outside of the barriers where you can pitch overnight. Motorhomers should also consider barrier closing times if leaving site in your vehicle for the evening.

Check out time is usually between 10am and 12 noon – advise staff if you will have to leave the site very early for any reason to make sure you can check out before you leave. Sites may also close for an extended lunch break, so if you're planning to arrive or check out around lunchtime check that the office will be open.

Pets on Campsites

Well behaved dogs are welcome on many sites, although you may have to prove that all of their vaccinations are up to date before they are allowed onto the site. Certain breeds of dogs are banned in some countries and other breeds will need to be muzzled and kept on a lead at all times. A list of breeds with restrictions can be found at www.caravanclub.co.uk/pets.

Sites usually charge for dogs and may limit the number allowed per pitch. On arrival make yourself aware of site rules regarding dogs, such as keeping them on a lead, muzzling them or not leaving them unattended in your outfit.

In popular tourist areas local regulations may ban dogs from beaches during the summer. Some dogs may find it difficult to cope with prolonged periods of hot weather if they are used to UK weather. Also watch out for diseases transmitted by ticks, caterpillars, mosquitoes or sandflies to which dogs from the UK have no natural resistance. Consult your vet about preventative treatment before you travel.

Visitors to southern Spain and Portugal should be aware of the danger of Pine Processionary Caterpillars from mid-winter to late spring. Dogs should be kept away from pine trees if possible or fitted with a muzzle that prevents the nose and mouth from touching the ground. This will also protect against poisoned bait sometimes used by farmers and hunters.

In the event that your pet is taken ill abroad a campsite should have information about local vets.

Most European countries require dogs to wear a collar identifying their owners at all times. If your dog goes missing, report the matter to the local police and the local branch of that country's animal welfare organisation.

See the Documents section of this book for more information about the Pet Travel Scheme.

Prices

Campsite prices per night (for an outfit and two adults) are shown in the site entries. If you stay on site after midday you may be charged for an extra day. Many campsites have a minimum amount for credit card transactions, meaning they can't be used to pay for overnight or short stays. Check which methods of payment are accepted when you check in.

Sites with automatic barriers may ask for a deposit for a swipe card to operate it.

Sites may impose extra charges for the use of facilities such as swimming pools, showers or laundry facilities. You may also be charged extra for dogs, Wi-Fi, tents and extra cars.

Often campsites have a daily discounted charg for children, other sites will charge a fixed rate per person, regardless of age.

Registering on Arrival

Local authority requirements mean you will usually have to produce an identity document on arrival, which will be retained by the site until you check out. If you don't want to leave you passport with reception then most sites will accept a camping document such as the Camping Key Europe (CKE) or Camping Card International (CCI) - if this is known site entrie are marked CKE/CCI.

CKE are available for Caravan Club members 1 purchase by calling 01342 336633 or are free to members if you take out the 'motoring' lev of cover from the Club's Red Pennant Oversea Holiday Insurance.

Camping La Torre Del Sol, Cambrils

General Advice

If you've visiting a new site see if it is possible to take a look round the site and facilities before booking in. If your pitch is allocated at check in ask to see it first to check the condition and access, as marked or hedged pitches can sometimes be difficult for large outfits. Riverside pitches can be very scenic but keep an eye on the water level; in periods of heavy rain this may rise rapidly.

A tourist tax, eco tax and/or rubbish tax may be imposed by local authorities in some European countries. VAT may also be payable on top of your campsite fees.

Speed limits on campsites are usually restricted to 10 km/h (6 mph). You may be asked to park your car in a separate area away from your caravan, particularly in the high season.

The use of the term 'statics' in the campsite reports in this guide may to long-term sea- sonal pitches, chalets, cottages, tour operators' fixed tents and cabins, as well as mobile homes.

Complaints

If a situation arises where you want to make a complaint, take it up with site staff or owners at the time. It is much better to make staff aware of a problem while something could be done to rectify the situation for the rest of your stay than to complain once you are home.

The Caravan Club has no control or influence over day to day campsite operations or administration of the sites listed in this guide. Therefore we aren't able to intervene in any dispute you should have with a campsite, unless the booking has been made through our Site Booking Service - see listings marked 'SBS' for sites we are able to book for you.

Portugal
Country Introduction

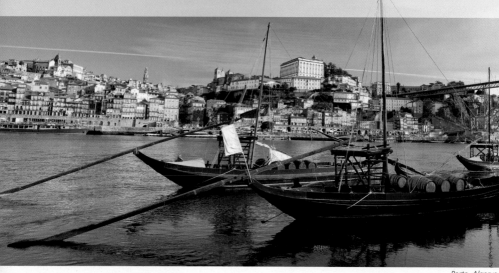

Porto, Algarve

Welcome to Portugal

With its mild climate, abundance of sunshine and miles of splendid beaches along the Atlantic Ocean, Portugal is the perfect holiday destination all year round.

The old white washed towns are great for exploring and stone churches and chapels create amazing pictures.

Country highlights

Portuguese cuisine is rich and varied and makes the most of abundant, locally grown produce; seafood is particularly good. The national speciality is bacalhau which is dried and salted cod.

As well as port, many excellent and inexpensive wines are produced, including the famous vinho verde.

During the last few days before Lent, Carnaval is held and livens up the country with outlandish costumes, parades and fun fairs. The biggest celebrations are in Lisbon, Loule, Nazare, Ovar and Viana do Castelo.

Major towns and cities

- Lisbon – the capital city of Portugal, it is one of the oldest cities and is full of history.
- Porto – a large city full of colourfully painted buildings and extravagant churches.
- Vila Nova de Gaia – a city well known for its caves where the famous Port wine is aged.
- Albufeira – with lots of sandy beaches, this city is very popular with tourists.

Attractions

- Oceanario de Lisboa – walk through breath taking exhibits and learn about the ocean.
- Pico do Arieiro – a stunning location with lots of paths to explore on the mountain.
- National Palace of Pena – a romantic palace with a gothic exterior and historical art.
- Cascais Old Town - a pretty and traditional resort with lots of little shops.

Find out more

www.visitportugal.com

Tel: (0)1 21 11 40 200 Portuguese Tourism

Country Information

Population (approx): 10.8 million

Capital: Lisbon (population approx 564,700)

Area: 92,951 sq km (inc Azores and Madeira)

Bordered by: Spain

Terrain: Rolling plains in south; mountainous and forested north of River Tagus

Climate: Temperate climate with no extremes of temperature; wet winters in the north influenced by the Gulf Stream; elsewhere Mediterranean with hot, dry summers and short, mild winters

Coastline: 1,793km

Highest Point (mainland Portugal): Monte Torre 1,993m

Language: Portuguese

Local Time: GMT or BST, i.e. the same as the UK all year

Currency: Euros divided into 100 cents; £1 = €1.26, €1 = £0.79 (September 2014)

Emergency numbers: Police 112; Fire brigade 112; Ambulance 112

Public Holidays 2015: Jan 1; Apr 3, 25; May 1; Jun 10 (National Day); Aug 15; Dec 8 (Immaculate Conception), 25.

Due to Austerity measures imposed by the Portuguese government, four dates which are usually Public Holidays in Portugal have been suspended for 5 years from 2013. These dates are: Corpus Christi (60 days after Easter), Oct 5 (Republic Day), Nov 1 (All Saints Day) and Dec 1 (Independence Day).
Other holidays and saints' days are celebrated according to region. School summer holidays run from the end of June to the end of August.

Camping and Caravanning

There are more than 200 campsites in Portugal, and many of these are situated along the coast. Sites are rated from 1 to 4 stars.

There are 22 privately owned campsites in the Orbitur chain. Caravanners can join the Orbitur Camping Club to obtain generous discounts off current rates. Senior citizens may join this Club free, otherwise the cost is €20. Membership can be arranged via any Orbitur site or on the Orbitur website. Their head office is at:

AVDA DA BOAVISTA 1681, 3º·SALAS 5 A 8
P-4100-132 PORTO
Tel: 00351 22 6061360 Fax: 00351 22 6063590
www.orbitur.com
orbiturporto@orbitur.pt

Casual/wild camping is not permitted.

Motorhomes

A number of local authorities now provide dedicated short stay areas for motorhomes called 'Áreas de Serviço'. It is rare that yours will be the only motorhome staying on such areas, but take sensible precautions and avoid any that are isolated.

Cycling

In Lisbon there are cycle lanes in Campo Grande gardens, also from Torre de Belém to Cais do Sodré (7km) along the River Tagus, and between Cascais and Guincho. Elsewhere in the country there are few cycle lanes.

Transportation of Bicycles

Legislation stipulates that the exterior dimensions of a vehicle should not be exceeded and, in practice, this means that only caravans or motorhomes are allowed to carry bicycles/ motorbikes at the rear of the vehicle. Bicycles may not extend beyond the width of the vehicle or more than 45cms from the back. However, bicycles may be transported on the roof of cars provided that an overall height of 4 metres is not exceeded. Cars carrying bicycles/motorbikes on the back may be subject to a fine.

If you are planning to travel from Spain to Portugal please note that slightly different regulations apply and these are set out in the Spain Country Introduction.

Electricity and Gas

Usually current on campsites varies between 6 and 15 amps. Plugs have two round pins. CEE connections are commonplace.

The full range of Campingaz cylinders is available.

Entry Formalities

Holders of British and Irish passports may visit Portugal for up to three months without a visa. For stays of over three months you will need to apply for a Registration Certificate from the local Camara Municipal (Town Hall) or from the nearest office of Servico de Estrangeiros e Fronteiras (immigration authority).

Medical Services

For treatment of minor conditions go to a pharmacy (farmacia). Staff are generally well trained and are qualified to dispense drugs, which may only be available on prescription in Britain. In large towns there is usually at least one pharmacy whose staff speak English, and all have information posted on the door indicating the nearest pharmacy open at night.

All municipalities have a health centre. State emergency health care and hospital treatment is free on production of a European Health Insurance Card (EHIC). You will have to pay for items such as X-rays, laboratory tests and prescribed medicines as well as dental treatment. Refunds can be claimed from local offices of the Administracão Regional de Saúde (regional health service).

For serious illness you can obtain the name of an English speaking doctor from the local police station or tourist office or from a British or American consulate. There is a private British hospital at Campo de Ourique, Rua Saraiva de Carvalho 49, 1269-098 Lisbon. Private treatment is expensive.

Normal precautions should be taken to avoid mosquito bites, including the use of insect repellents, especially at night.

Opening Hours

Banks – Mon-Fri 8.30am-3pm; some banks in city centres are open until 6pm.

Museums – Tue-Sun 10am-5pm/6pm; closed Mon and may close 12.30pm-2pm.

Post Offices – Mon-Fri 9am-6pm; may close for an hour at lunch.

Shops – Mon-Fri 9am-1pm & 3pm-7pm, Sat 9am-1pm; large supermarkets open Mon-Sun 9am/9.30am-10pm/11pm.

Safety and Security

The crime rate is comparatively low but pickpocketing, bag snatching and thefts from cars are common in major tourist areas. Be particularly vigilant on public transport, at crowded tourist sites and in public parks where it is wise to go in pairs. Keep car windows closed and doors locked while driving in urban areas at night. Pedestrians, particularly the elderly, are advised not to wear valuable jewellery or watches in public areas.

There has been an increase in reported cases of items stolen from vehicles in car parks. Thieves distract drivers by asking for directions, for example, or other information. Be cautious and alert if you are approached in this way in a car park. Do not leave valuables in an unattended car. Thieves often target foreign registered and hire cars.

Take care of your belongings at all times. Do not leave your bag on the chair beside you, under the table or hanging on your chair while you eat in a restaurant or café. Thieves often work in groups and create distractions with the aim of stealing.

Take extra care when crossing busy roads, especially late at night. This warning also applies to pedestrian crossings which are often badly lit and poorly marked.

Death by drowning occurs every year on Portuguese beaches. Warning flags should be taken very seriously. A red flag indicates danger and you should not enter the water when it is flying. If a yellow flag is flying you may paddle at the water's edge, but you may not swim. A green flag indicates that it is safe to swim, and a chequered flag means that the lifeguard is temporarily absent.

Do not swim from beaches which are not manned by lifeguards. The police are entitled to fine bathers who disobey warning flags.

During long, hot, dry periods forest fires occur frequently, especially in northern and central parts of the country. Take care when visiting or driving through woodland areas: ensure that cigarettes are extinguished properly, do not light barbecues, and do not leave empty bottles behind.

Both the Portuguese mainland and islands are susceptible to seismic activity. For more information and daily updates see the Portuguese Meteorological Office's website (English option), www.meteo.pt/pt/sismologia/actividade.

Portugal shares with the rest of Europe an underlying threat from terrorism. Attacks could be indiscriminate and against civilian targets in public places including tourist sites.

British Embassy
RUA DE SÃO BERNARDO 33,
1249-082 LISBOA
Tel: 21 392 4000
www.ukinportugal.fco.gov.uk

There are also British Consulates/Honorary Consulates in Porto and Portimão.

Irish Embassy
VENIDA DA LIBERDADE No 200, 4th FLOOR
1250-147 LISBON
Tel: 213 308 200
www.embassyofireland.pt

Documents

Driving Licence
All valid UK driving licences should be accepted in Portugal but holders of an older all green style licence are advised to update it to a photocard licence before travelling in order to avoid any local difficulties. Alternatively carry an International Driving Permit, available from the AA, the RAC or selected Post Offices.

Passport
The Portuguese authorities stipulate that proof of identity bearing the holder's photograph and signature, e.g. a passport or photocard licence, should be carried at all times. Failure to do so may incur a fine.

Vehicle(s)
When driving you must carry your vehicle registration certificate (V5C), proof of insurance and MOT certificate (if applicable). There are heavy on the spot fines for those who fail to do so.

Money

The major credit cards are widely accepted and there are cash machines (Multibanco) throughout the country. A tax of €0.50 is added to credit card transactions. Carry your credit card issuers'/banks' 24 hour UK contact numbers in case of loss or theft.

Motoring in Portugal

Many Portuguese drive erratically and vigilance is advised. By comparison with the UK, the accident rate is high. Particular blackspots are the N125 along the south coast, especially in the busy holiday season, and the coast road between Lisbon and Cascais. In rural areas you may encounter horse drawn carts and flocks of sheep or goats. Otherwise there are no special difficulties in driving except in Lisbon and Porto, which are unlimited 'free-for-alls'.

Accident Procedures

The police must be called in the case of injury or significant material damage.

Alcohol

The maximum permitted level of alcohol is 50 milligrams in 100 millilitres of blood, i.e. lower than permitted in the UK (80 milligrams). It is advisable to adopt the 'no drink-driving' rule at all times.

Breakdown Service

The Automovel Club de Portugal (ACP) operates a 24 hour breakdown service covering all roads in mainland Portugal. Its vehicles are coloured red and white. Emergency telephones are located at 2km intervals on main roads and motorways. To contact the ACP breakdown service call +351 219 429113 from a mobile or 707 509510 from a landline.

The breakdown service comprises on the spot repairs taking up to a maximum of 45 minutes and, if necessary, the towing of vehicles. The charges for breakdown assistance and towing vary according to distance, time of day and day of the week, plus motorway tolls if applicable. Payment by credit card is accepted.

Alternatively, on motorways breakdown vehicles belonging to the motorway companies (their emergency numbers are displayed on boards along the motorways) and police patrols (GNR/ Brigada de Trânsito) can assist motorists.

Essential Equipment

Reflective Jackets/Waistcoats

If your vehicle is immobilised on the carriageway you should wear a reflective jacket or waistcoat when getting out of your vehicle. This is a legal requirement for residents of Portugal and is recommended for visitors. Passengers who leave a vehicle, for example, to assist with a repair, should also wear one. Keep the jackets within easy reach inside your vehicle, not in the boot.

Warning Triangles

Use a warning triangle if, for any reason, a stationary vehicle is not visible for at least 100 metres. In addition, hazard warning lights must be used if a vehicle is causing an obstruction or danger to other road users.

Child Restraint System

Children under 12 years of age and less than 1.35m in height are not allowed to travel in the front passenger seat. They must be seated in a child restraint system adapted to their size and weight in the rear of the vehicle, unless the vehicle only has two seats, or if the vehicle is not fitted with seat belts.

Children under the age of 3 years old can be seated in the front passenger seat as long as they are in a suitable rear facing child restraint system and the airbag has been deactivated.

Fuel

Credit cards are accepted at most filling stations but a small extra charge may be added and a tax of €0.50 is added to credit card transactions. There are no automatic petrol pumps.

LPG (gáz liquido) is widely available – see www.portugalmania.com/transports/gpl-portugal.

Low Emission Zone

There is a Low Emission Zone in operation in Lisbon. There are 2 different zones within the city. In zone 1 vehicles must meet European Emission Standard 2 (EURO 2) and in zone 2 vehicles must

meet EURO 1 standard. For more information visit www.lowemissionzones.eu.

Mountain Roads and Passes

There are no mountain passes or tunnels in Portugal. Roads through the Serra da Estrela near Guarda and Covilha may be temporarily obstructed for short periods after heavy snow but otherwise motorists will encounter no difficulties in winter.

Parking

In most cases vehicles must be parked facing in the same direction as moving traffic. Parking is very limited in the centre of main towns and cities and 'blue zone' parking schemes operate. Illegally parked vehicles may be towed away or clamped. Parking in Portuguese is 'estacionamento'.

Priority

In general at intersections and road junctions, road users must give way to vehicles approaching from the right, unless signs indicate otherwise. At roundabouts vehicles already on the roundabout, i.e. on the left, have right of way.

Do not pass stationary trams at a tram stop until you are certain that all passengers have finished entering or leaving the tram and/or have reached the pavement at the side of the road.

Roads

Roads are surfaced with asphalt, concrete or stone setts. Main roads generally are well surfaced and may be three lanes wide, the middle lane being used for overtaking in either direction.

Roads in the south of the country are generally in good condition, but, despite recent extensive road improvement schemes, some sections in the north may still be in a poor state. All roads, with the exception of motorways, should be treated with care; even a good section may suddenly deteriorate and potholes may be a hazard. Roads in many towns and villages are often cobbled and rough.

Drivers entering Portugal from Zamora in Spain will notice an apparently shorter route on the

CL527/N221 road via Mogadouro. Although this is actually the signposted route, the road surface is poor in places and this route is not recommended for trailer caravans. The recommended route is via the N122/IP4 to Bragança.

Road Signs and Markings

Road signs conform to international standards. Road markings are white or yellow. Signs on motorways (auto-estrada) are blue and on regional roads they are white with black lettering. Roads are classified as follows:

Code	Road Type
AE	Motorways
IP	Principal routes
IC	Complementary routes
EN	National roads
EM	Municipal roads
CM	Other municipal roads

Signs you might encounter are as follows:

Portuguese	English Translation
Atalho	Detour
Entrada	Entrance
Estação de gasolina	Petrol station
Estacão de policia	Police station
Estacionamento	Parking
Estrada con portagem	Toll road
Saida	Exit

Speed Limits

	Open Road (km/h)	Motorway (km/h)
Car Solo	90-100	120
Car towing caravan/trailer	70-80	100
Motorhome under 3500kg	90-100	120
Motorhome 3500-7500kg	70-90	100

Drivers must maintain a speed between 40 km/h (25 mph) and 60 km/h (37 mph) on the 25th April Bridge over the River Tagus in Lisbon. Speed limits are electronically controlled.

Visitors who have held a driving licence for less than one year must not exceed 90 km/h (56 mph) on any road subject to higher limits.

In built-up areas there is a speed limit of 50 km/h.

It is prohibited to use a radar detector or to have one installed in a vehicle.

Towing

Motorhomes are permitted to tow a car on a four wheel trailer, i.e. with all four wheels of the car off the ground. Towing a car on an A-frame (two back wheels on the ground) is not permitted.

Traffic Jams

Traffic jams are most likely to be encountered around the two major cities of Lisbon and Porto and on roads to the coast, such as the A1 Lisbon-Porto and the A2 Lisbon-Setúbal motorways, which are very busy on Friday evenings and Saturday mornings. The peak periods for holiday traffic are the last weekend in June and the first and last weekends in July and August.

Around Lisbon bottlenecks occur on the bridges across the River Tagus, the N6 to Cascais, the A1 to Vila Franca de Xira, the N8 to Loures and on the N10 from Setúbal via Almada.

Around Porto you may find traffic jams on the IC1 on the Arribada Bridge and at Vila Nova de Gaia, the A28/IC1 from Póvoa de Varzim and near Vila de Conde, and on the N13, N14 and the N15.

Major motorways are equipped with suspended signs which indicate the recommended route to take when there is traffic congestion.

Traffic Lights

There is no amber signal after the red. A flashing amber light indicates 'caution' and a flashing or constant red light indicates 'stop'. In Lisbon there are separate traffic lights in bus lanes.

Violation of Traffic Regulations

Speeding, illegal parking and other infringements of traffic regulations are heavily penalised.

You may incur a fine for crossing a continuous single or double white or yellow line in the centre of the road when overtaking or when executing a left turn into or off a main road, despite the lack of any other 'no left turn' signs. If necessary, drive on to a roundabout or junction to turn, or turn right as directed by arrows.

The police are authorised to impose on the spot fines and a receipt must be given. Most police vehicles are now equipped with portable credit card machines to facilitate immediate payment of fines.

Motorways

Motorway Tolls

Portugal has more than 2,600km of motorways (auto-estradas), with tolls (portagem) payable on most sections. Take care not to use the 'Via Verde' green lanes reserved for motorists who subscribe to the automatic payment system – be sure to go through a ticket booth lane where applicable, or one equipped with the new electronic toll system.

Dual carriageways (auto vias) are toll free and look similar to motoways, but speed limits are lower.

It is permitted to spend the night on a motorway rest or service area with a caravan, although The Caravan Club does not recommend this practice for security reasons. It should be noted that toll tickets are only valid for 12 hours and fines are incurred if this period of time is exceeded.

Vehicle are classified for tolls as follows:

Class 1   Vehicle with or without trailer with height from front axle less than 1.10m.

Class 2   Vehicle with 2 axles, with or without trailer, with height from front axle over 1.10m.

Class 3   Vehicle or vehicle combination with 3 axles, with height from front axle over 1.10m.

Class 4*   Vehicle or vehicle combination with 4 or more axles with height from front axle over 1.10m.

* Drivers of high vehicles of the Range Rover/Jeep variety, together with some MPVs, and towing a twin axle caravan pay Class 4 tolls.

Electronic Tolls

An electronic toll collecting system was introduced in Portugal during 2010. The following motorways have tolls but no toll booths: A27, A28, A24, A41, A42, A25, A29, A23, A13, A8, A19, A33, A22 and parts of the A17 and A4. Tolls for these motorways can be paid by one of the following options:

If you are crossing the border from Spain on the A24, A25 or A22 or the A28 (via the EN13) then you can use the EASYToll welcome points. You can input your credit card details and the machine reads and then matches your credit/debit card to your number-plate, tolls are deducted automatically from your credit card, and the EASYToll machine will issue you a 30 day receipt as proof that you have paid.

If you are entering Portugal on a road that does not have an EASYToll machine you can register on-line or at a CTT post office and purchase either €5, €10, €20 or €40 worth of tolls, however, you only have 3 days in which to use the money you have pre-loaded. You can purchase a virtual prepaid ticket up to 6 times a year. For more information visit www.ctt.pt – you can select 'ENG' at the top left of the screen to see the site in English. In the 'Individuals' section, under 'Financial Services' select 'Tolls' and then in the left hand menu select 'Available services' – here you find information for Foreign Registered Licence Plates.

Alternatively you can get a temporary device (DT) available from some motorway service stations, post offices and Via Verde offices. A deposit of €27.50 is payable when you hire the DT and this is refundable when you return it to any of the outlets mentioned above. If you use a debit card, toll costs will automatically be debited from your card. If you pay cash you will be required to preload the DT. For further information see www.visitportugal.com and see the heading 'All about Portugal' then 'Useful Information'.

On motorways where this system applies you will see a sign: 'Lanço Com Portagem' or 'Electronic Toll Only', together with details of the tolls charged. Drivers caught using these roads without a DT will incur a minimum fine of €25.

The toll roads A1 to A15 and A21 continue to have manned toll booths. Most, but not all, accept credit cards or cash.

Toll Bridges

25th April Bridge and Vasco da Gama Bridge
The 2km long 25th April Bridge in Lisbon crosses the River Tagus. Tolls are charged for vehicles travelling in a south-north direction only. Tolls also apply on the Vasco da Gama Bridge, north of Lisbon, but again only to vehicles travelling in a south-north direction. Overhead panels indicate the maximum permitted speed in each lane and, when in use, override other speed limit signs.

In case of breakdown, or if you need assistance, you should try to stop on one of the emergency hard shoulder areas and wait inside your vehicle until a patrol arrives. Switch on your hazard warning lights. Emergency telephones are placed at frequent intervals. It is prohibited to carry out repairs, to push vehicles physically or to walk on the bridges.

Touring

Some English is spoken in large cities and tourist areas. Elsewhere a knowledge of French could be useful.

A Lisboa Card valid for 24, 48 or 72 hours, entitles the holder to free unrestricted access to public transport, including trains to Cascais and Sintra, free entry to a number of museums, monuments and other places of interest in Lisbon and surrounding areas, and discounts in shops and places offering services to tourists. It is obtainable from tourist information offices, travel agents, some hotels and Carris ticket booths, or from www.europeancitycards.com.

Do ensure when eating out that you understand exactly what you are paying for; appetisers put on the table are not free. Service is included in the bill, but it is customary to tip 5 to 10% of the total if you have received good service. Rules on smoking in restaurants and bars vary according to the size of the premises. The areas where clients are allowed to smoke are indicated by signs and there must be adequate ventilation. Each town in Portugal devotes several days in the year to local celebrations which are invariably lively and colourful. Carnivals and festivals during the period before Lent, during Holy Week and during the grape harvest can be particularly spectacular.

Public Transport

A passenger and vehicle ferry crosses the River Sado estuary from Setúbal to Tróia and there are frequent ferry and catamaran services for cars and passengers across the River Tagus from various points in Lisbon including Belém and Cais do Sodré.

Both Lisbon and Porto have metro systems operating from 6am to 1am. For routes and fares information see www.metrolisboa.pt and www.metrodoporto.pt (English versions).

Throughout the country buses are cheap, regular and mostly on time, with every town connected. In Lisbon the extensive bus and tram network is operated by Carris, together with one lift and three funiculars which tackle the city's steepest hills. Buy single journey tickets on board from bus drivers or buy a rechargeable 'Sete Colinas' or Via Viagem card for use on buses and the metro.

In Porto buy a 'Euro' bus ticket, which can be charged with various amounts, from metro stations and transport offices. Validate tickets for each journey at machines on the buses. Also available is an 'Andante' ticket which is valid on the metro and on buses. Porto also has a passenger lift and a funicular so that you can avoid the steep walk to and from the riverside.

Taxis are usually cream in colour. In cities they charge a standard, metered fare; outside they may run on the meter or charge a flat rate and are entitled to charge for the return fare. Agree a price for your journey before setting off.

ALANDROAL *C3* (13km S Rural) *38.60645, -7.34674*
Camping Rosário, Monte das Mimosas, Rosário, 7250-999 Alandroal [268 459566; info@campingrosario.com; www. campingrosario.com] Fr E exit IP7/A6 at Elvas W junc 9; at 3rd rndabt take exit sp Espanha, immed 1st R dir Juromenha & Redondo. Onto N373 until exit Rosário. Fr W exit IP7/A6 junc 8 at Borba onto N255 to Alandroal, then N373 E sp Elvas. After 1.5km turn R to Rosário & foll sp to site. Sm, hdstg, pt sl, pt shd; wc; chem disp; shwrs inc; el pnts (6A) €2.35; gas 2km; lndtte; shop 2km; tradsmn; rest; bar; playgrnd; pool; lake sw adj; boating; fishing; TV; wifi; no statics; dogs €1 (not acc Jul/Aug); Eng spkn; adv bkg; quiet; red long stay/low ssn; CKE/CCI. "Remote site beside Alqueva Dam; excel touring base; ltd to 50 people max; excel site; idyllic; peaceful; clean & well maintained; v helpful owner." 1 Mar-1 Oct. € 24.50   2014*

"There aren't many sites open at this time of year"

If you're travelling outside peak season remember to call ahead to check site opening dates – even if the entry says 'open all year'

⊞ **ALBUFEIRA** *B4* (1.5km NE Urban) *37.10617, -8.25395*
Camping Albufeira, Estrada de Ferreiras, 8200-555 Albufeira [289 587629 / 289 587630; fax 289 587633; geral@campingalbufeira.net / info@campingalbufeira. net; www.campingalbufeira.net] Exit IP1/E1 sp Albufeira onto N125/N395 dir Albufeira; camp on L, sp. V lge, some mkd pitch, pt sl, pt shd, wc; chem disp; mv service pnt; shwrs inc; el pnts (10-12A) €3; gas; lndtte; shop; supmkt; rest, snacks; bar; playgrnd; 3 pools; sand beach 1.5km; tennis; sports park; cycle hire; games area; games rm; disco (soundproofed); wifi; entmnt; TV; 20% statics; dogs; phone; bus adj; car wash; cash machine; security patrols; poss v cr; Eng spkn; no adv bkg; quiet; ccard acc; red long stay/low ssn/CKE/CCI. "Friendly, secure site; excel pool area/rest/bar; some pitches lge enough for US RVs; pitches on lower pt of site prone to flooding in heavy rain; conv beach & town; poss lge rallies during Jan-Apr; camp bus to town high ssn." ♦ € 24.65   2013*

⊞ **ALBUFEIRA** *B4* (10km W Urban) *37.11916, -8.35083*
Camping Canelas, Alcantarilha, 8365-908 Armação de Pêra [282 312612; fax 282 314719; turismovel@mail. telepac.pt; www.camping-canelas.com] Fr Lagos take N125, turn R (S) at Alcantarilha twd Armação de Pêra, site in 1.5km on R. Fr IP1/A22 Algarve coastal m'way, take Alcantarilha exit & turn L on N125 into vill, turn R at rndabt. Site on R in 1.5km just bef 2nd rndabt. V lge, hdg pitch, pt sl, shd; wc; chem disp; mv service pnt; shwrs; el pnts (5-10A) €3-3.50; gas; lndtte; shop; tradsmn; rest high ssn; snacks; bar; BBQ; playgrnd; 3 solar htd pools; sand beach 1.5km; tennis; games area; games rm; entmnt; TV rm; 5% statics; dogs €2; bus; phone; poss cr; Eng spkn; red low ssn/long stay; CKE/CCI. "Spacious, shady, much improved site; v popular in winter; vg security at ent; excel cent for Algarve." ♦ € 19.00   2011*

⊞ **ALBUFEIRA** *B4* (10.5km W Urban/Coastal) *37.10916, -8.35333* **Camping Armação de Pêra, 8365-184 Armação de Pêra [282 312260; fax 282 315379; geral@camping-armacao-pera.com; www.camping-armacao-pera.com]** Fr Lagos take N125 coast rd E. At Alcantarilha turn S onto N269-1 sp Armação de Pêra & Campismo. Site at 3rd rndabt in 2km on L. V lge, hdg pitch, pt sl, shd; wc; chem disp; mv service pnt; shwrs inc; el pnts (6-10A) €3-4; gas; lndtte (inc dryer); shop; rest, snacks; bar; playgrnd; pool & paddling pool; sand beach 500m; tennis; cycle hire; games area; games rm; internet; entmnt; TV rm; 25% statics; phone; bus adj; car wash; poss cr; Eng spkn; quiet; red low ssn; CKE/CCI. "Friendly, popular & attractive site; gd pool; min stay 3 days Oct-May; easy walk to town; interesting chapel of skulls at Alcantarilha; birdwatching in local lagoon; vg." ♦ € 20.50   2012*

⊞ **ALCACER DO SAL** *B3* (1km NW Rural) *38.38027, -8.51583* **Parque de Campismo Municipal de Alcácer do Sal, Olival do Outeiro, 7580-125 Alcácer do Sal [265 612303; fax 265 610079; cmalcacer@mail.telepac.pt]** Heading S on A2/IP1 turn L twd Alcácer do Sal on N5. Site on R 1km fr Alcácer do Sal. Sp at rndabt. Site behind supmkt. Sm, hdg/mkd pitch, pt sl, pt shd; wc; chem disp; mv service pnt; shwrs inc; el pnts (6-12A) €1.50; lndtte; shops 100m, rest, snacks & bar 50m; BBQ; playgrnd; pool, paddling pool adj; rv 1km; sand beach 24km; games area; internet; dogs; phone; bus 50m; clsd mid-Dec to mid-Jan; poss cr; Eng spkn; quiet; red low ssn; ccard acc; CKE/CCI. "Excel, clean facs; in rice growing area - major mosquito prob; historic town; spacious pitches; poss full in winter - rec phone ahead." ♦ ltd € 10.40   2011*

ALVOR see Portimao *B4*

"That's changed – Should I let The Club know?"

If you find something on site that's different from the site entry, fill in a report and let us know. See www.caravanclub.co.uk/europereport.

AMARANTE *C1* (1.5km NE Rural) *41.27805, -8.07027*
Camping Penedo da Rainha, Rua Pedro Alveollos, Gatão, 4600-099 Amarante [255 437630; fax 255 437353; ccporto@sapo.pt] Fr IP4 Vila Real to Porto foll sp to Amarante & N15. On N15 cross bdge for Porto & immed take R slip rd. Foll sp thro junc & up rv to site. Lge, some hdstg, pt sl, terr, shd; wc; chem disp; mv service pnt; shwrs inc; el pnts (4A) €1.50; gas 2km; lndtte; shop 100m & 2km; rest; snacks 100m; bar; playgrnd; sm pool & 3km; rv adj; fishing; canoeing; cycling; games rm; entmnt; TV; dogs; phone; bus to Porto fr Amarante; some Eng spkn; adv bkg; quiet; red low ssn/CKE/CCI. "Well-run site in steep woodland/parkland - take advice or survey rte bef driving to pitch; excel facs but some pitches far fr facs; few touring pitches; friendly, helpful recep; plenty of shade; conv Amarante old town & Douro Valley; Sat mkt." ♦ 1 Feb-30 Nov. € 12.50   2009*

ARCO DE BAULHE *C1* (1.5km NE Rural) *41.48659, -7.95845* **Arco Unipessoal, Lugar das Cruzes, 4860-067 Arco de Baúlhe (Costa Verde) [(351) 968176246; campismoarco@ hotmail.com]** Dir A7 exit 12 Mondm/Cabeceiras, 2nd R at rndabt dir Arco de Baulhe. Call and they will lead you in. V narr rd access, no mv's over 7mtrs. Med, terr, pt shd; wc; chem disp; shwr; el pnts (6A); lndtte; rest; bar; bbq; htd sw; paddling pool; rv; tv in bar; dogs; Eng spkn; adv bkg. "New site run by couple with 20 yrs experience; quiet; centrally located for historic towns & nature parks; gd rest; lovely well maintained site with view; excel facs; 100m fr vill cent; beautiful mountain area." 1 Apr-10 Oct. € 26.00   2014*

ARMACAO DE PERA see Albufeira *B4*

AVEIRO *B2* (6km SW Coastal) *40.59960, -8.74981* **Camping Costa Nova, Estrada da Vagueira, Quinta dos Patos, 3830-453 Ílhavo [234 393220; fax 234 394721; info@ campingcostanova.com; www.campingcostanova.com]** Site on Barra-Vagueira coast rd 1km on R after Costa Nova. V lge, mkd pitch, unshd; htd wc; chem disp; mv service pnt; shwrs inc; el pnts (2-6A) €2.40; gas; lndtte (inc dryer); shop; tradsmn; rest in ssn; snacks; bar; BBQ; playgrnd; pool 4km; sand beach; fishing; cycle hire; games area; games rm; internet; entmnt; TV rm; some statics; dogs €1.40; phone; poss cr; site clsd Jan; Eng spkn; adv bkg; quiet; ccard acc; red long stay; CKE/CCI. "Superb, peaceful site adj nature reserve; helpful staff; gd, modern facs; hot water to shwrs only; sm pitches; sep car park high ssn; vg." ♦ 21 Mar-31 Oct. € 23.30   2012*

⊞ **AVEIRO** *B2* (10km W Coastal) *40.63861, -8.74500* **Parque de Campismo Praia da Barra, Rua Diogo Cão 125, Praia da Barra, 3830-772 Gafanha da Nazaré [tel/fax (234) 369425; barra@cacampings.com; www.cacampings.com]** Fr Aveiro foll sp to Barra on A25/IP5; foll sp to site. Lge, mkd pitch, shd; wc (some cont); chem disp; mv service pnt; baby facs; shwrs inc; el pnts (6-10A) €2.50; gas; lndtte (inc dryer); shop; rest; bar; BBQ; playgrnd; pool 400m; sand beach 200m; cycle hire; games area; games rm; internet; entmnt; TV rm; 90% statics; dogs €1.80; phone; bus adj; recep open 0900-2200; Eng spkn; adv bkg; quiet; red low ssn; CKE/CCI. "Well-situated site with pitches in pine trees; old san facs." ♦ € 22.65   2013*

AVEIRO *B2* (8km NW Coastal/Rural) *40.70277, -8.7175* **Camping ORBITUR, N327, Km 20, 3800-901 São Jacinto [234 838284; fax 234 838122; infosjacinto@orbitur.pt; www.orbitur.pt]** Fr Porto take A29/IC1 S & exit sp Ovar onto N327. (Note long detour fr Aveiro itself by rd - 30+ km.) Site in trees to N of São Jacinto. Lge, mkd pitch, hdstg, terr, shd; wc; chem disp; mv service pnt; baby facs; shwrs inc; el pnts (5-15A) €3-4 (poss rev pol); gas; lndtte; sm shop & 5km; tradsmn; rest, snacks; bar; BBQ; playgrnd; pool 5km; sand beach 2.5km; fishing; TV; some statics; dogs €1.50; phone; bus; car wash; Eng spkn; adv bkg; quiet; red low ssn/long stay/snr citizens; ccard acc; CKE/CCI. "Excel site; best in area; gd children's park; 15 min to (car) ferry; gd, clean san facs." ♦ 1 Jun-30 Sep. € 27.00   2014*

⊞ **AVIS** *C3* (1km SW Rural) *39.05638, -7.91138* **Parque de Campismo da Albufeira do Maranhão, Clube Náutico de Avis, Albufeira do Maranhão, 7480-999 Avis [242 412452; fax 242 410099; parque_campismo@cm-avis.pt; www. cm-avis.pt/parquecampismo]** Fr N exit A23/IP6 at Abrantes onto N2 dir Ponte de Sor, then N244 to Avis. Fr S exit A6/IP7 N at junc 7 Estremoz or junc 4 Montemor onto N4 to Arraiolos, then onto N370 to Pavia & Avis. Site sp. V lge, mkd pitch, terr, pt shd; wc; chem disp; mv service pnt; shwrs inc; el pnts (16A) €2.60; gas 1km; lndry rm; rest adj; snacks; bar; playgrnd; pool complex adj; lake fishing & shgl beach adj; watersports; tennis; games area; games rm; TV; dogs €1; bus 1km; Eng spkn; adv bkg; quiet; red long stay; CKE/CCI. "V pleasant site on lakeside; interesting, historic town; gd walking area." ♦ € 14.00   2009*

⊞ **BEJA** *C4* (500m S Urban) *38.00777, -7.86222* **Parque de Campismo Municipal de Beja, Avda Vasco da Gama, 7800-397 Beja [tel/fax 284 311911; cmb.dcd@iol.pt; www.cm-beja.pt]** Fr S (N122) take 1st exit strt into Beja. In 600m turn R at island then L in 100m into Avda Vasco da Gama & foll sp for site on R in 300m - narr ent. Fr N on N122 take by-pass round town then 1st L after Intermarche supmkt, then as above. Lge, hdstg, shd, gravel pitches; wc; chem disp; shwrs inc; el pnts (6A) €1.85; supmkt 500m; rest 500m; snacks 200m; bar adj; pool, tennis & football stadium adj; bus 300m; rlwy stn 1.5km; poss noisy in ssn; red low ssn/CKE/CCI. "C'van storage facs; helpful staff; NH only." ♦ € 10.40   2013*

BRAGANCA *D1* (6km N Rural) *41.84361, -6.74722* **Inatel Parque Campismo Bragança, Estrada de Rabal, 5300-671 Meixedo [tel/fax 273 329409 / 001090; pc.braganca@ inatel.pt]** Fr Bragança N for 6km on N103.7 twd Spanish border. Site on R, sp Inatel. Med, hdstg, pt sl, terr, pt shd; wc; chem disp; shwrs inc; el pnts (6A) inc; gas; lndry rm; shop & 6km; tradsmn; rest in ssn; snacks; bar; playgrnd; fishing; cycle hire; dogs; bus; poss cr; Eng spkn; quiet but barking dogs. "On S boundary of National Park; rv runs thro site; friendly staff; gd rest; vg facs but site a little scruffy (June 2010); lovely location by rv." 1 Jun-15 Sep. € 16.80   2014*

⊞ **BRAGANCA** *D1* (10km W Rural) *41.84879, -6.86120* **Cepo Verde Camping, Gondesende, 5300-561 Bragança [273 999371; fax 273 323577; cepoverde@montesinho. com; www.bragancanet.pt/cepoverde]** Fr IP4 fr W take N103 fr Bragança for 8km. Site sp fr IP4 ring rd. R off N103, foll lane & turn R at sp. NB Camping sp to rd 103-7 leads to different site (Sabor) N of city. Med, mkd pitch, hdstg, terr, pt shd; wc; chem disp; shwrs inc; el pnts (6A) €2 (poss rev pol & long lead poss reg); shop; rest, snacks; bar; playgrnd; pool; dogs €1; phone; wifi; bus 1km; Eng spkn; adv bkg; quiet; CKE/CCI. "Remote, friendly, v pleasant, scenic site adj Montesinho National Park; clean but poorly maintained facs; vg value." ♦ € 20.00   2014*

BUDENS see Vila do Bispo *B4*

CABANAS TAVIRA see Tavira *C4*

⊞ **CALDAS DA RAINHA** *B3* (8km W Rural/Coastal) *39.43083, -9.20083* **Camping ORBITUR, Rua Maldonado Freitas, 2500-516 Foz do Arelho [262 978683; fax 262 978685; infofozarelho@orbitur.pt; www.orbitur.pt]** Take N360 fr Caldas da Raina twds Foz do Arelho. Site on L; well sp. Lge, mkd pitch, terr, shd; wc; chem disp; mv service pnt; shwrs; el pnts (5-15A) €3-4; gas; lndtte (inc dryer); shop; tradsmn; rest high ssn; snacks; bar; BBQ; playgrnd; htd pool high ssn; paddling pool; sand beach 2km; tennis; cycle hire; games rm; wifi; entmnt; cab/sat TV; 25% statics; dogs €1.50; car wash; Eng spkn; adv bkg; quiet; ccard acc; red low ssn; CKE/CCI. "Óbidos Lagoon nr; interesting walled town; attractive area; well-maintained, well-run site; excel san facs; excel touring base." ♦ € 24.60   2011*

"I like to fill in the reports as I travel from site to site"

You'll find report forms at the back of this guide, or you can fill them in online at www.caravaclub.co.uk/europereport.

⊞ **CAMINHA** *B1* (2km SW Coastal) *41.86611, -8.85888* **Camping ORBITUR-Caminha, Mata do Camarido, N13, Km 90, 4910-180 Caminha [258 921295; fax 258 921473; infocaminha@orbitur.pt; www.orbitur.pt]** Foll seafront rd N13/E1 fr Caminha dir Viana/Porto, at sp Foz do Minho turn R, site in approx 1km. Long o'fits take care at ent. Med, terr, shd; wc; mv service pnt; chem disp; shwrs inc; el pnts (5-15A) €3-4; gas; lndtte; shop (high ssn); rest (high ssn); snacks; bar; playgrnd; pool 2.5km; sand beach 150m; fishing; cycle hire; wifi; TV rm; 5% statics; dogs €1.50; Eng spkn; adv bkg; fairly quiet; ccard acc; red low ssn/long stay/snr citizens; CKE/CCI. "Pleasant, woodland site; care in shwrs - turn cold water on 1st as hot poss scalding; Gerês National Park & Viana do Castelo worth visit; poss to cycle to Caminha; vg site, nr attractive beach and sh walk to pleasant town." ♦ € 36.50   2014*

⊞ **CAMPO MAIOR** *C3* (1.5km E Rural) *39.00833, -7.04833* **Camping Rural Os Anjos, Estrada da Senhora da Saúde, 7370-150 Campo Maior [268 688138 or 965 236625 (mob); info@campingosanjos.com; www.campingosanjos.com]** Site sp fr Campo Maior; 1.5 km fr the Cent of Campo Maior; foll sp Parque de Campismo Rural. Sm, some hdstg, terr, pt shd; wc; chem disp; baby facs; shwrs inc; el pnts (6A) €2.60; lndtte; shop in town; tradsmn; bar; communal BBQ; pool; lake sw, fishing & watersports 8km; games area; games rm; wifi; TV rm; no statics; dogs €1 (max 1); phone; Eng spkn; adv bkg (15 Nov-15 Feb open with adv bkg only); quiet; red low ssn/long stay; CKE/CCI. "Excel, peaceful site; v helpful, friendly, Dutch owners; gd touring base for unspoiled, diverse area; conv Spanish border, Badajoz & Elvas; Campo Maior beautiful, white town; low ssn call or email bef arr." ♦ € 14.60   2013*

⊞ **CASCAIS** *A3* (5km NW Coastal/Urban) *38.72166, -9.46666* **Camping ORBITUR-Guincho, Lugar de Areia,EN 247-6, Guincho 2750-053 Cascais [(214) 870450; fax (214) 857413; infoguincho@orbitur.pt; www.orbitur. pt]** Fr Lisbon take A5 W, at end m'way foll sp twd Cascais. At 1st rndabt turn R sp Birre & Campismo. Foll sp for 2.5km. Steep traff calming hump - care needed. V lge, some hdg/mkd pitch, terr, shd; wc; chem disp; mv service pnt; baby facs; shwrs inc; el pnts (6A) €3-4; gas; lndtte (inc dryer); supmkt & 500m; rest, snacks; bar; BBQ; playgrnd; pool; sand beach 800m; watersports & fishing 1km; tennis; cycle hire; horseriding 500m; golf 3km; games rm; wifi; entmnt; cab/sat TV; 50% statics; dogs on lead €1.50; phone; car wash; Eng spkn; adv bkg; some rd noise; ccard acc; red low ssn/long stay/snr citizens; CKE/CCI. "Sandy, wooded site behind dunes; v busy high ssn; poss diff lge o'fits due trees; steep rd to beach; gd san facs, poss stretched high ssn; gd value rest; vg low ssn; buses to Cascais for train to Lisbon; beautiful coastline within 20 min walk." ♦ € 38.80   SBS - E10   2013*

CASTELO BRANCO *C2* (2.5km N Rural) *39.85777, -7.49361* **Camp Municipal Castelo Branco, Estrada Nacional 18, 6000-113 Castelo Branco [(272) 322577; fax (272) 322578; albigec@sm-castelobranco.pt; www.cm-castelobranco. pt]** Fr IP2 take Castelo Branco Norte, exit R on slip rd, L at 1st rndabt, site sp at 2nd rndabt. Turn L at T junc just bef Modelo supmkt, site 2km on L, well sp. Lge, pt sl, shd; wc; shwrs; chem disp; mv service pnt; el pnts (12A) €2.25; gas; lndtte; shop, rest, bar 2km; playgrnd; pool 4km; lake 500m; bus 100m; Eng spkn; quiet but some rd noise; CKE/CCI. "Useful NH on little used x-ing to Portugal; gd site but rds to it poor." 2 Jan-15 Nov. € 9.25   2013*

⊞ **CASTELO DE VIDE** *C3* (3km SW Rural) *39.39805, -7.48722* **Camping Quinta do Pomarinho, N246, Km 16.5, Castelo de Vide [965-755341 (mob); info@pomarinho.co.uk; www.pomarinho.com]** On N246 at km 16.5 by bus stop, turn into dirt track. Site in 500m. Sm, mkd pitch, hdstg, unshd; wc; chem disp; shwrs inc; el pnts (6-10A) €2.50-3.50; lndtte; shop 5km; tradsmn; pool; cycle hire; wifi; dogs; bus adj; Eng spkn; adv bkg; quiet. "On edge of Serra de São Mamede National Park; gd walking, fishing, birdwatching, cycling; vg." € 14.00   2009*

⊞ **CELORICO DE BASTO** *C1* (500m NW Rural) *41.39026, -8.00581* **Parque de Campismo de Celorico de Basto, Adaufe-Gemeos, 4890-361 Celorico de Basto [(255) 323340 or 964-064436 (mob); fax (255) 323341; geral@celoricodebastocamping.com; www. celoricodebastocamping.com]** E fr Guimarães exit A7/IC5 S sp Vila Nune (bef x-ing rv). Foll sp Fermil & Celorico de Basto, site sp. Rte narr and winding or take the N210 fr Amarente and foll sp to site. Med, mkd pitch, some hdstg, shd; wc; chem disp; mv service pnt; shwrs inc; el pnts (6-16A) €2-3.20; gas; lndtte (inc dryer); shop; tradsmn; rest; bar; BBQ; playgrnd; pool 500m; rv sw & fishing adj; games area; wifi; entmnt; TV rm; some statics; dogs €1.80; phone; quiet; ccard acc; red long stay/CKE/CCI. "Peaceful, well-run site; gd facs; gd cycling & walking; vg." ♦ € 16.00   2014*

PORTUGAL

⊞ **CHAVES** *C1* (4km S Rural) *41.70166, -7.50055* **Camp Municipal Quinta do Rebentão, Vila Nova de Veiga, 5400-764 Chaves [tel/fax 276 322733; ccchaves@sapo. pt]** Fr o'skts Chaves take N2 S. After about 3km in vill of Vila Nova de Veiga turn E at sp thro new estate, site in about 500m. Med, hdstg, terr, pt shd; wc; chem disp; mv service pnt; shwrs inc; el pnts (6A) €1.50; gas 4km; lndry rm; shop 1km; rest, snacks; bar; BBQ; pool adj; rv sw & fishing 4km; cycle hire; dogs; wifi; phone; bus 800m; site clsd Dec; Eng spkn; adv bkg; red CKE/CCI. "Gd site in lovely valley but remote; helpful staff; facs block quite a hike fr some terr pitches; Chaves interesting, historical Roman town." ♦ € 19.00   2014*

⊞ **COIMBRA** *B2* (1km SE Urban) *40.18888, -8.39944* **Camping Municipal Parque de Campismo de Coimbra, Rua de Escola, Alto do Areeiro, Santo António dos Olivais, 3030-011 Coimbra [tel/fax 239 086902; coimbra@ cacampings.com; www.cacampings.com]** Fr S on AP1/IP1 at junc 11 turn twd Lousa & in 1km turn twd Coimbra on IC2. In 9.5km turn R at rndabt onto Ponte Rainha, strt on at 3 rndabts along Avda Mendes Silva. Then turn R along Estrada des Beiras & cross rndabt to Rua de Escola. Or fr N17 dir Beira foll sp sports stadium/campismo. Fr N ent Coimbra on IC2, turn L onto ring rd & foll Campismo sps. V lge, terr, hdstg, pt sl, pt shd; htd wc; chem disp; mv service pnt; sauna; baby facs; shwrs inc; el pnts (6A) €2.70; gas; lndtte; shop; tradsmn; rest, snacks; bar; BBQ; playgrnd; pool adj; rv sw 300m; health club; tennis; cycle hire; games area; games rm; internet; TV rm; 10% statics; dogs €2.20; bus 100m; poss cr; Eng spkn; adv bkg; ccard acc; red long stay/low ssn/CKE/CCI. "Vg site & facs; v interesting, lively university town." ♦ € 16.00 (CChq acc)   2009*

⊞ **COIMBRAO** *B2* (NW Urban) *39.90027, -8.88805* **Camping Coimbrão, 185 Travessa do Gomes, 2425-452 Coimbrão [tel/fax 244 606007; campingcoimbrao@web.de]** Site down lane in vill cent. Care needed lge o'fits, but site worth the effort. Sm, unshd; wc; chem disp; mv service pnt; shwrs inc; el pnts (6-10A) €2.20-3.30; lndtte (inc dryer); tradsmn; shop & snacks 300m; BBQ; playgrnd; pool; sw, fishing, canoeing 4km; wifi; TV; no dogs; bus 200m; Eng spkn; quiet; office open 0800-1200 & 1500-2200; red long stay/low ssn. "Excel site; helpful & friendly staff; gd touring base." ♦ € 12.70   2010*

CORTEGACA see Espinho *B1*

COSTA DE CAPARICA see Lisboa *B3*

⊞ **COVILHA** *C2* (4km NW Rural) *40.28750, -7.52722* **Clube de Campismo do Pião, Rua 6 de Setembro 35, 356200-036 Covilhã [tel/fax 275 314312; campismopiao@hotmail. com]** App Covilhã, foll sp to cent, then sp to Penhas da Saúde/Seia; after 4km of gd but twisting climbing rd; site on L. Lge, terr, pt shd; wc; shwrs inc; el pnts (4-6A) €1.40; gas; shop; rest, snacks; bar; BBQ; playgrnd; pool; paddling pool; tennis; entmnt; TV; many statics; phone; bus adj; poss cr; Eng spkn; CKE/CCI. "Gd walking fr site; few touring pitches." ♦ € 11.30   2009*

DARQUE see Viana do Castelo *B1*

⊞ **ELVAS** *C3* (1.5km W Urban) *38.87305, -7.1800* **Parque de Campismo da Piedade, 7350-901 Elvas [268 628997 / 268 622877; fax 268 620729]** Exit IP7/E90 junc 9 or 12 & foll site sp dir Estremoz. Med, mkd pitch, hdstg, mostly sl, pt shd; wc; chem disp; shwrs inc; el pnts (16A) inc; gas; lndry rm; shop 200m; rest, snacks; bar; BBQ; playgrnd; dogs; phone; bus 500m; poss cr; CKE/CCI. "Attractive aqueduct & walls; Piedade church & relics adj; traditional shops; pleasant walk to town; v quiet site, even high ssn; adequate san facs; conv NH en rte Algarve." 1 Apr-15 Sep. € 16.50   2014*

ENTRE AMBOS OS RIOS see Ponte da Barca *B1*

⊞ **ERICEIRA** *B3* (1km N Coastal) *38.98055, -9.41861* **Camp Municipal Mil Regos, 2655-319 Ericeira [261 862706; fax 261 866798; info@ericeiracamping.com; www. ericeiracamping.com]** On N247 coast rd, well sp N of Ericeira. V lge, pt sl, pt shd; wc (some cont); own san rec; shwrs inc; el pnts (10A) €3.50; gas; shop; rest; playgrnd; 2 pools adj; beach 200m; fishing; internet; entmnt; 75% statics; phone; bus adj; quiet. "Busy site with sea views; improvements in hand (2009); uneven, sl pitches." ♦ € 24.50   2009*

> ## "We must tell The Club about that great site we found"
> Get your site reports in by mid-August and we'll do our best to get your updates into the next edition.

⊞ **ERMIDAS SADO** *B4* (7km NW Rural) *38.01805, -8.48500* **Camping Monte Naturista O Barão (Naturist), Foros do Barão, 7566-909 Ermidas-Sado [936710623 (mob); info@ montenaturista.com; www.montenaturista.com]** Fr A2 turn W onto N121 thro Ermidas-Sado twd Santiago do Cacém. At x-rds nr Arelãos turn R at bus stop (km 17.5) dir Barão. Site in 1km along unmade rd. Sm, mkd pitch, pt sl, pt shd; wc; chem disp; mv service pnt; baby facs; fam bthrm; shwrs inc; el pnts (6A) €3.20; lndry rm; shop 7.5km; tradsmn; meals on request; bar; BBQ; pool; games area; wifi; TV; 10% statics; dogs €1; bus 1.5km; Eng spkn; adv bkg; quiet; ccard acc; red long stay; INF/CKE/CCI. "Gd, peaceful 'retreat-type' site in beautiful wooded area; friendly atmosphere; spacious pitches - sun or shd." ♦ € 15.80   2010*

⊞ **ESPINHO** *B1* (10km S Coastal) *40.9400, -8.65833* **Camping Os Nortenhos, Praia de Cortegaça, 3885-278 Cortegaça [256 752199; fax 256 755177; clube.nortenhos@ netvisao.pt; http://cccosnortenhos.cidadevirtual.pt]** Fr Espinho foll rd thro Esmoriz twd Aveiro to Cortegaça vill. Turn R to beach (Praia), site on L at beach. At T-junc with pedestrian precinct in front turn L, take 2nd R then 2nd L. Other rtes diff. V lge, pt shd; wc (cont); shwrs; el pnts (6A); gas; shop; snacks; bar; playgrnd; sand beach adj; entmnt; TV; 95% statics; no dogs; phone; bus 500m; poss cr; quiet; ccard acc; CKE/CCI. "Ltd tourer pitches & poss v cr high ssn; facs ltd at w/end; conv Porto; guarded at ent; sun shelters over pitches." ♦ € 7.00   2009*

ESTELA see Povoa De Varzim *B1*

⊞ **EVORA** *C3* (2km SW Urban) *38.55722, -7.92583* **Camping Orbitur Evora, Estrada das Alcaçovas, Herdade Esparragosa, 7005-206 Évora [(266) 705190; fax (266) 709830; evora@orbitur.pt; www.orbitur.pt]** Fr N foll N18 & by-pass, then foll sps for Lisbon rd at each rndabt or traff lts. Fr town cent take N380 SW sp Alcaçovas, foll site sp, site in 2km. NB Narr gate to site. Med, mkd pitch, hdstg, pt sl, pt shd; wc; chem disp; mv service pnt; shwrs inc; el pnts (5-15A) €3.50-4.60 (long lead poss req); gas; lndtte; shop; supmkt 500m; tradsmn; snacks; bar; playgrnd; pool; paddling pool; tennis; games area; wifi; TV rm; dogs €2.20; phone; car wash; bus; rlwy stn 2km; Eng spkn; adv bkg; quiet; ccard acc; red low ssn/long stay/snr citizens; red CKE/CCI. "Conv town cent, Évora World Heritage site with wealth of monuments & prehistoric sites nrby; cycle path to town; free car parks just outside town walls; poss flooding some pitches after heavy rain." ♦ € 35.60   2014*

⊞ **EVORAMONTE** *C3* (3km NE Rural) *38.79276, -7.68701* **Camping Alentejo, Novo Horizonte, 7100-300 Evoramonte [268 959283 or 936 799249 (mob); info@ campingalentejo.com; www.campingalentejo.com]** Fr E exit A6/E90 junc 7 Estremoz onto N18 dir Evora. Site in 8km at km 236. Sm, terr, pt shd; wc; chem disp; mv service pnt; shwrs inc; el pnts (16A) €8; lndry rm; tradsmn; BBQ; horseriding; wifi; no statics;pool; dogs €1; bus adj; Eng spkn; adv bkg; quiet - some rd noise; CKE/CCI. "Excel site; gd birdwatching, v friendly and helpful owner." ♦ € 16.00   2012*

⊞ **FAO** *B1* (1km S Urban/Coastal) *41.50780, -8.77830* **Parque de Campismo de Barcelos, Rua São João de Deus, 4740-380 Fão [253 981777; fax 253 817786; contacto@ cccbarcelos.com; www.cccbarcelos.com]** Exit A28/IC1 junc 8 fr S or junc 9 fr N onto N13 thro Fão twd coast. Site sp off rd M501. Sm, pt shd; wc; chem disp; mv service pnt; baby facs; shwrs inc; el pnts (3A) €3; gas; lndtte; shop, snacks, bar high ssn; playgrnd; pool 5km; sand beach 800m; entmnt; TV; many statics; no dogs; bus 800m; quiet. "Gd site; Barcelos mkt Thurs." ♦ € 15.60   2009*

FERRAGUDO see Portimao *B4*

⊞ **FIGUEIRA DA FOZ** *B2* (4km S Coastal/Urban) *40.11861, -8.85666* **Camping ORBITUR-Gala, N109, Km 4, Gala, 3090-458 Figueira da Foz [233 431492; fax 233 431231; infogala@orbitur.pt; www.orbitur.pt]** Fr Figueira da Foz on N109 dir Leiria for 3.5km. After Gala site on R in approx 400m. Ignore sp on R 'Campismo' after long bdge. Lge, mkd pitch, hdstg, terr, shd; wc; chem disp; mv service pnt; shwrs; el pnts (6-10A) €3-4; gas; lndtte; shop; tradsmn; rest, snacks; bar; BBQ; playgrnd; htd pool high ssn; paddling pool; sand beach 400m; fishing 1km; tennis; games rm; wifi; entmnt; TV rm; many statics; dogs €1.50; phone; car wash; Eng spkn; adv bkg; red low ssn/long stay/snr citizens; ccard acc; CKE/CCI. "Gd, renovated site adj busy rd; luxury san facs (furthest fr recep); excel pool." ♦ € 29.00 (CChq acc)   2011*

⊞ **FIGUEIRA DA FOZ** *B2* (6km S Coastal) *40.14055, -8.86277* **Camping Foz do Mondego, Cabedelo-Gala, 3080-661 Figueira da Foz [233 402740/2; fax 233 402749; foz. mondego@fcmportugal.com; www.fcmportugal.com]** Fr S on N109 turn L bef bdge sp Gala. Foll site sp. V lge, mkd pitch; htd wc; chem disp; mv service pnt; baby facs; shwrs inc; el pnts (2A) inc; gas; lndtte; shop 2km; rest, snacks; bar; BBQ; playgrnd; sand beach adj; fishing; surfing; TV; 40% statics; dogs €0.50; phone; bus 1km; CKE/CCI. "Wonderful sea views but indus est adj; NH only." ♦ 14 Jan-13 Nov. € 16.40 2009*

FOZ DO ARELHO see Caldas da Rainha *B3*

FUZETA see Olhao *C4*

GAFANHA DA NAZARE see Aveiro *B2*

⊞ **GERES** *C1* (1km N Rural) *41.76305, -8.19111* **Parque de Campismo de Cerdeira, Rue de Cerdeira 400, Campo do Gerês, 4840-030 Terras do Bouro [(253) 351005; fax (253) 353315; info@parquecerdeira.com; www. parquecerdeira.com]** Fr N103 Braga-Chaves rd, 28km E of Braga turn N onto N304 at sp to Poussada. Cont N for 18km to Campo de Gerês. Site in 1km; well sp. V lge, shd; wc; chem disp; shwrs inc; el pnts (5-10A) €3.90-4.90; gas; lndry service; rest; bar; shop; playgrnd; lake sw; TV rm; cycle hire; fishing 2km; canoeing; few statics; dogs €3; bus 500m; entmnt; poss cr; quiet; Eng spkn; ccard acc; CKE/CCI. "Beautiful scenery; unspoilt area; fascinating old vills nrby & gd walking; ltd facs low ssn." ♦ € 30.75   2013*

GERES *C1* (2km N Rural) *41.73777, -8.15805* **Vidoeiro Camping, Lugar do Vidoeiro, 4845-081 Gerês [253 391289; aderepg@mail.telepac.pt]** NE fr Braga take N103 twds Chaves for 25km. 1km past Cerdeirinhas turn L twds Gerês onto N308. Site on L 2km after Caldos do Gerês. Steep rds with hairpins. Cross bdge & reservoir, foll camp sps. Lge, mkd pitch, hdstg, terr, pt shd; wc; chem disp; shwrs inc; el pnts (12A) €1.20; lndry rm; tradsmn; rest, bar 500m; BBQ; pool 500m, lake sw 500m; dogs €0.60; phone; quiet. "Attractive, wooded site in National Park; gd, clean facs; thermal spa in Gerês; diff access for lge o'fits, mountain rd." ♦ 15 May-15 Oct. € 17.00   2013*

⊞ **GOUVEIA** *C2* (6km NE Rural) *40.52083, -7.54149* **Camping Quinta das Cegonhas, Nabaínhos, 6290-122 Melo [tel/fax 238 745886; cegonhas@cegonhas.com; www.cegonhas.com]** Turn S at 114km post on N17 Seia-Celorico da Beira. Site sp thro Melo vill. Sm, pt shd; wc; chem disp; mv service pnt; shwrs; el pnts (6-10A) €3; lndtte; shop 300m; rest, snacks; bar; playgrnd; pool; entmnt; games rm; guided walks; TV; dogs €1.10; bus 400m; Eng spkn; adv bkg; quiet; red long stay/low ssn; CKE/CCI. "Vg, well-run, busy site in grnds of vill manor house; friendly Dutch owners; beautiful location conv Torre & Serra da Estrella; gd walks; highly rec." ♦ € 18.00   2013*

PORTUGAL

⊞ **GUARDA** C2 (500m SW Urban) 40.53861, -7.27944 **Camp Municipal da Guarda, Avda do Estádio Municipal, 6300-705 Guarda [271 221200; fax 271 210025]** Exit A23 junc 35 onto N18 to Guarda. Foll sp cent & sports centre. Site adj sports cent off rndabt. Med, hdstg, sl, shd; wc (some cont, own san rec); chem disp (wc); shwrs inc; el pnts (15A) €1.45; gas; lndry rm; shop; rest, snacks, bar high ssn; BBQ; playgrnd; pool 2km; TV; phone; bus adj; Eng spkn; poss noise fr rd & nrby nightclub; CKE/CCI. "Access to some pitches diff for c'vans, OK for m'vans; poss run down facs & site poss neglected low/mid ssn; walking dist to interesting town - highest in Portugal & poss v cold at night; music festival 1st week Sep." ♦ € 12.00   2014*

GUIMARAES B1 (6km SE Rural) 41.42833, -8.26861 **Camping Parque da Penha, Penha-Costa, 4800-026 Guimarães [tel/ fax 253 515912 or 253 515085; geral@turipenha.pt; www. turipenha.pt]** Take N101 SE fr Guimarães sp Felgueiras. Turn R at sp for Nascente/Penha. Site sp. Lge, hdstg, pt sl, terr, shd; wc; shwrs inc; el pnts (6A) €1.80; gas; shop; rest adj; snacks; bar; playgrnd; pool; fishing; no statics; no dogs; phone; wifi; bus 200m, teleferic (cable car) 200m; car wash; poss cr; Eng spkn; adv bkg; poss noisy; CKE/CCI. "Excel staff; gd san facs; lower terrs not suitable lge o'fits; densely wooded hilltop site; conv Guimaraes World Heritage site European City of Culture 2012; Cable car down to Guimaraes costs Euros 4.20 return." ♦ ltd 1 Apr-30 Sep. € 10.40   2011*

"I need an on-site restaurant"

We do our best to make sure site information is correct, but it is always best to check any must-have facilities are still available or will be open during your visit.

GUIMARAES C1 (2km W Rural) 41.46150, -8.01120 **Quinta Valbom, Quintã 4890-505 Ribas [351 253 653 048; info@ quintavalbom.nl; www.quintavalbom.nl]** Fr Guimaraes take A7 SE. Exit 11 onto N206 Fafe/Gandarela. Turn R bef tunnel twds Ribas. Foll blue & red signs of campsite. Med, mkd pitch, terr, pt shd; wc; shwrs inc; el pnts (10A); lndtte; tradsmn; bar; BBQ; pool; wifi; dogs ; bus 2km; twin axles; Eng spkn; poss cr; adv bkg; quiet; CCI. "Very nice site; friendly Dutch owners; quiet surroundings; lots of space in beautiful setting; if driving c'van, park at white chapel and call campsite for their 4WD assistance up last bit of steep hill." ♦ ltd 1 Apr-1 Oct. € 22.70   2014*

GUITIRIZ A2 (1km N Rural) 43.17850, -7.82640 **Camping El Mesón, 27305 Guitiriz (Lugo) [982-37 32 88; fax 626 50 91 40; elcampingelmeson@gmail.com; http:// elmesoncamping.wix.com/campingelmeson.]** On A6 NW fr Lugo, exit km 535 sp Guitiriz, site sp. Sm, mkd pitch, pt sl, pt shd; wc; chem disp (wc); baby facs; shwrs inc; el pnts (10A) €4.50; lndtte (inc dryer); gas; supmkt 1km; snack; bar; BBQ; playgrnd; rv sw 500m; phone; bus adj; quiet."Vg site." 15 Jun-15 Sep. € 17.00   2014*

⊞ **IDANHA A NOVA** C2 (8km NE Rural) 39.95027, -7.18777 **Camping ORBITUR-Barragem de Idanha-a-Nova, N354-1, Km 8, Barragem de Idanha-a-Nova, 6060 Idanha-a-Nova [(277) 202793; fax (277) 202945; infoidanha@orbitur. pt; www.orbitur.pt]** Exit IP2 at junc 25 sp Lardosa & foll sp Idanha-a-Nova on N18, then N233, N353. Thro Idanha & cross Rv Ponsul onto N354 to site. Avoid rte fr Castelo Branco via Ladoeiro as rd narr, steep & winding in places. Lge, mkd pitch, hdstg, terr, shd; wc; chem disp; mv service pnt; baby facs; shwrs inc; el pnts (6A) €3-4; gas; lndtte; shop; tradsmn; rest, snacks; bar; BBQ; playgrnd; htd pool; paddling pool; lake sw, fishing; watersports 150m; tennis; games rm; wifi; entmnt; cab/sat TV; 10% statics; dogs €1.50; phone; car wash; Eng spkn; adv bkg; quiet; red long stay/low ssn/snr citizens. "Uphill to town & supmkts; hot water to shwrs only; pitches poss diff - a mover req; level pitches at top of site; excel." ♦ € 29.40   2013*

ILHAVO see Aveiro B2

"Satellite navigation makes touring much easier"

Remember most sat navs don't know if you're towing or in a larger vehicle – always use yours alongside maps and site directions.

⊞ **LAGOS** B4 (1km SW Urban/Coastal) 37.09469, -8.67218 **Parque de Campismo da Trindade, Rossio da Trindade, 8601-908 Lagos [282 763893; fax 282 762885; info@ campingtrindade.com]** Fr Faro on N125 app Lagos, foll sp for Centro; drive 1.5km along front past BP stn, up hill to traff lts; turn L & foll Campismo sp to L. Cont to traff island & foll to bottom of hill, ent on R. Site adj football stadium. Sm, hdstg, terr, pt shd; wc; own san facs; chem disp; shwrs inc; el pnts (12A) €3.50; gas; lndtte; shop; rest, snacks; bar; playgrnd; pool 500m; sand beach 500m (steep steps); dogs €1; phone; poss cr; Eng spkn; rd noise; ccard acc; red long stay; CKE/CCI. "Gd beaches & cliff walks; clean san facs; gd size m'van pitches; conv walk into Lagos." ♦ € 16.70   2009*

⊞ **LAGOS** B4 (4km W Rural/Coastal) 37.10095, -8.73220 **Camping Turiscampo, N125 Espiche, 8600-109 Luz-Lagos [282 789265; fax 282 788578; info@turiscampo.com or reservas@turiscampo.com; www.turiscampo.com]** Exit A22/IC4 junc 1 to Lagos then N125 fr Lagos dir Sagres, site 3km on R. Lge, hdg/mkd pitch, some hdstg, pt sl, terr, shd; htd wc; chem disp; mv service pnt; baby facs; shwrs inc; el pnts (6A) inc - extra for 10A; gas; lndtte (inc dryer); supmkt; tradsmn; rest, snacks; bar; BBQ; playgrnds; pool; paddling pool; solarium; sand beach 2km; fishing 2.5km; tennis 2km; cycle hire; games area; games area; wifi; entmnt; TV rm; 25% statics; dogs €1.50; phone; bus to Lagos 100m; Eng spkn; adv bkg; quiet; ccard acc; red long stay/low ssn/CKE/ CCI. "Superb, well-run, busy site; v popular for winter stays & rallies; all facs (inc excel pool) open all yr; gd san facs; helpful staff; lovely vill, beach & views; varied & interesting area, Luz worth visit." ♦ € 35.50 (CChq acc) SBS - E07   2013*

See advert on next page

PORTUGAL

Camping Bungalow Park **Turiscampo**
www.turiscampo.com LAGOS ALGARVE PORTUGAL - OPEN ALL YEAR!
yelloh! VILLAGE

⊞ **LAGOS** *B4* (7km W Coastal/Urban) *37.10111, -8.71777*
Camping ORBITUR-Valverde, Estrada da Praia da Luz,
Valverde, 8600-148 Lagos [214 857400 or 282 789211; fax
214 857410; infovalverde@orbitur.pt; www.orbitur.pt]
Foll coast rd N125 fr Lagos to Sagres for 3km. Turn L at traff
lts sp Luz, site 2km on R, well sp. V lge, hdg/mkd pitch, hdstg,
terr, pt shd; wc; chem disp; mv service pnt; baby facs; shwrs
inc; el pnts (6A) €3.50-4.60; gas; lndtte (inc dryer); supmkt;
tradsmn; rest, snacks; bar; BBQ: playgrnd; pool; paddling pool;
sand beach 3km; tennis; sports facs; games area; games rm;
wifi; entmnt; cab/sat TV; many statics; dogs €2; bus; car wash;
Eng spkn; adv bkg; quiet; ccard acc; red low ssn/long stay/
snr citizens/Orbitur card; CKE/CCI. "Well-run site on mildly sl
grnd; v busy high ssn, spacious low ssn; friendly staff; modern,
clean san facs; pitches on sandy grnd, access poss tight due
trees; narr, busy rd to lovely beach/town; poss muddy in wet
weather." ♦ € 38.30   2011*

"There aren't many sites open at this time of year"

If you're travelling outside peak season
remember to call ahead to check site opening
dates – even if the entry says 'open all year'

⊞ **LAMAS DE MOURO** *C1* (1km S Rural) *42.04166, -8.20833*
Camping Lamas de Mouro, 4960-170 Lamas de Mouro
[(251) 466041; geral@camping-lamas.comEste endereço
de e-mail foi protegido contra spambots. Você deve
habilitar o JavaScript para visualizá-lo.; www.camping-
lamas.com] Fr N202 at Melgaço foll sp Peneda- Gerês National
Park, cont R to rd sp Porta de Lamas de Mouro. Cont 1km
past park info office, site on L in pine woods. Med, pt shd; wc;
chem disp; mv service pnt; shwrs inc; el pnts (10A) €3; lndry
rm; shop; tradsmn; rest, snacks; bar; cooking facs; playgrnd;
natural pool; dog €2; phone; bus 1km; poss cr; quiet; CKE/CCI.
"Ideal for walking in National Park." € 17.00   2013*

LAVRA see Porto *B1*

⊞ **LISBOA** *B3* (10km SW Coastal) *38.65111, -9.23777*
Camping ORBITUR-Costa de Caparica, Ave Afonso de
Albuquerque, Quinta de S. António, 2825-450 Costa
de Caparica [212 901366 or 903894; fax 212 900661;
infocaparica@orbitur.pt; www.orbitur.pt] Take A2/IP7 S
fr Lisbon; after Rv Tagus bdge turn W to Costa de Caparica. At
end of rd turn N twd Trafaria, & site on L. Well sp fr a'strada.
Lge, hdg/mkd pitch, terr, shd; wc; chem disp; mv service
pnt; shwrs inc; el pnts (6A) €3; gas; lndtte (inc dryer); shop;
tradsmn; rest, snacks; bar; BBQ; playgrnd; pool 800m; sand
beach 1km; fishing; tennis; games rm; wifi; entmnt; TV;
75% statics; dogs €1.50; phone; car wash; bus to Lisbon; Eng
spkn; adv bkg; some rd noise; ccard acc; red low ssn/long stay/
snr citizens/Orbitur card; CKE/CCI. "Gd, clean, well run site;
heavy traff into city; rec use free parking at Monument to the
Discoveries & tram to city cent; ferry to Belém; ltd facs low ssn;
pleasant, helpful staff." ♦ € 34.40 (CChq acc)   2012*

⊞ **LISBOA** *B3* (5km NW Urban) *38.72472, -9.20805*
Parque Municipal de Campismo de Monsanto, Estrada
da Circunvalação, 1400-061 Lisboa [(217) 628200;
fax (217) 628299; info@lisboacamping.com; www.
lisboacamping.com] Fr W on A5 foll sp Parque Florestal de
Monsanto/Buraca. Fr S on A2, cross toll bdge & foll sp for
Sintra; join expressway, foll up hill; site well sp; stay in RH
lane. Fr N on A1 pass airport, take Benfica exit & foll sp under
m'way to site. Site sp fr all major rds. Avoid rush hours! V lge,
mkd pitch, hdstg, pt sl, terr, pt shd; htd wc (cont); chem disp;
mv service pnt; 80% serviced pitches; baby facs; fam bthrm;
shwrs inc; el pnts (6-16A) inc; gas; lndtte; shop; tradsmn;
rest, snacks; bar; playgrnd; pool; sand beach 10km; tennis;
bank; PO; car wash; entmnt; TV rm; 5% statics; dogs free;
frequent bus to city; rlwy stn 3km; poss cr; Eng spkn; adv bkg;
some rd noise; red low ssn; ccard acc; red CKE/CCI. "Well
laid-out, spacious, guarded site in trees; ltd mv service pnt;
take care hygiene at chem disp/clean water tap; facs poss badly
maintained & stretched when site full; friendly, helpful staff; in
high ssn some o'fits placed on sloping forest area (quiet); few
pitches take awning; excel excursions booked at TO on site." ♦
€ 32.00   2013*

PORTUGAL

⊞ **LUSO** *B2* (1.5km S Rural) *40.38222, -8.38583* **Camping Luso, N336, Pampilhosa, Quinta do Vale do Jorge, 3050-246 Luso [231 930916; fax 231 930917; info@orbitur.pt]** S fr Luso on N336, sp. Lge, hdstg, pt sl, pt shd; wc; chem disp; mv service pnt; shwrs inc; el pnts (5-15A) €2.50; gas; lndtte; shop; tradsmn; rest, snacks; bar; playgrnd; pool 1km; sand beach 35km; tennis; games rm; TV rm; some statics; dogs €1.30; car wash; adv bkg; Eng spkn; quiet; red low ssn/long stay/snr citizens; ccard acc; CKE/CCI. "Excel site in wooded valley; vg san facs; some sm pitches unsuitable for c'vans + awnings; internet in vill; sh walk to interesting spa town; conv Coimbra." ♦ € 25.20   2011*

MARTINCHEL see Tomar *B2*

⊞ **MEDA** *2C* (0.5km N Urban) *40.96972, -7.25916* **Parque de Campismo Municipal, Av. Professor Adriano Vasco Rodrigues, 6430 Mêda [(351) 925 480 500/ (351) 279 883 270; campismo@cm-meda.pt; www.cm-meda.pt/turismo/Paginas/Parque_Camsimo.aspx]** Head N fr the cent of town, take 1st R, take 1st L & your dest will be on your L within the Meda Sports Complex. Sm; hdstg; pt shd; wc; chem disp; mv service pnt; child/baby facs; shwrs; shop; rest; pool; bar; snacks; WiFi; eng spkn. "Pt of the Municipal Sports Complex with facs avail; conv for town centre." ♦ ltd € 11.50   2014*

MEDAS GONDOMAR see Porto *B1*

MELO see Gouveia *C2*

⊞ **MIRA** *B2* (3km W Rural) *40.44728, -8.75723* **Camping Vila Caia, Travessa Da Carreira Do Tiro, Lagoa 3070-176 Mira [231 451524; fax 231 451861; vlcaia@portugalmail.com; www.vilacaia.com]** S fr Aveiro on N109 for 29km; at Mira take N334 for 5km. Site sp on R 500m W of Lagoa de Mira. Lge, hdstg, pt shd; wc (some cont); chem disp; mv service pnt; shwrs inc; el pnts (4A) €3; gas; lndtte; shop; rest, snacks; bar; playgrnd; pool; paddling pool; sand beach 3km; fishing; tennis; cycle hire; entmnt; TV; some statics; dogs €1.30; phone; bus adj; site clsd Dec; Eng spkn; no adv bkg; quiet, but poss noisy entmnt high ssn; ccard acc; red low ssn; CKE/CCI. "Gd site." ♦ € 20.00   2011*

MIRA *B2* (7km NW Coastal/Urban) *40.44472, -8.79888* **Camping ORBITUR-Mira, Estrada Florestal 1, Km 2, Dunas de Mira, 3070-792 Praia de Mira [231 471234; fax 231 472047; infomira@orbitur.pt; www.orbitur.pt]** Fr N109 in Mira turn W to Praia de Mira, foll site sp. Lge, hdg pitch, hdstg, shd; wc; chem disp; mv service pnt; shwrs inc; el pnts (5-15A) €3-4 (poss rev pol); gas; lndtte (inc dryer); shop (in ssn); tradsmn; rest, snacks, bar high ssn; playgrnd; pool 7km; sandy, surfing beach & dunes 800m; fishing; boating; wifi; entmnt; TV rm; 5% statics; dogs €1.50; phone; site clsd Dec; Eng spkn; adv bkg; poss noisy w/end; red low ssn/long stay/snr citizens; ccard acc; CKE/CCI. "Friendly, helpful staff; gd, clean, attractive site; excel surfing beach nr; suitable for cycling; nature reserve opp site." ♦ 1 Jan-16 Oct. € 26.70   2011*

MIRANDA DO DOURO *D1* (500m W Rural) *41.49861, -6.28444* **Campismo Municipal Santa Lúzia, Rua do Parque de Campismo, 5210-190 Miranda do Douro [273 431273 or 430020; fax 273 431075; mirdouro@mail.telepac.pt; www.cm-mdouro.pt]** Fr Spain on ZA324/N221, cross dam & thro town, site well sp. Do not enter walled town. Lge, pt sl, terr, pt shd; wc; chem disp; shwrs inc; el pnts (5A) €1.50; shop, rest & 1km; snacks, bar; playgrnd; pool 300m; phone; bus 500m; Eng spkn; quiet; CKE/CCI. "Simple, peaceful site; interesting ent into N Portugal; old walled town; spectacular rv gorge; boat trips; unrel opening dates." ♦ 1 Jun-30 Sep. € 9.50   2011*

MOGADOURO *D1* (1km S Rural) *41.33527, -6.71861* **Parque de Campismo da Quinta da Agueira, Complexo Desportivo, 5200-244 Mogadouro [279 340231 or 936-989202 (mob); fax 279 341874; campismo@mogadouro.pt; www.mogadouro.pt]** Fr Miranda do Douro on N221 or fr Bragança on IP2 to Macedo then N216 to Mogadouro. Site sp adj sports complex. Lge, shd; wc; chem disp; mv service pnt; shwrs inc; el pnts (15A) €2; gas; lndry rm; shop 1km; rest 200m; snacks; bar; BBQ; playgrnd; pool adj; waterslide; beach 15km; tennis; car wash; entmnt; internet; TV; dogs €1.50; phone; bus 300m; Eng spkn; adv bkg; quiet. "Brilliant site in lovely area; value for money; steep hill to town; gd touring base." ♦ 1 Apr-30 Sep. € 11.50   2013*

MONCARAPACHO see Olhao *C4*

⊞ **MONCHIQUE** *B4* (6km S Rural) **Parque Rural Caldas de Monchique, Barracão 190, 8550-213 Monchique [282 911502; fax 282 911503; valedacarrasqueira@sapo.pt; www.valedacarrasqueira.com]** Fr S exit A22 N onto N266, site sp on R in 11km. Fr N on N266 dir Portimão, thro Monchique, site on L. Well sp. M'vans only. Sm, mkd pitch, hdstg, unshd; wc; chem disp; mv service pnt; all serviced pitches; shwrs inc; el pnts (16A); lndtte; bar; BBQ; pool; dogs; no adv bkg; Eng spkn; quiet. "Excel, peaceful, scenic, clean site; excel san facs; helpful staff; poss taking c'vans in future." € 15.00   2009*

MONTALEGRE *C1* (10km S Rural) *41.75722, -7.81016* **Camping Penedones, 5470-235 Montalegre [276 510220; info@montalegre.com; www.montalegrehotel.com]** Fr N103 turn S at sp for Hotel Montalegre, site in 1km on lakeside. Well sp. Lge, some hdstg, pt shd; htd wc; chem disp; mv service pnt; shwrs inc; el pnts (6A) €2.10; lndry rm; rest, snacks; bar; playgrnd; lake sw; 10% statics; bus; quiet. "Beautiful situation; vg." 1 Apr-30 Sep. € 17.00   2010*

⊞ **MONTARGIL** *B3* (5km N Rural) *39.10083, -8.14472* **Camping ORBITUR, Baragem de Montargil, N2, 7425-017 Montargil [242 901207; fax 242 901220; infomontargil@orbitur.pt; www.orbitur.pt]** Fr N251 Coruche to Vimiero rd, turn N on N2, over dam at Barragem de Montargil. Fr Ponte de Sor S on N2 until 3km fr Montargil. Site clearly sp bet rd & lake. Med, mkd pitch, hdstg, terr, pt shd; wc; chem disp; mv service pnt; shwrs inc; el pnts (6-10A) €3-4; gas; lndtte; shop & 3km; tradsmn, rest, snacks; bar; BBQ; playgrnd; pool; paddling pool; rv beach adj; boating; watersports; fishing; tennis; games rm; wifi; entmnt; cab/sat TV; 60% statics; dogs €1.50; phone; car wash; Eng spkn; adv bkg; some rd noise; ccard acc; red low ssn/long stay/snr citizens; CKE/CCI. "Friendly site in beautiful area." ♦ € 26.70   2011*

⊞ **NAZARE** *B2* (2km N Rural) 39.62036, -9.05630 **Camping Vale Paraíso, N242, 2450-138 Nazaré [262 561800; fax 262 561900; info@valeparaiso.com; www.valeparaiso. com]** Site thro pine reserve on N242 fr Nazaré to Leiria. V lge, mkd pitch, hdstg, terr, shd; wc (some cont); chem disp; mv service pnt; baby facs; shwrs inc; el pnts (4-10A) €3; gas; lndtte (inc dryer); supmkt; rest, snacks; bar; playgrnd; pools; paddling pool; sand beach 2km; lake 1km; fishing; games area; games rm; cycle hire; wifi; TV rm; 20% statics; dogs €2; bus; site clsd 19-26 Dec; Eng spkn; adv bkg; quiet; ccard acc; red low ssn/long stay; CKE/CCI. "Gd, clean site; well run; gd security; pitches vary in size & price, & divided by concrete walls, poss not suitable lge o'fits, bus outside gates to Nazare, exit down steep hill." ♦ € 22.85   2011*

⊞ **NAZARE** *B2* (2km E Rural) 39.59777, -9.05611 **Camping ORBITUR-Valado, Rua dos Combatentes do Ultramar 2, EN8, Km 5, Valado, 2450-148 Nazaré-Alcobaca [262 561111; fax 262 561137; infovalado@orbitur.pt; www.orbitur.pt]** Site on N of rd to Alcobaça & Valado (N8-4), opp Monte de São Bartolomeu. Lge, mkd pitch, terr, sl, shd; wc; chem disp; mv service pnt; shwrs inc; el pnts (6A) €3-4; gas; lndtte; shop & 2km; tradsmn; rest, snacks; bar; BBQ; playgrnd; pool; sand beach 1.8km; tennis; games rm; wifi; TV rm; 10% statics; dogs €1.50; phone; car wash; Eng spkn; adv bkg; red low ssn/long stay/snr citizens; ccard acc. "Pleasant site in pine trees; v soft sand - tractor avail; helpful manager; visits to Fátima, Alcobaça, Balhala rec." ♦ 1 Jan-16 Oct. € 25.60 (CChq acc)   2010*

⊞ **ODEMIRA** *B4* (7km W Rural) 37.60565, -8.73786 **Zmar Eco Camping Resort & Spa, Herdade A-de-Mateus, N393/1, San Salvador, 7630-011 Odemira [(707) 200626 or (283) 690010; fax (283) 690014; info@zmar.eu; www. zmar.eu]** Fr N on A2 take IC33 dir Sines. Just bef ent Sines take IC4 to Cercal (sp Sul Algarve) then foll N390/393 & turn R dir Zambujeira do Mar, site sp. Med, mkd pitch, hdstg, pt shd; wc; chem disp; mv service pnt; baby facs; fam bthrm; sauna; shwrs inc; private bthrms avail; el pnts (10A) inc; lndtte; shop; rest, snacks; bar; BBQ; cooking facs; playgrnd; 2 pools (1 htd, covrd); paddling pool; sand beach 7km; tennis; cycle hire; games area; wellness cent; fitness rm; wifi; excursions; entmnt; TV rm; 17% statics; Eng spkn; adv bkg; dogs €2.50; twin-axles acc (rec check in adv); quiet; red low ssn. "Superb new site 2009 (eco resort) with excel facs; in national park; vg touring base." ♦ € 46.00 (4 persons) (CChq acc)   2013*

⊞ **ODIVELAS** *B3* (3km NE Rural) 38.18361, -8.10361 **Camping Markádia, Barragem de Odivelas, 7920-999 Alvito [(284) 763141; fax (284) 763102; markadia@ hotmail.com; www.markadia.com]** Fr Ferreira do Alentejo on N2 N twd Torrão. After Odivelas turn R onto N257 twd Alvito & turn R twd Barragem de Odivels. Site in 7km, clearly sp. Med, hdstg, pt sl, pt shd; wc; chem disp; mv service pnt; shwrs inc; el pnts (16A) inc; gas; lndtte (inc dryer); shop; tradsmn; rest, snacks; bar; playgrnd; pool 50m; paddling pool; sand beach, lake sw 500m; boating; fishing; horseriding; tennis; no dogs Jul-Aug; phone; car wash; adv bkg; v quiet; red low ssn/CKE/CCI. "Beautiful, secluded site on banks of reservoir; spacious pitches; gd rest; site lighting low but san facs well lit; excel walking, cycling, birdwatching; wonderful." ♦   € 32.00   2013*

⊞ **OLHAO** *C4* (10km NE Rural) **Camping Caravanas Algarve, Sitio da Cabeça Moncarapacho, 8700-618 Moncarapacho [(289) 791669]** Exit IP1/A22 sp Moncarapacho. In 2km turn L sp Fuzeta. At traff lts turn L & immed L opp supmkt in 1km. Turn R at site sp. Site on L. Sm, hdstg, pt sl, unshd; wc; chem disp; shwrs inc; el pnts (6A) inc; lndtte; shop, rest, snacks, bar 1.5km; sand beach 4km; 10% statics; dogs; poss cr; Eng spkn; adv bkg; quiet; 10% red CKE/CCI. "Situated on a farm in orange groves; pitches ltd in wet conditions; gd, modern san facs; gd security; Spanish border 35km; National Park Ria Formosa 4km; lovely popular site." € 10.00   2013*

⊞ **OLHAO** *C4* (10km NE Rural) **Campismo Casa Rosa, Apt 209 8700 Moncarapacho [(289) 794400 / (9191) 73132 (mob); fax (289) 792952; casarosa@sapo.pt; www.casarosa.eu.com]** Fr A22 (IP1) E twd Spain, leave at exit 15 Olhão/Moncarapacho. At rndabt take 2nd exit dir Moncarapacho. Cont past sp Moncarapacho Centro dir Olhão. In 1km at Lagoão, on L is Café Da Lagoão with its orange awning. Just past café is sp for Casa Rosa. Foll sp. Sm, hdstg, terr, unshd; htd wc ltd; chem disp; shwrs inc; el pnts (6A) inc; gas 3km; lndtte; rest; pool; shgl beach 6km; rv sw 6km; sat TV, wifi; dogs; Eng spkn; adv bkg; noise fr construction yard adj; CKE/CCI. "Excel CL-type site adj holiday apartments; adults only; helpful, friendly, Norwegian owners; evening meals avail; ideal for touring E Algarve; conv Spanish border; rec; 30% dep req, no refunds if leaving early; insufficient san facs, but still a gd site; drinkable water taps." ♦ ltd € 13.50   2013*

⊞ **OLHAO** *C4* (1.5km E Rural) 37.03527, -7.82250 **Camping Olhão, Pinheiros do Marim, 8700-912 Olhão [289 700300; fax 289 700390 or 700391; parque.campismo@sbsi.pt; www.sbsi.pt]** Turn S twd coast fr N125 1.5km E of Olhão by filling stn. Clearly sp on S side of N125, adj Ria Formosa National Park. V lge, hdg/mkd pitch, pt sl, shd; wc; chem disp; mv service pnt; shwrs inc; el pnts (6A) €1.90; gas; lndtte inc dryers; supmkt; tradsmn; rest; bar; playgrnd; pool; paddling pool; beach 1.5km; tennis; games rm; games area; cycle hire; horseriding 1km; internet; wifi; TV; 75% statics; dogs €1.60; phone; bus adj; rlwy stn 1.5km; sep car park for some pitches; car wash; security guard; Eng spkn; adv bkg; some rlwy noise; ccard acc; red long stay/low ssn; CKE/CCI. "Pleasant, helpful staff; excel pool; gd san facs; v popular long stay low ssn; many sm sandy pitches, some diff access for lge o'fits; gd for cycling, birdwatching; ferry to islands." ♦ € 24.00   2014*

⊞ **OLHAO** *C4* (9km E Coastal/Urban) 37.05294, -7.74484 **Parque Campismo de Fuzeta, 2 Rua do Liberdade, 8700-019 Fuzeta [289 793459; fax 289 794034; camping@ jf-fuseta.pt]** Fr N125 Olhão-Tavira rd, turn S at traff lts at Alfandanga sp Fuzeta & foll sp to site. Lge, some hdstg, pt shd; wc; chem disp; shwrs €0.25; el pnts (6-10A) inc; gas; lndtte; shop & 1km; rest adj; snacks; bar; BBQ; playgrnd adj; sand beach adj; internet; 5% statics; dogs; phone; train 500m; Eng spkn; no adv bkg; noise fr rd & adj bars; red long stay. "Pleasant staff; popular with long-stay m'vanners; elec cables run across site rds; poss flooding after heavy rain; clean san facs; gd security; attractive area & fishing port." ♦ ltd € 16.70   2010*

⊞ **OLIVEIRA DO HOSPITAL** *C2* (9km SE Rural) *40.34647, -7.80747* **Parque de Campisom de São Gião, 3400-570 São Gião [238 691154; fax 238 692451]** Fr N17 Guarda-Coimbra rd turn S almost opp N230 rd to Oliveira do Hospital, dir Sandomil. Site on R in about 3km over rv bdge. Lge, shd; wc; chem disp; shwrs; el pnts (6A) €1.50; gas; lndtte; shop, rest, snacks; bar; BBQ; playgrnd; pool 7km; fishing; phone; 50% statics; no dogs; bus adj; quiet. "Facs basic but clean; working water mill; app/exit long, steep, narr, lane."
€ 10.50   2009*

"That's changed – Should I let The Club know?"

If you find something on site that's different from the site entry, fill in a report and let us know. See www.caravanclub.co.uk/europereport.

⊞ **OLIVEIRA DO HOSPITAL** *C2* (10km NW Rural) *40.40550, -7.93100* **Camping Quinta das Oliveiras (Naturist), Rua de Estrada Nova, Andorinha, 3405-498 Travanca de Lagos [962 621287; fax 235 466007; campismo.nat@sapo.pt; www.quinta-das-oliveiras.com]** Fr Oliveira do Hospital foll N230 & N1314 to Travanca de Lagos. Then take N502 twd Midões. After 2km turn R on N1313 to Andorinha. Site on R 1.5km after Andorinha. Sm, pt sl, terr, pt shd; wc; chem disp; shwrs inc; el pnts (6A) €3.50; tradsmn; BBQ; playgrnd; pool; dogs €2; poss cr; Eng spkn; adv bkg; quiet; red low ssn; INF card. € 19.00   2009*

⊞ **ORTIGA** *C3* (1.5km SE Rural) *39.48277, -8.00305* **Parque Campismo de Ortiga, Estrada da Barragem, 6120-525 Ortiga [241 573464; fax 241 573482; campismo@cm-macao.pt]** Exit A23/IP6 junc 12 S to Ortiga. Thro Ortiga & foll site sp for 1.5km. Site beside dam. Sm, mkd pitch, hdstg, terr, pt shd; wc; chem disp; shwrs inc; el pnts (10A) €1.50; lndtte; shop 1km; rest, snacks, bar adj; BBQ; playgrnd; lake sw 100m; watersports; TV; 50% statics; dogs free; bus 1.5km; poss cr; Eng spkn; quiet; red low ssn; CKE/CCI; "Lovely site in gd position." ♦ € 11.00   2013*

PENACOVA *B2* (3km N Rural) *40.27916, -8.26805* **Camp Municipal de Vila Nova, Rua dos Barqueiros, Vila Nova, 3360-204 Penacova [239 477946; fax 239 474857; penaparque2@iol.pt]** IP3 fr Coimbra, exit junc 11, cross Rv Mondego N of Penacova & foll to sp to Vila Nova & site. Med, pt shd; wc; shwrs inc; el pnts (6A) €1; shop 50m; rest 150m; snacks; bar; BBQ; playgrnd; rv sw 200m; fishing; cycle hire; TV; no dogs; phone; bus 150m; Eng spkn; red CKE/CCI. "Open, attractive site." 1 Apr-30 Sep. € 10.80   2011*

PENELA *B2* (500m SE Rural) *40.02501, -8.38900* **Parque Municipal de Campismo de Panela, Rua do Convento de Santo Antonio, 3230-284 Penela [239 569256; fax 239 569400]** Fr Coimbra S on IC2, L at Condeixa a Nova, IC3 dir Penela. Thro vill foll sp to site. Sm, hstg, pt sl, terr, pt shd; wc; chem disp; shwrs €0.50; el pnts (6A) €0.50; shop, rest, snacks, bar 200m; pool 500m; some statics; no dogs; bus adj; some traff noise; CKE/CCI. "Attractive sm town; restful, clean, well-maintained site." ♦ ltd 1 Jun-30 Sep. € 4.50   2009*

⊞ **PENICHE** *B3* (1.5km NW Urban/Coastal) *39.36944, -9.39194* **Camping Peniche Praia, Estrada Marginal Norte, 2520 Peniche [262 783460; fax 262 784140; geral@ penichepraia.pt; www.penichepraia.pt]** Travel S on IP6 then take N114 sp Peniche; fr Lisbon N on N247 then N114 sp Peniche. Site on R on N114 1km bef Peniche. Med, hdg/mkd pitch, hdstg, unshd; wc; chem disp; mv service pnt; shwrs inc; el pnts (6A) inc; lndtte; shop 1.5km; tradsmn; rest, snacks, bar high ssn; BBQ; playgrnd; covrd pool; paddling pool; sand beach 1.5km; games rm; cycle hire; internet; entmnt; TV; dog €2.10; 30% statics; phone; bus 2km; car wash; poss cr; Eng spkn; adv bkg rec; red long stay/low ssn/CKE/CCI; "Vg site in lovely location; some sm pitches; rec, espec low ssn." € 18.30 2013*

POCO REDONDO see Tomar *B2*

PONTE DA BARCA *B1* (11km E Rural) *41.82376, -8.31723* **Camping Entre-Ambos-os-Rios, Lugar da Igreja, Entre-Ambos-os-Rios, 4980-613 Ponte da Barca [258 588361; fax 258 452450; aderepg@mail.telepac.pt; www.adere-pg.pt]** N203 E fr Ponte da Barca, pass ent sp for vill. Site sp N twd Rv Lima, after 1st bdge. Lge, pt sl, shd; wc; shwrs inc; el pnts (6A) €1.20; gas; lndry rm; shop, rest 300m; snacks; bar; playgrnd; canoeing; fishing; entmnt; TV; dogs €0.60; phone; bus 100m; adv bkg; CKE/CCI. "Beautiful, clean, well run & maintained site in pine trees; well situated for National Park; vg rest." 15 May-30 Sep. € 18.00   2014*

⊞ **PORTIMAO** *B4* (3km SE Coastal) *37.11301, -8.51096* **Camping Ferragudo, 8400-280 Ferragudo [282 461121; fax 282 461355; cclferragudo@clubecampismolisboa.pt; www.clubecampismolisboa.pt]** Leave N125 at sp Ferraguda, turn L at traff lts at end of Parchal vill onto N539. Foll sp to site. V lge, terr, pt shd; wc (some cont); mv service pnt; shwrs inc; el pnts (6A) inc; gas; lndry rm; shop, rest, snacks; bar; playgrnd; pool; sw & fishing 800m; entmnt; TV; 90% statics; no dogs; phone; bus 1km; v cr Jul/Aug; red low ssn; CKE/CCI. "Helpful staff; bus to Portimao at ent; shop/recep 1.5km fr pitches; unsuitable lge m'vans; housing bet site & beach." € 26.00   2010*

⊞ **PORTIMAO** *B4* (10km SW Rural) *37.13500, -8.59027* **Parque Campismo de Alvor (Formaly da Dourada), R Serpa Pinto 8500-053 Alvor [(282) 459178; fax (282) 459178; info@campingalvor.com; www. campingalvor.com]** Turn S at W end of N125 Portimão by-pass sp Alvor. Site on L in 4km bef ent town. V lge, pt sl, terr, shd; wc; chem disp; shwrs free; el pnts (6-16A) €3.-5.; gas; lndtte; shop high ssn; rest, snacks; bar; playgrnd; pool; paddling pool; sand beach 1km; fishing; sports area; entmnt; TV rm; dogs €2.50; bus adj; poss noisy from adjoining properties; red long stay/low ssn; CKE/CCI. "Friendly & helpful, family-run site; office poss unattended in winter, ltd facs & site untidy; excel rest; lovely town & beaches; Site much improved, never untidy (2013); v welcoming; popular with wintering Brits." ♦ € 21.50   2013*

PORTUGAL

⊞ **PORTO** *B1* (11km N Coastal) *41.2675, -8.71972* **Camping ORBITUR-Angeiras, Rua de Angeiras, Matosinhos, 4455-039 Lavra [229 270571 or 270634; fax 229 271178; infoangeiras@orbitur.pt; www.orbitur.pt]** Fr ICI/A28 take turn-off sp Lavra, site sp at end of slip rd. Site in approx 3km - app rd potholed & cobbled. Lge, pt sl, shd; wc (some cont); chem disp; mv service pnt; shwrs inc; el pnts (6A) €3-4 (check earth); gas; lndtte (inc dryer); shop; tradsmn; rest, snacks; bar; BBQ; playgrnd; pool; paddling pool; sand beach 400m; tennis; fishing; games area; games rm; wifi; entmnt; cab/sat TV; 70% statics; dogs €1.50; phone; bus to Porto at site ent; car wash; Eng spkn; adv bkg; red low ssn/long stay/snr citizens; ccard acc; CKE/CCI. "Friendly & helpful staff; clean, dated san facs; gd rest; gd pitches in trees at end of site but ltd space lge o'fits; ssnl statics all yr; fish & veg mkt in Matoshinhos." ♦ € 34.40 (CChq acc) 2014*

⊞ **PORTO** *B1* (16km SE Rural) *41.03972, -8.42666* **Campidouro Parque de Medas, Lugar do Gavinho, 4515-397 Medas-Gondomar [224 760162; fax 224 769082; geral@campidouro.pt]** Take N12 dir Gondomar off A1. Almost immed take R exit sp Entre-os-Rios. At rndabt pick up N108 & in approx 14km. Sp for Medas on R, thro hamlet & forest for 3km & foll sp for site on R. Long, steep app. New concrete access/site rds. Lge, mkd pitch, hdstg, terr, pt shd; wc; chem disp; mv service pnt; serviced pitches; shwrs inc; el pnts (3-6A) €2.73 (poss rev pol); gas; lndtte; shop, rest (w/end only low ssn); bar; playgrnd; pool & paddling pool; rv sw, fishing, boating; tennis; games rm; entmnt; TV rm; wifi; 90% statics; phone; bus to Porto; poss cr; quiet; ccard acc; red CKE/CCI. "Beautiful site on Rv Douro; helpful owners; gd rest; clean facs; sm level area (poss cr by rv & pool) for tourers - poss noisy at night & waterlogged after heavy rain; bus to Porto (just outside site) rec as parking diff (ltd buses at w/end)." € 27.35 2014*

⊞ **PORTO** *B1* (6km SW Coastal) *41.11055, -8.66083* **Camping Marisol, Rua Alto das Chaquedas 82, Canidelo, 400-356 Vila Nova de Gaia [227 135942; fax 227 126351]** Fr Porto ring rd IC1 take N109 exit sp Espinho. In 1km take exit Madalena. Site sp on coast rd. Med, hdg pitch, pt shd; wc; chem disp; mv service pnt; shwrs inc; el pnts (6A) €2.50; gas; lndry rm; shop; rest; bar; BBQ; playgrnd; pool 800m; sand beach adj; games area; car wash; TV; 50% statics; dogs €1.80; sandy pitches; bus 150m; poss cr; Eng spkn. "Conv for Porto; gd." ♦ € 17.00 2014*

⊞ **PORTO** *B1* (10km SW Coastal/Urban) *41.10777, -8.65611* **Camping ORBITUR-Madalena, Rua do Cerro 608, Praia da Madalena, 4405-736 Vila Nova de Gaia [(227) 122520; fax (227) 122534; infomadalena@orbitur.pt; www.orbitur. pt]** Fr Porto ring rd IC1/A44 take A29 exit dir Espinho. In 1km take exit slip rd sp Madalena opp Volvo agent. Watch for either 'Campismo' or 'Orbitur' sp to site along winding, cobbled rd. Lge, terr, pt sl, pt shd; wc (some cont); chem disp; mv service pnt; baby facs; shwrs inc; el pnts (6A) €4.60; gas; lndtte; shop; tradsmn; rest, snacks, bar in ssn; BBQ; playgrnd; pool; paddling pool; sand beach 250m; tennis; games area; games rm; wifi; entmnt; TV rm; 40% statics; dogs €2.20; phone; bus to Porto; car wash; Eng spkn; adv bkg; ccard acc; red low ssn/long stay/snr citizens; CKE/CCI. "Site in forest; restricted area for tourers; slight aircraft noise; some uneven pitches; poss ltd facs low ssn; excel bus to Porto cent fr site ent - do not take c'van into Porto; facs in need of refurb (2013)." ♦ € 35.00 2014*

⊞ **POVOA DE VARZIM** *B1* (13km N Coastal) *41.46277, -8.77277* **Camping ORBITUR-Rio Alto, EN13, Km 13, Lugar do Rio Alto, Estela, 4570-275 Póvoa de Varzim [252 615699; fax 252 615599; inforioalto@orbitur.pt; www.orbitur.pt]** Fr A28 exit Póvoa onto N13 N; turn L 1km N of Estela at yellow Golf sp by hotel, in 2km (cobbles) turn R to camp ent. V lge, some hdg/mkd pitch, unshd; wc; chem disp; mv service pnt; baby facs; shwrs inc; el pnts (5-15A) €3-4; gas; lndtte (inc dryer); shop; tradsmn; rest, snacks; bar; BBQ; playgrnd; pool high ssn; sand beach 150m; tennis; games area; games rm; golf adj; wifi; entmnt; cab/sat TV; 50% static/semi-statics; dogs €1.50; phone; bus 2km; car wash; poss cr; Eng spkn; adv bkg; poss cr; red low ssn/long stay/snr citizens; ccard acc; CKE/CCI. "Excel facs; helpful staff; vg rest on site; direct access to vg beach (steep sl); strong NW prevailing wind; excel touring base." ♦ € 29.00 (CChq acc) 2011*

PRAIA DE MIRA see Mira *B2*

> ## "I like to fill in the reports as I travel from site to site"
> You'll find report forms at the back of this guide, or you can fill them in online at www.caravaclub.co.uk/europereport.

PRAIA DE QUIAIOS *B2* (2km W Coastal) *40.2200, -8.88666* **Camping ORBITUR, Praia de Quiaios, 3080-515 Quiaios [233 919995; fax 233 919996; infoquiaios@orbitur.pt; www.orbitur.pt]** Fr N109 turn W onto N109-8 dir Quiaios, foll sp 3km to Praia de Quiaios & site. Lge, some mkd pitch, pt shd; wc; chem disp; mv service pnt; shwrs inc; el pnts (10A) €3-4; gas; lndtte; supmkt; tradsmn; rest, snacks; bar; BBQ; playgrnd; pool 500m; sand beach 500m; tennis; cycle hire; games rm; TV; entmnt; 20% statics; dogs €1.50; phone; car wash; Eng spkn; adv bkg; ccard acc; red low ssn/snr citizens/long stay; CKE/CCI. "Interesting historical area; vg touring base; peaceful site; hot water to shwrs only; care needed some pitches due soft sand." ♦ 1 Jan-16 Oct. € 21.20 2010*

⊞ **QUARTEIRA** *C4* (2km N Coastal/Urban) *37.06722, -8.08666* **Camping ORBITUR-Quarteira, Estrada da Fonte Santa, Ave Sá Carneira, 8125-618 Quarteira [289 302826 or 302821; fax 289 302822; infoquarteira@orbitur.pt; www.orbitur.pt]** Fr E & IP1/A22 take exit junc 12 at Loulé onto N396 to Quarteira; in 8.5km at rndabt by g'ge L along dual c'way. In 1km at traff lts fork R into site. No advance sp to site. V lge, mkd pitch, pt sl, terr, pt shd; wc; chem disp; mv service pnt; shwrs inc; el pnts (6A) €3-4 (long lead req some pitches); gas; lndtte (inc dryer); supmkt 200m; tradsmn; rest, snacks; bar; BBQ; playgrnd; pool; paddling pool; waterslide; sand beach 600m; tennis; games rm; wifi; entmnt; TV rm; 40% statics (tour ops); dogs €2; phone; bus 500m; car wash; Eng spkn; adv bkg; quiet; ccard acc; red low ssn/long stay/snr citizens; ccard acc; CKE/CCI. "Lovely site; popular winter long stay; narr site rds & tight turns; some o'hanging trees; some pitches diff lge o'fits; gd san facs; caterpillar problem Jan-Mar; easy walk to town; mkt Wed." ♦ € 30.00 2010*

ROSARIO see Alandroal *C3*

92 ⊞Site open all year   You can now fill in site reports online

⊞ **SAGRES** *B4* (2km W Coastal) *37.02305, -8.94555* **Camping ORBITUR-Sagres, Cerro das Moitas, 8650-998 Vila de Sagres [282 624371; fax 282 624445; infosagres@ orbitur.pt; www.orbitur.pt]** On N268 to Cape St Vincent; well sp. Lge, hdg/mkd pitch, hdstg, pt shd; wc; chem disp; mv service pnt; shwrs inc; el pnts (6-10A) €3-4; gas; lndtte (inc dryer); shop; rest, snacks; bar; BBQ; playgrnd; sand beach 2km; cycle hire; games rm; wifi; TV rm; dogs €1.50; car wash; Eng spkn; adv bkg; quiet; red long stay/low ssn/snr citizens; ccard acc. "Vg, clean, tidy site in pine trees; helpful staff; hot water to shwrs only; cliff walks." ♦ € 25.60 (CChq acc)   2012*

⊞ **SANTO ANTONIO DAS AREIAS** *C3* (1km SE Rural) *39.40992, -7.34075* **Camping Asseiceira, Asseiceira, 7330-204 Santo António das Areias [tel/fax (245) 992940 / (960) 150352 (mob); gary-campingasseiceira@hotmail.com; www. campingasseiceira.com]** Fr N246-1 turn off sp Marvão/Santo António das Areias. Turn L to Santo António das Areias then 1st R on ent town then immed R again, up sm hill to rndabt. At rndabt turn R then at next rndabt cont strt on. There is a petrol stn on R, cont down hill for 400m. Site on L. Sm, pt sl, pt shd; wc; chem disp; shwrs inc; el pnts (10A) €4; gas 500m; shop, rest 1km; snacks; bar; pool; wifi; no statics; dogs free; bus 1km; quiet; CKE/CCI. "Attractive area; peaceful, well-equipped, remote site among olive trees; clean, tidy; gd for walking, birdwatching; helpful, friendly, British owners; excel san facs, maintained to a high standard; nr Spanish border; excel; Ideal cent for walking, cycling, visit hilltop castle Marvao." ♦ ltd Apr -Sep. € 15.00   2013*

SAO GIAO see Oliveira do Hospital *C2*

SAO JACINTO see Aveiro *B2*

"We must tell The Club about that great site we found"

Get your site reports in by mid-August and we'll do our best to get your updates into the next edition.

⊞ **SAO MARCOS DA SERRA** *B4* (3km S Rural) *37.3350, -8.3467* **Campismo Rural Quinta Odelouca, Vale Grande de Baixo, CxP 644-S, 8375-215 São Marcos da Serra [282 361718; info@quintaodelouca.com; www. quintaodelouca.com]** Fr N (Ourique) on IC1 pass São Marcos da Serra & in approx 2.5km turn R & cross blue rlwy bdge. At bottom turn L & at cont until turn R for Vale Grande (paved rd changes to unmade). Foll sp to site. Fr S exit A22 junc 9 onto IC1 dir Ourique. Pass São Bartolomeu de Messines & at km 710.5 turn L & cross blue rlwy bdge, then as above. Sm, terr, pt shd; wc; chem disp; baby facs; shwrs inc; el pnts (10A) €2.10; lndtte; shop 3km; tradsmn; rest 2km; bar; BBQ; pool; lake sw; wifi; dogs €1; Eng spkn; adv bkg; quiet; CKE/CCI. "Helpful, friendly Dutch owners; phone ahead bet Nov & Feb; beautiful views; gd walks; vg." € 13.00   2009*

⊞ **SAO MARTINHO DO PORTO** *B2* (1.5km NE Coastal) *39.52280, -9.12310* **Parque de Campismo Colina do Sol, Serra dos Mangues, 2460-697 São Martinho do Porto [(262) 989764; fax (262) 989763; parque.colina.sol@clix. pt /geral@colinadosol.net; www.colinadosol.net]** Leave A8/IC1 SW at junc 21 onto N242 W to São Martinho, by-pass town on N242 dir Nazaré. Site on L. Lge, mkd pitch, hdstg, terr, pt shd; wc; chem disp; mv service pnt; shwrs inc; el pnts (6A) €2.75; gas; lndtte; shop high ssn; rest, snacks; bar; BBQ; playgrnd; pool; paddling pool; sand beach 2km; fishing; games area; games rm; TV; mobile homes/c'vans for hire; dogs €1; phone; bus 2km; site clsd at Xmas; poss cr; Eng spkn; adv bkg; quiet; ccard acc; CKE/CCI; "Gd touring base on attractive coastline; gd walking, cycling; vg san facs; excel site; san facs a bit tired (2013), water v hot." ♦ € 30.50   2013*

⊞ **SAO PEDRO DE MOEL** *B2* (2.2km N Urban/Coastal) *39.75861, -9.02583* **Camping ORBITUR-São Pedro de Moel, Rua Volta do Sete, São Pedro de Moel, 2430 Marinha Grande [244 599168; fax 244 599148; infospedro@orbitur. pt; www.orbitur.pt]** Site at end of rd fr Marinha Grande to beach; turn R at 1st rndabt on ent vill. Site S of lighthouse. V lge, some hdg/mkd pitch, hdstg, pt terr, shd; wc; chem disp; mv service pnt; shwrs inc; el pnts (6A) €3-4 (poss rev pol); gas; lndtte; shop; tradsmn; rest, snacks; bar; BBQ; playgrnd; htd pool; paddling pool; waterslide; sand beach 500m (heavy surf); fishing; tennis; cycle hire; games rm; wifi; entmnt; cab/sat TV; some statics; dogs €1.50; phone; car wash; poss cr; Eng spkn; adv bkg; quiet; red low ssn/long stay/snr citizens; ccard acc; CKE/CCI. "Friendly, well-run, clean site in pine woods; easy walk to shops, rests; gd cycling to beaches; São Pedro smart resort; ltd facs low ssn site in attractive area and well run." ♦ € 28.60   2011*

⊞ **SAO TEOTONIO** *B4* (7km W Coastal) *37.49497, -8.78667* **Camping Monte Carvalhal da Rocha, Praia do Carvalhal, 7630-569 S Teotónio [282 947293; fax 282 947294; geral@montecarvalhalr-turismo.com; www. montecarvalhaldarocha.com]** Turn W off N120 dir Brejão & Carvalhal; site in 4.5km. Site sp. Med, shd; wc; shwrs inc; el pnts (16A) inc; gas; lndtte; shop, rest, snacks, bar high ssn; BBQ; playgrnd; sand beach 500m; fishing; cycle hire; TV; some statics; no dogs; phone; bus 2km; car wash; Eng spkn; adv bkg; quiet; ccard acc; red low ssn. "Beautiful area; friendly, helpful staff." € 26.00   2012*

SAO TEOTONIO *B4* (7km W Coastal) *37.52560, -8.77560* **Parque de Campismo da Zambujeira, Praia da Zambujeira, 7630-740 Zambujeira do Mar [(283) 961172 / (935) 682790; fax (283) 961320; campingzambujeira@gmail.com; www. campingzambujeira.com.sapo.pt]** S on N120 twd Lagos, turn W when level with São Teotónio on unclassified rd to Zambujeira. Site on L in 7km, bef vill. V lge, pt sl, pt shd; wc; chem disp; mv service pnt; shwrs inc; el pnts (6-10A) €3.50; gas; shop, rest, snacks & bar high ssn; playgrnd; sand beach 1km; tennis; TV; dogs €4; phone; bus adj; Eng spkn; some rd noise; red low ssn/long stay. "Welcoming, friendly owners; in pleasant rural setting; hot water to shwrs only; sh walk to unspoilt vill with some shops & rest; cliff walks." 31Mar-31Dec. € 25.00   2013*

SATAO C2 (10km N Rural) 40.82280, -7.6961 **Camping Quinta Chave Grande, Rua do Barreiro 462, Casfreires, Ferreira d'Aves, 3560-043 Sátão [tel/fax 232 665552; info@chavegrande.com; www.chavegrande.com]** Leave IP5 Salamanca-Viseu rd onto N229 to Sátão, site sp in Satão - beyond Lamas. Med, terr, pt shd; wc; chem disp; baby facs; shwrs inc; el pnts (6A) €3.50; gas; lndtte; shop 3km; tradsmn; rest 3km; snacks; bar; playgrnd; pool; paddling pool; tennis; games area; games rm; internet; TV; dogs leashed €2.50; Eng spkn; quiet; red long stay. "Warm welcome fr friendly Dutch owners; gd facs; well organised BBQ's - friendly atmosphere; gd touring base; gd walks fr site; excel." 15 Mar-31 Oct. € 20.50   2013*

"I need an on-site restaurant"

We do our best to make sure site information is correct, but it is always best to check any must-have facilities are still available or will be open during your visit.

SERPA C4 (1km W Urban) 37.94090, -7.60404 **Parque Municipal de Campismo Serpa, Rua da Eira São Pedro, 7830-303 Serpa [284 544290; fax 284 540109]** Fr IP8 take 1st sp for town; site well sp fr most dirs - opp sw pool. Do not ent walled town. Med, pt sl, pt shd; wc; chem disp; shwrs inc; el pnts (6A) €1.25; gas; lndtte; shop 200m; rest, snacks, bar 50m; BBQ; daily mkt 500m; supmkt nr; pool adj; rv sw 5km; 20% statics; dogs; phone; wifi; adv bkg; some rd noise; no ccard acc; CKE/CCI. "Popular gd site; simple, high quality facs; interesting, historic town." ♦ € 10.06   2014*

SESIMBRA B3 (1km W Coastal) 38.43580, -9.11658 **Camp Municipal Forte do Cavalo, Porto de Abrigo, 2970 Sesimbra [212 288508; fax 212 288265; geral@cm-sesimbra.pt; www.cm-sesimbra.pt]** Fr Lisbon S on A2/IP7 turn S onto N378 to Sesimbra. Turn R immed after town ent sp Campismo & Porto. Fork R again sp Porto; L downhill at traff lts to avoid town cent. Turn R at sea front to site by lighthouse. Steep uphill app. V lge, pt sl, terr, shd; wc; shwrs inc; el pnts (6A) €2.15; gas; shop, rest 1km; snacks, bar 500m; BBQ; playgrnd; beach 800m; fishing; boating; no dogs; phone; bus 100m; poss cr; Eng spkn; no adv bkg; quiet; CKE/CCI. "Pitches ltd for tourers; gd views; lovely, unique fishing vill; castle worth visit; unrel opening dates (poss not open until Jun) - phone ahead." € 13.35   2010*

SETUBAL B3 (4km W Coastal) 38.50299, -8.92909 **Parque de Campismo do Outão, Estrada de Rasca, 2900-182 Setúbal [265 238318; fax 265 228098]** Fr Setúbal take coast rd W twd Outão, site on L. V lge, mkd pitch, hdstg, pt shd; wc (some cont); chem disp; shwrs inc; el pnts (5A) inc; gas; shop; rest; bar; playgrnd; sand beach adj; 90% statics; dogs €1.50; poss cr; Eng spkn; some rd noise; ccard acc; red low ssn; red CKE/CCI. "Few pitches for tourers; hdstg not suitable for awning; vacant static pitches sm & have kerb." ♦ € 19.80   2010*

TAVIRA C4 (5km E Rural/Coastal) 37.14506, -7.60223 **Camping Ria Formosa, Quinta da Gomeira, 8800-591 Cabanas-Tavira [tel/fax 281 328887; info@campingriaformosa.com; www.campingriaformosa.com]** Fr spain onto A22 take exit junc 17 (bef tolls) Fr N125 turn S at Conceição dir 'Cabanas Tavira' & 'Campismo'. Cross rlwy line & turn L to site, sp. V lge, mkd pitch, hdstg, terr, pt shd; htd wc; chem disp; mv service pnt; baby facs; shwrs inc; el pnts (16A) €3; gas; lndtte (inc dryer); shop; tradsmn; rest, snacks; bar; BBQ; playgrnd; pool; paddling pool; cycle hire; sand beach 1.2km; games area; wifi; TV rm; dogs €2; bus 100m; train 100m; car wash; Eng spkn; adv bkg; quiet; ccard acc; red long stay/CKE/CCI. "Excel, comfortable site; friendly, welcoming owner & staff; vg, modern san facs; various pitch sizes; cycle path to Tavira, excel facs." ♦ € 23.00   2014*

TOCHA B2 (7.5km W Coastal) 40.32777, -8.84027 **Camping Praia da Tocha, Rua dos Pescadores, Nossa Sra da Tocha, Praia da Tocha, 3060-691 Tocha [231 447112; tocha@cacampings.com; www.cacampings.com]** Fr N or S on N109, turn W onto N335 to Praia da Tocha, site sp. Med, pt shd; wc; chem disp; baby facs; shwrs; el pnts (4-6A) €1.85; gas; lndtte (inc dryer); shop, rest, snacks, bar high ssn; playgrnd; sand beach 200m; watersports; cycle hire; internet; TV rm; dogs €1.55; phone; bus adj; Eng spkn; adv bkg; quiet; CKE/CCI. "Well-maintained, pleasant site; helpful staff." ♦ € 11.80   2009*

TOMAR B2 (1km N Urban) 39.60694, -8.41027 **Campismo Parque Municipal, 2300-000 Tomar [249 329824; fax 249 322608; camping@cm-tomar.pt; www.cm-tomar. pt]** Fr S on N110 foll sp to town cent at far end of stadium. Fr N (Coimbra) on N110 turn R immed bef bdge. Site well sp fr all dirs. Med, mkd pitch, pt shd; htd wc; chem disp; mv service pnt; baby facs; shwrs inc; el pnts (10A) €1.40; lndry rm; tradsmn; shop, rest, snacks, bar in town; BBQ; playgrnd; pool adj; wifi; TV; no statics; dogs; phone adj; Eng spkn; adv bkg; quiet; red low ssn; ccard acc; CKE/CCI. "Useful base for touring Alcobaca, Batalha & historic monuments in Tomar; conv Fatima; Convento de Cristo worth visit; vg, popular, improved site; charming rvside town; easy access for lge vehicle; sh walk thro gdns to Knights Templar castle; free wifi nr recep; camp entry ticket gives free access to adj pool." € 18.00   2014*

"Satellite navigation makes touring much easier"

Remember most sat navs don't know if you're towing or in a larger vehicle – always use yours alongside maps and site directions.

TOMAR B2 (7km NE Rural) 39.63833, -8.33694 **Camping Pelinos, Casal das Aboboreiras, 2300-093 Tomar [249 301814; pelinos1@hotmail.com; www.campingpelinos.com]** N fr Tomar on N110, turn R to Calçadas at traff lts opp g'ge, foll site sp. Steep descent to site. Sm, terr, pt shd; wc; shwrs inc; el pnts (10A) €2; lndtte; rest, snacks; bar; BBQ (winter only); playgrnd; pool; lake sw; watersports; fishing 7km; TV; dogs; phone; bus 100m; Eng spkn; adv bkg; quiet; red low ssn; CKE/CCI. "Owner will assist taking o'fits in/out; vg." 15 Feb-15 Oct. € 11.50   2010*

⊞ **TOMAR** B2 (10km E Rural) *39.62538, -8.32166* **Camping Redondo, Rua do Casal Rei 6, 2300-035 Poço Redondo [tel/fax 249 376421; info@campingredondo.co.uk; www. campingredondo.com]** Fr N or S on N110, take IC3 for Tomar, then take exit at km97 Castelo do Bode/Tomar, dir Junceira. Foll site sp (red hearts) for 7km. Steep drop at site ent. Sm, pt sl, pt shd; wc; chem disp; mv service pnt; baby facs; shwrs inc; el pnts (6A) €2-2.30; lndtte; shop 2km; rest, snacks; bar; BBQ; playgrnd; pool; waterslide; lake beach 4.5km; sat TV; few statics; dogs €1; phone; bus; poss cr; Eng spkn; adv bkg; red low ssn; CKE/CCI. "Due steep drop at ent, site owner can tow c'vans out; peaceful site; friendly, helpful owners; excel walking area." € 13.60   2010*

TOMAR B2 (10km SE Rural) *39.53963, -8.31895* **Camping Castelo do Bode, 2200 Martinchel [241 849262; fax 241 849244; castelo.bode@fcmportugal.com]** S fr Tomar on N110, in approx 7km L onto N358-2 dir Barragem & Castelo do Bode. Site on L in 6km immed after dam; sh, steep app to ent. Med, mkd pitch, hdstg, terr, pt shd; wc (some cont); chem disp; shwrs inc; el pnts (6A) inc; supmkt 6km; tradsmn; rest, snacks 2km; bar; playgrnd; lake sw adj; boating; fishing; dogs €0.60; phone; bus to Tomar 1km; no adv bkg; quiet; CKE/CCI. "Site on edge of 60km long lake with excel watersports; old san facs, but clean; helpful staff; lge car park on ent Tomar - interesting town." ♦ 13 Jan-11 Nov. € 12.25   2011*

TRAVANCA DE LAGOS see Oliveira do Hospital C2

⊞ **VAGOS** B2 (8km W Rural) *40.55805, -8.74527* **Camping ORBITUR-Vagueira, Rua do Parque de Campismo, 3840-254 Gafanha da Boa-Hora [234 797526; fax 234 797093; infovagueira@orbitur.pt; www.orbitur.pt]** Fr Aveiro take N109 S twd Figuera da Foz. Turn R in Vagos vill. After 6km along narr poor rd, site on R bef reaching Vagueira vill. V lge, mkd pitch, shd; wc; chem disp; mv service pnt; baby facs; shwrs inc; el pnts (6-16A) €3-4; gas; lndtte; supmkt, tradsmn, rest, bar high ssn; playgrnd; pool 1km; sand beach 1.5km; fishing 1km; tennis; games area; games rm; cycle hire; wifi; entmnt; 90% statics; dogs €1.50; bus 500m; Eng spkn; adv bkg; quiet; ccard acc; red low ssn/snr citizens; CKE/ CCI. "V pleasant & well-run; friendly staff; poss diff access to pitches for lge o'fits; areas soft sand; gd touring base." ♦ € 21.20   2010*

VALVERDE see Lagos B4

⊞ **VIANA DO CASTELO** B1 (3km S Coastal) *41.67908, -8.82324* **Parque de Campismo Inatel do Cabedelo, Avda dos Trabalhadores, 4900-164 Darque [258 322042; fax 258 331502; pc.cabedelo@inatel.pt; www.inatel.pt]** Exit IC1 junc 11 to W sp Darque, Cabedelo, foll sp to site. Lge, mkd pitch, hdstg, pt sl, pt shd; wc (some cont); shwrs inc; el pnts (6A) inc; gas; lndtte; shop high ssn; tradsmn; snacks; bar; sand beach adj; entmnt; 30% statics; no dogs; phone; bus 100m; site clsd mid-Dec to mid-Jan; adv bkg; quiet; CKE/CCI. "V secure; gd for children; hourly ferry to Viana; spacious pitches under pines; poss poor facs low ssn & in need of refurb." ♦ € 12.50   2009*

⊞ **VIANA DO CASTELO** B1 (2km SW Coastal/Urban) *41.67888, -8.82583* **Camping ORBITUR-Viana do Castelo, Rua Diogo Álvares, Cabedelo, 4935-161 Darque [258 322167; fax 258 321946; infoviana@orbitur.pt; www. orbitur.pt]** Exit IC1 junc 11 to W sp Darque, Cabedelo, foll sp to site in park. Lge, mkd pitch, pt sl, shd; wc; chem disp; mv service pnt; shwrs inc; el pnts (5-15A) inc; gas; lndtte; shop; tradsmn; rest, snacks; bar; BBQ; playgrnd; htd pool; lge sand beach adj; surfing; fishing; wifi; entmnt; TV; dogs €2.20; phone; car wash; Eng spkn; adv bkg; quiet; red low ssn/long stay/snr citizens; ccard acc; CKE/CCI. "Site in pine woods; friendly staff; gd facs; plenty of shade; major festival in Viana 3rd w/end in Aug; lge mkt in town Fri; sm passenger ferry over Rv Lima to town high ssn; Santa Luzia worth visit." ♦ 23 Mar-30 Sep. € 38.00   2013*

⊞ **VILA DO BISPO** B4 (8km SE Coastal/Rural) *37.07542, -8.83133* **Quinta dos Carriços (Part Naturist), Praia de Salema, 8650-196 Budens [282 695201; fax 282 695122; quintacarrico@oninet.pt; www.quintadoscarricos.com]** Take N125 out of Lagos twd Sagres. In approx 14km at sp Salema, turn L & again immed L twd Salema. Site on R 300m. Lge, pt terr (tractor avail), pt shd; htd wc; chem disp; mv service pnt; shwrs €0.75; el pnts (6-10A) €3.90 (metered for long stay); gas; lndtte; shop; rest, snacks; bar; playgrnd; pool 1km; sand beach 1.5km; golf 1km; TV; 8% statics; dogs €2.45; phone; bus; Eng spkn; adv bkg (ess high ssn); noise fr adj quarry; ccard acc; red long stay/CKE/CCI. "Naturist section in sep valley; apartments avail on site; ltd pitches for lge o'fits; friendly Dutch owners; tractor avail to tow to terr; area of wild flowers in spring; beach 30 mins walk; buses pass ent for Lagos, beach & Sagres; excel." ♦ € 28.00   2012*

⊞ **VILA FLOR** C1 (2.5km SW Rural) *41.29420, -7.17180* **Camp Municipal de Vila Flor, Barragem do Peneireiro, 5360-303 Vila Flor [278 512350; fax 278 512380; cm.vila. flor@mail.telepac.pt; www.cm-vilaflor.pt]** Site is off N215, sp fr all dirs. V bumpy app rd - 12km. V lge, terr, pt shd; wc; chem disp (wc); shwrs inc; el pnts (16A) €1.50; gas; lndry rm; shop; snacks; bar; BBQ; playgrnd; pool adj; tennis adj; TV rm; 10% statics; dogs; phone; clsd 2300-0700 (1800-0800 low ssn); poss v cr; adv bkg; noisy high ssn; CKE/CCI. "Friendly staff; access to pitches diff." ♦ ltd € 9.40   2010*

VILA NOVA DE CACELA see Vila Real de Santo Antonio C4

VILA NOVA DE GAIA see Porto B1

⊞ **VILA NOVA DE MILFONTES** B4 (1km N Coastal) *37.73194, -8.78277* **Camping Milfontes, Apartado 81, 7645-300 Vila Nova de Milfontes [(283) 996140; fax (283) 996104; reservas@campingmilfontes.com; www. campingmilfontes.com]** S fr Sines on N120/IC4 for 22km; turn R at Cercal on N390 SW for Milfontes on banks of Rio Mira; clear sp. V lge, hdg/mkd pitch, pt shd; wc; chem disp; mv service pnt; shwrs inc; el pnts (6A) €3 (long lead poss req); gas; lndtte; shop; supmkt & mkt 5 mins walk; rest, snacks, bar high ssn; playgrnd; sand beach 800m; TV; many statics; phone; bus 600m; poss cr; quiet; ccard acc; red CKE/CCI. "Pitching poss diff for lge o'fits due trees & statics; nr fishing vill at mouth Rv Mira with beaches & sailing on rv; pleasant site." ♦ € 27.00   2013*

VILA REAL *C1* (500m NE Urban) *41.30361, -7.73694*
**Camping Vila Real, Rua Dr Manuel Cardona, 5000-558
Vila Real [259 324724]** On IP4/E82 take Vila Real N exit &
head S into town. Foll 'Centro' sp to Galp g'ge; at Galp g'ge
rndabt, turn L & in 30m turn L again. Site at end of rd in 400m.
Site sp fr all dirs. Lge, pt sl, terr, pt shd; wc; chem disp; baby
facs; shwrs inc; el pnts (6A) €2; gas; sm shop adj; tradsmn;
rest, snacks; bar; BBQ; playgrnd; pool complex adj; tennis;
10% statics; dogs; phone; bus 150m; poss cr; red CKE/CCI.
"Conv upper Douro; gd facs ltd when site full; gd mkt in town;
Lamego well worth a visit." ♦ 1 Mar-30 Nov. € 16.00 2011*

⊞ **VILA REAL DE SANTO ANTONIO** *C4* (10km W Rural)
37.18649, -7.55003 **Camping Caliço Park, Sitio do
Caliço, 8900-907 Vila Nova de Cacela [281 951195; fax
281 951977; transcampo@mail.telepac.pt]** On N side of
N125 Vila Real to Faro rd. Sp on main rd & in Vila Nova de
Cacela vill, visible fr rd. Lge, some hdstg, terr, pt sl, shd; wc;
chem disp; shwrs inc; el pnts (6A) €2.80; gas; lndtte (inc dryer);
shop; rest, snacks; bar; playgrnd; pool; sand beach 4km; cycle
hire; wifi; many statics; dogs €1.60; phone; bus/train 2km;
Eng spkn; adv bkg; noisy in ssn & rd noise; ccard acc; red long
stay/low ssn; CKE/CCI. "Friendly staff; not suitable for m'vans
or tourers in wet conditions - ltd touring pitches & poss diff
access; gd NH." € 17.00 2010*

VILAR DE MOUROS see Caminha *B1*

ZAMBUJEIRA DO MAR see Sao Teotonio *B4*

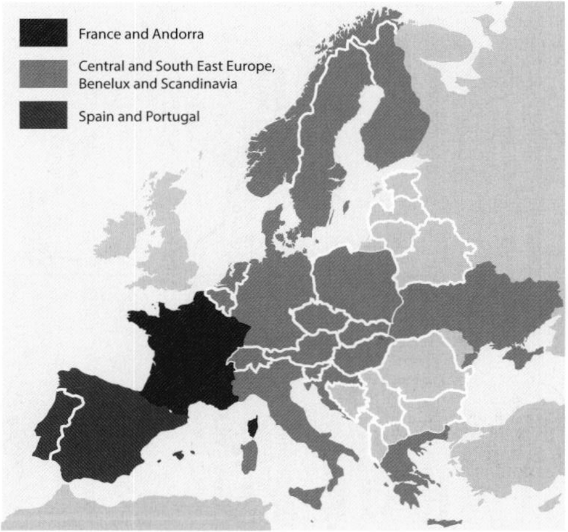
France and Andorra
Central and South East Europe, Benelux and Scandinavia
Spain and Portugal

Miranda do Douro to Vila Real de Santo António = 688km

	Aveiro	Beja	Braga	Bragança	Castelo Branco	Chaves	Coimbra	Elvas	Évora	Faro	Fundão	Guarda	Leiria	Lisboa (Lisbon)	Miranda do Douro	Mourão	Portalegre	Portimão	Porto	Sagres	Santarém	Setúbal	Sines	Valença	Viana do Castelo	Vila Formoso	Vila Real	Vila Real de Santo António	Vila Verde de Ficalho
Beja	408																												
Braga	129	500																											
Bragança	285	558	214																										
Castelo Branco	225	274	318	288																									
Chaves	235	630	140	106	341																								
Coimbra	77	339	186	298	156	260																							
Elvas	379	162	478	445	155	496	253																						
Évora	325	77	432	485	198	513	258	84																					
Faro	535	164	639	732	442	723	468	328	245																				
Fundão	227	317	263	253	43	175	150	198	239	483																			
Guarda	163	361	263	200	92	240	156	247	290	538	57																		
Leiria	143	276	248	368	174	327	77	252	201	417	199	230																	
Lisboa (Lisbon)	273	179	383	503	247	480	206	206	131	295	300	362	146																
Miranda do Douro	320	572	280	76	287	180	313	442	487	732	252	195	387	607															
Mourão	365	110	490	533	260	575	322	101	66	276	303	356	265	193	552														
Portalegre	258	180	365	382	94	440	191	64	105	351	136	185	167	216	382	173													
Portimão	508	105	607	680	379	725	443	267	185	61	465	476	381	295	682	215	288												
Porto	74	445	65	219	261	170	121	364	372	578	208	209	191	317	254	407	303	552											
Sagres	556	153	655	728	407	773	491	315	233	109	513	524	429	343	730	263	336	48	600										
Santarém	205	198	310	426	177	388	140	174	120	338	220	292	78	80	445	186	148	336	251	384									
Setúbal	309	144	418	525	261	500	240	171	96	260	347	391	182	47	576	161	195	260	355	308	113								
Sines	390	99	497	609	305	570	323	193	109	201	348	397	262	162	592	209	214	140	433	147	184	119							
Valença	180	560	66	280	373	208	241	529	487	696	365	316	297	436	352	544	418	658	116	706	364	466	548						
Viana do Castelo	147	520	50	264	342	192	196	437	446	651	314	283	263	395	340	509	379	625	77	673	322	423	507	51					
Vila Formoso	193	400	290	226	135	269	190	290	271	575	111	44	259	428	175	336	228	507	240	555	333	439	380	358	342				
Vila Real	163	560	95	119	268	643	190	425	448	641	222	166	262	412	188	510	363	660	100	708	321	432	506	165	150	200			
Vila Real de Santo António	594	120	693	688	396	815	529	284	200	66	560	492	463	350	688	234	308	126	639	174	400	312	264	761	728	535	742		
Vila Verde de Ficalho	465	60	560	626	334	680	399	222	140	230	377	430	338	241	627	68	246	182	511	230	261	204	160	622	583	460	614	183	
Viseu	84	445	191	220	171	173	89	326	341	547	77	77	161	330	234	401	259	650	132	698	219	321	404	255	237	107	99	562	501

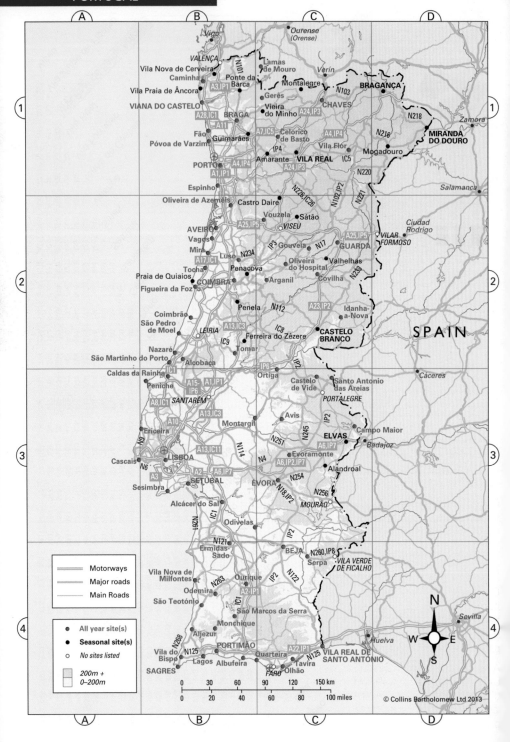

PORTUGAL

Spain
Country Introduction

Peniscola Village, Spain

Welcome to Spain

Famous for great sandy beaches, historic cities and a sunny climate, Spain is a popular destination for both summer and winter breaks.

The landscape offers everything from wide green meadows to snow capped mountains, along with the traditional seaside resorts the country is famous for.

One of the many places worth visiting is Spain's thriving capital city Madrid or the vibrant coastal city of Barcelona with its stunning architecture.

Country highlights

One of Spain's greatest attractions is undoubtedly its cuisine. Many regional specialities and traditional dishes have achieved worldwide fame, such as paella, gazpacho and tapas. Seafood in particular is excellent and plentiful.

A highlight of the food calendar in Spain is the La Tomatina Tomato Festival held on the streets of Buñol, in Valencia. The event, held on the last Wednesday in August, see thousands of participants throwing tomatoes at each other.

Major towns and cities

- Madrid – the capital city is full of amazing sights and beautiful buildings including the Almudena Cathedral.
- Barcelona – a very popular city with breathtaking castles and cathedrals.
- Alicante – home to one of the largest medieval fortresses in Spain, Castle of Santa Barbara.

Attractions

- Basilica of the Sagrada Familia – a unique modern cathedral with a beautiful interior.
- Prado Museum – a stunning museum housing a huge art collection.
- Plaza Nueva – located in the Old Town of Bilbao, a Neoclassical square with a variety of traditional restaurants and small stores.
- Alhambra - a beautiful palace that has stunning architecture and gardens.

Find out more

www.spain.info

Tel: (0)9 13 43 35 00 Spain Tourist Office

Country Information

Population (approx): 47.1 million

Capital: Madrid (population approx 3.2 million)

Area: 510,000 sq km (inc Balearic & Canary Islands)

Bordered by: Andorra, France, Portugal

Terrain: High, rugged central plateau, mountains to north and south

Climate: Temperate climate; hot summers, cold winters in the interior; more moderate summers and cool winters along the northern and eastern coasts; very hot summers and mild/warm winters along the southern coast

Coastline: 4,964km

Highest Point (mainland Spain): Mulhacén (Granada) 3,478m

Languages: Castilian Spanish, Catalan, Galician, Basque

Local Time: GMT or BST + 1, i.e. 1 hour ahead of the UK all year

Currency: Euros divided into 100 cents; £1 = €1.26, €1 = £0.79 (September 2014)

Emergency numbers: Police 092; Fire brigade 080; Ambulance (SAMUR) 061. Operators speak English. Civil Guard 062

Public Holidays 2015: Jan 1, 6; Apr 2, 3, 6; May 1; Aug 15; Oct 12 (National Holiday); Nov 1; Dec 6 (Constitution Day), 8, 25, 26.

Several other dates are celebrated for fiestas according to region. School summer holidays stretch from mid June to mid September.

Camping and Caravanning

There are more than 1,200 campsites in Spain with something to suit all tastes – from some of the best and biggest holiday parks in Europe, to a wealth of attractive small sites offering a personal, friendly welcome. Most campsites are located near the Mediterranean, especially on the Costa Brava and Costa del Sol, as well as in the Pyrenees and other areas of tourist interest. Campsites are indicated by blue road signs. In general pitch sizes are small at about 80 square metres.

Many popular coastal sites favoured for long winter stays may contain tightly packed pitches with long-term residents putting up large awnings, umbrellas and other secondary structures. Many sites allow pitches to be reserved from year to year, which can result in a tight knit community possibly biased to one nationality.

If planning to stay on sites in the popular coastal areas between late spring and October, or in January and February, it is advisable to arrive early in the afternoon or to book in advance.

Although many sites claim to be open all year this cannot be relied on. It is common for many 'all year' sites to open only at weekends during the winter and facilities may be very limited. If planning a visit out of season, always check first.

Motorhomes

A number of local authorities now provide dedicated or short stay areas for motorhomes called 'Áreas de Servicio'.

For details see the websites www.lapaca.org or www.viajarenautocaravana.com for a list of regions and towns in Spain and Andorra which have at least one of these areas.

It is rare that yours will be the only motorhome staying on such areas, but take sensible precautions and avoid any that are isolated.

Some motorhome service points are situated in motorway service areas. Use these only as a last resort and do not be tempted to park overnight. The risk of a break-in is high.

Recent visitors to tourist areas on Spain's Mediterranean coast report that the parking of motorhomes on public roads and, in some instances, in public parking areas, may be prohibited in an effort to discourage 'wild camping'. Specific areas where visitors have encountered this problem include Alicante, Dénia, Palamós and the Murcian coast. Police are frequently in evidence moving parked motorhomes on and it is understood that a number of owners of motorhomes have been fined for parking on sections of the beach belonging to the local authority.

Cycling

There are more than 1,800km of dedicated cycle paths in Spain, many of which follow disused railway tracks. Known as 'Vias Verdes' (Green Ways), they can be found mainly in northern Spain, in Andalucia, around Madrid and inland from the Costa Blanca. For more information see the website www.viasverdes.com or contact the Spanish Tourist Office.

There are cycle lanes in major cities and towns such as Barcelona, Bilbao, Córdoba, Madrid, Seville and Valencia. Madrid alone has over 100km of cycle lanes.

It is compulsory for all cyclists, regardless of age, to wear a safety helmet on all roads outside built-up areas. At night, in tunnels or in bad weather, bicycles must have front and rear lights and reflectors. Cyclists must also wear a reflective waistcoat or jacket while riding at night on roads outside built-up areas (to be visible from a distance of 150 metres) or when visibility is bad.

Strictly speaking, cyclists have right of way when motor vehicles wish to cross their path to turn left or right, but great care should always be taken. Do not proceed unless you are sure that a motorist is giving way.

Transportation of Bicycles
Spanish regulations stipulate that motor cycles or bicycles may be carried on the rear of a vehicle providing the rack to which the motorcycle or bicycle is fastened has been designed for the purpose. Lights, indicators, number plate and any signals made by the driver must not be obscured and the rack should not compromise the carrying vehicle's stability.

An overhanging load, such as bicycles, should not extend beyond the width of the vehicle but may exceed the length of the vehicle by up to 10% (up to 15% in the case of indivisible items). The load must be indicated by a 50cm x 50cm square panel with reflective red and white diagonal stripes. These panels may be purchased in the UK from motorhome or caravan dealers/accessory shops. There is currently no requirement for bicycle racks to be certified or pass a technical inspection.

If you are planning to travel from Spain to Portugal please note that slightly different official regulations apply. These are set out in the Portugal Country Introduction.

Electricity and Gas

The current on campsites should be a minimum of 4 amps but is usually more. Plugs have two round pins. Some campsites do not yet have CEE connections.

Campingaz is widely available in 901 and 907 cylinders. The Cepsa Company sells butane gas cylinders and regulators, which are available in large stores and petrol stations, and the Repsol Company sells butane cylinders at their petrol stations throughout the country.

French and Spanish butane and propane gas cylinders are understood to be widely available in Andorra.

Entry Formalities

Holders of valid British and Irish passports are permitted to stay up to three months without a visa. EU residents planning to stay longer are required to register in person at the Oficina de Extranjeros (Foreigners Office) in their province of residence or at a designated police station. You will be issued with a certificate confirming that the registration obligation has been fulfilled.

Dogs must be kept on a lead in public places and in a car they should be isolated from the driver by means of bars, netting or kept in a transport carrier.

Medical Services

Basic emergency health care is available free from practitioners in the Spanish National Health Service on production of a European Health Insurance Card (EHIC). Some health centres offer both private and state provided health care and you should ensure that staff are aware which service you require. In some parts of the country you may have to travel some distance to attend a surgery or health clinic operating within the state health service. It is probably quicker and more convenient to use a private clinic, but the Spanish health service will not refund any private health care charges.

In an emergency go to the casualty department (urgencias) of any major public hospital. Urgent treatment is free in a public ward on production of an EHIC; for other treatment you will have to pay a proportion of the cost.

Medicines prescribed by health service practitioners can be obtained from a pharmacy (farmacia) and there will be a charge unless you are an EU pensioner. In all major towns there is a 24 hour pharmacy.

Dental treatment is not generally provided under the state system and you will have to pay for treatment.

The Department of Health has two offices in Spain to deal with health care enquiries from British nationals visiting or residing in Spain. These are at the British Consultate offices in Alicante and Málaga, Tel: 965-21 60 22 or 952-35 23 00.

Opening Hours

Banks – Mon-Fri 8.30am/9am-2pm/2.30pm, Sat 9am-1pm (many banks are close Sat during summer).

Museums – Tue-Sat 9am/10am-1pm/2pm & 3pm/4pm-6pm/8pm. Sun 9am/10am-2pm; most close Mon.

Post Offices – Mon-Fri 8.30am-2.30pm & 5pm-8pm/8.30pm, Sat 9am/9.30am-1pm/1.30pm.

Shops – Mon-Sat 9am/10am-1.30pm/2pm & 4pm/4.30pm-8pm/8.30pm; department stores and shopping centres don't close for lunch.

Safety and Security

Street crime exists in many Spanish towns and holiday resorts and is occasionally accompanied by violence. Keep all valuable personal items such as cameras or jewellery out of sight. The authorities have stepped up the police presence in tourist areas but nevertheless, you should remain alert at all times (including at airports, train and bus stations, and even in supermarkets and their car parks).

In Madrid particular care should be taken in the Puerto de Sol and surrounding streets, including the Plaza Mayor, Retiro Park and Lavapies, and on the metro. In Barcelona this advice also applies to the Ramblas, Monjuic, Plaza Catalunya, Port Vell and Olympic Port areas. Be wary of approaches by strangers either asking directions or offering any kind of help. These approaches are sometimes ploys to distract attention while they or their accomplices make off with valuables and/or take note of credit card numbers for future illegal use.

A few incidents have been reported of visitors being approached by a bogus police officer asking to inspect wallets for fake euro notes, or to check their identity by keying their credit card PIN into an official looking piece of equipment carried by the officer. If in doubt ask to see a police officer's official identification, refuse to comply with the request and offer instead to go to the nearest police station.

Spanish police have set up an emergency number for holidaymakers with English speaking staff and offering round the clock assistance - call 902 10 2 112. An English speaking operator will take a statement about the incident, translate it into Spanish and fax or email it to the nearest police station. You still have to report in person to a police station if you have an accident, or have been robbed or swindled, and the helpline operator will advise you where to find the nearest one.

Motorists travelling on motorways – particularly those north and south of Barcelona, in the Alicante region, on the M30, M40 and M50 Madrid ring roads and on the A4 and A5 – should be wary of approaches by bogus policemen in plain clothes travelling in unmarked cars. In all traffic related matters police officers will be in uniform. Unmarked vehicles will have a flashing electronic sign in the rear window reading 'Policía' or 'Guardia Civil' and will normally have blue flashing lights incorporated into their headlights, which are activated when the police stop you.

In non-traffic related matters police officers may be in plain clothes but you have the right to ask to see identification. Genuine officers may ask you to show them your documents but would not request that you hand over your bag or wallet. If in any doubt, converse through the car window and telephone the police on 112 or the Guardia Civil on 062 and ask them for confirmation that the registration number of the vehicle corresponds to an official police vehicle.

On the A7 motorway between the La Junquera and Tarragona toll stations be alert for 'highway pirates' who flag down foreign registered and hire cars (the latter have a distinctive number plate), especially those towing caravans. Motorists are sometimes targeted in service areas, followed and subsequently tricked into stopping on the hard shoulder of the motorway. The usual ploy is for the driver or passenger in a passing vehicle, which may be 'official-looking', to suggest by gesture that there is something seriously wrong with a rear wheel or exhaust pipe (a tyre having been punctured earlier, for example, at a petrol station). The Club has received reports of the involvement of a second vehicle whose occupants also indicate a problem at the rear of your vehicle and gesture that you should pull over onto the hard shoulder. If flagged down by other motorists or a motorcyclist in this way, be extremely wary. Within the Barcelona urban area thieves may also employ the 'punctured tyre' tactic at traffic lights.

In instances such as this, the Spanish Tourist Office advises you not to pull over but to wait until you reach a service area or toll station. If you do get out of your car when flagged down take care it is locked while you check outside, even if someone is left inside. Car keys should never be left in the ignition. Be suspicious when parked in lay-bys or picnic areas, of approaches by other motorists asking for help.

Spain shares with the rest of Europe an underlying threat from terrorism. Attacks could be indiscriminate and against civilian targets in public places including tourist areas.

The Basque terrorist organisation, ETA, has been less active in recent years and on 20 October 2011 announced a "definitive cessation of armed activity." However you should always be vigilant and follow the instructions of local police and other authorities. British nationals are not a specific target for ETA terrorism but attacks could happen in places frequented by tourists.

Coast guards operate a beach flag system to indicate the general safety of beaches for swimming: red – danger / do not enter the water; yellow – take precautions; green – all clear. Coast guards operate on most of the popular beaches, so if in doubt, always ask. During the summer months stinging jellyfish frequent Mediterranean coastal waters.

There is a high risk of forest fires during the hottest months and you should avoid camping in areas with limited escape routes. Take care to avoid actions that could cause a fire, e.g. careless disposal of cigarette ends. It is possible that the Spanish government will introduce a total prohibition on the lighting of fires (including barbecues) in forest areas throughout Spain. Respect Spanish laws and customs. Parents should be aware that Spanish law defines anyone under the age of 18 as a minor, subject to parental control or adult supervision. Any unaccompanied minor coming to the attention of the local authorities for whatever reason is deemed to be vulnerable under the law and faces being taken into a minors centre for protection until a parent or suitable guardian can be found.

British Embassy & Consulate-General
TORRE ESPACIO, PASEO DE LA CASTELLANA 259D
28046 MADRID
Tel: 917 14 63 00
http://ukinspain.fco.gov.uk/en/

British Consulate-General
AVDA DIAGONAL 477-13, 08036 BARCELONA
Tel: 902 109 356

There are also British Consulates in Bilbao, Alicante and Málaga.

Irish Embassy
IRELAND HOUSE, PASEO DE LA CASTELLANA 46-4
28046 MADRID
Tel: 914 36 40 93
www.embassyofireland.es

There are also Irish Honorary Consulates in Alicante, Barcelona, Bilbao, El Ferrol, Málaga and Seville.

Customs Regulations

Alcohol and Tobacco
Under Spanish law the number of cigarettes which may be exported from Spain is set at eight hundred. Anything above this amount is regarded as a trade transaction which must be accompanied by the required documentation. Travellers caught with more than 800 cigarettes face seizure of the cigarettes and a large fine.

Documents

Driving Licence

The British EU format pink driving licence is recognised in Spain. Holders of the old style all green driving licence are advised to replace it with a photocard version. Alternatively, the old style licence may be accompanied by an International Driving Permit available from the AA, the RAC or selected Post Offices.

Passport

Visitors must be able to show some form of identity if requested to do so by the police and you should carry your passport or photocard licence at all times.

Vehicle(s)

When driving in Spain it is compulsory at all times to carry your driving licence, vehicle registration certificate (V5C), insurance certificate and MOT certificate (if applicable). Vehicles imported by a person other than the owner must have a letter of authority from the owner.

Money

All bank branches offer foreign currency exchange, as do many hotels and travel agents.

The major credit cards are widely accepted as a means of payment in shops, restaurants and petrol stations. Smaller retail outlets in non commercial areas may not accept payments by credit card – check before buying. When shopping carry your passport or photocard driving licence if paying with a credit card as you will almost certainly be asked for photographic proof of identity.

Keep a supply of loose change as you could be asked for it frequently in shops and at kiosks.

Motoring in Spain

Drivers should take particular care as driving standards can be erratic, e.g. excessive speed and dangerous overtaking, and the accident rate is higher than in the UK. Pedestrians should take particular care when crossing roads (even at zebra crossings) or walking along unlit roads at night.

Accidents

The Central Traffic Department runs an assistance service for victims of traffic accidents linked to an emergency telephone network along motorways and some roads. Motorists in need of help should ask for 'auxilio en carretera' (road assistance). The special ambulances used are connected by radio to hospitals participating in the scheme.

It is not necessary to call the emergency services in case of light injuries. A European Accident Statement should be completed and signed by both parties and, if conditions allow, photos of the vehicles and the location should be taken. If one of the drivers involved does not want to give his/her details, the other should call the police or Guardia Civil.

Alcohol

The maximum permitted level of alcohol is 50 milligrams in 100 millilitres of blood, i.e. less than in the UK (80 milligrams) and it reduces to 30 milligrams for drivers with less than two years experience, drivers of vehicles with more than 8 passenger seats and for drivers of vehicles over 3,500kg. After a traffic accident all road users involved have to undergo a breath test. Penalties for refusing a test or exceeding the legal limit are severe and may include immobilisation of vehicles, a large fine and suspension of your driving licence This limit applies to cyclists as well as drivers of private vehicles.

Breakdown Service

The motoring organisation, Real Automóvil Club de España (RACE), operates a breakdown service and assistance may be obtained 24 hours a day by telephoning the national centre in Madrid on 915 94 93 47. After hearing a message in Spanish press the number 1 to access the control room where English is spoken.

RACE's breakdown vehicles are blue and yellow and display the words 'RACE Asistencia' on the sides. This service provides on the spot minor repairs and towing to the nearest garage. Charges vary according to type of vehicle and time of day, but payment for road assistance must be made in cash.

Essential Equipment

Lights

Dipped headlights is now compulsory for all vehicles on all roads at night and in tunnels. Bulbs are more likely to fail with constant use and you are recommended to carry spares.

Dipped headlights must be used at all times on 'special' roads, e.g. temporary routes created at the time of road works such as the hard shoulder, or in a contra-flow lane.

Headlight flashing is only allowed to warn other road users about an accident or a road hazard, or to let the vehicle in front know that you intend to overtake.

Reflective Jacket/Waistcoat

If your vehicle is immobilised on the carriageway outside a built-up area at night, or in poor visibility, you must wear a reflective jacket or waistcoat when getting out of your vehicle. This rule also applies to passengers who may leave the vehicle, for example, to assist with a repair.

Reflectors/Marker Boards for Caravans

Any vehicle or vehicle combination, i.e. car plus caravan over 12 metres in length, must display at the rear of the towed vehicle two aluminium boards. These must have a yellow centre with a red outline, must be reflective and comply with ECE70 standards. These must be positioned between 50cm and 150cm off the ground and must be 500mm x 250mm or 565mm x 200mm in size. Alternatively a single horizontal reflector may be used measuring 1300mm x 250mm or 1130mm x 200mm.

To buy these aluminium marker boards (under Spanish regulations stickers are not acceptable) contact www.hgvdirect.co.uk, tel: 0845 6860008. Contact your local dealer or caravan manufacturer for advice on fitting them to your caravan.

Warning Triangles

All vehicles must carry warning triangles. They should be placed 50 metres behind and in front of broken down vehicles.

Child Restraint System

Children under the age of 12 years old and under the height of 1.35m must use a suitable child restraint system adapted for their size and weight (this does not apply in taxis in urban areas). Children measuring more than 1.35m in height may use an adult seatbelt.

Fuel

Credit cards are accepted at most petrol stations, but you should be prepared to pay cash if necessary in remote areas.

LPG (Autogas) can be purchased from some Repsol filling stations. Details of approximately 33 sales outlets throughout mainland Spain can be found on www.spainautogas.com.

Mountain Passes and Tunnels

Some passes are occasionally blocked in winter following heavy falls of snow. Check locally for information on road conditions.

Parking

Parking regulations vary depending on the area of a city or town, the time of day, the day of the week, and whether the date is odd or even. In many towns parking is permitted on one side of the street for the first half of the month and on the other side for the second half of the month. Signs marked '1-15' or '16-31' indicate these restrictions.

Yellow road markings indicate parking restrictions. Parking should be in the same direction as the traffic flow in one way streets or on the right hand side when there is two way traffic. Illegally parked vehicles may be towed away or clamped but, despite this, you will frequently encounter double and triple parking.

In large cities parking meters have been largely replaced by ticket machines and these are often located in areas known as 'zona azul', i.e. blue zones. The maximum period of parking is usually one and a half hours between 8am and 9pm. In the centre of some towns there is a 'zona O.R.A.' where parking is permitted for up to 90 minutes against tickets bought in tobacconists and other retail outlets.

In many small towns and villages it is advisable to park on the edge of town and walk to the centre, as many towns can be difficult to navigate due to narrow, congested streets.

Madrid

In Madrid, there is a regulated parking zone where parking spaces are shown by blue or green lines (called SER). Parking is limited to 1 or 2 hours in these areas for visitors and can be paid by means of ticket machines of by mobile phone.

Pedestrians

Jaywalking is not permitted. Pedestrians may not cross a road unless a traffic light is at red against the traffic, or a policeman gives permission. Offenders may be fined.

Priority and Overtaking

As a general rule traffic coming from the right has priority at intersections. When entering a main road from a secondary road drivers must give way to traffic from both directions. Traffic already on a roundabout (i.e. from the left) has priority over traffic joining it. Trams and emergency vehicles have priority at all times over other road users and you must not pass trams that are stationary while letting passengers on or off.

Motorists must give way to cyclists on a cycle lane, cycle crossing or other specially designated cycle track. They must also give way to cyclists when turning left or right.

You must use your indicators when overtaking. If a vehicle comes up behind you signalling that it wants to overtake and if the road ahead is clear, you must use your right indicator to acknowledge the situation.

Roads

There are approximately 14,000km of highways and dual carriageways. Roads marked AP (autopista) are generally toll roads and roads marked A (autovía) or N (nacional) are dual carriageways with motorway characteristics – but not necessarily with a central reservation – and are toll-free. In recent years some major national roads have been upgraded to Autovías and, therefore, have two identifying codes or have changed codes, e.g. the N-I from Madrid to Irún near the French border is now known as the A1 or Autovía del Norte. Autovías are often as fast as autopistas and are generally more scenic.

Roads managed by regional or local authorities are prefixed with the various identification letters such as C, CV, GR, L or T.

All national roads and roads of interest to tourists are generally in good condition, are well signposted, and driving is normally straightforward. Hills often tend to be longer and steeper than in parts of the UK and some of the coastal roads are very winding, so traffic flows at the speed of the slowest lorry.

As far as accidents are concerned the N340 coast road, especially between Málaga and Fuengirola, is notorious, as are the Madrid ring roads, and special vigilance is necessary.

Road humps are making an appearance on Spanish roads and recent visitors report that they may be high, putting low stabilisers at risk.

Andorra

The main road to Barcelona from Andorra is the C14/C1412/N141b via Ponts and Calaf. It has a good surface and avoids any high passes. The N260 along the south side of Andorra via Puigcerda and La Seo de Urgel also has a good surface.

Road Signs and Markings

Road signs conform to international standards. Lines and markings are white. Place names may appear both in standard (Castilian) Spanish and in a local form, e.g. Gerona/Girona, San Sebastián/Donostia, Jávea/Xàbio, and road atlases and maps usually show both.

You may encounter the following signs:

Spanish	English Translation
Carretera de peaje	Toll road
Ceda el paso	Give way
Cuidado	Caution
Curva peligrosa	Dangerous bend
Despacio	Slow
Desviación	Detour
Dirección única	One-way street
Embotellamiento	Traffic jam

Spanish	English Translation
Estacionamiento prohibido	No parking
Estrechamiento	Narrow lane
Gravillas	Loose chippings/gravel
Inicio	Start
Obras	Roadworks
Paso prohibido	No entry
Peligro	Danger
Prioridad	Right of way
Salida	Exit
Todas direcciones	All directions

Many non motorway roads have a continuous white line on the near (verge) side of the carriageway. Any narrow lane between this line and the side of the carriageway is intended primarily for pedestrians and cyclists and not for use as a hard shoulder.

A continuous line also indicates 'no stopping' even if it is possible to park entirely off the road and it should be treated as a double white line and not crossed except in a serious emergency. If your vehicle breaks down on a road where there is a continuous white line along the verge, it should not be left unattended as this is illegal and an on the spot fine may be levied.

Many road junctions have a continuous white centre line along the main road. This line must not be crossed to execute a left turn, despite the lack of any other 'no left turn' signs. If necessary, drive on to a 'cambio de sentido' (change of direction) sign to turn.

Traffic police are keen to enforce both the above regulations.

Watch out for traffic lights which may be mounted high above the road and hard to spot. The international three colour traffic light system is used in Spain. Green, amber and red arrows are used on traffic lights at some intersections.

Speed Limits

	Open Road (km/h)	Motorway (km/h)
Car Solo	90-100	120
Car towing caravan/trailer	70-80	80
Motorhome under 3500kg	70-80	90
Motorhome 3500-7500kg	70-80	90

In built-up areas speed is limited to 50km/h (31mph) except where signs indicate a lower limit. Reduce your speed to 20km/h (13mph) in residential areas. On motorways and dual carriageways in built-up areas, speed is limited to 80km/h (50mph) except where indicated by signs.

Outside built-up areas motorhomes under 3500kg are limited to 100km/h (62mph) and those over 3500kg are limited to 90km/h (56 mph) on motorways and dual carriageways. On other main roads motorhomes under 3500kg are limited to 80-90km/h (50-56mph) and those over 3500kg are limited to 80km/h (50mph)

It is prohibited to own, transport or use radar detectors.

Foreign Registered Vehicles

When a radar camera detects a foreign registered vehicle exceeding the speed limit, a picture of the vehicle and its number plate will be sent not only to the relevant traffic department, but also to the nearest Guardia Civil mobile patrol. The patrol will then stop the speeding vehicle and impose an on the spot fine which non-residents must pay immediately, otherwise the vehicle will be confiscated until the fine is paid.

This is to prevent offenders flouting the law and avoiding paying their fines, as pursuing them is proving costly and complicated for the Spanish authorities.

Towing

Motorhomes are prohibited from towing a car unless the car is on a special towing trailer with all four wheels of the car off the ground.

Any towing combination in excess of 10 metres in length must keep at least 50 metres from the vehicle in front except in built-up areas, on roads where overtaking is prohibited, or where there are several lanes in the same direction.

Traffic Jams

Roads around the large cities such as Madrid, Barcelona, Zaragoza, Valencia and Seville are extremely busy on Friday afternoons when residents leave for the mountains or coast, and again on Sunday evenings when they return. The coastal roads along the Costa Brava and the Costa Dorada may also be congested. The coast road south of Torrevieja is frequently heavily congested as a result of extensive holiday home construction.

Summer holidays extend from mid June to mid September and the busiest periods are the last weekend in July, the first weekend in August and the period around the Assumption holiday in mid August.

Traffic jams occur on the busy AP7 from the French border to Barcelona during the peak summer holiday period. An alternative route now exists from Malgrat de Mar along the coast to Barcelona using the C32 where tolls are lower than on the AP7.

The Autovía de la Cataluña Central (C25) provides a rapid east-west link between Gerona and Lleida via Vic, Manresa and Tàrrega. There is fast access from Madrid to La Coruña in the far north-west via the A6/AP6.

Information on road conditions, traffic delays, etc can be found on http://infocar.dgt.es/etraffic.

Violation of Traffic Regulations

The police are empowered to impose on the spot fines. Visiting motorists must pay immediately otherwise a vehicle will be confiscated until the fine is paid. An official receipt should be obtained. An appeal may be made within 15 days and there are instructions on the back of the receipt in English. RACE can provide legal advice – tel: 902 40 45 45.

Motorways

The Spanish motorway system has been subject to considerable expansion in recent years with more motorways under construction or planned. The main sections are along the Mediterranean coast, across the north of the country and around Madrid. Tolls are charged on most autopistas but many sections are toll-free, as are autovias. Exits on autopistas are numbered consecutively from Madrid. Exits on autovias are numbered according to the kilometre point from Madrid.

Many different companies operate within the motorway network, each setting their own tolls which may vary according to the time of day and classification of vehicles. For an overview of the motorway network (in English) see www.aseta.es. This website has links to the numerous motorway companies where you will be able to view routes and tolls (generally shown in Spanish only). Tolls are payable in cash or by credit card.

Avoid signposted 'Via T' lanes showing a circular sign with a white capital T on a blue background where toll collection is by electronic device only. Square 'Via T' signs are displayed above mixed lanes where other forms of payment are also accepted.

Rest areas with parking facilities, petrol stations and restaurants or cafés are strategically placed and are well signposted. Emergency telephones are located at 2km intervals.

Motorway signs near Barcelona are confusing. To avoid the city traffic when heading south, follow signs for Barcelona, but the moment signs for Tarragona appear follow these and ignore Barcelona signs.

Touring

A fixed price menu or 'menú del dia' invariably offers good value. Service is generally included in restaurant bills but a tip of approximately €1 per person up to 10% of the bill is appropriate if you have received good service. Smoking is not allowed in indoor public places, including bars, restaurants and cafés.

Spain is one of the world's top wine producers, enjoying a great variety of high quality wines of which cava, rioja and sherry are probably the best known. Local beer is low in alcohol content and is generally drunk as an aperitif to accompany tapas.

Perhaps due to the benign climate and long hours of sunshine, Spaniards tend to get up later and stay out later at night than their European neighbours. Out of the main tourist season and in 'non-touristy' areas it may be difficult to find a restaurant open in the evening before 9pm.

Taking a siesta is still common practice, although it is now usual for businesses to stay open during the traditional siesta hours.

Spain's many different cultural and regional influences are responsible for the variety and originality of fiestas held each year. Over 200 have been classified as 'of interest to tourists' while others have gained international fame, such as La Tomatina mass tomato throwing battle held each year in August in Buñol near Valencia. A full list of fiestas can be obtained from the Spanish Tourist Office, www.spain.info/uk or from provincial tourist offices. In addition, every year each town celebrates its local Saint's Day which is always a very happy and colourful occasion.

The Madrid Card, valid for one, two or three days, gives free use of public transport, free entry to various attractions and museums, including the Prado, Reina Sofia and Thyssen-Bornemisza collection, as well as free tours and discounts at restaurants and shows. You can buy the card from www.madridcard.com or by visiting the City Tourist Office in Plaza Mayor, or on Madrid Visión tour buses. Similar generous discounts can be obtained with the Barcelona Card, valid from two to five days, which can be purchased from tourist offices or online at www.barcelonaturisme.com. Other tourist cards are available in Burgos, Córdoba, Seville and Zaragoza.

The region of Valencia and the Balearic Islands are prone to severe storms and torrential rainfall between September and November and are probably best avoided at that time. Monitor national and regional weather on www.wmo.int.

Gibraltar

For information on Gibraltar contact:
GIBRALTAR GOVERNMENT TOURIST OFFICE
150 STRAND, LONDON WC2R 1JA
Tel: 020 7836 0777
www.gibraltar.gov.uk
info@gibraltar.gov.uk

There are no campsites on the Rock, the nearest being at San Roque and La Línea de la Concepción in Spain. The only direct access to Gibraltar from Spain is via the border at La Línea which is open 24 hours a day. You may cross on foot and it is also possible to take cars or motorhomes to Gibraltar.

A valid British passport is required for all British nationals visiting Gibraltar. Nationals of other countries should check entry requirements with the Gibraltar Government Tourist Office.

There is currently no charge for visitors to enter Gibraltar but Spanish border checks can cause delays and you should be prepared for long queues. As roads in the town are extremely narrow and bridges low, it is advisable to park on the outskirts. Visitors advise against leaving vehicles on the Spanish side of the border owing to the high risk of break-ins.

An attraction to taking the car into Gibraltar includes English style supermarkets and a wide variety of competitively priced goods free of VAT. The currency is sterling and British notes and coins circulate alongside Gibraltar pounds and pence, but note that Gibraltar notes and coins are not accepted in the UK. Scottish and Northern Irish notes are not generally accepted in Gibraltar. Euros are accepted but the exchange rate may not be favourable.

Disabled visitors to Gibraltar may obtain a temporary parking permit from the police station on production of evidence confirming their disability. This permit allows parking for up to two hours (between 8am and 10pm) in parking places reserved for disabled people.

Violence or street crime is rare but there have been reports of people walking from La Línea to Gibraltar at night being attacked and robbed.

If you need emergency medical attention while on a visit to Gibraltar, treatment at primary healthcare centres is free to UK passport holders under the local medical scheme. Non UK nationals need a European Health Insurance Card (EHIC). You are not eligible for free treatment if you go to Gibraltar specifically to be treated for a condition which arose elsewhere, e.g in Spain.

Public Transport

Madrid boasts an extensive and efficient public transport network including a metro system, suburban railways and bus routes. You can purchase a pack of ten tickets which offer better value than single tickets. In addition, tourist travel passes for use on all public transport are available from metro stations, tourist offices and travel agencies and are valid for one to seven days – you will need to present your passport when buying them. Single tickets must be validated before travel. For more information see www.ctm-madrid.es.

Metro systems also operate in Barcelona, Bilbao, Seville and Valencia and a few cities operate tram services including La Coruña, Valencia, Barcelona and Bilbao.
The Valencia service links Alicante, Benidorm and Dénia.

Various operators run year round ferry services from Spain to North Africa, the Balearic Islands and the Canary Islands. All enquiries should be made through their UK agent:

SOUTHERN FERRIES
22 SUSSEX STREET, LONDON SW1V 4RW
Tel: 0844 8157785, Fax: 0844 815 7795
www.southernferries.co.uk
mail@southernferries.co.uk

Park Guell, Barcelona

ABEJAR *3C1* (800m NW Rural) *41.81645, -2.78869*
Camping El Concurso, Ctra Abejar-Molinos de Duero s/n, Km 1, N234, 42146 Abejar (Soria) [975-37 33 61; fax 975-37 33 96; info@campingelconcurso.com; www. campingelconcurso.com] N234 W fr Soria to Abejar. Turn onto rd CL117 dir Molinos de Duero, site on L. Lge, mkd pitch, pt sl, pt shd; wc; chem disp; mv service pnt; shwrs inc; el pnts (5A) inc; gas; lndtte; shop & 500m; tradsmn; rest, snacks; bar; BBQ; playgrnd; pool; paddling pool; lake 2km; some statics; dogs; phone; poss cr & noisy in ssn; ccard acc; CKE/CCI. "Nr lake & National Park; v beautiful; gd san facs; not suitable m'van due slope." ◆ ltd Easter-12 Oct. € 19.50   2009*

"There aren't many sites open at this time of year"

If you're travelling outside peak season remember to call ahead to check site opening dates – even if the entry says 'open all year'

ABIZANDA *3B2* (5km N Rural) *42.28087, 0.19740*
Fundación Ligüerre de Cinca, Ctra A138, Km 28, 22393 Abizanda (Huesca) [974-50 08 00; fax 974-50 08 30; info@ liguerredecinca.com; www.liguerredecinca.com] A138 N fr Barbastro, site sp at km 29, or S fr Ainsa site sp at km 27, 18km S of Ainsa. Med, hdg/mkd pitch, terr, shd; wc; chem disp; shwrs inc; baby rm; el pnts (10A) inc; gas; lndtte; shop, rest, snacks, bar high ssn; playgrnd; pool; lake sw 1km; watersports; tennis; cycle hire; games rm; horseriding; car wash; 10% statics; dogs; phone; poss cr; Eng spkn; adv bkg; quiet; ccard acc; red long stay; CKE/CCI. "Excel facs, ltd low ssn; highly rec; site in 2 parts sep by ravine, bottom terr muddy in wet; trees may be diff for lge o'fits; helpful staff; lovely site; nearest shops at Ainsa; conv Ordesa & Monte Perdido National Park." € 29.00   2010*

AGER *3B2* (300m W Rural) *42.00277, 0.76472* **Camping Val d'Àger, Calle Afores s/n, 25691 Ager (Lleida) [973-45 52 00; fax 973-45 52 02; iniciatives@valldager.com; www.campingvalldager.com/]** Fr C13 turn W onto L904/ C12 twd L'Ametlla & Àger. Cross Rv Noguera, site sp on L. Med, terr, pt shd; wc; chem disp; shwrs inc; el pnts €5.70; lndtte; shop & 800m; rest, snacks; bar; BBQ; playgrnd; pool high ssn; paddling pool; games area; games rm; wifi; some statics; dogs €3.60; adv bkg; quiet. "Mountain views; high o'fits rec to park nr recep (due trees); vg, peaceful site." ◆ € 22.00   2009*

AGUILAR DE CAMPOO *1B4* (27.8km SW Rural) *42.58977, - 4.33260* **Camping Fuente De Los Caños, Fuente Los Canos,34400 Herrera De Pisuerga (Palencia) [639- 81 34 69]** Fr N take A67 take exit mkd Herrera de Pisuerga a Olmos de Ojeda/P-227, turn R onto Av de Eusebio Salvador Merino, turn R onto Lugar de la Fuente los Canos, site will be on the L. Sm site; pt shd; chem disp; wc; shwr; el pts (3A); rv adj; lndry rm; playgrnd; pool; fishing; cycle hire; walking. "Suitable for a NH." € 19.00   2011*

AGUILAR DE CAMPOO *1B4* (3km W Rural) *42.78694, -4.30222* **Monte Royal Camping, Carretera Virgen del Llano 34800 Aguilar de Campóo (Palencia) [979-18 10 07; info@campingmonteroyal.com; www. campingmonteroyal.com]** App site fr S on N611 fr Palencia. At Aguilar de Campóo turn W at S end of rv bdge at S end of town. Site on L in 3km; sp at edge of reservoir. Fr N take 3rd exit fr rndabt on N611. Do not tow thro town. Lge, mkd pitch, pt sl, shd; wc; chem disp (wc); baby facs; shwrs €0.60; el pnts (6A) inc; gas; lndtte; shops 3km; rest in ssn; bar; playgrnd; sand beach nr lake; watersports; horseriding; fishing; TV; 20% statics; dogs; phone; ccard acc; CKE/CCI. "Useful, peaceful NH 2 hrs fr Santander; ltd/basic facs low ssn & poss stretched high ssn - in need of maintenance (2010); barking dogs poss problem; friendly staff; gd walking, cycling & birdwatching in National Park; unrel opening dates low ssn." ◆ € 22.00   2014*

AGUILAS *4G1* (4km NE Rural) *37.42638, -1.55083* **Camping Águilas, Ctra Cabo Cope, Los Geráneos, 30880 Águilas (Murcia) [968-41 92 05; fax 968-41 92 82; info@ campingaguilas.es; www.campingaguilas.es]** Fr A7 N of Lorca take C3211 dir Águilas. On joining N332 turn L & foll sp L to Calabardina/Cabo Cope; site on L within 3km. Med, mkd pitch, hdstg, pt shd; wc; chem disp; mv service pnt; shwrs inc; el pnts (10A) €5; gas; lndtte; shop high ssn; rest, snacks; bar; playgrnd; pool; sand beach 4km; tennis; wifi; 30% statics; dogs €1; phone; site poss clsd last 2 weeks May & Sep; Eng spkn; adv bkg; quiet; red low ssn/long stay; ccard acc; red low ssn; CKE/CCI. "All pitches shaded with trees or netting; clean facs; helpful staff; popular winter long stay; excel." € 39.00   2010*

"That's changed – Should I let The Club know?"

If you find something on site that's different from the site entry, fill in a report and let us know. See www.caravanclub.co.uk/europereport.

AGUILAS *4G1* (2km SW Coastal) *37.3925, -1.61111* **Camping Bellavista, Ctra de Vera, Km 3, 30880 Águilas (Murcia) [tel/fax 968-44 91 51; info@campingbellavista. com; www.campingbellavista]** Site on N332 Águilas to Vera rd on R at top of sh, steep hill, 100m after R turn to El Cocon. Well mkd by flags. Fr S by N332 on L 400m after fuel stn, after v sharp corner. Sm, hdg pitch, hdstg, pt sl, pt shd; wc; chem disp; mv service pnt; shwrs inc; el pnts (10A) €5.20 or metered; gas; lndtte (inc dryer); sm shop; tradsmn; rest adj; snacks; BBQ; playgrnd; pool; sand beach 300m; cycle hire; wifi; some statics; dogs €2.50; poss cr; Eng spkn; adv bkg; quiet; ccard acc; red long stay/low ssn; CKE/CCI. "Gd autumn/winter stay; clean, tidy site with excel facs; ltd pitches for lge o'fits; helpful owner; fine views; rd noise at 1 end; excel town & vg beaches; v secure site." € 33.65   2014*

Check any essential information with the site before you travel   *Last year of report   **111**

⊞ **AINSA** *3B2* (2.5km N Rural) *42.43555, 0.13583* **Camping Peña Montañesa, Ctra Ainsa-Bielsa, Km 2.3, 22360 Labuerda (Huesca) [974-50 00 32; fax 974-50 09 91; info@ penamontanesa.com; www.penamontanesa.com]** E fr Huesca on N240 for approx 50km, turn N onto N123 just after Barbastro twd Ainsa. In 8km turn onto A138 N for Ainsa & Bielsa. Or fr Bielsa Tunnel to A138 S to Ainsa & Bielsa, site sp. NB: Bielsa Tunnel sometimes clsd bet Oct & Easter due to weather. Lge, mkd pitch, shd; htd wc; chem disp; mv service pnt; baby facs; sauna; shwrs inc; el pnts (6A) inc; gas; lndtte (inc dryer); supmkt; rest, snacks; bar; BBQ (gas/elec only); playgrnd; htd pools (1 covrd); lake sw 2km; fishing; canoeing; tennis; cycle hire; horseriding; games area; games rm; wifi; entmnt; TV; 30% statics; dogs €4.25; no c'vans/m'vans over 10m; phone; adv bkg; quiet, poss some noise fr local festival mid-Aug; ccard acc; red low ssn; CKE/CCI. "Situated by fast-flowing rv; v friendly staff; Eng spkn; gd, clean san facs; pitching poss diff due trees; nr beautiful medieval town of Ainsa & Ordesa National Park; excel." ♦ € 39.00 SBS - E12   2014*

See advertisement

AINSA *3B2* (10km N Rural) *42.50916, 0.12777* **Camping Valle de Añisclo, Ctra Añisclo, Km 2, 22363 Puyarruego (Huesca) [974-50 50 96; info@valleanisclo.com; www. staragon.com/campingvalleanisclo/]** N fr Ainsa on A138, at Escalona turn L onto HU631 dir Puyarruego. In 2km cross bdge, site on R at ent to vill. Med, mkd pitch, pt sl, pt shd; htd wc; chem disp; mv service pnt; baby facs; shwrs inc; el pnts (6A) €4.55; lndtte; shop; rest, snacks; bar; playgrnd; rv adj; wifi; poss €1.65; phone; Eng spkn; adv bkg; quiet; red low ssn. "Excel walking & birdwatching - nightingales; helpful owners; excel." Easter-15 Oct. € 19.00   2011*

AINSA *3B2* (1km E Rural) *42.41944, 0.15111* **Camping Ainsa, Ctra Ainsa-Campo, 22330 Ainsa (Huesca) [974-50 02 60; fax 974-50 03 61; info@campingainsa.com; www.campingainsa.com]** Fr Ainsa take N260 E dir Pueyo de Araguás, cross rv bdge, site sp L in 200m. Foll lane to site. Sm, terr, pt shd; wc; baby facs; shwrs inc; el pnts €4.75; gas; lndtte; shop 1km; rest, snacks bar high ssn; playgrnd; pool; games rm; wifi; TV; 50% statics; dogs €2.20; phone; poss cr; some indus noise mornings; ccard acc; red low ssn; CKE/CCI. "Pleasant, welcoming, well-maintained site; fine view of old city & some pitches mountain views; vg san facs; not suitable lge o'fits; gd pool." Holy Week-30 Oct. € 24.25   2014*

⊞ **AINSA** *3B2* (6km NW Rural) *42.43004, 0.07881* **Camping Boltaña, Ctra N260, Km 442, Ctra Margudgued, 22340 Boltaña (Huesca) [974-50 23 47; fax 974-50 20 23; info@ campingboltana.com; www.campingboltana.com]** Fr Ainsa head twd Boltaña, turn L over rv & foll sp. Site is 2km E of Boltaña, final 300m on single track rd. Med, mkd pitch, pt sl, terr, pt shd; htd wc; chem disp; mv service pnt; baby facs; shwrs inc; el pnts (4-10A) €6.40; gas; lndtte (inc dryer); shop & 2km; tradsmn; rest, snacks; bar; playgrnd; pool; paddling pool; fishing 600m; tennis 1km; cycle hire; horseriding 500m; games area; cycle hire; adventure sports; wifi; 30% statics; dogs €3.25; phone; clsd 15 Dec-15 Jan; poss cr; Eng spkn; adv bkg; poss noisy; ccard acc; red low ssn. "Conv Ordesa National Park; san facs stretched high ssn; friendly, helpful staff; Ainsa old town worth visit; excel." ♦ ltd € 29.00 (CChq acc)   2010*

ALBANYA *3B3* (2.4km W Rural) *42.30630, 2.70970* **Camping Bassegoda Park, Camí Camp de l'Illa, 17733 Albanyà (Gerona) [972-54 20 20; fax 972-54 20 21; info@ bassegodapark.com; www.bassegodapark.com]** Fr France exit AP7/E15 junc 3 onto GI510 to Albanyà. At end of rd turn R, site on rvside. Fr S exit AP7 junc 4 dir Terrades, then Albanyà. App poss diff for lge o'fits. Med, hdg pitch, hdstg, pt shd; htd wc; chem disp; mv waste; baby facs; shwrs inc; el pnts (10A) €6.75; lndtte (inc dryer); shop; tradsmn; rest, snacks; bar; BBQ; playgrnd; pool; fishing; trekking; hill walking; mountain biking; cycle hire; games area; games rm; wifi; entmnt; TV rm; 8% statics; dogs €4.75 (1 only); phone; Eng spkn; adv bkg; quiet; ccard add; red low ssn/snr citizens/CKE/CCI. "Excel site surrounded by woods, rvs & streams; excel san facs; well worth a detour." ♦ 1 Mar-11 Dec. € 28.65 (CChq acc)   2010*

ALBARRACIN *3D1* (2km E Rural) *40.41228, -1.42788* **Camp Municipal Ciudad de Albarracín, Camino de Gea s/n, 44100 Albarracín (Teruel) [tel/fax 978-71 01 97 or 657-49 84 33 (mob); campingalbarracin5@hotmail.com; www. campingalbarracin.com]** Fr Teruel take A1512 to Albarracín. Go thro vill, foll camping sps. Med, mkd pitch, pt sl, pt shd; wc; chem disp; baby facs; shwrs inc; el pnts (16A) €3.85; gas; lndtte; shop & adj; tradsmn; snacks; bar; BBQ; playgrnd; pool adj in ssn; wifi; some statics; dogs; phone; poss cr; adv bkg; quiet; ccard acc; CKE/CCI. "Gd site; immac san facs; narr pitches poss diff for lge o'fits; sports cent adj; gd touring base & gd walking fr site; rec; friendly staff." 15 Mar-3 Nov. € 16.00   2013*

ALBERCA, LA *1D3* (2km N Rural) *40.50915, -6.12312*
**Camping Al-Bereka, Ctra Salamanca-La Alberca, Km
75.6, 37624 La Alberca (Salamanca) [923-41 51 95; www.
albereka.com]** Fr Salamanca S on N630/E803 take C515 to
Mogarraz, then SA202 to La Alberca. Site on L at km 75.6 bef
vill. Rte fr Ciudad Real OK but bumpy in places. Med, mkd
pitch, terr, shd; wc; chem disp; shwrs inc; el pnts (3-6A) €3.50;
Indtte; shop; rest, snacks; bar; BBQ; playgrnd; pool; paddling
pool; TV; some statics; dogs; quiet; ccard acc; CKE/CCI. "Gd,
quiet site; helpful owner; beautiful countryside; La Alberca
medieval vill with abbey." ♦ 15 Mar-31 Oct. € 21.40   2009*

ALBERCA, LA *1D3* (6km N Rural) *40.52112, -6.13756*
**Camping Sierra de Francia, Ctra Salamanca-La Alberca,
Km 73, 37623 El Caserito (Salamanca) [923-45 40 81; fax
923-45 40 01; info@campingsierradefrancia.com; www.
campingsierradefrancia.com]** Fr Cuidad Rodrigo take C515.
Turn R at El Cabaco, site on L in approx 2km. Med, hdg/mkd
pitch, shd; wc; shwrs; mv service pnt; el pnts (3-6A) €3.75; gas;
Indtte; shop; rest; bar; BBQ; playgrnd; pool; paddling pool;
cycle hire; horseriding; wifi; some statics; dogs free; quiet;
ccard acc. "Conv 'living history' vill of La Alberca & Monasterio
San Juan de la Peña; excel views." ♦ ltd Holy Week-15 Sep.
€ 18.40   2009*

⊞ **ALCALA DE LOS GAZULES** *2H3* (4km E Rural) *36.46403,
-5.66482* **Camping Los Gazules, Ctra de Patrite, Km 4,
11180 Alcalá de los Gazules (Cádiz) [956-42 04 86; fax
956-42 03 88; camping@losgazules.e.telefonica.net;
www.campinglosgazules.com]** Fr N exit A381 at 1st junc to
Alcalá, proceed thro town to 1st rndabt & turn L onto A375/
A2304 dir Ubriqu, site sp strt ahead in 1km onto CA2115
dir Patrite on v sharp L. Fr S exit A381 at 1st sp for Acalá. At
rndabt turn R onto A375/A2304 dir Ubrique. Then as above.
Med, mkd pitch, pt sl, pt shd; wc; chem disp (wc); mv service
pnt; shwrs inc; el pnts (10A) €5.25 (poss rev pol); Indtte; shop;
rest; bar; playgrnd; pool; cycle hire; TV rm; 90% statics; dog
€2; phone; adv bkg; red long stay/low ssn; CKE/CCI. "Well-
maintained, upgraded site; take care canopy frames; sm pitches
& tight turns & kerbs on site; friendly, helpful staff; ltd facs
low ssn; ltd touring pitches; attractive town with v narr rds,
leave car in park at bottom & walk; gd walking, birdwatching."
€ 34.85   2013*

⊞ **ALCANAR** *3D2* (4km NE Coastal) *40.53986, 0.52071*
**Camping Estanyet, Paseo del Marjal s/n 43870, Les
Cases d'Alcanar (Catalonia) [tel/fax 977-73 72 68; http://
fr.campings.com/camping-estanyet-les-cases-dalcanar/]**
Leave Alcanar to N340 at ILes Cases D'Alcanar foll camping
signs. Fr AP7 Junc 41 fr N or Junc 43 fr S. Med, hdg pitch;
hdstg; pt shd; htd wc; chem disp (wc); shwrs inc; baby facs;
el pnts (10A) €6.50; Indtte; ltd shop high ssn; tradsmn; rest,
snacks; bar; BBQ (charcoal); playgrnd; pool high ssn; shgl beach
adj; 10% statics; phone; dogs €3.50; poss cr; adv bkg; ccard
acc; CKE/CCI. "Gd; friendly owners; but ltd facs esp low ssn."
1 Apr-30 Sep. € 40.42   2013*

⊞ **ALCARAZ** *4F1* (6km E Rural) *38.67301, -2.40462*
**Camping Sierra de Peñascosa, Ctra Peñascosa-
Bogarra, Km 1, 02313 Peñascosa (Albacete) [967-
38 25 21; info@campingsierrapenascosa.com; www.
campingsierrapenascosa.com]** Fr N322 turn E bet km posts
279 & 280 sp Peñascosa. In vill foll site sp for 1km beyond vill.
Gravel access track & narr ent. Sm, mkd pitch, hdstg, terr, shd;
wc; chem disp; shwrs; el pnts (6A) €4; gas; Indtte; shop; rest
high ssn; snacks; bar; playgrnd; pool; cycle hire; dogs €2; open
w/end in winter; v quiet; ccard acc; CKE/CCI. "Not suitable
lge o'fits or faint-hearted; pitches sm, uneven & amongst
trees - care needed when manoeuvring; historical sites nr." ♦
€ 21.00   2009*

⊞ **ALCOSSEBRE** *3D2* (2.5km NE Coastal/Rural) *40.27016,
0.30646* **Camping Ribamar, Partida Ribamar s/n, 12579
Alcossebre (Castellón) [964-76 11 63; fax 964-76 14 84;
info@campingribamar.com; www.campingribamar.com]**
Exit AP7 at junc 44 into N340 & foll sp to Alcossebre, then dir
Sierra de Irta & Las Fuentes. Turn in dir of sea & foll sp to site
in 2km - pt rough rd. Med, hdg/mkd pitch, hdstg, pt sl, terr,
pt shd; wc; chem disp; mv service pnt; baby facs; shwrs inc;
el pnts (10A) €4.40 (metered for long stay); gas; Indtte (inc
dryer); shop; tradsmn; supmkt 2km; rest; bar; playgrnd; pool;
sand beach 100m; paddling pool; tennis; games area; games
rm; wifi; entmnt; TV rm; 25% statics; dogs €1.70; poss cr; Eng
spkn; adv bkg; quiet; red long stay/low ssn; CKE/CCI. "Excel,
refurbished tidy site in 'natural park'; warm welcome; realistic
pitch sizes; variable prices; excel san facs; beware caterpillars
in spring - poss dangerous for dogs." ♦ € 42.50 SBS - W04
2011*

See advertisement

⊞ **ALCOSSEBRE** *3D2* (2.5km S Coastal) *40.22138, 0.26888* **Camping Playa Tropicana, Camino de l'atall s/n, 12579 Alcossebre (Castellón) [964-41 24 63; fax 964 41 28 05; info@playatropicana.com; www.playatropicana.com]** Fr AP7 exit junc 44 onto N340 dir Barcelona. After 3km at km 1018 turn on CV142 twd Alcossebre. Just bef ent town turn R sp 'Platjes Capicorb', turn R at beach in 2.5km, site on R. Lge, mkd pitch, pt terr, pt shd; htd wc; chem disp; baby facs; some serviced pitches; shwrs inc; el pnts (10A) €4.50; gas; lndtte; supmkt; rest, snacks; bar; playgrnd; pool; sand beach adj; watersports; cycle & kayak hire; games area; beauty salon; cinema rm; wifi; entmnt; TV; car wash; 10% statics; no dogs; poss cr; Eng spkn; adv bkg rec high ssn; quiet; ccard acc; ACSI acc red low ssn/long stay & special offers; various pitch prices. "Excel facs & security; superb well-run site; vg low ssn; poss rallies Jan-Apr; management v helpful; poss flooding after heavy rain; pitch access poss diff lge o'fits due narr access rds & high kerbs; take fly swat!" ♦ € 56.00   2013*

"I like to fill in the reports as I travel from site to site"

You'll find report forms at the back of this guide, or you can fill them in online at www.caravaclub.co.uk/europereport.

⊞ **ALGAMITAS** *2G3* (3km SW Rural) *37.01934, -5.17440* **Camping El Peñon, Ctra Algámitas-Pruna, Km 3, 41661 Algámitas (Sevilla) [955-85 53 00; info@campingalgamitas.com]** Fr A92 turn S at junc 41 (Arahal) to Morón de la Frontera on A8125. Fr Morón take A406 & A363 dir Pruna. At 1st rndabt at ent Pruna turn L onto SE9225 to Algámitas. Site on L in approx 10km - steep app rd. Sm, hdg/mkd pitch, hdstg, pt shd; wc; chem disp (wc); mv service rnt; shwrs inc; el pnts (16A) €3.32; gas; lndtte (inc dryer); shop 3km; rest; bar; BBQ; playgrnd; pool; games area; 50% statics; dogs; site clsd 13-24 Nov; adv bkg; quiet; cc acc; CKE/CCI. "Conv Seville, Ronda & white vills; walking, hiking & horseriding fr site; excel rest; excel, clean san facs; vg site - worth effort to find." ♦ ltd € 15.00   2009*

⊞ **ALHAMA DE MURCIA** *4F1* (6km NW Rural) *37.88888, -1.49333* **Camping Sierra Espuña, El Berro, 30848 Alhama de Murcia (Murcia) [968-66 80 38; fax 968-66 80 79; camping@campingsierraespuna.com; www.campingsierraespuna.com]** Exit A7 junc 627 or 631 to Alhama de Murcia & take C3315 sp Gebas & Mula. Ignore 1st sp to site & after Gebas foll sp to site sp El Berro, site on edge of vill. 15km by rd fr Alhama - narr, twisty & steep in parts, diff for lge o'fits & m'vans over 7.5m. Med, hdstg, terr, pt shd; wc; chem disp; baby facs; shwrs; el pnts (6A) €4.28 (poss rev pol); gas; lndtte; shop 200m; rest in vill; snacks; bar; playgrnd; pool; tennis; minigolf; organised activities; wifi; 30% statics; dogs €2.14; phone; adv bkg; quiet but poss noise w/end; red long stay; ccard acc; CKE/CCI. "In Sierra Espu a National Park on edge of unspoilt vill; gd walking, climbing, mountain biking area; friendly staff; highly rec." ♦ € 17.20   2009*

⊞ **ALHAURIN DE LA TORRE** *2H4* (4km W Rural) *36.65174, -4.61064* **Camping Malaga Monte Parc, 29130 Alhaurín de la Torre (Málaga) [tel/fax 951-29 60 28; info@malagamonteparc.com; www.malagamonteparc.com]** W fr Málaga on AP7 or N340 take exit for Churriana/Alhaurín de la Torre. Thro Alhaurín de la Torre take A404 W sp Alhaurín el Grande, site on R, sp. Sm, hdg/mkd pitch, hdstg, pt sl, shd; htd wc (cont); chem disp; shwrs inc; el pnts (6A) inc; lndtte; shop 4km; rest, snacks; bar; BBQ; pool; golf nrby; wifi; TV; some statics; dogs €1.70; bus 200m; Eng spkn; adv bkg; quiet; ccard acc; red low ssn; CKE/CCI. "Vg site; well-appointed, clean san facs; friendly Welsh owner; all facs open all year; sm pitches; gd position to tour Costa Del Sol." ♦ ltd € 25.32   2014*

"We must tell The Club about that great site we found"

Get your site reports in by mid-August and we'll do our best to get your updates into the next edition.

⊞ **ALICANTE** *4F2* (10km NE Coastal) *38.41333, -0.40556* **Camping Bon Sol, Camino Real de Villajoyosa 35, Playa Muchavista, 03560 El Campello (Alicante) [tel/fax 965-94 13 83; bonsol@infonegocio.com; www.infonegocio.com/bonsol]** Exit AP7 N of Alicante at junc 67 onto N332 sp Playa San Juan; on reaching coast rd turn N twds El Campello; site sp. Sm, mkd pitch, hdstg, pt shd, all serviced pitches; wc; chem disp; shwrs; el pnts (4A) €4.50; lndtte; shop; rest; bar; sand beach; 50% statics; adv bkg; ccard acc; red long stay/low ssn; CKE/CCI. "Diff ent for long o'fits; helpful staff; noisy at w/end; poss cold shwrs; vg." ♦ € 31.50   2011*

"I need an on-site restaurant"

We do our best to make sure site information is correct, but it is always best to check any must-have facilities are still available or will be open during your visit.

⊞ **ALLARIZ** *1B2* (1.5km W Rural) *42.18443, -7.81811* **Camping Os Invernadeiros, Ctra Allariz-Celanova, Km 3, 32660 Allariz (Ourense) [988-44 01 26; fax 988-44 20 06; reatur@allariz.com]** Well sp off N525 Orense-Xinzo rd & fr A52. Steep descent to site off rd OU300. Height limit 2.85m adj recep - use gate to R. Sm, pt shd; wc; shwrs inc; el pnts €4; gas; lndtte; shop; snacks; bar; playgrnd; pool 1.5km; horseriding; cycle hire; some statics; dogs €2; bus 1.8km; Eng spkn; quiet; red long stay; ccard acc; CKE/CCI. "Vg; steep slope into site, level exit is avail; site combined with horseriding stable; rv walk adj." € 21.00   2011*

ALMAYATE see Torre del Mar *2H4*

⊞ **ALMERIA** *4G1* (23km SE Coastal/Rural) *36.80187, -2.24471* **Camping Cabo de Gata, Ctra Cabo de Gata s/n, Cortijo Ferrón, 04150 Cabo de Gata (Almería) [950-16 04 43; fax 950-91 68 21; info@campingcabodegata. com; www.campingcabodegata.com]** Exit m'way N340/344/E15 junc 460 or 467 sp Cabo de Gata, foll sp to site. Lge, hdg/mkd pitch, shd; wc; chem disp; baby facs; shwrs inc; el pnts (6-16A) €4.60; gas; lndtte; supmkt high ssn; tradsmn; rest, snacks; bar; BBQ; playgrnd; pool; diving cent; sand beach 900m; tennis; games area; games rm; excursions; cycle hire; wifi; TV; some statics; dogs €2.80; bus 1km; Eng spkn; adv bkg; quiet; ccard acc; red long stay/low ssn/CKE/CCI. "M'vans with solar panels/TV aerials take care sun shades; gd cycling, birdwatching esp flamingoes; popular at w/end; isolated, dry area of Spain with many interesting features; warm winters; excel site." ♦ € 41.05   2014*

⊞ **ALMERIA** *4G1* (4km W Coastal) *36.82560, -2.51685* **Camping La Garrofa, Ctra N340a, Km 435.4, 04002 Almería [tel/fax 950-23 57 70; info@lagarrofa.com; www. lagarrofa.com]** Site sp on coast rd bet Almería & Aguadulce. Med, mkd pitch, pt sl, shd; wc; chem disp; mv service pnt; shwrs inc; el pnts (6-10A) €4.30-4.90; gas; lndtte; shop; rest, snacks; bar; playgrnd; shgl beach adj; games area; wifi; 10% statics; dogs €2.40; phone; bus adj; sep car park; quiet; red low ssn/long stay; CKE/CCI. "V pleasant site adj eucalyptus grove; helpful staff; modern, clean facs; sm pitches, not rec lge o'fits; vg." ♦ € 20.50   2014*

⊞ **ALMERIA** *4G1* (10km W Coastal) *36.79738, -2.59128* **Camping Roquetas, Ctra Los Parrales s/n, 04740 Roquetas de Mar (Almería) [950-34 38 09; fax 950-34 25 25; info@ campingroquetas.com; www.campingroquetas.com]** Fr A7 take exit 429; ahead at rndabt A391 sp Roquetas. Turn L at rndabt sp camping & foll sp to site. V lge, pt shd; wc; chem disp; mv service pnt; shwrs inc; el pnts (10-15A) €6.35-7.45; gas; lndtte; shop; snacks; bar; 2 pools; paddling pool; shgl beach 400m; tennis; wifi; TV rm; 10% statics; dogs €2.25; phone; bus 1km; Eng spkn; adv bkg rec high ssn; quiet; ccard acc; red low ssn/long stay/CKE/CCI. "Double-size pitches in winter; helpful staff; gd clean facs; tidy site but poss dusty; artificial shade; many long term visitors in winter." ♦ € 32.00   2014*

⊞ **ALMUNECAR** *2H4* (6km W Coastal) *36.73954, -3.75358* **Nuevo Camping La Herradura, Paseo Andrés Segovia s/n (Peña Parda), 18690 La Herradura (Granada) [958-64 06 34; fax 958-64 06 42; laherradura@neuvocamping. com; www.nuevocamping.com]** Turn S off N340 sp La Herradura & foll rd to seafront. Turn R to end of beach rd. Site not well sp. Avoid town cent due narr rds. Med, mkd pitch, pt terr, pt shd; wc; chem disp; mv service pnt; serviced pitches; shwrs inc; el pnts (5A) €3.50; gas 500m; lndtte; shop, rest, snacks, bar adj; playgrnd; shgl beach adj; 20% statics; dogs €1.50; phone; bus 300m; poss v cr; adv bkg; quiet; red low ssn/long stay; CKE/CCI. "Friendly, attractive site in avocado orchard; mountain views some pitches; height restriction lge m'vans; some sm pitches - v tight to manoeuvre; vg san facs but ltd low ssn; popular winter long stay." ♦ € 22.00 2010*

⊞ **ALTEA** *4F2* (4km S Coastal) *38.57751, -0.06440* **Camping Cap-Blanch, Playa de Albir, 03530 Altea (Alicante) [965-84 59 46; fax 965-84 45 56; capblanch@ctv.es; www. camping-capblanch.com]** Exit AP7/E15 junc 64 Altea-Collosa onto N332, site bet Altea & Benidorm, dir Albir. 'No entry' sps on prom rd do not apply to access to site. Lge, pt shd, hdstg; wc; chem disp; mv service pnt; baby facs; shwrs inc; el pnts (5-10A) €3.50; gas; shop 100m; lndtte (inc dryer); rest; bar; playgrnd; shgl beach adj; watersports; tennis; golf 5km; wifi; TV; some statics; dogs free; phone; poss cr; Eng spkn; no adv bkg; quiet; ccard acc; red low ssn/long stay. "V cr in winter with long stay campers; lge pitches; Altea mkt Tues; buses to Benidorm & Altea; handy for lovely beach; most pitches hdstg on pebbles." ♦ € 25.00   2011*

⊞ **AMETLLA DE MAR, L'** *3C2* (2.5km S Coastal) *40.86493, 0.77860* **Camping L'Ametlla Village Platja, Paratge de Santes Creus s/n, 43860 L'Ametlla de Mar (Tarragona) [977-26 77 84; fax 977-26 78 68; info@campingametlla. com; www.campingametlla.com]** Exit AP7 junc 39, fork R as soon as cross m'way. Foll site sp for 3km - 1 v sharp, steep bend. Lge, hdg/mkd pitch, hdstg, terr, pt shd; htd wc; chem disp; mv service pnt; baby facs; shwrs inc; el pnts (5-10A) inc; gas; lndtte; shop high ssn; rest, snacks; bar; tradsmn; BBQ; playgrnd; pool; paddling pool; shgl beach 400m; diving cent; games area; games rm; fitness rm; cycle hire; wifi; entmnt; TV rm; some statics; dogs free; phone; Eng spkn; adv bkg; some rd & rlwy noise; ccard acc; red low ssn/long stay; CKE/CCI. "Conv Port Aventura & Ebro Delta National Park; excel site & facs; excel site; can cycle into vill with mkt." ♦ € 47.60   2013*

> ## "Satellite navigation makes touring much easier"
>
> Remember most sat navs don't know if you're towing or in a larger vehicle – always use yours alongside maps and site directions.

⊞ **ARANDA DE DUERO** *1C4* (3km N Rural) *41.70138, -3.68666* **Camping Costajan, Ctra A1/E5, Km 164-165, 09400 Aranda de Duero (Burgos) [947-50 20 70; fax 947-51 13 54; campingcostajan@camping-costajan.com]** Sp on A1/E5 Madrid-Burgos rd, N'bound exit km 164 Aranda Norte, S'bound exit km 165 & foll sp to Aranda & site 500m on R. Med, pt sl, shd; htd wc; chem disp; mv service pnt; shwrs inc; el pnts (10A) €5 (poss rev pol &/or no earth); gas; lndtte; shop; tradsmn; supmkt 3km; rest high ssn; snacks; bar; BBQ; playgrnd; pool high ssn; tennis; games area; wifi; 10% statics; dogs €2; phone; bus 2km; Eng spkn; adv bkg; quiet, but some traff noise; red low ssn but ltd facs; CKE/CCI. "Lovely site under pine trees; poultry farm adj; diff pitch access due trees & sandy soil; friendly, helpful owner; site poss clsd low ssn - phone ahead to check; many facs clsd low ssn & gate clsd o'night until 0800; recep poss open evening only low ssn; poss cold/tepid shwrs low ssn; gd winter NH; vg site for dogs." € 27.00 2014*

⊞ **ARANJUEZ** *1D4* (1.5km NE Rural) *40.04222, -3.59944*
Camping International Aranjuez, Calle Soto del
Rebollo s/n, 28300 Aranjuez (Madrid) [918-91 13 95;
fax 918-92 04 06; info@campingaranjuez.com; www.
campingaranjuez.com] Fr N (Madrid) turn off A4 exit 37
onto M305. After ent town turn L bef rv, after petrol stn
on R. Take L lane & watch for site sp on L, also mkd M305
Madrid. Site in 500m on R. (If missed cont around cobbled
rndabt & back twd Madrid.) Fr S turn off A4 for Aranjuez
& foll Palacio Real sp. Join M305 & foll sp for Madrid &
camping site. Site on Rv Tajo. Warning: rd surface rolls,
take it slowly on app to site & ent gate tight. Lge, hdg/
mkd pitch, pt sl, unshd; htd wc; chem disp; mv service pnt;
some serviced pitches; baby facs; shwrs inc; el pnts (16A)
€4 (poss no earth, rev pol); gas; lndtte (inc dryer); shop;
hypmkt 3km; rest, snacks; bar; playgrnd; pool & paddling
pool; rv fishing; canoe & cycle hire; games area; wifi;
entmnt; some statics; dogs free; phone; quiet; ccard acc;
red low ssn/long stay; CKE/CCI. "Well-maintained site; gd
san facs; rest vg value; some lge pitches - access poss diff
due trees; some uneven pitches - care req when pitching;
pleasant town - World Heritage site; conv Madrid by train;
excel site; free train to Royal Palace each morning." ♦
€ 41.80
2014*

See advertisement

⊞ **ARENAS DEL REY** *2G4* (5km N Rural) *36.99439,
-3.88064* Camping Los Bermejales, Km 360, Embalse
Los Bermejales, 18129 Arenas del Rey (Granada) [958-
35 91 90; fax 958-35 93 36; camping@losbermejales.com;
www.losbermejales.com] On A44/E902 S fr Granada, exit
at junc 139 dir La Malahá onto A385. In approx 10km, turn L
onto A338 dir Alhama de Granada & foll sp for site. Fr A92 foll
sp Alhama de Granada, then Embalse Los Bermejales. Med,
mkd pitch, hdstg, terr, pt shd; wc; chem disp; mv service pnt;
shwrs inc; el pnts (9A) €2.67; gas; lndtte; shop; rest, snacks;
bar; BBQ; playgrnd; pool; lake sw & sand/shgl beach adj;
fishing (licence req); pedalos; tennis; TV rm; 50% statics; dogs;
phone; poss cr high ssn; little Eng spkn; adv bkg; quiet. "Ideal
base for touring Granada; Roman baths 12km at Alhama de
Granada." ♦ € 16.70   2011*

ARENAS, LAS *1A4* (1km E Rural) *43.30083, -4.80500*
Camping Naranjo de Bulnes, Ctra Cangas de Onís-Panes,
Km 32.5, 33554 Arenas de Cabrales (Asturias) [tel/fax
985-84 65 78; info@campingnaranjodebulnes.com; www.
campingnaranjodebulnes.com] Fr Unquera on N634, take
N621 S to Panes, AS114 23km to Las Arenas. Site E of vill of
Las Arenas de Cabrales, both sides of rd. V lge, mkd pitch, pt
sl, pt terr, pt shd; wc; chem disp; baby facs; shwrs inc; el pnts
(10A) €3.50 (poss rev pol); gas; lndtte; shop; rest, snacks; bar;
playgrnd; internet; TV rm; bus 100m; poss cr; rd noise; ccard
acc. "Beautifully-situated site by rv; delightful vill; attractive,
rustic-style san facs - hot water to shwrs only, not basins or
sinks; wcs up steps; poss poor security; conv Picos de Europa;
mountain-climbing school; excursions; walking; excel cheese
festival last Sun in Aug." 1 Mar-30 Sept. € 25.60   2012*

ARIJA *1A4* (1km N Rural) *43.00064, -3.94492* Camping
Playa de Arija, Avda Gran Via, 09570 Arija (Burgos) [942-
77 33 00; fax 942-77 32 72; info @ campingplayadearija
Sodot null. Com; www.campingplayadearija.com] Fr W on
A67 at Reinosa along S side of Embalse del Ebro. Go thro Arija
& take 1st L after x-ing bdge. Go under rlwy bdge, site well sp
on peninsula N of vill on lakeside. Or fr E on N623 turn W onto
BU642 to Arija & turn R to peninsula & site. NB Rd fr W under
repair 2009 & in poor condition. Lge, shd; wc; chem disp; mv
service pnt; baby facs; shwrs inc; el pnts (5A) €3; lndtte; shop;
rest; bar; BBQ; playgrnd; lake sw & beach; watersports; games
area; 10% statics; dogs; phone; bus 1km; quiet; CKE/CCI.
"Gd new site; gd birdwatching; low ssn phone ahead for site
opening times." Easter-15 Sep. € 14.00   2013*

⊞ **ARNES** *3C2* (1km NE Rural) *40.9186, 0.2678* Camping Els
Ports, Ctra Tortosa T330, Km 2, 43597 Arnes (Tarragona)
[tel/fax 977-43 55 60; elsports@hotmail.com] Exit AP7 at
junc Tortosa onto C12 sp Gandesa. Turn W onto T333 at El
Pinell de Brai, then T330 to site. Med, pt shd; htd wc; shwrs
inc; el pnts €4.20; lndtte; rest; bar; pool; paddling pool; games
area; cycle hire; horseriding 3km; entmnt; TV rm; some statics;
no dogs; phone; bus 1km; quiet; ccard acc. "Nr nature reserve
& many sports activities; excel walking/mountain cycling; basic
san facs; poss smells fr adj pig units (2009); rock pegs req."
♦ ltd € 18.40   2009*

AURITZ *3A1* (3km SW Rural) *42.97302, -1.35248* **Camping Urrobi, Ctra Pamplona-Valcarlos, Km 42, 31694 Espinal-Auritzberri (Navarra) [tel/fax 948-76 02 00; info@ campingurrobi.com; www.campingurrobi.com]** NE fr Pamplona on N135 twd Valcarlos thro Erro; 1.5km after Auritzberri (Espinal) turn R on N172. Site on N172 at junc with N135 opp picnic area. Med, pt shd; wc; chem disp; mv service pnt; shwrs inc; el pnts (5A) €4.90; gas; lndtte; shop; tradsmn; supmkt 1.5km; rest, snacks; bar; BBQ; playgrnd; pool; rv adj; tennis; cycle hire; horseriding; wifi; 20% statics; phone; Eng spkn; adv bkg; quiet; ccard acc; CKE/CCI. "Excel, busy site & facs; solar htd water - hot water to shwrs only; walks in surrounding hills; ltd facs low ssn; poss youth groups." ♦ 1 Apr-31 Oct. € 20.00   2010*

AVIN see Cangas de Onis *1A3*

⊞ **AYERBE** *3B2* (1km NE Rural) *42.28211, -0.67536* **Camping La Banera, Ctra Loarre Km.1, 22800 Ayerbe (Huesca) [tel/fax 974-38 02 42 / 659-16 15 90 (mob); labanera@ gmail.com; www.campinglabanera.com]** Take A132 NW fr Huesca fr Pamplona. Turn R at 1st x-rds at ent to Ayerbe sp Loarre & Camping. Site 1km on R on A1206. Med, mkd pitch, terr, pt shd; wc; chem disp (wc); baby facs; fam bthrm; shwrs inc; el pnts (6A) €2.60; gas; lndtte; shop 1km; rest, snacks; bar; cooking facs; TV rm; dogs €2; some Eng spkn; adv bkg; quiet; ccard acc; red long stay; CKE/CCI. "Friendly, pleasant, well-maintained, peaceful, family-run site; facs clean; pitches poss muddy after rain; helpful owners; wonderful views; close to Loarre Castle; care req by high o'fits as many low trees; area famous for Griffon Vultures which inhabit tall cliffs nr Loarre." ♦ € 17.50   2014*

⊞ **AYERBE** *3B2* (10km NE Rural) *42.31989, -0.61848* **Camping Castillo de Loarre, Ctra del Castillo s/n, 22809 Loarre (Huesca) [tel/fax 974-38 27 22; info@ campingloarre.com; www.campingloarre.com]** NW on A132 fr Huesca, turn R at ent to Ayerbe to Loare sp Castillo de Loarre. Pass 1st site on R (La Banera) & foll sp to castle past Loarre vill on L; site on L. App rd steep & twisting. Med, pt sl, pt shd; wc; chem disp; shwrs inc; el pnts (6A) €4.50; gas; lndtte; shop; tradsmn; rest, snacks; bar; playgrnd; sm pool; cycle hire; 10% statics; dogs; phone; site clsd Feb; poss cr; Eng spkn; quiet; ccard acc; CKE/CCI. "Elevated site in almond grove; superb scenery & views, esp fr pitches on far L of site; excel birdwatching - many vultures/eagles; site open w/end in winter; busy high ssn & w/ends; pitching poss diff lge o'fits due low trees; worth the journey." ♦ € 16.00   2010*

BAIONA *1B2* (5km NE Urban/Coastal) *42.13861, -8.80916* **Camping Playa América, Ctra Vigo-Baiona, Km 9.250,Aptdo. Correos 3105 - 36350 Nigrán (Pontevedra) [986-36 54 03 or 986-36 71 61; fax 986-36 54 04; oficina@ campingplayaamerica.com; www.campingplayaamerica. com]** Sp on rd PO552 fr all dirs (Vigo/Baiona) nr beach. Med, mkd pitch, pt shd; wc; chem disp; mv service pnt; baby facs; shwrs inc; el pnts (6A) €5.; gas; lndtte; shop; tradsmn; rest, snacks; bar; BBQ; playgrnd; pool; paddling pool; sand beach 300m; cycle hire; 60% statics; dogs; bus 500m; poss cr; Eng spkn; adv bkg; CKE/CCI. "Friendly staff; pleasant, wooded site; gd." ♦ 16 Mar-15 Oct. € 25.45   2013*

⊞ **BAIONA** *1B2* (1km E Coastal) *42.11416, -8.82611* **Camping Bayona Playa, Ctra Vigo-Baiona, Km 19, Sabarís, 36393 Baiona (Pontevedra) [986-35 00 35; fax 986-35 29 52; campingbayona@campingbayona.com; www. campingbayona.com]** Fr Vigo on PO552 sp Baiona. Or fr A57 exit Baiona & foll sp Vigo & site sp. Lge, mkd pitch, pt shd; wc; chem disp; mv service pnt; shwrs inc; el pnts (3A) €4.80; gas; lndtte; shop; rest, snacks; bar; playgrnd; pool; waterslide; sand beach adj; 50% statics; dogs; phone; poss cr; adv bkg (ess high ssn); quiet; red low ssn/long stay; CKE/CCI. "Area of outstanding natural beauty with sea on 3 sides; well-organised site; excel, clean san facs; avoid access w/end as v busy; ltd facs low ssn; tight access to sm pitches high ssn; gd cycle track to town; replica of ship 'La Pinta' in harbour." ♦ € 28.40   2011*

⊞ **BALAGUER** *3C2* (8km N Rural) *41.86030, 0.83250* **Camping La Noguera, Partida de la Solana s/n, 25615 Sant Llorenç de Montgai (Lleida) [973-42 03 34; fax 973-42 02 12; info@campinglanoguera.com; www. campinglanoguera.com]** Fr Lleida, take N11 ring rd & exit at km 467 onto C13 NE dir Andorra & Balaguer. Head for Balaguer town cent, cross rv & turn R onto LV9047 dir Gerb. Site on L in 8km thro Gerb. App fr Camarasa not rec. Lge, mkd pitch, hdstg, terr, pt shd; wc; chem disp; mv service pnt; baby facs; shwrs inc; el pnts (6A) €5.15; gas; lndtte; supmkt; tradsmn; rest, snacks; bar; BBQ; playgrnd; pool; games area; TV rm; 80% statics; dogs €3.50; phone; poss cr; Eng spkn; adv bkg; quiet; ccard acc; red long stay; CKE/CCI. "Next to lake & nature reserve; gd cycling; poss diff lge o'fits; friendly warden; gd facs." ♦ ltd € 45.80   2014*

BANOS DE FORTUNA see Fortuna *4F1*

BANOS DE MONTEMAYOR see Béjar *1D3*

⊞ **BANYOLES** *3B3* (2km W Rural) *42.12071, 2.74690* **Camping Caravaning El Llac, Ctra Circumvallació de l'Estany s/n, 17834 Porqueres (Gerona) [tel/fax 972-57 03 05; info@campingllac.com; www.campingllac.com]** Exit AP7 junc 6 to Banyoles. Go strt thro town (do not use by-pass) & exit town at end of lake in 1.6km. Use R-hand layby to turn L sp Porqueres. Site on R in 2.5km. Lge, mkd pitch, pt shd; chem disp; wc; shwrs; el pnts (6A) €4.60; lndtte; shop; snacks; bar; pool; lake sw; wifi; 80% statics; dogs €2.30; bus 1km; site clsd mid-Dec to mid-Jan; poss cr; quiet but noisy rest/disco adj in high ssn; red long stay/low ssn. "Immac, ltd facs low ssn & stretched high ssn; sm pitches bet trees; pleasant walk around lake to town; site muddy when wet." ♦ € 22.00   2009*

BARBATE see Vejer de la Frontera *2H3*

BARCELONA See sites listed under El Masnou, Gavà and Sitges.

BARREIROS/REINANTE see Foz *1A2*

⊞ **BEAS DE GRANADA** 2G4 (750m N Rural) 37.22416, -3.48805 **Camping Alto de Viñuelas, Ctra de Beas de Granada s/n, 18184 Beas de Granada (Granada) [958-54 60 23; fax 958-54 53 57; info@campingaltodevinuelas. com; www.campingaltodevinuelas.com]** E fr Granada on A92, exit junc 256 & foll sp to Beas de Granada. Site well sp on L in 1.5km. Sm, mkd pitch, terr, pt shd; htd wc; chem disp; mv service pnt; shwrs inc; el pnts (5A) €3.50; lndtte (inc dryer); shop; rest, snacks; bar; BBQ; playgrnd; pool; wifi; 10% statics; dogs; bus to Granada at gate; Eng spkn; red long stay; CKE/CCI. "In beautiful area; views fr all pitches; 4X4 trip to adj natural park; gd; conv for night halt." € 26.00 (CChq acc)   2014*

BEGUR 3B3 (1.5km S Rural) 41.94040, 3.19890 **Camping Begur, Ctra d'Esclanyà, Km 2, 17255 Begur (Gerona) [972-62 32 01; fax 972-62 45 66; info@campingbegur.com; www.campingbegur.com]** Exit AP7/E15 junc 6 Gerona onto C66 dir La Bisbal & Palamós. At x-rds to Pals turn L dir Begur then turn R twd Esclanyà, site on R, clearly sp. Slope to site ent. Lge, mkd pitch, hdstg, shd; wc; chem disp; mv service pnt; baby facs; serviced pitches; shwrs inc; el pnts (10A) inc; lndtte; supmkt; rest, snacks; bar; BBQ; playgrnd; pool; paddling pool; sand/shgl beach 2km; tennis; cycle hire; games area; games rm; gym; wifi; entmnt; 14% statics; dogs €6.50; phone; bus adj; Eng spkn; adv bkg; red long stay/snr citizens/CKE/CCI. "Excel, peaceful site; narr site rds poss diff lge o'fits; adj castle & magnificent views; excel touring base." ♦ 15 Apr-25 Sep. € 43.00   2010*

BEJAR 1D3 (6km S Rural) 40.36344, -5.74918 **Camping Cinco Castaños, Ctra de la Sierra s/n, 37710 Candelario (Salamanca) [923-41 32 04; fax 923-41 32 82; profetur@ candelariohotel.com; www.candelariohotel.com]** Fr Béjar foll sp Candelario on C515/SA220, site sp on N side of vill. Steep bends & narr aprd rd. Sm, mkd pitch, pt sl, pt shd; htd wc; chem disp (wc); baby facs; shwrs inc; el pnts (6A) €3.15; gas; lndtte; shop 500m; rest; bar; playgrnd; pool high ssn; no dogs; bus 500m; phone; quiet; CKE/CCI. "Mountain vill; friendly owner; no facs in winter; no lge o'fits as steep site." ♦ Holy Week-15 Oct. € 18.50   2011*

⊞ **BEJAR** 1D3 (15km SW Rural) 40.28560, -5.88182 **Camping Las Cañadas, Ctra N630, Km 432, 10750 Baños de Montemayor (Cáceres) [927-48 11 26; fax 927-48 13 14; info@campinglascanadas.com; www.campinglascanadas. com]** Fr S turn off A630 m'way at 437km stone to Heruns then take old N630 twd Béjar. Site at 432km stone, behind 'Hervas Peil' (leather goods shop). Fr N exit A66 junc 427 thro Baños for 3km to site at km432 on R. Lge, mkd pitch, pt sl, shd (net shdg); htd wc; chem disp; mv service pnt; baby facs; shwrs inc; el pnts (5A) €4; gas; lndtte; shop; rest, snacks; bar; playgrnd; pool; paddling pool; fishing; tennis; cycle hire; games area; TV rm; 60% statics; dogs; poss cr; Eng spkn; quiet but rd noise; ccard acc; red long stay/low ssn; CKE/CCI. "Gd san facs but poss cold shwrs; high vehicles take care o'hanging trees; gd walking country; NH/sh stay." ♦ ltd € 17.35 (CChq acc) 2009*

⊞ **BELLVER DE CERDANYA** 3B3 (2km E Rural) 42.37163, 1.80674 **Camping Bellver, Ctra N260, Km 193.7, 17539 Isòvol (Gerona) [973-51 02 39; fax 973-51 07 19; campingbellver@campingbellver.com; www. campingbellver.com]** On N260 fr Puigcerdà to Bellver; site on L, well sp. Lge, mkd pitch, shd; htd wc; chem disp (wc); shwrs inc; el pnts (5A) €3.50; gas; lndtte; rest, snacks; bar; playgrnd; pool; 90% statics; dogs; phone; poss cr; Eng spkn; quiet; ccard acc; CKE/CCI. "Friendly, helpful staff; lovely pitches along rv; san facs immac; v quiet low ssn; gd NH for Andorra." € 19.20   2011*

⊞ **BELLVER DE CERDANYA** 3B3 (1km W Rural) 42.37110, 1.73625 **Camping La Cerdanya, Ctra N260, Km 200, 25737 Prullans (Lleida) [973-51 02 62; fax 973-51 06 72; cerdanya@prullans.net; www.prullans.net/camping]** Fr Andorra frontier on N260, site sp. Lge, mkd pitch, shd; wc; baby facs; mv service pnt; shwrs inc; el pnts (4A) €5.15; gas; lndtte; shop; rest, snacks; playgrnd; pool; paddling pool; games area; internet; entmnt; 80% statics; dogs €3.45; phone; bus 1km; poss cr; adv bkg; quiet; red long stay; ccard acc. ♦ € 20.60   2011*

"There aren't many sites open at this time of year"

If you're travelling outside peak season remember to call ahead to check site opening dates – even if the entry says 'open all year'

BENABARRE 3B2 (500m N Urban) 42.1103, 0.4811 **Camping Benabarre, 22580 Benabarre (Huesca) [974-54 35 72; fax 974-54 34 32; aytobenabarre@aragon.es]** Fr N230 S, turn L after 2nd camping sp over bdge & into vill. Ignore brown camping sp (pt of riding cent). Med, some hdstg, pt shd; wc; shwrs inc; el pnts (10A) inc; shops 500m; bar; pool; tennis; no statics; bus 600m; phone; quiet. "Excel, friendly, simple site; gd facs; gd value for money; v quiet low ssn; warden calls 1700; mkt on Fri; lovely vill with excel chocolate shop; conv Graus & mountains - a real find." 1 Apr-30 Sep. € 14.50   2012*

⊞ **BENICARLO** 3D2 (1.5km NE Urban/Coastal) 40.42611, 0.43777 **Camping La Alegría del Mar, Ctra N340, Km 1046, Calle Playa Norte, 12580 Benicarló (Castellón) [964-47 08 71; info@campingalegria.com; www. campingalegria.com]** Sp off main N340 app Benicarló. Take slip rd mkd Service, go under underpass, turn R on exit & cont twd town, then turn at camp sp by Peugeot dealers. Sm, mkd pitch, pt shd; htd wc; shwrs; el pnts (4-6A) €4.70; gas; lndtte; shop 500m; rest, snacks; bar; playgrnd; sm pool; beach adj; games rm; wifi; some statics; dogs; phone; bus 800m; poss cr; quiet but rd noise at night & poss cockerels!; red long stay/low ssn; ccard acc. "British owners; access to complete variable, poss diff in ssn; vg, clean san facs; Xmas & New Year packages; phone ahead to reserve pitch; excel." € 22.00   2009*

⊞ **BENICASSIM** *3D2* (500m NE Coastal) *40.05709, 0.07429*
**Camping Bonterra Park, Avda de Barcelona 47, 12560
Benicàssim (Castellón) [964 30 00 07; fax 964 10 06 69;
info@bonterrapark.com; www.bonterrapark.com]** Fr N
exit AP7 junc 45 onto N340 dir Benicàssim. In approx 7km
turn R to Benicàssim/Centro Urba; strt ahead to traff lts,
then turn L, site on L 500m after going under rlwy bdge.
Lge, mkd pitch, hdstg, pt sl, shd; htd wc; chem disp; mv
service pnt; some serviced pitches; baby facs; shwrs inc; el
pnts (6-10) inc; gas; lndtte (inc dryer); shop; rest, snacks; bar;
BBQ; playgrnd; 2 pools (1 covrd & htd); paddling pool; sand
beach 300m; tennis; cycle hire; gym; entmnt; games area;
wifi; games/TV rm; 15% statics; dogs €2.24 (not acc Jul/Aug);
no c'vans/m'vans over 10m; phone; train; sep car park; Eng
spkn; adv bkg; rd noise; ccard acc; red long stay/low ssn/CKE/
CCI. "Fabulous site in gd location; excel cycle tracks & public
transport; lovely beach; reasonable sized pitches; well-kept &
well-run; clean modern san facs; access to some pitches poss
diff due to trees; sun shades some pitches; winter festival 3rd
wk Jan; Harley Davidson rallies Jan & Sep, check in adv; highly
rec; flat rd to town; excel facs; ACSI card acc." ♦ € 66.45
SBS - E19   2013*

⊞ **BENICASSIM** *3D2* (4.5km NW Coastal) *40.05908, 0.08515*
**Camping Azahar, Ptda Villaroig s/n, 12560 Benicàssim
(Castellón) [964-30 35 51; fax 964-30 25 12; info@
campingazahar.es; www.campingazahar.es]** Fr AP7 junc
45 take N340 twd València; in 5km L at top of hill (do not turn
R to go-karting); foll sp. Turn R under rlwy bdge opp Hotel
Voramar. Lge, mkd pitch, pt sl, terr, unshd; htd wc; chem
disp; mv service pnt; baby facs; shwrs inc; el pnts (4-6A) €2.90
(long leads poss req); gas; lndtte; rest, snacks; bar; playgrnd;
pool; sand beach 300m across rd; tennis at hotel; cycle hire;
25% statics; dogs €4.07; phone; bus adj; poss cr high ssn;
Eng spkn; bus adj; adv bkg; ccard acc; red long stay/low ssn/
snr citizens; CKE/CCI. "Popular site, esp in winter; poss noisy
high ssn; access poss diff for m'vans & lge o'fits; poss uneven
pitches; organised events; gd walking & cycling; gd touring
base." ♦ ltd € 40.00   2013*

⊞ **BENIDORM** *4F2* (2km N Coastal) *38.56926, -0.09328*
**Camping Almafrá, Partida de Cabut 25, 03503 Benidorm
(Alicante) [tel/fax 965-88 90 75; info@campingalmafra.
es; www.campingalmafra.es]** Exit AP7/E15 junc 65 onto
N332 N. Foll sp Alfaz del Pi, site sp. Lge, mkd pitch, unshd; htd
wc; sauna; baby facs; sauna; private san facs avail; shwrs inc;
el pnts (16A); lndtte (inc dryer); shop; rest, snacks; bar; BBQ;
playgrnd; 2 htd pools (1 covrd); paddling pool; jacuzzi; tennis;
wellness/fitness cent; games area; gym; wifi; entmnt; sat TV;
30% statics; no dogs; adv bkg; quiet; red long stay/low ssn/
CKE/CCI. ♦ (CChq acc)   2010*

⊞ **BENIDORM** *4F2* (2km N Urban) **Camping Villamar, Ctra
del Albir, Km 0.300, 03503 Benidorm (Alicante) [966-
81 12 55; fax 966-81 35 40; camping@ampingvillamar.
com; www.campingvillamar.com]** Exit AP7 junc 65. Down
hill twd town, turn L at traff lts into Ctra Valenciana, turn R
where 2 petrol stns either side of rd, site on L. V lge, mkd
pitch, terr, pt shd; wc; chem disp; serviced pitches; shwrs;
el pnts €3.50; gas; lndtte; shop; rest; bar; playgrnd; 2 pools
(1 covrd/htd); sand beach 2km; entmnt; games rm; sat TV;
phone; no dogs; adv bkg; quiet; red long stay/low ssn. "Excel
site, esp winter; gd security; v welcoming; gd walking area."
♦ € 28.00   2012*

See advertisement

⊞ **BENIDORM** *4F2* (1.5km NE Urban) *38.54833, -0.09851*
**Camping El Raco, Avda Dr Severo Ochoa, 19 Racó de
Loix, 03503 Benidorm (Alicante) [965-86 85 52; fax 965-
86 85 44; info@campingraco.com; www.campingraco.
com]** Turn off A7 m'way at junc 65 then L onto A332; take
turning sp Benidorm Levante Beach; ignore others; L at 1st
traff lghts; strt on at next traff lts, El Raco 1km on R. Lge, hdg/
mkd pitch, hdstg, pt sl, pt shd; wc; chem disp; 50% serviced
pitches; baby facs; shwrs inc; el pnts (10A) metered; gas; lndtte
(inc dryer); shop; rest, snacks; bar; BBQ; playgrnd; 2 pools (1
htd, covrd); beach 1.5km; games area; Eng spkn; wifi; TV; dogs
€1.15; 30% statics; bus; poss v cr in winter; quiet; red low
ssn; CKE/CCI. "Excel site; popular winter long stay but strictly
applied rules about leaving c'van unoccupied; el pnts metered
for long stay; friendly helpful staff; two pin adaptor needed for
elec conn." ♦ € 34.00   2014*

www.turismodecastellon.com

⊞ **BENIDORM** *4F2* (3km NE Urban) *38.56024, -0.09844*
Camping Benisol, Avda de la Comunidad Valenciana
s/n, 03500 Benidorm (Alicante) [965-85 16 73; fax
965-86 08 95; campingbenisol@yahoo.es; www.
campingbenisol.com] Exit AP7/E15 junc 65 onto N332. Foll
sp Benidorm, Playa Levante (avoid by-pass). Dangerous rd on
ent to sit; site ent easy to miss. Lge, hdg pitch, hdstg, shd; wc;
chem disp; serviced pitches; shwrs inc; el pnts (4-6A) €2.80;
gas; lndtte; shop & rest (high ssn); snacks; bar; playgrnd; pool
(hgh ssn); sand beach 4km; TV; 85% statics; dogs; phone; bus
to Benidorm; poss cr; Eng spkn; adv bkg with dep; some rd
noise; red long stay/low ssn; CKE/CCI. "Helpful staff; well-run,
clean site; many permanent residents." ♦ € 27.20   2011*

⊞ **BENIDORM** *4F2* (3km NE Coastal) *38.54438, -0.10325*
Camping La Torreta, Avda Dr Severo Ochoa 11, 03500
Benidorm (Alicante) [965-85 46 68; fax 965-80 26 53;
campinglatorreta@gmail.com] Exit AP7/E15 junc 65 onto
N332. Foll sp Playa Levante, site sp. Lge, mkd pitch, hdstg, pt
sl, terr, pt shd (bamboo shades); wc (some cont); chem disp;
mv service pnt; shwrs inc; el pnts (10A) €3.40; gas; lndtte (inc
dryer); shop; rest, snacks; bar; playgrnd; pool; paddling pool;
sand beach 1km; wifi; 10% statics; dogs; bus; no adv bkg;
quiet; red long stay; CKE/CCI. "Take care siting if heavy rain;
some pitches v sm; popular with long stay winter visitors." ♦
€ 29.00   2010*

⊞ **BENIDORM** *4F2* (1km E Coastal) *38.5449, -0.10696*
Camping Villasol, Avda Bernat de Sarriá 13, 03500
Benidorm (Alicante) [965-85 04 22; fax 966-80 64 20;
info@camping-villasol.com; www.camping-villasol.com]
Leave AP7 at junc 65 onto N332 dir Alicante; take exit into
Benidorm sp Levante. Turn L at traff lts just past Camping
Titus, then in 200m R at lts into Avda Albir. Site on R in 1km.
Care - dip at ent, poss grounding. V lge, mkd pitch, hdstg,
shd; htd wc; chem disp; baby facs; shwrs inc; el pnts (5A)
€4.28; lndtte; supmkt; rest, snacks; bar; playgrnd; 2 pools (1
htd, covrd); sand beach 300m; games area; wifi; sat TV all
pitches; medical service; currency exchange; 5% statics; no
dogs; phone; adv bkg; Eng spkn; quiet; ccard acc; red low
ssn/long stay. "Excel, well-kept site espec in winter; some sm
pitches; friendly staff." ♦ € 32.00   2013*

See advertisement

⊞ **BERCEO** *1B4* (200m SE Rural) *42.33565, -2.85335*
Camping Berceo, El Molino s/n, 26327 Berceo (La Rioja)
[941-37 32 27; fax 941-37 32 01; camping.berceo@fer.es]
Fr E on N120 foll sp Tricio, San Millan de la Cogolla on LR136/
LR206. Fr W foll sp Villar de Torre & San Millan. In Berceo foll
sp sw pools & site. Med, hdg/mkd pitch, hdstg, pt sl, shd; htd
wc; chem disp; baby facs; fam bthrm; shwrs inc; el pnts (7A)
€4.70; lndtte (inc dryer); shop; tradsmn; rest, snacks; bar;
playgrnd; pool; paddling pool; cycle hire; wifi; TV; 50% statics;
phone; bus 200m; adv bkg; quiet; red long stay; CKE/CCI.
"Excel base for Rioja vineyards; gd site." ♦ € 30.65   2010*

BESALU *3B3* (2km E Rural) *42.20952, 2.73682* **Camping
Masia Can Coromines, Ctra N260, Km 60, 17851 Maià
del Montcal (Gerona) [tel/fax 972-59 11 08; coromines@
grn.es; www.cancoromines.com]** NW fr Gerona on C66 to
Besalú. Turn R sp Figueras (N260) for 2.5km. At 60km sp turn
into driveway on L opp fountain for approx 300m. Narr app &
ent. Site is 1km W of Maià. Narr site ent poss diff lge o'fits. Sm,
pt shd; wc; serviced pitch; shwrs €0.50; el pnts (10-15A) €3;
gas; lndtte; shop 2.5km; rest high ssn; snacks; bar; playgrnd;
pool; cycle hire; internet; some statics; dogs €2.90; Eng
spkn; adv bkg; quiet with some rd noise; ccard acc; CKE/CCI.
"Friendly, family-run site in beautiful area; gd walks; facs poss
stretched when site full." ♦ 1 Apr-4 Nov. € 20.40   2011*

BIELSA *3B2* (7km W Rural) *42.65176, 0.14076* **Camping
Pineta, Ctra del Parador, Km 7, 22350 Bielsa (Huesca)
[974-50 10 89; fax 974-50 11 84; info@campingpineta.
com; www.campingpineta.com]** Fr A138 in Bielsa turn W
& foll sp for Parador Monte Perdido & Valle de Pineta. Site on
L after 8km (ignore previous campsite off rd). Lge, terr, pt sl,
pt shd; wc; chem disp; mv service pnt; baby facs; shwrs inc; el
pnts (6A) €5. (poss rev pol); gas; lndtte (inc dryer); shop & 8km;
rest, snacks; bar; BBQ; playgrnd; pool; games area; cycle hire;
dog €2.50; some statics; phone; ccard acc; CKE/CCI. "Well-
maintained site; clean facs; glorious location in National Park."
1 Apr-15 Oct. € 36.20   2013*

⊞ BIESCAS 3B2 (1km SE Rural) 42.61944, -0.30416 **Camping Gavín**, Ctra N260, Km 502.5, 22639 Gavín (Huesca) [974-48 50 90 or 659-47 95 51; fax 974-48 50 17; info@campinggavin.com; www.campinggavin.com] Take N330/A23/E7 N fr Huesca twd Sabiñánigo then N260 twd Biescas & Valle de Tena. Ignore all sp to Biescas on N260 until R turn at g'ge. Drive over blue bdge & foll sp Gavín & site. Site is at km 502.5 fr Huesca, bet Biescas & Gavín. Lge, mkd pitch, terr, pt shd; htd wc; chem disp; mv service pnt; baby facs; fam bthrm; shwrs inc; el pnts (10A) inc; gas; lndtte (inc dryer); shop; tradsmn; rest, snacks; bar; playgrnd; pool; tennis; cycle hire in National Park; wifi; TV rm; 40% statics; dogs inc; phone; bus 1km; adv bkg; quiet; CKE/CCI. "Wonderful, scenic site nr Ordesa National Park; poss diff access to pitches for lge o'fits & m'vans; superb htd san facs; Eng spkn; immac kept site; excel; superb site inc rest pitches with views, gd for walking." ♦ € 52.00   2014*

"That's changed – Should I let The Club know?"

If you find something on site that's different from the site entry, fill in a report and let us know. See www.caravanclub.co.uk/europereport.

⊞ BILBAO 1A4 (14km N Coastal) 43.38916, -2.98444 **Camping Sopelana**, Ctra Bilbao-Plentzia, Km 18, Playa Atxabiribil 30, 48600 Sopelana (Vizcaya) [946-76 19 81/ 649-11 57 51; fax 944-21 50 10; recepcion@campingsopelana.com; www.campingsopelana.com] In Bilbao cross rv by m'way bdge sp to airport, foll 637/634 N twd & Plentzia. Cont thro Sopelana & foll sp on L. Med, hdg pitch, sl, terr; wc (some cont); own san; chem disp; mv service pnt; baby facs; shwrs; el pnts (10A) €4.50; gas; lndtte; shop, rest (w/end only low ssn); snacks; bar; playgrnd; pool; sand beach 200m; 70% statics; poss cr; Eng spkn; adv bkg ess high ssn; quiet but noise fr disco adj; red long stay; CKE/CCI. "Poss stong sea winds; ltd space for tourers; pitches sm, poss flooded after heavy rain & poss diff due narr, steep site rds; ltd facs low ssn & poss unclean; poss no hot water for shwrs; helpful manager; site used by local workers; poor security in city cent/Guggenheim car park; poss clsd low ssn - phone ahead to check; NH/sh stay only; check open dates." ♦ € 34.50   2013*

BLANES 3C3 (1km S Coastal) 41.65944, 2.77972 **Camping Bella Terra**, Avda Vila de Madrid 35-40, 17300 Blanes (Gerona) [972-34 80 17 or 972-34 80 23; fax 972-34 82 75; info@campingbellaterra.com; www.campingbellaterra.com] Exit A7 junc 9 via Lloret or junc 10 via Tordera. On app Blanes, all campsites are sp at rndabts; all sites along same rd. V lge, mkd pitch, hdstg, pt sl, shd; wc; chem disp; mv service pnt; baby facs; shwrs inc; el pnts (5A) inc; gas; lndtte (inc dryer); shop; tradsmn; rest, snacks; bar; BBQ; playgrnd; pools; sand beach adj; tennis; games area; games rm; cycle hire; wifi; entmnt; TV rm; 15% statics; dogs €4.50; Eng spkn; quiet; ccard acc; red long stay/low ssn/CKE/CCI. "Split site - 1 side has pool, 1 side adj beach; pitches on pool side lger; vg site with excel facs." ♦ 27 Mar-26 Sep. € 42.40   2010*

⊞ BLANES 3C3 (1km S Coastal) 41.65933, 2.77000 **Camping Blanes**, Avda Vila de Madrid 33, 17300 Blanes (Gerona) [972-33 15 91; fax 972-33 70 63; info@campingblanes.com; www.campingblanes.com] Fr N on AP7/E15 exit junc 9 onto NII dir Barcelona & foll sp Blanes. Fr S to end of C32, then NII dir Blanes. On app Blanes, foll camping sps & Playa S'Abanell - all campsites are sp at rndabts; all sites along same rd. Site adj Hotel Blau-Mar. Lge, mkd pitch, shd; wc; chem disp; mv service pnt; shwrs inc; shop; el pnts (5A) inc; gas; lndtte; supmkt; snacks high ssn; bar; playgrnd; pool; solarium; dir access to sand beach; watersports; cycle hire; games rm; wifi; entmnt; dogs; phone; bus; poss cr; Eng spkn; quiet; ccard acc; red low ssn. "Excel site, espec low ssn; helpful owner; narr site rds; easy walk to town cent; trains to Barcelona & Gerona." ♦ € 37.00 2011*

See advertisement

BLANES 3C3 (1km S Coastal) 41.6550, 2.77861 **Camping El Pinar Beach**, Avda Villa de Madrid s/n, 17300 Blanes (Gerona) [972-33 10 83; fax 972-33 11 00; camping@elpinarbeach.com; www.elpinarbeach.com] Exit AP7/E15 junc 9 dir Malgrat. On app Blanes, all campsites are sp at rndabts; all sites along same rd. V lge, mkd pitch, shd; wc; chem disp; mv service pnt; baby facs; shwrs inc; el pnts (5A) inc; lndtte; shop; rest, snacks; bar; BBQ; playgrnd; pool; paddling pool; sand beach adj; games area; entmnt; excursions; internet; TV; 10% statics; dogs €2; phone; adv bkg; ccard acc; red long stay/low ssn/CKE/CCI. "V pleasant site; gd facs; lovely beach; lots to do." ♦ ltd 27 Mar-26 Sep. € 36.00   2010*

⊞ **BLANES** *3C3* (1.5km SW Urban/Coastal) *41.66305, 2.78083* **Camping La Masia, Calle Cristòfor Colon 44, 17300 Blanes (Gerona) [972-33 10 13; fax 972-33 31 28; info@campinglamasia.com; www.campinglamasia.com]** Fr A7 exit junc 9 sp Lloret de Mar, then Blanes. At Blanes foll sp Blanes Sur (Playa) & Campings, site immed past Camping S'Abanell, well sp. V lge, hdstg, pt shd; htd wc; chem disp; mv service pnt; 25% serviced pitches; sauna; steam rm; baby facs; shwrs inc; el pnts (3-5A) inc; lndtte (inc dryer); shop; rest, snacks; bar; playgrnd; 2 pools (1 htd, covrd); paddling pool; sand beach nrby; watersports; tennis 500m; weights rm; wellness cent; games area; games rm; wifi; entmnt; TV rm; 90% statics; dogs; site clsd mid-Dec to mid-Jan; poss cr; Eng spkn; adv bkg; poss noisy at w/ends; red long stay/low ssn; CKE/CCI. "Well-maintained site; excel, clean facs; helpful staff." ♦ € 38.50 (CChq acc)   2009*

BLANES *3C3* (1.5km SW Coastal) *41.66206, 2.78046* **Camping Solmar, Calle Cristòfor Colom 48, 17300 Blanes (Gerona) [972-34 80 34; fax 972-34 82 83; campingsolmar@campingsolmar.com; www.campingsolmar.com]** Fr N on AP7/E15 exit junc 9 onto NII dir Barcelona & foll sp Blanes. Fr S to end of C32, then NII dir Blanes. On app Blanes, foll camping sps. Lge, hdg/mkd pitch, shd; wc; chem disp; mv service pnt; baby facs; shwrs inc; el pnts (6A) inc; lndtte (inc dryer); shop; rest, snacks; bar; BBQ; playgrnd; 2 pools; paddling pool; sand beach 150m; tennis; games area; games rm; wifi; entmnt; some statics; dogs free; bus 100m; adv bkg; quiet; ccard acc; red long stay/low ssn/CKE/CCI. "Excel site & facs." ♦ 2 Apr-12 Oct. € 39.45 2011*

BOCA DE HUERGANO see Riaño *1A3*

⊞ **BOCAIRENT** *4F2* (9km E Rural) *38.75332, -0.54957* **Camping Mariola, Ctra Bocairent-Alcoy, Km 9, 46880 Bocairent (València) [962-13 51 60; info@campingmariola.com; www.campingmariola.com]** Fr N330 turn E at Villena onto CV81. N of Banyeres & bef Bocairent turn E sp Alcoi up narr, steep hill with some diff turns & sheer drops; site sp. Lge, hdstg, pt shd; htd wc (cont); chem disp; child/baby fac; mv service pnt; shwrs inc; el pnts (6A) inc; lndtte; shop; rest, snacks; bar; BBQ; cooking facs; playgrnd; pool; paddling pool; games area; games rm; bicycles; entmnt; wifi; TV (bar); twin axle acc; Eng spkn; adv bkg acc; 50% statics; phone; ccard acc; CKE/CCI. "In Mariola mountains; gd walking; superb tranquil location in Sierra Mariola National Park, excel walking & cycling, great for dogs, friendly family atmosphere." ♦ ltd € 22.00   2013*

BOLTANA see Ainsa *3B2*

BONANSA see Pont de Suert *3B2*

⊞ **BOSSOST** *3B2* (3km SE Rural) *42.74921, 0.70071* **Camping Prado Verde, Ctra de Lleida a Francia, N230, Km 173, 25551 Era Bordeta/La Bordeta de Vilamòs (Lleida) [tel/fax 973-64 71 72; info@campingpradoverde.es; www.campingpradoverde.es]** On N230 at km 173 on banks of Rv Garona. Med, shd; htd wc; mv service pnt; baby facs; shwrs; el pnts (6A) €5.50; lndtte (inc dryer); shop & 3km; rest, snacks; bar; playgrnd; pool; paddling pool; fishing; cycle hire; wifi; TV; some statics; dogs; bus; quiet; ccard acc; CKE/CCI. "V pleasant NH." € 22.00   2010*

BROTO *3B2* (1.2km W Rural) *42.59779, -0.13072* **Camping Oto, Afueras s/n, 22370 Oto-Valle De Broto (Huesca) [974-48 60 75; fax 974-48 63 47; info@campingoto.com; www.campingoto.com]** On N260 foll camp sp on N o'skts of Broto. Diff app thro vill but poss. Lge, pt sl, pt shd; wc; chem disp; baby facs; shwrs inc; el pnts (10A) €3.80 (poss no earth); gas; lndtte; shop; snacks; bar; BBQ; playgrnd; pool; paddling pool; entmnt; adv bkg; quiet; ccard acc. "Excel, clean san facs; excel bar & café; friendly owner; pitches below pool rec; some noise fr adj youth site; conv Ordesa National Park; gd site, pleasant." 5 Mar-15 Oct. € 30.20   2013*

⊞ **BROTO** *3B2* (6km W Rural) *42.61576, -0.15432* **Camping Viu, Ctra N260, Biescas-Ordesa, Km 484.2, 22378 Viu de Linás (Huesca) [974-48 63 01; fax 974-48 63 73; info@campingviu.com; www.campingviu.com]** Lies on N260, 4km W of Broto. Fr Broto, N for 2km on rd 135; turn W twd Biesca at junc with Torla rd; site approx 4km on R. Med, sl, pt shd; htd wc; chem disp; mv service pnt; shwrs inc; el pnts (5-8A) €4.20; gas; lndtte; shop; rest; BBQ; playgrnd; games rm; cycle hire; horseriding; walking, skiing & climbing adj; car wash; phone; adv bkg; quiet; ccard acc; CKE/CCI. "Friendly owners; gd home cooking; fine views; highly rec; clean, modern san facs; poss not suitable for lge o'fits." € 17.40   2011*

BURGOS () **Camping -Motel Pecon del Conde,**   2011*

⊞ **BURGOS** *1B4* (2.5km E Rural) *42.34111, -3.65777* **Camp Municipal Fuentes Blancas, Ctra Cartuja Miraflores, Km 3.5, 09193 Burgos [tel/fax 947-48 60 16; info@campingburgos.com; www.campingburgos.com]** E or W on A1 exit junc 238 & cont twd Burgos. Strt over 1st rndabt, then turn R sp Cortes. Look for yellow sps to site. Fr N (N627 or N623) on entering Burgos keep in R hand lane. Foll signs Cartuja miraflores & yellow camp signs. Lge, mkd pitch, shd; some htd wc; chem disp; mv service pnt; baby facs; shwrs inc; el pnts (6A) inc; gas; lndtte; shop high ssn & 3km; rest, snacks; bar; playgrnd; pool high ssn; games area; wifi; 10% statics; dogs €2.17; phone; bus at gate; poss cr; Eng spkn; quiet; ccard acc; "Clean facs but refurb req (2010); neat, roomy, well-maintained site adj woodland; some sm pitches; ltd facs low ssn; poss v muddy in wet; easy access town car parks or cycle/rv walk; Burgos lovely town; NH." € 35.50   2014*

CABO DE GATA see Almería *4G1*

⊞ **CABRERA, LA** *1D4* (1km SW Rural) *40.85797, -3.61580* **Camping Pico de la Miel, Ctra A-1 Salida 57, 28751 La Cabrera (Madrid) [918-68 80 82 or 918-68 95 07; fax 918-68 85 41; pico-miel@picodelamiel.com / info@picodelamiel.com; www.picodelamiel.com]** Fr Madrid on A1/E5, exit junc 57 sp La Cabrera. Turn L at rndabt, site sp. Lge, mkd pitch, pt sl, pt shd; htd wc; chem disp; shwrs inc; el pnts (10A) €4.45; gas; lndtte (inc dryer); shop high ssn; supmkt 1km; rest, snacks, bar high ssn & w/end; playgrnd; Olympic-size pool; paddling pool; sailing; fishing; windsurfing; tennis; games area; squash; mountain-climbing; car wash; 75% statics; dogs; phone; v cr high ssn & w/end; some Eng spkn; adv bkg; quiet; ccard acc; red long stay/low ssn/CKE/CCI. "Attractive walking country; conv Madrid; ltd touring area not v attractive; some pitches have low sun shades; excel san facs; ltd facs low ssn." ♦ ltd € 43.00   2014*

CABRERA, LA *1D4* (15km SW Rural) *40.80821, -3.69106*
Camping Piscis, Ctra Guadalix de la Sierra a Navalafuente, Km 3, 28729 Navalafuente (Madrid) [918-43 22 68; fax 918-43 22 53; campiscis@campiscis.com; www.campiscis.com] Fr A1/E5 exit junc 50 onto M608 dir Guidalix de la Sierra, foll sp to Navalafuente & site. Lge, hdg pitch, hdstg, pt sl, pt shd; wc; chem disp; shwrs €0.30; el pnts (5A) €4.85 (long lead req); gas; lndtte; shop 6km; rest, snacks; bar; playgrnd; pool; paddling pool; watersports 10km; tennis; games area; 75% statics; quiet; adv bkg; Eng spkn; ccard acc; red low ssn; CKE/CCI. "Mountain views; walking; bus to Madrid daily outside gate; spacious pitches but uneven; rough site rds." ♦ 15 Jun-15 Sep. € 24.20   2010*

"I like to fill in the reports as I travel from site to site"

You'll find report forms at the back of this guide, or you can fill them in online at www.caravaclub.co.uk/europereport.

⊞ **CACERES** *2E3* (4km NW Urban) *39.29190, -6.2446*
Camp Municipal Ciudad de Cáceres, Ctra N630, Km 549.5, 10005 Cáceres [927-23 31 00; fax 927- 23 58 96; info@campingcaceres.com; www.campingcaceres.com] Fr Cáceres ring rd take N630 dir Salamanca. At 1st rndbt turn R sp Via de Servicio with camping symbol. Foll sp 500m to site. Or fr N exit A66 junc 545 onto N630 twd Cáceres. At 2nd rndabt turn L sp Via de Servicio, site on L adj football stadium. Med, mkd pitch, hdstg, terr, unshd; wc; chem disp; mv service pnt; individual san facs each pitch; shwrs inc; el pnts (10-16A) €4.50; gas; lndtte; shop; rest, snacks; bar; BBQ; playgrnd; pool high ssn; paddling pool; games area; wifi; TV; 15% statics; dogs; bus 500m over footbdge; Eng spkn; adv bkg; distant noise fr indus est nrby; ccard acc; ACSI acc; red low ssn/CKE/CCI. "Vg, well-run site; excel facs; vg value rest; gd bus service to and fr interesting old town with many historical bldgs; excel site with ensuite facs at each pitch; location not pretty adj to football stadium & indus est; town to far to walk." € 32.00   2014*

CADAQUES *3B3* (1km N Coastal) *42.29172, 3.28260*
Camping Cadaqués, Ctra Port Lligat 17, 17488 Cadaqués (Girona) [972-25 81 26; fax 972-15 93 83; info@campingcadaques.com; www.spain.info] At ent to town, turn L at rdbt (3rd exit) sp thro narr rds, site in about 1.5km on L. NB App to Cadaqués on busy, narr mountain rds, not suitable lge o'fits. If raining, rds only towable with 4x4. Lge, mkd pitch, sl, pt shd; wc; chem disp; shwrs; el pnts (5A) €5.95; gas; lndtte; shop; rest, snacks; bar; playgrnd; pool; paddling pool; shgl beach 600m; no dogs; sep car park; poss cr; Eng spkn; no adv bkg; quiet; ccard acc. "Cadaqués home of Salvador Dali; sm pitches; medical facs high ssn; san facs poss poor low ssn; fair, red facs in LS next to m'way so poss noisy but gd for en-route stop." Easter-17 Sep. € 35.00   2013*

CADAVEDO see Luarca *1A3*

⊞ **CALATAYUD** *3C1* (15km N Rural) *41.44666, -1.55805*
Camping Saviñan Parc, Ctra El Frasno-Mores, Km 7, 50299 Saviñan (Zaragoza) [tel/fax 976-82 54 23] Exit A2/E90 (Zaragoza-Madrid) at km 255 to T-junc. Turn R to Saviñan for 6km, foll sps to site 1km S. Lge, hdstg, terr, pt shd; wc; chem disp; mv service pnt; shwrs inc; el pnts (6-10A) €4.20; gas; lndtte; shop; playgrnd; pool high ssn; tennis; horseriding; 50% statics; dogs €2.70; phone; site clsd Jan; quiet; ccard acc; CKE/CCI. "Beautiful scenery & views; some sm narr pitches; rec identify pitch location to avoid stop/start on hill; terr pitches have steep, unfenced edges; many pitches with sunscreen frames & diff to manoeuvre long o'fits; modern facs block but cold in winter & poss stretched high ssn; hot water to some shwrs only; gates poss clsd low ssn - use intercom; site poss clsd Feb." € 24.00   2014*

⊞ **CALDES DE MONTBUI** *3C3* (2km N Rural) *41.6442, 2.1564* **Camping El Pasqualet, Ctra Sant Sebastià de Montmajor, Km 0.3, 08140 Caldes de Montbui (Barcelona) [938-65 46 95; fax 938-65 38 96; elpasqualet@elpasqualet.com; www.elpasqualet.com]** N fr Caldes on C59 dir Montmajor, site sp on L off rd BV1243. Med, terr, pt shd; wc; chem disp; mv service pnt; baby facs; shwrs inc; el pnts (4A) €6.90; gas; lndtte (inc dryer); shop 2km; tradsmn; rest, snacks; bar; playgrnd; pool; games area; TV rm; 80% statics; dogs €2.60; bus 2km; site clsd mid-Dec to mid-Jan; poss cr; adv bkg; quiet. "Beautiful area; ltd touring pitches; facs poss stretched high ssn." ♦ € 26.40   2010*

CALELLA *3C3* (2km NE Coastal) *41.61774, 2.67680* **Camping Caballo de Mar, Passeig Maritim s/n, 08397 Pineda de Mar (Barcelona) [937-67 17 06; fax 937-67 16 15; info@caballodemar.com; www.caballodemar.com]** Fr N exit AP7 junc 9 & immed turn R onto NII dir Barcelona. Foll sp Pineda de Mar & turn L twd Paseo Maritimo. Fr S on C32 exit 122 dir Pineda de Mar & foll dir Paseo Maritimo. Lge site, sm mkd pitch, shd; wc; chem disp; baby facs; shwrs inc; el pnts (3-6A) €3.40-4.40; gas; lndtte; shop high ssn; tradsmn; rest, snacks; bar; BBQ; playgrnd; pool; sand beach adj; games area; games rm; entmnt; internet; 10% statics; dogs €2.20; rlwy stn 2km (Barcelona 30 mins); Eng spkn; adv bkg; quiet; ccard acc; red long stay/CKE/CCI. "Excursions arranged; gd touring base & conv Barcelona; gd, modern facs; excel; pitches sm for twin axle; noise fr locals on site." ♦ 31 Mar-30 Sep. € 33.70 (CChq acc)   2012*

⊞ **CALELLA** *3C3* (1km S Coastal) *41.60722, 2.63973*
Camping Botànic Bona Vista Kim, Ctra N11, Km 665.8, 08370 Calella de la Costa (Barcelona) [937-69 24 88; fax 937-69 58 04; info@botanic-bonavista.net; www.botanic-bonavista.net] A19/C32 exit sp Calella onto NII coast rd, site is sp S of Calella on R. Care needed on busy rd & sp almost on top of turning (adj Camp Roca Grossa). Lge, mkd pitch, hdstg, terr, pt shd; shwrs inc; wc; chem disp; mv service pnt; sauna; shwrs inc; el pnts (6A) €7.80 (rev pol); lndtte; supmkt; rest, snacks; bar; BBQ/picnic area; playgrnd; pool; paddling pool; sand beach adj; solarium; jacuzzi; TV; 20% statics; dogs €5.90; phone; poss cr; Eng spkn; adv bkg; some rd noise; ccard acc; CKE/CCI. "Steep access rd to site - owner prefers to tow c'vans with 4x4; poss diff v lge m'vans; all pitches have sea view; friendly owner; clean facs; train to Barcelona fr St Pol (2km)." ♦ € 30.80   2010*

SPAIN

CALELLA 3C3 (1km SW Coastal) 41.60635, 2.63890 **Camping Roca Grossa, Ctra N-11, Km 665, 08370 Calella (Barcelona) [937-69 12 97; fax 937-66 15 56; rocagrossa@rocagrossa. com; www.rocagrossa.com]** Situated off rd N11 at km stone 665, site sp. V steep access rd to site. Lge, sl, terr, shd; wc; chem disp; mv service pnt; shwrs inc; el pnts (6A) €6; gas; lndtte; shop & rest at ent; snacks; bar; games rm; TV rm; pool; playgrnd; beach adj; windsurfing; tennis; statics; phone; dogs €4.20; adv bkg; Eng spkn; ccard acc. "V friendly, family-run site; steep - tractor pull avail - but level pitches; clean modern facs; excel pool & playgrnd on top of hill; scenic drive to Tossa de Mar; conv for Barcelona." 1 Apr-30 Sep. € 28.40   2010*

CALIG 3D2 (1km NW Rural) 40.45183, 0.35211 **Camping L'Orangeraie, Camino Peniscola-Calig, 12589 Càlig [34 964 765 059; fax 34 964 765 460; info@camping-lorangeraie.es]** On AP7 exit 43 Benicarlo-Peniscola. 1st R at rndabt to Calig then foll sp to campsite. Fr N340 exit N232 to Morella, then after 1.5km turn L to Calig CV135, foll sp to campsite. Med, hdg pitch, mkd pitch, terr, pt shd; wc; chem disp; mv service pnt; baby facs; el pnts (10A); lndtte; shop; snack; bar; BBQ; playgrnd; pool; waterslide; paddling pool; sandy beach 8km; games area; entmnt; wifi; 15% statics; dogs €2.50; bus 1km; twin axles; Eng spkn; adv bkg; quiet. "Excel site". ♦ ltd 1 Apr-12 Oct. € 41.00   2014*

⊞ **CALLOSA D'EN SARRIA** 4F2 (6km NE Rural) 38.65450, -0.09246 **Camping Fonts d'Algar, Ptda Segarra, 03510 Callosa d'en Sarrià (Alicante) [639-52 03 65 or 699-11 26 88 (mob); campingalgar@hotmail.com; www. campingfontsdalgar.co.uk]** Exit A7 junc 64 & take CV755 NW dir Alcoi to Collosa. In Callosa take CV715 N & in 2km turn R at sp Fonts d'Algar. Steep, narr rd bef site on R. Med, hdstg, terr, unshd; wc; chem disp; shwrs inc; el pnts (5-16A) €4.50; shop & shop 6km; rest, snacks; bar; BBQ; sand beach 15km; entmnt; some statics; dogs; Eng spkn; quiet. "Mountain views; cactus garden & waterfalls nr; site being improved (2010)." € 23.00   2010*

CALONGE see Playa de Aro 3B3

⊞ **CALPE** 4F2 (300m NE Urban/Coastal) 38.64488, 0.05604 **Camping CalpeMar, Calle Eslovenia 3, 03710 Calpe (Alicante) [tel/fax 965-87 55 76; info@campingcalpemar. com; www.campingcalpemar.com]** Exit AP7/E15 junc 63 onto N332 & foll sp, take slip rd sp Calpe Norte & foll dual c'way CV746 round Calpe twd Peñón d'Ifach. At rndabt nr police stn with metal statues turn L, then L at next rndabt, over next rndabt, site 200m on R. Med, hdg/mkd pitch, hdstg, unshd; htd wc; chem disp; baby facs; all serviced pitches; shwrs inc; el pnts (10A) inc (metered for long stay); lndtte (inc dryer); ice; shop 500m; tradsmn; rest, snacks; bar; BBQ; playgrnd; pool; sand beach 300m; games area; games rm; entmnt; Spanish lessons; car wash; dog wash; wifi; TV rm; 3% statics; dogs free; phone; extra lge pitches avail at additional charge; bus adj; sep car park; Eng spkn; adv bkg; quiet; ccard acc; red long stay/low ssn; CKE/CCI. "High standard site; well-kept & laid out; gd security; excel; gd for long stay, friendly staff close to beach and Lidl." ♦ € 36.00 2012*

See advertisement

"We must tell The Club about that great site we found"

Get your site reports in by mid-August and we'll do our best to get your updates into the next edition.

⊞ **CAMARASA** 3B2 (23km N Rural) 42.00416, 0.86583 **Camping Zodiac, Ctra C13, Km 66, La Baronia de Sant Oïsme, 25621 Camarasa (Lleida) [tel/fax 973-45 50 03; zodiac@campingzodiac.com; www.campingzodiac.com]** Fr C13 Lleida to Balaguer. N of Balaguer take C13 & foll sp for Camarasa, then dir Tremp & site. Steep, winding but scenic app rd. Med, hdstg, pt sl, terr, pt shd; wc; chem disp; baby facs; shwrs; el pnts (5A) €4.60; shop; lndtte; rest, snacks; bar; playgrnd; pool; rv sw adj; tennis; TV; 90% statics; phone; Eng spkn; quiet; ccard acc. "Site on reservoir; poss untidy, shabby low ssn; some sm pitches diff due trees; excel views & walks; Terradets Pass 2km." ♦ ltd € 18.80   2011*

CAMBRILS See also sites listed under Salou.

SPAIN

⊞ **CAMBRILS** *3C2* (1km N Rural) *41.07928, 1.06661*
Camping Àmfora d'Arcs, Ctra N340, Km 1145, 43391 Vinyols i Els Arcs (Tarragona) [977-36 12 11; fax 977-79 50 75; info@amforadarcs.com; www.amforadarcs.com] Exit AP7 junc 37 onto N340 E & watch for km sps, site bet 1145 & 1146km. Lge, hdg pitch, hdstg, pt shd; wc; chem disp; shwrs inc; el pnts (5A) inc; gas; lndtte; supmkt opp; rest high ssn; bar; playgrnd; pool; beach 1.5km; 60% statics; dogs €4.50; phone; bus 300m; site poss clsd Xmas; poss cr; Eng spkn; adv bkg; noisy espec at w/end; ccard acc; red long stay/low ssn; CKE/CCI. "Sm pitches." € 34.50   2009*

CAMBRILS *3C2* (1.5km N Urban/Coastal) *41.06500, 1.08361*
Camping Playa Cambrils Don Camilo, Carrer Oleastrum 2, Ctra Cambrils-Salou, Km 1.5, 43850 Cambrils (Tarragona) [977-36 14 90; fax 977-36 49 88; camping@playacambrils.com; www.playacambrils.com] Exit A7 junc 37 dir Cambrils & N340. Turn L onto N340 then R dir port then L onto coast rd. Site sp on L at rndabt after rv bdge 100m bef watch tower on R, approx 2km fr port. V lge, hdg/mkd pitch, shd; wc; chem disp; baby facs; shwrs inc; el pnts (5A) inc; gas; lndtte (inc dryer); supmkt; rest, snacks; bar; playgrnd; htd pool; paddling pool; sand beach adj; tennis; games rm; boat hire; cycle hire; watersports; entmnt; children's club; cinema; wifi; TV rm; 25% statics; bus 200m; cash machine; doctor; 24-hr security; dogs €4.35; Eng spkn; adv bkg ess high ssn; some rd & rlwy noise; ccard acc; red long stay/low ssn/CKE/CCI. "Helpful, friendly staff; sports activities avail; Port Aventura 5km; vg site." ♦ 15 Mar-12 Oct. € 43.35 (CChq acc) 2011*

See advertisement

CAMBRILS *3C2* (2km S Coastal) *41.05533, 1.02333* **Camping Joan**, Urbanització La Dorada, Passeig Marítim 88, 43850 Cambrils (Tarragona) [977-36 46 04; fax 977-79 42 14; info@campingjoan.com; www.campingjoan.com] Exit AP7 junc 37 onto N340, S dir València. Turn off at km 1.141 & Hotel Daurada, foll site sp. Lge, hdg/mkd pitch, hdstg, terr, shd; htd wc; chem disp; mv service pnt; baby facs; shwrs inc; el pnts (5A) €4.40; gas; lndtte; supmkt; rest, snacks; bar; BBQ; playgrnd; pool & paddling pool; sand beach adj; watersports; fishing; cycle hire; games area; games rm; wifi; entmnt; sat TV; 16% statics; dogs €3.10; phone; currency exchange; car wash; Eng spkn; adv bkg; quiet; red low ssn/long stay/CKE/CCI. "Conv Port Aventura; gd family site; v clean san facs; friendly welcome; some sm pitches; gd beach; vg." ♦ 27 Mar-5 Nov. € 30.00   2009*

CAMBRILS *3C2* (5km SW Coastal) *41.04694, 1.00361*
Camping Oasis Mar, Ctra de València N340, Km 1139, 43892 Montroig (Tarragona) [977-17 95 95; fax 977-17 95 16; info@oasismar.com; www.oasismar.com] Fr AP7 exit 37; N340 Tarragona-València rd, at Montroig, km 1139. Lge, mkd pitch, pt shd; wc; chem disp; shwrs inc; baby facs; el pnts (5A) €5; gas; lndtte; shop; rest, snacks; bar; BBQ; playgrnd; pool; sand beach adj; watersports; 30% statics; dogs €5.08 Eng spkn; red long stay/low ssn. "Excel site by super beach; friendly, helpful owners; gd facs; busy at w/end when statics occupied; vg." 1 Mar-31 Oct. € 30.00   2009*

CAMBRILS *3C2* (8km SW Coastal) *41.03333, 0.96777*
Playa Montroig Camping Resort, N340, Km1.136, 43300 Montroig (Tarragona) [977 810 637; fax 977 811 411; info@playamontroig.com; www.playamontroig.com] Exit AP7 junc 37, W onto N340. Site has own dir access onto N340 bet Cambrils & L'Hospitalet de L'Infant, well sp fr Cambrils. V lge, mkd pitch, pt sl, shd; htd wc; chem disp; mv service pnt; serviced pitches; baby facs; shwrs inc; el pnts (10A) inc; gas; lndtte; supmkt; rest, snacks; bars; playgrnd; 3 htd pools; sand beach adj; tennis; games area; games rm; skateboard track; many sports; cycle hire; golf 3km; cash machine; doctor; wifi; entmnt; 30% statics; no dogs; phone; Eng spkn; adv bkg; some rd & rlwy noise; ccard acc; red snr citizens/low ssn/CKE/CCI. "Magnificent, clean, secure site; private, swept beach; some sm pitches & low branches; 4 grades pitch/price; highly rec." ♦ 1 Apr-30 Oct. € 68.00   2011*

⊞ **CAMBRILS** *3C2* (1.8km W Urban/Coastal) *41.06550, 1.04460* **Camping La Llosa**, Ctra N340 Barcelona a Valencia, Km 1143, 43850 Cambrils (Tarragona) [977-36 26 15; fax 977-79 11 80; info@camping-lallosa.com; www.camping-lallosa.com] Exit A7/E15 at junc 37 & join N340 S. Head S into Cambrils (ignore L turn to cent) & at island turn R. Site sp on L within 100m. Fr N exit junc 35 onto N340. Strt over at x-rds, then L over rlwy bdge at end of rd, strt to site. V lge, hdstg, shd; wc; shwrs inc; el pnts (5A) €5; gas; lndtte; shop; rest, snacks; bar; playgrnd; pool; sand beach; entmnt high ssn; car wash; 50% statics; dogs €3.50; phone; bus 500m; poss cr; Eng spkn; some rd & rlwy noise; ccard acc; red long stay/low ssn. "Interesting fishing port; gd facs; excel pool; gd supmkt nrby; poss diff siting for m'vans due low trees; excel winter NH." ♦ € 62.00   2014*

CAMBRILS *3C2* (8km W Coastal) *41.03717, 0.97622*
**Camping La Torre del Sol, Ctra N340, Km 1.136,
Miami-Playa, 43300 Montroig Del Camp (Tarragona)
[977 810 486; fax 977-81 13 06; info@latorredelsol.com;
www.latorredelsol.com]** Leave A7 València/Barcelona
m'way at junc 37 & foll sp Cambrils. After 1.5km join N340
coast rd S for 6km. Watch for site sp 4km bef Miami Playa.
Fr S exit AP7 junc 38, foll sp Cambrils on N340. Site on R
4km after Miami Playa. Site ent narr, alt ent avail for lge
o'fits. V lge, hdg/mkd pitch, shd; wc; chem disp; mv service
pnt; baby facs; sauna; shwrs inc; el pnts (6A) inc (10A avail);
gas; lndtte (inc dryer); supmkt; tradsmn; rest, snacks; bar;
BBQ; playgrnd; 2 htd pools; paddling pool; whirlpool; jacuzzi;
direct access private sand beach; tennis; squash; pitch 'n'
putt; 80% statics; dogs €1.30; phone; Eng spkn; adv bkg;
gym; skateboard zone; golf 4km; cinema; disco; games rm;
wifi; entmnt; TV; 40% statics; no dogs; poss v cr; Eng spkn;
adv bkg; quiet, but some rd/rlwy noise & disco; ccard acc;
red low ssn. "Attractive well-guarded site for all ages; sandy
pitches; gd, clean san facs; steps to facs for disabled; access to
pitches poss diff lge o'fits due trees & narr site rds; radios/TVs
to be used inside vans only; conv Port Aventura, Aquaparc,
Aquopolis; highly rec, can't praise site enough; excel." ♦
15 Mar-30 Oct. € 52.00 (CChq acc) SBS - E14   2011*

See advert on previous page

⊞ **CAMPELL** *4E2* (1km S Rural) *38.77672, -0.10529* **Camping
Vall de Laguar, Carrer Sant Antoni 24, 03791 La Vall de
Laguar (Alicante) [965-57 74 90 or 699-77 35 09; info@
campinglaguar.com; www.campinglaguar.com]** Exit A7
junc 62 sp Ondara. Turn L to Orba onto CV733 dir Benimaurell
& foll sp to Vall de Laguar. In Campell vill (narr rds) fork L &
foll site sp uphill (narr rd). Steep ent to site. Lge o'fits ignore sp
in vill & turn R to Fleix vill. In Fleix turn L to main rd, downhill
to site sp at hairpin. Diff app. Med, mkd pitch, hdstg, terr, pt
shd; htd wc; chem disp; shwrs inc; el pnts (5-10A) €2.75; gas;
lndtte; shop 500m; rest, snacks; bar; BBQ; pool; sand beach
18km; 50% statics; dogs €1.30; phone; Eng spkn; adv bkg;
quiet; ccard acc; red low ssn/long stay; CKE/CCI. "Sm pitches
diff for lge o'fits; m'vans 7.50m max; excel home-cooked food
in rest; ideal site for walkers; mountain views; friendly owners
live on site; excel but rec sm o'fits & m'vans only." ♦ ltd
€ 21.50   2009*

CAMPELLO, EL see Alicante *4F2*

⊞ **CAMPRODON** *3B3* (2km S Rural) *42.29010, 2.36230*
**Camping Vall de Camprodon, Les Planes d'en Xenturri,
Ctra Ripoll-Campródon, C38, Km 7.5, 17867 Campródon
[972-74 05 07; fax 972-13 06 32; info@valldecamprodon.
net; www.valldecamprodon.net]** Fr Gerona W on C66/C26
to Sant Pau de Segúries. Turn N onto C38 to Campródon, site
sp. Access over bdge weight limit 3,5000 kg. Lge, mkd pitch,
pt shd; htd wc; mv service pnt; baby facs; shwrs; el pnts (4-10)
€4.20-9.10 (poss rev pol); lndtte (inc dryer); shop; rest, snacks;
bar; BBQ; playgrnd; pool; paddling pool; rv fishing; tennis;
games area; horseriding; wifi; entmnt; TV; 90% statics; dogs
€5; bus 200m; o'night m'van area (no san facs); adv bkg; quiet.
"Campródon attractive vill; lovely scenery; peaceful site; helpful
staff; ltd facs low ssn." ♦ € 31.40 (CChq acc)   2011*

CANDAS see Gijon *1A3*

CANDELARIO see Béjar *1D3*

CANET DE MAR *3C3* (1.5km E Coastal) *41.59086, 2.59195*
**Camping Globo Rojo, Ctra N11, Km 660.9, 08360 Canet
de Mar (Barcelona) [tel/fax 937-94 11 43; camping@
globo-rojo.com; www.globo-rojo.com]** On N11 500m N
of Canet de Mar. Site clearly sp on L. Gd access. Med, hdg/
mkd pitch, hdstg, shd; wc; chem disp; baby facs; shwrs; el pnts
(10A) €6; gas; lndtte; shop; tradsmn; rest, snacks; bar; BBQ;
playgrnd; pool; paddling pool; shgl beach & watersports adj;
tennis; games area; horseriding 2km; cycle hire; internet; TV
rm; 80% statics; dogs €5.50; phone; sep car park; Eng spkn;
adv bkg; rd noise; ccard acc; red low ssn/CKE/CCI. "Excel
facs; friendly, family-run site; busy w/end; slightly run down
area; conv Barcelona by train (40km)." ♦ 1 Apr-30 Sep.
€ 42.00   2010*

⊞ **CANGAS DE ONIS** *1A3* (16km E Rural) *43.33527,
-4.94777* **Camping Picos de Europa, Avin-Onís, 33556
Avin, [985-84 40 70; fax 985-84 42 40; info@picos-europa.
com; www.picos-europa.com]** E80, exit 307. Dir Posada A5-
115. Loc on the rd Onis-Carrena, 15km fr Cangas de Onis and
10 km fr Carrena, foll sps. Med, hdg/mkd pitch, terr, pt shd;
wc; chem disp; baby facs; shwrs inc; el pnts (6A) €3.80; gas;
lndtte (inc dryer); shop; rest, snacks; bar; pool; beach 20km;
horseriding; canoeing on local rvs; some statics; phone; poss cr;
Eng spkn; adv bkg; some rd noise & goat bells; ccard not acc;
CKE/CCI. "Owners v helpful; beautiful, busy, well-run site; vg
value rest; modern san facs; poss diff access due narr site rds
& cr; some sm pitches - lge o'fits may need 2; conv local caves,
mountains, National Park, beaches; highly rec." € 21.75 2013*

CANGAS DE ONIS *1A3* (3km SE Rural) *43.34715, -5.08362*
**Camping Covadonga, 33589 Soto de Cangas (Asturias)
[tel/fax 985-94 00 97; info@camping-covadonga.com;
www.camping-covadonga.com]** N625 fr Arriondas to
Cangas de Onis, then AS114 twds Covadonga & Panes, cont
thro town sp Covadonga. At rndabt take 2nd exit sp Cabrales,
site on R in 100m. Access tight. Med, mkd pitch, pt shd; wc;
chem disp; shwrs; el pnts (10A) €3.50 (no earth); lndtte (inc
dryer); shop; supmkt in town; rest, snacks; bar; bus adj; poss cr;
adv bkg; quiet, but slight rd noise; red long stay; CKE/CCI. "Sm
pitches; take care with access; site rds narr; 17 uneven steps
to san facs; conv for Picos de Europa." Holy Week & 15 Jun-
30 Sep. € 21.20   2009*

CAPMANY see Figueres *3B3*

CARAVIA ALTA see Colunga *1A3*

CARBALLINO *1B2* (1.5km W Rural) **Camp Municipal
Arenteiro, Parque Etnográfico do Arenteiro s/n, 32500 O
Carballiño (Ourense) [988-27 38 09; camping@carballino.
org; www.campingarenteiro.carballino.org]** N fr Ourense
on N541, just beyond km 29, turn L at Godas do Rio at site
sp. Site in 1km on L. Sm, mkd pitch, shd; wc; chem disp; mv
service pnt; shwrs inc; el pnts (10A) €2.50; lndry rm; shop
& 1.5km; rest, snacks; bar; BBQ; playgrnd; dogs; Eng spkn;
quiet; red CKE/CCI. "In Ribeiro wine area among well-wooded
mountains; vg mkd walks; highly rec." ♦ Holy Week & 1 May-
30 Sep. € 12.50   2010*

⊞ **CARBALLO** *1A2* (6km N Coastal) *43.29556, -8.65528*
Camping Baldayo, Ctra Coruña- Arteyo, 15684 Carballo
(La Coruña) [981-73 95 29] Loc in Rebordelos, access via
AC-514. Sm, pt sl, terr, pt shd; wc; chem disp; shwrs; el pnts
€1.50; lndtte; shop; snacks; bar; playgrnd; sand beach 500m;
95% statics; no dogs; phone; poss cr; quiet. "Sm pitches &
narr camp rds poss diff lge o'fits; poss unkempt low ssn."
€ 15.20   2012*

CARCHUNA see Motril *2H4*

⊞ **CARIDAD, LA (EL FRANCO)** *1A3* (1km SE Coastal)
43.54795, -6.80701 **Camping Playa de Castelló,**
Ctra N634, Santander-La Coruña, Km 532, 33758 La
Caridad (El Franca) (Asturias) [985-47 82 77; contacto@
campingcastello.com; www.campingcastello.com/] On
N634/E70 Santander dir La Coruña, turn N at km 532. Site in
200m fr N634, sp fr each dir. Sm, mkd pitch, pt shd; wc; chem
disp; baby facs; shwrs inc; el pnts (2-5A) €3; gas; lndtte; shop,
tradsmn, bar high ssn only; BBQ; playgrnd; shgl beach 800m;
internet; some statics; dogs €1; bus 200m; Eng spkn; adv bkg;
quiet; red long stay/CKE/CCI. "A green oasis with character;
gd." Holy Week & 1 Jun-30 Sep. € 23.00   2012*

⊞ **CARIDAD, LA (EL FRANCO)** *1A3* (3.6km W Rural)
43.55635, -6.86218 **Camping A Grandella, Ctra N634, Km**
536.9 (Desvío San Juan de Prendonés), 33746 Valdepares
(Asturias) [607-85 49 00/661-35 28 70 (mob); camping@
campingagrandella.com] Sp fr N634/E70. Med, pt shd;
wc; chem disp; shwrs inc; el pnts €3.50; lndtte; snacks; bar;
playgrnd; bus 200m; some statics; dogs €1; site clsd mid-
Dec to mid-Jan; quiet. "Attractive little site; well-situated."
€ 18.00   2012*

⊞ **CARLOTA, LA** *2G3* (1km NE Rural) *37.68321, -4.91891*
Camping Carlos III, Ctra de Madrid-Cádiz Km 430.5, 14100
La Carlota (Córdoba) [957-30 03 38; fax 957-30 06 97;
camping@campingcarlosiii.com; www.campingcarlosiii.
com] Approx 25km SW fr Córdoba on A4/E5, exit at km 432
turning L under autovia. Turn L at rndabt on main rd, site
well sp on L in 800m. Lge, mkd pitch, hdstg, pt sl &
htd wc (some cont); chem disp; shwrs inc; el pnts (5-10A) €4;
gas; lndtte; shop; rest; bar; BBQ; playgrnd; pool; horseriding;
30% statics; dogs; phone; Eng spkn; adv bkg; ccard acc; red
long stay; CKE/CCI. "V efficient, well-run site; less cr than
Córdoba municipal site; excel pool; gd, clean facs; if pitched
under mulberry trees, poss staining fr berries; bus to Córdoba
every 2 hrs." ◆ € 20.85   2010*

⊞ **CARRION DE LOS CONDES** *1B4* (400m W Rural)
42.33694, -4.60638 **Camping El Edén, Ctra Vigo-Logroño,**
Km 200, 34120 Carrión de los Condes (Palencia) [979-
88 11 52; administracion@campingeleden.es; www.
campingeleden.es] Exit A231 to Carrión, turn L immed onto
N120 sp Burgos & ent town fr NE. Site sp E & W ents to town
off N120 adj Rv Carrión at El Plantio. App poorly sp down narr
rds to rv. Suggest park nr Café España & check rte on foot.
Med, mkd pitch, pt shd; wc; shwrs; mv service pnt; el pnts (5A)
€3.50; gas; lndtte; rest; bar; playgrnd; dogs; bus 500m; ccard
acc. "Pleasant walk to town; basic rvside site; recep in bar/rest;
site open w/ends only low ssn; fair NH; quite lively in high ssn."
◆ € 22.00   2014*

⊞ **CARTAGENA** *4G1* (10km SW Coastal/Rural) *37.58611,*
-1.0675 **Camping Naturista El Portús (Naturist), 30393**
Cartagena (Murcia) [968-55 30 52; fax 968-55 30 53;
elportus@elportus.com; www.elportus.com] Fr N332
Cartagena to Mazarrón rd take E20 to Canteras. In Canteras
turn R onto E22 sp Isla Plana & in 500m turn L onto E21 sp
Galifa/El Portús. In 2km at rndabt, site ent on L. Lge, mkd pitch;
some hdstg, pt shd; wc; chem disp; mv service pnt; shwrs inc;
el pnts (6A) inc; gas; lndtte (inc dryer); shop; rest, snacks; bar;
playgrnd; htd, covrd pool & paddling pool; shgl beach adj;
tennis; games area; gym; spa; golf 15km; internet; entmnt;
30% statics; dogs €4.80; phone; bus 1km; poss cr; Eng spkn;
ccard acc; red low ssn/long stay; INF card req. "Restful low
ssn; gd situation; many long-stay winter visitors; helpful staff;
random pitching & poss untidy site; Cartagena interesting old
town." ◆ ltd € 40.80   2009*

CASPE *3C2* (12km NE Rural) *41.28883, 0.05733* **Lake Caspe**
Camping, Ctra N211, Km 286.7, 50700 Caspe (Zaragoza)
[976-63 41 74 or 689-99 64 30 (mob); fax 976-63 41 87;
lakecaspe@lakecaspe.com; www.campinglakecaspe.com]
Fr E leave AP2 or N11 at Fraga & foll N211 dir Caspe to site.
Fr W take N232 fr Zaragoza then A1404 & A221 E thro Caspe
to site in 16km on L at km 286.7, sp. Med, hdg/mkd pitch,
hdstg, pt shd; wc; chem disp; baby facs; shwrs inc; el pnts
(5-10A) €5.60; gas; lndtte; shop; rest, snacks; bar; playgrnd;
pool high ssn; fishing; sailing; 10% statics; dogs €3.75; phone;
poss cr; Eng spkn; adv bkg; quiet; CKE/CCI. "Gd, well-run,
scenic site but isolated (come prepared); avoid on public hols;
site rds gravelled but muddy after rain; sm pitches nr lake; gd
watersports; mosquitoes; beware low branches." 1Mar-10 Nov.
€ 36.80   2013*

CASTANARES DE LA RIOJA see Haro *1B4*

CASTELLBO see Seo de Urgel *3B3*

CASTELLO D'EMPURIES *3B3* (4km NE Rural) *42.26460,*
3.10160 **Camping Mas Nou, Ctra Mas Nou 7, Km 38,**
17486 Castelló d'Empúries (Gerona) [972-45 41 75;
fax 972-45 43 58; info@campingmasnou.com; www.
campingmasnou.com] On m'way A7 exit 3 if coming
fr France & exit 4 fr Barcelona dir Roses (E) C260. Site on L at
ent to Empuriabrava - use rndabt to turn. Lge, shd, mkd pitch;
htd wc; chem disp; mv service point; baby facs; shwrs inc; el
pnts (10A) €4.90; lndtte (inc dryer); shops 200m; rest, snacks;
bar; BBQ; playgrnd; pool; beach 2.5km; tennis; games area;
wifi; entmnt; TV; 5% statics; dogs €2.35; phone; Eng spkn;
red long stay/low ssn; ccard acc; CKE/CCI. "Aqua Park 4km,
Dali Museum 10km; gd touring base; helpful staff; well-run
site; excel, clean san facs; sports activities & children's club; gd
cycling; excel." ◆ 31 Mar-30 Sep. € 38.70 (CChq acc) 2011*

CASTELLO D'EMPURIES *3B3* (4km SE Coastal) *42.20725, 3.10026* **Camping Nautic Almatá, Aiguamolls de l'Empordà, 17486 Castelló d'Empúries (Gerona)** [972-45 44 77; fax 972-45 46 86; info@almata.com; www.almata.com] Fr A7 m'way exit 3; foll sp to Roses. After 12km turn S for Sant Pere Pescador & site on L in 5km. Site clearly sp on rd Castelló d'Empúries-Sant Pere Pescador. Lge, pt shd; wc; chem disp; shwrs inc; el pnts (10A) inc; rest; gas; shop; lndtte; playgrnd; pool; sand beach adj; sailing school; tennis; games area; horseriding; cycle hire; TV; disco bar on beach; entmnt; dogs €6.40; poss cr; adv bkg; quiet; red low ssn. "Excel, clean facs; ample pitches; sports facs inc in price; helpful staff; direct access to nature reserve; waterside pitches rec." ♦ 16 May-20 Sep. € 59.00   2011*

CASTELLO D'EMPURIES *3B3* (1km S Coastal) *42.25563, 3.13791* **Camping Castell Mar, Ctra Roses-Figueres, Km 40.5, Playa de la Rubina, 17486 Castelló d'Empúries (Gerona)** [972-45 08 22; fax 972-45 23 30; cmar@campingparks.com; www.campingparks.com] Exit A7 at junc 3 sp Figueres; turn L onto C260 sp Roses, after traff lts cont twd Roses, turn R down side of rest La Llar for 1.5km, foll sp Playa de la Rubina. Lge, hdg/mkd pitch, pt shd; wc; chem disp; serviced pitches; baby facs; shwrs inc; el pnts (6-10A) inc; gas; lndtte (inc dryer); shop; tradsmn; rest, snacks; bar; BBQ; playgrnd; pool; paddling pool; sand beach 100m; games rm; entmnt; sat TV; 30% statics; dogs; phone; Eng spkn; adv bkg; quiet; red low ssn; CKE/CCI. "Pitches poss unsuitable lge o'fits; gd location; excel for families." ♦ 22 May-19 Sep. € 52.00   2013*

CASTELLO D'EMPURIES *3B3* (5km S Coastal) *42.23735, 3.12121* **Camping-Caravaning Laguna, Platja Can Turias, 17486 Castelló d'Empúries (Gerona)** [972-45 05 53; fax 972-45 07 99; info@campinglaguna.com] Exit AP7 junc 4 dir Roses. After 12km at rndabt take 3rd exit, site sp. Site in 4km; rough app track. V lge, mkd pitch, pt shd; wc; chem disp; mv service pnt; some serviced pitches (inc gas); baby facs; shwrs inc; el pnts (5A) inc; gas; lndtte; supmkt; rest, snacks; bar; playgrnd; htd beach; sailing; watersports; tennis; games area; multisports area; cycle hire; horseriding; wifi; entmnt; 4% statics; dogs €2; Eng spkn; adv bkg; quiet; red snr citizens/long stay/low ssn; ccard acc; CKE/CCI. "Clean, modern san facs; gd birdwatching; excel." ♦ 5 Apr-31 Oct. € 49.70   2010*

CASTRO URDIALES *1A4* (1km N Coastal) *43.39000, -3.24194* **Camping de Castro, Barrio Campijo, 39700 Castro Urdiales (Cantabria)** [942-86 74 23; fax 942-63 07 25; info@campingdecastro.com] Fr Bilbao turn off A8 at 2nd Castro Urdiales sp, km 151. Camp sp on R by bullring. V narr, steep lanes to site - no passing places, great care req. Lge, pt sl, pt terr, unshd; wc; shwrs inc; el pnts (6A) €3; lndtte; shop; rest; bar; playgrnd; pool; sand beach 1km; 90% statics; dogs; phone; bus; poss cr; Eng spkn; adv bkg; quiet; CKE/CCI. "Gd, clean facs; conv NH for ferries; ltd touring pitches; narr, long, steep single track ent; great views over Bilbao bay." ♦ ltd 13 Feb-10 Dec. € 39.60   2014*

CASTROJERIZ *1B4* (1km NE Rural) *42.29102, -4.13165* **Camping Camino de Santiago, Calle Virgen del Manzano s/n, 09110 Castrojeriz (Burgos)** [947-37 72 55 or 658-96 67 43 (mob); fax 947-37 72 36; info@campingcamino.com; www.campingcamino.com] Fr N A62/E80 junc 40 dir Los Balbases, Vallunquera & Castrojeriz - narr, uneven rd. In 16 km ent Castrojeriz, sp fr BU400 where you turn onto BU404. Once on BU404 proceed for approx 500yds to next rndabt, take 2nd exit. Site 1m on the L. Fr S A62, exit 68 twds Torquemada, then take P412, then BU4085 to Castrojeriz. Do not go thro town, as rd are narr. Med, hdg/mkd pitch, pt sl, shd; wc (some cont); chem disp (wc); shwrs inc; el pnts (5-10A) €4 (poss no earth); lndtte (inc dryer); shop 1km; rest, snacks; bar; games area; games rm; internet; TV rm; dogs €2; bus 200m; some Eng spkn; quiet; CKE/CCI. "Lovely site; helpful owner; pilgrims' refuge on site; some diff sm pitches; vg; site ent narr; excel bird watching tours on req; san facs dated." ♦ ltd 15 Mar-15 Nov. € 32.00   2014*

CASTROPOL see Ribadeo *1A2*

CEE *1A1* (6km NW Coastal) *42.94555, -9.21861* **Camping Ruta Finisterre, Ctra La Coruña-Finisterre, Km 6, Playa de Estorde, 15270 Cée (La Coruña)** [tel/fax 981-74 63 02; www.rutafinisterre.com] Foll sp thro Cée & Corcubión on rd AC445 twd Finisterre; site easily seen on R of rd (no thro rd). Lge, mkd pitch, terr, shd; wc; chem disp; shwrs inc; el pnts (10A) €4; gas; lndtte; shop & 1km; rest, snacks; bar; playgrnd; sand beach 100m; dogs €3.70; phone; bus adj; poss cr; Eng spkn; adv bkg; some rd noise; ccard acc; CKE/CCI. "Family-run site in pine trees - check access to pitch & el pnts bef positioning; gd, clean facs; 5km to Finisterre; clean beach adj; peaceful." ♦ Holy Week & 1 Jun-10 Sep. € 23.00   2010*

CERVERA DE PISUERGA *1B4* (500m W Rural) *42.87135, -4.50332* **Camping Fuentes Carrionas, La Bárcena s/n, 34840 Cervera de Pisuerga (Palencia)** [979-87 04 24; fax 979-12 30 76; campingfuentescarrionas@hotmail.com] Fr Aguilar de Campóo on CL626 pass thro Cervera foll sp CL627 Potes. Site sp on L bef rv bdge. Med, mkd pitch, pt shd; wc; chem disp; shwrs inc; el pnts €3.50; lndtte; shop 500m; rest 500m; bar; tennis; games area; 80% statics; bus 100m; quiet; CKE/CCI. "Gd walking in nature reserve; conv Casa del Osos bear info cent." ♦ ltd Holy Week-30 Sep. € 21.00 2009*

⊞ **CIUDAD RODRIGO** *1D3* (1km SW Rural) *40.59206, -6.53445* **Camping La Pesquera, Ctra Cáceres-Arrabal, Km 424, Huerta La Toma, 37500 Ciudad Rodrigo (Salamanca)** [tel/fax 923-48 13 48; campinglapesquera@hotmail.com; www.campinglapesquera.com] Fr Salamanca on A62/E80 exit junc 332. Look for tent sp on R & turn R, then 1st L & foll round until site on rvside. Med, mkd pitch, pt shd; wc; shwrs inc; el pnts (6A) inc; lndtte; shop; snacks; rv sw; fishing adj; wifi; TV; dogs free; phone; poss cr; no adv bkg; quiet; ccard acc; CKE/CCI. "Medieval walled city worth visit - easy walk over Roman bdge; gd san facs; gd, improved site; friendly nice sm site, gd for NH; vg site." ♦ € 22.50   2011*

⊞ CLARIANA *3B3* (4km NE Rural) *41.95878, 1.60361*
Camping La Ribera, Pantà de Sant Ponç, 25290 Clariana
de Cardener (Lleida) [tel/fax 973-48 25 52; info@
campinglaribera.com; www.campinglaribera.com]
Fr Solsona S on C55, turn L onto C26 at km 71. Go 2.7km, site
sp immed bef Sant Ponç Dam. Lge, mkd pitch, hdstg, pt shd;
wc; chem disp; baby facs; shwrs; el pnts (4-10A) €4.60-8.45;
lndtte; shop; snacks; bar; playgrnd; pool; paddling pool; lake
sw & beach 500m; tennis; games area; TV; 95% statics; dogs;
bus 2.5km; phone; quiet. "Excel facs; gd site; narr pitches." ♦
€ 27.48   2014*

⊞ COLOMBRES *1A4* (3km SW Rural) *43.37074, -4.56799*
Camping Colombres, Ctra El Peral A Noriega Kml
- 33590 Colombres (Ribadedeva) [985 412 244; fax
985 413 056; campingcolombres@hotmail.com; www.
campingcolombres.com] E70/A8 Santander-Oviede, between
283 & 284km markers, shop L turn opp petrol stn. Site to
L 1km. Med; mkd pitch; terr; pt shd; htd wc; chem disp
dedicated point; mv service pnt; child/baby facs; shwr(s) inc; el
pnts (6A) €4.20; lndtte (inc dryer); shop; rest, snacks; bar; BBQ
sep area; playgrnd; pool; sandy beach (3km); games area; wifi;
5% statics; dogs free; twin axles; Eng spkn; quiet; ccard acc;
red low ssn; CKE/CCI; "Quiet, peaceful site in rural setting with
fine mountain views; v helpful owners; nice pool; excel san
facs; well kept & clean; immac, modern san facs; gd walking."
♦ € 37.70   2014*

COLUNGA *1A3* (1km N Coastal) *43.49972, -5.26527*
Camping Costa Verde, Playa La Griega de Colunga, 33320
Colunga (Asturias) [tel/fax 985-85 63 73] N632 coast rd,
fr E turn R twd Lastres in cent of Colunga; site 1km on R. Med,
mkd pitch, unshd; wc; chem disp; mv service pnt; baby facs;
shwrs; el pnts (5A) €3.50 - €5.20 (poss rev pol); gas; lndtte;
shop; rest; bar; BBQ; playgrnd; sand beach 500m; games
area; cycle hire; 50% statics; dogs €3; bus 500m; adv bkg;
quiet but some rd noise; ccard acc; CKE/CCI. "Beautiful sandy
beach; lovely views to mountains & sea; poss noise some fr rd
& resident static owners; some site access rds used for winter
storage; gd, plentiful facs; ltd hot water low ssn; friendly,
welcoming staff; pleasant town." Easter & 1 Jun-30 Sep.
€ 19.25   2011*

COLUNGA *1A3* (8km E Coastal) *43.47160, -5.18434* Camping
Arenal de Moris, Ctra de la Playa s/n, 33344 Caravia Alta
(Asturias) [985-85 30 97; fax 985-85 31 37; camoris@
desdeasturias.com; www.arenaldemoris.com] Fr E70/A8
exit junc 337 onto N632 to Caravia Alta, site clearly sp. Lge,
mkd pitch, terr, pt shd; wc; chem disp; shwrs inc; el pnts (5A)
€4.50; lndtte; shop; rest, snacks; bar; playgrnd; pool; sand
beach 500m; tennis; 10% statics; bus 1.5km; adv bkg; quiet
but rd noise; ccard acc; CKE/CCI. "Lovely views to mountains
& sea; well-kept, well-run site; excel, clean san facs."
Easter-20 Sep. € 24.00   2009*

COMA RUGA see Vendrell, El *3C3*

COMILLAS *1A4* (1km E Coastal) *43.38583, -4.28444*
Camping de Comillas, 39520 Comillas (Cantabria) [942-
72 00 74; fax 942-21 52 06; info@campingcomillas.com;
www.campingcomillas.com] Site on coast rd CA131 at
E end of Comillas by-pass. App fr Santillana or San Vicente
avoids town cent & narr streets. Lge, hdg/mkd pitch, pt sl, pt
shd; wc; chem disp; shwrs inc; el pnts (5A) €3.85; lndtte (inc
dryer); shop; tradsmn; rest 1km; snacks; bar; playgrnd; sand
beach 800m; TV; dogs; phone; poss cr; adv bkg; quiet; CKE/
CCI. "Clean, ltd facs low ssn (hot water to shwrs only); vg site
in gd position with views; easy walk to interesting town; gd
but rocky beach across rd; helpful owner; pitches inbetween 2
rds." Holy Week & 1 Jun-30 Sep. € 34.00   2013*

COMILLAS *1A4* (3km E Rural) *43.38328, -4.24689* Camping
El Helguero, 39527 Ruiloba (Cantabria) [942-72 21 24; fax
942-72 10 20; reservas@campingelhelguero.com; www.
campingelhelguero.com] Exit A8 junc 249 dir Comillas onto
CA135 to km 7. Turn dir Ruiloba onto CA359 & thro Ruiloba
& La Iglesia, fork R uphill. Site sp. Lge, mkd pitch, pt sl, pt shd;
htd wc; chem disp; mv service pnt; baby facs; shwrs inc; el pnts
(6A) €4.35; lndtte (inc dryer); shop, rest, snacks, bar in ssn;
playgrnd; pool; paddling pool; sand beach 3km; tennis 300m;
cycle hire; wifi; many statics; dogs; night security; poss v cr
high ssn; Eng spkn; poss noisy high ssn; ccard acc; CKE/CCI.
"Attractive site, gd touring cent; clean facs but some in need of
refurb; helpful staff; sm pitches poss muddy in wet." ♦ 1 Apr-
30 Sep. € 39.55 (CChq acc)   2014*

COMILLAS *1A4* (3km W Rural/Coastal) *43.3858, -4.3361*
Camping Rodero, Ctra Comillas-St Vicente, Km 5,
39528 Oyambre (Cantabria) [942-72 20 40; fax 942-
72 26 29; rodero@campingrodero-oyambre.es; www.
campingrodero-oyambre.es] Exit A8 dir San Vicente de la
Barquera, cross bdge over estuary & take R fork nr km27.5.
Site just off C131 bet San Vicente & Comillas, sp. Lge, mkd
pitch, pt sl, terr, pt shd; wc; chem disp; mv service pnt; shwrs
inc; el pnts (6A) €3; gas; lndtte; shop; tradsmn; rest, snacks;
bar; playgrnd; pool; sand beach 200m; games area; wifi;
10% statics; no dogs; phone; bus 200m; poss v cr; adv bkg;
ccard acc; CKE/CCI. "Lovely views; on top of hill; friendly
owners; site noisy but happy - owner puts Dutch/British in
quieter part; sm pitches; poss run down low ssn." ♦ 15 Mar-
30 Sep. € 29.00   2014*

⊞ CONIL DE LA FRONTERA *2H3* (3km N Coastal) *36.30206,
-6.13082* Camping Cala del Aceite (Naturist), Ctra del
Puerto Pesquero, Km 4, 11140 Conil de la Frontera (Cádiz)
[956-44 29 50; fax 956-44 09 72; info@caladelaceite.com;
www.caladelaceite.com] Exit A48 junc 26 dir Conil. In 2km
at rndabt foll sp Puerto Pesquero along CA3208 & CA4202.
Site sp. V lge, mkd pitch, pt shd; wc; chem disp;sauna; shwrs
inc; el pnts (10A) €5.50; gas; lndtte; supmkt; rest, snacks; bar;
playgrnd; pool; beach 500m; jacuzzi & steam rm; sep naturist
area on site; dogs €3; phone; poss cr; Eng spkn; adv bkg; quiet;
red long stay; CKE/CCI. "Friendly, helpful staff; interesting
region; gd cliff-top walking; lge pitches; long stay winter offers;
gd, modern san facs." ♦ Holy Week-31 Oct. € 30.60   2011*

SPAIN

⊞ **CONIL DE LA FRONTERA** 2H3 (3km NE Rural) 36.31061, -6.11276 **Camping Roche, Carril de Pilahito s/n, N340km 19.2, 11149 Conil de la Frontera (Cádiz) [956-44 22 16; fax 956-44 26 24; info@campingroche.com; www. campingroche.com]** Exit A48 junc 15 Conil Norte. Site sp on N340 dir Algeciras. Lge, mkd pitch, hdstg, pt shd; wc; chem disp; mv service pnt; el pnts (10A) €5; lndtte; shop; rest, snacks; bar; BBQ low ssn; playgrnd; pool; paddling pool; sand beach 2.5km; tennis; games area; games rm; TV; 20% statics; dogs €3.75; Eng spkn; adv bkg; quiet; ccard acc; red low ssn/ long stay; special monthly rates. "V pleasant, peaceful site in pine woods; all-weather pitches; friendly, helpful staff; clean san facs; superb beaches nr; excel facs; lack of adequate management." ◆ € 36.60 SBS - W02   2014*

> ## "Satellite navigation makes touring much easier"
> Remember most sat navs don't know if you're towing or in a larger vehicle – always use yours alongside maps and site directions.

⊞ **CONIL DE LA FRONTERA** 2H3 (1.3km NW Rural/Coastal) 36.29340, -6.09626 **Camping La Rosaleda, Ctra del Pradillo, Km 1.3, 11140 Conil de la Frontera (Cádiz) [956-44 33 27; fax 956-44 33 85; info@campinglarosaleda.com; www.campinglarosaleda.com]** Exit A48 junc 26 dir Conil. In 2km at rndabt foll sp Puerto Pesquero along CA3208. Site sp on R. Lge, mkd pitch, some hdstg, pt sl, terr, pt shd; wc; chem disp; mv service pnt; shwrs inc; el pnts (5-10A) inc; gas; lndtte; shop & 1.3km; tradsmn; rest, snacks; bar; playgrnd; pool; sand beach 1.3km; entmnt; internet; 10% statics; no dogs 15 Jun-15 Sep, otherwise in sep area €5; phone; car wash; Eng spkn; adv bkg; quiet; red low ssn/long stay; CKE/CCI. "Well-run site; friendly, helpful staff; gd social atmosphere; poss noisy w/end; sm pitches not suitable lge o'fits but double-length pitches avail; poss travellers; pitches soft/muddy when wet; lge rally on site in winter; gd walking & cycling; sea views; historical, interesting area; conv Seville, Cádiz, Jerez, day trips Morocco; If low occupancy, facs maybe clsd and excursions cancelled." ◆ € 38.50   2013*

⊞ **CORDOBA** 2F3 (8km N Rural) 37.96138, -4.81361 **Camping Los Villares, Ctra Los Villares, Km 7.5, 14071 Córdoba) [957-33 01 45; fax 957-33 14 55; campingvillares@latinmail.com]** Best app fr N on N432: turn W onto CP45 1km N of Cerro Muriano at km 254. Site on R after approx 7km shortly after golf club. Last 5-6km of app rd v narr & steep, but well-engineered. Badly sp, easy to miss. Or fr city cent foll sp for Parador until past municipal site on R. Shortly after, turn L onto CP45 & foll sp Parque Forestal Los Villares, then as above. Sm, hdstg, sl, shd; wc; chem disp; shwrs inc; el pnts (15A) €4.30 (poss rev pol); gas; lndry rm; shop; rest & bar (high ssn); some statics; no dogs; bus 1km; quiet; red long stay; CKE/CCI. "In nature reserve; peaceful; cooler than Córdoba city with beautiful walks, views & wildlife; sm, close pitches; basic facs (v ltd & poss unclean low ssn); mainly sl site in trees; strictly run; suitable as NH; take care electrics; poss no drinking water/hot water." ◆ € 17.70   2014*

⊞ **CORDOBA** 2F3 (1km NW Urban) 37.90063, -4.7875 **Camp Municipal El Brillante, Avda del Brillante 50, 14012 Córdoba [957-40 38 36; fax 957-28 21 65; elbrillante@ campings.net; www.campingelbrillante.com]** Fr N1V take Badejoz turning N432. Take rd Córdoba N & foll sp to Parador. Turn R into Paseo del Brilliante which leads into Avda del Brilliante; white grilleblock wall surrounds site. Alt, foll sp for 'Macdonalds Brilliante.' Site on R 400m beyond Macdonalds on main rd going uphill away fr town cent. Site poorly sp. Med, hdg/mkd pitch, hdstg, pt shd; wc; chem disp; mv service pnt; serviced pitches; shwrs inc; el pnts (6-10A) €5.50 (poss no earth); gas; lndtte (inc dryer); shop; tradsmn; hypmkt nrby; rest, snacks high ssn; bar; playgrnd; pool adj in ssn; dogs free; phone; bus adj; poss cr; Eng spkn; no adv bkg; quiet but traff noise & barking dogs off site; ccard not acc; CKE/CCI. "Well-run, busy, clean site; rec arr bef 1500; friendly staff; sun shades over pitches; easy walk/gd bus to town; poss cramped pitches - diff lge o'fits; poss travellers low ssn (noisy); gd for wheelchair users; highly rec; easy walk to beautiful city." ◆ € 39.50   2014*

CORUNA, A see Coruña, La 1A2

CORUNA, LA 1A2 (5km E Coastal) 43.34305, -8.35722 **Camping Bastiagueiro, Playa de Bastiagueiro, 15110 Oleiros (La Coruña) [981-61 48 78; fax 981-26 60 08]** Exit La Coruña by NVI twd Betanzos. After bdge, take AC173 sp Santa Cruz. At 3rd rndabt, take 3rd exit sp Camping. In 100m, turn R up narr rd. Site on R in 150m. Sm, pt shd; wc (some cont); chem disp; shwrs inc; el pnts (6A) €4; gas; lndtte; shop; snacks; bar; playgrnd; sand beach 500m; dogs; phone; bus 300m; o'night area for m'vans; poss cr; adv bkg; quiet; CKE/ CCI. "Friendly owners; lovely views of beach; care req thro narr ent gate, sharp turn & steep exit; poss feral cats on site & facs poss unclean in winter; some refurb needed." Easter & 1 Jun-30 Sep. € 20.00   2010*

> ## "There aren't many sites open at this time of year"
> If you're travelling outside peak season remember to call ahead to check site opening dates – even if the entry says 'open all year'

CORUNA, LA 1A2 (9km E Rural) 43.34806, -8.33592 **Camping Los Manzanos, Olieros, 15179 Santa Cruz (La Coruña) [981-61 48 25; info@camping-losmanzanos.com; www.camping-losmanzanos.com]** App La Coruña fr E on NVI, bef bdge take AC173 sp Santa Cruz. Turn R at 2nd traff lts in Santa Cruz cent (by petrol stn), foll sp, site on L. Fr AP9/ E1 exit junc 3, turn R onto NVI dir Lugo. Take L fork dir Santa Cruz/La Coruña, then foll sp Meiras. Site sp. Lge, pt shd; wc; chem disp; shwrs; el pnts (6A) €4.80; gas; lndtte (inc dryer); shop; rest, snacks; bar; playgrnd; pool; TV; 10% statics; dogs free; phone; adv bkg (day bef arr only); ccard acc; CKE/CCI. "Lovely site; steep slope into site, level exit is avail; helpful owners; hilly 1km walk to Santa Cruz for bus to La Coruña or park at Torre de Hércules (lighthouse) & take tram; gd rest; conv for Santiago de Compostela; excel." Easter-30 Sep. € 25.60   2013*

⊞ **COTORIOS** *4F1* (2km E Rural) *38.05255, -2.83996*
**Camping Llanos de Arance, Ctra Sierra de Cazorla/Beas de
Segura, Km 22, 23478 Cotoríos (Jaén) [953-71 31 39; fax
953-71 30 36; arancell@inicia.es; www.llanosdearance.
com]** Fr Jaén-Albecete rd N322 turn E onto A1305 N of
Villanueva del Arzobispo sp El Tranco. In 26km to El Tranco
lake, turn R & cross over embankment. Cotoríos at km stone
53, approx 25km on shore of lake & Río Guadalaquivir. App
fr Cazorla or Beas definitely not rec if towing. Lge, shd; wc;
shwrs; el pnts (5A) €3.21; gas; shops 1.5km; rest, snacks;
bar; BBQ; playgrnd; pool; 2% statics; no dogs; phone; poss
cr; quiet; ccard acc; red low ssn; CKE/CCI. "Lovely site; excel
walks & bird life, boar & wild life in Cazorla National Park."
€ 21.40   2014*

COVARRUBIAS *1B4* (500m E Rural) *42.05944, -3.51527*
**Camping Covarrubias, Ctra Hortigüela, 09346 Covarrubias
(Burgos) [947-40 64 17; fax 983-29 58 41; proatur@
proatur.com; www.proatur.com]** Take N1/E5 or N234 S
fr Burgos, turn onto BU905 after approx 35km. Site sp on
BU905. Lge, mkd pitch, pt sl, pt shd; wc; shwrs; el pnts (12A)
€3.90; gas; lndtte; shop 500m; rest; bar; playgrnd; pool &
paddling pool; 90% statics; phone; poss cr; "Ltd facs low ssn;
pitches poss muddy after rain; charming vill; poss vultures;
phone to confirm if open." € 18.50   2013*

> ## "That's changed – Should
> ## I let The Club know?"
>
> If you find something on site that's different from
> the site entry, fill in a report and let us know. See
> www.caravanclub.co.uk/europereport.

CREIXELL *3C3* (2.9km E Coastal) *41.16512, 1.45800* **Camping
La Plana, Ctra N340, Km 1182, 43839 Creixell (Tarragona)
[977-80 03 04; fax 977-66 36 63]** Site sp at Creixell off N340.
Med, hdstg, shd; wc; chem disp; shwrs inc; el pnts inc; gas;
lndtte; shop, rest, snacks; bar; sand beach adj; poss cr; Eng
spkn; adv bkg; some rlwy noise. "Vg, v clean site; v helpful &
pleasant owners." 1 May-30 Sep. € 21.00   2011*

CREIXELL *3C3* (1km S Coastal) *41.15714, 1.44137* **Camping
Gavina Platja, Ctra N340, Km 1181, Platja Creixell, 43839
Creixell de Mar (Tarragona) [977-80 15 03; fax 977-
80 05 27; info@gavina.net; www.gavina.net]** Exit AP7 junc
31 (Coma-Ruga) onto N340 dir Tarragona. At km 1181 turn
R twd Playa de Creixel via undergnd passage. Site 1km S of
Creixell, adj beach - foll sp Creixell Platja. Lge, mkd pitch, pt
shd; wc; chem disp; baby facs; fam bthrm; shwrs inc; el pnts
(6A) €4.50; gas; lndtte; shop; rest, snacks; bar; playgrnd; sand
beach adj; watersports; tennis; wifi; entmnt; 20% statics; dogs;
poss cr; adv bkg rec Jul/Aug; some train noise; ccard acc; red
long stay; CKE/CCI. "Rest o'looks beach; Port Aventura 20km."
♦ 4 Apr-31 Oct. € 34.50   2009*

CREVILLENT see Elche *4F2*

⊞ **CUBILLAS DE SANTA MARTA** *1C4* (4km S Rural)
41.80511, -4.58776 **Camping Cubillas, Ctra N620, Km 102,
47290 Cubillas de Santa Marta (Valladolid) [983-58 50 02;
fax 983-58 50 16; info@campingcubillas.com; www.
campingcubillas.com]** A-62 Exit 102 Cubillas de Santa Marta.
Fr N foll slip rd and cross rd to Cubillas de Santa Marta the
site is on the R in 200 metres. Fr S take Exit 102 take 5th exit
off rndabt, cross over m'way and then site on R in 200
metres. Lge, some hdg/mkd pitch, pt sl, unshd; wc; chem disp;
mv service pnt; shwrs inc; el pnts (6-10A) €4-5.80; gas; lndtte;
sm shop; tradsmn; rest; snacks & bar in ssn; BBQ; playgrnd;
pool; entmnt; 50% statics; dogs €2; phone; site clsd 18 Dec-10
Jan; Eng spkn; ccard acc; red long stay/low ssn; CKE/CCI. "Ltd
space for tourers; conv visit Palencia & Valladolid; rd & m'way,
rlwy & disco noise at w/end until v late; v ltd facs low ssn; NH
only." ♦ ltd € 26.00   2014*

CUDILLERO *1A3* (2.5km SE Rural) *43.55416, -6.12944*
**Camping Cudillero, Ctra Playa de Aguilar, Aronces,
33150 El Pito (Asturias) [tel/fax 985-59 06 63; info@
campingcudillero.com; www.campingcudillero.com]** Exit
N632 (E70) sp El Pito. Turn L at rndabt sp Cudillero & in 300m
at end of wall turn R at site sp, cont for 1km, site on L. Do not
app thro Cudillero; streets v narr & steep; much traffic. Med,
hdg/mkd pitch, pt shd; wc; chem disp; baby facs; shwrs inc;
el pnts (3-5A) €4.05; gas; lndtte; shop; snacks high ssn; bar;
playgrnd; htd pool; sand beach 1.2km; games area; entmnt
high ssn; wifi; TV; no statics; dogs €2.15; phone; bus 1km; adv
bkg; quiet; CKE/CCI. "Excel, well-maintained, well laid-out site;
some generous pitches; gd san facs; steep walk to beach & vill;
v helpful staff; excel facs; vill worth a visit, parking on quay but
narr rds." ♦ 11 Apr-15 Sep. € 42.00   2014*

CUDILLERO *1A3* (2km S Rural) *43.55555, -6.13777* **Camping
L'Amuravela, El Pito, 33150 Cudillero (Asturias) [tel/
fax 985-59 09 95; camping@lamuravela.com; www.
lamuravela.com]** Exit N632 (E70) sp El Pito. Turn L at rndabt
sp Cudillero & in approx 1km turn R at site sp. Do not app
thro Cudillero; streets v narr & steep; much traffic. Med, mkd
pitch, pt sl, unshd; wc; chem disp; mv service pnt; shwrs inc; el
pnts €4.10; gas; shop; snacks; bar; pool; paddling pool; sand
beach 2km; 50% statics (sep area); dogs €1; poss cr; ccard acc
high ssn. "Pleasant, well-maintained site; gd clean facs; hillside
walks into Cudillero, attractive fishing vill with gd fish rests; red
facs low ssn & poss only open w/ends, surroundings excel."
Holy Week & 1 Jun-30 Sep. € 24.60   2011*

CUENCA *3D1* (8km N Rural) *40.12694, -2.14194* **Camping
Cuenca, Ctra Tragacete, Km8, 16147 Cuenca [tel/
fax 969-23 16 56; info@campingcuenca.com; www.
campingcuenca.com]** Fr Madrid take N400/A40 dir Cuenca
& exit sp 'Ciudad Encantada' & Valdecabras on CM2110.
In 7.5km turn R onto CM2105, site on R in 1.5km. Foll sp
'Nalimiento des Rio Jucar'. Lge, pt sl, pt terr, pt shd; wc; chem
disp; mv service pnt; shwrs inc; el pnts (6-10A) €4; gas; lndtte;
shop; snacks; bar; playgrnd; pool high ssn; jacuzzi; tennis;
games area; 15% statics; dogs €1; phone; poss cr esp Easter w/
end; Eng spkn; adv bkg; quiet; CKE/CCI. "Pleasant, well-kept,
green site; gd touring cent; friendly, helpful staff; excel san
facs but ltd low ssn; interesting rock formations at Ciudad
Encantada." ♦ 19 Mar-11 Oct. € 20.80   2013*

CUEVAS DEL ALMANZORA see Garrucha *4G1*

DEBA 3A1 (6km E Coastal) 43.29436, -2.32853 **Camping Itxaspe, N634, Km 38, 20829 Itziar (Guipúzcoa) [tel/fax 943-19 93 77; itxaspe@hotmail.es; www.campingitxaspe. com]** Exit A8 junc 13 dir Deba; at main rd turn L up hill, in 400m at x-rds turn L, site in 2km - narr, winding rd. NB Do not go into Itziar vill. Sm, mkd pitch, pt sl, pt shd; wc; chem disp; baby facs; shwrs; el pnts (5A) €4; gas; shop; rest, bar adj; BBQ; playgrnd; pool; solarium; shgl beach 4km; wifi; some statics; bus 2km; adv bkg; quiet; red low ssn; CKE/CCI. "Excel site; helpful owner; w/ends busy; sea views; Coastal geology is UNESCO site, walking fr site superb." ♦ ltd 1 Apr-30 Sep. € 35.60   2012*

DEBA 3A1 (5km W Coastal) 43.30577, -2.37789 **Camping Aitzeta, Ctra Deba-Guernica, Km. 3.5, C6212, 20930 Mutriku (Guipúzcoa) [943-60 33 56; fax 943-60 31 06; www.campingseuskadi.com/aitzeta]** On N634 San Sebastián-Bilbao rd thro Deba & on o'skts turn R over rv sp Mutriku. Site on L after 3km on narr & winding rd up sh steep climb. Med, mkd pitch, terr, pt shd; wc; chem disp (wc); shwrs inc; el pnts (4A) €3; gas; lndry rm; sm shop; rest 300m; snacks; bar; playgrnd; sand beach 1km; dogs; bus 500m; phone; quiet; CKE/CCI. "Easy reach of Bilbao ferry; sea views; gd, well-run, clean site; not suitable lge o'fits for tourers; helpful staff; walk to town." ♦ ltd 1 May-30 Sep. € 21.00   2010*

"I like to fill in the reports as I travel from site to site"

You'll find report forms at the back of this guide, or you can fill them in online at www.caravaclub.co.uk/europereport.

DELTEBRE 3D2 (8km E Coastal) 40.72041, 0.84849 **Camping L'Aube, Afores s/n, 43580 Deltebre (Tarragona) [977-26 70 66; fax 977-26 75 05; campinglaube@hotmail.com; www.campinglaube.com]** Exit AP7 junc 40 or 41 onto N340 dir Deltebre. Fr Deltebre foll T340 sp Riumar for 8km. At info kiosk branch R, site sp 1km on R. Lge, mkd pitch, hdstg, pt shd; wc; chem disp; mv service pnt; shwrs inc; el pnts (3-10A) €2.80-5; lndtte; shop; rest; bar; snacks; pool; playgrnd; phone; sand beach adj; 40% statics; poss cr low ssn; red long stay; CKE/CCI. "At edge of Ebro Delta National Park; excel birdwatching; ltd facs in winter." ♦ ltd 1 Mar-31 Oct. € 16.00   2011*

DELTEBRE 3D2 (10km SE Coastal) 40.65681, 0.77971 **Camping Eucaliptus, Playa Eucaliptus s/n, 43870 Amposta (Tarragona) [tel/fax 977-47 90 46; eucaliptus@ campingeucaliptus.com; www.campingeucaliptus.com]** Exit AP7/E15 at junc 41. Foll sp to Amposta but do not go into town. Take sp for Els Muntells on TV3405 then Eucaliptus beach. Site on R 100m fr beach. Lge, mkd pitch, pt shd; wc; chem disp; shwrs; el pnts (5A) €4.30; gas; lndtte; shops; rest, snacks; bar; BBQ area; playgrnd; pool; paddling pool; sand beach adj; fishing; watersports; cycling; entmnt; 40% statics; dogs €2.40; poss cr; adv bkg; noisy w/end & high ssn; red long stay; CKE/CCI. "Vg, well-run, peaceful site; gd facs; gd bar/ rest; excel birdwatching; poss mosquito prob." ♦ Holy Week-27 Sep. € 24.00   2009*

⊞ **DENIA** 4E2 (3.5km SE Coastal) 38.82968, 0.14767 **Camping Los Pinos, Ctra Dénia-Les Rotes, Km 3, Les Rotes, 03700 Dénia (Alicante) [tel/fax 965-78 26 98; lospinosdenia@gmail.com; www.lospinosdenia.com]** Fr N332 foll sp to Dénia in dir of coast. Turn R sp Les Rotes/ Jávea, then L twrds Les Rotes. Foll site sp turn L into narr access rd poss diff lge o'fits. Med, mkd pitch, pt shd; wc; chem disp; shwrs inc; el pnts (6-10A) €3.20; gas; lndtte; shop adj; tradsmn; BBQ; cooking facs; playgrnd; shgl beach adj; internet; TV rm; 25% statics; dogs €3; phone; bus 100m; poss cr; Eng spkn; adv bkg; quiet; red long stays/low ssn; ccard acc; CKE/ CCI. "Friendly, well-run, clean, tidy site but san facs tired (Mar 09); excel value; access some pitches poss diff due trees - not suitable lge o'fits or m'vans; many long-stay winter residents; cycle path into Dénia; social rm with log fire; naturist beach 1km, private but rocky shore." ♦ € 26.40   2012*

⊞ **DENIA** 4E2 (9km W Rural/Coastal) 38.86750, -0.01615 **Camping Los Llanos, Partida Deveses 32, 03700 Dénia (Alicante) [965-75 51 88 or 649-45 51 58; fax 965-75 54 25; losllanos@losllanos.net; www.losllanos.net]** Exit AP7 junc 62 dir Dénia onto CV725. At lge rndabt turn L & foll sp to site along N332a. Med, pt shd; wc; chem disp; mv service pnt; shwrs inc; el pnts (10A) €3.50; lndtte; shop & 2km; rest 500m; snacks; bar; playgrnd; pool; paddling pool; sand beach 150m; wifi; 30% statics; dogs €2; phone; bus 100m; poss cr; adv bkg; quiet; ccard acc; red long stay. "Pleasant site; gd, modern san facs; gd touring base; friendly, helpful staff; vg." € 25.00   2009*

DOS HERMANAS 2G3 (1km W Urban) 37.27731, -5.93722 **Camping Villsom, Ctra Sevilla/Cádiz A4, Km 554.8, 41700 Dos Hermanas (Sevilla) [tel/fax 954-72 08 28; campingvillsom@hotmail.com]** On main Seville-Cádiz NIV rd travelling fr Seville take exit at km. 555 sp Dos Hermanos-Isla Menor. At the rndabt turn R (SE-3205 Isla Menor) to site 80 m. on R. Lge, hdg/mkd pitch, hdstg, pt sl, pt shd; wc (some cont); chem disp; shwrs inc; el pnts (10A) €3.65 (poss no earth); gas; lndtte; sm shop; hypmkt 1km; snacks in ssn; bar; playgrnd; pool in ssn; wifi; bus to Seville 300m (over bdge & rndabt); site clsd 25 Dec-9 Jan; poss cr; Eng spkn; adv bkg; rd noise; ccard acc; CKE/CCI. "Adv bkg rec Holy Week; helpful staff; clean, tidy, well-run site; vg; san facs, ltd low ssn; height barrier at Carrefour hypmkt - ent via deliveries; no twin axles; wifi only in office & bar area." 10 Jan-23 Dec. € 35.50   2014*

⊞ **ELCHE** 4F2 (7km S Rural) 38.17770, -0.80876 **Marjal Costa Blanca Eco Camping Resort, AP-7 Salida 730, 03330 Crevillent (Comunidad Valenciana) [965-48 49 45; camping@marjalcostablanca.com; www. marjalcostablanca.com]** Fr A7/E15 merge onto AP7 (sp Murcia), take exit 730; site sp fr exit. V lge, hdg/mkd pitch, hdstg, pt shd; wc; chem disp; baby facs; shwrs; serviced pitches; el pnts (16A) inc; gas; lndtte (inc dryer); supmkt; rests; snacks; bar; BBQ; playgrnd; htd pool complex; wellness cent with fitness studio, htd pools, saunas, physiotherapy & spa; lake sw; tennis; car wash; hairdresser; doctor's surgery; games area; games rm; bike hire; entmnt; wifi; TV; 30% statics; tour ops; dogs €2.20; phone; Eng spkn; twin axle acc; adv bkg; ccard acc; lge pitches extra charge; red low ssn; CCI. "Superb site; gd security; excel facs; new site, trees and hedges need time to grow; excel, immac san facs." ♦ € 53.00 (CChq acc) SBS - W05   2014*

SPAIN

⊞ **ELCHE** *4F2* (10km SW Urban) *38.24055, -0.81194*
Camping Las Palmeras, Ctra Murcia-Alicante, Km 45.3,
03330 Crevillent (Alicante) [965-40 01 88 or 966-68 06 30;
fax 966-68 06 64; laspalmeras@laspalmeras-sl.com;
www.laspalmeras-sl.com] Exit A7 junc 726/77 onto N340
to Crevillent. Immed bef traff lts take slip rd into rest parking/
service area. Site on R, access rd down side of rest. Med, mkd
pitch, hdstg, pt shd; wc; chem disp; shwrs inc; el pnts (6A)
inc; lndtte; supmkt adj; rest, snacks; bar; pool; paddling pool;
10% statics; dogs free; ccard acc; CKE/CCI. "Useful NH; report
to recep in hotel; helpful staff; gd cent for touring Murcia; gd
rest in hotel; gd, modern san facs; excel." € 45.00   2011*

⊞ **ESCALA, L'** *3B3* (2km SE Coastal) *42.11048, 3.16378*
Camping Cala Montgó, Avda Montgó s/n, 17130 L'Escala
(Gerona) [972-77 08 66; fax 972-77 43 40; calamontgo@
betsa.es; www.betsa.es] Exit AP7 junc 4 Figueres onto C31
dir Torroella de Montgri. Foll sp L'Escala & Montgó to site. V
lge, pt sl, pt shd; wc; chem disp; baby facs; shwrs inc; el pnts
(5A) €4.10; gas; lndtte; shop; tradsmn; rest; bar; playgrnd;
pool; paddling pool; sand beach 200m; fishing; sports area;
cycle hire; 30% statics; dogs; poss cr; adv bkg; quiet; ccard
not acc; red low ssn; CKE/CCI. "Nr trad fishing vill; facs ltd/
run down; quiet low ssn; exposed, poss windy & dusty site." ♦
€ 36.00   2009*

ESCALA, L' *3B3* (500m S Urban/Coastal) *42.1211, 3.1346*
Camping L'Escala, Camí Ample 21, 17130 L'Escala
(Gerona) [972-77 00 84; fax 972-77 00 08; info@
campinglescala.com; www.campinglescala.com] Exit
AP7 junc 5 onto Gl623 dir L'Escala; at o'skts of L'Escala, at
1st rndabt (with yellow sign Gl623 on top of rd dir sp) turn
L dir L'Escala & Ruïnes Empúries; at 2nd rndabt go str on dir
L'Escala-Riells, then foll site sp. Do not app thro town. Med,
hdg/mkd pitch, pt shd; wc; chem disp; all serviced pitches;
baby facs; shwrs inc; el pnts (6A) inc; gas; lndtte; supmkt;
tradsmn; rest 100m; snacks; bar; BBQ; playgrnd; beach 300m;
TV; 20% statics; no dogs; phone; car wash; poss cr; Eng spkn;
adv bkg; quiet; red low ssn; CKE/CCI. "Access to sm pitches
poss diff lge o'fits; helpful, friendly staff; vg, modern san facs;
Empúrias ruins 5km; vg." ♦ 12 Apr-21 Sep. € 44.50   2014*

ESCALA, L' *3B3* (1km S Coastal) *42.1134, 3.1443* **Camping**
Maite, Avda Montó, Playa de Riells, 17130 L'Escala
(Gerona) [tel/fax 972-77 05 44; www.campingmaite.com]
Exit A7 junc 5 dir L'Escala. Thro town dir Riells to rndabt with
supmkts on each corner, turn R to site. Lge, mkd pitch, some
terr, shd; wc; chem disp; mv service pnt; shwrs inc; el pnts (6A)
€4.30; gas; shop adj; rest; bar; playgrnd; beach 200m; TV; bus
1km; adv bkg; red long stay; ccard acc; CKE/CCI. "Well-run
site; quiet oasis in busy resort; steep site rds; some pitches narr
access." ♦ 1 Jun-15 Sep. € 20.80   2011*

ESCALA, L' *3B3* (2km S Coastal) *42.11027, 3.16555* **Camping**
Illa Mateua, Avda Montgó 260, 17130 L'Escala (Gerona)
[972-77 02 00 or 77 17 95; fax 972-77 20 31; info@
campingillamateua.com; www.campingillamateua.com]
On N11 thro Figueras, approx 3km on L sp C31 L'Escala; in
town foll sp for Montgó & Paradis. Lge, terr, pt shd; wc; chem
disp; mv service pnt; baby facs; shwrs inc; el pnts (5A) inc;
gas; lndtte; shop; rest; bar; playgrnd; 2 pools; sand beach adj;
watersports; tennis; games area; entmnt; 5% statics; dogs
€3.60; Eng spkn; adv bkg ess high ssn; quiet; red low ssn/long
stay; CKE/CCI. "V well-run site; spacious pitches; excel san facs;
gd beach; no depth marking in pool; excel rest." ♦ ltd 11 Mar-
20 Oct. € 58.40   2013*

ESCALA, L' *3B3* (3km S Coastal) *42.10512, 3.15843*
Camping Neus, Cala Montgó, 17130 L'Escala (Gerona)
[972-77 04 03 or 972-20 86 67; fax 972-77 27 51 or 972-
22 24 09; info@campingneus.com; www.campingneus.
com] Exit AP7 junc 5 twd L'Escala then turn R twd Cala
Montgó & foll sp. Med, mkd pitch, pt sl, pt terr, shd; wc;
chem disp; mv service pnt; baby facs; shwrs inc; el pnts (6A)
€4; gas; lndtte; shop; snacks; bar; playgrnd; pool; paddling
pool; sand beach 850m; fishing; tennis; car wash; internet;
entmnt; TV rm; 15% statics; dogs €2; phone; bus 500m;
Eng spkn; adv bkg; quiet; ccard acc; red low ssn/long stay;
CKE/CCI. "Pleasant, clean site in pine forest; gd san facs; lge
pitches; vg." 28 May-19 Sep. € 39.00   2009*

See advertisement

⊞ **ESCORIAL, EL** *1D4* (6km NE Rural) *40.62630, -4.09970*
Camping-Caravaning El Escorial, Ctra Guadarrama
a El Escorial, Km 3.5, 28280 El Escorial (Madrid)
[918 90 24 12 / 02 01 49 00; fax 918 96 10 62; info@
campingelescorial.com; www.campingelescorial.com]
Exit AP6 NW of Madrid junc 47 El Escorial/Guadarrama, onto
M505 & foll sp to El Escorial, site on L at km stone 3,500 -
long o'fits rec cont to rndabt (1km) to turn & app site on R. V
lge, mkd pitch, some hdstg, pt shd; htd wc; chem disp; baby
facs; shwrs inc; el pnts (5A) inc (long cable rec); gas; lndtte;
shop; rest, snacks & bar in ssn & w/end; BBQ; hypmkt 5km;
BBQ; playgrnd; 3 pools high ssn; tennis; horseriding 7km;
games rm; cash machine; wifi; entmnt; TV; 80% statics (sep
area); dogs free; c'vans/m'vans over 8m must reserve lge pitch
with elec, water & drainage; adv bkg; some Eng spkn; poss cr
& noisy at w/end; ccard acc. "Excel, busy site; mountain views;
helpful staff; clean facs; gd security; sm pitches poss diff due
trees; o'head canopies poss diff for tall o'fits; facs ltd low ssn;
trains & buses to Madrid nr; Valle de Los Caídos & Palace at
El Escorial well worth visit; easy parking in town for m'vans if
go in early; mkt Wed; stunning scenery, nesting storks." ♦
€ 50.50 SBS - E13   2014*

See advertisement

ESCULLOS, LOS see Nijar *4G1*

ESPINAL see Auritz *3A1*

ESTARTIT, L' *3B3* (500m Urban/Coastal) *42.04808, 3.1871*
Camping La Sirena, Calle La Platera s/n, 17258 L'Estartit
(Gerona) [972-75 15 42; fax 972-75 09 44; info@camping-
lasirena.com; www.camping-lasirena.com] Fr Torroella foll
sp to L'Estartit on rd GI641. On o'skts of vill turn R at Els Jocs
amusements, site on L 200m. Lge, pt shd; wc; chem disp; baby
facs; shwrs inc; el pnts (6-10A) €5 (poss long lead req); gas;
lndtte (inc dryer); shop; rest, snacks; bar; BBQ; playgrnd; htd
pool; paddling pool; sand beach adj; scuba diving; internet;
money exchange; car wash; TV; 10% statics; dogs €2.50; bus
adj; Eng spkn; quiet; red long stay/low ssn; CKE/CCI. "Sm
pitches, diff lge o'fits; poss long walk to beach; v ltd facs low
ssn; gd value boat trips; nature reserve adj." ♦ Easter-12 Oct.
€ 26.00   2009*

ESTARTIT, L' *3B3* (1.2km NE Coastal) *42.05670, 3.19785*
Camping Estartit, Calle Villa Primevera 12, 17258
L'Estartit (Gerona) [972-75 19 09; fax 972-75 09 91; www.
campingestartit.com] Exit AP7 junc 6 onto C66, then take
G642 dir Torroella de Montgri & L'Estartit; fork L on ent
L'Estartit, foll site sps. Med, pt sl, shd; htd wc; chem disp; baby
facs; shwrs ; el pnts (6A) €3.73; gas; lndtte; shop; rest adj;
snacks; bar; playgrnd; htd pool; paddling pool; sand beach
400m; 15% statics; no dogs 20/6-20/8; phone; poss
cr; Eng spkn; red long stay. "Friendly staff; 100m fr vill cent; gd
security; gd walks adj nature reserve; bar/rest & night club adj;
facs poss stretched high ssn." 1 Apr-30 Sep. € 24.00   2011*

ESTARTIT, L' *3B3* (1km S Coastal) *42.04972, 3.18416*
Camping El Molino, Camino del Ter, 17258 L'Estartit (Gerona) [tel/fax 972-75 06 29] Fr N11 junc 5, take rd to L'Escala. Foll sp to Torroella de Montgri, then L'Estartit. Ent town & foll sp, site on rd Gl 641. V lge, hdg pitch, pt sl, pt shd; wc; mv service pnt; shwrs; el pnts (6A) €3.60; gas; lndtte; supmkt high ssn & 2km; rest; bar; playgrnd; sand beach 1km; games rm; internet; bus 1km; poss cr; adv bkg. "Site in 2 parts - 1 in shd, 1 at beach unshd; gd facs; quiet location outside busy town." 1 Apr-30 Sep. € 28.00   2014*

⊞ **ESTARTIT, L'** *3B3* (2km S Coastal) *42.04250, 3.18333*
Camping Les Medes, Paratge Camp de l'Arbre s/n, 17258 L'Estartit (Gerona) [972-75 18 05; fax 972-75 04 13; info@campinglesmedes.com; www.campinglesmedes. com] Fr Torroella foll sp to L'Estartit. In vill turn R at town name sp (sp Urb Estartit Oeste), foll rd for 1.5km, turn R, site well sp. Lge, mkd pitch, shd; htd wc; chem disp; mv service pnt; serviced pitches; baby facs; sauna; shwrs inc; el pnts (6A) €4.60; gas; lndtte; shop; rest, snacks; bar; playgrnd; htd indoor/outdoor pools; sand beach 800m; watersports; solarium; tennis; games area; horseriding 400m; cycle hire; car wash; games rm; wifi; entmnt; TV; 7% statics; no dogs high ssn otherwise €2.60; phone; site clsd Nov; poss cr; Eng spkn; adv bkg; quiet; red long stay/low ssn (pay on arr); CKE/CCI. "Excel, popular, family-run & well organised site; helpful staff; gd clean facs & constant hot water; gd for children; no twin-axle vans high ssn - by arrangement low ssn; conv National Park; well mkd foot & cycle paths." ♦ € 36.00   2011*

See advertisement

ESTARTIT, L' *3B3* (1km W Coastal) *42.05035, 3.18023*
Camping Castell Montgri, Ctra de Torroella, Km 4.7, 17258 L'Estartit (Gerona) [972-75 16 30; fax 972-75 09 06; cmontgri@campingparks.com; www.campingparks.com] Exit A7 junc 5 onto Gl 623 dir L'Escala. Foll sp on rd C252 fr Torroella de Montgri to L'Estartit. Site on L clearly sp. V lge, hdg pitch, terr, hdstg, shd; wc; mv service pnt; chem disp; baby facs; shwrs inc; el pnts (10A) inc; gas; lndtte (inc dryer); shop; rest, snacks; bar; playgrnd; 3 pools; waterslide; beach 1km; tennis; games area; watersports; wifi; entmnt; TV; car wash; money exchange; 30% statics; dogs free; phone; poss cr; adv bkg; red long stay/low ssn. "Gd views; help given to get to pitch; excel site." ♦ 12 May-30 Sep. € 62.00   2011*

ESTARTIT, L' *3B3* (1km W Coastal) *42.04907, 3.18385*
Camping L'Empordà, Ctra Torroella-L'Estartit, Km 4.8, 17258 L'Estartit (Gerona) [972-75 06 49; fax 972-75 14 30; info@campingemporda.com; www.campingemporda. com] Exit AP7 junc 5 onto Gl623 dir L'Escala. Bef L'Escala turn S onto C31 dir Torroella de Montgri, then at Torroella take rd Gl641 dir L'Estartit. Site bet L'Estartit & Torroella, opp Castell Montgri. Lge, hdg/mkd pitch, pt shd; wc; chem disp; shwrs inc; baby facs; el pnts (6A) €4.70; gas; lndtte; shop; snacks; bar; playgrnd; pool; paddling pool; sand beach 1km; tennis; entmnt; organised walks; wifi; TV; dogs €2.80; phone; bus 70m; car wash; poss cr; adv bkg; quiet; red low ssn/long stay; CKE/CCI. "Family-run, pleasant & helpful; easy walking dist town cent; lge pitches." ♦ 2 Apr-12 Oct. € 26.00   2011*

⊞ **ESTELLA** *3B1* (2km S Rural) *42.65695, -2.01761* **Camping Lizarra, Paraje de Ordoiz s/n, 31200 Estella (Navarra) [948-55 17 33; fax 948-55 47 55; info@campinglizarra.com; www.campinglizarra.com]** N111 Pamplona to Logroño. Leave N111 sp Estella, turn R at T-junc, bear R at traff lts & turn R immed after rd tunnel, site sp. Pass factory, site on L in 1.5km. Well sp thro town. Lge, mkd pitch, wide terr, pt sl, unshd; htd wc; chem disp; mv service pnt; baby facs; shwrs inc; el pnts (6A) inc; gas; lndtte; shop high ssn; rest, snacks; bar; BBQ; playgrnd; pool; 80% w/end statics; phone; bus at w/end; site clsd mid-Dec to early Jan; poss cr; Eng spkn; noisy; ccard acc; CKE/CCI. "Poss school parties; no hdstg; poss muddy when wet; interesting old town; excel birdwatching in hills; on rte Camino de Compostela; unrel opening low ssn." ♦ € 25.25   2011*

⊞ **ESTEPAR** *1B4* (2km NE Rural) *42.29233, -3.85097*
Camping Cabia, Ctra Burgos-Valladolid, Km 15.2, 09192 Cabia/Cavia (Burgos) [947-41 20 78] Site 15km SW of Burgos on N side of A62/E80, adj Hotel Rio Cabia. Ent via Campsa petrol stn, W'bound exit 17, E'bound exit 16, cross over & re-join m'way. Ignore camp sp at exit 18 (1-way). Med, pt shd; wc; chem disp; shwrs inc; el pnts (6A) inc; shops 15km & basic supplies fr rest; rest; bar; playgrnd; few statics; dogs; constant rd noise; ccard acc; CKE/CCI. "Friendly, helpful owner; gd rest; conv for m'way for Portugal but poorly sp fr W; poss v muddy in winter; refurbed san facs; NH only." € 14.00 2012*

Check any essential information with the site before you travel   *Last year of report

SPAIN

⊞ **ESTEPONA** 2H3 (7km E Coastal) 36.45436, -5.08105
Camping Parque Tropical, Ctra N340, Km 162,
29680 Estepona (Málaga) [tel/fax 952-79 36 18;
parquetropicalcamping@hotmail.com; www.
campingparquetropical.com] On N side of N340 at km 162,
200m off main rd. Med, hdg/mkd pitch, terr, pt shd; wc; chem
disp; mv service pnt; serviced pitch; shwrs inc; el pnts (10A)
€4; gas; lndtte; shop; rest, snacks; bar; sm playgrnd; htd, covrd
pool; sand/shgl beach 1km; golf, horseriding nrby; wildlife park
1km; 10% statics; dogs €2; phone; bus 400m; poss cr; Eng
spkn; adv bkg; rd noise; red low ssn/long stay; CKE/CCI. "Site
run down (Feb 09); facs in need of update; helpful owners." ♦
€ 27.00   2009*

ETXARRI ARANATZ 3B1 (2km N Rural) 42.91255, -2.07919
Camping Etxarri, Parase Dambolintxulo, 31820
Etxarri-Aranatz (Navarra) [tel/fax 948-46 05 37; info@
campingetxarri.com; www.campingetxarri.com] Fr N exit
A15 at junc 112 to join A10 W dir Vitoria/Gasteiz. Exit at junc
19 onto NA120; go thro Etxarri vill, turn L & cross bdge, then
take rd over rlwy. Turn L, site sp. Med, hdg pitch, pt shd; wc;
chem disp; shwrs inc; el pnts (6A) €5.50; gas; lndtte; shop;
rest; bar; BBQ; pool; playgrnd; sports area; archery; horseriding;
cycling; wifi; entmnt; 90% statics; dogs €2.15; phone; poss
cr; Eng spkn; ccard acc; red low ssn; CKE/CCI. "Gd, wooded
site; gd walks; interesting area; helpful owner; conv NH to/
fr Pyrenees; youth hostel & resident workers on site; san facs
gd; various pitch sizes & shapes, some diff lge o'fits; NH only."
01 Mar-05 Oct. € 38.20   2014*

EUSA see Pamplona 3B1

FARGA DE MOLES, LA see Seo de Urgel 3B3

⊞ **FIGUERES** 3B3 (1km N Urban) 42.28311, 2.94978
Camping Pous, Ctra N11A, Km 8.5, 17600 Figueres
(Gerona) [972-67 54 96; fax 972-67 50 57; hostalandrol@
wanadoo.es] Fr N exit AP7/E15 at junc 3 & join N11. Then foll
N11A S twd Figueres. Site on L in 2km, ent adj Hostal Androl.
Fr S exit junc 4 onto NII to N of town. At rndabt (access to
AP7 junc 3) foll NII S, then as above. Site recep in hotel. No
access to N11A fr junc 4. Med, mkd pitch, pt sl, shd; wc; chem
disp; shwrs inc; el pnts (10A) €3; shop 1km; rest, snacks; bar;
playgrnd; few statics; dogs €3; bus adj; Eng spkn; quiet with
some rd noise; ccard acc. "Gd, clean site but san facs slightly
run down & ltd/unisex low ssn; easy access; pleasant owner;
excel rest; 30 min walk to town (busy main rd, no pavements)
& Dali museum; 18km fr Roses on coast." ♦ € 25.00   2014*

⊞ **FIGUERES** 3B3 (12km N Rural) 42.37305, 2.91305
Camping Les Pedres, Calle Vendador s/n, 17750 Capmany
(Gerona) [972-54 91 92 or 686 01 12 23 (mob); info@
campinglespedres.net; www.campinglespedres.net] S
fr French border on N11, turn L sp Capmany, L again in 2km
at site sp & foll site sp. Med, mkd pitch, pt sl, pt shd; htd wc;
chem disp; shwrs inc; el pnts (6-10A) €4.50; lndry rm; shop
1km; rest, snacks; bar; pool; sand beach 25km; 20% statics;
dogs; phone; Eng spkn; adv bkg; quiet; ccard acc; red low ssn;
CKE/CCI. "Helpful Dutch owner; lovely views; gd touring &
walking cent; gd winter NH." ♦ € 39.40   2013*

FIGUERES 3B3 (8km NE Rural) 42.33902, 3.06758 Camping
Vell Empordà, Ctra Roses-La Jonquera s/n, 17780
Garriguella (Gerona) [972-53 02 00 or 972-57 06 31 (LS);
fax 972-55 23 43; vellemporda@vellemporda.com; www.
vellemporda.com] On A7/E11 exit junc 3 onto N260 NE dir
Llançà. Nr km 26 marker, turn R sp Garriguella, then L at T-junc
N twd Garriguella. Site on R shortly bef vill. Lge, hdg/mkd pitch,
hdstg, terr, shd; htd wc; chem disp; mv service pnt; baby facs;
shwrs inc; el pnts (6-10A) inc; gas; lndtte; shop; rest, snacks;
bar; BBQ; playgrnd; pool; paddling pool; sand beach 6km;
games area; games rm; entmnt; internet; TV; 20% statics; dogs
€4.50; phone; Eng spkn; adv bkg; quiet; ccard acc; red long
stay/low ssn; CKE/CCI. "Conv N Costa Brava away fr cr beaches
& sites; 20 mins to sea at Llançà; o'hanging trees poss diff high
vehicles; excel." ♦ 1 Feb-15 Dec. € 35.40   2011*

⊞ **FIGUERES** 3B3 (15km NW Rural) 42.31444, 2.77638
Camping La Fradera, Pedramala, 17732 Sant Llorenç de la
Muga (Gerona) [tel/fax 972-54 20 54; camping.fradera@
teleline.es; www.terra.es/personal2/camping.fradera]
Fr cent Figueres take N260 W dir Olot. After 1km turn R at
mini-rndabt (supmkt on L), pass police stn to rd junc, strt on
& cross over A7 m'way & pass thro Llers & Terrades to Sant
Llorenç. Site 1km past vill on L. Med, mkd pitch, pt shd; wc;
chem disp; shwrs inc; el pnts (6A) €2.67; lndtte; shop 2km;
tradsmn; snacks; rest in vill; playgrnd; htd pool; rv sw 1km; few
statics; poss cr; Eng spkn; adv bkg; quiet; ccard acc; red long
stay. "Vg site in delightful vill in foothills of Pyrenees; fiesta 2nd
w/end Aug; pleasant staff; gates clsd low ssn - phone owner."
♦ ltd € 19.26   2011*

FORNELLS DE LA SELVA see Gerona 3B3

⊞ **FORTUNA** 4F1 (3km N Rural) 38.20562, -1.10712
Camping Fuente, Camino de la Bocamina s/n,
30709 Baños de Fortuna (Murcia) [968-68 50 17;
fax 968 68 51 25; info@campingfuente.com; www.
campingfuente.com] Fr Murcia on A7/E15 turn L onto C3223
sp Fortuna. After 19km turn onto A21 & foll sp Baños de
Fortuna, then sp 'Complejo Hotelero La Fuente'. Avoid towing
thro vill, if poss. Med, mkd pitch, hdstg, pt sl, unshd; htd
wc; chem disp; private san facs some pitches; shwrs; el pnts
(10-16A) €2.20 or metered; possrev pol; gas; lndtte (inc dryer);
shop; tradsmn; rest, snacks; bar; BBQ; playgrnd; htd pool, spa,
jacuzzi; wifi; some statics; dogs €1.10; phone; bus 200m; adv
bkg; ccard acc; red long stay; CKE/CCI. "Gd san facs; excel
pool & rest; secure o'flow parking area; many long-stay winter
visitors - adv bkg rec; ltd recep hrs low ssn; poss sulphurous
smell fr thermal baths." ♦ € 17.50   2013*

⊞ **FORTUNA** 4F1 (3km N Rural) 38.20666, -1.11194
Camping Las Palmeras, 30709 Baños de Fortuna (Murcia)
[tel/fax 968-68 60 95] Exit A7 junc 83 Fortuna; cont on
C3223 thro Fortuna to Los Baños; turn R & foll sp. Concealed
R turn on crest at beg of vill. Med, mkd pitch, pt shd; wc;
chem disp (wc); shwrs; el pnts (6-10A) €2.20-3 or metered;
gas; lndtte; shops 300m; tradsmn; rest, snacks; bar; natural
hot water mineral pool 200m; some statics; dogs €0.54; poss
cr; quiet; adv bkg acc; red long stay; ccard acc; CKE/CCI. "Gd
value, friendly site; gd, modern san facs; gd rest; lge pitches;
poss tatty statics; thermal baths also at Archena (15km)." ♦ ltd
€ 11.88   2010*

⊞ FOZ *1A2* (7km E Coastal) *43.55416, -7.17000* **Camping Playa Reinante Anosa Casa, Estrada da Costa 42, 27279 Barreiros/Reinante (Lugo) [tel/fax 982-13 40 05; info@ campinganosacasa.com; www.campinganosacasa.com]** E fr Barreiros on N634, exit rd at Reinante opp Hotel Casa Amadora, turn R at beach, site on R. Sm, unshd; wc; chem disp; shwrs €1; el pnts €4.50; gas; lndtte; shop, rest, snacks, bar 500m; BBQ; sand beach adj; wifi; 10% statics; dogs €5; bus/train 900m; quiet. "Owners & location make up for basic facs in need of upgrading; excel coastal walking fr site." ♦ ltd € 18.00   2009*

⊞ FOZ *1A2* (11.9km E Coastal) *43.55525, -7.20019* **Camping Benquerencia, 27792 Benquerencia-Barreiros (Lugo) [982-12 44 50 or 679-15 87 88 (mob); contactol@ campingbenquerencia.com; www.campingbenquerencia. com]** Fr junc of N642 & N634 S of Foz; E twd Ribadeo; in 1km past Barreiros at km stone 566 turn L at site sp. Site on R in 1.5km. Med, mkd pitch, pt sl, pt shd; wc; shwrs inc; el pnts (6A) €3.50; gas; lndtte; shop in ssn & 2km; rest; bar; playgrnd; sand beach 400m; tennis; games area; phone; quiet; ccard acc; CKE/CCI. "Hot water to shwrs only; NH only." € 18.50 2009*

FOZ *1A2* (2.5km NW Coastal/Rural) *43.58678, -7.28356* **Camping San Rafael, Playa de Peizas, 27789 Foz (Lugo) [tel/fax 982-13 22 18; info@campingsanrafael.com; www. campingsanrafael.com]** N fr Foz on N642, site sp on R. Med, pt sl, unshd; wc; chem disp; mv service pnt; shwrs inc; el pnts (5A) €4.50; gas; lndtte; shop; tradsmn; rest, snacks; bar; sand beach adj; games area; wifi; dogs €1; bus 200m; poss cr; adv bkg; quiet; 15% red long stay; ccard acc; CKE/CCI. "Peaceful, spacious site; basic facs; hot water to shwrs only; take care electrics; pay night bef dep." 1 Apr-30 Sep. € 17.55   2009*

⊞ **FRAGA** *3C2* (1km SE Urban) *41.51738, 0.35553* **Camping Fraga, Calle Major 22, Km 437, Ptda Vincanet s/n, 22520 Fraga (Huesca) [974-34 52 12; info@campingfraga.com; www.campingfraga.com]** Fr W pass thro Fraga town on N11. After about 500m turn R at mini rbdt into indus est just past petrol stn. Turn R again in indus est, foll site sp. Fr E turn L into indus est at mini rdbt just bef petrol stn. NB steep app poss v diff lge o'fits. Sm, mkd pitch, hdstg, terr, pt shd; wc; chem disp; mv service pnt; shwrs inc; el pnts (6A) €3.20 (rev pol & poss long lead req); lndtte; hypmkt 1km; tradsmn; rest, snacks; bar; playgrnd; pool; TV rm; some statics; dogs €2.70; phone; bus 1km; poss cr; adv bkg; red low ssn; CKE/CCI. "Conv NH bet Zaragoza & Tarragona; unspoilt town in beautiful area; rec not to hook-up if in transit - ltd reliable el pnts; chem disps placed between pitches; NH only." ♦ € 22.70   2011*

FRANCA, LA *1A4* (1km NW Coastal) *43.39250, -4.57722* **Camping Las Hortensias, Ctra N634, Km 286, 33590 Colombres/Ribadedeva (Asturias) [985-41 24 42; fax 985-41 21 53; lashortensias@campinglashortensias.com; www.campinglashortensias.com]** Fr N634 on leaving vill of La Franca, at km286 foll sp 'Playa de la Franca' & cont past 1st site & thro car park to end of rd. Med, mkd pitch, pt sl, pt terr, pt shd; wc; chem disp; baby facs; shwrs inc; el pnts (6-10A) €5; gas; lndtte; shop; rest, snacks, bar adj; playgrnd; sand beach adj; tennis; cycle hire; phone; dogs (but not on beach) €5; bus 800m; poss cr; Eng spkn; adv bkg; ccard acc; red low ssn/CKE/ CCI. "Beautiful location nr scenic beach; sea views fr top terr pitches; vg." 5 Jun-30 Sep. € 28.50   2011*

FRESNEDA, LA *3C2* (2.5km SW Rural) *40.90705, 0.06166* **Camping La Fresneda, Partida Vall del Pi, 44596 La Fresneda (Teruel) [978-85 40 85; info@campinglafresneda. com; www.campinglafresneda.com]** Fr Alcañiz S on N232 dir Morella; in 15km turn L onto A231 then A231 twd Valjunquera to La Fresneda; cont thro vill; in 2.5km turn R onto site rd. Site sp fr vill. Sm, hdg/mkd pitch, terr, pt shd; wc; chem disp; baby facs; shwrs inc; el pnts (6A) inc; gas 2.5km; lndtte; tradsmn; rest, snacks; bar; plunge pool; wifi; no dogs; phone; poss cr; Eng spkn; quiet; ccard acc; red long stay; CKE/CCI. "Narr site rds, poss diff lge o'fits; various pitch sizes; gd; adv bkg adv; v helpful owners." ♦ 15 Mar-15 Oct. € 24.50   2012*

⊞ **FUENGIROLA** *2H4* (9km W Coastal) *36.48943, -4.71813* **Camping Los Jarales, Ctra N340, Km 197 Calahonda, 29650 Mijas-Costa (Málaga) [tel/fax 952-93 00 03; www. campinglosjarales.com]** Fr Fuengirola take N340 W twd Marbella, turn at km 197 stone; site located to N of rd. Lge, mkd pitch, hdstg, pt sl, pt shd; wc; chem disp; serviced pitch; shwrs inc; el pnts (5A) €3.25; gas; lndtte; shop adj; rest, snacks; bar; playgrnd; pool; sand beach 400m; tennis; TV; no dogs; bus adj; poss cr; Eng spkn; adv bkg; rd noise; red long stay/ CKE/CCI. "Well-run site; buses to Marbella & Fuengirola." ♦ € 21.43   2011*

"We must tell The Club about that great site we found"

Get your site reports in by mid-August and we'll do our best to get your updates into the next edition.

⊞ **FUENTE DE PIEDRA** *2G4* (700m S Rural) *37.12905, -4.73315* **Camping Fuente de Pedra, Calle Campillos 88-90, 29520 Fuente de Piedra (Málaga) [952-73 52 94; fax 952-73 54 61; info@camping-rural.com; www.camping-rural.com]** Turn off A92 at km 132 sp Fuente de Piedra. Sp fr vill cent. Or to avoid town turn N fr A384 just W of turn for Bobadilla Estación, sp Sierra de Yeguas. In 2km turn R into nature reserve, cont for approx 3km, site on L at end of town. Sm, mkd pitch, hdstg, pt sl, terr, pt shd; wc; shwrs inc; el pnts (10A) €5; gas; lndry rm; shop; rest, snacks; bar; BBQ; playgrnd; pool in ssn; internet; 25% statics; dogs €3; phone; bus 500m; Eng spkn; poss noise fr adj public pool; ccard acc; red long stay/ low ssn/CKE/CCI. "Mostly sm, narr pitches, but some avail for o'fits up to 7m; gd rest; san facs dated & poss stretched; adj lge lake with flamingoes; gd." ♦ ltd € 22.00   2009*

FUENTE DE SAN ESTABAN, LA *1D3* (1km E Rural) *40.79128, -6.24384* **Camping El Cruce, 37200 La Fuente de San Esteban (Salamanca) [923-44 01 30; campingelcruce@ yahoo.es; www.campingelcruce.com]** On A62/E80 (Salamanca-Portugal) take exit 293 into vill & foll signs immed behind hotel on S side of rd. Fr E watch for sp 'Cambio de Sentido' to cross main rd. Med, pt shd; wc; chem disp; shwrs; el pnts (6A) €3.50 (poss no earth); rest adj; snacks; bar; playgrnd; wifi; Eng spkn; some rd noise; ccard acc; CKE/CCI. "Conv NH/sh stay en rte Portugal; friendly." ♦ 1 May-30 Sep. € 15.00   2013*

⊞ **FUENTEHERIDOS** *2F3* (600m SW Rural) *37.9050, -6.6742*
**Camping El Madroñal, Ctra Fuenteheridos-Castaño
del Robledo, Km 0.6, 21292 Fuenteheridos (Huelva)
[959-50 12 01; castillo@campingelmadronal.com; www.
campingelmadronal.com]** Fr Zafra S on N435n turn L onto
N433 sp Aracena, ignore first R to Fuenteheridos vill, camp
sp R at next x-rd 500m on R. At rndabt take 2nd exit. Avoid
Fuenteheridos vill - narr rds. Med, mkd pitch, pt sl, pt shd; wc;
chem disp; shwrs; el pnts €3.20; gas; lndry rm; shop & 600m;
snacks, bar high ssn; BBQ; 2 pools; cycle hire; horseriding;
80% statics; dogs; phone; bus 1km; car wash; quiet; CKE/CCI.
"Tranquil site in National Park of Sierra de Aracena; pitches
among chestnut trees - poss diff lge o'fits or m'vans & poss sl &
uneven; o'hanging trees on site rds; scruffy, pitches not clearly
mkd; beautiful vill 1km away, worth a visit." € 13.20   2014*

GALENDE see Puebla de Sanabria *1B3*

> ## "I need an on-site restaurant"
>
> We do our best to make sure site
> information is correct, but it is always best
> to check any must-have facilities are still
> available or will be open during your visit.

⊞ **GALLARDOS, LOS** *4G1* (4km N Rural) *37.18448,
-1.92408* **Camping Los Gallardos, 04280 Los Gallardos
(Almería) [950-52 83 24; fax 950-46 95 96; reception@
campinglosgallardos.com; www.campinglosgallardos.
com]** Fr N leave A7/E15 at junc 525; foll sp to Los Gallardos;
take 1st R after approx 800m pass under a'route; turn L
into site ent. Med, mkd pitch, hdstg, pt shd; wc; chem disp;
serviced pitch; mv service pnt; shwrs inc; el pnts (10A) €3; gas;
lndtte; supmkt; rest (clsd Thurs); snacks; bar; pool; sand beach
10km; 2 grass bowling greens; golf; tennis adj; dogs €2.25;
40% statics; poss v cr; m'way noise; adv bkg; reds long stay/
low ssn; ccard acc; CKE/CCI. "British owned; 90% British
clientele low ssn; gd social atmosphere; sep drinking water
supply nr recep; prone to flooding wet weather; facs tired; poss
cr in winter; friendly staff." ♦ € 20.00   2014*

⊞ **GANDIA** *4E2* (2km N Coastal) *38.98613, -0.16352*
**Camping L'Alqueria, Avda del Grau s/n; 46730 Grao
de Gandía (València) [962-84 04 70; fax 962-84 10 63;
lalqueria@lalqueria.com; www.lalqueria.com]** Fr N on A7/
AP7 exit 60 onto N332 dir Grao de Gandía. Site sp on rd bet
Gandía & seafront. Fr S exit junc 61 & foll sp to beaches. Lge,
mkd pitch, hdstg, pt shd; htd wc; chem disp; mv service pnt;
baby facs; shwrs inc; el pnts (10A) €5.94; gas; lndtte; shop;
rest adj; snacks; bar; playgrnd; htd, covrd pool; jacuzzi; sand
beach 1km; games area; cycle hire; wifi; entmnt; 30% statics
inc disabled accessible; sm dogs (under 10kg) €1.90; phone;
bus; adv bkg; quiet; ccard acc; red long stay/snr citizens;
CKE/CCI. "Pleasant site; helpful family owners; lovely pool;
easy walk to town & stn; excel beach nrby; bus & train to
Valencia." ♦ € 36.00   2010*

See advertisement

⊞ **GARGANTILLA DEL LOZOYA** *1C4* (2km SW Rural)
40.9503, -3.7294 **Camping Monte Holiday, Ctra C604, Km
8.8, 28739 Gargantilla del Lozoya (Madrid) [918-69 52 78;
fax 918-69 52 78; monteholiday@monteholiday.com;
www.monteholiday.com]** Fr N on A1/E5 Burgos-Madrid
rd turn R on M604 at km stone 69 sp Rascafría; in 8km turn
R immed after rlwy bdge & then L up track in 300m, foll site
sp. Do not ent vill. Lge, terr, pt sl, pt shd; wc; chem disp; mv
service pnt; baby facs; shwrs inc; el pnts (7A) €4.30 (poss
rev pol); lndtte (inc dryer); shop 6km; rest; bar; pool; wifi;
80% statics; bus 500m; phone; little Eng spkn; adv bkg; quiet;
ccard acc; red CKE/CCI. "Interesting, friendly site; vg san facs;
gd views; easy to find; some facs clsd low ssn; lovely area but
site isolated in winter & poss heavy snow; conv NH fr m'way
& for Madrid & Segovia; excel wooded site; v rural but well
worth the sh drive fr the N1 E5; clean; lovely surroundings." ♦
€ 41.70 (CChq acc) SBS - E04   2014*

GARRIGUELLA see Figueres *3B3*

⊞ **GARRUCHA** *4G1* (6km N Coastal) *37.23785, -1.79911*
Camping Cuevas Mar, Ctra Garrucha-Villaricos s/n, 04618 Palomares-Cuevas de Almanzora (Almería) [tel/fax 950-46 73 82; www.campingcuevasmar.com] Exit A7 at junc 537 sp Cuevas del Almanzora & take A1200 sp Vera. In 2km turn L onto AL7101 (ALP118) sp Palomares & take 2nd exit at rndabt immed bef Palomares, site on L in 1.5km. Fr S exit A7 at junc 520, by-pass Garrucha, site on L in 6km. Med, hdg/ mkd pitch, hdstg, pt shd; wc; chem disp; mv service pnt; baby facs; shwrs inc; el pnts (6A) €4.20; gas 3km; lndtte (inc dryer); shop; tradsmn; rest 500m; bar; BBQ; playgrnd; pool; jacuzzi; sand/shgl beach 350m; wifi; 10% statics; dogs €2; bus adj; poss cr; adv bkg; red low ssn/long stay; CKE/CCI. "Immac, well-maintained site; lge pitches; friendly owner; vg san facs; only 1 tap for drinking water; cycle track adj; beautiful coastline; mosquito problem; Fri mkt Garrucha; popular long stay site." ♦ ltd € 33.20   2011*

GAVA *3C3* (5km S Coastal) *41.27245, 2.04250* **Camping Tres Estrellas, C31, Km 186.2, 08850 Gavà (Barcelona) [936-33 06 37; fax 936-33 15 25; info@camping3estrellas.com; www.camping3estrellas.com]** Fr S take C31 (Castelldefels to Barcelona), exit 13. Site at km 186.2 300m past rd bdge. Fr N foll Barcelona airport sp, then C31 junc 13 Gavà-Mar slip rd immed under rd bdge. Cross m'way, turn R then R again to join m'way heading N for 400m. Lge, mkd pitch, pt sl, pt shd; htd wc; chem disp; mv service pnt; baby facs; shwrs inc; el pnts (5A) €6.56 (poss rev pol &/or no earth); gas; lndtte (inc dryer); shop; rest, snacks; bar; BBQ; playgrnd; htd pool; sand beach adj; tennis; internet; entmnt; TV; 20% statics; dogs €4.90; phone; bus to Barcelona 400m; poss cr; Eng spkn; adv bkg; aircraft & rd noise & w/end noise fr disco nrby; ccard acc; red snr citizens/CKE/CCI. "20 min by bus to Barcelona cent; poss smells fr stagnant stream in corner of site; poss mosquitoes." ♦ 15 Mar-15 Oct. € 52.50   2013*

GERONA *3B3* (8km S Rural) *41.9224, 2.82864* **Camping Can Toni Manescal, Ctra de la Barceloneta, 17458 Fornells de la Selva (Gerona) [972-47 61 17; fax 972-47 67 35; campinggirona@campinggirona.com; www.campinggirona.com]** Fr N leave AP7 at junc 7 onto N11 dir Barcelona. In 2km turn L to Fornells de la Selva; in vill turn L at church (sp); over rv; in 1km bear R & site on L in 400m. NB Narr rd in Fornells vill not poss lge o'fits. Sm, mkd pitch, pt sl, pt shd; wc; chem disp; baby facs; shwrs inc; el pnts (5A) inc (poss long lead req); gas; lndtte; shop, rest 2km; snacks, bar 4km; playgrnd; pool; sand beach 23km; dogs; bus 1.5km; train nr; Eng spkn; adv bkg; quiet; ccard acc; CKE/CCI. "Pleasant, open site on farm; gd base for lovely medieval city Gerona - foll bus stn sp for gd, secure m'van parking; welcoming & helpful owners; lge pitches; ltd san facs; excel cycle path into Gerona, along old rlwy line; Gerona mid-May flower festival rec; gd touring base away fr cr coastal sites." 1 Jun-30 Sep. € 23.00   2012*

GETAFE see Madrid *1D4*

⊞ **GIJON** *1A3* (9.5km NW Coastal) *43.58343, -5.75713* **Camping Perlora, Ctra Candás, Km 12, Perán, 33491 Candás (Asturias) [tel/fax 985-87 00 48; recepcion@ campingperlora.com; www.campingperlora.com]** Exit A8 dir Candás; in 9km at rndabt turn R sp Perlora (AS118). At sea turn L sp Candás, site on R. Avoid Sat mkt day. Med, mkd pitch, pt sl, terr, unshd; wc; chem disp; some serviced pitches; shwrs inc; el pnts (5A) €3.50; gas; lndtte (inc dryer); shop; rest; playgrnd; sand beach 1km; tennis; watersports; fishing; wifi; 80% statics; dogs free; phone; bus adj; poss cr; Eng spkn; quiet; ccard not acc; red long stay. "Excel; helpful staff; attractive, well-kept site on dramatic headland; ltd space for tourers; vg san facs; ltd low ssn; easy walk to Candás; gem of a site; train (5 mins)." ♦ € 21.00   2014*

GIJON *1A3* (13km NW Coastal) *43.57575, -5.74530* **Camping Buenavista, Ctra Dormon-Perlora s/n, Carreño, 33491 Perlora (Asturias) [tel/fax 985-87 17 93; buenavista@ campingbuenavista.com; www.campingbuenavista.com]** Fr Gijón take AS19 sp Tremañes & foll rd for approx 5km. On sharp L bend take exit on R (Avilés) & immed L onto AS239 sp Candás/Perlora, site sp. Med, terr, pt shd; wc; chem disp; shwrs; el pnts inc; gas; lndtte; shop; rest, snacks; bar; playgrnd; sand beach 500m; 70% statics; bus 200m; site open w/end only out of ssn & clsd Dec & Jan; poss cr; noisy; CKE/CCI. "Oviedo historic town worth a visit; quite steep pull-out, need gd power/weight ratio." 15 Jun-15 Sep. € 22.70   2011*

GIRONELLA *3B3* (500m S Rural) *42.01378, 1.87849* **Camping Gironella, Ctra C16/E9, Km 86.750 Entrada Sud Gironella, 08680 Gironella (Barcelona) [938-25 15 29; fax 938-22 97 37; informacio@campinggironella.com; www. campinggironella.cat]** Site is bet Berga & Puig-reig on C16/ E9. Well sp. Med, hdg/mkd pitch, hdstg, pt shd; wc; chem disp; serviced pitch; baby facs; shwrs inc; el pnts (3-10A) €2.75-7; gas; lndtte; shop; tradsmn; rest, snacks; bar; playgrnd; htd pool; games rm; entmnt; TV rm; 90% statics; dogs €1; phone; bus 600m; poss cr; Eng spkn; adv bkg; quiet; CKE/ CCI. "Pleasant site; friendly staff; ltd touring pitches (phone ahead); conv NH." ♦ Holy Week, 1 Jul-15 Sep & w/e low ssn. € 18.00   2011*

GORLIZ *1A4* (700m N Coastal) *43.41782, -2.93626* **Camping Arrien, Uresarantze Bidea, 48630 Gorliz (Bizkaia) [946-77 19 11; fax 946-77 44 80; recepcion@campinggorliz.com; www.campinggorliz.com]** Fr Bilbao foll m'way to Getxo, then 637/634 thro Sopelana & Plentzia to Gorliz. In Gorliz turn L at 1st rndabt, foll sps for site, pass TO on R, then R at next rndabt, strt over next, site on L adj sports cent/running track. Not sp locally. Lge, pt sl, pt shd; wc; chem disp; shwrs inc; el pnts (3-5A) €4.20; lndtte; gas; shop; rest, snacks; bar; BBQ; playgrnd; sand beach 700m; 60% statics; dogs €1; phone; bus 150m; poss cr; Eng spkn; ccard acc; red long stay/CKE/CCI. "Useful base for Bilbao & ferry (approx 1hr); bus to Plentzia every 20 mins, fr there can get metro to Bilbao; friendly, helpful staff; poss shortage of hot water." 1 Mar-31 Oct. € 30.85   2013*

SPAIN

GRANADA *2G4* (4km N Rural) *37.24194, -3.63333* **Camping Granada, Cerro de la Cruz s/n, 18210 Peligros (Granada) [tel/fax 958-34 05 48; pruizlopez1953@yahoo.es]** S on A44 fr Jaén twd Granada; take exit 121 & foll sp Peligros. Turn L at rndabt after 1km by Spar shop, site access rd 300m on R. Single track access 1km. Med, hdstg, terr, pt shd; wc; chem disp; shwrs inc; el pnts (5A) €4.32; gas; lndtte; shop; rest; bar; playgrnd; pool; tennis; dogs €1.30; bus 1km; poss cr; some Eng spkn; adv bkg; quiet; ccard acc; CKE/CCI. "Friendly, helpful owners; well-run site in olive grove; vg facs; superb views; gd access for m'vans but poss diff for v lge o'fits; pitches poss uneven & muddy after rain; site rds & access steep; conv Alhambra - book tickets at recep." ♦ ltd Holy Week & 1 Jul-30 Sep. € 24.62   2009*

⊞ **GRANADA** *2G4* (4km N Urban) *37.19832, -3.61166* **Camping Motel Sierra Nevada, Avda de Madrid 107, 18014 Granada [958-15 00 62; fax 958-15 09 54; campingmotel@terra.es; www.campingsierranevada.com]** App Granada S-bound on A44 & exit at junc 123, foll dir Granada. Site on R in 1.5km just beyond bus stn & opp El Campo supmkt, well sp. Lge, shd; wc; chem disp; mv service pnt; baby facs; shwrs inc; el pnts (6A) €4.20; gas; lndtte (inc dryer); supmkt opp; rest, snacks; BBQ; playgrnd; 2 pools adj; sports facs; wifi; dogs; bus to city cent 500m; poss cr (arr early); Eng spkn; noisy at w/end; ccard acc; CKE/CCI. "V helpful staff; excel san facs, but poss ltd low ssn; motel rms avail; can book Alhambra tickets at recep (24 hrs notice); conv city; excel site." ♦ € 40.20   2014*

GRANADA *2G4* (9km E Rural) *37.16083, -3.45555* **Camping Cubillas, Ctra Bailén-Motril, Km 115, 18220 Albolote (Granada) [958-45 34 08]** Exit A44/E902 junc 116 dir El Chaparral, site sp. Sm, mkd pitch, pt sl, pt shd; wc; chem disp; mv service pnt; shwrs inc; el pnts (5-10A) €2.50; gas; shop; snacks; bar; lake sw; playgrnd; boating & fishing adj; dogs; quiet; 10% red long stay & CKE/CCI. "Useful NH for Granada; some birdwatching; friendly staff; ltd facs low ssn." ♦ 9 May-13 Dec. € 17.20   2009*

⊞ **GRANADA** *2G4* (13km E Rural) *37.16085, -3.45388* **Camping Las Lomas, 11 Ctra de Güejar-Sierra, Km 6, 18160 Güejar-Sierra (Granada) [958-48 47 42; fax 958-48 40 00; info@campinglaslomas.com; www.campinglaslomas.com]** Fr A44 exit onto by-pass 'Ronda Sur', then exit onto A395 sp Sierra Nevada. In approx 4km exit sp Cenes, turn under A395 to T-junc & turn R sp Güejar-Sierra, Embalse de Canales. After approx 3km turn L at sp Güejar-Sierra & site. Site on R 6.5km up winding mountain rd. Med, hdg/mkd pitch, terr, pt shd; htd wc; chem disp; mv service pnt; baby facs; fam bthrm; shwrs inc; el pnts (10A) €4 (poss no earth/rev pol); gas; lndtte (inc dryer); shop; rest, snacks; bar; playgrnd; pool; paddling pool; waterskiing nrby; wifi; dogs free; bus adj; poss cr; Eng spkn; adv bkg ess; quiet; red long stay; ccard acc; CKE/CCI. "Helpful, friendly owners; well-run site; conv Granada (bus at gate); access diff for lge o'fits; excel san facs; gd shop & rest; beautiful mountain scenery; excel site." ♦ ltd € 40.00   2014*

⊞ **GRANADA** *2G4* (3km SE Urban) *37.12444, -3.58611* **Camping Reina Isabel, Calle de Laurel de la Reina, 18140 La Zubia (Granada) [958-59 00 41; fax 958-59 11 91; info@reinaisabelcamping.com; www.reinaisabelcamping.com]** Exit A44 nr Granada at junc sp Ronda Sur, dir Sierra Nevada, Alhambra, then exit 2 sp La Zubia. Foll site sp approx 1.2km on R; narr ent set back fr rd. Med, hdg pitch, hdstg, pt shd; htd wc; chem disp; mv service pnt; baby facs; shwrs inc; el pnts (5A)poss rev pol €4.20; gas; lndtte; shop; supmkt 1km; tradsmn; snacks; bar; pool high ssn; internet; TV; dogs free; phone; bus to Granada cent; Eng spkn; poss cr; adv bkg rec at all times; quiet except during festival in May; ccard acc; red long stay/low ssn; red CKE/CCI. "Well-run, busy site; poss shwrs v hot/cold - warn children; helpful staff; ltd touring pitches & sm; poss student groups; conv Alhambra (order tickets at site), shwr block not heated." ♦ € 24.80   2011*

⊞ **GRANADA** *2G4* (12km S Rural) *37.06785, -3.65176* **Camping Suspiro del Moro, 107 Avda de Madrid, 18630 Otura (Granada) [tel/fax 958-55 54 11; info@campingsuspirodelmoro.com; www.campingsuspirodelmoro.com]** On A44/E902 dir Motril, exit junc 139. Foll camp sp fr W side of rndabt; site visible at top of slight rise on W side of A44, 1km S of Otura. Med, mkd pitch, hdstg, shd; wc; chem disp; mv service pnt; el pnts (5A) €3 (poss no earth); gas; lndry rm; shop; snacks & rest in ssn; bar; playgrnd; lge pool; tennis; games area; 10% statics; phone; bus to Granada adj; Eng spkn; rd noise & noisy rest at w/end; red low ssn; ccard acc; CKE/CCI. "Decent site; reasonable pitches; quiet low ssn; clean facs but inadequate for site this size." ♦ ltd € 19.00   2011*

⊞ **GRAUS** *3B2* (6km S Rural) *42.13069, 0.30980* **Camping Bellavista & Subenuix, Embalse de Barasona, Ctra Graus N123, Km 23, 22435 La Puebla de Castro (Huesca) [974-54 51 13; fax 974 34 70 71; info@hotelcampingbellavista.com; www.hotelcampingbellavista.com]** Fr E on N230/N123 ignore 1st sp for Graus. Cont to 2nd sp 'El Grado/Graus' & turn R. Site on L in 1km adj hotel. Med, mkd pitch, terr, pt shd; htd wc; chem disp; shwrs inc; el pnts (10A) €4.50; gas; lndtte; shop; rest, snacks; bar; playgrnd; pool; lake sw adj; watersports; boat hire; fishing; tennis; horseriding; wifi; entmnt; TV rm; 50% statics; dogs €1; phone; Eng spkn; adv bkg; noisy at w/end; red low ssn; ccard acc; CKE/CCI. "Helpful staff; sm pitches; excel rest; beautiful position above lake with sandy beach; mountain views; gd NH." € 18.60   2011*

GRAUS *3B2* (5km SW Rural) *42.13130, 0.30871* **Camping Lago Barasona, Ctra Barbastro-Graus, N123A, Km 25, 22435 La Puebla de Castro (Huesca) [974-54 51 48 or 974-24 69 06; fax 974-54 52 28; info@lagobarasona.com; www.lagobarasona.com]** Fr E on N123, ignore 1st sp for Graus. Cont to 2nd sp 'El Grado/Graus/Benasque' & turn R. Site on L in 2km. Lge, hdg/mkd pitch, hdstg, sl, terr, shd; htd wc; chem disp; mv service pnt; baby facs; shwrs inc; el pnts (6A) inc; gas; lndtte (inc dryer); shop; tradsmn; rest, snacks; bar; BBQ; playgrnd; 2 pools; paddling pool; lake beach & sw 100m; watersports; sailing; tennis; fitness rm; horseriding 1km; wifi; entmnt; TV rm; 15% statics; dogs €3; Eng spkn; adv bkg; quiet; ccard acc; red long stay; CKE/CCI. "Excel, well-equipped site; lge pitches; helpful staff; adj reservoir water levels likely to drop; highly rec." ♦ 1 Mar-12 Dec. € 36.80   2011*

GUADALUPE *2E3* (1.5km S Rural) *39.44232, -5.31708*
Camping Las Villuercas, Ctra Villanueva-Huerta del Río, Km 2, 10140 Guadalupe (Cáceres) [927-36 71 39; fax 927-36 70 28; www.campinglasvilluercasguadalupe.es] Exit A5/E90 at junc 178 onto EX118 to Guadalupe. Do not ent town. Site sp on R at rndabt at foot of hill. Med, shd; wc; shwrs; el pnts €2.50 (poss no earth/rev pol); lndtte; shop; rest; bar; playgrnd; pool; tennis; ccard acc. "Vg; helpful owners; ltd facs low ssn; some pitches sm & poss not avail in wet weather; nr famous monastery." 1 Mar-15 Dec. € 14.50   2012*

"Satellite navigation makes touring much easier"

Remember most sat navs don't know if you're towing or in a larger vehicle – always use yours alongside maps and site directions.

⊞ **GUARDAMAR DEL SEGURA** *4F2* (2km N Rural/Coastal) *38.10916, -0.65472* Camping Marjal, Ctra N332, Km 73.4, 03140 Guardamar del Segura (Alicante) [966-72 70 70; fax 966-72 66 95; camping@marjal.com; www.campingmarjal. com] Fr N exit A7 junc 72 sp Aeropuerto/Santa Pola; in 5km turn R onto N332 sp Santa Pola/Cartagena, U-turn at km 73.4, site sp on R at km 73.5. Fr S exit AP7 at junc 740 onto CV91 twd Guardamar. In 9km join N332 twd Alicante, site on R at next rndabt. Lge, hdg/mkd pitch, hdstg, pt shd; all serviced pitches; wc; chem disp; baby facs; sauna; shwrs inc; el pnts (16A) €3 or metered; gas; lndtte (inc dryer); supmkt; rest; snacks & bar; BBQ; playgrnd; 2 htd pools (1 covrd); tropical water park; sand beaches 1km (inc naturist); lake sw 15km; tennis; sports cent; cycle hire; wifi; entmnt; TV rm; 18% statics; dogs €2.20; phone; recep 0800-2100; adv bkg rec; Eng spkn; quiet; red long stay/low ssn; ccard acc; CKE/CCI. "Fantastic facs; friendly, helpful staff; excel family entmnt & activities; excel; well sign-posted; lge shower cubicles; highly rec." ♦ € 77.00   2014*

GUARDIOLA DE BERGUEDA *3B3* (3.5km SW Rural) *42.21602, 1.83705* Camping El Berguedà, Ctra B400, Km 3.5, 08694 Guardiola de Berguedà (Barcelona) [938-22 74 32; info@ campingbergueda.com; www.campingbergueda.com] On C16 S take B400 W dir Saldes. Site is approx 10km S of Cadí Tunnel. Med, mkd pitch, some hdstg, terr, pt shd; wc; chem disp; baby facs; shwrs; el pnts (6A) €3.90 (poss rev pol); gas; lndtte; shop; tradsmn; rest, snacks; bar; BBQ; playgrnd; pool; paddling pool; games area; games rm; TV; some statics; phone; dogs; Eng spkn; quiet; CKE/CCI. "Helpful staff; vg clean san facs; beautiful, remote situation; gd walking; poss open w/ ends in winter; highly rec; spectacular mountains/scenery; gd touring area; rec Gaudi's Garden in La Pobla." ♦ 1 Apr-1 Nov. € 39.30   2014*

GUEJAR SIERRA see Granada *2G4*

HARO *1B4* (600m N Urban) *42.57900, -2.85153* Camping de Haro, Avda Miranda 1, 26200 Haro (La Rioja) [941-31 27 37; fax 941-31 20 68; campingdeharo@fer.es; www. campingdeharo.com] Fr N or S on N124 take exit sp A68 Vitoria/Logrono & Haro. In 500m at rndabt take 1st exit, under rlwy bdge, cont to site on R immed bef rv bdge. Fr AP68 exit junc 9 to town; at 2nd rndabt turn L onto LR111 (sp Logroño). Immed after rv bdge turn sharp L & foll site sp. Avoid cont into town cent. Med, hdg/mkd pitch, pt shd; htd wc; chem disp; mv service pnt; shwrs inc (am only in winter); el pnts (6A) €4.40; gas; lndtte (inc dryer); shop & 600m; snacks; bar; BBQ; playgrnd; htd pool high ssn; wifi; 70% statics; dogs €3; phone; bus 800m; car wash; site clsd 9 Dec-13 Jan; poss cr; Eng spkn; adv bkg; quiet (not w/end), some rv noise; red low ssn; ccard acc; CKE/CCI. "Clean, tidy site - peaceful low ssn; friendly owner; some sm pitches & diff turns; excel facs; statics busy at w/ends; conv Rioja 'bodegas' & Bilbao & Santander ferries; conv NH recep clsd 1300-1500 no entry then due to security barrier; excel NH for Santander/Bilbao; lge o'night area with electric." ♦ 25 Jan-8 Dec. € 37.40 SBS - E02   2014*

⊞ **HARO** *1B4* (10km SW Rural) *42.53017, -2.92173* Camping De La Rioja, Ctra de Haro/Santo Domingo de la Calzada, Km 8.5, 26240 Castañares de la Rioja (La Rioja) [941-30 01 74; fax 941-30 01 56; info@campingdelarioja.com] Exit AP68 junc 9, take rd twd Santo Domingo de la Calzada. Foll by-pass round Casalarreina, site on R nr rvside just past vill on rd LR111. Lge, hdg pitch, pt shd; htd wc; chem disp; shwrs; el pnts (4A) €3.90 (poss rev pol); gas; lndtte (inc dryer); sm shop; rest, snacks; bar; pool high ssn; tennis; cycle hire; entmnt; dogs; clsd 10 Dec-8 Jan; 90% statics; dogs; bus adj; site clsd 9 Dec-11 Jan; poss cr; adv bkg; noisy high ssn; ccard acc. "Fair site but fairly isolated; basic san facs but clean; ltd facs in winter; sm pitches; conv for Rioja wine cents; Bilbao ferry." € 26.80   2009*

"There aren't many sites open at this time of year"

If you're travelling outside peak season remember to call ahead to check site opening dates – even if the entry says 'open all year'

⊞ **HECHO** *3B1* (1km S Rural) *42.73222, -0.75305* Camping Valle de Hecho, Ctra Puente La Reina-Hecho s/n, 22720 Hecho (Huesca) [974-37 53 61; fax 976-27 78 42; campinghecho@campinghecho.com; www. campinghecho.com] Leave Jaca W on N240. After 25km turn N on A176 at Puente La Reina de Jaca. Site on W of rd, o'skts of Hecho/Echo. Med, mkd pitch, pt sl, pt shd; htd wc; chem disp; mv service pnt; shwrs inc; el pnts (5-15A) €4.20; gas; lndtte; shop; rest, snacks; bar; playgrnd; pool; games area; 50% statics; dogs; phone; bus 200m; quiet; ccard acc; CKE/ CCI. "Pleasant site in foothills of Pyrenees; excel, clean facs but poss inadequate hot water; gd birdwatching area; Hecho fascinating vill; shop & bar poss clsd low ssn except w/end; v ltd facs low ssn; not suitable lge o'fits." € 22.35   2010*

HERRADURA, LA see Almuñécar *2H4*

HONDARRIBIA see Irun *3A1*

⊞ **HORCAJO DE LOS MONTES** 2E4 (200m E Rural)
39.32440, -4.6358 **Camping Mirador de Cabañeros, Calle
Cañada Real Segoviana s/n, 13110 Horcajo de los Montes
(Ciudad Real) [926 77 54 39; fax 926 77 50 03; info@
campingcabaneros.com; www.campingcabaneros.com]** At
km 53 off CM4103 Horcajo-Alcoba rd, 200m fr vill. CM4106
to Horcajo fr NW poor in parts. Med, mkd pitch, hdstg, terr,
pt shd; htd wc; chem disp; mv service pnt; baby facs; shwrs;
el pnts (6A) €4.20; gas; shop 500m; rest; bar; BBQ; playgrnd;
pool; rv sw 12km; games area; games rm; tennis 500m; cycle
hire; entmnt; TV; 10% statics; dogs €2; phone; adv bkg rec
high ssn; quiet; red long stay/low ssn; ccard acc; CKE/CCI.
"Beside Cabañeros National Park; beautiful views; rd fr S much
better." ♦ € 32.40 (CChq acc)   2013*

HORNOS 4F1 (9km SW Rural) 38.18666, -2.77277
**Camping Montillana Rural, Ctra Tranco-Hornos A319,
km 78.5, 23292 Hornos de Segura (Jaén) [953-12 61 94
or 680-15 21 10; jrescalvor@hotmail.com; www.
campingmontillana.es]** Fr N on N322 take A310 then A317
S then A319 dir Tranco & Cazorla. Site nr km 78.5, ent by
1st turning. Fr S on N322 take A6202 N of Villaneuva del
Arzobispo. In 26km at Tranco turn L onto A319 & nr km 78.5
ent by 1st turning up slight hill. Sm, mkd pitch, hdstg, terr,
pt shd; wc; chem disp; shwrs inc; el pnts (10A) €3.20; lndtte;
shop; tradsmn; rest, snacks; bar; pool; lake adj; 5% statics;
dogs; phone; some Eng spkn; adv bkg; quiet; CKE/CCI.
"Beautiful area; conv Segura de la Sierra, Cazorla National
Park; much wildlife; friendly, helpful staff; gd site." 19 Mar-
30 Sep. € 16.00   2013*

HOSPITAL DE ORBIGO 1B3 (1.3km N Urban) 42.4664,
-5.8836 **Camp Municipal Don Suero, 24286 Hospital de
Órbigo (León) [987-36 10 18; fax 987-38 82 36; camping@
hospitaldeorbigo.com; www.hospitaldeorbigo.com]** N120
rd fr León to Astorga, km 30. Site well sp fr N120. Narr streets
in Hospital. Med, hdg pitch, pt shd; wc; shwrs; el pnts (6A)
€1.90; lndtte (inc dryer); shop, bar high ssn; rest adj; BBQ; pool
adj; bus to León nr; 50% statics; dogs; bus 1km; poss open w/
end only mid Apr-May; phone; poss cr; Eng spkn; ccard acc;
CKE/CCI. "Statics v busy w/ends, facs stretched; poss noisy;
phone ahead to check site open if travelling close to opening/
closing dates." ♦ Holy Week-30 Sep. € 14.40   2009*

⊞ **HOSPITALET DE L'INFANT, L'** 3C2 (2km S Coastal)
40.97750, 0.90361 **Camping Cala d'Oques, Via Augusta
s/n, 43890 L'Hospitalet de l'Infant (Tarragona) [977-
82 32 54; fax 977-82 06 91; info@caladoques.com; www.
caladoques.com]** Exit AP7 junc 38 onto N340. Take rd sp
L'Hospitalet de l'Infant at km 1128. Lge, terr, shd; htd wc; mv
service pnt; baby facs; shwrs; el pnts (10A) €4.95; gas; lndtte;
shop; rest; bar; playgrnd; sand/shgl beach adj (naturist beaches
nr); wifi; entmnt; dogs €3.40; poss cr; Eng spkn; some rlwy
& rd noise; ltd facs low ssn; red snr citizens/long stay/low ssn;
CKE/CCI. "Friendly, relaxing site; clean, modern san facs; well
kept site; vg rest; sea views; poss v windy; conv Aquapolis &
Port Aventura; mkd mountain walks; vg NH & longer stay."
€ 38.00   2011*

HOSPITALET DE L'INFANT, L' *3C2* (2km S Coastal) *40.97722, 0.90083* **Camping El Templo del Sol (Naturist), Poligon 14-15, Playa del Torn, 43890 L'Hospitalet de l'Infant (Tarragona) [977-82 34 34; fax 977-82 34 64; info@eltemplodelsol.com; www.eltemplodelsol.com]** Leave A7 at exit 38 or N340 twds town cent. Turn R (S) along coast rd for 2km. Ignore 1st camp sp on L, site 200m further on L. Lge, hdg/mkd pitch, pt sl, pt shd; wc; chem disp; serviced pitch; shwrs inc; el pnts (6A) inc; gas; lndtte; shop; rest, snacks; bar; playgrnd; pools; solar-energy park; jacuzzi; official naturist san/shgl beach adj; cinema/theatre; TV rm; 5% statics; poss cr; Eng spkn; adv bkg (dep); some rlwy noise rear of site; ccard acc; red long stay/low ssn; INF card. "Excel naturist site; no dogs, radios or TV on pitches; lge private wash/shwr rms; pitches v tight - take care o'hanging branches; conv Port Aventura; mosquito problem; poss strong winds - take care with awnings." ♦ 1 Apr-22 Oct. € 43.35 2009*

See advertisement

HOYOS DEL ESPINO *1D3* (4km E Rural) *40.34313, -5.13131* **Camping Navagredos, Ctra de Valdecasas, 05635 Navarredonda de Gredos (Ávila) [920-20 74 76; fax 983-29 58 41; proatur@proatur.com]** Fr N take N502 S. Then W on C500 twd El Barco. Site sp in Navarredonda on L in 2km, just bef petrol stn. Steep app rd with bends. Med, pt sl, pt shd; wc; chem disp; mv service pnt; baby facs; shwrs inc; el pnts (10A) €3.90; lndtte; shops 2km; tradsmn; rest & snacks in ssn; bar; BBQ; internet; phone; quiet. "Excel walking in Gredos mountains; some facs poorly maintained low ssn; steep slope to san facs; site open w/ends until mid-Nov." ♦ Easter-12 Oct. € 17.35   2010*

HOYOS DEL ESPINO *1D3* (1.5km S Rural) *40.34055, -5.17527* **Camping Gredos, Ctra Plataforma, Km.1.8, 05634 Hoyos del Espino (Ávila) [920-20 75 85; campingredos@ campingredos.com; www.campingredos.com]** Fr N110 turn E at El Barco onto AV941 for approx 41km; at Hoyos del Espino turn S twd Plataforma de Gredos. Site on R in 1.8km. Or fr N502 turn W onto AV941 dir Parador de Gredos to Hoyos del Espino, then as above. Sm, pt sl, shd; wc; chem disp; shwrs inc; el pnts €2.90; gas; lndtte; shop 1km; snacks; playgrnd; rv sw adj; cycle hire; horseriding; adv bkg; quiet; CKE/ CCI. "Lovely mountain scenery; beautiful loc in forest nr rv, san facs basic, mountain walks." ♦ Holy Week & 1 May-1 Oct. € 16.00   2012*

HUESCA *3B2* (1.5km SW Urban) *42.13725, -0.41900* **Camping San Jorge, Calle Ricardo del Arco s/n, 22004 Huesca [tel/fax 974-22 74 16; contacto@campingsanjorge. com; www.campingsanjorge.com]** Exit A23 S of town at km 568 & head N twd town cent. Site well sp adj municipal pool & leisure facs. Med, shd; wc; chem disp (wc); shwrs inc; el pnts (10A) €4; lndtte; shop; snacks; bar; 2 pools; internet; dogs; bus 300m; ccard acc; CKE/CCI. "Grassy pitches poss flooded after heavy rain; san facs gd but poss stretched high ssn; vg pool; friendly; conv town cent; gd supmkt 250m; gd NH." 15 Mar-15 Oct. € 21.00   2014*

⊞ **HUMILLADERO** *2G4* (500m S Rural) *37.10750, -4.69611* **Camping La Sierrecilla, Avda de Clara Campoamor s/n, 29531 Humilladero (Málaga) [951-19 90 90 or 693-82 81 99 (mob); fax 952-83 43 73; info@lasierrecilla.com; www.lasierrecilla.com]** Exit A92 junc 138 onto A7280 twd Humilladero. At vill ent turn L at 1st rndabt, site visible. Med, mkd pitch, terr, hdstg, pt sl, pt shd; htd wc; chem disp; mv service pnt; fam bathrm; baby facs; serviced pitches; shwrs inc; el pnts (16A) €3.50; lndtte; shop 1km; rest, snacks; bar; BBQ; playgrnd; htd pool; paddling pool; wifi; entmnt; 10% statics; dogs €1.50; Eng spkn; adv bkg; quiet; CKE/CCI. "Excel new site; gd modern, san facs; vg touring base; gd walking; horseriding, caving, archery high ssn; Fuentepiedra lagoon nrby; new trees planted, still need a year or so to give much shade, but attractive none the less." ♦ € 32.00   2014*

⊞ **IRUN** *3A1* (2km N Rural) *43.36638, -1.80436* **Camping Jaizkibel, Ctra Guadalupe Km 22, 20280 Hondarribia (Guipúzcoa) [943-64 16 79; fax 943-64 26 53; jaizkibel@ campingseuskadi.com; www.campingseuskadi.com/ jaizkibel]** Fr Hondarribia/Fuenterrabia inner ring rd foll sp to site below old town wall. Do not ent town. Med, hdg pitch, pt hdstg, terr, pt shd; wc; baby facs; shwrs; el pnts (6A) €4.35 (check earth); lndtte; tradsmn; rest; bar; BBQ; playgrnd; sand beach 1.5km; tennis; wifi; 90% statics; no dogs; phone; bus 1km; Eng spkn; adv bkg; quiet; red low ssn; ccard acc; CKE/ CCI. "Easy 20 mins walk to historic town; scenic area; gd walking; gd touring base but ltd turning space for tourers; clean facs; gd rest & bar." € 31.25   2014*

⊞ **IRUN** *3A1* (3km S Rural) *43.31540, -1.87419* **Camping Oliden, Ctra NI Madrid-Irún, Km 470, 20180 Oiartzun (Guipúzcoa) [943-49 07 28; oliden@campingseuskadi. com]** On S side of N1 at E end of vill. Lge, pt sl, pt shd; wc; chem disp; mv service pnt; shwrs; el pnts (5A) €3.53; lndtte (inc dryer); shops adj; rest; bar; playgrnd; pool in ssn; beach 10km; bus 200m; some statics; rlwy & factory noise; red CKE/ CCI. "Steps to shwrs; grass pitches v wet low ssn; NH only." € 17.80   2009*

⊞ **IRUN** *3A1* (6km W Coastal) *43.37629, -1.79939* **Camping Faro de Higuer, Ctra. Del Faro, 58, 20280 Hondarribia [943 64 10 08; fax 943 64 01 50; faro@campingseuskadi. com; www.campingseuskadi.com]** Fr AP8 exit at junc 2 Irun. Foll signs for airport. At rndabt after airport take 2nd exit, cross two more rndabts. 2nd exit at next 2 rndabts. Cont uphill to lighthouse & foll signs for Faro. Med, hdg pitch, mkd pitch, pt sl, terr, unshd; wc; chem disp; mv service pnt; baby facs; fam bthrm; shwrs; el pnts (10A) €5.20; lndtte (inc dryer); shop; rest; snack; bar; BBQ; cooking facs; playgrnd; pool; waterslide; paddling pool; beach adj; games area; games rm; bike hire; entmnt; wifi; tv rm; 50% statics; dogs €1.20; phone; poss cr; Eng spkn; adv bkg; noisy. "Vg site on top of winding rd, is v busy outside; sep ent & exit; exit has low stone arch, be careful when leaving." ♦ € 26.00   2014*

SPAIN

⊞ **ISABA** *3B1* (13km E Rural) *42.87495, -0.81985* **Camping Zuriza, Ctra Anso-Zuriza, Km 14, 22728 Ansó (Huesca)** [tel/fax 974-37 01 96; campingzuriza@valledeanso.com; http://campingzuriza.valledeanso.com] On NA1370 N fr Isaba, turn R in 4km onto NA2000 to Zuriza. Foll sp to site. Fr Ansó, take HUV2024 N to Zuriza. Foll sp to site; narr, rough rd not rec for underpowered o'fits. Lge, pt sl, pt shd; wc; some serviced pitches; shwrs inc; el pnts €6.00; lndtte; shop; tradsmn; rest; bar; playgrnd; 50% statics; phone; quiet; ccard acc; CKE/CCI. "Beautiful, remote valley; no vill at Zuriza, nearest vills Isaba & Ansó; no direct rte to France; superb location for walking." € 18.00   2011*

ISLA *1A4* (4km SW Rural) *43.46446, -3.60773* **Camping Los Molinos de Bareyo, 39170 Bareyo (Cantabria)** [942-67 05 69; losmolinosdebareyo@ceoecant.es; www. campingsonline.com/molinosdebareyo/] Exit A8 at km 185 & foll sp for Beranga, Noja. Bef Noja at rndabt take L for Ajo, site sp on L up hill. Do not confuse with Cmp Los Molinos in Noja. V lge, mkd pitch, terr, pt shd; htd wc; chem disp; shwrs inc; el pnts (3A) €3.60; lndtte; shop; rest, snacks; bar; BBQ; playgrnd; htd pool; sand beach 4km; tennis; games area; TV rm; 60% statics; dogs; phone; bus 1km; site clsd mid Dec-end Jan; poss cr; Eng spkn; adv bkg; CKE/CCI. "Vg site on hill with views of coast; lively but not o'crowded high ssn." ♦ 1 Jun-30 Sep. € 22.50   2010*

ISLA *1A4* (1km NW Coastal) *43.50261, -3.54351* **Camping Playa de Isla, Calle Ardanal 1, 39195 Isla (Cantabria)** [tel/fax 942-67 93 61; consultas@playadeisla.com; www. playadeisla.com] Turn off A8/E70 at km 185 Beranga sp Noja & Isla. Foll sp Isla. In town to beach, site sp to L. Then in 100m keep R along narr seafront lane (main rd bends L) for 1km (rd looks like dead end). Med, mkd pitch, pt sl, terr, pt shd; wc; chem disp; shwrs inc; el pnts (3A) €4.50; gas; lndtte; shop & 1km; snacks; bar; playgrnd; sand beach adj; 90% statics; no dogs; phone; bus 1km; poss cr; quiet; ccard acc; CKE/CCI. "Beautiful situation; ltd touring pitches; busy at w/end." Easter-30 Sep. € 26.45   2013*

⊞ **ISLA CRISTINA** *2G2* (4km E Coastal) *37.20555, -7.26722* **Camping Playa Taray, Ctra La Antilla-Isla Cristina, Km 9, 21430 La Redondela (Huelva)** [959-34 11 02; fax 959-34 11 96; www.campingtaray.com] Fr W exit A49 sp Isla Cristina & go thro town heading E. Fr E exit A49 at km 117 sp Lepe. In Lepe turn S on H4116 to La Antilla, then R on coast rd to Isla Cristina & site. Lge, pt shd; wc; mv service pnt; shwrs; el pnts (10) €4.28; gas; lndtte; shop; bar; rest; playrnd; sand beach adj; some statics; phone; dogs; bus; quiet; ccard acc; red long stay/low ssn; CKE/CCI. "Gd birdwatching, cycling; less cr than other sites in area in winter; poss untidy low ssn & ltd facs; poss diff for lge o'fits; friendly, helpful owner." ♦ € 19.00   2011*

ISLA PLANA see Puerto de Mazarrón *4G1*

ISLARES see Oriñón *1A4*

ITZIAR see Deba *3A1*

⊞ **IZNATE** *2G4* (1km NE Rural) *36.78449, -4.17442* **Camping Rural Iznate, Ctra Iznate-Benamocarra s/n, 29792 Iznate (Málaga)** [tel/fax 952-53 56 13; info@campingiznate.com; www.campingiznate.com] Exit A7/E15 junc 265 dir Cajiz & Iznate. Med, mkd pitch, hdstg, unshd; wc; chem disp; shwrs; el pnts (5-16A) €3-3.50 (poss no earth); gas; lndtte; shop; rest, snacks; bar; pool; shgl beach 8km; wifi; some statics; dogs €2.10; bus adj; Eng spkn; quiet; red long stay/low ssn. "Beautiful scenery & mountain villages; conv Vélez-Málaga & Torre del Mar; pleasant owners; many ssnl static c'vans - scruffy low ssn." € 17.70   2010*

⊞ **JACA** *3B2* (2km W Urban) *42.56416, -0.57027* **Camping Victoria, Avda de la Victoria 34, 22700 Jaca (Huesca)** [974-35 70 08; fax 974-35 70 09; victoria@campings.net; www. campingvictoria.es] Fr Jaca cent take N240 dir Pamplona, site on R. Med, mkd pitch, pt shd; wc; chem disp; mv service pnt; shwrs inc; el pnts (10A) €5; lndtte; snacks; bar; BBQ; playgrnd; htd pool high ssn; 80% statics; dogs; bus adj; quiet. "Basic facs, but clean & well-maintained; friendly staff; conv NH/sh stay Somport Pass." € 22.00   2012*

> ## "That's changed – Should I let The Club know?"
>
> If you find something on site that's different from the site entry, fill in a report and let us know. See www.caravanclub.co.uk/europereport.

JARANDILLA DE LA VERA *1D3* (2km W Rural) *40.12723, -5.69318* **Camping Yuste, Ctra EX203, Km 47, 10440 Aldeanueva de la Vera (Cáceres)** [927-57 26 59] Fr Plasencia head E on EX203 following sp for Parador, site at km stone 47 in Aldeanueva de la Vera. Clearly sp down narr rd. Med, pt sl, pt shd; wc; shwrs; el pnts (5A) inc; gas; lndry rm; shop; rest, snacks; bar; BBQ; pool; rv fishing; tennis; games rm; TV; bus 500m; phone; quiet. "Simple, well-maintained, attractive site." 15 Mar-15 Sep. € 24.80   2010*

⊞ **JAVEA/XABIA** *4E2* (1km S Rural) *38.78333, 0.17294* **Camping Jávea, Camí de la Fontana 10, 03730 Jávea (Alicante)** [965-79 10 70; fax 966-46 05 07; info@ campingjavea.es; www.camping-javea.com] Exit N332 for Jávea on A132, cont in dir Port on CV734. At rndabt & Lidl supmkt, take slip rd to R immed after rv bdge sp Arenal Platjas & Cap de la Nau. Strt on at next rndabt to site sp & slip rd 100m sp Autocine. If you miss slip rd go back fr next rndabt. Lge, mkd pitch, pt shd; wc ltd; chem disp; baby facs; shwrs inc; el pnts (8A) €4.56 (long lead rec); gas; lndtte; shop 500m; tradsmn; rest, snacks; bar; BBQ; playgrnd; pool; paddling pool; sand beach 1.5km; tennis; games area; internet; 15% statics; dogs €2; adv bkg; quiet; red low ssn/long stay; ccard acc; CKE/CCI. "Excel site & rest; variable pitch sizes/prices; some lge pitches - lge o'fits rec phone ahead; gd, clean san facs; mountain views; helpful staff; m'vans beware low trees; gd cycling." ♦ € 27.20   2012*

See advertisement

⊞ **JAVEA/XABIA** *4E2* (3km S Coastal) *38.77058, 0.18207*
**Camping El Naranjal, Cami dels Morers 15, 03730
Jávea (Alicante) [965-79 29 89; fax 966-46 02 56; delfi@
campingelnaranjal.com; www.campingelnaranjal.com]**
Exit A7 junc 62 or 63 onto N332 València/Alicante rd. Exit at
Gata de Gorgos to Jávea. Foll sp Camping Jávea/Camping El
Naranjal. Access rd by tennis club, foll sp. Med, mkd pitch,
hdstg, pt shd; htd wc; chem disp; mv service pnt; baby facs;
shwrs inc; el pnts (10A) €4.05 (poss rev pol); gas; lndtte (inc
dryer); shop; tradsmn; rest, snacks; bar; BBQ; playgrnd; pool;
paddling pool; sand beach 500m; tennis 300m; cycle hire;
games rm; golf 3km; wifi; TV rm; 35% statics; dogs free;
phone; bus 500m; adv bkg; Eng spkn; quiet; ccard acc; red
long stay/low ssn/CKE/CCI. "Gd scenery & beach; pitches poss
tight lge o'fits; excel rest; immac facs; tourist info - tickets sold;
rec." ♦ € 26.00   2010*

LABUERDA see Ainsa *3B2*

LAREDO *1A4* (500m W Urban/Coastal) *43.40888, -3.43277*
**Camping Carlos V, Avnda Los Derechos Humanos 15, Ctra
Residencial Playa, 39770 Laredo (Cantabria) [tel/fax 942-
60 55 93]** Leave A8 at junc 172 to Laredo, foll yellow camping
sp, site on W side of town. Med, mkd pitch, pt shd; wc; mv
service pnt; baby facs; shwrs inc; el pnts €2.60; gas; lndtte;
shop & 100m; rest; bar; playgrnd; sand beach 200m; dogs
€2.14; bus 100m; poss cr; noisy; CKE/CCI. "Well sheltered
& lively resort; sm area for tourers; gd, clean, modern facs."
6 May-30 Sep. € 25.00   2012*

LAREDO *1A4* (2km W Coastal) *43.41176, -3.45329* **Camping
Playa del Regatón, El Sable 8, 39770 Laredo (Cantabria)
[tel/fax 942-60 69 95; info@campingplayaregaton.com;
www.campingplayaregaton.com]** Fr W leave A8 junc 172,
under m'way to rndabt & take exit sp Calle Rep Colombia. In
800m turn L at traff lts, in further 800m turn L onto tarmac rd
to end, passing other sites. Fr E leave at junc 172, at 1st rndabt
take 2nd exit sp Centro Comercial N634 Colindres. At next
rndabt take exit Calle Rep Colombia, then as above. Lge, mkd
pitch; pt shd; wc; chem disp; mv service pnt; shwrs inc; el pnts
(6A) €4.30; gas; lndtte; shop; rest; bar; sand beach adj & 3km;
horseriding mr; wifi; 75% statics; no dogs; bus 600m; Eng
spkn; adv bkg; quiet; ccard acc; red long stay/CKE/CCI. "Clean
site; sep area for tourers; wash up facs (cold water) every pitch;
gd, modern facs; gd NH/sh stay (check opening times of office
for el pnt release)." ♦ 1 Apr-25 Sep. € 30.05   2011*

LEKEITIO *3A1* (3km S Coastal) *43.35071, -2.49260* **Camping
Leagi, Calle Barrio Leagi s/n, 48289 Mendexa (Vizcaya)
[946-84 23 52; fax 946-24 34 20; leagi@campingleagi.
com; www.campingleagi.com]** Fr San Sebastian leave A8/
N634 at Deba twd Ondarroa. At Ondarroa do not turn into
town, but cont on BI633 beyond Berriatua, then turn R onto
BI3405 to Lekeitio. Fr Bilbao leave A8/N634 at Durango & foll
B1633 twd Ondarroa. Turn L after Markina onto BI3405 to
Lekeitio - do not go via Ondarroa, foll sp to Mendexa & site.
Steep climb to site & v steep tarmac ent to site. Only suitable
for o'fits with v high power/weight ratio. Med, mkd pitch, pt
sl, unshd; wc; chem disp; mv service pnt; serviced pitch; shwrs
inc; el pnts (5A) €3.90 (rev pol); lndtte; shop; rest, snacks; bar;
playgrnd; sand beach 1km; many statics; dogs; bus 1.5km; cr
& noisy high ssn; ccard acc (over €50); CKE/CCI. "Ltd facs low
ssn; tractor tow avail up to site ent; beautiful scenery; excel
local beach; lovely town; gd views; gd walkingsan facs under
pressure due to many tents; bus to Bilbao & Gurnika." 28 Feb-
9 Nov. € 36.20   2014*

LEKUNBERRI *3A1* (500m SE Rural) *43.00043, -1.88831* **Aralar
Camping, Plazaola 9, 31870 Lekunberri (Navarra) [tel/
fax 948-50 40 11 or 948-50 40 49; info@campingaralar.
com; www.campingaralar.com]** Exit fr AP15 at junc
124 dir Lukunberri & foll sp for site. Site on R after v sharp
downhill turn. Med, all hdstg, pt sl, terr, pt shd; htd wc;
chem disp; shwrs inc; el pnts (5A) €4.65; gas; lndtte; shop;
rest, snacks; bar; playgrnd; pool; cycle hire; horseriding; TV;
dogs €2.95; 70% statics; phone; some Eng spkn; quiet;
ccard acc. "Beautiful scenery & mountain walks; only 14 sm
touring pitches; avoid Pamplona mid-Aug during bull-run; site
also open at w/end & long w/end all year except Jan/Feb."
Holy Week & 1 Jun-30 Sep. € 22.50   2009*

LEON *1B3* (3km SE Urban) *42.5900, -5.5331* **Camping
Ciudad de León, Ctra N601, 24195 Golpejar de la
Sobarriba [tel/fax 987-26 90 86; camping_leon@yahoo.es;
www.vivaleon.com/campingleon.htm]** SE fr León on N601
twds Valladolid, L at top of hill at rndabt & Opel g'ge & foll
site sp Golpejar de la Sobarriba; 500m after radio masts turn R
at site sp. Narr track to site ent. Sm, pt sl, shd; wc; chem disp;
shwrs inc; el pnts inc (6A) €3.60; gas; lndtte; shop; rest, snacks;
bar; playgrnd; pool; paddling pool; tennis; cycle hire; dogs
€1.50; bus 200m; quiet; adv bkg; poss cr; Eng spkn; CKE/CCI.
"Clean, pleasant site; helpful, welcoming staff; access some
sm pitches poss diff; easy access to León." ♦ 1 Jun-20 Sep.
€ 23.25   2014*

LEON 1B3 (12km SW Urban) 42.51250, -5.77472
Camping Camino de Santiago, Ctra N120, Km 324.4, 24392 Villadangos del Páramo (León) [tel/fax 987-68 02 53; info@campingcaminodesantiago.com; www. campingcaminodesantiago.com] Access fr N120 to W of vill, site sp on R (take care fast, o'taking traff). Fr E turn L in town & foll sp to site. Lge, mkd pitch, pt shd; wc; chem disp; mv service pnt; baby facs; shwrs inc; el pnts €3.90; gas; lndtte; shop; rest, snacks; bar; pool; wifi; 50% statics; dogs; phone; bus 300m; poss cr; adv bkg; rd noise; ccard acc; red long stay; CKE/CCI. "Poss no hot water low ssn; facs tired; pleasant, helpful staff; mosquitoes; vill church worth visit; gd NH." ♦ 23 Mar-30 Sep. € 18.60   2013*

⊞ **LINEA DE LA CONCEPCION, LA** 2H3 (S Urban/Coastal) 36.19167, -5.3350 **Camping Sureuropa, Camino de Sobrevela s/n, 11300 La Línea de la Concepción (Cádiz) [956-64 35 87; fax 956-64 30 59; info@campingsureuropa. es; www.campingsureuropa.com]** Fr AP7, ext junc 124. Use junc124 fr both dirs. Just bef Gibraltar turn R up lane, in 200m turn L into site. Fr N on AP7, exit junc 124 onto A383 dir La Línea; foll sp Santa Margarita thro to beach. Foll rd to R along sea front, site in approx 1km - no advance sp. App rd to site off coast rd poss floods after heavy rain. Med, hdg/mkd pitch, hdstg, pt shd; wc; chem disp; shwrs inc; el pnts €4.30; lndtte; bar; sand beach 500m; sports club adj;no statics; clsd 21 Dec-7 Jan; no dogs; phone; bus 1.5km; site clsd 20 Dec-7 Jan; poss cr; Eng spkn; adv bkg; quiet but noise fr adj sports club; no ccard acc; CKE/CCI. "Clean, flat, pretty site; vg, modern san facs; sm pitches & tight site rds poss diff twin-axles & l'ge o'fits; ideal for Gibraltar 4km; stay ltd to 4 days; Wi-Fi in camp recep only; Sh stay only." ♦ € 18.60   2014*

LLAFRANC see Palafrugell 3B3

LLANES 1A4 (8km E Coastal) 43.39948, -4.65350 **Camping La Paz, Ctra N634, Km 292, 33597 Playa de Vidiago (Asturias) [tel/fax 985-41 12 35; delfin@campinglapaz. com; www.campinglapaz.eu]** Take Fr A8/N634/E70 turn R at sp to site bet km stone 292 & 293 bef Vidiago.Site access via narr 1km lane. Stop bef bdge & park on R, staff will tow to pitch. Narr site ent & steep access to pitches. Lge, mkd pitch, terr, shd; wc; chem disp; mv service pnt; baby facs; shwrs inc; el pnts (9A) €4.82 (poss rev pol); gas; lndtte (inc dryer); shop; rest; bar; BBQ; playgrnd; sand beach adj; fishing; watersports; horseriding; mountain sports; golf 4km; games rm; wifi; TV; no statics; dogs €2.51; phone; poss cr w/end; Eng spkn; adv bkg; quiet; ccard acc; CKE/CCI. "Exceptionally helpful owner & staff; sm pitches; gd, modern san facs; excel views; cliff top rest; superb beaches in area." ♦ Easter-30 Sep. € 42.00   2011*

LLANES 1A4 (2km W Coastal) 43.42500, -4.78944
Camping Las Conchas de Póo, Ctra General, 33509 Póo de Llanes (Asturias) [tel/fax 985-40 22 90 / 674-16 58 79(mob); campinglasconchas@gmail.com; www. campinglasconchas.com] Exit A8/E70 at Llanes West junc 307 & foll sp. Site on rd AS263. Med, sl, terr, pt shd; wc; chem disp; baby facs; shwrs; el pnts (5A) €3.20; lndtte (inc dryer); shop (only in high ssn); rest; bar; playgrnd; sand beach adj; 50% statics; dogs; bus adj; phone; bus; quiet. "Pleasant site; footpath to lovely beach; lovely coastal walk to Celorio; stn in Poo vill." 1 Jun-15 Sep. € 23.00   2014*

LLANES 1A4 (5km W Coastal) 43.43471, -4.81810 **Camping Playa de Troenzo, Ctra de Celerio-Barro, 33595 Celorio (Asturias) [985-40 16 72; fax 985-74 07 23; troenzo@ telepolis.com]** Fr E take E70/A8 exit at junc 300 to Celorio. At T-junc with AS263 turn L dir Celorio & Llanes. Turn L on N9 (Celorio) thro vill & foll sp to Barro. Site on R after 500m (after Maria Elena site). Lge, terr, pt shd; wc; chem disp; mv service pnt; shwrs inc; el pnts (6A) €2.51; gas; lndtte; rest, snacks; bar; playgrnd; sand beach 400m; 90% statics; dogs; phone; wifi; poss cr; Eng spkn; adv bkg; CKE/CCI. "Lovely, old town; most pitches sm; for pitches with sea views go thro statics to end of site; gd, modern facs; gd rests in town; nr harbour." 16 Feb-19 Dec. € 21.00   2014*

LLAVORSI 3B2 (8km N Rural) 42.56004, 1.22810 **Camping Del Cardós, Ctra Llavorsí-Tavascan, Km 85, 25570 Ribera de Cardós (Lleida) [973-62 31 12; fax 973-62 31 83; info@ campingdelcardos.com; www.campingdelcardos.com]** Take L504 fr Llavorsi dir Ribera de Cardós for 9km; site on R on ent vill. Med, mkd pitch, pt shd; wc; chem disp; mv service pnt; shwrs; el pnts (4-6A) €5.30; gas; lndtte (inc dryer); shop; tradsmn; rest; playgrnd; pool; 2 paddling pools; fishing; games area; TV rm; 5% statics; dogs €3.60; Eng spkn; quiet; CKE/ CCI. "By side of rv, v quiet low ssn; excel." 1 Apr-20 Oct. € 24.00   2009*

⊞ **LLAVORSI** 3B2 (9km N Rural) 42.56890, 1.23040
Camping La Borda del Pubill, Ctra de Tavescan, Km 9.5, 25570 Ribera de Cardós (Lleida) [973-62 30 80; fax 973-62 30 28; info@campinglabordadelpubill.com; www. campinglabordadelpubill.com] Fr France on A64 exit junc 17 at Montréjeau & head twd Spanish border. At Vielha turn E onto C28/C1412 to Llavorsí, then L504 to Ribera. Fr S take N260 fr Tremp to Llavorsí, then L504 to site. Lge, pt shd; htd wc; baby facs; shwrs; el pnts €5.30; gas; lndtte; shop, rest high ssn; snacks; bar; playgrnd; htd pool; paddling pool; rv sw & fishing; kayaking; trekking; adventure sports; quad bike hire; horseriding; skiing 30km; games area; games rm; TV; 10% statics; dogs €3; phone; car wash; adv bkg; quiet; ccard acc. "In beautiful area; excel walking; gd rest." ♦ € 24.00   2009*

LLORET DE MAR 3B3 (1km S Coastal) 41.6973, 2.8217 **Camping Tucan, Ctra Blanes-Lloret, 17310 Lloret de Mar (Gerona) [972-36 99 65; fax 972-36 00 79; info@ campingtucan.com; www.campingtucan.com]** Fr N exit AP7 junc 9 onto C35 twd Sant Feliu then C63 on R sp Lloret de Mar. At x-rds foll sp Blanes, site on R. Fr S take last exit fr C32 & foll sp Lloret de Mar, site on L, sp. Lge, mkd pitch, terr, shd; wc; chem disp; baby facs; shwrs inc; el pnts (3-6A) €3.40-4.40; gas; lndtte; shop; rest, snacks; bar; BBQ; playgrnd; pool; paddling pool; sand beach 600m; games area; golf 500m; entmnt; internet; TV rm; 25% statics; dogs €2; phone; bus; car wash; Eng spkn; adv bkg; quiet; ccard acc; red long stay/ snr citizens/CKE/CCI. "Well-appointed site; friendly staff." ♦ 1 Apr-30 Sep. € 27.80   2011*

⊞ **LLORET DE MAR** *3B3* (1km SW Coastal) *41.6984, 2.8265*
**Camping Santa Elena-Ciutat, Ctra Blanes/Lloret, 17310
Lloret de Mar (Gerona) [972-36 40 09; fax 972-36 79 54;
santaelana@betsa.es; www.betsa.es]** Exit A7 junc 9 dir
Lloret. In Lloret take Blanes rd, site sp at km 10.5 on rd GI
682. V lge, pt sl; wc; baby facs; shwrs; el pnts (5A) €3.90; gas;
lndtte; shop; rest, snacks; bar; playgrnd; pool; paddling pool;
shgl beach 600m; games area; phone; cash machine; poss cr;
Eng spkn; quiet low ssn; red facs low ssn; CKE/CCI. "Ideal for
teenagers." ♦ € 34.60   2011*

⊞ **LOBOS, LOS** *4G1* (2km NE Rural) **Camping Hierbabuena,
Los Lobos, 04610 Cuevas del Almanzora (Almería) [tel/
fax 950-16 86 97 or 629-68 81 53 (mob)]** S fr Lorca on A7;
at Cuevas del Almanzora turn L onto A332 to Los Lobos - do
not ent vill; 400m after junc with A1201 (dir El Largo & Pulpí)
turn L & foll gravel rd to site in 1km. Sm, mkd pitch, hdstg, pt
shd; htd wc; chem disp; baby facs; shwrs inc; el pnts (6-10A)
inc; gas (Spanish only); lndtte; supmkt & rest 5km; snacks &
bar 500m; BBQ; playgrnd; sand beach 5km; 75% statics (sep
area); dogs free; Eng spkn; adv bkg; quiet; ccard not acc; red
long stay. "Gd for long winter stay; friendly British owners;
lge pitches; pretty & interesting area; excel choice of beaches;
gd walking, cycling & sightseeing; vg security; excel." ♦
€ 25.45   2011*

⊞ **LOGRONO** *3B1* (500m N Urban) *42.47187, -2.45164*
**Camping La Playa, Avda de la Playa 6, 26006 Logroño
(La Rioja) [941-25 22 53; fax 941-25 86 61; info@
campinglaplaya.com; www.campinglaplaya.com]** Leave
Logroño by bdge 'Puente de Piedra' on N111, then turn L
at rndabt into Camino de las Norias. Site well sp in town &
fr N111, adj sports cent Las Norias, on N side of Rv Ebro. Med,
hdg pitch, shd; wc; mv service pnt; shwrs inc; el pnts (5A)
€4.80; gas; lndtte (inc dryer); shop; snacks, bar in ssn; playgrnd;
pool; rv sw adj; tennis; 80% statics; dogs €2; red CKE/CCI.
"Sh walk to town cent; ltd facs low ssn & site poss clsd; vg; nr
rest." ♦ € 25.00   2014*

LOGRONO *3B1* (10km W Rural) *42.41613, -2.55169* **Camping
Navarrete, Ctra La Navarrete-Entrena, Km 1.5, 26370
Navarrete (La Rioja) [941-44 01 69; fax 941-44 06 39;
campingnavarrete@fer.es; www.campingnavarrete.
com]** Fr AP68 exit junc 11, at end slip rd turn L onto LR137
to Navarrete. Foll sp thro town for Entrena (S) on LR137 dir
Entrena. Site 1km on R. Lge, mkd pitch, pt shd; wc; chem disp;
mv service pnt; baby facs; shwrs inc; el pnts (6A) €4.40; gas;
lndtte; shop; snacks; bar; BBQ; playgrnd; pool & paddling pool;
tennis; horseriding; car wash; wifi; 95% statics; dogs €2.40;
site clsd 10 Dec-12 Jan; bus 1.3km; Eng spkn; noisy at w/end;
ccard acc; red low ssn/long stay. "Professionally run, clean, tidy
site; excel san facs; helpful staff; some sm pitches; Bilbao ferry
2 hrs via m'way; gd NH; interesting area; highly rec." 16 Jan-
14 Dec. € 42.00   2014*

⊞ **LORCA** *4G1* (8km W Rural) *37.62861, -1.74888*
**Camping La Torrecilla, Ctra Granada-LaTorrecilla,
30817 Lorca (Murcia) [968-44 21 36; fax 968-44 21 96;
campinglatorrecilla@hotmail.com]** Leave A7/E15 at junc 585.
In 1km turn L, site well sp. Med, mkd pitch, hdstg, pt sl, pt
shd; htd wc; chem disp; mv service pnt; shwrs inc; el pnts (6A)
€3.88; gas; lndtte; shop 2km; tradsmn; rest, snacks; bar; BBQ;
playgrnd; pool; tennis; games area; TV rm; 95% statics; dogs;
phone; bus 1km; poss cr; Eng spkn; quiet; ccard acc; red long
stay. "Ltd touring pitches & el pts; friendly, helpful staff; excel
pool; vg san facs." ♦ € 20.32   2013*

⊞ **LUARCA** *1A3* (1km NE Coastal) *43.54914, -6.52426*
**Camping Los Cantiles, Ctra N634, Km 502.7, 33700 Luarca
(Asturias) [985-64 09 38; fax 984-11 14 58; cantiles@
campingloscantiles.com; www.campingloscantiles.com]**
On A8 exit junc 467 (sp Luarca/Barcia/Almuña, At rndabt foll
sp to Luarca, after petrol stn turn R, foll sp to site. Not rec to
ent town fr W. Not rec to foll SatNav as may take you up v
steep & narr rd. On leaving site, retrace to main rd - do not
tow thro Luarca. Med, hdg pitch, pt shd; wc; chem disp; baby
facs; shwrs inc; el pnts inc (3-6A) €2-2.50; gas; lndtte; shop;
tradsmn; rest high ssn; snacks; bar; pool 300m; shgl beach at
foot of cliff; dogs €1; phone; poss cr; Eng spkn; adv bkg; quiet;
red long stay; CKE/CCI. "Site on cliff top; some narr side rds;
pitches soft after rain; steep climb down to beach; 30 min walk
to interesting town & port; wonderful setting; san fac's ok,
water in shwrs v hot." ♦ € 29.40   2013*

⊞ **LUARCA** *1A3* (12km E Rural/Coastal) *43.54898,
-6.38420* **Camping La Regalina, Ctra de la Playa s/n,
33788 Cadavedo (Asturias) [tel/fax 985-64 50 56; info@
laregalina.com]** Fr N632 dir Cadavedo, km126. Site well sp.
Med, pt shd; wc; chem disp; shwrs inc; el pnts (5-8A) €2.30;
gas; shop; rest, snacks; bar; pool; beach 1km; TV; 10% statics;
dogs €3; phone; bus 600m; adv bkg; quiet; ccard acc high ssn;
red long stay. "Scenic area; pretty vill; ltd facs low ssn; gd."
€ 21.00   2009*

LUARCA *1A3* (2km W Coastal) *43.55116, -6.55310* **Camping
Playa de Taurán, 33700 Luarca (Asturias) [tel/fax 985-
64 12 72 or 619-88 43 06 (mob); tauran@campingtauran.
com; www.campingtauran.com]** Exit A8/N634 junc 471 sp
Luarca, El Chano. Cont 3.5km on long, narr, rough access rd.
Rd thro Luarca unsuitable for c'vans. Med, some hdg pitch, pt
sl, pt shd; wc; chem disp; mv service pnt; baby facs; shwrs inc;
el pnts (10A) €3.50; gas; lndtte; shop; tradsmn; rest, snacks;
bar; BBQ; pool; paddling pool; shgl beach 200m; sand beach
2km; cycle hire; phone; dogs €1; quiet; red long stay. "Sea
& mountain views; off beaten track; conv fishing & hill vills;
peaceful, restful, attractive, well-kept site; steep access to
beach; excel." 1 Apr-30 Sep. € 18.50   2013*

LUGO *1B2* (25km S Rural) *42.78683, 7.84516* **A Peneda, Edil Luis Garcia Rojo 38, 27560 Monterroso [tel/fax 34 98 23 77 501; aged@aged-sl.com]** Fr Lugo on N540, take N640 sp to Monterroso. Sp in ctr of town, go down to rv. Sm, hdg pitch, pt shd; wc; chem disp; mv service pnt; baby facs; shwr inc; el pnts (6A); tradsmn; rest; snacks; bar; playgrnd; 1% statics; poss cr; adv bkg; quiet; CCI. "Very pretty, nr rv and excel picnic facs; helpful staff, ltd Eng; excel site." ♦ 30 Mar-24 Sep. € 28.00   2014*

LUMBIER *3B1* (500m W Rural) *42.6500, -1.3119* **Camping Iturbero, Ctra N240 Pamplona-Huesca, 31440 Lumbier (Navarra) [948-88 04 05; fax 948-88 04 14; iturbero@ campingiturbero.com; www.campingiturbero.com]** SE fr Pamplona on N240 twds Yesa Reservoir. In 30km L on NA150 twds Lumbier. In 3.5km immed bef Lumbier turn R at rndabt then over bdge, 1st L to site, adj sw pool. Well sp fr N240. Med, hdg/mkd pitch, some hdstg, pt shd; wc; chem disp; mv service pnt; shwrs inc; el pnts (5A) €4.95; gas; lndtte; shop 1km; rest, snacks; bar; BBQ; playgrnd; pool 100m; tennis; hang-gliding; 25% statics; dogs; bus 1km; quiet; CKE/CCI. "Beautiful, well-kept site; clean, basic facs; excel touring base; open w/end only Dec-Easter (poss fr Sep) but clsd 19 Dec-19 Feb; eagles & vultures in gorge & seen fr site; helpful staff; Lumbier lovely sm town." 15 Mar-15 Dec. € 35.50   2014*

> **"We must tell The Club about that great site we found"**
>
> Get your site reports in by mid-August and we'll do our best to get your updates into the next edition.

⊞ **LUMBRALES** *1C3* (6km NE Rural) *40.95750, -6.65611* **Camping La Hojita, Ctra de Fregeneda, Km 89, 37240 Lumbrales (Salamanca) [923-16 92 68 or 655-91 95 80 (mob); camping_la_hojita@hotmail.com; www. campinglahojita.com]** Fr Salamanca or fr Portuguese border, site sp on CL517. Sm, mkd pitch, shd; wc; chem disp; mv service pnt; baby facs; shwrs inc; el pnts (10A) €3.15; lndtte; shop 2km; rest, snacks; bar; BBQ; playgrnd; pool; some statics; Eng spkn; quiet; red long stay. "Excel, tranquil site." 1 Apr-1 Nov. € 18.00   2009*

MACANET DE CABRENYS *3B3* (1km S Rural) *42.37314, 2.75419* **Camping Maçanet de Cabrenys, Mas Roquet s/n, 17720 Maçanet de Cabrenys (Gerona) [667-77 66 48 (mob); info@campingmassanet.com; www. campingmassanet.com]** Fr N, exit AP7 junc 2 at La Jonquera onto N-II dir Figueres; at km 767 turn R onto GI-502/GI-503 dir Maçanet de Cabrenys; turn L 500m bef vill; site sp. Or fr S, exit AP7 junc 4 at Figueres onto N-II dir France; at km 766 turn L onto GI-502 dir Maçanet de Cabrenys; then as above. Sm, mkd pitch, some hdstg, sl, terr, pt shd; htd wc; chem disp; mv service pnt; baby facs; shwrs; el pnts (10A) €6.50; gas; lndtte; sm shop & 2km; tradsmn; ltd rest, snacks; bar; BBQ; playgrnd; pool; cycle hire; cycle rtes fr site; games rm; wifi; TV; some statics; dogs €5.50; Eng spkn; quiet; adv bkg; ccard acc; red low ssn; CKE/CCI. ♦ 1 Mar-31 Dec. € 30.00   2013*

⊞ **MADRID** *1D4* (8km NE Urban) *40.45361, -3.60333* **Camping Osuna, Calle de los Jardines de Aranjuez, Avda de Logroño s/n, 28042 Madrid [917-41 05 10; fax 913-20 63 65; camping.osuna.madrid@microgest.es]** Fr M40, travelling S clockwise (anti-clockwise fr N or E) exit junc 8 at Canillejas sp 'Avda de Logroño'. Turn L under m'way, then R under rlwy, immed after turn R at traff lts. Site on L corner - white painted wall. Travelling N, leave M40 at junc 7 (no turn off at junc 8) sp Avda 25 Sep, U-turn at km 7, head S to junc 8, then as above. Med, hdg/mkd pitch, pt sl, pt shd; wc; chem disp; shwrs inc; el pnts (6A) €4.85 (long lead rec); lndtte; shop 600m; playgrnd; metro to town 600m; 10% statics; dogs free; phone; poss cr; rd & aircraft noise; Eng spkn; red low ssn; CKE/CCI. "Sm pitches poss diff lge o'fits; poss neglected low ssn & facs tired (June 2010); poss travellers; conv city cent." ♦ ltd € 26.50   2014*

⊞ **MADRID** *1D4* (13km S Urban) *40.31805, -3.68888* **Camping Alpha, Ctra de Andalucía N-IV, Km 12.4, 28906 Getafe (Madrid) [916-95 80 69; fax 916-83 16 59; info@ campingalpha.com; www.campingalpha.com]** Fr S on A4/E5 twd Madrid, leave at km 12B to W dir Ocaña & foll sp. Fr N on A4/E5 at km 13B to change dir back onto A4; then exit 12B sp 'Polígono Industrial Los Olivos' to site. Lge, hdstg, hdg pitch, pt shd; wc; chem disp; mv service pnt; shwrs inc; el pnts (15A) €5.90 (poss no earth); lndtte; shop; rest, snacks; bar; playgrnd; pool high ssn; tennis; games area; 20% statics; dogs; phone; poss cr; Eng spkn; adv bkg; ccard acc; red CKE/CCI. "Lorry depot adj; poss vehicle movements 24 hrs but minimal noise; bus & metro to Madrid 30-40 mins; sm pitches poss tight for space; vg, clean facs; helpful staff; NH or sh stay." € 28.00   2011*

⊞ **MADRIGAL DE LA VERA** *1D3* (500m E Rural) *40.14864, -5.35769* **Camping Alardos, Ctra Madrigal-Candeleda, 10480 Madrigal de la Vera (Cáceres) [tel/fax 927-56 50 66; mirceavd@hotmail.com; www.campingalardos.es]** Fr Jarandilla take EX203 E to Madrigal. Site sp in vill nr rv bdge. Med, mkd pitch, pt shd; wc; chem disp; shwrs inc; el pnts (6-10A) €4; lndtte; shop & 1km; rest, snacks; bar; BBQ; playgrnd; pool; rv sw adj; TV; 10% statics; no dogs; phone; poss cr Jul/Aug; Eng spkn; adv bkg; ccard not acc. "Friendly owners; superb site; ltd facs low ssn; beautiful scenery; excel touring area; ancient Celtic settlement at El Raso 5km." € 24.60   2013*

⊞ **MAMOLA, LA** *2H4* (500m W Coastal) *36.74062, -3.29976* **Camping Castillo de Baños, Castillo de Baños, 18750 La Mamola (Granada) [958-82 95 28; fax 958-82 97 68; info@ campingcastillo.com; www.campingcastillo.com]** Fr E on A7/E15 exit km 360.4 sp Camping/Rest El Paraiso/Castillo de Baños, site on L after rest at ent to vill. Fr W exit km 359.3. Lge, mkd pitch, hdstg, pt shd; wc; chem disp; mv service pnt; shwrs inc; el pnts (5A) €4; gas; lndtte (inc dryer); shop; tradsmn; rest, snacks; bar; playgrnd; pool; private shgl beach adj; fishing; cycle hire; entmnt; internet; Eng spkn; dogs €2.50; bus 200m; adv bkg; ccard acc; quiet; red low ssn/CKE/CCI. "Poss rallies low ssn." ♦ € 23.50   2010*

SPAIN

⊞ **LA MANGA DEL MAR MENOR** *4G2* (27.7km E Urban) *37.6244, -0.7447* **Caravaning La Manga, Autovia Cartagena - La Manga, exit 11, E-30370 La Manga del Mar Menor** [968-56 30 19; fax 968-543426; lamanga@caravaning.es; www.caravaning.es] Take Autovia CT-32 fr Cartagena to La Manga; take exit 800B twds El Algar/Murcia; keep L, merge onto Autovia MU312; cont to foll MU-312; cont onto Ctra a La Manga & cont onto Av Gran Via; site clearly sp. Lge, hdg, hdstg; pt shd; wc; chem disp; mv service pnt; serviced pitches; baby facs; shwrs inc; el pnts (10A) inc; lndtte (inc dryer); supmkt; rest, snacks; bar; BBQ; playgrnd; pools; beach; gym; sauna; jacuzzi; outdoor fitness course; tennis; watersports; cycle hire & horseridng nrby; games rm; entmnt; wifi; some statics; dogs €1.45.; Eng spkn; adv bkg; bus to Murcia and Cartagena; recep open 24 hrs; ccard acc. "Open air cinema & children's programme high ssn; lovely location & gd for golfers; Mar Menor well worth visiting; v gd rest; helpful staff." € 37.70 			 2013*

See advertisement

⊞ **MANGA DEL MAR MENOR, LA** *4G2* (2km W Coastal) *37.62455, -0.74300* **Camping La Manga, Ctra El Algar/Cabo de Palos, Km 12, 30386 La Manga del Mar Menor (Murcia)** [968-56 30 14 or 56 30 19; fax 968-56 34 26; lamanga@caravaning.es / reservas@caravaning.es; www.caravaning.es] Leave MU312 junc 11 sp Playa Honda; over dual c'way then turn R. Site sp fr La Manga. Ent visible beside dual c'way with flags flying. V lge, hdg/mkd pitch, hdstg, pt shd; htd wc; chem disp; mv service pnt; sauna; serviced pitches; shwrs inc; el pnts (10A) metered; gas; lndtte (inc dryer); supmkt; rest, snacks; bar; BBQ; playgrnd; 2 pools (1 htd, covrd); paddling pool; direct access sand beach; fishing; watersports; windsurfing; horseriding; jacuzzi; gym; tennis; cinema; games rm; wifi; entmnt; cab TV/TV rm; 30% statics; dogs €1.40; no c'vans/m'vans over 12m; phone; poss cr; Eng spkn; adv bkg ess; ccard acc; red long stay/low ssn. "Immac, busy, popular site; Mar Menor shallow & warm lagoon; gd for families; some narr site rds & trees - rec park in car park on arr & walk to find pitch; gd walking; mountain biking; bird sanctuary; poss lge rallies on site Dec-Mar; excel; Friendly site." ♦ € 35.60 (CChq acc) SBS - E16 			 2013*

"I need an on-site restaurant"

We do our best to make sure site information is correct, but it is always best to check any must-have facilities are still available or will be open during your visit.

⊞ **MANZANARES EL REAL** *1D4* (8km NE Rural) *40.74278, -3.81583* **Camping La Fresneda, Ctra M608, Km 19.5, 28791 Soto del Real (Madrid)** [tel/fax 918-47 65 23] Fr AP6/NV1 turn NE at Collado-Villalba onto M608 to Cerceda & Manzanares el Real. Foll rd round lake to Soto del Real, site sp at km 19.5. Med, shd; wc; chem disp; baby facs; shwrs €0.15; el pnts (6A) €3.50; gas; lndtte; shop; snacks; bar; playgrnd; pool; tennis; dogs €3; phone; rd noise; ccard acc. ♦ € 24.00 			 2009*

"Satellite navigation makes touring much easier"

Remember most sat navs don't know if you're towing or in a larger vehicle – always use yours alongside maps and site directions.

⊞ **MANZANERA** *3D2* (1km NE Rural) *40.06266, -0.82629* **Camping Villa de Manzanera, Partida Las Bateas s/n, Ctra 1514, Km 10.5, 44420 Manzanera (Teruel)** [978-78 18 19 or 978-78 17 48; fax 978-78 17 09; reservas@campingmanzanera.com] Exit junc 76 fr A23 onto N234 dir Sarrión. Nr Mora turn onto A1514 at site sp. Site on L by petrol stn bef vill. Med, mkd pitch, unshd; htd wc; chem disp; baby facs; shwrs inc; el pnts (10A) €4.20; gas; lndtte; shop 1km; rest, snacks; bar; playgrnd; pool; 80% statics; no dogs; phone; bus 300m; poss cr; poss noisy; ccard acc; CKE/CCI. "Site v run down & unclean (Jan 2011); nr wintersports area; ltd touring pitches bet seasonal statics - some pitches worn & uneven; ltd facs in winter & site poss clsd; pay at filling stn adj; NH only if desperate." ♦ ltd € 21.00 			 2011*

SPAIN

LA BUGANVILLA CAMPING Costa del Sol MARBELLA Spain

GPS N 36°30'11'' W 4°48'12''

4.3ha 300T (60-90m2) ⊙16A

€14 1/1 - 15/7 1/9 - 31/12
7-6 14-11 21-17

Ctra, Nacional 340 Km. 188.8 - E-29660

+34 952 831973

info@campingbuganvilla.com
www.campingbuganvilla.com

⊞ **MARBELLA** 2H3 (7km E Coastal) 36.50259, -4.80413
**Camping La Buganvilla, Ctra N340, Km 188.8, 29600
Marbella (Málaga) [952-83 19 73 or 952-83 19 74; fax
952-83 56 21; info@campingbuganvilla.com; www.
campingbuganvilla.com]** E fr Marbella for 6km on N340/
E15 twds Málaga. Pass site & cross over m'way at Elviria &
foll site sp. Fr Málaga exit R off autovia immed after 189km
marker. Lge, terr, shd; pt sl; wc; chem disp; shwrs; el pnts
(10A) €4.80; gas; lndtte; shop & 250m; rest; bar & sun terr;
playgrnd; pool; sand beach 350m; games rm; wifi; TV; phone;
dogs €4 (not acc Jul/Aug); Eng spkn; adv bkg; poss noisy at w/
end; red long stay/snr citizens; ccard acc; CKE/CCI. "Relaxed,
conv site; helpful staff; excel beach; facs being upgraded
(2014)." ♦ € 48.60   2014*

See advertisement

"There aren't many sites open at this time of year"

If you're travelling outside peak season
remember to call ahead to check site opening
dates – even if the entry says 'open all year'

⊞ **MARBELLA** 2H3 (10km E Coastal) 36.49111, -4.76416
**Camping Marbella Playa, Ctra N340, Km 192.8,
29600 Marbella (Málaga) [952-83 39 98; fax 952-
83 39 99; recepcion@campingmarbella.com; www.
campingmarbella.com]** Fr Marbella on A7/N340 coast rd (not
AP7/E15 toll m'way) & site is on R bef 193 km stone & just bef
pedestrian bdge over A7/N340, sp 'to beach'. Fr Málaga U-turn
on m'way as follows: pass 192km mark & immed take R slip
rd to Elviria to turn L over bdge, back onto A7/N340. Turn R
bef next bdge. Lge, mkd pitch, hdstg, pt shd; wc; chem disp;
mv service pnt; baby facs; shwrs; el pnts (10A) €4; gas; lndry
service; supmkt; rest, snacks; bar; BBQ; playgrnd; pool; sand
beach adj; watersports; tennis 50m; wifi; TV; dogs; phone;
bus nr; poss v cr; rd noise; ccard acc; red low ssn/long stay/
snr citizens/CKE/CCI. "Pitches tight; clean facs but tired; gd
supmkt; friendly, helpful manager; gd base Costa del Sol; noisy
peak ssn & w/ends, espec Sat nights." ♦ € 26.00   2010*

⊞ **MARBELLA** 2H3 (12km E Coastal) 36.48881, -4.74294
**Kawan Village Cabopino, Ctra N340/A7, Km 194.7,
29600 Marbella (Málaga) [tel/fax 952-83 43 73; info@
campingcabopino.com; www.campingcabopino.com]**
Fr E site is on N side of N340/A7; turn R at km 195 'Salida
Cabopino' past petrol stn, site on R at rndabt. Fr W on A7
turn R at 'Salida Cabopino' km 194.7, go over bdge to
rndabt, site strt over. NB Do not take sm exit fr A7 immed
at 1st Cabopino sp. Lge, mkd pitch, pt sl, pt shd; wc; chem
disp; mv service pnt; baby facs; shwrs inc; el pnts (6-10A)
inc (poss long lead req); lndtte (inc dryer); shop; rest, snacks;
bar; BBQ (gas/elec); playgrnd; 2 pools (1 covrd); sand beach/
dunes 200m; watersports; marina 300m; games area; archery;
golf driving range; wifi; games/TV rm; 50% statics; dogs €2;
no c'vans/m'vans over 11m high ssn; bus 100m; Eng spkn;
rd noise & lge groups w/enders; ccard acc; red low ssn; CKE/
CCI. "V pleasant site set in pine woodland; busy, particularly
w/end; varied pitch size, poss diff access lge o'fits; blocks req
some pitches; gd, clean san facs; feral cats on site (2009)." ♦
€ 48.00 (CChq acc) SBS - E21   2014*

"That's changed – Should I let The Club know?"

If you find something on site that's different from
the site entry, fill in a report and let us know. See
www.caravanclub.co.uk/europereport.

⊞ **MARIA** 4G1 (8km W Rural) 37.70823, -2.23609
**Camping Sierra de María, Ctra María a Orce, Km 7,
Paraje La Piza, 04838 María (Málaga) [950-16 70 45
or 660-26 64 74 (mob); fax 950-48 54 16; info@
campingsierrademaria.com; www.campingsierrademaria.
com]** Exit A92 at junc 408 to Vélez Rubio, Vélez Blanco &
María. Foll A317 to María & cont dir Huéscar & Orce. Site on
R. Med, mkd pitch, pt sl, pt shd; wc; chem disp; shwrs; el pnts
(6-10A) €3.75; shop high ssn; rest; bar; cycle hire; horseriding;
some statics; dogs; adv bkg; quiet; ccard acc; CKE/CCI. "Lovely,
peaceful, ecological site in mountains; much wildlife; variable
pitch sizes; facs poss stretched high ssn; v cold in winter." ♦
€ 16.20   2011*

⊞ **MARINA, LA** *4F2* (1.5km S Coastal) *38.12972, -0.65000*
Camping Internacional La Marina, Ctra N332a, Km
76, 03194 La Marina (Alicante) [965-41 92 00; fax
965-41 91 10; info@campinglamarina.com; www.
campinglamarina.com] Fr N332 S of La Marina turn E twd
sea at rndabt onto Camino del Cementerio. At next rndabt
turn S onto N332a & foll site sp along Avda de l'Alegría. V lge,
hdg/mkd pitch, hdstg, terr, shd; htd wc; chem disp; mv service
pnt; 50% serviced pitches; baby facs; fam bthrm; sauna;
solarium; shwrs inc; el pnts (10A) €3.21; gas; lndtte (inc dryer);
supmkt; rest, snacks; bars; playgrnd; 2 pools (1 htd/covrd);
waterslides; sand beach 500m; fishing; watersports; tennis;
games area; games rm; fitness cent; entmnt; disco; wifi; TV rm;
10% statics; dogs €2.14; phone; bus 50m; car wash; security;
Eng spkn; adv bkg; ccard acc; various pitch sizes/prices; red
long stay/low ssn; CKE/CCI. "Popular winter site - almost full
late Feb; v busy w/end; clean, high quality facs; bus fr gate; gd
security; excel rest; gd site." ◆ € 69.80   2014*

See advertisement

"I like to fill in the reports as I travel from site to site"

You'll find report forms at the back of
this guide, or you can fill them in online at
www.caravaclub.co.uk/europereport.

⊞ **MASNOU, EL** *3C3* (750m W Coastal) *41.4753,
2.3033* Camping Masnou, Ctra NII, Km 633, Carrer de
Camil Fabra 33, 08320 El Masnou (Barcelona) [tel/
fax 935-55 15 03; masnou@campingsonline.es; www.
campingmasnoubarcelona.com] App site fr N on N11. Pass
El Masnou rlwy stn on L & go strt on at traff lts. Site on R on
N11 after km 633. Not clearly sp. Med, pt sl, shd; wc; mv
service pnt; shwrs inc; el pnts €5.88; shop, snacks, bar high ssn;
BBQ; playgrnd; pool high ssn; sand beach opp; internet; dogs;
phone; bus 300m; train to Barcelona nr; poss v cr; Eng spkn;
rd & rlwy noise; ccard acc; CKE/CCI; "Gd pitches, no awnings;
some sm pitches, poss shared; facs vg, though poss stretched
when site busy; no restriction on NH vehicle movements; well-
run, friendly site but tired; gd service low ssn; rlwy line bet site
& excel beach - subway avail; excel train service to Barcelona;
excel pool." ◆ ltd € 33.70   2013*

MATARO *3C3* (3km E Coastal) *41.55060, 2.48330* Camping
Barcelona, Ctra NII, Km 650, 08304 Mataró (Barcelona)
[937-90 47 20; fax 937-41 02 82; info@campingbarcelona.
com; www.campingbarcelona.com] Exit AP7 onto C60 sp
Mataró. Turn N onto NII dir Gerona, site sp on L after rndabt.
Lge, mkd pitch, hdstg, shd; wc; chem disp; mv service pnt;
baby facs; shwrs inc; el pnts (6A) €5.50; gas; lndtte; shop;
rest, snacks; bar; playgrnd; pool; paddling pool; sand beach
1.5km; games area; games rm; animal farm; wifi; entmnt; TV;
5% statics; dogs €4; shuttle bus to beach & town; Eng spkn;
adv bkg; rd noise; ccard acc; red long stay/low ssn; CKE/CCI.
"Conv Barcelona 28km; pleasant site; friendly, welcoming
staff." ◆ 4 Mar-1 Nov. € 45.70   2013*

SPAIN

⊞ **MAZAGON** 2G2 (10km E Coastal) 37.09855, -6.72650
Camping Doñana Playa, Ctra San Juan del Puerto-
Matalascañas, Km 34.6, 21130 Mazagón (Huelva) [959-
53 62 81; fax 959-53 63 13; info@campingdonana.com;
www.campingdonana.com] Fr A49 exit junc 48 at Bullullos
del Condado onto A483 sp El Rocio, Matalascañas. At coast
turn R sp Mazagón, site on L in 16km. V lge, mkd pitch, hdstg,
pt shd; wc; chem disp; shwrs inc; el pnts (6A) €5.20; shop, rest,
snacks; bar; playgrnd; pool; sand beach 300m; watersports;
tennis; games area; cycle hire; entmnt; some statics; dogs
€4.10; bus 500m; site clsd 14 Dec-14 Jan; adv bkg; quiet but
v noisy Fri/Sat nights; red low ssn; CKE/CCI. "Pleasant site
amongst pine trees but lack of site care low ssn; ltd low ssn; lge
pitches but poss soft sand; new (2014) lge shwr block on lower
pt of site." ♦ € 48.20   2014*

MENDEXA see Lekeitio 3A1

"We must tell The Club about that great site we found"

Get your site reports in by mid-August
and we'll do our best to get your updates
into the next edition.

⊞ **MENDIGORRIA** 3B1 (500m SW Rural) 42.62416, -1.84277
Camping El Molino, Ctra Larraga, 31150 Mendigorría
(Navarra) [948-34 06 04; fax 948-34 00 82; info@
campingelmolino.com; www.campingelmolino.com]
Fr Pamplona on N111 turn L at 25km in Puente la Reina onto
NA601 sp Mendigorría. Site sp thro vill dir Larraga. Med,
some mkd pitch, pt shd; wc; chem disp; serviced pitches; baby
facs; shwrs inc; el pnts (6A) inc; gas; lndtte (inc dryer); shop;
tradsmn; rest, snacks; bar; BBQ; playgrnd; pool; paddling pool;
waterslide; canoe hire; tennis; games area; wifi; TV; statics (sep
area); dogs; phone; poss cr at w/end; clsd 23 Dec-14 Jan &
poss Mon-Thurs fr Nov to Feb, phone ahead to check; adv bkg;
poss v noisy at w/end; ccard acc; CKE/CCI. "Gd clean san facs;
solar water heating - water poss only warm; vg leisure facs;
v ltd facs low ssn; for early am dep low ssn, pay night bef &
obtain barrier key; friendly, helpful staff; lovely medieval vill."
♦ 7 Jan-22 Dec. € 38.00   2013*

MEQUINENZA 3C2 (Urban) 41.37833, 0.30555 Camp
Municipal Octogesa, Ctra Alcanyís-Fraga s/n, Km 314,
50170 Mequinenza (Zaragoza) [974-46 44 31; fax 974-
46 50 31; rai@fuibol.e.telefonica.net; www.fuibol.net] Exit
AP2 junc 4 onto N211 S. On ent Mequinenza just reach pwooded
area on L, turn L thro break in service rd, site well sp. Tight
ent poss unsuitable lge o'fits. Med, hdg/mkd pitch, terr, pt
shd; wc; chem disp (wc); shwrs inc; el pnts (6A) €3.90; lndtte;
shop 1km; rest, snacks; bar; BBQ; playgrnd; 2 pools high ssn;
tennis; dogs; phone; Eng spkn; adv bkg; quiet but noise fr arr
of fishing parties; ccard acc; CKE/CCI. "Site pt of complex on
bank of Rv Segre; base for fishing trips - equipment supplied;
sm pitches unsuitable lge o'fits; NH only." 15 Feb-15 Nov.
€ 17.70   2009*

⊞ **MERIDA** 2E3 (2km SE Urban) 38.93558, -6.30426
Camping Mérida, Avda de la Reina Sofia s/n, 06800
Mérida (Badajoz) [924-30 34 53; fax 924-30 03 98;
proexcam@jet.es; http://personales.jet.es/proexcam/
principal.htm] Fr E on A5/E90 exit junc 333/334 to Mérida,
site on L in 2km. Fr W on A5/E90 exit junc 346, site sp. Fr N
exit A66/E803 at junc 617 onto A5 E. Leave at junc 334, site
on L in 1km twd Mérida. Fr S on A66-E803 app Mérida, foll
Cáceres sp onto bypass to E; at lge rndabt turn R sp Madrid;
site on R after 2km. Med, mkd pitch, pt sl, pt shd; wc; chem
disp; shwrs inc; el pnts (6A) €3.20 (long lead poss req & poss
rev pol); gas; lndtte; ltd shop high ssn & 3km; hypmkt 6km;
rest, snacks; bar; pool; paddling pool; TV; some statics; dogs;
phone; no bus; quiet but some rd noise; CKE/CCI. "Roman
remains & National Museum of Roman Art worth visit; poss diff
lge o'fits manoeuvring onto pitch due trees & soft grnd after
rain; facs tired; gd seafood rest; ltd facs low ssn; conv NH; taxi
to town costs 5-9 euros; new san facs; grass pitches; bread can
be ordered fr rest." ♦ € 29.00   2014*

⊞ **MIAJADAS** 2E3 (10km SW Rural) 39.09599, -6.01333
Camping-Restaurant El 301, Ctra Madrid-Lisbon, Km 301,
10100 Miajadas (Cáceres) [927-34 79 14; camping301@
hotmail.com] Leave A5/E90 just bef km stone 301 & foll sp
'Via de Servicio' with rest & camping symbols; site in 500m.
Med, pt shd; wc; chem disp; shwrs inc; el pnts (8A) €4 (poss
no earth); gas; lndtte; shop; rest, snacks; bar; playgrnd; pool;
TV; phone; m'way noise & dogs; ccard acc; CKE/CCI. "Well-
maintained, clean site; grass pitches; OK wheelchair users but
steps to pool; gd NH." € 16.20   2010*

MIJAS COSTA see Fuengirola 2H4

MOIXENT 4E2 (12km N Rural) 38.96488, -0.79917
Camping Sierra Natura (Naturist), Finca El Tejarico, Ctra
Moixent-Navalón, Km 11.5, 46810 Enguera (València)
[962-25 30 26; fax 962-25 30 20; info@sierranatura.com;
www.sierranatura.com] Exit A35 fr N exit junc 23 or junc
23 fr S onto CV589 sp Navalón. At 11.5km turn R sp Sierra
Natura - gd rd surface but narr & some steep, tight hairpin
bends (owners arrange convoys on request). Fr E on N340 exit
junc 18 (do not take junc 14). Sm, pt sl, pt shd; wc; chem disp;
baby facs; sauna; shwrs inc; el pnts (10A) €5.20; lndry rm; shop
& 12 km; rest, snacks; bar; playgrnd; pool; 10% statics; dogs
€4.55; phone; poss cr; Eng spkn; adv bkg; quiet; red long stay.
"Tranquil, family-run site in remote area; unusual architecture;
stunning mountain scenery; nature walks on site; excel pool &
rest complex." ♦ ltd 1 Mar-30 Oct. € 19.00   2011*

⊞ **MOJACAR** 4G1 (3.5km S Coastal) 37.12656, -1.83250
Camping El Cantal di Mojácar, Ctra Garrucha-Carboneras,
04638 Mojácar (Almería) [950-47 82 04; fax 950-47 23 93;
campingelcantal@hotmail.com] Fr N on coast rd AL5105,
site on R 800m after Parador, opp 25km sp.Or exit A7 junc 520
sp Mojácar Parador. Foll Parador sps by-passing Mojácar, to
site. Med, hdstg, pt shd; wc; chem disp; mv service pnt; shwrs
inc; el pnts (15A) €3; gas; lndry rm; shop 500m; tradsmn; shops
adj; rest, snacks; bar adj; BBQ; sand beach adj; 5% statics;
dogs; phone; bus; poss v cr; some rd noise; red long stay/
low ssn; CKE/CCI. "Pitches quite lge, not mkd; lge o'fits rec
use pitches at front of site; busy site; staff unhelpful, quite
expensive; facs run down." ♦ € 30.00   2014*

⊞ **MOJACAR** *4G1* (9km S Rural) *37.06536, -1.86864*
**Camping Sopalmo, Sopalmo, 04638 Mojácar
(Almería) [950-47 84 13; fax 950-47 30 02;
info@campingsopalmoelcortijillo.com; www.
campingsopalmoelcortijillo.com]** Exit A7/E15 at junc 520
onto AL6111 sp Mojácar. Fr Mojácar turn S onto A1203/
AL5105 dir Carboneras, site sp on W of rd about 1km S of El
Agua del Medio. Sm, mkd pitch, hdstg, pt shd; wc; chem disp
(wc); shwrs; el pnts (15A) €3; gas; lndtte; sm shop (high ssn);
tradsmn; rest, snacks 6km; bar; shgl beach 1.7km; internet;
10% statics; dogs €1; Eng spkn; adv bkg; some rd noise; ccard
not acc; red low ssn; CKE/CCI. "Clean, pleasant, popular site;
remote & peaceful; friendly owner; gd walking in National Park;
lovely san facs." ♦ € 29.00   2012*

⊞ **MOJACAR** *4G1* (4km SW Coastal) *37.08888, -1.85599*
**Camping Cueva Negra, Camino Lotaza, 2, 04638
Mojácar (Almería) [950-47 58 55; fax 950-47 57 11; info@
campingcuevanegra.es; www.campingcuevanegra.es]**
Leave N340/E15 at junc 520 for AL151 twd Mojácar Playa.
Turn R onto coastal rd. Site 500m fr Hotel Marina on R. App rd
diff lge o'fits.m'vans due grounding. Take care dip at site ent.
Med, hdg/mkd pitch, all hdstg, terr, unshd; wc; chem disp; mv
service pnt; shwrs inc; el pnts (22A) €3.30; gas; lndtte; shop;
tradsmn; rest, snacks; bar; covrd pool; jacuzzi; sand beach adj;
entmnt; TV; 5% statics; dogs €1.90; poss cr; adv bkg; quiet;
red 30+ days; CKE/CCI. "Well-kept, beautifully laid-out site;
clean san facs but some basic; pleasant atmosphere; gd touring
base; facs stretched when site full." ♦ € 28.60   2011*

⊞ **MOJACAR** *4G1* (500m W Rural) *37.14083, -1.85916*
**Camping El Quinto, Ctra Mojácar-Turre, 04638
Mojácar (Almería) [950-47 87 04; fax 950-47 21 48;
campingelquinto@hotmail.com]** Fr A7/E15 exit 520 sp Turre
& Mojácar. Site on R in approx 13km at bottom of Mojácar
vill. Sm, hdg/mkd pitch, hdstg, pt shd; wc; chem disp; mv
service pnt; shwrs inc; el pnts (6-10A) €3.21; gas; lndtte; shop;
tradsmn; rest 3km; snacks; bar; BBQ; playgrnd; pool; sand
beach 3km; dogs €1; phone; poss cr; Eng spkn; adv bkg; quiet
but some rd noise; red long stay; CKE/CCI. "Neat, tidy site; mkt
Wed; close National Park; excel beaches; metered 6A elect for
long winter stay; popular in winter, poss cr & facs stretched;
security barrier; poss mosquitoes; drinking water ltd to 5L a
time." ♦ € 20.50   2012*

⊞ **MOJACAR** *4G1* (5km W Rural) *37.16394, -1.89361*
**Canada Camping, 04639 Turre (Almería) [627-
76 39 08 (mob); canadacampingmojacar@yahoo.co.uk]**
Exit A7/E15 at junc 525 & foll sp Los Gallardos on N340A.
After approx 3km turn L at sp Turre & Garrucha onto A370. In
3.5km slow down at green sp 'Kapunda' & turn R in 300m at
sp 'Casa Bruns'. Site in 100m - bumpy access. Sm, hdg/mkd
pitch, hdstg, unshd; wc; chem disp; mv service pnt; shwrs inc;
el pnts (6A) €3.50; lndry rm; shop, rest, snacks, bar 4km; BBQ;
no statics; dogs; adv bkg; quiet - some rd noise. "Gd, British-
owned, adults-only site; friendly atmosphere; lge pitches;
mountain views." € 10.00   2010*

⊞ **MONASTERIO DE RODILLA** *1B4* (800m NE Rural)
42.4604, -3.4581 **Camping Picon del Conde, Ctra N1
Madrid-Irún, Km 263, 09292 Monasterio de Rodilla
(Burgos) [tel/fax 947-59 43 55; info@picondelconde.
com; www.picondelconde.com]** Fr A1 join N1 at exit 2 or
3, site is on N1 at km marker 263 - behind motel. Easy to miss
in heavy traff. Med, hdg/mkd pitch, shd; htd wc; chem disp;
shwrs inc; el pnts (5A) €3.60; gas; lndry rm; shop; rest, snacks;
bar; playgrnd; pool; 75% statics; dogs; phone; rd noise; ccard
acc; CKE/CCI. "Ltd facs low ssn; poss migrant workers; caution
el pnts; new grnd floor san facs 2009; site muddy in wet
weather; friendly staff; 2 hrs drive fr Bilbao ferry; gd NH." ♦
€ 14.60   2011*

⊞ **MONCOFA** *3D2* (2km E Coastal/Urban) *39.80861,
-0.12805* **Camping Monmar, Camino Serratelles s/n,
12593 Platja de Moncófa (Castellón) [tel/fax 964-58 85 92;
campingmonmar@hotmail.com]** Exit 49 fr A7 or N340, foll
sp Moncófa Platja passing thro Moncófa & foll sp beach &
tourist info thro 1-way system. Site sp, adj Aqua Park. Lge, hdg
pitch, hdstg, pt shd; htd wc; chem disp; all serviced pitches;
baby facs; shwrs inc; el pnts (6A) inc; gas; lndtte (inc dryer);
shop & 1km; tradsmn; rest, snacks; bar; BBQ; playgrnd; pool;
sand/shgl beach 200m; entmnt; internet; 80% statics; no dogs;
phone; bus 300m; poss v cr; Eng spkn; adv bkg; quiet; ccard
acc; red low ssn/long stay; CKE/CCI. "Helpful owner & staff;
rallies on site Dec-Apr; mini-bus to stn & excursions; sunshades
over pitches poss diff high o'fits; excel clean, tidy site." ♦
€ 45.00   2014*

⊞ **MONCOFA** *3D2* (2km S Coastal) *39.78138, -0.14888*
**Camping Los Naranjos, Camino Cabres, Km 950.8, 12593
Moncófa (Castellón) [964-58 03 37; fax 964-76 62 37;
info@campinglosnaranjos.com]** Fr N340 at km post 950.8
turn L at site sp, site 1km on R. Med, mkd pitch, hdstg, pt shd;
wc; chem disp; mv service pnt; shwrs inc; el pnts (10A) €5.35;
gas; lndtte; shop; tradsmn; rest, snacks; bar; playgrnd; pool;
paddling pool; beach 300m; games area; 20% statics; phone;
bus 1.5km; poss cr; adv bkg; quiet; red low ssn/long stay.
"Gd." € 27.00   2010*

⊞ **MONTBLANC** *3C2* (1.5km NE Rural) *41.37743, 1.18511*
**Camping Montblanc Park, Ctra Prenafeta, Km 1.8, 43400
Montblanc (Tarragona) [977-86 25 44; fax 977-86 05 39;
montblancpark@franceloc.fr; www.montblancpark.com]**
Exit AP2 junc 9 sp Montblanc; foll sp Montblanc/Prenafeta/
TV2421; site on L on TV2421. Med, hdg pitch, pt sl, terr, pt
shd; htd wc; chem disp; mv service pnt; baby facs; shwrs inc;
el pnts (10A) inc; lndtte; shop; tradsmn; rest, snacks; bar;
BBQ; playgrnd; pool; paddling pool; wifi; entmnt; 50% statics;
dogs €4.50; phone; Eng spkn; adv bkg; ccard acc; red long
stay/snr citizens; CKE/CCI. "Excel site; excel facs; lovely area;
many static pitches only suitable for o'fits up to 7m; Cistercian
monesteries nrby; conv NH Andorra." ♦ ltd € 39.50   2014*

MONTROIG see Cambrils *3C2*

SPAIN

MONZON *3B2* (5.7km NE Rural) *41.93673, 0.24146* **Camping Almunia, Calle del Nao 10, 22420 Almunia de san Juan [696-77 18 51; camping-almunia@hotmail.com; www. camping-almunia.es]** Foll the A-22 to Monzón. Turn R onto the A-1237 to campsite. Sm, hdstg, terr, pt shd; wc; chem disp; mv service pnt; child/baby facs; fam bthrm; shwrs; el (6A) €4; lndtte; BBQ; playgrnd; pool; wifi; twin axle acc; adv bkg acc; "Friendly German couple; Monzon splendid medieval castle to visit; conv NH." ♦ € 13.00   2013*

⊞ **MORATALLA** *4F1* (8km NW Rural) *38.21162, -1.94444* **Camping La Puerta, Ctra del Canal, Paraje de la Puerta, 30440 Moratalla (Murcia) [tel/fax 968-73 00 08; info@ campinglapuerta.com; www.campinglapuerta.com]** Fr Murcia take C415 dir Mula & Caravaca. Foll sp Moratalla & site. Lge, mkd pitch, pt sl, terr, shd; htd wc; chem disp; shwrs inc; el pnts (10A) €5.30; gas; lndtte (inc dryer); shop; tradsmn; rest, snacks; bar; BBQ; playgrnd; pool; tennis; games area; internet; TV rm; statics; dogs €1.20; adv bkg; quiet; ccard acc. "Busy at w/ends." ♦ € 18.80   2011*

⊞ **MORELLA** *3D2* (2km NE Rural) *40.62401, -0.09141* **Motor Caravan Parking, 12300 Morella (Castellón)** Exit N232 at sp (m'van emptying). Sm, hdstg, pt shd; chem disp; mv service pnt; water; quiet. "Free of charge; stay up to 72 hrs; clean; superb location; lge m'vans acc; excel Aire with fine views of hilltop town of Morella (floodlit at night), clean, well maintained."   2013*

⊞ **MOTILLA DEL PALANCAR** *4E1* (10km NW Rural) *39.61241, -2.10185* **Camping Pantapino, Paraje de Hontanar, s/n, 16115 Olmedilla de Alarcón (Cuenca) [969-33 92 33 or 676-47 86 11 (mob); fax 969-33 92 44; pantapino@hotmail.com]** Fr cent of Motilla foll NIII; turn NW onto rd CM2100 at sp for Valverde de Júcar; site on L just bef 12km marker. Med, mkd pitch, pt sl, pt shd; wc; chem disp; mv service pnt; serviced pitches; baby facs; shwrs inc; el pnts (6A) €4; gas; lndtte; shop; rest, bar high ssn; BBQ; playgrnd; pool; tennis; games area; horseriding; cycle hire; 40% statics; dogs €1.50; adv bkg; quiet; ltd facs low ssn; ccard acc; 10% red CKE/CCI. "Clean, attractive site but tatty statics; poor facs; gd size pitches; resident owners hospitable; poss clsd in winter - phone ahead to check; vg; san facs old but clean; gd NH; poss problem with earth on elec." ♦ € 18.00   2014*

⊞ **MOTRIL** *2H4* (12km SE Coastal) *36.70066, -3.44032* **Camping Don Cactus, N340, Km 343, 18730 Carchuna (Granada) [958-62 31 09; fax 958-62 42 94; camping@ doncactus.com; www.doncactus.com]** On N340 SE fr Motril 1km W of Calahonda. Foll site sp. Lge, hdg/mkd pitch, hdstg, shd; wc; chem disp; mv service pnt; shwrs; el pnts (5A) €4.50; gas; lndtte; supmkt; rest, snacks; bar; BBQ; playgrnd; pool; shgl beach adj; tennis; archery; golf 6km; wifi; entmnt; TV rm; 60% statics; dogs €2.50 (not acc Jul & Aug); poss cr; no adv bkg; quiet; ccard acc; red long stay/low ssn; CKE/CCI. "Many greenhouses around site (unobtrusive); some sm pitches not rec lge o'fits; clean san facs; gd pool & rest; helpful staff; popular winter long stay; gd NH." ♦ € 28.50   2010*

⊞ **MUNDAKA** *3A1* (1km N Coastal) *43.4094, -2.7003* **Camping Portuondo, Ctra Amorebieta-Bermeo, Km 43, 48360 Mundaka (Bilbao) [946-87 77 01; fax 946-87 78 28; recepcion@campingportuondo.com; www. campingportuondo.com]** Leave E70 E of Bilbao onto B1631 to Bermeo. Keep on coast rd dir Mundaka, site 1km on L. Ess to app fr Bermeo due to steep ent. Do not drive past recep until booked in due steep access. Med, terr, pt shd; wc; shwrs inc; el pnts (6A) €4.20; lndtte; rest, snacks; bar; playgrnd; pool; paddling pool; beach 500m; 30% statics; site clsd Jan-mid Feb; dogs; train 800m; poss v cr w/ends; adv bkg rec; ccard acc. "Excel clean, modern facs; pitches tight not suitable for lge o'fits; popular with surfers; conv Bilbao by train; site suitable sm m'vans only." € 35.05   2012*

MUROS *1B1* (3km SSW Coastal) *42.76072, -9.06222* **A'Vouga, Ctra Mouros-Finisterre, km 3 15291 Louro [tel/ fax 34 98 18 26 115; avouga@hotmail.es]** On Coast rd fr Muros (3km) on L side. Med, mkd pitch, pt sl, unshd; htd wc; chem disp; mv service pnt; baby facs; shwrs inc; el pnts (6A); lndtte (inc dryer); shops 3km; tradsmn; rest; snacks; bar; BBQ; beach adj; games rm; entmnt; wifi; tv rm; 10% statics; dogs; phone; twin axles; poss cr; Eng spkn; adv bkg; quiet; ccard acc. "Excel site & rest; seaviews; friendly & helpful staff; rec; guided walking tours." 1 Mar-31 Oct. € 38.00   2014*

MUROS *1B1* (500m W Coastal/Rural) *42.76176, -9.07365* **Camping San Francisco, Camino de Convento 21, 15291 Louro-Muros (La Coruña) [981-82 61 48; fax 981-57 19 16; campinglouro@yahoo.es; www.campinglouro.com]** Fr Muros cont on C550 coast rd for 3km to San Francisco vill. Site sp to R up narr rd. Med, mkd pitch, pt shd; htd wc; chem disp; mv service pnt; shwrs; el pnts (5-8A) inc; gas; lndtte; rest, snacks; bar; sand beach 200m; playgrnd; dogs; phone; bus 300m; Eng spkn; adv bkg; quiet; ccard acc; CKE/CCI. "Pleasant site in walled monastery garden; gd, clean facs; vg sm rest; sh walk to lovely beach; excel security; unspoilt area." ♦ 22 Jun-7 Sep. € 27.60   2009*

MUROS *1B1* (7km W Coastal) *42.76100, 9.11100* **Camping Ancoradoiro, Ctra Corcubión-Muros, Km.7.2, 15250 Louro (La Coruña) [981-87 88 97; fax 981-87 85 50; wolfgang@ mundo-r.com; www.rc-ancoradoiro.com/camping]** Foll AC550 W fr Muros. Site on L (S), well sp. Immed inside ent arch, to thro gate on L. Med, hdg/mkd pitch, terr, pt shd; wc; chem disp; shwrs inc; el pnts (6-15A) €3.50; lndtte; shop adj; rest; snacks; bar adj; playgrnd; sand beach 500m; watersports; entmnt; no statics; no dogs; bus 500m; phone; poss cr; adv bkg; quiet; CKE/CCI. "Excel, lovely, well-run, well-kept site; superb friendly site on headland bet 2 sandy beaches; welcoming owner; excel rest; excel san facs; poss diff for lge o'fits; beautiful beaches; scenic area." 15 Mar-15 Sep. € 22.00   2014*

MUTRIKU see Deba *3A1*

⊞ **MUXIA** *1A1* (10km E Coastal) *43.1164, -9.1583* **Camping Playa Barreira Leis, Playa Berreira, Leis, 15124 Camariñas-Muxia (La Coruña) [tel/fax 981-73 03 04; playaleis@yahoo.es]** Fr Ponte do Porto turn L sp Muxia; foll camp sp. Site is 1st after Leis vill on R. Med, mkd pitch, terr, pt shd; wc; chem disp; shwrs inc; el pnts €3.50; lndtte; shop; rest; bar; BBQ; playgrnd; sand beach 100m; dogs €1; TV; quiet; ccard acc; CKE/CCI. "Beautiful situation on wooded hillside; dir acces to gd beach; ltd, poorly maintained facs low ssn; mkt in Muxia Thurs." € 16.00   2012*

NAJERA *3B1* (500m S Urban) *42.41183, -2.73168* **Camping El Ruedo, San Julián 24, 26300 Nájera (La Rioja) [941-36 01 02; www.campingslarioja.es]** Take Nájera town dirs off N120. In town turn L bef x-ing bdge. Site sp. Sm, pt shd; htd wc; chem disp; shwrs inc; el pnts (10-16A) €3 (rev pol & poss no earth); gas; lndtte; shop; rest; snacks; bar; playgrnd; pool 1km; entmnt; TV; phone; bus 200m; poss cr; adv bkg; quiet; ccard acc; CKE/CCI. "Pleasant site in quiet location, don't be put off by 1st impression of town; monastery worth visit, some pitches in former bullring." 1 Apr-10 Sep. € 21.00   2013*

⊞ **NAVAJAS** *3D2* (1km W Rural) *39.87489, -0.51034* **Camping Altomira, Carretera, CV-213 Navajas Km. 1, E-12470 Navajas (Castellón) [964-71 32 11; fax 964-71 35 12; reservas@campingaltomira.com; www.campingaltomira.com]** Exit A23/N234 at junc 33 to rndabt & take CV214 dir Navajas. In approx 2km turn L onto CV213, site on L just past R turn into vill, sp. Med, hdstg, terr, pt shd; htd wc; chem disp; serviced pitches; baby facs; shwrs; el pnts (3-6A) €3.80; gas; lndtte (inc dryer); shop; tradsmn; rest; snacks; bar; BBQ; playgrnd; pool; paddling pool; tennis; cycle hire; wifi; TV; 70% statics; dogs; phone; bus 500m; adv bkg; poss noisy w/end & public hols; ccard acc; red low ssn/long stay/CKE/CCI. "Friendly welcome; panoramic views fr upper level (steep app) but not rec for lge o'fits due tight bends & ramped access/kerb to some pitches; gd birdwatching, walking, cycling; excel san facs; some sm pitches poss diff for lge o'fits without motor mover; poss clsd low ssn - phone ahead to check; useful NH & longer; excel." ♦ € 36.20 (CChq acc)   2014*

NAVALAFUENTE see Cabrera, La *1D4*

NAVARREDONDA DE GREDOS see Hoyos del Espino *1D3*

NAVARRETE see Logroño *3B1*

⊞ **NEGRAS, LAS** *4G1* (1km N Coastal) *36.87243, -2.00674* **Camping Náutico La Caleta, Parque Natural Cabo de Gata, 04116 Las Negras (Almería) [tel/fax 950-52 52 37; campinglacaleta@gmail.com]** Exit N344 at km stone 487 twd Las Negras. Site sp at ent to vill on R. Med, hdg pitch, hdstg, shd; wc; chem disp; shwrs inc; el pnts (10A) inc; gas; lndtte; shop & 1km; tradsmn; rest; snacks; bar; playgrnd; pool (high ssn); sand/shgl beach adj; cycle hire; dogs €3.20; phone; bus 300m; poss cr; quiet; red long stay/low ssn; CKE/CCI. "Lge o'fits need care on steep app rd; vans over 2.50m take care sun shades on pitches; gd walking area; lovely site in lovely area." ♦ € 30.80   2010*

⊞ **NERJA** *2H4* (4km E Rural) *36.76035, -3.83490* **Nerja Camping, Ctra Vieja Almeria, Km 296.5, Camp de Maro, 29787 Nerja (Málaga) [952-52 97 14; fax 952-52 96 96; nerjacamping5@hotmail.com]** On N340, cont past sp on L for 200m around RH corner, bef turning round over broken white line. Foll partly surfaced rd to site on hillside. Fr Almuñécar on N340, site on R approx 20km. Med, pt sl, terr, pt shd; wc; chem disp; shwrs inc; el pnts (5A) €3.75 (check earth); gas; lndry rm; shops; tradsmn; rest, snacks; bar; playgrnd; sm pool; sand beach 2km; cycle hire; site clsd Oct; Eng spkn; adv bkg rec; rd noise; red long stay/low ssn/CKE/CCI. "5 mins to Nerja caves; mkt Tue; annual carnival 15 May; diff access lge o'fits; gd horseriding; site rds steep but gd surface; gd views; friendly owners." ♦ ltd € 23.80   2011*

⊞ **NIJAR** *4G1* (23km SE Coastal) *36.80298, -2.07768* **Camping Los Escullos San José, Paraje de los Escullos s/n, 04118 Los Escullos (Almería) [950-38 98 11; fax 950-38 98 10; info@losescullossanjose.com; www.losescullossanjose.com]** Fr E on E15/A7 exit 479 sp San Isidro; fr W exit junc 471 sp San José. Foll sp San José on AL3108 & after passing La Boca de los Frailes turn L onto AL4200 sp Los Escullos & site. After 3km turn R to site, ent on R in 1km - take care unmkd speed bumps. Lge, mkd pitch, hdstg, pt sl, shd; wc; chem disp; mv service pnt; baby facs; sauna; private san facs avail; shwrs inc; el pnts (10A) €5.10; gas; lndtte (inc dryer); shop; rest, snacks; bar; playgrnd; pool; beach 700m; watersports; diving; tennis; cycle hire; fitness rm; wifi; entmnt; TV rm; 40% statics; dogs €2.60; Eng spkn; adv bkg; ccard acc; red long stay/CKE/CCI. "Well-run, rustic, attractive site in National Park; many secluded beaches & walks; excel for watersports; vg pool & rest; clean facs; helpful staff; pitches poss flood in heavy rain." ♦ € 30.00 (CChq acc)   2010*

⊞ **NOIA** *1B2* (5km SW Coastal) *42.77198, -8.93761* **Camping Punta Batuda, Playa Hornanda, 15970 Porto do Son (La Coruña) [981-76 65 42; camping@puntabatuda.com; www.puntabatuda.com]** Fr Santiago take C543 twd Noia, then AC550 5km SW to Porto do Son. Site R approx 1km after Boa. Lge, mkd pitch, terr, pt shd; htd wc; chem disp; shwrs inc; el pnts (3A) €3.74 (poss rev pol); gas; lndtte; shop; rest w/end only; snacks; bar; tradsmn; playgrnd; htd pool w/end only; sand beach adj; tennis; 50% statics; some Eng spkn; adv bkg; quiet; red long stay/low ssn; CKE/CCI. "Wonderful views; exposed to elements & poss windy; ltd facs low ssn; hot water to shwrs only; some pitches v steep &/or sm; gd facs; naturist beach 5km S." ♦ € 23.60   2012*

NOJA *1A4* (N Coastal) *43.48525, -3.53918* **Camping Los Molinos, Playa del Ris, 39180 Noja (Cantabria) [942-63 04 26; fax 942-63 07 25; campinglosmolinos@campinglosmolinos.com; www.campinglosmolinos.com]** Exit A8 at km 185. Go N & foll sp to Noja, then L at Playa del Ris. Site sp. V lge, hdg pitch, pt shd; wc; chem disp; mv service pnt; shwrs; baby facs; el pnts (3A) €3.60; gas; lndtte; shop; rest, snacks; bar; BBQ; playgrnd; pool; paddling pool; sand beach 500m; tennis; car wash; entmnt; 75% statics; dogs; poss cr; Eng spkn; adv bkg; ccard not acc; CKE/CCI. "Gd site; lovely beach; some noise fr karting circuit until late evening but noise levels strictly curtailed at midnight." ♦ 1 Jun-30 Sep. € 30.00   2010*

NOJA *1A4* (700m N Coastal) *43.49011, -3.53636* **Camping Playa Joyel, Playa del Ris, 39180 Noja (Cantabria) [942-63 00 81; fax 942-63 12 94; info@playayoyel.com; www. playayoyel.com]** Fr Santander or Bilbao foll sp A8/E70 (toll-free). Approx 15km E of Solares exit m'way junc 185 at Beranga onto CA147 N twd Noja & coast. On o'skirts of Noja turn L sp Playa del Ris, (sm brown sp) foll rd approx 1.5km to rndabt, site sp to L, 500m fr rndabt. Fr Santander take S10 for approx 8km, then join A8/E70. V lge, mkd pitch, pt sl, pt shd; wc; chem disp; mv service pnt; baby facs; shwrs inc; el pnts (6A) inc; gas; lndtte (inc dryer); supmkt; tradsmn; rest, snacks; bar; BBQ (gas/charcoal/elec); playgrnd; pool; paddling pool; jacuzzi; direct access to sand beach adj; windsurfing; sailing; tennis; hairdresser; car wash; cash dispenser; wifi; entmnt; games/TV rm; 40% statics; no dogs; no c'vans/m'vans over 8m high ssn; phone; recep 0800-2200; poss v cr w/end & high ssn; Eng spkn; adv bkg; ccard acc; quiet at night; red low ssn/snr citizens; CKE/CCI. "Well-organised site on sheltered bay; v busy high ssn; pleasant staff; gd, clean facs; superb pool & beach; some narr site rds with kerbs; midnight silence enforced; highly rec." ♦ 11 Apr-27 Sep. € 58.40 SBS - E05   2014*

⊞ **NOJA** *1A4* (1.9km NW Coastal) *43.49294, -3.5248* **Camping Playa de Ris, Paseo Maritimo 2, Avda de Ris, 39180 Noja [942-63 04 15]** Fr A8 take exit 185, at rdbt 3rd exit onto N634, at next rdbt take exit CA147, turn R CA452, turn R onto Barrio de Castillo San Pedro CA147, turn L onto Av de los Ris/CA451 turn R onto Paseo de Maritimo. Sm, pt shd; wc; chem disp (wc); shwr inc; lndry rm; shop 500m; snacks; bar; pool adj; sandy beach 200m; 50% statics; no dogs; poss cr; no twin-axles; CKE/CCI. "Conv for Santander ferry; poss tight for lge o'fits." € 24.34   2011*

NUEVALOS *3C1* (300m N Rural) *41.21846, -1.79211* **Camping Lago Park, Ctra De Alhama de Aragón a Cillas, Km 39, 50210 Nuévalos (Zaragoza) [tel/fax 976-84 90 38; info@campinglagopark.com; www.campinglagopark. com]** Fr E on A2/E90 exit junc 231 to Nuévalos, turn R sp Madrid. Site 1.5km on L when ent Nuévalos. Fr W exit junc 204, site well sp. Steep ent fr rd. V lge, hdg/mkd pitch, terr, pt shd; wc; chem disp; child/baby facs; shwrs inc; el pnts (10A) €5.40; gas; lndtte; shop 500m; rest, snacks high ssn; bar 500m; BBQ; playgrnd; pool; lake nrby; fishing; boating; games area; some statics; dogs free; bus 500m; poss cr; adv bkg; quiet but noisy w/end high ssn; red long stay; CKE/CCI. "Nr Monasterio de Piedra & Tranquera Lake; excel facs on top terr, but stretched high ssn & poss long, steepish walk; ltd facs low ssn; gd birdwatching; only site in area; gd." 1 Apr-30 Oct. € 27.50 (CChq acc)   2010*

⊞ **O GROVE** *1B2* (2km SW Coastal) *42.48305, -8.89083* **Camping Moreiras, Reboredo 26, 36989 O Grove (Pontevedra) [986-73 16 91; campingmoreiras@ campingmoreiras.com; www.campingmoreiras.com]** Exit AP9 junc 119 W onto AG41 dir Sangenjo to Pedriñán; then foll sp N to O Grove, site sp, adj aquarium. Med, hdg/mkd pitch, shd; htd wc; chem disp; mv service pnt; baby facs; shwrs; el pnts €4.50; lndtte (inc dryer); shop; rest, snacks; bar; BBQ; playgrnd; sand beach adj; watersports; cycle hire; games area; golf 3km; wifi; some statics; no dogs; adv bkg; quiet. € 23.20   2010*

⊞ **OCHAGAVIA** *3A1* (500m S Rural) *42.90777, -1.08750* **Camping Osate, Ctra Salazar s/n, 31680 Ochagavia (Navarra) [tel/fax 948-89 01 84; info@campingosate. net; www.campingosate.net]** On N135 SE fr Auritz, turn L onto NA140 & cont for 24km bef turning L twd Ochagavia on NA140. Site sp in 2km on R, 500m bef vill. Med, mkd pitch, pt shd; wc; chem disp; some serviced pitches; shwrs inc; el pnts (4A) €5.50; gas; lndtte; shop; rest high ssn; snacks; bar; BBQ; Eng spkn; 50% statics; dogs €2; quiet but poss noise fr bar (open to public). "Attractive, remote vill; gd, well-maintained site; touring pitches under trees, sep fr statics; facs ltd & poss stretched high ssn; site clsd 3 Nov-15 Dec & rec phone ahead low ssn." € 22.45   2014*

⊞ **OLITE** *3B1* (2km S Rural) *42.48083, -1.67756* **Camping Ciudad de Olite, Ctra N115, Tafalla-Peralta, Km 2.3, 31390 Olite [948-74 10 14; fax 948-74 06 04; info@ campingdeolite.com; www.campingdeolite.com]** Fr Pamplona S on AP15 exit 50 twd Olite. At rndabt turn L, then in 300m turn R onto NA115, site sp on L past Netto in 2km. Lge, mkd pitch, pt shd; wc; chem disp; mv service pnt; serviced pitches; baby facs; shwrs inc; el pnts (5A) inc; lndtte; shop 2km; rest; bar; playgrnd; htd pool (caps ess); tennis; entmnt; games area; 95% statics; dogs €1; poss cr; Eng spkn; phone; poss noisy at w/ends; ccard acc; CKE/CCI. "Close to m'way; ltd space & facs for tourers; site mostly used by Spanish for w/ends; site bleak in winter; narr site rds; Olite historic vill with fairytale castle; neglected facs (2009); ltd el pnts; NH only, 35 min walk thro fields to Olite, friendly owners." ♦ ltd € 21.50   2011*

⊞ **OLIVA** *4E2* (2km E Coastal) *38.93278, -0.09778* **Camping Kiko Park, Calle Assagador de Carro 2, 46780 Playa de Oliva (València) [962-85 09 05; fax 962-85 43 20; kikopark@kikopark.com; www.kikopark.com]** Exit AP7/ E15 junc 61; fr toll turn R at T-junc onto N332.At rndabt turn L foll sp Platjas; next rdbt take 1st exit sp Platja; next rdbt foll sp Kiko Park . Do not drive thro Oliva. Access poss diff on app rds due humps. Lge, hdg/mkd pitch, hdstg, shd; htd wc; chem disp; mv service pnt; some serviced pitches; baby facs; fam bthrm; shwrs inc; el pnts (16A) inc; gas; lndtte (inc dryer); supmkt; rest, snacks; bar; BBQ; playgrnd; 2 pools (1 covrd); paddling pool; whirlpool; spa; direct access to sand beach adj; watersports; windsurfing school; fishing; golf & horseriding nrby; tennis; games area; cycle hire; games rm; beauty centre; cash machine; wifi; entmnt; dogs €3.10; phone; pitch price variable (lge pitches avail); Eng spkn; adv bkg; quiet; ccard acc; red snr cititzens/long stay/low ssn; red CKE/CCI. "Gd, family-run site; v helpful staff; vg, clean san facs; excel rest in Michelin Guide; access tight to some pitches." ♦ € 66.20 SBS - E20   2014*

See advertisement

OLIVA *4E2* (4km E Coastal) *38.90759, -0.06722* **Camping Azul, 46780 Playa de Oliva (València) [962-85 41 06; fax 962-85 40 96; campingazul@ctv.es; www.campingazul. com]** Exit A7/E15 junc 61; fr toll turn R at T-junc onto N332. Drive S thro Oliva, site sp, turn twds sea at km 209.8. Narr access rd. Med, mkd pitch, pt shd; wc; mv service pnt; shwrs inc; el pnts (10A) €3.20; gas; lndtte; shop; rest; bar; playgrnd; cycle hire; games area; golf 1km; wifi; entmnt; 20% statics; dogs free; no adv bkg; ccard acc; red long stay/low ssn. "Gd site but constant barking dogs fr adj houses; san facs tired." ♦ 1 Mar-1 Nov. € 25.60   2010*

"Satellite navigation makes touring much easier"

Remember most sat navs don't know if you're towing or in a larger vehicle – always use yours alongside maps and site directions.

⊞ **OLIVA** *4E2* (3km SE Coastal) *38.90555, -0.06666* **Eurocamping, Ctra València-Oliva, Partida Rabdells s/n, 46780 Playa de Oliva (València) [962-85 40 98; fax 962-85 17 53; info@eurocamping-es.com; www.eurocamping-es.com]** Fr N exit AP7/E15 junc 61 onto N332 dir Alicante. Drive S thro Oliva & exit N332 km 209.9 sp 'urbanización'. At v lge hotel Oliva Nova Golf take 3rd exit at rndabt sp Oliva & foll camping sp to site. Fr S exit AP7 junc 62 onto N332 dir València, exit at km 209 sp 'urbanización', then as above. Lge, hdg/mkd pitch, hdstg, pt shd; htd wc; chem disp; mv service pnt; baby facs; shwrs inc; el pnts (6-10A) €4.64-6.70; gas; lndtte (inc dryer); shop; tradsmn; rest; snacks; bar; BBQ; playgrnd; sand beach adj; cycle hire; wifi; entmnt; TV; dogs €2.16; phone; poss cr; quiet but some noise fr adj bar; ccard acc; red long stay/low ssn/CKE/CCI. "Gd facs; busy, well-maintained, clean site adj housing development; helpful British owners; beautiful clean beach; gd rest; gd beach walks; cycle rte thro orange groves to town; pitch far fr recep if poss, night noise fr generators 1700-2400; recep clsd 1400-1600; highly rec; rest stretched; busy site." ♦ € 44.39 (CChq acc)   2012*

⊞ **OLIVA** *4E2* (3km S Coastal) *38.89444, -0.05361* **Camping Olé, Partida Aigua Morta s/n, 46780 Playa de Oliva (València) [962-85 75 17; fax 962-85 75 16; campingole@ hotmail.com; www.camping-ole.com]** Exit AP7/E15 junc 61 onto N332 dir Valencia/Oliva. At km 209 (bef bdge) turn R sp 'Urbanización. At 1st rndabt, take 2nd exit past golf club ent, then 1st exit at next rndabt, turn L sp ' Camping Olé' & others. Site down narr rd on L. Lge, hdg/mkd pitch, hdstg, pt shd; htd wc; chem disp; baby facs; shwrs inc; el pnts (6-10A) €5.74; gas; lndtte (inc dryer); supmkt; rest, snacks; bar; BBQ; playgrnd; pool; sand beach adj; fishing; tennis 600m; cycle hire; games rm; horseriding 2km; golf adj; wifi; entmnt; 15% statics; dogs €3.15; phone; Eng spkn; adv bkg; quiet; ccard acc; red long stay/low ssn; CKE/CCI. "Many sports & activities; direct access to beach; Excel site; rest across rd v nice; gd value; pool only opens 1st July." ♦ € 50.25   2014*

⊞ **OLOT** *3B3* (3km SE Rural) *42.15722, 2.51694* **Camping Fageda, Batet de la Serra, Ctra Olot-Santa Pau, Km 3.8, 17800 Olot (Gerona) [tel/fax 972-27 12 39; info@ campinglafageda.com; www.campinglafageda.com]** Fr Figueras exit A26 sp Olot E twd town cent. Pick up & foll sp Santa Pau on rd GI524. Site in 3.8km. Med, mkd pitch, pt sl, terr, pt shd; htd wc; chem disp; shwrs inc; el pnts (10A) €3.50 (poss rev pol); gas; lndtte; shop; snacks; rest & bar high ssn; playgrnd; htd pool high ssn; wifi; 90% statics (sep area); dogs; phone; Eng spkn; adv bkg; quiet; ccard acc; CKE/CCI. "In beautiful area with extinct volcanoes & forests; isolated, pretty site; few visitors low ssn; friendly, helpful staff; diff access to water pnts for m'vans." ♦ € 21.05   2011*

⊞ **OLVERA** *2H3* (4.2km E Rural) *36.93905, -5.21719* **Camping Pueblo Blanco, Ctra N384, Km 69, 11690 Olvera (Cadiz) [619 45 35 34; fax 952 83 43 73; info@ campingpuebloblanco.com; www.campingpuebloblanco. com]** Bet Antequera and Jerez de la Frontera, on the A384, at 69km marker. About 3km bef Olvera on the R. Wide driveway 600m to the top. Lge, terr, pt sl, unshd; wc; chem disp; mv service pnt; child/baby facs; shwrs, el (16A) €4; shop; rest, bar; BBQ; playgrnd; poolgames area; games rm; entmnt high ssn; wifi; tv srm; 12 bungalows; dog €1.50; Eng spkn; adv bkg acc, red long stay. "Site has 360 degree mountain views; ideal for walking; bird watching and Pueblo Blanco; vg site, but not quite finished." ♦ € 27.50   2013*

⊞ **ORGIVA** 2G4 (2km S Rural) 36.88852, -3.41837 **Camping Órgiva, Ctra A348, Km 18.9, 18400 Órgiva (Granada) [tel/fax 958-78 43 07; campingorgiva@descubrelaalpujarra.com; www.descubrelaalpujarra.com]** Fr N or S on Granada-Motril rd suggest avoid A348 via Lanjarón (narr & congested). Fr N323/A44 turn E nr km 179, 1km S of lge dam sp Vélez de Benaudalla, over multi-arch bdge, turn L sp Órgiva. Foll rd (easy climb) turn L after sh tunnel over rv bdge; site 2nd building on R. Sm, pt sl, pt shd; wc; chem disp; serviced pitches; baby facs; shwrs inc; el pnts (10A) €3.82 (rev pol); gas; lndtte; supmkt 2km; rest, snacks; bar; playgrnd; pool; shgl beach 30km; bus 2km; adv bkg; ccard acc; some Eng spkn; red low ssn/long stay; ccard acc; red long stay/CKE/CCI. "Immac san facs; excel, friendly site; some sm pitches; vg value rest open all yr; magnificent scenery; gd base for mountains & coast; Thurs mkt in town; fiesta 27 Sep-1 Oct; pleasant walk thro orange & almond groves to vill; loyalty discounts & gd red for longer stays." ♦ € 18.80   2011*

⊞ **ORGIVA** 2G4 (2km NW Rural) 36.90420, -3.43880 **Camping Puerta de la Alpujarra, Ctra Lanjarón-Órgiva (Las Barreras), 18418 Órgiva (Granada) [tel/fax 958-78 44 50; puertalpujarra@yahoo.es; www.campingpuertadelaalpujarra.com]** Fr Órgiva take A348 to Lanjarón. Site on L in 2km. Lanjarón poss diff for long o'fits. Med, mkd pitch, hdstg, terr, pt shd; wc; chem disp; mv service pnt; shwrs inc; el pnts (16A) €3.50; gas 2km; lndtte; shop; rest; bar; playgrnd; pool, paddling pool high ssn; entmnt; few statics; dogs free; phone; bus adj; poss cr; Eng spkn; adv bkg; quiet; ccard acc; 10% red 7+ days. "Scenic area with gd views fr site; steepish access to pitches; excel walking; ltd facs & staff low ssn." ♦ € 30.00   2010*

ORIHUELA DEL TREMEDAL 3D1 (1km S Rural) 40.54784, -1.65095 **Camping Caimodorro, Camino Fuente de los Colladillos s/n, 44366 Orihuela del Tremedal (Teruel) [978-71 43 55 or 686-92 21 53 (mob); campingcaimodorro@gmail.com; www.campingcaimodorro.com]** Fr Albarracin on A1512 head twd Orihuela. Turn R twd vill & R after petrol stn, sp. Sm, unshd; wc; shwrs; el pnts €3.30; lndtte (inc dryer); shop; snacks; bar; pool; paddling pool; wifi; dogs; some statics; phone; bus 600m; Eng spkn; ccard acc. "Elevated, breezy situation o'looking mountain vill; lovely scenery; gd touring base; friendly owner; v quiet low ssn." 1 Apr-31 Oct. € 13.40   2009*

ORINON 1A4 (2km E Coastal) 43.40361, -3.31027 **Camping Playa Arenillas, Ctra Santander-Bilbao, Km 64, 39798 Islares (Cantabria) [tel/fax 942-86 31 52 or 609-44-21-67 (mob); cueva@mundivia.es; www.campingplayaarenillas.com]** Exit A8 at km 156 Islares. Turn W on N634. Site on R at W end of Islares. Steep ent & sharp turn into site, exit less steep. Lge, mkd pitch, pt shd; wc; chem disp; mv service pnt; baby facs; shwrs inc; el pnts (5A) €4.63 (poss no earth); gas; lndtte; shop; tradsmn; rest adj; snacks; bar; BBQ; playgrnd; sand beach 100m; horseriding; cycle hire; games area; TV; 40% statics; no dogs; phone; bus 500m; poss cr; adv bkg rec Jul/Aug; some rd noise; ccard acc; CKE/CCI. "Facs ltd low ssn & stretched in ssn; facs constantly cleaned; hot water to shwrs and washing up; rec arr early for choice of own pitch; conv Guggenheim Museum; excel NH for Bilbao ferry." 1 Apr-30 Sep. € 25.62   2014*

ORINON 1A4 (500m NW Rural/Coastal) 43.39944, -3.32805 **Camping Oriñón, 39797 Oriñón (Cantabria) [tel/fax 942-87 86 30; info@campingorinon.com; www.campingorinon.com]** Exit A8/E70 at km 160 to Oriñón. Adj holiday vill. Med, mkd pitch, pt sl, unshd; wc; chem disp; mv service pnt; shwrs inc; el pnts (4A) €4; gas; lndtte (inc dryer); shop; rest, snacks; bar; playgrnd; sand beach adj; internet; TV; 90% statics; dogs; phone; bus 1km; Eng spkn; quiet; red long stay. "Excel surfing beach adj; clean site; no hot water to wash basins; helpful staff; conv Bilbao ferry." ♦ ltd Holy Week & 1 Jun-30 Sep. € 20.00   2009*

ORIO see Zarautz 3A1

⊞ **OROPESA** 3D2 (4.2km N Coastal) 40.12125, 0.15848 **Camping Didota, Avenida de la Didota s/n, 12594 Oropesa del Mar (Castellón) [964 31 95 51; fax 964 31 98 47; info@campingdidota.es; www.campingdidota.es]** N on rd E-15 fr València to Barcelona, bear L at exit 45 sp Oropesa del Mar. Turn L onto N-340. Turn R at next exit, then cont strt at rndabt onto on Avenida La Ratlla. Foll camping signs. Med, pt shd; wc; shwrs inc; chem disp; el pnts (6-10A) €4.30; child/baby facs; lndtte; shop; rest, snacks; meals; gas; pool; sand beach; playgrnd; dogs; some statics; poss cr; ccard acc; adv bkg; "Gd site, helpful friendly staff; excel pool." ♦ € 33.70   2014*

See advertisement

⊞ **OROPESA** *3D2* (3km NE Coastal) *40.12786, 0.16088*
Camping Torre La Sal 1, Camí L'Atall s/n, 12595 Ribera de Cabanes (Castellón) [964-31 95 96; fax 964-31 96 29; info@campingtorrelasal.com; www.campingtorrelasal. com] Leave AP7 at exit 44 or 45 & take N340 twd Tarragona. Foll camp sp fr km 1000.1 stone. Do not confuse with Torre La Sal 2 or Torre Maria. Lge, hdg/mkd pitch, hdstg, pt shd; htd wc; chem disp; mv service pnt; baby facs; shwrs inc; el pnts (10A) €4.20; gas; lndtte; shop adj; rest, snacks, bar; BBQ; playgrnd; htd, covrd pool; paddling pool; sand/shgl beach adj; tennis; games area; wifi; TV rm; 10% statics; dogs (except Jul/ Aug); phone adj; bus 200m; poss cr; Eng spkn; adv bkg; quiet; ccard acc; red long stay/snr citizens; CKE/CCI. "Clean, well-maintained, peaceful site; elec metered for long stays; night security guard." ♦ ltd € 24.00   2010*

⊞ **OROPESA** *3D2* (3.5km NE Coastal) *40.1275, 0.15972*
Camping Torre La Sal 2, Cami L'Atall s/n, 12595 Ribera de Cabanes (Castellón) [964-31 95 67; fax 964-31 97 44; camping@torrelasal2.com; www.torrelasal2.com] Leave AP7 at exit 45 & take N340 twd Tarragona. Foll camp sp fr km 1000 stone. Site adj Torre La Sal 1. Lge, hdg/mkd pitch, hdstg, pt shd; htd wc; chem disp; sauna; serviced pitch; shwrs inc; el pnts (10A) inc; gas; lndtte; shop; tradsmn; supmkt adj & 1km; rest, snacks; bar; playgrnd; shgl beach adj; 4 pools (2 htd & covrd); tennis; games area; wifi; entmnt; library; wifi; TV rm; some statics; dogs free; Eng spkn; adv bkg; quiet; red long stay/ low ssn/snr citizens; CKE/CCI. "Vg, clean, peaceful, well-run site; lger pitches nr pool; more mature c'vanners v welcome; many dogs; poss diff for lge o'fits & m'vans; excel rest; excel beach with dunes; excel site, spotless facs, highly rec." ♦ € 50.77   2013*

"There aren't many sites open at this time of year"
If you're travelling outside peak season remember to call ahead to check site opening dates – even if the entry says 'open all year'

⊞ **OSSA DE MONTIEL** *4E1* (10km SW Rural) *38.93717, -2.84744* **Camping Los Batanes, Ctra Lagunas de Ruidera, Km 8, 02611 Ossa de Montiel (Albacete) [926-69 90 76; fax 926-69 91 71; camping@losbatanes.com; www. losbatanes.com]** Fr Munera twd Ossa de Montiel on N430. In Ossa foll sp in vill to site in 10km. Fr Manzanares on N430 app to Ruidera, cross bdge; turn immed R alongside lagoon, camp at 12km. Lge, pt shd; htd wc; chem disp; mv service pnt; shwrs; el pnts (5A) €3.10; lndtte; shops 10km; tradsmn; rest 200m; snacks; bar; playgrnd; pool, paddling pool high ssn; lake sw adj; cycle hire; TV; 10% statics; dogs €2; phone; site clsd 28 Dec-2 Jan; Eng spkn; adv bkg; noisy at w/end; ccard acc; red CKE/CCI. "Lovely area of natural lakes; excel birdwatching & walking; friendly owners; low ssn phone to check open." ♦ € 24.00   2011*

OTURA see Granada *2G4*

PALAFRUGELL *3B3* (5km E Coastal) *41.9005, 3.1893* **Kim's Camping, Calle Font d'en Xeco s/n, 17211 Llafranc (Gerona) [972-30 11 56; fax 972-61 08 94; info@ campingkims.com; www.campingkims.com]** Exit AP7 at junc 6 Gerona Nord if coming fr France, or junc 9 fr S dir Palamós. Foll sp for Palafrugell, Playa Llafranc. Site is 500m N of Llafranc. Lge, hdg/mkd pitch, hdstg, pl sl, terr, shd; wc; chem disp; baby facs; shwrs inc; el pnts (6A) inc; gas; lndtte; shop; rest, snacks; bar; BBQ (gas only); playgrnd; 2 pools; sand beach 500m; watersports; tennis 500m; games rm; games area; cycle hire 500m; golf 10km; wifi; entmnt; excursions; TV; 10% statics; dogs; phone; guarded; poss cr; Eng spkn; adv bkg; quiet; ccard acc; red low ssn/long stay; red CKE/CCI. "Excel, well-organised, friendly site; steep site rds, new 2nd ent fr dual c'way fr Palafrugell to llafranc for lge o'fits & steps to rd to beach; discount in high ssn for stays over 1 wk; excel, modern san facs." ♦ 30 Mar-30 Sep. € 50.80   2013*

"That's changed – Should I let The Club know?"
If you find something on site that's different from the site entry, fill in a report and let us know. See www.caravanclub.co.uk/europereport.

PALAFRUGELL *3B3* (5km SE Rural) *41.89694, 3.18250* **Camping La Siesta, Chopitea 110, 17210 Calella de Palafrugell (Gerona) [972-61 51 16; fax 972-61 44 16; info@campinglasiesta.com; www.campingzodiac.com]** Fr C66/C31 main rd Gerona-Palamós turn E at rndabt onto GI6546 & foll sp Calella - Avda del Mar. Site on R just bef Calella dir Llafranc. V lge, mkd pitch, pt sl, pt shd; wc; chem disp; shwrs inc; el pnts (6A) inc; gas; lndtte (inc dryer); shops; rest, snacks; 2 bars; no BBQ; playgrnd; 2 lge pools; waterslide; beach 1.3km; tennis; horseriding; wifi; entmnt; 80% statics; no dogs; bus; site open w/ends Nov-March & clsd Xmas to 8 Jan; Eng spkn; adv bkg; noisy at w/end; red low ssn. "Excel beaches at Llafranc & Calella de Palafrugell; mkt at Palafrugell; many beaches & coves adj; narr, winding paths thro pines to pitches; most vans have to be manhandled onto pitches." ♦ Easter-31 Oct. € 52.70   2011*

PALAFRUGELL *3B3* (5km S Coastal) *41.88831, 3.18013* **Camping Moby Dick, Carrer de la Costa Verda 16-28, 17210 Calella de Palafrugell (Gerona) [972-61 43 07; fax 972-61 49 40; info@campingmobydick.com; www. campingmobydick.com]** Fr Palafrugell foll sps to Calella. At rndabt just bef Calella turn R, then 4th L, site clearly sp on R. Med, hdstg, sl, terr, pt shd; wc; chem disp; mv service pnts; baby facs; shwrs inc; el pnts (6-10A) €4.05; lndtte; shop; supmkt 100m; rest 100m; snacks; bar; playgrnd; shgl beach 100m; TV; 15% statics; dogs €3.30; phone; bus 100m; poss cr; Eng spkn; adv bkg; quiet; ccard acc; CKE/CCI. ♦ 1 Apr-30 Sep. € 23.40   2009*

PALAMOS *3B3* (1km N Coastal) *41.85695, 3.13801* **Camping Internacional Palamós, Camí Cap de Planes s/n, 17230 Palamós (Gerona) [972-31 47 36; fax 972-31 76 26; info@ internacionalpalamos.com; www.internacionalpalamos. com]** Fr N leave AP7 at junc 6 to Palamós on C66. Fr Palafrugell turn L 16m after overhead sp to Sant Feliu-Palamós at sm sp La Fosca & camp sites. Winding app thro La Fosca. Fr S, take exit 9 dir Sant Feliu & Lloret, then C65/C31 to Santa Christina-Palamós, then La Fosca. Lge, pt shd; wc (mainly cont); chem disp; mv service pnt; baby facs; serviced pitches; private bthrms avail; shwrs inc; el pnts; (5A) inc; lndtte; shop; rest, snacks; bar; playgrnd; pool; paddling pool; sand beach 300m; solarium; windsurfing, sailing & diving 1km; cycle hire; golf 15km; wifi; TV rm; car wash; 20% statics; phone; bus 600m; quiet. "Attractive site; superb san facs; some sm pitches on steep access rds - check bef pitching; highly rec; lovely area." ♦ 16 Apr-30 Nov. € 42.50 (CChq acc)   2011*

PALAMOS *3B3* (1km N Coastal) *41.85044, 3.13873* **Camping Palamós, Ctra La Fosca 12, 17230 Palamós (Gerona) [972-31 42 96; fax 972-60 11 00; campingpal@grn.es; www. campingpalamos.com]** App Palamós on C66/C31 fr Gerona & Palafrugell turn L 16m after overhead sp Sant Feliu-Palamós at sm sp La Fosca & campsites. Lge, pt sl, terr, pt shd; wc; shwrs; baby facs; el pnts (4A) €2.70; gas; lndtte; shop; rest 400m; playgrnd; 2 htd pools; shgl/rocky beach adj; tennis; golf; internet; 30% statics; dogs €2; phone; ccard acc. ♦ 27 Mar-30 Sep. € 40.00   2013*

PALAMOS *3B3* (2km N Coastal) *41.87277, 3.15055* **Camping Benelux, Paratge Torre Mirona s/n, 17230 Palamós (Gerona) [972-31 55 75; fax 972-60 19 01; cbenelux@ cbenelux.com; www.cbenelux.com]** Turn E off Palamós-La Bisbal rd (C66/C31) at junc 328. Site in 800m on minor metalled rd, twd sea at Playa del Castell. Lge, hdstg, pt sl, pt shd; wc; chem disp; mv service pnt; shwrs inc; el pnts (6A) €4.30; gas; lndtte; shop; tradsmn; supmkt; rest (w/end only low ssn); snacks; bar; playgrnd; pool; sand beach 1km; safe dep; car wash; currency exchange; TV; 50% statics; dogs; poss cr; Eng spkn; adv bkg; noisy at w/end; red low ssn/long stay; ccard acc; CKE/CCI. "In pine woods; many long stay British/Dutch; friendly owner; clean facs poss ltd low ssn; poss flooding in heavy rain; rough grnd." ♦ ltd Easter-30 Sep. € 43.20   2012*

PALAMOS *3B3* (2km N Coastal) *41.86263, 3.14315* **Camping Caravanning Kings, Ctra de la Fosca, s/n 17230 Palamós (Gerona) [972-31 75 11; fax 972-31 77 42; info@ campingkings.com; www.campingkings.com]** App Palamós on C66/C31 fr Gerona & Palafrugell, turn L immed after o'head sp Sant Felui-Palamós at sm sp La Fosca & campsites. Lge, pt sl, pt shd; wc; shwrs; el pnts (6A) inc; lndtte; supmkt; rest; bar; playgrnd; pool; spa; beach 200m; cycle hire; games rm; wifi; entmnt; dogs €2.70; adv bkg; quiet; ccard acc; red low ssn. "Upmkt recep building; helpful staff; clean modern san facs; super pool; gd walking & cycling; thoroughly rec." 2 Apr-18 Sep. € 48.40   2010*

PALAMOS *3B3* (3km SW Coastal) *41.84598, 3.09460* **Camping Costa Brava, Avda Unió s/n, 17252 Sant Antoni de Calonge (Gerona) [tel/fax 972-65 02 22; campingcostabrava@campingcostabrava.net; www. campingcostabrava.net]** Foll sp St Antoni de Calonge fr C31, site sp. Lge, mkd pitch, shd; wc; chem disp; baby facs; shwrs inc; el pnts (4A) €3.80; lndtte; shop adj; rest, snacks; bar; BBQ; playgrnd; pool & child pool; sand beach 300m; watersports; games rm; entmnt; car wash; dogs; phone; bus; poss cr; adv bkg; quiet; ccard acc. "Well-managed, family-run site; sm pitches; clean san facs; rec arr early high ssn to secure pitch; pleasant, helpful owners." ♦ 1 Jun-15 Sep. € 22.75   2011*

PALAMOS *3B3* (2.5km W Rural) *41.88194, 3.14083* **Camping Castell Park, Ctra C31 Palamós-Palafrugell, Km 328, 17253 Vall-Llobrega (Gerona) [tel/fax 972-31 52 63; info@ campingcastellpark.com; www.campingcastellpark.com]** Exit m'way at junc 6 & take C66/C31 to Palamós. Site on R sp after 40km marker. Lge, mkd pitch, terr, shd; wc (some cont); chem disp; baby facs; shwrs inc; el pnts (3A) inc; gas; lndtte; supmkt; rest, snacks; bar; BBQ; playgrnd; pool; paddling pool; sand beach 2.5km; cycle hire; golf 11km; games rm; internet; entmnt; TV rm; some statics; dogs; bus 700m; Eng spkn; adv bkg; quiet; red long stay/low ssn/snr citizens; CKE/CCI. "Pleasant, quiet family site with friendly atmosphere & gd welcome; rallies & single c'vanners welcome; c'van storage avail." ♦ 27 Mar-12 Sep. € 34.00   2009*

PALAMOS *3B3* (3km W Coastal) *41.84700, 3.09861* **Eurocamping, Avda de Catalunya 15, 17252 Sant Antoni de Calonge (Gerona) [972-65 08 79; fax 972-66 19 87; info@euro-camping.com; www.euro-camping.com]** Exit A7 junc 6 dir Palamós on C66 & Sant Feliu C31. Take exit Sant Antoni; on ent Sant Antoni turn R at 1st rndabt. Visible fr main rd at cent of Sant Antoni. V lge, hdg/mkd pitch, shd; wc; chem disp; mv service pnt; 20% serviced pitches; baby facs; shwrs inc; el pnts (5A) inc; lndtte; supmkt; rest, snacks; bar; BBQ; playgrnd; 2 pools & paddling pool; waterpark; sand beach 300m; waterpark 5km; tennis; golf 7km; games area; games rm; fitness rm; doctor Jul & Aug; car wash; entmnt high ssn; wifi; TV rm; 15% statics; dogs €4; phone; Eng spkn; adv bkg; quiet; ccard acc; red long stay/low ssn. "Excel facs for families; lots to do in area; excel." ♦ 16 Apr-18 Sep. € 48.25   2010*

PALS *3B3* (6km NE Coastal) *41.98132, 3.20125* **Camping Inter Pals, Avda Mediterránea s/n, Km 45, 17256 Playa de Pals (Gerona) [972-63 61 79; fax 972-66 74 76; interpals@ interpals.com; www.interpals.com]** Exit A7 junc 6 dir Palamós onto C66. Turn N sp Pals & foll sp Playa/Platja de Pals, pass Camping Neptune sp on L then Golf Aparthotel on R. At rndbt take 2nd exit, site clearly sp on L approx 500m. Lge, pt sl, terr, shd; htd wc; chem disp; mv service pnt; baby facs; shwrs inc; el pnts (5-10A) inc; lndtte (inc dryer); supmkt nr; rest, snacks; bar; playgrnd; pool; paddling pool; sand beach 600m (naturist beach 1km); watersports; tennis; cycle hire; games area; golf 1km; wifi; entmnt; TV; 20% statics; dogs €3.50; phone; adv bkg; quiet; red snr citizens/CKE/CCI. "Lovely, well-maintained site in pine forest; poss diff lge o'fits - lge pitches at lower end of site; modern, well-maintained facs." ♦ 1 Apr-25 Sep. € 55.60 (CChq acc)   2014*

PALS *3B3* (4km E Rural) *41.98555, 3.18194* **Camping Cypsela, Rodors 7, 17256 Playa de Pals (Gerona) [972-66 76 96; fax 972-66 73 00; info@cypsela.com; www.cypsela.com]** Exit AP7 junc 6, rd C66 dir Palamós. 7km fr La Bisbal take dir Pals & foll sp Playa/Platja de Pals, site sp. V lge, hdg/mkd pitch, hdstg, shd; wc; chem disp; mv service pnt; 25% serviced pitches; child/baby facs; private bthrms avail; shwrs inc; el pnts (6-10A) inc; gas; lndtte; supmkt; rest, snacks; bar; BBQ; playgrnd; pool; sand beach 1.5km; tennis; mini-golf & other sports; cycle hire; golf 1km; games rm; wifi; entmnt; TV rm; free bus to beach; 30% statics; no dogs; Eng spkn; adv bkg; ccard acc; red long stay/low ssn/CKE/CCI. "Noise levels controlled after midnight; excel san facs; 4 grades of pitch/price (highest price shown); vg site." ♦ 14 May-15 Sep. € 58.00   2012*

"I like to fill in the reports as I travel from site to site"

You'll find report forms at the back of this guide, or you can fill them in online at www.caravaclub.co.uk/europereport.

⊞ **PAMPLONA** *3B1* (7km N Rural) *42.85776, -1.62250* **Camping Ezcaba, Ctra a Francia, km 2,5, 31194 Eusa-Oricain (Navarre) [948-33 03 15; fax 948-33 13 16; info@campingezcaba.com; www.campingezcaba.com]** Fr N leave AP15 onto NA30 (N ring rd) to N121A sp Francia/Iruña. Pass Arre & Oricáin, turn L foll site sp 500m on R dir Berriosuso. Site on R in 500m - fairly steep ent. Or fr S leave AP15 onto NA32 (E by-pass) to N121A sp Francia/Iruña, then as above. Med, mkd pitch, pt sl, pt shd; wc; shwrs inc; el pnts (10A) €5.50; gas; lndtte (inc dryer); shop; rest, snacks; bar; playgrnd; pool; horseriding; tennis; wifi; dogs €2.95; phone; bus 1km; poss cr; adv bkg; rd noise; red low ssn. "Helpful, friendly staff; sm pitches unsuitable lge o'fits & poss diff due trees, esp when site full; attractive setting; gd pool, bar & rest; ltd facs low ssn & poss long walk to san facs; in winter use as NH only; phone to check open low ssn; cycle track to Pamplona; quiet rural site; gd facs not htd." ♦ € 38.65   2013*

PEDROSILLO EL RALO see Salamanca *1C3*

PELIGROS see Granada *2G4*

PENAFIEL *1C4* (2km SW Rural) *41.59538, -4.12811* **Camping Riberduero, Avda Polideportivo 51, 47300 Peñafiel [tel/fax 983-88 16 37; camping@campingpenafiel.com; www.campingpenafiel.com]** Fr Valladolid 56km or Aranda de Duero 38km on N122. In Peñafiel take VA223 dir Cuéllar, foll sp to sports cent/camping. Med, mkd pitch, hdstg, shd; htd wc; chem disp; mv service pnt; baby facs; fam bthrm; shwrs inc; el pnts (5A) €3.50; gas; lndtte; shop; rest, snacks; bar; playgrnd; pool; rv 1km; cycle hire; TV; 20% statics; dogs €1.50; phone; bus 1km; site open w/end only low ssn; poss cr; Eng spkn; adv bkg; quiet; ccard acc; 10% red 15 days. "Excel, well-kept site; interesting, historical area; ideal for wheelchair users; sm pitches and access diff due to trees." ♦ Holy Week & 1 Apr-30 Sep. € 18.50   2013*

PENASCOSA see Alcaraz *4F1*

⊞ **PENISCOLA** *3D2* (500m N Coastal) *40.37694, 0.39222* **Camping El Cid, Azagador de la Cruz s/n, 12598 Peñíscola (Castellón) [964-48 03 80; fax 964-46 76 02; info@campingelcid.com; www.campingelcid.com]** Exit A7 at junc 43. Take N340 sp València for sh dist, turn L sp Peñíscola. Approx 2km look for yellow sp to site. Narr site ent - rec loop o'fit rnd in rd & ent thro R-hand site of security barrier. Med, mkd pitch, shd; wc; chem disp; shwrs inc; el pnts (10A) €4.50; gas; lndtte; shop; supmkt; rest, snacks; bar; playgrnd; pool; paddling pool; sand beach 500m; 50% statics; poss cr; ccard acc; red long stay/low ssn; CKE/CCI. "Vg, well-run site; popular with Spanish families; friendly staff." € 27.00   2009*

⊞ **PENISCOLA** *3D2* (500m N Coastal) *40.36222, 0.39583* **Camping Ferrer, Avda Estación 27, 12598 Peñiscola (Castellón) [964-48 92 23; fax 964-48 91 44; campingferrer@campingferrer.com; www.campingferrer.com]** Exit AP7 onto CV141 twd Peñiscola, site sp on R, adj Consum supmkt. Med, hdstg, terr, pt shd; htd wc; chem disp; mv service pnt; baby facs; shwrs inc; el pnts (6A) €3; lndry rm; shop adj; rest, snacks; bar; BBQ; playgrnd; pool; sand beach 500m; games rm; wifi; entmnt; some statics; dogs; bus 700m; adv bkg; poss rd noise; cc acc; red long stay; CKE/CCI. "Conv NH; vg, family run site; level pitches but access poss diff due trees." € 22.00   2010*

"We must tell The Club about that great site we found"

Get your site reports in by mid-August and we'll do our best to get your updates into the next edition.

⊞ **PENISCOLA** *3D2* (1km N Coastal) *40.37152, 0.40269* **Camping El Edén, Ctra CS501 Benicarló-Peñíscola Km 6, 12598 Peñíscola (Castellón) [964-48 05 62; fax 964-48 98 28; camping@camping-eden.com; www.camping-eden.com]** Exit AP7 junc 43 onto N340 & CV141 dir Peñíscola. Take 3rd exit off rndabt on seafront, L at mini-rndabt, L after Hotel del Mar. Rec avoid Sat Nav rte across marshes fr Peñíscola. Lge, hdg/mkd pitch, pt shd; htd wc; chem disp; mv service pnt; baby facs; shwrs inc; el pnts (10A) inc; gas; service lndtte; shop 300m; rest, snacks; bar; playgrnd; pool; paddling pool; sand/shgl beach adj; wifi; 40% statics; dogs €0.75; bus adj; cash dispenser; poss cr; no adv bkg; rd noise in ssn; ccard acc; red long stay/low ssn; ACSI acc; "San facs refurbished & v clean; beach adj cleaned daily; gd security; excel pool; easy access to sandy/gravel pitches but many sm trees poss diff for awnings or high m'vans; poss vicious mosquitoes at dusk; easy walk/cycle to town; 4 diff sizes of pitch (some with tap, sink & drain) with different prices; ltd facs low ssn; excel." ♦ € 71.00   2013*

⊞ **PENISCOLA** *3D2* (2km NW Rural) *40.40158, 0.38116*
Camping Spa Natura Resort, Partida Villarroyos s/n,
Playa Montana, 12598 Peñíscola-Benicarló (Castellón)
[964-47 54 80; fax 964-78 50 51; info@spanaturaresort.
com; www.spanaturaresort.com] Exit AP7 junc 43, within
50m of toll booths turn R immed then immed L & foll site sp
twd Benicarló (NB R turn is on slip rd). Fr N340 take CV141 to
Peñíscola. Cross m'way bdge & immed turn L; site sp. Med,
mkd pitch, hdstg, shd; htd wc; chem disp; mv service pnt;
serviced pitches; sauna; baby facs; shwrs inc; el pnts (6A) inc;
gas; lndtte (inc dryer); tradsmn; rest, snacks; bar; BBQ area;
playgrnd; pool; htd pool; waterslide; paddling pool; spa;
wellness centre; jacuzzi; sand beach 2.5km; tennis; cycle hire;
gym; games area; games rm; wifi; entmnt; TV rm; 50% statics;
dogs €3 (free low ssn); twin-axles acc (rec check in adv);
phone; bus 600m; c'van storage; car wash; Eng spkn; adv bkg;
some rd noise; ccard acc; red low ssn/long stay/snr citizens/
CKE/CCI. "Vg site; helpful, enthusiastic staff; gd clean san
facs; wide range of facs; gd cycling." ♦ € 40.00 (CChq acc)
SBS - E23   2013*

"I need an on-site restaurant"

We do our best to make sure site
information is correct, but it is always best
to check any must-have facilities are still
available or will be open during your visit.

⊞ **PILAR DE LA HORADADA** *4F2* (4km NE Coastal)
37.87916, -0.76555 **Lo Monte Camping & Caravaning,**
Avenida Comunidada Valenciana No 157 CP 03190
[00 34 966 766 782; fax 00 34 966 746 536; info@
campinglomonte-alicante.es; www.campinglomonte-
alicante.es] Exit 770 of AP7 dir Pilar de la Horadada; take
the 1st L. Med, mkd/hdg pitch; htd wc; chem disp; serviced
pitches; baby facs; shwrs inc; el pnts (16) €0.40; lndtte; shop;
rest; bar; BBQ; playgrnd; htd, covrd pool; beach 1km; bike hire;
gym/wellness centre; entmnt; wifi; dogs €1; adv bkg; ccard acc;
CKE/CCI. "New site; superb facs; great location - lots of golf &
gd for walking; rec; excel." ♦ € 35.00   2014*

PINEDA DE MAR see Calella *3C3*

PINEDA, LA see Salou *3C2*

PITRES *2G4* (500m SW Rural) *36.93178, -3.33268* **Camping**
El Balcón de Pitres, Ctra Órgiva-Ugijar, Km 51, 18414
Pitres (Granada) [958-76 61 11; fax 958-80 44 53; info@
balcondepitres.com; www.balcondepitres.com] S
fr Granada on A44/E902, turn E onto A348 for 22km. At
Órgiva take A4132 dir Trevélez to Pitres to site. Ask at rest in
vill for dirs. Sm, terr, shd; wc; chem disp; el pnts (10A) €4.28;
gas; lndtte; shop; rest, snacks; bar; playgrnd; pool; cycle hire;
some statics; bus 600m; poss cr Aug; quiet; red long
stay; ccard acc; CKE/CCI. "Site in unspoilt Alpujarras region of
Sierra Nevada mountains; fine scenery & wildlife; site on steep
hillside; poss diff lge o'fits; san facs at top of hill - own san facs
saves climb." 1 Mar-31 Oct. € 32.00 (3 persons)   2011*

⊞ **PLASENCIA** *1D3* (4km NE Urban) *40.04348, -6.05751*
Camping La Chopera, Ctra N110, Km 401.3, Valle
del Jerte, 10600 Plasencia (Caceres) [tel/fax 927-
41 66 60; lachopera@campinglachopera.com; www.
campinglachopera.com] In Plasencia on N630 turn E on
N110 sp Ávila & foll sp indus est & sp to site. Med, shd; wc;
serviced pitches; chem disp; baby facs; shwrs inc; el pnts (6A)
inc; gas; lndtte; shop; rest; bar; BBQ; playgrnd; pool; paddling
pool; tennis; cycle hire; wifi; dogs; quiet but w/end disco; ccard
acc; CKE/CCI. "Peaceful & spacious; much birdsong; conv
Manfragüe National Park (breeding of black/Egyptian vultures,
black storks, imperial eagles); excel pool & modern facs; helpful
owners." ♦ 1 Mar-30 Sep. € 30.00   2011*

⊞ **PLASENCIA** *1D3* (10km SE Rural) *39.94361, -6.08444*
Camping Parque Natural Monfragüe, Ctra Plasencia-
Trujillo, Km 10, 10680 Malpartida de Plasencia
(Cáceres) [tel/fax 927- 45 92 33 / 605 94 08 78 (mob);
campingmonfrague@hotmail.com; www.
campingmonfrague.com] Fr N on A66/N630 by-pass
town, 5km S of town at flyover junc take EXA1 (EX108) sp
Navalmoral de la Mata. In 6km turn R onto EX208 dir Trujillo,
site on L in 5km. Med, hdg pitch, pt sl, terr, pt shd; htd wc;
chem disp; mv service pnt; baby facs; shwrs inc; el pnts (5-15A)
€4; gas; lndtte (inc dryer); shop; tradsmn; rest, snacks; bar;
BBQ; playgrnd; pool high ssn; tennis; games area; archery; cycle
hire; rambling; 4x4 off-rd; horseriding; wifi; TV rm; 10% statics;
dogs; phone; Eng spkn; no adv bkg; quiet; ccard acc; red long
stay/cash/CKE/CCI; "Friendly staff; vg, clean facs; gd rest; clean,
tidy, busy site but poss dusty - hoses avail; 10km to National
Park (birdwatching trips); many birds on site; excel year round
base; new san facs; staff helpful; discounted fees must be paid
in cash." ♦ € 28.00 (CChq acc)   2014*

"Satellite navigation makes touring much easier"

Remember most sat navs don't know if
you're towing or in a larger vehicle – always
use yours alongside maps and site directions.

PLAYA DE ARO *3B3* (2km N Coastal) *41.83116, 3.08366*
Camping Cala Gogo, Avda Andorra 13, 17251 Calonge
(Gerona) [972-65 15 64; fax 972-65 05 53; calagogo@
calagogo.es; www.calagogo.es] Exit AP7 junc 6 dir Palamós/
Sant Feliu. Fr Palamós take C253 coast rd S twd Sant Antoni,
site on R 2km fr Playa de Aro, sp. Lge, pt sl, pt terr, pt shd;
wc; chem disp; mv service pnt; serviced pitch; baby facs; shwrs
inc; el pnts (10A) inc; gas; lndtte (inc dryer); supmkt; rest; bar;
snacks; bar; BBQ; playgrnds; htd pool; paddling pool; sand
beach adj; boat hire; diving school; games area; games rm;
tennis; cycle hire; golf 4km; wifi; entmnt; TV; no dogs 3/7-21/8
(otherwise €2); Eng spkn; adv bkg; quiet; red long stay/low ssn.
"Clean & recently upgraded san facs; rest/bar with terrace; site
terraced into pinewood on steep hillside; excel family site." ♦
16 Apr-18 Sep. € 52.00   2011*

Càmping TREUMAL Costa Brava

YOU WILL FIND US ON THE BEACH ...

Apdo. Correos nº 348 17250 PLATJA D'ARO (GIRONA)
TLF. (0034) 972 65 10 95   FAX. (0034) 972 65 16 71   E mail: Info@campingtreumal.com
www.campingtreumal.com

⊞ **PLAYA DE ARO** *3B3* (2km N Coastal) *41.83333, 3.08416* Camping Internacional Calonge, Avda d'Andorra s/n, Ctra 253, Km 47, 17251 Calonge (Gerona) [972-65 12 33 or 972-65 14 64; fax 972-65 25 07; info@intercalonge.com; www.intercalonge.com] Fr A7 exit junc 6 onto C66 dir La Bisbal, Palamós & Playa de Aro; 3km bef Palamós foll sp St Antoni de Calonge. At 2nd rndbt bear R onto C253 dir Sant Feliu, site on R in 3km. V lge, mkd pitch, terr, shd; htd wc; chem disp; mv service pnt; some serviced pitches; baby facs; shwrs inc; el pnts (5A) inc; gas; lndtte; supmkt; rest, snacks; bar; BBQ; playgrnd; 2 pools; paddling pool; solarium; sand/shgl beach adj; tennis; extensive sports facs; wifi; entmnt; TV rm; 30% statics; phone; dogs €4.20; Eng spkn; adv bkg; poss noisy high ssn; ccard acc; red low ssn/long stay; CKE/CCI. "On side of steep hill - parking poss diff at times; conv Dali Museum; Roman ruins; gd security; superb facs; excel site." ♦ € 49.35   2011*

"There aren't many sites open at this time of year"

If you're travelling outside peak season remember to call ahead to check site opening dates – even if the entry says 'open all year'

PLAYA DE ARO *3B3* (2km N Coastal) *41.83666, 3.08722* Camping Treumal, Ctra Playa de Aro/Palamós, C253, Km 47.5, 17250 Playa de Arro (Gerona) [972-65 10 95; fax 972-65 16 71; info@campingtreumal.com; www.campingtreumal.com] Exit m'way at junc 6, 7 or 9 dir Sant Feliu de Guixols to Playa de Aro; site is sp at km 47.5 fr C253 coast rd SW of Palamós. Lge, mkd pitch, terr, shd; wc; baby facs; shwrs inc; chem disp; mv service pnt; el pnts (10A) inc; gas; lndtte; supmkt; tradsmn; rest, snacks; bar; playgrnd; sm pool; sand beach adj; fishing; tennis 1km; games rm; sports facs; cycle hire; golf 5km; wifi; entmnt; 25% statics; no dogs; phone; car wash; Eng spkn; adv bkg; quiet; ccard acc; red low ssn; CKE/CCI. "Peaceful site in pine trees; excel san facs; manhandling poss req onto terr pitches; gd beach." ♦ 31 Mar-30 Sep. € 49.30   2011*

See advertisement

PLAYA DE ARO *3B3* (2km N Rural) *41.81116, 3.01821* Yelloh! Village Mas Sant Josep, Ctra Santa Cristina-Playa de Aro, Km 2, 17246 Santa Cristina de Aro (Gerona) [972-83 51 08; fax 972-83 70 18; info@campingmassantjosep.com; www.campingmassantjosep.com or www.yellohvillage.co.uk] Fr A7/E15 take exit 7 dir Sant Feliu de Guixols to Santa Christina town. Take old rd dir Playa de Aro, site in 2km. V lge, mkd pitch, shd; htd wc; chem disp; mv service pnt; baby facs; serviced pitches; sauna; shwrs inc; el pnts (10A) inc; gas; lndtte (inc dryer); shop; rest, snacks; bar; BBQ; playgrnd; lge pools; sand beach 3.5km; tennis; games rm; games area; mini-golf & assorted sports; cycle hire; entmnt; golf 4km; internet; TV rm; 60% statics; dogs €4; Eng spkn; adv bkg; quiet; ccard acc; red low ssn; CKE/CCI. "Generous pitches; excel." ♦ 15 Apr-11 Sep. € 47.00   2010*

PLAYA DE ARO *3B3* (1km S Coastal) *41.81416, 3.04444* Camping Valldaro, Carrer del Camí Vell 63, 17250 Playa de Aro (Gerona) [972-81 75 15; fax 972-81 66 62; info@valldaro.com; www.valldaro.com] Exit A7 junc 7 onto C65 dir Sant Feliu. Turn L onto C31 for Playa de Aro thro Castillo de Aro & site on R, 1km fr Playa at km 4.2. V lge, pt shd; htd wc; chem disp; mv service pnt; baby facs; shwrs inc; el pnts (5A) inc; gas; lndtte (inc dryer); shop; rest, snacks; bar; playgrnd; 2 pools; paddling pool; waterslides; beach 1km; watersports; tennis; horseriding 2km; golf 3km; games area; cycle hire; wifi; entmnt; 50% statics; dogs €2.90; phone; extra for lger pitch; adv bkg; red long stay. "Excel family site; some lge pitches; many facs." ♦ 1 Apr-25 Sep. € 48.00 (CChq acc)   2010*

PLAYA DE ARO *3B3* (2km S Coastal) *41.8098, 3.0466* Camping Riembau, Calle Santiago Rusiñol s/n, 17250 Playa de Aro (Gerona) [972-81 71 23; fax 972-82 52 10; camping@riembau.com; www.riembau.com] Fr Gerona take C250 thro Llagostera, turn for Playa de Aro. Fr Playa de Aro take C253 twd Sant Feliu. Site access rd 2km on R. V lge, pt shd; wc; chem disp; baby facs; shwrs inc; el pnts (5A) inc; gas; lndtte; rest, snacks; bar; shop; beach 800m; 2 pools (1 indoor); playgrnd; tennis; fitness cent; games area; games rm; entmnt; internet; 40% statics; phone; adv bkg; some rd noise. ♦ Easter-30 Sep. € 36.00   2011*

PLAYA DE OLIVA see Oliva *4E2*

PLAYA DE PALS see Pals *3B3*

PLAYA DE PINEDO see Valencia *4E2*

PLAYA DE VIDIAGO see Llanes *1A4*

PLAYA TAMARIT see Tarragona *3C3*

POBLA DE SEGUR, LA *3B2* (3km NE Rural) *42.2602, 0.9862* Camping Collegats, Ctra N260, Km 306, 25500 La Pobla de Segur (Lleida) [973-68 07 14; fax 973-68 14 02; camping@ collegats.com; www.collegats.com] Fr Tremp N to La Pobla on N260. Site sp in town at traff lts, turn R onto N260 dir Sort. Ent by hairpin bend. Last section of rd narr & rough. Med, mkd pitch, shd; wc; chem disp; shwrs; el pnts €5; gas; lndtte; shop & 4km; tradsmn; snacks; bar; BBQ; playgrnd; pool; games area; some statics (sep area); dogs; poss cr; Eng spkn; quiet; CKE/ CCI. "Clean facs; site not suitable lge o'fits; twin-axle vans not acc; conv NH." ♦ 1 Apr-31 Oct. € 20.00   2011*

⊞ **POBOLEDA** *3C2* (300m SW Rural) *41.23298, 0.84305* Camping Poboleda, Plaça Les Casetes s/n, 43376 Poboleda (Tarragona) [tel/fax 977-82 71 97; poboleda@ campingsonline.com; www.campingpoboleda.com] By-pass Reus W of Tarragona on T11/N420 then turn N onto C242 sp Les Borges del Camp. Go thro Alforja over Col d'Alforja & turn L onto T207 to Poboleda & foll camping sp in vill. Alt rd 50m W called Calle Major though steep on exit fr site. Med, mkd pitch, terr, pt shd; htd wc; chem disp; baby facs; fam bthrm; el pnts (4A) inc; lndry rm; shop, rest, snacks, bar in vill; pool; lake sw 8km; tennis; wifi; TV; no statics; dogs; phone; Eng spkn; quiet; ccard acc; CKE/CCI. "In heart of welcoming vill in mountain setting; friendly, helpful owner; not suitable lge o'fits as access thro vill." ♦ € 32.67   2011*

POLA DE SOMIEDO *1A3* (250m E Rural) *43.09222, -6.25222* Camping La Pomerada de Somiedo, 33840 Pola de Somiedo (Asturias) [985-76 34 04; csomiedo@ infonegocio.com] W fr Oviedo on A63, turn S onto AS15/ AS227 to Augasmestas & Pola de Somiedo. Site adj Hotel Alba, sp fr vill. Route on steep, winding, mountain rd - suitable sm, powerful o'fits only. Sm, mkd pitch, pt shd; wc; chem disp; mv service pnt; shwrs inc; el pnts €4.20; shop, rest bar in vill; quiet. "Mountain views; nr national park." 1 Apr-31 Dec. € 19.00   2009*

⊞ **PONFERRADA** *1B3* (10km W Rural) *42.56160, 6.74590* Camping El Bierzo, 24550 Villamartín de la Abadia (León) [tel/fax 987-56 25 15; info@campingbierzo.com; www. campingbierzo.com] Exit A6 junc 399 dir Carracedelo; after rndabt turn onto NV1 & foll sp Villamartín. Bef ent Villamartín turn L & foll site sp. Med, pt shd; wc; chem disp; mv service pnt (ltd); shwrs inc; el pnts (3A) €3.78; shops 2km; rest; bar; playgrnd; 90% statics; dogs €1.73; phone; bus 1km; adv bkg; quiet; ccard not acc; CKE/CCI; "Attractive, rvside site in pleasant area; gd facs; friendly, helpful owner takes pride in his site; Roman & medieval attractions nr." ♦ ltd € 25.50   2013*

PONT D'ARROS see Vielha *3B2*

⊞ **PONT DE BAR, EL** *3B3* (2.6km E Rural) *42.37458, 1.63687* Camping Pont d'Ardaix, N260, Km 210, 25723 El Pont de Bar (Lleida) [973-38 40 98; fax 973-38 41 15; pontdardaix@ clior.es; www.pontdardaix.com] On Seo de Urgel-Puigcerdà rd, N260, at rear of bar/rest Pont d'Ardaix. Med, terr, pt shd; wc; mv service pnt; shwrs inc; el pnts (3-5A) €5.10-7.10; gas; lndtte; shop & 4km; rest; bar; playgrnd; pool; 80% statics; dogs €5.30; phone; Eng spkn; quiet; CKE/CCI; "In pleasant valley on bank of Rv Segre; touring pitches on rv bank; site poss scruffy & unkempt low ssn; gd NH; vill 2.5km away." ♦ € 20.60   2011*

PONT DE SUERT *3B2* (4km N Rural) *42.43083, 0.73861* Camping Can Roig, Ctra Boí, Km 0.5, 25520 El Pont de Suert [973-69 05 02; fax 973-69 12 06; info@ campingcanroig.com; www.campingcanroig.com] N of Pont de Suert on N230 turn NE onto L500 dir Caldes de Boí. Site in 1km. App narr for 100m. Med, mkd pitch, hdstg, pt sl, pt shd; wc; chem disp; shwrs inc; el pnts (5A) €5.15; gas; lndtte; shop & 3km; snacks; bar; playgrnd; paddling pool; 5% statics; dogs €3.60; adv bkg; quiet; ccard acc. "NH en rte S; beautiful valley; informal, friendly, quirky site (free range poultry); v relaxed atmosphere; helpful owner; fabulous valley & national park with thermal springs." 1 Mar-31 Oct. € 20.60   2013*

⊞ **PONT DE SUERT** *3B2* (5.5km N Rural) *42.44833, 0.71027* Camping Alta Ribagorça, Ctra Les Bordes s/n, Km 131, 25520 Pont de Suert (Lleida) [973-69 05 21; fax 973-69 06 97; ana.uma@hotmail.com] Fr N on N230 site sp S of Vilaller on S1km, mkd pitch, terr, pt shd; htd wc; chem disp; shwrs inc; el pnts (5A) inc; lndtte; rest; bar; playgrnd; pool; 10% statics; dogs; Eng spkn; rd noise. "Fair NH." € 19.50   2009*

⊞ **PONT DE SUERT** *3B2* (16km NE Rural) *42.51900, 8.84600* Camping Taüll, Ctra Taüll s/n, 25528 Taüll (Lleida) [973 69 61 74; www.campingtaull.com] Fr Pont de Suert 3km N on N230 then NE on L500 dir Caldes de Boí. In 13km turn R into Taüll. Site sp on R. Sm, pt sl, terr, pt shd; htd wc; chem disp; baby facs; shwrs inc; el pnts €6; lndry rm; shop, rest, bar 300m; 30% statics; dogs €3; clsd 15 Oct-15 Nov; poss cr; quiet; CKE/CCI. "Excel facs; taxis into National Park avail; ltd touring pitches; suitable sm m'vans only; many bars & rest in pretty vill." € 28.50   2014*

⊞ **PONT DE SUERT** *3B2* (5km NW Rural) *42.43944, 0.69860* Camping Baliera, Ctra N260, Km 355.5, Castejón de Sos, 22523 Bonansa (Huesca) [974-55 40 16; fax 974-55 40 99; info@baliera.com; www.baliera.com] N fr Pont de Suert on N230 turn L opp petrol stn onto N260 sp Castejón de Sos. In 1km turn L onto A1605 sp Bonansa, site on L immed over rv bdge. Site sp fr N230. Lge, mkd pitch, pt sl, terr, shd; htd wc; chem disp; mv service pnt; baby facs; shwrs inc; el pnts (5-10A) €5; gas; lndtte (inc dryer); shop; tradsmn; rest in ssn; snacks; bar; BBQ; playgrnd; pool; paddling pool; rv fishing; lake sw 10km; cycle hire; horseriding 4km; golf 4km; weights rm; wifi; sat TV; 50% statics; dogs €3.80; phone; site clsd Nov & Xmas; poss cr; Eng spkn; quiet; ccard acc; red low ssn; CKE/ CCI. "Excel, well-run, peaceful site in parkland setting; walking in summer, skiing in winter; excel cent for touring; conv Vielha tunnel; all facs up steps; pt of site v sl; helpful owner proud of his site; clean facs, some rvside pitches." ♦ € 32.40 (CChq acc)   2014*

PORT DE LA SELVA, EL *3B3* (2km N Coastal) *42.34222, 3.18333* **Camping Port de la Vall, Ctra Port de Llançà, 17489 El Port de la Selva (Gerona) [972-38 71 86; fax 972-12 63 08; portdelavall@terra.es]** On coast rd fr French border at Llançà take GI612 twd El Port de la Selva. Site on L, easily seen. Lge, pt shd; wc; shwrs; el pnts (3-5A) €5.65; gas; lndtte; shop; rest, snacks; bar; playgrnd; shgl beach adj; internet; some statics; dogs €2.95; phone; poss cr; adv bkg; poss noisy; ccard acc; red low ssn. "Easy 1/2 hr walk to harbour; gd site; sm pitches & low branches poss diff - check bef siting." 1 Mar-15 Oct. € 43.00 (4 persons) 2011*

PORT DE LA SELVA, EL *3B3* (1km S Coastal) *42.32641, 3.20480* **Camping Port de la Selva, Ctra Cadaqués s/n, Km 1, 17489 El Port de la Selva (Gerona) [972-38 72 87 or 972-38 73 86; info@campingselva.com; www.campingselva.com]** Exit A7 junc 3 or 4 onto N260 to Llança, then take GI 612 to El Port de la Selva. On ent town turn R twd Cadaqués, site in R in 1km. Med, mkd pitch, pt shd; wc; chem disp (wc); shwrs inc; el pnts (4A) inc (poss no earth); lndtte; shop & 1km; rest, snacks, bar 1km; playgrnd; pool; sand/shgl beach 1km; games area; TV; 25% statics; dogs €2.50; poss cr; adv bkg; quiet; ccard not acc; red low ssn; CKE/CCI. "Excel for coastal & hill walking; well-run site; gd, clean facs; gd beach; pleasant, attractive vill; poss diff for lge m'vans due low branches." 1 Jun-15 Sep. € 37.00 2010*

PORT DE LA SELVA, EL *3B3* (1km SW Coastal) *42.33462, 3.19683* **Camping L'Arola, Ctra. Llança-El Port de la Selva, 17489 El Port de la Selva (Gerona) [972-38 70 05; fax 972-12 60 81]** Off N11 at Figueras, sp to Llançà on N260. In 20km turn R to El Port de la Selva. Site on L (N side of coast rd) bef town. Sm, hdstg, unshd; wc; chem disp; shwrs; el pnts (10A) €5; lndry rm; shops 1km; tradsmn; rest, snacks, bar; shgl beach adj; 5% statics; dogs €3.21; bus; poss cr; adv bkg; ccard acc; CKE/CCI. "Nr sm, pleasant town with gd shops, rests, harbour, amusements for all ages; scenic beauty; v friendly owner." ♦ ltd 1 Jun-30 Sep. € 21.50 2010*

POTES *1A4* (1km W Rural) *43.15527, -4.63694* **Camping La Viorna, Ctra Santo Toribio, Km 1, Mieses, 39570 Potes (Cantabria) [942-73 20 21; fax 942-73 21 01; info@campinglaviorna.com; www.campinglaviorna.com]** Exit N634 at junc 272 onto N621 dir Panes & Potes - narr, winding rd (passable for c'vans). Fr Potes take rd to Fuente Dé sp Espinama; in 1km turn L sp Toribio. Site on R in 1km, sp fr Potes. Med, mkd pitch, terr, pt shd; htd wc; chem disp; mv service pnt; baby facs; shwrs inc; el pnts (6A) €3.40 (poss rev pol); lndtte (inc dryer); shop & 2km; tradsmn; rest, snacks; bar; BBQ; playgrnd; pool high ssn; paddling pool; cycle hire; wifi; bus 1km; poss cr; Eng spkn; adv bkg; quiet; ccard acc; CKE/CCI; "Lovely views; gd walks; friendly, family-run, clean, tidy site; gd pool; ideal Picos de Europa; conv cable car, 4x4 tours, trekking; mkt on Mon; festival mid-Sep v noisy; some pitches diff in wet & diff lge o'fits; excel." ♦ 1 Apr-31 Oct. € 23.87 2014*

POTES *1A4* (3km W Rural) *43.15742, -4.65617* **Camping La Isla-Picos de Europa, Ctra Potes-Fuente Dé, 39586 Turieno (Cantabria) [tel/fax 942-73 08 96; campicoseuropa@terra.es; www.liebanaypicosdeeuropa.com]** Take N521 W fr Potes twd Espinama, site on R in 3km thro vill of Turieno (app Potes fr N). Med, mkd pitch, pt sl, shd; wc; chem disp; mv service pnt; shwrs inc; el pnts (6A) €3.60 (poss rev pol); gas; lndtte; shop; tradsmn; rest; bar; BBQ; playgrnd; pool (caps req); walking; horseriding; cycling; 4x4 touring; hang-gliding; mountain treks in area; wifi; some statics; phone; poss cr; Eng spkn; adv bkg; poss noisy high ssn; ccard acc; red long stay; CKE/CCI. "Delightful, family-run site; friendly, helpful owners; gd san facs; conv cable car & mountain walks (map fr recep); many trees & low branches; rec early am dep to avoid coaches on gorge rd; highly rec; Lovely loc, gd facs." Easter-31 Oct. € 20.50 2012*

POTES *1A4* (5km W Rural) *43.15527, -4.68333* **Camping San Pelayo, Ruta Potes-Fuente Dé, Km 5, 39587 San Pelayo (Cantabria) [tel/fax 942-73 30 87; info@campingsanpelayo.com; www.campingsanpelayo.com]** Take CA185 W fr Potes twd Espinama, site on R in 5km, 2km past Camping La Isla. Med, mkd pitch, pt sl, pt shd; wc; chem disp; shwrs inc; el pnts (6A) inc; lndtte (inc dryer); shop; rest, snacks; bar; playgrnd; pool; paddling pool; cycle hire; games rm; wifi; TV; bus; poss cr; adv bkg; quiet, but noise fr bar; ccard acc high ssn; red long stay; CKE/CCI. "Friendly, helpful owner; some sm pitches; conv mountain walking; excel pool." Easter-15 Oct. € 17.20 2010*

PRADES see Vilanova de Prades *3C2*

PUEBLA DE CASTRO, LA see Graus *3B2*

PUEBLA DE SANABRIA *1B3* (500m S Rural) *42.04930, -6.63068* **Camping Isla de Puebla-DELETED, Pago de Barregas s/n, 49300 Puebla de Sanabria (Zamora) [980-56 79 54; fax 980-56 79 55; c.isladepuebla@hotmail.com; www.isladepuebla.com]** Fr Portugal border on C622, at ent to Puebla de Sanabria foll sp down sh track twd rv. Fr N525 ent vill & foll sp Isla de Puebla. Med, mkd pitch, pt shd; wc; chem disp;mv service pnt; shwrs inc; el pnts (10-16A) €4.90-6; gas; lndtte (inc dryer); shop; rest, snacks; bar; BBQ; playgrnd; pool; trout-fishing; games area; some statics; dogs; bus 200m; adv bkg; quiet; red long stay; ccard acc; CKE/CCI. "Vg, modern san facs; interesting town; vg for nature lovers; friendly, helpful staff; vg rest in old mill; facs ltd low ssn." Holy Week-30 Sep. € 18.00 2012*

PUEBLA DE SANABRIA *1B3* (10km NW Rural) *42.13111, -6.70111* **Camping El Folgoso, Ctra Puebla de Sanabria-San Martin de Castañeda, Km 13, 49361 Vigo de Sanabria (Zamora) [980-62 67 74; fax 980-62 68 00; info@.campingelfolgoso.com; www.campingelfolgoso.com/]** Exit A52 sp Puebla de Sanabria & foll sp for Lago/Vigo de Sanabria thro Puente de Sanabria & Galende; site 2km beyond vill of Galende; sp. Med, pt sl, terr, shd; wc; chem disp; shwrs €1; el pnts (5A) €2.50; gas; lndtte; shop high ssn; rest high ssn; snacks; bar; playgrnd; cycle hire; statics; phone; ccard acc. "Lovely setting beside lake, and woods, v cold in winter." ♦ ltd 1 Apr-31 Oct. € 18.00 2012*

SPAIN

PUEBLA DE SANABRIA *1B3* (10km NW Rural) *42.11778, -6.69116* **Camping Peña Gullón, Ctra Puebla de Santabria-Ribadelago, Km 11.5, Lago de Sanabria, 49360 Galende (Zamora) [980-62 67 72]** Fr Puebla de Sanabria foll sp for Lago de Sanabria. Site 3km beyond vill of Galende clearly sp. Lge, pt shd; wc; shwrs inc; el pnts (15A) €2.51; gas; lndtte; shop in ssn; rest; playgrnd; lake adj; poss cr; quiet; red long stay; CKE/CCI. "Site in nature park 35km fr Portugal's Montesinho Park; rec arr by 1200; beautiful area; excel site." 28 Jun-31 Aug. € 17.00   2011*

⊞ **PUERTO DE MAZARRON** *4G1* (3km NE Rural/Coastal) *37.58981, -1.22881* **Camping Las Torres, Ctra N332, Cartagena-Mazarrón, Km 29, 30860 Puerto de Mazarrón (Murcia) [968-59 52 25; fax 968 59 55 16; info@campinglastorres.com; www.campinglastorres.com]** Fr N on A7/E15 exit junc 627 onto MU602, then MU603 to Mazarrón. At junc with N322 turn L to Puerto de Mazarrón & foll Cartagena sp until site sps. Lge, hdg/mkd pitch, terr, hdstg, pt shd; wc; chem disp; mv service pnt; 40% serviced pitch; baby facs; shwrs inc; el pnts (6A) inc; gas; lndtte; rest (w/end only); snacks; bar; sm shop & 3km; playgrnd; 2 pools (1 htd, covrd); sand/shgl beach 2km; tennis; cycle hire; wifi; entmnt; sat TV; 60% statics; dogs; phone; bus 1km; Eng spkn; adv bkg rec in winter; poss noisy; ccard acc; red low ssn/long stay; CKE/CCI. "Unspoilt coastline; busy at w/end; well-managed, family site; poss full in winter; excel pool; sm pitches." ♦ € 24.50   2010*

⊞ **PUERTO DE MAZARRON** *4G1* (5km NE Coastal) *37.5800, -1.1950* **Camping Los Madriles, Ctra a la Azohía 60, Km 4.5, 30868 Isla Plana (Murcia) [968-15 21 51; fax 968-15 20 92; info@campinglosmadriles.com; www.campinglosmadriles.com]** Fr Cartagena on N332 dir Puerto de Mazarrón. Turn L at rd junc sp La Azohía (32km). Site in 4km sp. Fr Murcia on E15/N340 dir Lorca exit junc 627 onto MU603 to Mazarrón, then foll sp. (Do not use rd fr Cartagena unless powerful tow vehicle/gd weight differential - use rte fr m'way thro Mazarrón). Lge, hdg/mkd pitch, hdstg, pt sl, pt shd; wc; chem disp; mv service pnt; serviced pitches; shwrs inc; el pnts (10A) €5; gas; lndtte; shop; rest high ssn; bar; playgrnd; 2 htd pools; jacuzzi; shgl beach 500m; games area; wifi; no dogs; bus; poss cr; Eng spkn; adv bkg (fr Oct for min 2 months only); quiet; ccard acc high ssn; red long stay/low ssn/CKE/CCI. "Clean, well-run, v popular winter site; adv bkg ess fr Oct; some sm pitches, some with sea views; sl bet terrs; 3 days min stay high ssn; v helpful staff; excel." ♦ € 48.55   2014*

⊞ **PUERTO DE MAZARRON** *4G1* (2km E Rural/Coastal) *37.56777, -1.2300* **Camping Los Delfines, Ctra Isla Plana-Playa El Mojon, 30860 Puerto de Mazarrón (Murcia) [tel/fax 968-59 45 27; www.campinglosdelfines.com]** Fr N332 turn S sp La Azohía & Isla Plana. Site on L in 3km. Med, mkd pitch, hdstg, pt sl, pt shd; htd wc; chem disp; mv service pnt; serviced pitches; baby facs; private san facs avail; shwrs inc; el pnts (5A) €3; gas; lndtte; tradsmn; snacks & bar high ssn; BBQ; playgrnd; shgl beach adj; TV; 5% statics; dogs €3; quiet; poss cr; Eng spkn; phone; red long stay; CKE/CCI. "Gd sized pitches; popular low ssn." ♦ € 40.80   2009*

⊞ **PUERTO DE MAZARRON** *4G1* (5km SW Coastal) *37.56388, -1.30388* **Camping Playa de Mazarrón, Ctra Mazarrón-Bolnuevo, Bolnuevo, 30877 Mazarrón (Murcia) [968-15 06 60; fax 968-15 08 37; camping@playamazarron.com; www.playamazarron.com]** Take Bolnuevo rd fr Mazarrón, at rndabt go strt, site immed on L. Lge, mkd pitch, hdstg, pt shd; wc; 90% serviced pitches; chem disp; mv service pnt; shwrs inc; el pnts (5A) €4; gas; lndtte; shop, rest (high ssn); snacks, bar; playgrnd; sand beach adj; tennis; games area; internet; TV; dogs free; bus; phone; poss v cr; adv bkg; red long stay/low ssn; ccard acc. "Some lge pitches but tight turning for lge o'fits; friendly staff; metal-framed sunshades in ssn on most pitches but low for m'vans; poss poor daytime security; gd for wheelchair users; popular & v cr in winter - many long stay visitors." ♦ € 36.85   2011*

⊞ **PUERTO DE SANTA MARIA, EL** *2H3* (2km SW Coastal) *36.58768, -6.24092* **Camping Playa Las Dunas de San Antón, Paseo Maritimo La Puntilla s/n, 11500 El Puerto de Santa María (Cádiz) [956-87 22 10; fax 956-86 01 17; info@lasdunascamping.com; www.lasdunascamping.com]** Fr N or S exit A4 at El Puerto de Sta María. Foll site sp carefully to avoid narr rds of town cent. Site 2-3km S of marina & leisure complex of Puerto Sherry. Alternatively, fr A4 take Rota rd & look for sp to site & Hotel Playa Las Dunas. Site better sp fr this dir & avoids town. Lge, pt sl, pt shd; wc; chem disp; mv service pnt; shwrs inc; el pnts (5-10A) €3.10-5.89; gas; lndtte; shop (high ssn); tradsmn; snacks; bar; playgrnd; pool adj; sand beach 50m; sports facs; wifi; internet; 30% statics; phone; guarded; poss cr; adv bkg rec; poss noisy disco w/end; red facs low ssn; ccard acc; CKE/CCI. "Friendly staff; conv Cádiz & Jerez sherry region, birdwatching areas & beaches; conv ferry or catamaran to Cádiz; facs poss stretched high ssn; there is hot water in bthrms and washing up area but only the basins on one side of each rm; pitches quiet away fr rd; take care caterpillars in spring - poss dangerous to dogs; dusty site but staff water rds." ♦ € 10.32   2013*

PUIGCERDA *3B3* (2km NE Rural) *42.44156, 1.94174* **Camping Stel, Ctra de Llívia s/n, 17520 Puigcerdà (Gerona) [972-88 23 61; fax 972-14 04 19; puigcerda@stel.es; www.stel.es]** Fr France head for Bourg-Madame on N820 (N20) or N116. Cross border dir Llívia on N154, site is 1km after rndabt on L. Lge, mkd pitch, terr, pt shd; htd wc; chem disp; mv service pnt; baby facs; shwrs; el pnts (7A) €4.50; lndtte (inc dryer); shop; rest, snacks; bar; BBQ; playgrnd; htd pool; paddling pool; canoeing; watersports; archery; cycle hire; games area; golf 4km; wifi; entmnt; TV rm; 10% statics; dogs; site open w/ends only in winter; Eng spkn; adv bkg; some rd noise; ccard acc. "Pitches on upper terr quieter; superb scenery; sep area for campers with pets; gd walking, cycling." ♦ 3 Jun-11 Sep. € 36.40 (CChq acc)   2011*

PUYARRUEGO see Ainsa *3B2*

QUEVEDA see Santillana del Mar *1A4*

RIANO 1A3 (7km E Rural) 42.97361, -4.92000 **Camping Alto Esla, Ctra León-Santander, 24911 Boca de Huérgano (León) [987-74 01 39; camping@altoesla.eu; www. altoesla.eu]** SW on N621 fr Potes just past junc with LE241 at Boca de Huérgano. Site on L. (See Picos de Europa in Mountain Passes & Tunnels in the section Planning & Travelling at front of guide). Sm, pt sl, pt shd; wc; chem disp; mv service pnt; el pnts (5A) €2.68 (poss rev pol); lndtte; shops 500m; bus 300m; bar; phone; quiet; ccard acc; CKE/CCI. "Lovely setting; superb views; attractive site; ltd el pnts; excel san facs." ♦ 26 Jun-8 Sep. € 17.76   2011*

⊞ **RIAZA** 1C4 (1.5km W Rural) 41.26995, -3.49750 **Camping Riaza, Ctra de la Estación s/n, 40500 Riaza (Segovia) [tel/fax 921-55 05 80; info@camping-riaza.com; www. camping-riaza.com]** Fr N exit A1/E5 junc 104, fr S exit 103 onto N110 N. In 12km turn R at rndabt on ent to town, site on L. Lge, hdg pitch, unshd; htd wc; chem disp; mv service pnt; baby facs; shwrs inc; el pnts (15A) €4.70; lndtte (inc dryer); shop; rest, snacks; bar; BBQ; playgrnd; pool; paddling pool; games area; games rm; internet; some statics; dogs free; phone; bus 900m; Eng spkn; adv bkg; quiet. "Vg site; various pitch sizes - some lge; excel san facs; easy access to/fr Santander or Bilbao; beautiful little town." ♦ € 40.30 2014*

RIBADEO 1A2 (4km E Coastal) 43.55097, -6.99699 **Camping Playa Peñarronda, Playa de Peñarronda-Barres, 33794 Castropol (Asturias) [tel/fax 985-62 30 22; campingpenarrondacb@hotmail.com; www. campingplayapenarronda.com]** Exit A8 at km 498 onto N640 dir Lugo/Barres; turn R approx 500m and then foll site sp for 2km. Med, mkd pitch, pt shd; wc; chem disp; mv service pnt; shwrs inc; el pnts (6A) €4 (poss rev pol); gas; lndtte; shop; rest, snacks; bar; BBQ; playgrnd; sand beach adj; games area; cycle hire; some statics; phone; Eng spkn; quiet; red long stay; CKE/CCI. "Beautifully-kept, delightful, clean, friendly, family-run site on 'Blue Flag' beach; rec arr early to get pitch; facs clean; gd cycling along coastal paths to & to Ribadeo; ltd facs low ssn, sm pitches; gd sized pitches, little shd." Holy Week-25 Sep. € 23.60   2012*

RIBADEO 1A2 (3km W Rural) 43.53722, -7.08472 **Camping Ribadeo, Ctra Ribadeo-La Coruña, Km 2, 27700 Ribadeo (Lugo) [982-13 11 68; fax 982-13 11 67; www. campingribadeo.com]** W fr Ribadeo on N634/E70 twd La Coruña, in 2km pass sp Camping Ribadeo. Ignore 1st camping sp, take next L in 1.4km. Lge, mkd pitch, pt shd; wc; chem disp; mv service pnt; shwrs inc; el pnts (3A) €3.20 (rev pol); gas 4km; lndtte; shop; tradsmn; rest, snacks; bar; BBQ; playgrnd; pool; sand beach 2km; no dogs; bus 500m; quiet; red for 10+ days; CKE/CCI. "Gd NH; friendly, family owners; gd san facs, request hot water for shwrs; everything immac; highly rec; many interesting local features." Holy Week & 1 Jun-30 Sep. € 19.00   2010*

RIBADESELLA 1A3 (4km W Rural) 43.46258, -5.08725 **Camping Ribadesella, Sebreño s/n, 33560 Ribadesella (Asturias) [tel/fax 985 858293 / 985 857721; info@ camping-ribadesella.com; www.camping-ribadesella.com]** W fr Ribadesella take N632. After 2km fork L up hill. Site on L after 2km. Poss diff for lge o'fits & alt rte fr Ribadesella vill to site to avoid steep uphill turn can be used. Lge, mkd pitch, pt sl, pt terr, pt shd; wc; chem disp; baby facs; shwrs inc; el pnts (5A) €4.80; gas; lndtte; shop, rest, snacks, bar; BBQ; playgrnd; htd, covrd pool; sand beach 4km; tennis; games area; games rm; dog €2.50; poss cr; adv bkg; quiet; ccard acc; red low ssn/ long stay;CKE/CCI. "Clean san facs; some sm pitches; attractive fishing vill; prehistoric cave paintings nrby." ♦ Easter-26 Sep. € 28.20   2013*

⊞ **RIBADESELLA** 1A3 (8km W Coastal/Rural) 43.47472, -5.13416 **Camping Playa de Vega, Vega, 33345 Ribadesella (Asturias) [985-86 04 06; fax 985-85 76 62; campingplayadevega@hotmail.com; www. campingplayadevega.com]** Fr A8 exit junc 333 sp Ribadesella W, thro Bones. At rndabt cont W dir Caravia, turn R opp quarry sp Playa de Vega. Fr cent of Ribadesella (poss congestion) W on N632. Cont for 5km past turning to autovia. Turn R at sp Vega & site. Med, hdg pitch, pt terr, pt shd; wc; chem disp; serviced pitch; shwrs inc; el pnts €3.50; lndtte; shop; beach rest, snacks; bar; BBQ; sand beach 400m; TV; dogs; bus 700m; phone; quiet; ccard acc; CKE/CCI. "Sh walk to vg beach thro orchards; sm pitches not suitable lge o'fits; poss overgrown low ssn; Immac san facs; a gem of a site." € 21.00 2012*

⊞ **RIBEIRA** 1B2 (7km N Rural) 42.62100, -8.98600 **Camping Ría de Arosa II, Oleiros, 15993 Santa Eugenia (Uxía) de Ribeira (La Coruña) [981- 86 59 11; fax 981-86 55 55; info@camping.riadearosa.com; www.campingriadearosa. com]** Exit AP9 junc 93 Padrón & take N550 then AC305/ VG11 to Ribeira. Then take AC550 to Oleiros to site, well sp. V lge, hdg/mkd pitch, shd; htd wc; chem disp; mv service pnt; baby facs; shwrs inc; el pnts (6A) inc; gas; lndtte; supmkt; rest, snacks; bar; BBQ; playgrnd; pool; sand beach 7km; fishing; tennis; games area; games rm; wifi; TV; some statics; dogs €2.50; phone; Eng spkn; adv bkg; quiet; ccard acc; red low ssn;CKE/CCI. "Beautiful area; helpful, friendly staff; excel." ♦ € 38.00   2013*

RIBEIRA 1B2 (8km NE Coastal) 42.58852, -8.92465 **Camping Ría de Arosa I, Playa de Cabío s/n, 15940 Puebla (Pobra) do Caramiñal (La Coruña) [981-83 22 22; fax 981-83 32 93; playa@campingriadearosa.com; www. campingriadearosa.com]** Exit AP9/E1 junc 93 or N550 at Padrón onto VG11 along N side of Ría de Arosa into Puebla do Caramiñal. Site is 1.5km S of Pobra, sp fr town. Lge, pt shd; wc; chem disp; mv service pnt; shwrs; el pnts (6A) €4.60; gas; lndtte; shop; rest, snacks; bar; playgrnd; sand beach adj; watersports; cycle hire; internet; TV; some statics; dogs €2.50; phone; poss cr; adv bkg; quiet; ccard acc. 13 Mar-15 Oct. € 24.00   2010*

RIBERA DE CARDOS see Llavorsí 3B2

SPAIN

⊞ **RIBES DE FRESER** *3B3* (500m NE Rural) *42.31260, 2.17570* **Camping Vall de Ribes, Ctra de Pardines, Km 0.5, 17534 Ribes de Freser (Girona) [972-72 88 20 / 620-78 39 20; fax 972 93 12 96; info@campingvallderibes.com; www. campingvallderibes.com]** N fr Ripoll on N152; turn E at Ribes de Freser; site beyond town dir Pardines. Site nr town but 1km by rd. App rd narr. Med, mkd pitch, terr, pt shd; htd wc; chem disp; shwrs inc; el pnts (6A) €4.30; lndry rm; shop 500m; rest; bar; playgrnd; pool; 50% statics; dog €4.60; train 500m; quiet;CKE/CCI. "Gd, basic site; steep footpath fr site to town; 10-20 min walk to stn; cog rlwy train to Núria a 'must' - spectacular gorge, gd walking & interesting exhibitions; sm/ med o'fits only; poss unkempt statics low ssn; spectacular walk down fr the Vall de Nuria to Queralbs." € 22.85   2013*

RIOPAR *4F1* (7.6km E Rural) *38.48960, -2.34588* **Campsite Rio Mundo, Ctra Comarcal 412, km 205, 02449 Mesones (Albacete) [967-43 32 30; fax 967-43 32 87; riomundo@ campingriomundo.com; www.campingriomundo.com]** On N322 Albacete-Bailén, turn off at Reolid dir Riópar. Camp site 7km past Riópar on side rd on L (km-marker 205) (Mesones). Med, mkd pitch, hdstg; shd; wc; chem disp; mv service pnt; shwrs inc; lndry rm; gas; shop; rest, snacks; bar; BBQ; playgrnd; pool; cycle hire; fishing; games area; wifi; dogs €3.40; Eng spkn; adv bkg; quiet; ccard acc; red low ssn;CKE/CCI; "Well run site in mountainous nature reserve by Rv Mundo; gd dogs walks; spotless san facs." ♦ ltd 20 Mar-13 Oct. € 35.55   2011*

⊞ **RIPOLL** *3B3* (2km N Rural) *42.21995, 2.17505* **Camping Ripollés, Ctra Barcelona/Puigcerdà, Km 109.3, 17500 Ripoll (Gerona) [972-70 37 70; fax 972-70 35 54]** At km 109.3 up hill N fr town; well sp. Steep access rd. Med, mkd pitch, pt sl, pt shd; htd wc; chem disp; mv service pnt; baby facs; shwrs inc; el pnts €4; lndtte; shop 2km; rest, snacks; bar; BBQ; playgrnd; pool; tennis; 20% statics; dogs €2.80; phone; adv bkg; quiet; ccard acc;CKE/CCI. "V pleasant; gd bar/rest; not suitable med/lge o'fits." ♦ € 19.00   2011*

RIPOLL *3B3* (1km S Rural) *42.18218, 2.19552* **Camping Solana del Ter, Ctra Barcelona-Puigcerdà, C17, Km 92.5, 17500 Ripoll (Gerona) [972-70 10 62; fax 972-71 43 43; camping@solanadelter.com; www.solanadelter.com]** Site sp S of Ripoll on N152 behind hotel & rest. Med, mkd pitch, hdstg, pt shd; htd wc; chem disp; baby facs; shwrs inc; el pnts (4A) €5.90; lndtte; shop; rest, snacks; bar; playgrnd; pool high ssn only; paddling pool; tennis; TV; Eng spkn; phone; some rd & rlwy noise; ccard acc;CKE/CCI. "Historic monastery in town; scenic drives nr." Holy Week-15 Oct. € 27.30   2010*

⊞ **RIPOLL** *3B3* (6km NW Rural) *42.23522, 2.11797* **Camping Molí Serradell, 17530 Campdevànol (Gerona) [tel/fax 972-73 09 27; calrei@teleline.es]** Fr Ripoll N on N152; L onto GI401 dir Gombrèn; site on L in 4km. NB 2nd site. Sm, pt shd; htd wc; chem disp; mv service pnt; shwrs inc; el pnts €4.50; lndtte (in dryer); shop; tradsmn; rest; 75% statics; poss cr; quiet; red low ssn; CKE/CCI. € 25.40   2009*

⊞ **ROCIO, EL** *2G3* (1km N Rural) *37.14194, -6.49250* **Camping La Aldea, Ctra del Rocío, Km 25, 21750 El Rocío,Almonte (Huelva) [959-44 26 77; fax 959-44 25 82; info@campinglaaldea.com; www.campinglaaldea.com]** Fr A49 turn S at junc 48 onto A483 by-passing Almonte, site sp just bef El Rócio rndabt. Fr W (Portugal) turn off at junc 60 to A484 to Almonte, then A483. Lge, hdg/mkd pitch, hdstg, pt shd; htd wc; chem disp; mv service pnt; baby facs; shwrs inc; el pnts (10A) €6.50; gas; lndtte (inc dryer); shop; tradsmn; rest, snacks; bar; BBQ; playgrnd; htd pool high ssn; sand beach 16km; horseriding nrby; van washing facs; wifi; 30% statics; dogs €3; phone; bus 500m; poss cr; Eng spkn; adv bkg; rd/ motocross noise; red long stay/low ssn; ccard acc;CKE/CCI; "Well-appointed & maintained site; winter rallies; excel san facs; friendly, helpful staff; tight turns on site; most pitches have kerb or gully; pitches soft after rain; gd birdwatching (lagoon 1km); interesting town; avoid festival (in May-7 weeks after Easter.) when town cr & site charges higher; poss windy; excel birdwatching nrby." ♦ ltd € 42.50   2014*

RODA DE BARA *3C3* (2km E Coastal) *41.17003, 1.46427* **Campsite Stel Cat 1., Ctra N340, Km 1182, 43883 Roda de Barà (Tarragona) [977-80 20 02; fax 977-80 05 25; rodadebara@stel.es; www.stel.es]** Exit AP7 junc 31, foll sps for Tarragona on N340. Site on L immed after Arco de Barà. Lge, mkd pitch, pt shd; wc; chem disp; mv service pnt; baby facs; htd private bthrms avail; shwrs inc; el pnts (5A) inc; gas; lndtte (inc dryer); shop; rest, snacks; bar; BBQ; playgrnd; htd pool; waterslides; sand beach adj; watersports; tennis; sports & entmnt; cycle hire; games area; golf 20km; wifi; TV; 10% statics; no dogs; phone; poss cr; adv bkg; some rd/rlwy noise; red long stay/low ssn;CKE/CCI. "Some sm pitches; excel, well maintained site;1st class san facs; 2 mins walk from sandy beach; more expensive than some but worth the money." ♦ 7 Apr-25 Sep. € 57.40   2011*

⊞ **RODA DE BARA** *3C3* (3km E Coastal/Rural) *41.17034, 1.46708* **Camping Arc de Barà, N340, Km 1182, 43883 Roda de Barà (Tarragona) [977-80 09 02; camping@ campingarcdebara.com; www.campingarcdebara. com]** Exit AP7 junc 31 or 32, foll sp Arc de Barà on N340 dir Tarragona. Site on L after 5km shortly after Camping Park Playa Barà. NB When app fr N ess to use 'Cambia de Sentido' just after Arc de Barà (old arch). Lge, shd; htd wc; chem disp; baby facs; shwrs inc; el pnts (5A) €3.50; gas; lndtte (inc dryer); shop high ssn; supmkt 200m; rest, snacks; bar; BBQ; pool; paddling pool; sand beach adj; games area; 75% statics in sep area; dogs €2.80; phone; bus adj; site clsd Nov; poss cr; Eng spkn; rlwy noise; ccard acc;CKE/CCI. "Ltd number sm touring pitches; gd, clean NH en rte Alicante; phone ahead winter/low ssn to check open, minimum price in high ssn 01/07 - 31/08." ♦ € 28.00 (3 persons)   2011*

RONDA *2H3* (4km NE Rural) *36.76600, -5.11900* **Camping El Cortijo, Ctra Campillos, Km 4.5, 29400 Ronda (Málaga) [952-87 07 46; fax 952-87 30 82; elcortijo@ hermanosmacias.com; www.hermanosmacias.com]** Fr Ronda by-pass take A367 twd Campillos. Site on L after 4.5km opp new development 'Hacienda Los Pinos'. Med, mkd pitch, pt shd; wc; chem disp; mv service pnt; serviced pitches; baby facs; shwrs inc; el pnts inc; lndtte; shop; rest; bar; playgrnd; pool; tennis; games area; cycle hire; 5% statics; dogs; phone; Eng spkn; some rd noise; CKE/CCI. "Friendly, helpful owner; conv NH." ♦ 1 Apr-15 Oct. € 16.00   2011*

⊞ **RONDA** *2H3* (1km S Rural) *36.72111, -5.17166*
**Camping El Sur, Ctra Ronda-Algeciras Km 1.5, 29400
Ronda (Málaga) [952-87 59 39; fax 952-87 70 54; info@
campingelsur.com; www.campingelsur.com]** Site on W
side of A369 dir Algeciras. Do not tow thro Ronda. Med, mkd
pitch, hdstg, terr, sl, pt shd; htd wc; chem disp; mv service pnt;
baby facs; shwrs inc; el pnts (5-10A) €4.30-5.35 (poss rev pol
&/or no earth); lndtte; shop; rest adj; snacks; bar; playgrnd;
pool high ssn; wifi; dogs €1.70; phone; poss cr; Eng spkn; adv
bkg; quiet; red long stay/low ssn; CKE/CCI. "Gd rd fr coast with
spectacular views; long haul for lge o'fits; busy family-run site
in lovely setting; conv National Parks & Pileta Caves; poss diff
access some pitches due trees & high kerbs; hard, rocky grnd;
san facs poss stretched high ssn; easy walk to town; friendly
staff; vg rest; excel." ♦ € 24.40   2014*

ROQUETAS DE MAR see Almería *4G1*

ROSES *3B3* (200m SW Coastal) *42.26888, 3.1525* **Camping
Rodas, Calle Punta Falconera 62,17480 Roses (Gerona)
[972-25 76 17; fax 972-15 24 66; info@campingrodas.
com; www.campingrodas.com]** On Figueras-Roses rd, at
o'skts of Roses sp on R after supmkt. Lge, hdg/mkd pitch, pt
shd; wc; chem disp; serviced pitches; shwrs inc; el pnts (6A)
inc; gas; lndtte; shop adj; tradsmn; rest, snacks; bar; lndtte;
sm playgrnd; htd pool; paddling pool; sand beach 600m; bus
1km; poss cr; Eng spkn; adv bkg; quiet; ccard acc; CKE/CCI.
"Well-run site; site rds all tarmac; Roses gd cent for region."
1 Jun-30 Sep. € 31.50   2009*

ROSES *3B3* (1km W Urban/Coastal) *42.26638, 3.16305*
**Camping Joncar Mar, Ctra Figueres s/n, 17480 Roses
(Gerona) [tel/fax 972-25 67 02; info@campingjoncarmar.
com; www.campingjoncarmar.com]** At Figueres take C260
W for Roses. On ent Roses turn sharp R at last rndabt at end of
dual c'way. Site on both sides or rd - go to R (better) side, park
& report to recep on L. Lge, pt sl, pt shd; htd wc; chem disp;
baby facs; shwrs; el pnts (6-10A) €4.40 (poss no earth); gas;
lndtte; shop; rest; bar; playgrnd; pool; sand beach 150m; golf
15km; entmnt; games rm; internet; 15% statics; dogs €2.40;
phone; bus 500m; poss cr; Eng spkn; adv bkg; rd noise; ccard
acc; red low ssn/long stay. "Conv walk into Roses; hotels &
apartment blocks bet site & beach; poss cramped/tight pitches;
narr rds; vg value low ssn; new san facs under construction
2009." 1 Jan-31 Oct. € 27.75   2010*

ROSES *3B3* (2km W Coastal) *42.26638, 3.15611* **Camping
Salatà, Port Reig s/n, 17480 Roses (Gerona) [972-25 60 86;
fax 972-15 02 33; info@campingsalata.com; www.
campingsalata.com]** App Roses on rd C260. On ent Roses
take 1st R after Roses sp & Caprabo supmkt. Lge, mkd pitch,
hdstg, pt shd; htd wc; chem disp; baby facs; shwrs inc; el
pnts (6-10A) inc; gas; lndtte (inc dryer); shop; tradsmn; rest,
snacks; bar; playgrnd; htd pool high ssn; sand beach 200m;
wifi; 10% statics; dogs €2.80 (not acc Jul/Aug); phone; poss
cr; Eng spkn; adv bkg; red long stay/low ssn; ccard acc; CKE/
CCI. "Vg area for sub-aqua sports; vg clean facs; red facs
low ssn; pleasant walk/cycle to town." ♦ 19 Feb-13 Nov.
€ 45.00   2011*

ROTA see Puerto de Santa María, El *2H3*

RUILOBA see Comillas *1A4*

⊞ **SABINANIGO** *3B2* (6km N Rural) *42.55694, -0.33722*
**Camping Valle de Tena, Ctra N260, Km 512.6, 22600
Senegüe (Huesca). [974-48 09 77 / 974-48 03 02; correo@
campingvalledetena.com; www.campingvalledetena.
com]** Fr Jaca take N330, in 12km turn L onto N260 dir Biescas.
In 5km ignore site sp Sorripas, cont for 500m to site on L - new
ent at far end. Lge, mkd pitch, terr, unshd; htd wc; chem
disp; mv service pnt; serviced pitches; baby facs; shwrs inc; el
pnts (6A) €6; lndtte; shop; rest, snacks; bar; playgrnd; pool;
paddling pool; sports facs; hiking & rv rafting nr; entmnt;
internet; TV rm; 60% statics; dogs €2.70; phone; Eng spkn;
adv bkg; rd noise during day but quiet at night; "Helpful staff;
steep, narr site rd; sm pitches; excel, busy NH to/fr France;
beautiful area; in reach of ski runs; v busy." € 21.00   2013*

⊞ **SACEDON** *3D1* (500m E Rural) *40.48148, -2.72700*
**Camp Municipal Ecomillans, Camino Sacedón 15, 19120
Sacedón (Guadalajara) [949-35 10 18, 949 35 17 80;
fax 949-35 10 73; ecomillans63@hotmail.com; www.
campingsacedon.com]** Fr E on N320 exit km220, foll Sacedón
& site sp; site on L. Fr W exit km 222. Med, mkd pitch,
hdstg, pt sl, shd; wc (cont); shwrs; el pnts €5; lndry rm; shop
500m; lake sw 1km; quiet. "NH only in area of few sites; sm
pitches; san facs v poor; low ssn phone to check open." ♦
€ 15.55   2013*

⊞ **SAGUNTO** *4E2* (7km NE Coastal) *39.72027, -0.19166*
**Camping Malvarrosa de Corinto, Playa Malvarrosa de
Corinto, 46500 Sagunto (València) [962-60 89 06; fax 962-
60 89 43; camalva@live.com; www.malvacorinto.com]**
Exit 49 fr A7 onto N340, foll dir Almenara-Casa Blanca. Turn
E twd Port de Sagunto & Canet d'en Berenguer on CV320.
Site poorly sp. Lge, pt shd; wc; chem disp; sauna; shwrs inc;
el pnts (5-10A) €4.40; gas; lndtte; shop & 5km; rest, snacks;
bar; BBQ; playgrnd; sand & shgl beach adj; tennis; horseriding;
gym; 85% statics; dogs €2.70; phone; poss cr; Eng spkn; quiet;
red ow ssn/long stay; CKE/CCI. "Lovely site under palm trees;
friendly, helpful owners; gd facs; many feral cats & owners'
dogs on site; excel pitches adj beach; ltd touring pitches but
access to some poss diff; ltd facs & poss neglected low ssn; no
local transport." € 19.00   2010*

SALAMANCA *1C3* (4.5km NE Rural) *40.97611, -5.60472*
**Camping Don Quijote, Ctra Aldealengua, Km 1930, 37193
Cabrerizos (Salamanca) [923-20 90 52; fax 923-20 97 87;
info@campingdonquijote.com; www.campingdonquijote.
com]** Fr Madrid or fr S cross Rv Tormes by most easterly bdge
to join inner ring rd. Foll Paseo de Canalejas for 800m to Plaza
España. Turn R onto SA804 Avda de los Comuneros & strt on
for 5km. Site ent 2km after town boundary sp. Fr other dirs,
head into city & foll inner ring rd to Plaza España. Site well
sp fr rv & ring rd. Med, hdg/mkd pitch, hdstg, pt shd; wc;
chem disp; mv service pnt; baby facs; shwrs inc; el pnts (10A)
€4.50 (poss earth fault, 2010); lndtte; shop; supmkt 3km; rest,
snacks; bar; playgrnd; pool; paddling pool; beach 200m; rv
fishing; wifi; 10% statics; dogs; phone; bus; poss cr w/end; adv
bkg; quiet; red CKE/CCI; "Gd rv walks; conv city cent - easy
cycle ride; basic, clean facs; 45 mins cycle ride to town along rv;
rv Tormes flows alongside site with pleasant walks." ♦ 1 Mar-
31 Oct. € 31.00 (CChq acc)   2014*

⊞ **SALAMANCA** *1C3* (12km NE Rural) *41.05805, -5.54611* Camping Olimpia, Ctra de Gomecello, Km 3.150, 37427 Pedrosillo el Ralo (Salamanca) [923-08 08 54 or 620-46 12 07; fax 923-35 44 26; info@campingolimpia.com; www.campingolimpia.com] Exit A62 junc 225 dir Pedrosillo el Ralo & La Vellés, strt over rndabt, site sp. Sm, hdg pitch, pt shd; htd wc; chem disp; shwrs inc; el pnts €3; lndtte (inc dryer); tradsmn; rest, snacks; bar; no statics; dogs €1; phone; bus 300m; site clsed 8-16 Sep; Eng spkn; adv bkg; some rd nois; CKE/CCI. "Helpful & pleasant owner; really gd 2 course meal for €10 (2014); handy fr rd with little noise & easy to park; poss open w/ends only low ssn; excel; grass pitches." € 20.00   2014*

"That's changed – Should I let The Club know?"

If you find something on site that's different from the site entry, fill in a report and let us know. See www.caravanclub.co.uk/europereport.

⊞ **SALAMANCA** *1C3* (4km E Urban) *40.94722, -5.6150* Camping Regio, Ctra Ávila-Madrid, Km 4, 37900 Santa Marta de Tormes (Salamanca) [923-13 88 88; fax 923-13 80 44; recepcion@campingregio.com; www.campingregio.com] Fr E on SA20/N501 outer ring rd, pass hotel/camping sp visible on L & exit Sta Marta de Tormes, site directly behind Hotel Regio. Foll sp to hotel. Lge, mkd pitch, pt sl, pt shd; wc; chem disp; mv service pnt; baby facs; shwrs inc; el pnts (10A) €3.95 (no earth); gas; lndtte; shop & 1km; hypmkt 3km; rest, snacks in hotel; bar; playgrnd; hotel pool high ssn; cycle hire; wifi (at adj hotel); TV; 5% statics; dogs; phone; bus to Salamanca; car wash; poss cr; Eng spkn; quiet; ccard acc; CKE/CCI. "In low ssn stop at 24hr hotel recep; poss no hdstg in wet conditions; conv en rte Portugal; refurbished facs to excel standard; site poss untidy, & ltd security in low ssn; spacious pitches but some poss tight for lge o'fits; take care lge brick markers when reversing; hourly bus in and out of city; excel pool; vg; facs up to gd standard." ♦ € 29.30   2014*

⊞ **SALAMANCA** *1C3* (3km NW Rural) *40.99945, -5.67916* Camping Ruta de la Plata, Ctra de Villamayor, 37184 Villares de la Reina (Salamanca) [tel/fax 923-28 95 74; recepcion@campingrutadelaplata.com; www.campingrutadelaplata.com] Fr N on A62/E80 Salamanca by-pass, exit junc 238 & foll sp Villamayor. Site on R about 800m after rndabt at stadium 'Helmántico'. Avoid SA300 - speed bumps. Fr S exit junc 240. Med, some hdg/mkd pitch, terr, pt sl, pt shd; htd wc; chem disp; mv service pnt; shwrs inc; el pnts (6A) €2.90; gas; lndtte; shop & 1km; tradsmn; snacks; bar; playgrnd; pool high ssn; golf 3km; TV rm; dogs €1.50; bus to city at gate; poss cr; rd noise; red snr citizen/CKE/CCI. "Family-owned site; some gd, san facs tired (poss unhtd in winter); ltd facs low ssn; less site care low ssn & probs with el pnts; conv NH; helpful owners; bus stop at camp gate, every hr." ♦ ltd € 26.80   2014*

⊞ **SALDES** *3B3* (3km E Rural) *42.2280, 1.7594* Camping Repos del Pedraforca, Ctra B400, Km 13.5, 08697 Saldes (Barcelona) [938-25 80 44; fax 938-25 80 61; pedra@campingpedraforca.com; www.campingpedraforca.com] S fr Puigcerdà on C1411 for 35km, turn R at B400, site on L in 13.5km. Lge, mkd pitch, pt sl, shd; htd wc; chem disp; mv service pnt; baby facs; sauna; shwrs inc; el pnts (3-10A) €4.50-6.95; lndtte (inc dryer); shop; tradsmn; rest, snacks high ssn; bar; playgrnd; 2 htd pools (1 covrd); paddling pool; cycle hire; gym; wifi; entmnt; TV rm; 50% statics; dogs €2.50; phone; Eng spkn; some rd noise; adv bkg; red long stay; ccard acc; CKE/CCI. "Tow to pitches avail; vg walking; in heart of nature reserve; poss diff ent long o'fits; lger, sunnier pitches on R of site; excel." ♦ € 29.30 (CChq acc)   2010*

⊞ **SALOU** *3C2* (2km NE Coastal) *41.08840, 1.18270* Camping La Pineda de Salou, Ctra Tarragona-Salou, Km 5, 43481 La Pineda-Vilaseca (Tarragona) [977-37 30 80; fax 977-37 30 81; info@campinglapineda.com; www.campinglapineda.com] Exit A7 junc 35 dir Salou, Vilaseca & Port Aventura. Foll sp Port Aventura then La Pineda/Platjes on rd TV 3148. Med, mkd pitch, pt shd; htd wc; baby facs; chem disp; sauna; shwrs; el pnts (5A) €4.80; gas; lndtte; shop; rest, snacks; bar; playgrnd; pool & paddling pool; spa cent; beach 400m; watersports; fishing; tennis; horseriding; cycle hire; mini club; tourist info; entmnt; TV; some statics; dogs €4 (not acc mid-Jul to mid-Aug); phone; ccard acc; red low ssn. "Conv Port Aventura & Tarragona." € 45.30   2009*

SALOU *3C2* (1km S Urban/Coastal) *41.0752, 1.1176* Camping Sanguí, Paseo Miramar-Plaza Venus, 43840 Salou (Tarragona) [977-38 16 41; fax 977-38 46 16; mail@sanguli.es; www.sanguli.es] Exit AP7/E15 junc 35. At 1st rndbt take dir to Salou (Plaça Europa), at 2nd rndabt foll site sp. V lge, mkd pitch, hdstg, pt sl, shd; htd wc; chem disp; mv service pnt; some serviced pitches; baby facs; shwrs inc; el pnts (10A) inc; gas; lndtte; shop; 2 supmkts; rest, snacks; bar; BBQ; playgrnd; 3 pools & 3 paddling pools; waterslide; jacuzzi; sand beach 50m; games area; tennis; games rm; fitness rm; entmnt; excursions; cinema; youth club; mini-club; amphitheatre; wifi; TV; dogs; 35% statics; phone; bus; car wash; Eng spkn; adv bkg rec Jul-Aug; some rlwy noise; red low ssn/long stay/snr citizens; ccard acc; CKE/CCI. "Quiet end of Salou nr Cambrils & 3km Port Aventura; site facs recently updated/upgraded; excel, well-maintained site." ♦ 4 Apr-2 Nov. € 78.00   2014*

See advertisement

SAN FULGENCIO *4F2* (7km ENE Coastal) *38.12094, -0.65982* Camper Park San Fulgencio, Calle Mar Cantábrico 7 Centro Comercial las Dunas (Alicante) [966-72 53 17 / 679-62 26 93; infosol@camperparksanfulgencio.com; www.camperparksanfulgencio.com] Fr N on AP7, take exit 740 twd Guardamar; At rndabt exit onto CV-91. 2nd exit at next rndabt then 3rd exit at another rndabt and stay on CV91. Take 1st exit at rndabt onto N-332, merge onto N332 and go thro 1 rndabt. At next rndabt take 3rd exit onto Calle Mar Cantabrico, go thro next rndabt and site is on the L. Sm, unshaded, hdstg; wc; chem disp; mv service pnt; shwrs; el pnts (5A) inc; lndtte; 1.75km to wooden area & sea; wifi; bus to Alicante 150m; Eng spkn; "Sm m'van only site; gd facs; friendly helpful owner; gd atmosphere; Sat mkt; vg." € 14.00   2013*

SAN MIGUEL DE SALINAS see Torrevieja *4F2*

CAMPING RESORT
Sangulí Salou
★★★★★

KT-000090

Passeig Miramar - Plaça Venus · 43840 SALOU :: TEL. 0034 977 38 16 41

SPAIN

⊞ **SAN SEBASTIAN/DONOSTIA** *3A1* (5km NW Rural) *43.30458, -2.04588* **Camping Igueldo, Paseo Padre Orkolaga 69, 20008 San Sebastián (Guipúzcoa) [943-21 45 02; fax 943-28 04 11; info@campingigueldo.com; www.campingigueldo.com]** Fr W on A8, leave m'way at junc 9 twd city cent, take 1st R & R at rndabt onto Avda de Tolosa sp Ondarreta. At sea front turn hard L at rndabt sp to site (Avda Satrústegui) & foll sp up steep hill 4km to site. Fr E exit junc 8 then as above. Site sp as Garoa Camping Bungalows. Steep app poss diff for lge o'fits. Lge, hdg/mkd pitch, terr, pt shd, 40% serviced pitches; wc; chem disp; baby facs; shwrs inc; el pnts (10A) inc; gas; lndtte; shop; rest, bar high ssn; playgrnd; pool 5km; sand beach 5km; TV; phone; bus to city adj; poss cr/noisy; Eng spkn; red long stay/low ssn; CKE/CCI. "Gd, clean facs; sm pitches poss diff; spectacular views; pitches muddy when wet; excel rest 1km (open in winter)." ♦ € 33.50   2012*

SAN TIRSO DE ABRES *1A2* (450m N Rural) *43.41352, -7.14141* **Amaido, El Llano, 33774 San Tirso de Abres [985-47 63 94; fax 985-47 63 94; amaido@amaido.com; www.amaido.com]** Head N on A6 twds Lugo & exit 497 for N-640 twds Oviedo/Lugo Centro cidade. At rndabt take 4th exit onto N-640, turn R at LU-P-6104, turn R onto Vegas, then take 2nd L. Site at end of rd. Med, hdg pitch, terr, pt shd, wc; chem disp; mv service pnt; baby facs; fam bthrm; shwrs; el pnts (6A); lndtte; shop; bbq; playgrnd; games area; bike hire; wifi; tv rm; dogs; twin axles; adv bkg; red low ssn. "Lovely wooded site set in a circle around facs; farm animals; vg site." ♦ ltd 10 Apr-15 Sep. € 27.75   2014*

SAN VICENTE DE LA BARQUERA *1A4* (1km E Coastal) *43.38901, -4.3853* **Camping El Rosal, Ctra de la Playa s/n, 39540 San Vicente de la Barquera (Cantabria) [942-71 01 65; fax 942-71 00 11; info@campingelrosal.com; www.campingelrosal.com]** Fr A8 km 264, foll sp San Vicente. Turn R over bdge then 1st L (site sp) immed at end of bdge; keep L & foll sp to site. Barier height 3.1mtrs. Med, mkd pitch, pt sl, terr, pt shd; wc; chem disp; shwrs; el pnts (6A) €4.80; gas; lndtte; shop; rest, snacks; bar; sand beach adj; wifi; phone; poss cr; Eng spkn; adv bkg; quiet; ccard acc; red low ssn/long stay; CKE/CCI. "Lovely site in pine wood o'looking bay; surfing beach; some modern, clean facs; helpful staff; vg rest; easy walk or cycle ride to interesting town; Sat mkt; no hot water at sinks." ♦ 1 Apr-30 Sep. € 27.00   2014*

SAN VICENTE DE LA BARQUERA *1A4* (5km E Coastal) *43.38529, -4.33831* **Camping Playa de Oyambre, Finca Peña Gerra, 39540 San Vicente de la Barquera (Cantabria) [942-71 14 61; fax 942-71 15 30; camping@oyambre.com; www.oyambre.com]** E70/A8 Santander-Oviedo, exit sp 264 S. Vicente de la Barquera, then N634 for 3 km to Comillas exit on the Ctra La Revilla-Comillas (CA 131) between km posts 27 and 28. Lge, mkd pitch, terr, pt sl, pt shd; wc; chem disp; mv service pnt; shwrs inc; el pnts (10A) €4.55; gas; lndtte; shop & 5km; tradsmn; rest, snacks; bar; pool; beach 800m; playgrnd, wifi; 40% statics; bus 200m; Eng spkn; adv bkg; ccard acc; CKE/CCI. "V well-kept site; clean, helpful owner; quiet week days low ssn; gd base for N coast & Picos de Europa; 4x4 avail to tow to pitch if wet; some sm pitches & rd noise some pitches; conv Santander ferry; immac san facs." 1 Mar - 28 Sep. € 37.50   2014*

SANT ANTONI DE CALONGE see Palamós *3B3*

"I like to fill in the reports as I travel from site to site"

You'll find report forms at the back of this guide, or you can fill them in online at www.caravaclub.co.uk/europereport.

SANT FELIU DE GUIXOLS *3B3* (1km N Urban/Coastal) *41.78611, 3.04111* **Camping Sant Pol, Ctra Dr Fleming 1, 17220 Sant Feliu de Guixols (Gerona) [972-32 72 69 or 972-20 86 67; fax 972-32 72 11 or 972-22 24 09; info@campingsantpol.cat; www.campingsantpol.cat]** Exit AP7 junc 7 onto C31 dir Sant Feliu. At km 312 take dir S'Agaro; at rndabt foll sp to site. Med, hdg/mkd pitch, terr, shd; htd wc; chem disp; mv service pnt; some serviced pitches; baby facs; shwrs inc; el pnts (10A) €4; lndtte; shop; rest; bar; BBQ; playgrnd; 3 htd pools; sand beach 350m; games rm; cycle hire; wifi; 30% statics; dogs €2; sep car park; Eng spkn; adv bkg; quiet - some rd noise; ccard acc; red long stay/snr citizens/CKE/CCI. "Vg, well-run site; excel facs; lovely pool; cycle track to Gerona." ♦ 26 Mar-12 Dec. € 53.00   2009*

See advertisement

SANT JOAN DE LES ABADESSES see Sant Pau de Segúries *3B3*

SPAIN

⊞ **SANT JORDI** *3D2* (1.5km S Rural) **Camping Maestrat Park, 12320 Sant Jordi (Castellón) [964-86 08 89 or 679-29 87 95 (mob); info@maestratpark.es; www. maestratpark.es]** Exit AP7 junc 42 onto CV11 to Sant Rafel del Riu. At rndabt with fuel stn take CV11 to Traiguera; then at rndabt take 1st exit onto N232 dir Vinarós & at next rndabt take 2nd exit sp Calig. Site 2km on L. Med, hdg/mkd pitch, hdstg, pt sl, pt shd; wc; chem disp; mv service pnt; baby facs; shwrs inc; el pnts (10A) €4.50; lndtte (inc dryer); shop; snacks; bar; BBQ; playgrnd; pool; paddling pool; beach 10km; games rm; cycle hire; internet; wifi; TV; 25% statics; dogs; phone; twin axles; Eng spkn; adv bkg; quiet; red long stay/low ssn; CKE/CCI. "Excel; club memb owner; excel for v lge o'fits." ♦ € 20.00   2014*

SANT LLORENC DE LA MUGA see Figueres *3B3*

⊞ **SANT PAU DE SEGURIES** *3B3* (500m S Rural) *42.26292, 2.36913* **Camping Els Roures, Avda del Mariner 34, 17864 Sant Pau de Segúries (Gerona) [972-74 70 00; fax 972-74 71 09; info@elsroures.com; www.elsroures.com]** On C38/C26 Campródon S twd Ripoll for 6km. In Sant Pau turn L 50m after traff lts. Site on R after 400m. Lge, mkd pitch, terr, shd; wc; mv service pnt; baby facs; shwrs inc; el pnts (4-8A) €3.20-6.50; gas; lndtte; shop; rest; bar; playgrnd; 2 pools; tennis; cinema; games rm; gym; internet; 80% statics; dogs €3.50; phone; bus 200m; poss cr; some noise; CKE/CCI. "Gd." ♦ € 26.00   2011*

⊞ **SANT PAU DE SEGURIES** *3B3* (4km SW Rural) *42.25549, 2.35081* **Camping Abadesses, Ctra Camprodón, Km 14.6, 17860 Sant Joan de les Abadesses (Gerona) [630-14 36 06; fax 972-70 20 69; info@campingabadesses.com; www. campingabadesses.com]** Fr Ripoll take C26 in dir Sant Joan, site approx 4km on R after vill. Steep access. Sm, mkd pitch, terr, unshd; htd wc; baby facs; shwrs; el pnts (6A) €2.88; gas; lndtte; shop; snacks; bar; playgrnd; pool; games area; wifi; 70% statics; dogs €3.21; bus 150m; quiet; ccard acc. "Vg facs; gd views fr most pitches; steep access to recep; poss diff access around terraces." ♦ € 22.00   2011*

SANT PERE PESCADOR *3B3* (200m E Rural) *42.18747, 3.08891* **Camping Riu, Ctra de la Playa s/n, 17470 Sant Pere Pescador (Gerona) [972-52 02 16; fax 972-55 04 69; info@campingriu.com; www.campingriu.com]** Fr N exit AP7 junc 4 dir L'Escala & foll sp Sant Pere Pescador, then turn L twds coast, site on L. Fr S exit AP7 junc 5 dir L'Escala, then as above & turn R to beaches & site. Lge, mkd pitch, shd; wc; chem disp; baby facs; shwrs inc; el pnts (5A) €3.90; gas; lndtte; shop & 300m; rest, snacks; bar; BBQ; playgrnd; pool; sand beach 2km; rv fishing adj; kayak hire; games area; entmnt; internet; 5% statics; dogs €3.40; Eng spkn; adv bkg; quiet; ccard acc; red long stay; CKE/CCI. "Excel boating facs & fishing on site; gd situation; site rec." ♦ 4 Apr-19 Sep. € 38.00   2009*

SPAIN

SANT PERE PESCADOR *3B3* (1km E Coastal) *42.18908, 3.1080* **Camping La Gaviota, Ctra de la Playa s/n, 17470 Sant Pere Pescador (Gerona) [972-52 05 69; fax 972-55 03 48; info@lagaviota.com; www.lagaviota.com]** Exit 5 fr A7 dir Sant Martí d'Empúries, site at end of beach rd. Med, hdg/mkd pitch, pt shd; wc; chem disp; baby facs; shwrs inc; el pnts (5A) €3.70; gas; lndtte; shop; rest; bar; playgrnd; direct access sand beach 50m; games rm; internet; 20% statics; phone; dogs €4; poss cr; Eng spkn; adv bkg; quiet; ccard acc; red long stay; CKE/CCI. "V friendly owners; gd, clean site; excel facs & constant hot water; some sm pitches & narr site rds; poss ltd access for lge o'fits; take care o'hanging trees; poss mosquito problem." ♦ 19 Mar-24 Oct. € 38.00   2009*

"We must tell The Club about that great site we found"

Get your site reports in by mid-August and we'll do our best to get your updates into the next edition.

SANT PERE PESCADOR *3B3* (1km SE Coastal) *42.18180, 3.10403* **Camping L'Àmfora, Avda Josep Tarradellas 2, 17470 Sant Pere Pescador (Gerona) [972-52 05 40; fax 972-52 05 39; info@campingamfora.com; www.campingamfora.com]** Fr N exit junc 3 fr AP7 onto N11 fro Figueres/Roses. At junc with C260 foll sp Castelló d'Empúries & Roses. At Castelló turn R at rndabt sp Sant Pere Pescador then foll sp to L'Àmfora. Fr S exit junc 5 fr AP7 onto GI 623/GI 624 to Sant Pere Pescador. V lge, hdg/mkd pitch, pt shd; htd wc; chem disp; mv service pnt; serviced pitches; baby facs; private san facs avail; shwrs inc; el pnts (10A) inc; gas; lndtte (inc dryer); ice; supmkt; rest, snacks; bar; BBQ (charcoal/elec); playgrnd; 4 pools; waterslide; paddling pool; sand beach adj; windsurf school; fishing; tennis; horseriding 5km; cycle hire; entmnt; wifi; games/TV rm; 15% statics; dogs €4.95; no c'vans/m'vans over 10m Apr-Sep; phone; adv bkg; Eng spkn; quiet; ccard not acc; red long stay/low ssn/snr citizens/CKE/CCI. "Excel, well-run, clean site; helpful staff; immac san facs; gd rest; poss flooding on some pitches when wet; Parque Acuatico 18km." ♦ 14 Apr-27 Sep. € 60.40 (CChq acc) SBS - E22   2014*

See advert on previous page

SANT PERE PESCADOR *3B3* (2km SE Coastal) *42.16194, 3.10888* **Camping Las Dunas, 17470 Sant Pere Pescador (Gerona) (Postal Address: Aptdo Correos 23, 17130 L'Escala) [972-52 17 17 or 01205 366856 (UK); fax 972-55 00 46; campinglasdunas.com; www.campinglasdunas.com]** Exit AP7 junc 5 dir Viladamat & L'Escala; 2km bef L'Escala turn L for Sant Martí d'Empúries, turn L bef ent vill for 2km, camp sp. V lge, mkd pitch, pt sl, pt shd; wc; chem disp; mv service pnt; baby facs; serviced pitches; shwrs inc; el pnts (6A) inc; gas; lndtte (inc dryer); kiosk; supmkt; souvenir shop; rest, snacks; bar; BBQ; playgrnd; pool; paddling pool; sand beach adj; watersports; tennis; games area; games rm; money exchange; cash machines; doctor; wifi; entmnt; TV; 5% statics; dogs €4.50; phone; quiet; adv bkg (ess high ssn); Eng spkn; red low ssn; CKE/CCI. "Greco-Roman ruins in Empúries; gd sized pitches - extra for serviced; busy, popular site; excel, clean facs; vg site." ♦ 17 May-19 Sep. € 56.50   2014*

See advert on the inside back cover

SANT PERE PESCADOR *3B3* (3km SE Coastal) *42.17701, 3.10833* **Camping Aquarius, Camí Sant Martí d'Empúries, 17470 Sant Pere Pescador (Gerona) [972-52 00 03; fax 972-55 02 16; camping@aquarius.es; www.aquarius.es]** Fr AP7 m'way exit 3 on N11, foll sp to Figueres. Join C260, after 7km at rndabt at Castello d'Empúries turn R to Sant Pere Pescador. Cross rv bdge in vill, L at 1st rndabt & foll camp sp. Turn R at next rndabt, then 2nd L to site. Lge, pt shd; wc; chem disp; mv service pnt; serviced pitches; baby facs; fam bthrm; shwrs; el pnts (6-15A) €4.-8.; gas; lndtte; supmkt; rest, snacks; bar; 2 playgrnds; sand beach adj; nursery in ssn; games rm; games area; car wash; internet; some statics; dogs €4.10; phone; cash point; poss cr; Eng spkn; adv bkg (ess Jul/Aug); quiet; ccard not acc; red low ssn/long stay/snr citizens (except Jul/Aug)/CKE/CCI; "Immac, well-run site; helpful staff; vg rest; windsurfing; vast beach; recycling facs; Excel site, highly rec, gd value ACSI site; wind gets v high." ♦ ltd 15 Mar-2 Nov. € 56.70   2013*

See advertisement

The Club takes you further – for less!

SPAIN

SANT PERE PESCADOR *3B3* (1.3km S Coastal) *42.18816, 3.10265* **Camping Las Palmeras, Ctra de la Platja 9, 17470 Sant Pere Pescador (Gerona)** [972-52 05 06; fax 972-55 02 85; info@campinglaspalmeras.com; www.campinglaspalmeras.com] Exit AP7 junc 3 or 4 at Figueras onto C260 dir Roses/Cadaqués rd. After 8km at Castelló d'Empúries turn S for Sant Pere Pescador & cont twd beach. Site on R of rd. Lge, mkd pitch, shd; wc; chem disp; mv service pnt; some serviced pitches; baby facs; shwrs inc; el pnts (5-16A) €3.90; gas; lndtte (inc dryer); shop; rest, snacks; bar; playgrnd; htd pool; paddling pool; sand beach 200m; tennis; cycle hire; games area; games rm; wifi; entmnt; TV; dogs €4.50; phone; cash point; poss cr; Eng spkn; adv bkg; quiet; red low ssn/CKE/CCI. "Pleasant site; helpful, friendly staff; superb, clean san facs; gd cycle tracks; nature reserve nrby; excel." ♦ 15 Apr-5 Nov. € 47.70   2010*

See advertisement

"I need an on-site restaurant"

We do our best to make sure site information is correct, but it is always best to check any must-have facilities are still available or will be open during your visit.

SANT PERE PESCADOR *3B3* (4km S Rural/Coastal) *42.15222, 3.11166* **Camping La Ballena Alegre, Ctra Sant Martí d'Empúries, 17470 Sant Pere Pescador (Gerona)** [902-51 05 20; fax 902 51 05 21; info2@ballena-alegre.com; www.ballena-alegre.com] Fr A7 exit 5, dir L'Escala to rd GI 623, km 18.5. At 1st rndabt turn L dir Sant Martí d'Empúries, site on R in 1km. V lge, mkd pitch, hdstg, terr, unshd; htd wc; chem disp; mv service pnt; some serviced pitches; baby facs; shwrs inc; el pnts (10A) inc; gas; lndtte (inc dryer); supmkt; tradsmn; rest, snacks; bar; BBQ; playgrnd; 3 pools; sand beach adj; watersports; tennis; games area; games rm; fitness rm; cycle hire; money exchange; surf shop; doctor; wifi; entmnt; TV rm; 10% statics; dogs €4.75; poss cr; Eng spkn; adv bkg; quiet; ccard not acc; red low ssn/snr citizens/long stay; CKE/CCI. "Excel site; superb facs." ♦ 14 May-26 Sep. € 56.00   2010*

"Satellite navigation makes touring much easier"

Remember most sat navs don't know if you're towing or in a larger vehicle – always use yours alongside maps and site directions.

⊞ **SANT QUIRZE SAFAJA** *3C3* (2km E Rural) *41.72297, 2.16888* **Camping L'Illa, Ctra Sant Feliu de Codina-Centelles, Km 3.9, 08189 Sant Quirze Safaja (Barcelona)** [938-66 25 26; fax 935-72 96 21; info@campinglilla.com; www.campinglilla.com] N fr Sabadell on C1413 to Caldes de Montbui; then twds Moià on C59. Turn R at vill sp, cont thro vill to T-junc, site ent opp junc. Lge, mkd pitch, hdstg, terr, pt shd; htd wc; chem disp; shwrs inc; el pnts (6A) €5.50; gas; lndtte; rest, snacks; bar; sm shop; tradsmn; playgrnd; pool; paddling pool; games area; games rm; TV; 50% statics; dogs €5; phone; bus 100m; site clsd mid-Dec to mid-Jan; Eng spkn; adv bkg; CKE/CCI. "Easy drive to Barcelona; poss open w/end only low ssn." € 28.00   2010*

⊞ **SANTA CILIA DE JACA** *3B2* (3km W Rural) *42.55556, -0.75616* **Camping Los Pirineos, Ctra Pamplona N240, Km 300.5, 22791 Santa Cilia de Jaca (Huesca)** [tel/fax 974-37 73 51; info@campingpirineos.es; www.campingpirineos.es] Fr Jaca on N240 twd Pamplona. Site on R after Santa Cilia de Jaca, clearly sp. Lge, hdg/mkd pitch, hdstg, terr, shd; wc; chem disp; mv service pnt; baby facs; shwrs inc; el pnts (5A) €6 (check for earth); gas; lndtte; shop; rest, snacks; bar; playgrnd; pool in ssn; paddling pool; tennis; games area; 30% statics; dogs; phone; site clsd Nov & open w/ends only low ssn; Eng spkn; adv bkg; some rd noise; ccard acc; red low ssn; CKE/CCI. "Excel site in lovely area; ltd access for tourers & some pitches diff lge o'fits; gd bar/rest on site; on Caminho de Santiago pilgrim rte; conv NH." ♦ € 26.00   2009*

SANTA CRISTINA DE ARO see Playa de Aro *3B3*

SANTA CRUZ see Coruña, La *1A2*

⊞ **SANTA ELENA** *2F4* (350m E Rural) *38.34305, -3.53611*
Camping Despeñaperros, Calle Infanta Elena s/n, Junto a
Autovia de Andulucia, Km 257, 23213 Santa Elena (Jaén)
[tel/fax 953-66 41 92; info@campingdespenaperros.com;
www.campingdespenaperros.com] Leave A4/E5 at junc
257 or 259, site well sp to N side of vill nr municipal leisure
complex. Med, mkd pitch, hdstg, pt shd; wc; chem disp; mv
service pnt; all serviced pitches; shwrs inc; el pnts (10A) €4.25
(poss rev pol); gas; lndtte; sm shop; tradsmn; rest high ssn;
snacks; bar; playgrnd; pool; internet; wifi; TV & tel points all
pitches; dogs free; many statics; phone; bus 500m; adv bkg;
poss noisy w/end high ssn; ccard acc; red long stay/CKE/CCI.
"Gd winter NH in wooded location; gd size pitches but muddy
if wet; gd walking area, perfect for dogs; friendly, helpful staff;
clean san facs; disabled facs wc only; conv national park &
m'way; gd rest; sh walk to vill & shops; site v rural; beautiful
area." ♦ ltd € 32.00   2014*

SANTA MARINA DE VALDEON *1A3* (500m N Rural)
43.13638, -4.89472 Camping El Cares, El Cardo, 24915
Santa Marina de Valdeón (León) [tel/fax 987-74 26 76;
campingelcares@hotmail.com] Fr S take N621 to Portilla
de la Reina. Turn L onto LE243 to Santa Marina. Turn L thro
vill, just beyond vill turn L at camping sp. Vill street is narr &
narr bdge 2.55m on app to site. Do not attempt to app fr N
if towing - 4km of single track rd fr Posada. Med, terr, pt shd;
wc; chem disp; shwrs; el pnts (5A) €3.20; lndtte (inc dryer);
shop; tradsmn; rest; bar; 10% statics; dogs €2.10; phone; bus
1km; quiet; ccard acc; CKE/CCI. "Lovely, scenic site high in
mountains; gd base for Cares Gorge; friendly, helpful staff;
gd views; tight access - not rec if towing or lge m'van." ♦
Holy Week & 15 Jun-16 Sep. € 18.85   2010*

SANTA MARTA DE TORMES see Salamanca *1C3*

⊞ **SANTA PAU** *3B3* (2km E Rural) *42.15204, 2.54713*
Camping Ecològic Lava, Ctra Olot-Santa Pau, Km 7, 17811
Santa Pau (Gerona) [972-68 03 58; fax 972-68 03 15;
vacances@i-santapau.com; www.i-santapau.com] Take
rd GI 524 fr Olot, site at top of hill, well sp & visible fr rd. Lge,
mkd pitch, pt shd; wc; chem disp (wc); shwrs inc; baby facs; el
pnts €4.20; gas; lndtte; shop 2km; tradsmn; rest, snacks; bar;
playgrnd; pool; horseriding adj; dogs; phone; Eng spkn; adv
bkg; quiet; ccard acc. "V helpful staff; gd facs; v interesting,
unspoilt area & town; in Garrotxa Parc Naturel volcanic region;
v busy with tourists all ssn; walks sp fr site; Pyrenees museum
in Olot; tourist train fr site to volcano; excel rests in medieval
town." € 24.50   2011*

⊞ **SANTA POLA** *4F2* (1km NW Urban/Coastal) *38.20105,
-0.56983* Camping Bahía de Santa Pola, Ctra de Elche
s/n, Km. 11, 03130 Santa Pola (Alicante) [965-41 10 12;
fax 965-41 67 90; campingbahia@gmail.com; www.
campingbahia.com] Exit A7 junc 72 dir airport, cont to N332
& turn R dir Cartagena. At rndabt take exit sp Elx/Elche onto
CV865, site 100m on R. Lge, mkd pitch, hdstg, pt shd; htd wc;
chem disp; mv service pnt; baby facs; shwrs inc; el pnts (10A)
€3; gas; lndtte (inc dryer); shop; supmkt; rest; playgrnd; pool;
sand beach 1km; sat TV; 50% statics; dogs; phone; bus adj;
Eng spkn; adv bkg; rd noise; ccard acc; red long stay/low ssn/
CKE/CCI. "Helpful, friendly manager; well-organised site; sm
pitches; recep in red building facing ent; excel san facs; site rds
steep; attractive coastal cycle path." ♦ € 34.00   2014*

⊞ **SANTAELLA** *2G3* (5km N Rural) *37.62263, -4.85950*
Camping La Campiña, La Guijarrosa-Santaella, 14547
Santaella (Córdoba) [957-31 53 03; fax 957-31 51 58;
info@campinglacampina.com; www.campinglacampina.
com] Fr A4/E5 leave at km 441 onto A386 rd dir La Rambla to
Santaella for 11km, turn L onto A379 for 5km & foll sp. Sm,
mkd pitch, hdstg, pt sl, pt shd; wc; chem disp; baby facs; shwrs
inc; el pnts (10A) €4; gas; lndtte; shop & 6km; rest, snacks; bar;
BBQ; playgrnd; pool; TV; dogs €2; bus at gate to Córdoba; Eng
spkn; adv bkg; rd noise; ccard acc; red long stay/low ssn; CKE/
CCI. "Fine views; friendly, warm welcome; popular, family-run
site; many pitches sm for lge o'fits; guided walks; poss clsd
winter - phone to check." ♦ € 20.50   2009*

⊞ **SANTANDER** *1A4* (12km E Rural) *43.44777, -3.72861*
Camping Somo Parque, Ctra Somo-Suesa s/n, 39150
Suesa-Ribamontán al Mar (Cantabria) [tel/fax 942-
51 03 09; somoparque@somoparque.com; www.
somoparque.com] Fr car ferry foll sp Bilbao. After approx 8km
turn L over bdge sp Pontejos & Somo. After Pedreña climb hill
at Somo Playa & take 1st R sp Suesa. Foll site sp. Med, pt shd;
wc; chem disp; shwrs & bath; el pnts (6A) €3 (poss rev pol);
gas; shop; snacks; bar; playgrnd; beach 1.5km; 99% statics;
site clsd 16 Dec-31 Jan; some Eng spkn; quiet; CKE/CCI.
"Friendly owners; peaceful rural setting; sm ferry bet Somo
& Santander; poss unkempt low ssn & poss clsd; NH only."
€ 23.00   2012*

SANTANDER *1A4* (6km W Coastal) *43.47678, -3.87303*
Camping Virgen del Mar, Ctra Santander-Liencres, San
Román-Corbán s/n, 39000 Santander (Cantabria) [942-
34 24 25; fax 942-32 24 90; cvirdmar@ceoecant.es; www.
campingvirgendelmar.com] Fr ferry turn R, then L up to
football stadium, L again leads strt into San Román. If app fr W,
take A67 (El Sardinero) then S20, leave at junc 2 dir Liencres,
strt on. Site well sp. Lge, mkd pitch, pt shd; wc; chem disp; mv
service pnt; shwrs; el pnts (4-10A) €4; lndtte; shop; supmkt
2km; rest, snacks; bar; playgrnd; pool; sand beach 300m; no
dogs; bus 500m; adv bkg; quiet; red long stay; CKE/CCI. "Basic
facs, poss ltd hot water; some sm pitches not suitable lge
o'fits; site adj cemetary; phone in low ssn to check site open;
expensive low ssn." ♦ ltd 1 Mar-10 Dec. € 28.00   2014*

⊞ **SANTANDER** *1A4* (2km NW Coastal) *43.46762, -3.89925*
Camping Costa San Juan, Avda San Juan de la Canal s/n,
39110 Soto de la Marina (Cantabria) [tel/fax 942-57 95 80
or 629-30 36 86; info@hotelcostasanjuan.com; www.
hotelcostasanjuan.com] Fr A67 take S20 twds Bilbao, exit
junc 2 & foll sp Liencres. In 2km at Irish pub turn 1st R to Playa
San Juan de la Canal, site behind hotel on L. Sm, pt shd; wc;
shwrs inc; el pnts (3-6A) €3.20 (poss rev pol); rest; bar; sand
beach 400m;wifi; TV rm; 90% statics; no dogs; bus 600m;
poss cr; quiet. "NH for ferry; muddy in wet; poss diff lge
o'fits; gd coastal walks; 2 pin adaptor needed for elec conn."
€ 28.70   2014*

SANTANDER 1A4 (6km NW Coastal) 43.48916, -3.79361
**Camping Cabo Mayor, Avda. del Faro s/n, 39012
Santander (Cantabria) [tel/fax 942-39 15 42; info@
cabomayor.com; www.cabomayor.com]** Sp thro town
but not v clearly. On waterfront (turn R if arr by ferry). At lge
junc do not foll quayside, take uphill rd (resort type prom) &
foll sp for Faro de Cabo Mayor. Site 200m bef lighthouse on
L. Lge, mkd pitch, terr, unshd; wc; chem disp (wc); baby facs;
shwrs inc; el pnts (5A) inc; gas; lndtte; shop, rest, snacks; bar;
playgrnd; pool high ssn; many beaches adj; TV; 10% statics;
no dogs; phone; wifi; poss cr; Eng spkn; no ccards; CKE/CCI.
"Med to lge pitches; site popular with lge youth groups high
ssn; shwrs clsd 2230-0800; conv ferry; pitches priced by size,
pleasant coastal walk to Sardinero beachs; gd NH." ♦ 1 Apr-
14 Oct. € 34.20   2014*

⊞ **SANTIAGO DE COMPOSTELA** 1A2 (2km E Urban)
42.88972, -8.52444 **Camping As Cancelas, Rua do Xullo
25, 35, 15704 Santiago de Compostela (La Coruña)
[981-58 02 66 or 981-58 04 76; fax 981-57 55 53; info@
campingascancelas.com; www.campingascancelas.com]**
Exit AP9 junc 67 & foll sp Santiago. At rndabt with lge service
stn turn L sp 'camping' & foll sp to site turning L at McDonalds.
Site adj Guardia Civil barracks - poorly sp. Lge, mkd pitch,
terr, pt sl, shd; wc; chem disp; baby facs; shwrs inc; el pnts
(6A) €4.60; gas; lndtte; shop, rest, snacks & bar in ssn; BBQ;
playgrnd; pool & paddling pool high ssn; wifi; entmnt; TV;
dogs; phone; bus 100m; poss v cr; Eng spkn; quiet; red low
ssn; CKE/CCI. "Busy site - conv for pilgrims; rec arr early high
ssn; some sm pitches poss diff c'vans & steep ascent; clean san
facs but stretched when site busy; gd rest; bus 100m fr gate
avoids steep 15 min walk back fr town (low ssn adequate car
parks in town); poss interference with car/c'van electrics fr local
transmitter - if problems report to site recep; low ssn recep in
bar; arr in sq by Cathedral at 1100 for Thanksgiving service at
1200." ♦ € 43.80   2014*

SANTIAGO DE COMPOSTELA 1A2 (4km E Urban) 42.88694,
-8.49027 **Camping Monte do Gozo, Ctra Aeropuerto,
Km 2, 15820 Santiago de Compostela (La Coruña)
[981-55 89 42 or 902-93 24 24; fax 981-56 28 92; info@
cvacaciones-montedogozo.com; www.cvacaciones-
montedogozo.com]** Site sp on 'old' rd N634 (not new
autovia) into town fr E, nr San Marcos. Do not confuse with
pilgrim site nr to city. Foll sp 'Ciudad de Vacaciones'. Lge, pt
sl, shd; wc; chem disp; shwrs; el pnts €5 (poss rev pol); gas;
lndtte; shop; rest; bar; playgrnd; 2 pools; tennis; cycle hire;
20% statics; no dogs; phone; bus 1km; ccard acc. 1 Jul-
31 Aug. € 22.00   2011*

SANTILLANA DEL MAR 1A4 (3km E Rural) 43.38222,
-4.08305 **Camping Altamira, Barrio Las Quintas s/n, 39330
Queveda (Cantabria) [942-84 01 81; fax 942-26 01 55;
altamiracamping@yahoo.es]** Clear sp to Santillana fr A67;
site on R 3km bef vill. Med, mkd pitch, pt sl, terr, unshd; wc;
shwrs; el pnts (3A)- (5A) €2 (poss rev pol); gas; lndtte; sm
shop; rest; bar; pool; sand beach 8km; horseriding; TV rm;
30% statics; bus 100m; poss cr; Eng spkn; adv bkg ess high
ssn; ccard acc in ssn; CKE/CCI; "Pleasant site; ltd facs low
ssn; nr Altimira cave paintings; easy access Santander ferry
on m'way; gd coastal walks; open w/end only Nov-Mar - rec
phone ahead; excel." 10 Mar-7 Dec. € 21.40   2013*

⊞ **SANTILLANA DEL MAR** 1A4 (500m W Rural) 43.39333,
-4.11222 **Camping Santillana del Mar, Ctra de Comillas
s/n, 39330 Santillana del Mar (Cantabria) [942-81 82 50;
fax 942-84 01 83; www.campingsantillana.com]** Fr W exit
A8 junc 230 Santillana-Comillas, then foll sp Santillana & site
on rd CA131. Fr E exit A67 junc 187 & foll sp Santillana. Turn
R onto CA131, site on R up hill after vill. Lge, sl, terr, pt shd;
wc; chem disp (wc); mv service pnt; baby facs; shwrs inc; el
pnts (6A) inc (poss rev pol); gas; lndtte (inc dryer); shop; rest,
snacks; bar; playgrnd; pool; paddling pool; beach 5km; tennis;
cycle hire; horseriding; golf 15km; entmnt; internet; car wash;
cash machine; 20% statics; dogs; bus 300m; phone; poss cr;
Eng spkn; some rd noise; CKE/CCI. "Useful site in beautiful
historic vill; gd san facs; hot water only in shwrs; diff access
to fresh water & to mv disposal point; narr, winding access
rds, projecting trees & kerbs to some pitches - not rec lge
o'fits or twin-axles; poss muddy low ssn & pitches rutted; poss
travellers; gd views; lovely walk to town; poor facs (2014);
NH." ♦ ltd € 30.00 (CChq acc)   2014*

SANXENXO 1B2 (2km E Coastal) 42.39638, -8.77777
**Camping Airiños do Mar, Playa de Areas, O Grove,
36960 Sanxenxo (Pontevedra) [tel/fax 986-72 31 54]**
Fr Pontevedra take P0308 W twd Sanxenxo & O Grove. Turn L
at km post 65; site sp on S side of rd. Access rd needs care in
negotiation. Sm, mkd pitch, pt shd; wc; shwrs inc; el pnts (16A)
€4.81; gas; lndtte; shop; rest; bar; beach adj; bus adj; poss cr;
Eng spkn; adv bkg; quiet. "Not suitable for m'vans over 2.50m
high; c'vans over 6m may need help of staff at ent; bar & rest
o'look beach; lovely views." 1 Jun-30 Sep. € 24.60   2011*

SANXENXO 1B2 (4km W Rural/Coastal) 42.39944, -8.85472
**Camping Suavila, Playa de Montalvo 76-77, 36970
Portonovo (Pontevedra) [tel/fax 986-72 37 60; suavila@
terra.es; www.campingzodiac.com]** Fr Sanxenxo take P0308
W; at km 57.5 site sp on L. Med, mkd pitch, shd; wc; serviced
pitches; baby facs; shwrs inc; el pnts (6A) €3.75; gas; lndtte;
shop; tradsmn; rest, snacks; bar; BBQ; playgrnd; sand beach;
TV rm; phone; adv bkg; ccard acc; red long stay; quiet; CKE/
CCI. "Warm welcome; friendly owner; sm pitches in 1 pt of
site." ♦ ltd Holy Week-30 Sep. € 19.00   2011*

⊞ **SANXENXO** 1B2 (3km NW Coastal) 42.41777, -8.87555
**Camping Monte Cabo, Soutullo 174, 36990 Noalla
(Pontevedra) [tel/fax 986-74 41 41; info@montecabo.com;
www.montecabo.com]** Fr AP9 exit junc 119 onto upgraded
VRG4.1 dir Sanxenxo. Ignore sp for Sanxenxo until rndabt sp
A Toxa/La Toja, where turn L onto P308. Cont to Fontenla
supmkt on R - minor rd to site just bef supmkt. Rd P308 fr AP9
junc 129 best avoided. Sm, mkd pitch, terr, pt shd; wc; chem
disp; mv service pnt; shwrs inc; el pnts €3.90; lndtte (inc dryer);
shop & 500m; tradsmn; rest, snacks; bar; playgrnd; sand beach
250m; TV; 10% statics; phone; bus 600m; poss cr; Eng spkn;
adv bkg; quiet; ccard acc; red long stay/low ssn; CKE/CCI.
"Peaceful, friendly site set above sm beach (access via steep
path) with views; sm pitches; beautiful coastline & interesting
historical sites; vg." € 23.20   2011*

SANXENXO *1B2* (3km NW Coastal) *42.39254, -8.84517*
Camping Playa Paxariñas, Ctra C550, Km 2.3 Lanzada-Portonovo, 36960 Sanxenxo (Pontevedra) [986-72 30 55; fax 986-72 13 56; info@campingpaxarinas.com; www.campingpaxarinas.com] Fr Pontevedra W on P0308 coast rd; 3km after Sanxenxo. Site thro hotel on L at bend. Site poorly sp. Fr AP9 fr N exit junc 119 onto VRG41 & exit for Sanxenxo. Turn R at 3rd rndabt for Portonovo to site in dir O Grove. Do not turn L to port area on ent Portonovo. Lge, mkd pitch, pt sl, terr, shd; wc; chem disp; baby facs; shwrs inc; el pnts (5A) €4.75; gas; lndtte (inc dryer); shop; snacks; bar; BBQ; playgrnd; sand beach adj; wifi; TV; 25% statics; dogs; phone; bus adj; Eng spkn; adv bkg; quiet; ccard acc; red long stay/CKE/CCI. "Site in gd position; secluded beaches; views over estuary; take care high kerbs on pitches; excel san facs - ltd facs low ssn & poss clsd; lovely unspoilt site; plenty of shd." ♦ 17 Mar-15 Oct. € 41.65 2014*

SAVINAN see Calatayud *3C1*

SAX *4F2* (5km NW Rural) **Camping Gwen & Michael, Colonia de Santa Eulalia 1, 03630 Sax (Alicante) [965-47 44 19 or 01202 291587 (UK)]** Exit A31 at junc 48 & foll sp for Santa Eulalia, site on R just bef vill sq. Rec phone prior to arr. Sm, hdg pitch, hdstg, unshd; wc; chem disp; fam bthrm; shwrs inc; el pnts (3A) €1; lndtte; shops 6km; bar 100m; no statics; dogs; quiet. "Vg CL-type site; friendly British owners; beautiful area; gd NH & touring base." 15 Mar-30 Nov. € 14.00 2009*

SEGOVIA *1C4* (3km SE Urban) *40.93138, -4.09250* **Camping El Acueducto, Ctra de la Granja, 40004 Segovia [tel/fax 921-42 50 00; informacion@campingacueducto.com; www.campingacueducto.com]** Turn off Segovia by-pass N110/SG20 at La Granja exit, but head twd Segovia on DL601. Site in approx 500m off dual c'way just bef Restaurante Lago. Lge, mkd pitch, pt sl, pt shd; wc; chem disp; mv service pnt; shwrs inc; el pnts (6-10A) €5; gas; lndtte; sm shop; mkt 1km; rest adj; bar; BBQ; playgrnd; pool & paddling pool high ssn; cycle hire; wifi; some statics; dogs; phone; bus 150m; poss cr; m'way noise; CKE/CCI. "Excel; helpful staff; lovely views; clean facs; gates locked 0000-0800; gd bus service; some pitches sm & diff for lge o'fits; city a 'must' to visit." ♦ ltd 1 Apr-30 Sep. € 29.60 2014*

SENA DE LUNA *1A3* (1km S Rural) *42.92181, -5.96153*
Camping Río Luna, Ctra de Abelgas s/n, 24145 Sena de Luna (León) [987-59 77 14; lunacamp@telefonica.net; www.campingrioluna.com] S fr Oviedo on AP66, at junc 93 turn W onto CL626 to Sena de Luna in approx 5km. Site on L, sp. Med, pt shd; htd wc; chem disp; mv service pnt; shwrs inc; el pnts (5A) €3.50; lndtte; tradsmn; snacks; bar; BBQ; rv sw adj; internet; TV; dogs; phone; adv bkg; quiet; ccard acc. "Vg, scenic site; walking, climbing; cent for wild boar & wolves." ♦ Easter & 1 May-30 Sep. € 15.00 2010*

SENEGUE see Sabiñánigo *3B2*

⊞ **SEO DE URGEL** *3B3* (8km N Rural) *42.42777, 1.46333*
Camping Frontera, Ctra de Andorra, Km 8, 25799 La Farga de Moles (Lleida) [973-35 14 27; fax 973-35 33 40; info@fronterapark.com; www.fronterapark.com] Sp on N145 about 300m fr Spanish Customs sheds. Access poss diff. Suggest app fr N - turn in front Customs sheds if coming fr S. Lge, mkd pitch, hdstg, pt sl, pt shd; htd wc; chem disp; mv service pnt; baby facs; shwrs inc; el pnts (10A) €5.40; gas; lndtte (inc dryer); hypmkt 2km; tradsmn; rest, snacks; bar; playgrnd; pool; paddling pool; internet; TV rm; 90% statics; dogs €3.60; phone; car wash; poss cr; adv bkg; noisy; CKE/CCI. "Ideal for shopping in Andorra; winter skiing; beautiful situation but poss dusty; sm pitches; helpful owners." ♦ € 23.00 (CChq acc) 2011*

⊞ **SEO DE URGEL** *3B3* (3km SW Urban) *42.34777, 1.43055* **Camping Gran Sol, Ctra N260, Km 230, 25711 Montferrer (Lleida) [973-35 13 32; fax 973-35 55 40; info@campingransol.com; www.campinggransol.com]** S fr Seo de Urgel on N260/C1313 twds Lerida/Lleida. Site approx 3km on L fr town. Med, pt shd; wc; chem disp (wc); shwrs inc; el pnts (6A) €5.85; gas; lndtte; shop; rest; playgrnd; pool; some statics; dogs free; bus 100m; some Eng spkn; adv bkg; some rd noise; CKE/CCI. "Gd site & facs (poss stretched if full); conv for Andorra; beautiful vills & mountain scenery; in low ssn phone to check site open; gd NH." ♦ € 21.60 2010*

SEO DE URGEL *3B3* (8.5km NW Rural) *42.37388, 1.35777*
Camping Castellbò- Buchaca, Ctra Lerida-Puigcerdà 127, 25712 Castellbò (Lleida) [973-35 21 55] Leave Seo de Urgel on N260/1313 twd Lerida. In approx 3km turn N sp Castellbò. Thro vill & site on L, well sp. Steep, narr, winding rd, partly unfenced - not suitable car+c'van o'fits or lge m'vans. Sm, mkd pitch, pt sl, pt shd; wc; chem disp (wc); shwrs inc; el pnts (5A) €5.85; lndtte; shop; snacks; playgrnd; pool; dogs €3.60; phone; poss cr; adv bkg; quiet; "CL-type site in beautiful surroundings; friendly recep; Basic fac's." 1 May-30 Sep. € 30.00 2013*

SEVILLA See site listed under Dos Hermanas.

SITGES *3C3* (2km SW Urban/Coastal) *41.23351, 1.78111*
Camping Bungalow Park El Garrofer, Ctra C246A, Km 39, 08870 Sitges (Barcelona) [93 894 17 80; fax 93 811 06 23; info@garroferpark.com; www.garroferpark.com] Exit 26 on the C-32 dir St. Pere de Ribes, at 1st rndabt take 1st exit, at 2nd rndabt take 2nd exit, foll rd C-31 to campsite. V lge, hdg/mkd pitch, hdstg, pt shd; htd wc; chem disp; mv service pnt; baby facs; shwrs inc; serviced pitches; el pnts (5-10A) €4.10 (poss rev pol); gas; lndtte; shop; rest, snacks; bar; playgrnd; pool; shgl beach 900m; windsurfing; tennis 800m; horseriding; cycle hire; games area; games rm; car wash; wifi; entmnt; TV; 80% statics; dogs €2.65; phone; bus adj (to Barcelona); recep open 0800-2100; site clsd 19 Dec-27 Jan to tourers; poss cr; Eng spkn; adv bkg; ccard acc; red snr citizen/low ssn; CKE/CCI. "Great location, conv Barcelona, bus adj; sep area for m'vans; pleasant staff; gd level site; quiet; gd old & new facs." ♦ 28 Feb-14 Dec. € 49.60 2014*

SITGES *3C3* (1.5km W Urban/Coastal) *41.2328, 1.78511*
Camping Sitges, Ctra Comarcal 246, Km 38, 08870 Sitges (Barcelona) [938-94 10 80; fax 938-94 98 52; info@ campingsitges.com; www.campingsitges.com] Fr AP7/E15 exit junc 28 or 29 dir Sitges. Site on R after El Garrofer, sp. If app fr Sitges go round rndabt 1 more exit than sp, & immed take slip rd - avoids a L turn. Lge, mkd pitch, hdstg, pt shd; htd wc; chem disp; baby facs; shwrs inc; el pnts (4A) €4.80; gas; lndtte; shop; rest, snacks; bar; BBQ; playgrnd; pool high ssn; paddling pool; sand beach 800m; wifi; 30% statics; dogs; phone; bus 300m; train 1.5km; poss cr; Eng spkn; quiet but some rlwy noise; ccard acc; red long stay/low ssn. "Well-maintained, clean site; friendly staff; excel, clean san facs; some pitches v sm; m'vans with trailers not acc; gd pool, rest & shop; rec arr early as v popular & busy, espec w/ends; gd security." ♦ 1 Mar-20 Oct. € 26.50   2010*

SOPELANA see Bilbao *1A4*

"There aren't many sites open at this time of year"

If you're travelling outside peak season remember to call ahead to check site opening dates – even if the entry says 'open all year'

SORIA *3C1* (2km SW Rural) *41.74588, -2.48456* **Camping Fuente de la Teja, Ctra Madrid-Soria, Km 223, 42004 Soria [tel/fax 975-22 29 67; camping@fuentedelateja.com; www.fuentedelateja.com]** Fr N on N111 (Soria by-pass) 2km S of junc with N122 (500m S of Km 223) take exit for Quintana Redondo, site sp. Fr Soria on NIII dir Madrid sp just past km 223. Turn R into site app rd. Fr S on N111 stake exit for Quintana Redondo & foll site sp. Med, mkd pitch, pt sl, pt shd; wc; chem disp; baby facs; shwrs inc; el pnts (6A) €3 (poss no earth); gas; lndtte; hypmkt 3km; tradsmn; rest, snacks; bar; playgrnd; pool high ssn; TV rm; wifi; few statics; dogs; phone; poss cr; adv bkg; some rd noise; ccard acc; CKE/CCI. "Vg site; excel, gd for NH; vg san facs; interesting town; phone ahead to check site poss open bet Oct & Easter; easy access to site; pitches around 100sqm, suits o'fits upto 10m; quiet; friendly staff." ♦ ltd 1 Mar-31 Oct. € 30.00   2014*

SOTO DEL REAL see Manzanares el Real *1D4*

⊞ **TABERNAS** *4G1* (8km E Rural) **Camping Oro Verde, Piezas de Algarra s/n, 04200 Tabernas (Almería) [687-62 99 96]** Fr N340A turn S onto ALP112 sp Turrillas. Turn R in 100m into narr tarmac lane bet villas, site on L in 600m, not well sp. Sm, pt shd; wc; chem disp; shwrs inc; el pnts (6-10A) inc (poss long lead req); gas; lndtte; shop 1km; rest, bar nrby in hotel; BBQ; pool; sand beach 40km; dogs; adv bkg; quiet; red long stay; CKE/CCI. "In sm olive grove; beautiful views; pitches muddy in wet; basic san facs; friendly British owners; 'Mini-Hollywood' 7km where many Westerns filmed; conv Sorbas & Guadix caves; excel." ♦ € 16.00   2011*

TALARN see Tremp *3B2*

TAMARIT see Tarragona *3C3*

⊞ **TAPIA DE CASARIEGO** *1A3* (2km W Rural) *43.54870, -6.97436* **Camping El Carbayin, La Penela, 33740 [tel/fax 985-62 37 09; www.campingelcarbayin.com/]** Take N634/ E70 (old coast rd parallel to A8-E70) to Serantes, foll sp to site bet N634 and sea. Sm, mkd pitch, pt sl, pt shd; wc; chem disp; baby facs; shwrs inc; el pnts (3A) €3; lndtte; shop; rest; bar; playgrnd; sand beach 1km; fishing; watersports; some statics; bus 400m; phone; adv bkg; quiet; ccard acc; CKE/CCI. "Gd for coastal walks & trips to mountains; gd; new san facs." ♦ € 19.50   2013*

TAPIA DE CASARIEGO *1A3* (3km W Coastal) *43.56394, -6.95247* **Camping Playa de Tapia, La Reburdia, 33740 Tapia de Casariego (Asturias) [tel/fax 985-47 27 21; www.campingelcarbayin.com/]** Loc on N634. Site in vill of Serantes, halfway btw Tapia de Casareigo and Ribadeo. Med, hdg/mkd pitch, pt sl, pt shd; wc; chem disp; mv service pnt; child/baby facs; shwrs inc; el pnts (16A) €4.06; gas; lndtte (inc dryer); shop; rest; bar; hi ssn only; sand beach 1m; wifi; dogs; bus 800m; phone; Eng spkn; adv bkg; quiet; CKE/CCI. "Gd access; busy, well-maintained, friendly site; o'looking coast & harbour; poss ltd hot water; walking dist to delightful town." ♦ Holy Week & 1 Jun-15 Sep. € 32.70   2012*

⊞ **TARIFA** *2H3* (11km W Coastal) *36.07027, -5.69305* **Camping El Jardín de las Dunas, Ctra N340, Km 74, 11380 Punta Paloma (Cádiz) [956-68 91 01; fax 956-69 91 06; info@lasdunascamping.com; www.campingjdunas. com]** W on N340 fr Tarifa, L at sp Punta Paloma. Turn L 300m after Camping Paloma, site in 500m. Lge, hdg pitch, pt shd; wc; chem disp; serviced pitches; baby facs; shwrs inc; el pnts (6A) €5.16; lndtte; shop; rest, snacks; bar; playgrnd; beach 50m; entmnt; TV rm; no dogs; phone; noisy; ccard acc; red low ssn. "Poss strong winds; unsuitable lge o'fits due tight turns & trees; modern facs; poss muddy when wet." ♦ € 35.00   2014*

⊞ **TARIFA** *2H3* (3km NW Coastal) *36.04277, -5.62972* **Camping Rió Jara, Ctra N340, km 81, 11380 Tarifa (Andalucia) [tel/fax 956-68 05 70; campingriojara@terra. com]** Site on S of N340 Cádiz-Algeciras rd at km post 81.2; 3km after Tarifa; clearly visible & sp. Med, mkd pitch, pt shd; wc (some cont); chem disp; mv service pnt; shwrs inc; el pnts (10A) €4; gas; lndtte (inc dryer); shop; tradsmn; rest, snacks; bar; playgrnd; sand beach 200m; fishing; wifi; dogs €3.50; poss cr; adv bkg; rd noise; ccard acc; red low ssn; CKE/CCI. "Gd, clean, well-kept site; friendly recep; long, narr pitches diff for awnings; daily trips to N Africa; gd windsurfing nrby; poss strong winds; mosquitoes in summer." ♦ € 45.00   2014*

TARIFA *2H3* (6km NW Coastal) *36.05468, -5.64977* **Camping Tarifa, N340, Km 78.87, Los Lances, 11380 Tarifa (Cádiz) [tel/fax 956-68 47 78; info@campingtarifa.es; www. campingtarifa.es]** Site on R of Cádiz-Málaga rd N340. Med, mkd pitch, hdstg, shd; wc; chem disp; mv service pnt; serviced pitch; baby facs; shwrs inc; el pnts (5A) €3.50; gas; lndtte; shop; rest, snacks; bar; playgrnd; pool; sand beach adj; wifi; no dogs; phone; car wash; Eng spkn; adv bkg; quiet; red long stay & low ssn; ccard acc. "Vg; ideal for windsurfing; immed access to beach; lovely site with beautiful pool; v secure - fenced & locked at night; some pitches sm & poss diff access due bends, trees & kerbs; conv ferry to Morocco; poss strong winds." ♦ 1 Mar-31 Oct. € 33.20 (CChq acc)   2009*

⊞ **TARIFA** *2H3* (10km NW Coastal) *36.06908, 5.68036*
Camping Valdevaqueros, Ctra N340 km 75,5
11380 Tarifa [34 956 684 174; fax 34 956 681 898;
info@campingvaldevaqueros.com; www.
campingvaldevaqueros.com] Campsite is sp 9km fr Tarifa
on the N340 twds Cadiz. Lge, pt sl, pt shd; wc; chem disp;
mv service pnt; shwrs; el pnts (6A); shop; tradsmn; rest; bar;
playgrnd; pool; paddling pool; sandy beach 1km; games area;
bike hire; entmnt; wifi; tv; 50% statics; dogs; phone; Eng spkn;
adv bkg. "Excel site; watersports nrby." € 43.00   2014*

⊞ **TARIFA** *2H3* (11km NW Coastal) *36.07621, -5.69336*
Camping Paloma, Ctra Cádiz-Málaga, Km 74, Punta
Paloma, 11380 Tarifa (Cádiz) [956-68 42 03; fax
956-68 18 80; campingpaloma@yahoo.es; www.
campingpaloma.com] Fr Tarifa on N340, site on L at 74km
stone sp Punta Paloma, site on R. Lge, mkd pitch, hdstg, pt
sl, terr, pt shd; wc (some cont); chem disp; mv service pnt;
shwrs inc; el pnts (6A) €4.28; gas; lndtte; shop; rest, snacks;
bar; playgrnd; high ssn; sand beach 1km; watersports;
windsurfing; horseriding; cycle hire; 20% statics; bus 200m;
poss cr; Eng spkn; no adv bkg; quiet; ccard acc; red long stay/
low ssn; CKE/CCI. "Well-run site; vg facs; peaceful away fr busy
rds; lge o'fits poss diff due low trees; trips to N Africa & whale-
watching; mountain views." ♦ ltd € 21.47   2009*

TARRAGONA *3C3* (600m NE Urban Coastal) *40.88707,
0.80630* **Camping Nautic, Calle Libertat s/n, 43860**
L'Ametlla de Mar Tarragona [34 977 493 031; fax
34 977 456 110; info@campingnautic.com; www.
campingnautic.com] Fr N340 exit at km 1113 sp L'Ametlla
de Mar (or A7 exit 39). Over rlwy bdge, foll rd to L. Turn R
after park and TO on R, foll signs to campsite. Lge, hdstg, terr,
pt shd; wc; chem disp; mv service pnt; baby facs; shwrs; el
pnts; lndtte (inc dryer); shop; rest; snack; bar; playgrnd; pool;
paddling pool; beach; games area; wifi; tv; 25% statics; dogs;
phone; bus 500m; train 700m; Eng spkn; adv bkg; no ccard
acc; CCI. "Vg site; tennis court; 5 mins to attractive town with
rest & sm supermkts; lge Mercadona outsite town; site on
different levels". ♦ 15 Mar-15 Oct. € 50.20   2014*

TARRAGONA *3C3* (4km NE Coastal) *41.13082, 1.30345*
Camping Las Salinas, Ctra N340, Km 1168, Playa Larga,
43007 Tarragona [977-20 76 28] Access via N340 bet km
1167 & 1168. Med, shd; wc; shwrs; el pnts €3.74; gas; lndtte;
shop; snacks; bar; beach adj; some statics; poss cr;
rlwy noise. Holy Week & 15 May-30 Sep. € 29.20   2011*

TARRAGONA *3C3* (5km NE Coastal) *41.13019, 1.31170*
Camping Las Palmeras, N340, Km 1168, 43080 Tarragona
[977-20 80 81; fax 977-20 78 17; laspalmeras@
laspalmeras.com; www.laspalmeras.com] Exit AP7 at junc
32 (sp Altafulla). After about 5km on N340 twd Tarragona take
sp L turn at crest of hill. Site sp. V lge, mkd pitch, pt shd; wc;
chem disp; baby facs; shwrs inc; el pnts (6A) inc; gas; lndtte
(inc dryer); shop; tradsmn; rest, snacks; bar; playgrnd; pool;
paddling pool; sand beach adj; naturist beach 1km; tennis;
games area; games rm; wifi; entmnt; some statics; dogs €5;
phone; poss cr; rlwy noise; ccard acc; red long stay/snr citizens/
low ssn; CKE/CCI. "Gd beach; ideal for families; poss mosquito
prob; many sporting facs; gd, clean san facs; friendly, helpful
staff; supmkt 5km; excel site." ♦ 2 Apr-12 Oct. € 45.00
(CChq acc)   2012*

TARRAGONA *3C3* (7km NE Coastal) *41.12887, 1.34415*
Camping Torre de la Mora, Ctra N340, Km 1171, 43008
Tarragona-Tamarit [977-65 02 77; fax 977-65 28 58; info@
torredelamora.com; www.torredelamora.com] Fr AP7 exit
junc 32 (sp Altafulla), at rndabt take La Mora rd. Then foll site
sp. After approx 1km turn R, L at T-junc, site on R. Lge, hdstg,
terr, pt shd; wc; chem disp; mv service pnt; baby facs; shwrs
inc; el pnts (6A) €5.20; gas; lndtte; shop & 1km; tradsmn; rest,
snacks; bar; playgrnd; pool; sand beach adj; tennis; sports club
adj; golf 2km; entmnt; internet; 50% statics; dogs €3.65; bus
200m; Eng spkn; adv bkg; quiet away fr rd & rlwy; ccard acc;
red long stay; CKE/CCI. "Improved, clean site set in attractive
bay with fine beach; excel pool; conv Tarragona & Port
Aventura; sports club adj; various pitch sizes, some v sm." ♦
18 Mar-31 Oct.   2013*

TAULL see Pont de Suert *3B2*

TIEMBLO, EL *1D4* (8km W Rural) *40.40700, -4.57400*
Camping Valle de Iruelas, Las Cruceras, 05110 Barraco
(Ávila) [918-62 50 59; fax 918-62 53 95; iruelas@
valledeiruelas.com; www.valledeiruelas.com] Fr N403 turn
off at sp Reserva Natural Valle de Iruelas. After x-ing dam foll
sp Las Cruceras & camping. In 5km foll sp La Rinconada, site in
1km. Med, hdg/mkd pitch, terr, shd; wc; chem disp; baby facs;
shwrs inc; el pnts €5; lndtte; supmkt; rest; bar; playgrnd; pool;
paddling pool; canoeing; horseriding; bird hide; quiet; CKE/
CCI. "Pleasant, woodland site with wildlife." ♦ Easter-31 Aug.
€ 26.00   2009*

**"That's changed – Should
I let The Club know?"**

If you find something on site that's different from
the site entry, fill in a report and let us know. See
www.caravanclub.co.uk/europereport.

⊞ **TOLEDO** *1D4* (2km W Rural) *39.86530, -4.04714*
Camping El Greco, Ctra Pueblo Montalban, Km.0.7, 45004
Toledo [tel/fax 925-22 00 90; campingelgreco@telefonica.
net; www.campingelgreco.es] Site on CM4000 fr Toledo
dir La Puebla de Montalbán & Talavera. When app, avoid town
cent, keep to N outside of old town & watch for camping sp.
Or use outer ring rd. Diff to find. Med, hdg/mkd pitch, hdstg,
pt sl, pt shd; htd wc; chem disp; mv service pnt; shwrs inc;
el pnts (6A) €4.30 (poss rev pol); gas; lndtte; shop; tradsmn;
bar; BBQ; playgrnd; pool; paddling pool; games area; dogs;
bus to town; train to Madrid fr town; phone; wifi; Eng spkn;
ccard acc; CKE/CCI. "Clean, tidy, well-maintained; all pitches
on gravel; easy parking on o'skts - adj Puerta de San Martín
rec - or bus; some pitches poss tight; san facs clean; lovely,
scenic situation; excel rest; friendly, helpful owners; vg; dusty."
€ 42.00   2014*

TORDESILLAS *1C3* (1km SW Urban) *41.49653, -5.00614* Kawan Village El Astral, Camino de Pollos 8, 47100 Tordesillas (Valladolid) [tel/fax 983-77 09 53; info@campingelastral.es; www.campingelastral.com] Fr NE on A62/E80 thro town turn L at rndabt over rv & immed after bdge turn R dir Salamanca & almost immed R again into narr gravel track (bef Parador) & foll rd to site; foll camping sp & Parador. Poorly sp. Fr A6 exit sp Tordesillas & take A62. Cross bdge out of town & foll site sp. Med, hdg/mkd pitch, hdstg, pt shd; htd wc; chem disp; mv service pnt; baby facs; shwrs inc; el pnts (5A-10A) €3.60-5 (rev pol); gas; lndtte (inc dryer); shop; supmkt in town; rest, snacks; bar; playgrnd; pool in ssn; rv fishing; tennis; cycle hire; wifi; TV rm; 10% statics; dogs €2.35; phone; site open w/end Mar & Oct; Eng spkn; quiet, but some traff noise; ccard acc; CKE/CCI. "V helpful owners & staff; easy walk to interesting town; pleasant site by rv; vg, modern, clean san facs & excel facs; vg rest; popular NH; excel site in every way, facs superb; various size pitches." ♦ 1 Mar-31 Oct. € 41.40 (CChq acc) SBS - E03   2014*

TORLA *3B2* (2km N Rural) *42.63948, -0.10948* Camping Ordesa, Ctra de Ordesa s/n, 22376 Torla (Huesca) [974-11 77 21; fax 974-48 63 47; infocamping@campingordesa.es; www.campingordesa.es] Fr Ainsa on N260 twd Torla. Pass Torla turn R onto A135 (Valle de Ordesa twd Ordesa National Park). Site 2km N of Torla, adj Hotel Ordesa. Med, pt shd; wc; chem disp; serviced pitch; baby facs; shwrs; el pnts (6A) €5.50; gas 2km; lndtte; shop 2km, tradsmn; rest high ssn; bar; playgrnd; pool; tennis; wifi (in adj hotel); some statics (sep area); dogs €3; phone; bus 1km; poss cr; Eng spkn; adv bkg (ess Jul/Aug); quiet; red low ssn; ccard acc; CKE/CCI. "V scenic; recep in adj Hotel Ordesa; excel rest; helpful staff; facs poss stretched w/end; long, narr pitches & lge trees on access rd poss diff lge o'fits; ltd facs low ssn; no access to National Park by car Jul/Aug, shuttlebus fr Torla." 28 Mar-30 Sep. € 31.70   2013*

"I like to fill in the reports as I travel from site to site"

You'll find report forms at the back of this guide, or you can fill them in online at www.caravaclub.co.uk/europereport.

TORLA *3B2* (8km N Rural) *42.67721, -0.12337* Camping Valle de Bujaruelo, 22376 Torla (Huesca) [974-48 63 48; info@campingvalledebujaruelo.com; www.campingvalledebujaruelo.com] N fr Torla on A135, turn L at El Puente de los Navarros onto unmade rd for 3.8km. Unsuitable lge m'vans & c'vans. Med, mkd pitch, terr, pt shd; htd wc; chem disp; mv service pnt; shwrs inc; el pnts (6A) €4.50; gas; lndtte; shop (high ssn) & 8km; rest, snacks; bar; BBQ; some statics; dogs €2; poss cr; Eng spkn; adv bkg; quiet. "In beautiful, peaceful valley in Ordesa National Park; superb views & walking." ♦ Easter-15 Oct. € 19.00   2010*

⊞ **TORRE DEL MAR** *2H4* (1km SW Coastal) *36.7342, -4.1003* Camping Torre del Mar, Paseo Maritimo s/n, 29740 Torre del Mar (Málaga) [952-54 02 24; fax 952-54 04 31; info@campingtorredelmar.com / campingtorredelmar@hotmail.com; www.campingtorredelmar.com] Fr N340 coast rd, at rndabt at W end of town with 'correos' on corner turn twds sea sp Faro, Torre del Mar. At rndabt with lighthouse adj turn R, then 2nd R, site adj big hotel, ent bet lge stone pillars (no name sp). Lge, hdg/mkd pitch, hdstg, shd; wc; chem disp; mv service pnt; serviced pitches; shwrs inc; el pnts (15A) €4.40 (long lead req); gas; lndtte; shop on site & 500m; rest, snacks, bar nrby in ssn; playgrnd; pool & paddling pool; sandy/shgl beach 50m; tennis; sat TV; 39% statics; phone; poss cr all year; quiet but noise fr adj football pitch; red low ssn/long stay; CKE/CCI. "Tidy, clean, friendly, well-run site; some sm pitches; rds tight; gd, clean san facs; popular low ssn; constant hot water." ♦ € 43.60   2014*

"We must tell The Club about that great site we found"

Get your site reports in by mid-August and we'll do our best to get your updates into the next edition.

⊞ **TORRE DEL MAR** *2H4* (1km W Coastal) *36.72976, -4.10285* Camping Laguna Playa, Prolongación Paseo Maritimo s/n, 29740 Torre del Mar (Málaga) [952-54 06 31; fax 952-54 04 84; info@lagunaplaya.com; www.lagunaplaya.com] Fr N340 coast rd, at rndabt at W end of town with 'correos' on corner turn twds sea sp Faro, Torre del Mar. At rndabt with lighthouse adj turn R, then 2nd R, site sp in 400m. Med, pt shd; wc; chem disp; mv service pnt; shwrs inc; el pnts (5-10A) €3.70; gas; lndtte; shop; rest, snacks; bar; playgrnd; pool; sand beach 1km; 80% statics; dogs; poss cr; Eng spkn; adv bkg; quiet; red low ssn. "Popular low ssn; sm pitches; excel, clean san facs; gd location, easy walk to town; NH only." € 29.00   2013*

⊞ **TORRE DEL MAR** *2H4* (2km W Coastal) *36.72660, -4.11330* Camping Naturista Almanat (Naturist), Ctra de la Torre Alta, Km 269, 29749 Almayate (Málaga) [952-55 64 62; fax 952-55 62 71; info@almanat.de; www.almanat.de] Exit E15/N340 junc 274 sp Vélez Málaga for Torre del Mar. Exit Torre del Mar on coast rd sp Málaga. In 2km bef lge black bull on R on hill & bef water tower turn L at sp. If rd not clear cont to next turning point & return in dir Torre del Mar & turn R to site at km 269. Site well sp. Lge, hdg/mkd pitch, hdstg (gravel), pt shd; htd wc; chem disp; mv service pnt (on request); sauna; shwrs inc; el pnts (10-16A) €3.90; gas; lndtte; shop; rest; bar; BBQ; playgrnd; pool; jacuzzi; sand/shgl beach adj; tennis; wifi; entmnt; cinema; games area; gym; golf 10km; some statics; dogs €2.70; phone; bus 500m; poss cr; Eng spkn; adv bkg; quiet but poss noise fr birdscarer; ccard acc; red long stay/low ssn/snr citizens up to 50%; INF card. "Superb facs; popular & highly rec; reasonable dist Seville, Granada, Córdoba; easy walk/cycle to town; emergency exit poss kept locked; sm pitches & narr site rds diff for lge o'fits." ♦ € 21.00   2009*

TORRE DEL MAR *2H4* (3km W Coastal) *36.72526, -4.13532* Camping Almayate Costa, Ctra N340, Km 267, 29749 Almayate Bajo (Málaga) [952-55 62 89; fax 952-55 63 10; almayatecosta@campings.net; www.campings.net/ almayatecosta] E fr Málaga on N340/E15 coast rd. Exit junc 258 dir Almería, site on R 3km bef Torre del Mar. Easy access. Lge, mkd pitch, hdstg, shd; wc; chem disp; mv service pnt; shwrs inc; el pnts (10A) €5.10; gas; lndtte; supmkt; bar; BBQ; playgrnd; pool; sand beach 50m; games rm; golf 7km; no dogs; car wash; phone; Eng spkn; adv bkg; quiet but some rd noise; ccard acc; red long stay/low ssn; CKE/CCI. "Helpful manager; pitches nr beach tight for lge o'fits & access rds poss diff; vg resort; excel." ♦ 15 Mar-30 Sep. € 43.50   2013*

"I need an on-site restaurant"

We do our best to make sure site information is correct, but it is always best to check any must-have facilities are still available or will be open during your visit.

⊞ **TORREVIEJA** *4F2* (7km SW Rural) *37.97500, -0.75111* Camping Florantilles, Ctra San Miguel de Salinas-Torrevieja, 03193 San Miguel de Salinas (Alicante) [965-72 04 56; fax 966-72 32 50; camping@campingflorantilles. com; www.campingflorantilles.com] Exit AP7 junc 758 onto CV95, sp Orihuela, Torrevieja Sud. Turn R at rndabt & after 300m turn R again, site immed on L. Or if travelling on N332 S past Alicante airport twd Torrevieja. Leave Torrevieja by-pass sp Torrevieja, San Miguel. Turn R onto CV95 & foll for 3km thro urbanisation 'Los Balcones', then cont for 500m, under by-pass, round rndabt & up hill, site sp on R. Lge, hdg/mkd, hdstg, terr, pt shd; wc; chem disp; mv service pnt; shwrs inc; el pnts (10A) inc; gas; lndtte; supmkt; snacks; bar; BBQ; playgrnd; pool & paddling pool (high ssn); 3 golf courses nrby; sand beach 5km; horseriding 10km; fitness studio/keep fit classes; workshops: calligraphy, card making, drawing/painting, reiki, sound therapy etc; basic Spanish classes; walking club; games/ TV rm; 20% statics; no dogs; no c'vans/m'vans over 10m; recep clsd 1330-1630; adv bkg; rd noise; ccard acc; red low ssn; CKE/ CCI. "Popular, British owned site; friendly staff; many long-stay visitors & all year c'vans; suitable mature couples; own transport ess; gd cyling, both flat & hilly; conv hot spa baths at Fortuna & salt lakes." ♦ € 30.05 SBS - E11   2011*

TORROELLA DE MONTGRI *3B3* (6km SE Coastal) *42.01111, 3.18833* Camping El Delfin Verde, Ctra Torroella de Montgrí-Palafrugell, Km 4, 17257 Torroella de Montgrí (Gerona) [972-75 84 54; fax 972-76 00 70; info@ eldelfinverde.com; www.eldelfinverde.com] Fr N leave A7 at junc 5 dir L'Escala. At Viladamat turn R onto C31 sp La Bisbal. After a few km turn L twd Torroella de Montgrí. At rndabt foll sp for Pals (also sp El Delfin Verde). At the flags turn L sp Els Mas Pinell. Foll site sp for 5km. V lge, mkd pitch, pt shd, pt shd; wc; chem disp; mv service pnt; baby facs; shwrs inc; el pnts (6A) inc; lndtte (inc dryer); supmkt; rests; snacks; 3 bars; BBQ; playgrnd; pool; sand beach adj; fishing; tennis; horseriding 4km; cycle hire; windsurfing; sportsgrnd; hairdresser; money exchange; games rm; entmnt; disco; wifi; TV; 40% statics (sep area); winter storage; no dogs 18/7-21/8, at low ssn €4; no c'vans/m'vans over 8m high ssn; poss cr; quiet; ccard acc; red low ssn; CKE/CCI. "Superb, gd value site; excel pool; wide range of facs; clean, modern san facs; all water de-salinated fr fresh water production plant; bottled water rec for drinking & cooking; mkt Mon." ♦ 17 May-20 Sep. € 58.00 SBS - E01   2011*

⊞ **TORROX COSTA** *2H4* (2km NNW Urban) *36.73944, -3.94972* Camping El Pino, Urbanización Torrox Park s/n, 29793 Torrox Costa (Málaga) [952-53 00 06; fax 952-53 25 78; info@campingelpino.com; www. campingelpino.com] Exit A7 at km 285, turn S at 1st rndabt, turn L at 2nd rndabt & foll sp Torrox Costa N340; in 1.5km at rndabt turn R to Torrox Costa, then L onto rndabt sp Nerja, site well sp in 4km. App rd steep with S bends. Fr N340 fr Torrox Costa foll sp Torrox Park, site sp. Lge, mkd pitch, terr, shd; wc; chem disp; shwrs inc; el pnts €3.80 (long lead req); gas; lndtte (inc dryer); shop; rest, snacks adj; bar; BBQ; playgrnd; 2 pools; sand beach 800m; games area; golf 8km; wifi; 35% statics; dogs €2.50; phone; car wash; Eng spkn; red low ssn/long sta/CKE/CCI. "Gd size pitches but high kerbs; narr ent/exit; gd hill walks; conv Malaga; Nerja caves, Ronda; gd touring base; noise fr rd and bar; san facs adequate." ♦ € 18.00   2013*

See advertisement

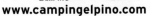

TOSSA DE MAR *3B3* (500m N Coastal) *41.72885, 2.92584*
Camping Can Martí, Avda Pau Casals s/n, 17320 Tossa de Mar (Gerona) [972-34 08 51; fax 972-34 24 61; campingcanmarti@terra.es; www.campingcanmarti.net] Exit AP7 junc 9 dir Vidreras & take C35 dir Llagostera. Turn R at rndabt dir GI681 to coast, then GI682 to site. Mountain rd fr Sant Feliu not rec. V lge, mkd pitch, pt shd; wc; chem disp; baby facs; shwrs inc; el pnts (10A) €3; gas; lndtte; shop; rest, snacks; bar; playgrnd; pool & paddling pool; shgl beach 500m; fishing; tennis; horseriding; 10% statics; dogs free; phone; car wash; sep car park; Eng spkn; no adv bkg; quiet; red long stay/low ssn/CKE/CCI. "Helpful, friendly staff; facs clean." ♦ 15 May-15 Sep. € 32.00   2009*

TOSSA DE MAR *3B3* (4km NE Coastal) *41.73627, 2.94683*
Camping Pola, Ctra Tossa-Sant Feliu, Km 4, 17320 Tossa de Mar (Gerona) [972-34 10 50; campingpola@giverola.es; www.camping-pola.es] Exit AP7 junc 9 onto C35 dir Sant Feliu de Guíxols. In approx 9km turn R onto GI681 dir Tossa de Mar. In Tossa take GI GE682 dir Sant Feliu. Narr, winding rd but gd. Site sp. Lge, pt sl, pt shd; wc; shwrs inc; el pnts (15A) inc; gas; lndtte (inc dryer); shop; rest; bar; playgrnd; pool; paddling pool; sand beach adj; tennis; games area; entmnt; some statics; dogs €3.50; bus 500m; sep car park high ssn; adv bkg; ccard acc. "Site deep in narr coastal inlet with excel beach; few British visitors; san facs old but clean; gd." 1 Jun-30 Sep. € 44.80   2009*

⊞ **TOTANA** *4G1* (2km SW Rural) *37.74645, -1.51933*
Camping Totana, Ctra N340, Km 614, 30850 Totana (Murcia) [tel/fax 968-42 48 64; info@campingtotana.es; www.campingtotana.es] Fr N340/E15 exit at km 612 fr N. Fr S exit km 609. Foll Totana rd, site 2km on R. Sl ent. Sm, hdg/mkd pitch, hdstg, terr, pt shd; wc; chem disp; shwrs inc; el pnts (6A) €3; shop on site & 4km; rest, bar high ssn; BBQ; playgrnd; pool high ssn; games rm; entmnt; 90% statics; dogs €2; Eng spkn; red long stay; CKE/CCI. "Access to sm pitches tight due trees; helpful owners; tidy site; ltd privacy in shwrs; vg NH." € 16.00   2011*

TREMP *3B2* (4km N Rural) *42.18872, 0.92152* Camping Gaset, Ctra C13, Km 91, 25630 Talarn (Lleida) [973-65 07 37; fax 973-65 01 02; campingaset@pallarsjussa.net; www.pallarsjussa.net/gaset/] Fr Tremp, take C13/N260 N sp Talarn. Site clearly visible on R on lakeside. Lge, pt sl, terr, pt shd; wc; chem disp; shwrs; el pnts (4A) €5.30; lndtte; shop; rest 4km; snacks; bar; BBQ; playgrnd; pool; paddling pool; sand beach & lake sw; fishing; tennis; games area; wifi; 15% statics; dogs €3.60; phone; poss cr; quiet; ccard acc. "Picturesque setting; some sm pitches." 1 Apr-15 Oct. € 24.50   2010*

⊞ **TREVELEZ** *2G4* (1km E Rural) *36.99195, -3.27026*
Camping Trevélez, Ctra Órgiva-Trevélez, Km 1, 18417 Trevélez (Granada) [tel/fax 958-85 87 35 or 625-50-27-69 (mob); info@campingtrevelez.net; www.campingtrevelez.net] Fr Granada on A44/E902 exit junc 164 onto A348 dir Lanjarón, Pampaneira. Cont for approx 50km to on A4132 to Trevélez, site sp. Med, mkd pitch, terr, pt shd; htd wc; chem disp; mv service pnt; shwrs inc; el pnts (9A) €3.50; gas; lndtte; shop; tradsmn; rest, snacks; bar; playgrnd; pool; rv 1km; entmnt; wifi; few statics; dogs; phone; bus adj; poss cr; Eng spkn; adv bkg; quiet; red long stay. "Excel site; helpful, welcoming owners; access to Mulhacén (highest mountain mainland Spain); lots of hiking." ♦ € 27.30   2011*

TURIENO see Potes *1A4*

UCERO see Burgo de Osma, El *1C4*

UNQUERA *1A4* (3km N Coastal) *43.39127, -4.50986*
Camping Las Arenas, Ctra Unquera-Pechón, Km. 2, 39594 Pechón (Cantabria) [tel/fax 942-71 71 88; info@campinglasarenas.com; www.campinglasarenas.com] Exit A8/E70 at km 272 sp Unquera. At rndabt foll CA380 sp Pechón, climb narr winding rd to site ent at top on L. Lge, pt sl, terr, pt shd; wc; chem disp; shwrs inc; el pnts (5A) €3.95 (poss rev pol); gas; lndtte (inc dryer); rest; shop on site & 3km; bar; playgrnd; pool; shgl beach adj; fishing; cycle hire; internet; no statics; dogs; poss cr & noisy; Eng spkn; quiet; ccard acc; CKE/CCI. "Magnificent position on terr cliffs; peaceful, well-kept & clean; immac, modern san facs; helpful staff." 1 Jun-30 Sep. € 30.40   2010*

⊞ **VALDEAVELLANO DE TERA** *3B1* (1km NW Rural)
41.94523, -2.58837 Camping Entrerrobles, Ctra de Molinos de Razón s/n, 42165 Valdeavellano de Tera (Soria) [975-18 08 00; fax 975-18 08 76; entreobbles@hotmail.com; www.entrerrobles.freeservers.com] S fr Logroño on N111, after Almarza turn R onto SO-820 to Valdeavellano. In 10km turn R at site sp, site on R in 1km. Med, mkd pitch, pt sl, pt shd; htd wc; chem disp; baby facs; shwrs inc; el pnts (6A) €5; lndtte (inc dryer); tradsmn; rest, snacks; bar; playgrnd; pool; games area; cycle hire; TV rm; 8% statics; dogs; phone; Eng spkn; adv bkg; quiet; ccard acc; red CKE/CCI. "Excel touring base; attractive area but isolated (come prepared); friendly staff; new san facs." ♦ € 19.00   2009*

VALDOVINO *1A2* (700m W Coastal) *43.61222, -8.14916*
Camping Valdoviño, Ctra Ferrol-Cedeira, Km 13, 15552 Valdoviño (La Coruña) [981-48 70 76; fax 981-48 61 31] Fr Ortigueira on C642; turn W onto C646 sp Cadeira then Ferrol; turn R at camping sp, down hill R again, site on R almost on beach. Med, terr, pt shd; wc; chem disp; baby facs; shwrs inc; el pnts (15A) inc; gas; lndtte; shop; rest; bar; snacks; playgrnd; sand beach adj; playgrnd; wifi; TV; some statics; no dogs; bus adj; poss cr; quiet; Eng spkn; CKE/CCI. "Pleasant, busy site nr lge beach with lagoon & cliffs but poss windy; locality run down; vg rest." ♦ 10 Apr-30 Sep. € 28.50 2009*

VALENCIA *4E2* (9km S Coastal) *39.39638, -0.33250* Camping Coll Vert, Ctra Nazaret-Oliva, Km 7.5, 46012 Playa de Pinedo (València) [961-83 00 36; fax 961-83 00 40; info@collvertcamping.com; www.collvertcamping.com] Fr S on V31 turn R onto V30 sp Pinedo. After approx 1km turn R onto V15/CV500 sp El Salar to exit El Salar Platjes. Turn L at rndabt, site on L in 1km. Fr N bypass València on A7/E15 & after junc 524 turn N twd València onto V31, then as above. Turn L at rndabt, site in 1km on L. Med, hdg/mkd pitch, shd; wc; shwrs inc; el pnts 4.81 6A; gas; lndtte; shop; bar; BBQ; playgrnd; pool; paddling pool; sand beach 500m; games area; entmnt; 20% statics; dogs €4.28; phone; bus to city & marine park; car wash; poss cr; Eng spkn; adv bkg; quiet; some rd noise; ccard acc; red long stay. "Hourly bus service fr outside site to cent of València & marine park; helpful, friendly staff; San facs need update sm pitches; Conv for F1." ♦ 16 Feb-14 Dec. € 22.00   2014*

⊞ **VALENCIA** *4E2* (9.5km S Urban/Coastal) **Camping Park El Saler, Ctra del Riu 548, 46012 El Saler (València) [tel/ fax 961-83 02 44; info@campingparkelsaler.com; www. campingparkelsaler.com]** Fr València foll coast rd or V15 to El Saler. Site adj rndabt just N of El Saler. Med, hdg/mkd pitch, hdstg, pt shd; wc; chem disp; shwrs inc; el pnts (6A) inc; End spkn; lndtte; shop; rest; bar; pool; sand beach 300m; 50% statics; dogs; phone; bus at gate; poss cr; rd noise; CKE/ CCI. "Very conv València - hourly bus; tow pin adaptor needed for conn cable; narr pitches & ent." € 25.00   2014*

⊞ **VALENCIA** *4E2* (16km S Rural) *39.32302, -0.30940* **Camping Devesa Gardens, Ctra El Saler, Km 13, 46012 València [961-61 11 36; fax 961-61 11 05; alojamiento@ devesagardens.com; www.devesagardens.com]** S fr València on CV500, site well sp on R 4km S of El Saler. Med, mkd pitch, hdstg, pt shd; htd wc; chem disp; mv service pnt; baby facs; el pnts (7-15A) €5; gas; lndtte; supmkt (high ssn) & 4km; rest; bar; BBQ; playgrnd; pool; beach 700m; tennis; lake canoeing; horseriding; 70% statics; no dogs; phone; bus to València; quiet; adv bkg; ccard acc. "Friendly staff; warden needed to connect to el pnts; site has own zoo (clsd low ssn); excel." ♦ € 22.70   2011*

VALENCIA DE DON JUAN see Villamañán *1B3*

VALL LLOBREGA see Palamós *3B3*

⊞ **VALLE DE CABUERNIGA** *1A4* (1km NE Rural) *43.22800, 4.28900* **Camping El Molino de Cabuérniga, Sopeña, 39510 Cabuérniga (Cantabria) [942-70 62 59; fax 942-70 62 78; cmcabuerniga@campingcabuerniga.com; www. campingcabuerniga.com]** Sopeña is 55 km. SW of Santander. Fr A8 (Santander - Oviedo) take 249 exit and join N634 to Cabezón de la Sal. Turn SW on CA180 twds Reinosa for 11 km. to Sopeña (site sp to L). Turn into vill (car req - low bldgs), cont bearing R foll sp to site. Med, shd; wc; shwrs inc; el pnts (3A) 2.67 (check earth); gas; lndtte; sm shop; snacks; bar; playgrnd; rv 200m; fishing; tennis; dogs €1.50; phone; bus 500m; adv bkg; quiet; ccard acc; CKE/CCI. "Excel site & facs on edge of vill; no shops in vicinity, but gd location, rds to site narr in places." ♦ € 23.00   2013*

VECILLA, LA *1B3* (1km N Rural) *42.85806, -5.41155* **Camping La Cota, Ctra Valdelugueros, LE321, Km 19, 24840 La Vecilla (León) [987-74 10 91; lacota@campinglacota.com; www.campinglacota.com]** Fr N630 turn E onto CL626 at La Robla, 17km to La Vecilla. Site sp in vill. Med, mkd pitch; wc; chem disp; baby facs; shwrs inc; el pnts €3.50; lndry rm; snacks; bar; games area; wifi; 50% statics; open w/ends out of ssn; train nr; quiet; ccard acc. "Pleasant site under poplar trees - poss diff to manoeuvre lge o'fits; gd walking, climbing nr; interesting mountain area; NH only." 23 Mar-30 Sep. € 21.00   2013*

⊞ **VEJER DE LA FRONTERA** *2H3* (10km S Coastal) *36.20084, -6.03506* **Camping Pinar San José, Ctra de Vejer-Caños de Meca, Km 10.2, Zahora 17, 11159 Barbate (Cadiz) [956-43 70 30; fax 956-43 71 74; info@campingpinarsanjose. com; www.campingpinarsanjose.com]** Fr A48/N340 exit junc 36 onto A314 to Barbate, then foll dir Los Caños de Meca. Turn R at seashore rd dir Zahora. Site on L, 2km beyond town. Med, mkd pitch, shd; wc; chem disp; mv service pnt; fam bthrm; shwrs; el pnts inc; lndtte; shop; rest; playgrnd; pool; paddling pool; sand beach 700m; tennis; games area; wifi; satellite TV; some statics; dogs €2 (low ssn only); adv bkg; quiet. "Excel, modern facs." ♦ € 64.00   2013*

VELEZ MALAGA *2G4* (16.2km NNW Rural) *36.87383, -4.18527* **Camping Rural Presa la Vinuela, Carretera A-356, Km 30 La Viñuela Málaga [952-55 45 62; fax 952-55 45 70; campingpresalavinuela@hotmail.com; www. campinglavinuela.es]** Site is on A356 N of Velez Malaga adjoining the W shore of la Vinuela lake. Fr junc with A402, foll sp to Colmenar/Los Romanes. Stay on A356(don't turn off into Los Romanes). Site is on R approx 2.5km after turn for Los Romanes, next to rest El Pantano. Sm, hed/mkd pitch, hdstg, terr, pt shd; wc; chem disp; shwr; el pnts (5A); lndtte; shop; rest; café; snack; bar; pool; games area; games rm; wifi; tv; 20% statics; dogs €1.10; Eng spkn; adv bkg; red low ssn. "Excel site". 1 Jan-30 Sep. € 21.00   2014*

VENDRELL, EL *3C3* (2km S Coastal) *41.18312, 1.53593* **Camping Sant Salvador, Avda Palfuriana 68, 43880 Sant Salvador (Tarragona) [tel/fax 977-68 08 04; campingsantsalvador@troc.es; www. campingsantsalvador.com]** Exit A7 junc 31 onto N340, after 1km turn L. Site bet Calafell & Coma-Ruga. Lge, pt shd; wc; chem disp; baby facs; shwrs inc; el pnts (4A) €5; gas; lndtte; shop; rest; bar; playgrnd; beach; 75% statics; dogs €2.50; bus adj; poss cr; ccard acc; red long stay/low ssn; CKE/CCI. "Secure site; not suitable lge o'fits; conv Safari Park & Port Aventura." ♦ 26 Mar-3 Oct. € 29.20   2010*

VENDRELL, EL *3C3* (7km SW Coastal) *41.17752, 1.50132* **Camping Francàs, Ctra N340, Km 1185.5, 43880 Coma-Ruga (Tarragona) [977-68 07 25; fax 977-68 47 73; info@ campingfrancas.net; www.campingfrancas.net]** Exit N340 at km stone 303 to Comarruga. Lge, mkd pitch, shd; wc; chem disp; baby facs; shwrs; el pnts €3.65; lndtte; shop; rest, snacks; bar; BBQ; playgrnd; sand beach adj; watersports; fishing; games area; car wash; wifi; entmnt; some statics; dogs; bus 100m; car wash; adv bkg; quiet. "Pleasant site." ♦ Easter-1 Sep. € 24.50   2010*

VIELHA *3B2* (6km N Rural) *42.73638, 0.76083* **Camping Artiganè, Ctra N230, Km 171, Val d'Arán, 25537 Pont d'Arròs (Lleida) [tel/fax 973-64 03 38; info@ campingartigane.com; www.campingartigane.com]** Fr French border head S on N230 for 15km. Fr Vielha head N to France & turn L at Pont d'Arròs. Site on main rd by rv. Lge, pt sl, pt shd; wc; chem disp; baby facs; shwrs inc; el pnts (10A) €4.50; gas; lndry rm; shop; rest, snacks, bar in high ssn; BBQ; playgrnd; htd pool; games area; golf; 5% statics; dogs €3.25; bus adj; phone; poss cr; quiet; CKE/CCI. "Scenic area - wild flowers, butterflies; friendly warden; low ssn site yourself - warden calls; simple/v basic facs, poss stretched when site full." ♦ Holy Week-15 Oct. € 25.00   2011*

SPAIN

⊞ **VIELHA** *3B2* (7km N Rural) *42.73649, 0.74640* **Camping Verneda, Ctra Francia N230, Km 171, 25537 Pont d'Arròs (Lleida) [973-64 10 24; fax 973-64 32 18; info@ campingverneda.com; www.campingverneda.com]** Fr Lerida N on N230 twd Spain/France border, site on R adj N230, 2km W of Pont d'Arròs on rvside, 1km after Camping Artigane. Med, pt shd; wc; chem disp; baby facs; shwrs inc; el pnts (4A) €3.90; gas; lndtte; rest, snacks; bar; playgrnd; pool; horseriding; games rm; cycle hire; entmnt; TV; 10% statics; dogs €2.50; adv bkg; Eng spkn; ccard acc; CKE/CCI. "Gd area for walking; site open w/end rest of year; well-run site; gd facs." € 25.00   2011*

"Satellite navigation makes touring much easier"

Remember most sat navs don't know if you're towing or in a larger vehicle – always use yours alongside maps and site directions.

VIELHA *3B2* (6km SE Rural) *42.70005, 0.87060* **Camping Era Yerla D'Arties, Ctra C142, Vielha-Baquiera s/n, 25599 Arties (Lleida) [973-64 16 02; fax 973-64 30 53; yerla@ coac.net; www.aranweb.com/yerla]** Fr Vielha take C28 dir Baquiera, site sp. Turn R at rndabt into Arties, site in 30m on R. Med, shd; htd wc; chem disp; baby facs; shwrs inc; el pnts (4-10A) €4.25-5.15; gas; lndtte; shop & rest nrby; snacks; bar; pool; skiing nr; some statics; bus 200m; phone; quiet; ccard acc; CKE/CCI. "Pleasant site & vill; ideal for ski resort; san facs gd; gd walking; OK for sh stay." 1 Dec-14 Sep. € 23.70   2012*

VILAGARCIA DE AROUSA *1B2* (4km NE Coastal) *42.63527, -8.75555* **Camping Río Ulla, Bamio, 36612 Vilagarcía de Arousa (Pontevedra) [tel/fax 986-50 54 30; 986505430@ telefonica.net; www.campingrioulla.com]** Fr N exit A9 at km 93 dir Pontecesures & take PO548 twd Vilagarcía de Arousa. Thro Catoira & in 5km turn R at traff lts at top of hill, site in 500m. Med, hdg/mkd pitch, pt shd; wc; chem disp; mv service pnt; baby facs; shwrs inc; el pnts (10A) €4; lndtte; shop; rest, snacks; bar; BBQ; playgrnd; pool; paddling pool; sand beach adj; games area; TV; 10% statics; bus 200m; Eng spkn; adv bkg; rd & rlwy noise; ccard acc; CKE/CCI. "Helpful owners; excel, clean facs." ♦ Holy Week & 1 Jun-15 Sep. € 20.00   2009*

⊞ **VILALLONGA DE TER** *3B3* (500m NW Rural) *42.33406, 2.30705* **Camping Conca de Ter, Ctra Setcases s/n, Km 5.4, 17869 Vilallonga de Ter (Gerona) [972-74 06 29; fax 972-13 01 71; concater@concater.com; www.concater.com]** Exit C38 at Camprodón; at Vilallonga de Ter do NOT turn off into vill but stay on main rd; site on L. Lge, mkd pitch, hdstg, pt shd; htd wc; chem disp; shwrs inc; el pnts (5-15A) €3.50-6.54; lndtte (inc dryer); shop; rest; bar; pool; paddling pool; games area; games rm; ski lift 15km; entmnt; 95% statics; dogs €4.30; poss cr; Eng spkn; ccard acc; CKE/CCI. "Pitches sm & cr together; gd." ♦ € 31.00   2010*

⊞ **VILANOVA DE PRADES** *3C2* (500m NE Rural) *41.34890, 0.95860* **Camping Parc de Vacances Serra de Prades, Calle Sant Antoni s/n, 43439 Vilanova de Prades (Tarragona) [tel/fax 977-86 90 50; info@serradeprades.com; www. serradeprades.com]** Fr AP2 take exit 8 (L'Albi) or 9 (Montblanc), foll C240 to Vimbodi. At km 47.5 take TV7004 for 10km to Vilanova de Prades. Site ent on R immed after rndabt at ent to vill. Lge, some hdg/mkd pitch, terr, pt shd; wc; chem disp; mv service pnt; baby facs; shwrs inc; el pnts (6A) €5.80 (poss long lead req) gas; lndtte (inc dryer); basic shop on site & 8km; tradsmn; rest, snacks; bar; BBQ; playgrnd; htd pool; lake sw 20km; tennis; games area; games rm; wifi; TV rm; many statics; dogs; phone; Eng spkn; adv bkg high ssn; quiet; red long stay/CKE/CCI. "Well-maintained, well-run, scenic, friendly site; clean facs; sm pitches; access some pitches diff due steep, gravel site rds & storm gullies; conv Barcelona; vg touring base/NH." ♦ € 27.20 (CChq acc)   2009*

⊞ **VILANOVA DE PRADES** *3C2* (4km S Rural) *41.31129, 0.98020* **Camping Prades, Ctra T701, Km 6.850, 43364 Prades (Tarragona) [977-86 82 70; camping@ campingprades.com; www.campingprades.com]** Fr S take N420 W fr Reus, C242 N to Albarca, T701 E to Prades. Fr N exit AP2/E90 junc 9 Montblanc; N240 to Vimbodi; TV7004 to Vilanova de Prades; L at rndabt to Prades; go thro town, site on R in 500m. Narr rds & hairpins fr both dirs. Lge, mkd pitch, pt shd; wc; chem disp; mv service pnt; baby facs; shwrs; el pnts (3A) €5.50; gas; lndtte; shop; tradsmn; rest, snacks; bar; playgrnd; pool; paddling pool; cycle hire; wifi; entmnt; TV rm; 60% statics; phone; bus 200m; poss cr; adv bkg; ccard acc; CKE/CCI. "Beautiful area; in walking dist of lovely, tranquil old town; excel, helpful staff." ♦ € 30.75   2011*

"There aren't many sites open at this time of year"

If you're travelling outside peak season remember to call ahead to check site opening dates – even if the entry says 'open all year'

VILANOVA I LA GELTRU *3C3* (5km SW Coastal) *41.19988, 1.64339* **Camping La Rueda, Ctra C31, Km 146.2, 08880 Cubelles (Barcelona) [938-95 02 07; fax 938-95 03 47; larueda@la-rueda.com; www.la-rueda.com]** Exit A7 junc 29 then take C15 dir Vilanova onto autopista C32 & take exit 13 dir Cunit. Site is 2.5km S of Cubelles on C31 at km stone 146.2. Lge, mkd pitch, shd; htd wc; chem disp; mv service pnt; shwrs inc; el pnts (4A) €6.90; gas; lndtte; shop; rest, snacks; bar; sand beach 100m; playgrnd; pool; tennis; horseriding; watersports; fishing; entmnt; car wash; 12% statics; dogs €3.70; phone; bus; train; Eng spkn; adv bkg; quiet; red long stay/low ssn; ccard acc; red CKE/CCI. "Conv Port Aventura & Barcelona; vg family site." 16 Apr-11 Sep. € 34.50   2010*

⊞ **VILANOVA I LA GELTRU** *3C3* (3km NW Urban) *41.23190, 1.69075* **Camping Vilanova Park, Ctra Arboç, Km 2.5, 08800 Vilanova i la Geltru (Barcelona) [938-93 34 02; fax 938-93 55 28; info@vilanovapark.com; www.vilanovapark.com]** Fr N on AP7 exit junc 29 onto C15 dir Vilanova; then take C31 dir Cubelles. Leave at 153km exit dir Vilanova Oeste/L'Arboç to site. Fr W on C32/A16 take Vilanova-Sant Pere de Ribes exit. Take C31 & at 153km exit take BV2115 dir L'Arboc to site. Fr AP7 W leave at exit 31 onto the C32 (A16); take exit 16 (Vilanova-L'Arboc exit) onto BV2115 to site. Parked cars may block loop & obscure site sp. V lge, hdg/mkd pitch, hdstg, terr, pt shd; htd wc; chem disp; mv service pnt; some serviced pitches; baby facs; fam bthrm; sauna; shwrs inc; el pnts (10A) inc (poss rev pol); gas; lndtte (inc dryer); supmkt; tradsmn; rest, snacks; bar; BBQ (gas/elec); playgrnd; 2 pools (1 htd covrd) & fountains; paddling pool; jacuzzi & spa; fitness cent; sand beach 3km; lake sw 2km; fishing; tennis; cycle hire; mini golf and jumping pillow for children due to open in 2012; horseriding 500m; golf 1km; games rm; wifi; entmnt; TV rm; 50% statics; dogs €12.50; phone; bus directly fr campsite to Barcelona; poss cr; Eng spkn; adv bkg ess high ssn; ccard acc; red snr citizens/low ssn/long stay; CKE/CCI. "Gd for children; excel san facs; gd rest & bar; gd winter facs; helpful staff; gd security; some sm pitches with diff access due trees or ramps; conv bus/train Barcelona, Tarragona, Port Aventura & coast; mkt Sat; excel site; superb." ♦ € 61.30 (CChq acc) SBS - E08 2013*

See advertisement

VILLADANGOS DEL PARAMO see León *1B3*

⊞ **VILLAFRANCA** *2F4* (1.5km S Rural) *42.26333, -1.73861* **Camping Bardenas, Ctra NA-660 PK 13.4, 31330 Villafranca [34 94 88 46 191; info@campingbardenas.com; www.campingbardenas.com]** Fr N leave AP15 at Junc 29 onto NA660 sp Villafranca. Site on R 1.5km S of town. Med, hdstg, unshd; htd wc; chem disp; baby facs; shwr; lndtte (inc dryer); shop; rest; bar; BBQ; pool; games rm; 30% statics; ccard acc; CCI. "Gd site for winter stopover en rte to S. Spain; some rd noise; facs ltd in severe weather; excel rest." € 36.50 2014*

⊞ **VILLAFRANCA DE CORDOBA** *2F4* (1km W Rural) *37.95333, -4.54710* **Camping La Albolafia, Camino de la Vega s/n, 14420 Villafranca de Córdoba (Córdoba) [tel/fax 957-19 08 35; informacion@campingalbolafia.com; www.campingalbolafia.com]** Exit A4/E5 junc 377, cross rv & at rndabt turn L & foll sp to site in 2km. Beware humps in app rd. Med, hdg/mkd pitch, hdstg, pt shd; wc; chem disp; mv service pnt; shwrs inc; el pnts (10A) €4.20 (long lead poss req); lndtte (inc dryer); shop; rest, snacks; bar; BBQ; playgrnd; pool; wifi; TV; some statics; dogs €2.80; bus to Córdoba 500m; phone; Eng spkn; quiet; CKE/CCI. "V pleasant, well-run, friendly, clean site; watersports park nrby; bar and rest clsd end May." ♦ € 24.20 2013*

⊞ **VILLAMANAN** *1B3* (1km SE Rural) *42.31403, -5.57290* **Camping Palazuelo, 24680 Villamañán (León) [tel/fax 987-76 82 10]** Fr N630 Salamanca-León turn SE at Villamañán onto C621 dir Valencia de Don Juan. Site on R in 1km behind hotel. Med, pt shd; wc; shwrs inc; el pnts (10A) €2.50; lndtte; shop 1km; rest, snacks; pool; quiet but some rd noise; ccard acc. "NH only; neglected & run down low ssn, poss unclean; ltd privacy in shwrs; Valencia de Don Juan worth visit." € 19.00 2009*

VILLAMANAN *1B3* (6km SE Rural) *42.29527, -5.53777* **Camping Pico Verde, Ctra Mayorga-Astorga, Km 27.6, 24200 Valencia de Don Juan (León) [tel/fax 987-75 05 25; campingpicoverd@terra.es]** Fr N630 S, turn E at km 32.2 onto C621 sp Valencia de Don Juan. Site in 4km on R. Med, mkd pitch, wc; shwrs inc; el pnts (6A) inc; lndtte; shop on site & 1km; rest; snacks 1km; playgrnd; covrd pool; paddling pool; tennis; 25% statics; dogs free; quiet; red CKE/CCI. "Friendly, helpful staff; conv León; picturesque vill; sw caps to be worn in pool; phone ahead to check site open if travelling close to opening/closing dates." ♦ 15 Jun-8 Sep. € 20.21 2014*

VILLAMARTIN DE LA ABADIA see Ponferrada *1B3*

SPAIN

VILLANANE *1B4* (3km S Rural) *42.84221, -3.06867* **Camping Angosto, Ctra Villanañe-Angosto 2, 01425 Villanañe (Gipuzkoa) [945-35 32 71; fax 945-35 30 41; info@ camping-angosto.com; www.camping-angosto.com]** S fr Bilbao on AP68 exit at vill of Pobes & take rd to W sp Espejo. Turn L 2.4km N of Espejo dir Villanañe, lane to site 400m on R. Med, some mkd pitch, pt shd; htd wc; chem disp; baby facs; shwrs inc; el pnts €4.15 (long cable poss req - supplied by site); lndtte; shop; rest, snacks; bar; BBQ; playgrnd; htd, covrd pool; entmnt; TV; 50% statics; dogs; phone; poss cr w/ends; Eng spkn; quiet. "Beautiful area; friendly staff; open site - mkd pitches rec if poss; gd rest; conv NH fr Bilbao; wonderful site; in low ssn site seems close but call nbr on gate." ♦ 15 Feb-30 Nov. € 23.70   2014*

⊞ **VILLARGORDO DEL CABRIEL** *4E1* (3km NW Rural) *39.5525, -1.47444* **Kiko Park Rural, Ctra Embalse de Contreras, Km 3, 46317 Villargordo del Cabriel (València) [962-13 90 82; fax 962-13 93 37; kikoparkrural@kikopark. com; www.kikopark.com/rural]** A3/E901 València-Madrid, exit junc 255 to Villargordo del Cabriel, foll sp to site. Med, mkd pitch, hdstg, terr, pt shd; wc; chem disp; mv service pnt; some serviced pitches; shwrs inc; el pnts (6A) €3.70; gas; lndtte (inc dryer); shop; tradsmn; rest, snacks; bar; pool; lake sw 1km; canoeing; watersports; fishing; horseriding; white water rafting; cycle hire; TV; some statics; dogs €0.80; some rlwy noise; Eng spkn; adv bkg rec high ssn; ccard acc; red long stay/low ssn/snr citizens; red CKE/CCI. "Beautiful location; superb, well-run, peaceful site; lge pitches; gd walking; vg rest; many activities; helpful staff." ♦ € 41.70   2013*

VILLAVICIOSA *1A3* (8km NE Rural) *43.50900, -5.33600* **Camping La Rasa, Ctra La Busta-Selorio, 33316 Villaviciosa (Asturias) [985-89 15 29; info@campinglarase.com; www. campinglarase.com]** Fr A8 exit km 353 sp Lastres/Venta del Pobre. In approx 500m foll site sp, cross bdge over m'way to site. Lge, hdg/mkd pitch, sl, unshd; wc; chem disp; mv service pnt; serviced pitches; shwrs inc; el pnts (6A) €3.10; lndtte; sm shop; snacks; bar; playgrnd; pool; sand beach 7km; 60% statics; dogs €2.80; phone; site open w/end low ssn/winter; Eng spkn; red low ssn; CKE/CCI. "Pleasant, friendly site; beautiful countryside; conv m'way & coast; tight access rds to sm pitches." ♦ 15 Jun-15 Sep. € 22.80   2009*

VILLAVICIOSA *1A3* (15km NW Rural) *43.5400, -5.52638* **Camping Playa España, Playa de España, Quintes, 33300 Villaviciosa (Asturias) [tel/fax 985-89 42 73; camping@ campingplayaespana.es; www.campingplayaespana. es]** Exit A8 onto N632/AS256 dir Quintes then Villaverde. Site approx 12km fr Villaviciosa & 10km fr Gijón. Last 3km of app rd narr & steep with sharp bends. Med, pt shd; wc; chem disp; shwrs; el pnts €4.25 (poss rev pol); gas; lndtte; shop; snacks; bar; beach 200m; dogs €3; phone; quiet; ccard acc. "Gd site; lovely coast & scenery with mountains behind; clean; vg san facs." Holy Week & 16 May-19 Sep. € 24.60   2010*

⊞ **VINAROS** *3D2* (5km N Coastal) *40.49363, 0.48504* **Camping Vinarós, Ctra N340, Km 1054, 12500 Vinarós (Castellón) [964-40 24 24; fax 964-45 53 28; info@ campingvinaros.com; www.campingvinaros.com]** Fr N exit AP7 junc 42 onto N238 dir Vinarós. At junc with N340 turn L dir Tarragona, site on R at km 1054. Fr S exit AP7 junc 43. Lge, hdg/mkd pitch, hdstg, pt shd; htd wc; chem disp; mv service pnt; 85% serviced pitches; baby facs; shwrs inc; el pnts (6A) €6; gas; lndtte; shop 500m; tradsmn; rest adj; snacks; bar; playgrnd; pool; sand/shgl beach 1km; wifi; 15% statics; dogs €3; phone; bus adj; currency exchange; poss cr; Eng spkn; adv bkg - rec high ssn; quiet but some rd noise; ccard acc; red long stay/low ssn; CKE/CCI. "Excel gd value, busy, well-run site; many long-stay winter residents; spacious pitches; vg clean, modern san facs; el volts poss v low in evening; gd rest; friendly, helpful staff; rec use bottled water; Peñíscola Castle & Morello worth a visit; easy cycle to town." ♦ ltd € 50.00   2013*

VINUELA *2G4* (7.5km NW Rural) *36.87383, -4.18527* **Camping Presa La Viñuela, Ctra A356, km 30 29712 Viñuela [952-55 45 62; fax 952-55 45 70; campingpresalavinuela@hotmail.com; www. campinglavinuela.es]** Site on A356 N of Velez Malaga adjoining the W shore of la Vinuela lake. Fr junc with A402, foll sp to Colmenar & Los Romanes. Stay on A356 (don't turn off into Los Romanes). Site is on R approx 2.5km after the turn for Los Romanes, next to El Pantano rest. Sm, mkd pitch, hdstg, terr, pt shd; wc; chem disp; shwrs; el pnts (5A); lndtte; shop; rest; café; bar; pool; games area; games rm; wifi; tv in bar; 20% statics; dogs €1.10; Eng spkn; adv bkg; red low ssn. "Excel site." 1 Jan-30 Sep. € 21.00   2014*

VINUESA *3B1* (2km N Rural) *41.9272, -2.7650* **Camping Cobijo, Ctra Laguna Negra, Km 2, 42150 Vinuesa (Soria) [tel/fax 975-37 83 31; recepcion@campingcobijo.com; www.campingcobijo.com]** Travelling W fr Soria to Burgos, at Abejar R on SO840. by-pass Abejar cont to Vinuesa. Well sp fr there. Lge, pt sl, pt shd; wc; chem disp; baby facs; shwrs inc; el pnts (3-6A) €4-5.70 (long cead poss req); gas; lndtte; shop; rest, snacks; bar high ssn; BBQ; playgrnd; pool; cycle hire; internet; 10% statics; dogs; phone; poss cr w/end; Eng spkn; phone; quiet; ccard acc; CKE/CCI. "Friendly staff; clean, attractive site; some pitches in wooded area poss diff lge o'fits; special elec connector supplied (deposit); ltd bar & rest low ssn, excel rests in town; gd walks." ♦ Holy Week-2 Nov. € 17.00   2009*

⊞ **VITORIA/GASTEIZ** *3B1* (3km W Rural) *42.8314, -2.7225* **Camping Ibaya, Nacional 102, Km 346.5, Zuazo de Vitoria 01195 Vitoria/Gasteiz (Alava) [945-14 76 20; fax 627-07 43 99; info@campingibaia.com; www.campingibaia. com]** Fr A1 take exit 343 sp N102/A3302. At rndabt foll sp N102 Vitoria/Gasteiz. At next rndabt take 3rd exit & immed turn L twd filling stn. Site ent on R in 100m, sp. Sm, mkd pitch, hdstg, pt sl, pt shd; wc; chem disp; shwrs; el pnts (5A) €5.40; gas; lndry rm; sm shop; supmkt 2km; rest adj; snacks; bar; BBQ; playgrnd; wifi; 5-10% statics; dogs; phone; poss cr; Eng spkn; rd noise; CKE/CCI. "NH only; gd, modern san facs; phone ahead to check open low ssn; fair site." € 29.50   2014*

VIU DE LINAS see Broto *3B2*

VIVEIRO *1A2* (500m NW Coastal) *43.66812, -7.59998*
**Camping Vivero, Cantarrana s/n, Covas, 27850 Viveiro
(Lugo) [982-56 00 04; fax 982-56 00 84; campingvivero@
gmail.com]** Fr E twd El Ferrol on rd LU862, turn R in town
over rv bdge & bear R & foll yellow camping sp. Site in 500m
adj football stadium in Covas, sp. Fr W go into town on 1-way
system & re-cross rv on parallel bdge to access rd to site. Site
not well sp - foll stadium sp. Med, shd; wc; chem disp; shwrs
inc; el pnts (10A) €4.30; lndtte; shop & 1.5km; snacks; bar;
beach 500m; wifi; phone; bus adj; o'night area for m'vans;
ccard acc. "Sh walk to interesting old town, outstanding
craft pottery at sharp RH bend on Lugo rd; vg clean site."
Easter & 1 Jun-30 Sep. € 17.00   2011*

"I like to fill in the reports as I travel from site to site"

You'll find report forms at the back of
this guide, or you can fill them in online at
www.caravaclub.co.uk/europereport.

VIVER *3D2* (3.5km W Rural) *39.90944, -0.61833* **Camping
Villa de Viver, Camino Benaval s/n, 12460 Viver
(Castellón) [964-14 13 34; info@campingviver.com;
www.campingviver.com]** Fr Sagunto on A23 dir Terual,
approx 10km fr Segorbe turn L sp Jérica, Viver. Thro vill dir
Teresa, site sp W of Viver at end of single track lane in approx
2.8km (yellow sp) - poss diff for car+c'van, OK m'vans. Med,
hdg pitch, terr, pt shd; htd wc; chem disp; mv service pnt;
some serviced pitches; shwrs inc; el pnts (6A) €3.80; lndtte;
shop 3.5km; tradsmn; rest, snacks; bar; playgrnd; pool; TV;
10% statics; dogs €3.10; phone; Eng spkn; adv bkg; quiet; red
long stay; ccard acc; CKE/CCI. "Improved site; lovely situation -
worth the effort." ♦ 1Mar-1 Nov. € 19.20   2013*

☐ **ZARAGOZA** *3C1* (3km S Urban) *41.63766, -0.94227*
**Camping Ciudad de Zaragoza, Calle San Juan Bautista
de la Salle s/n, 50012 Zaragoza [876-24 14 95; fax
876-24 12 86; info@campingzaragoza.com; www.
campingzaragoza.com]** Fr S on A23 foll Adva Gómez Laguna,
turn L at 2nd rndabt, in 500m bear R in order to turn L at
rndabt, site on R in 750m, sp. Fr all other dirs take Z40 ring rd
dir Teruel, then Adva Gómez Laguna twd city, then as above.
Site well sp. Med, mkd pitch, hdstg, pt sl, unshd; htd wc; chem
disp; mv service pnt; baby facs; shwrs inc; el pnts (10A) €4.85;
lndtte (inc dryer); shop; rest, snacks; bar; BBQ; playgrnd; pool;
tennis; games area; wifi; 50% statics; dogs €3.04; poss cr;
Eng spkn; adv bkg; poss noisy (campers & daytime aircraft).
"Modern san facs but poss unclean low ssn & pt htd; poss
travellers; unattractive, but conv site in suburbs; gd sh stay; gd
food at bar; helpful staff." € 38.20   2014*

☐ **ZARAUTZ** *3A1* (2.5km E Coastal) *43.28958, -2.14603*
**Gran Camping Zarautz, Monte Talaimendi s/n,
20800 Zarautz (Guipúzkoa) [943-83 12 38; fax 943-
13 24 86; info@grancampingzarautz.com; www.
grancampingzarautz.com]** Exit A8 junc 11 Zarautz, strt on
at 1st & 2nd rndabt after toll & foll site sp. On N634 fr San
Sebastián to Zarautz, R at rndabt. On N634 fr Bilbao to Zarautz
L at rndabt. Lge, hdg/mkd pitch, hdstg, pt sl, terr, pt shd; htd
wc; chem disp; mv service pnt; shwrs inc; el pnts (6A) inc; gas;
lndtte (inc dryer); shop; tradsmn; rest; bar; BBQ; playgrnd;
beach 1km (steep walk); games rm; golf 1km; wifi; TV rm;
50% statics; phone; train/bus to Bilbao & San Sebastian; poss
cr; Eng spkn; no adv bkg; ccard acc; CKE/CCI. "Site on cliff
o'looking bay; excel beach, gd base for coast & mountains;
helpful, friendly staff; some pitches sm with steep access &
o'looked fr terr above; sans facs upgraded but poor standard
and insufficient when cr; excel rest; pitches poss muddy; NH for
Bilbao ferry; rec arr early to secure pitch; v steep walk to beach;
gd for NH; excel train service to San Sebastian; gd shop on
site." ♦ € 37.25 (CChq acc)   2014*

"We must tell The Club about that great site we found"

Get your site reports in by mid-August
and we'll do our best to get your updates
into the next edition.

ZARAUTZ *3A1* (4km E Coastal) *43.27777, -2.12305* **Camping
Playa de Orio, 20810 Orio (Guipúzkoa) [943-83 48 01; fax
943-13 34 33; info@oriokanpina.com; www.oriokanpina.
com]** Fr E on A8 exit junc 33 & at rndabt foll sp Orio, Kanpin &
Playa. Site on R. Or to avoid town cent cross bdge & foll N634
for 1km, turn L at sp Orio & camping, turn R at rndabt to site.
Lge, mkd pitch, pt sl, pt shd; wc; chem disp; mv service pnt;
baby facs; shwrs inc; el pnts (5A) inc; gas; lndtte (inc dryer);
shop high ssn; tradsmn; rest adj; snacks; bar; playgrnd; pool
high ssn; paddling pool; sand beach adj; tennis; 50% statics
(sep area); no dogs; phone; car wash; poss cr at w/end; Eng
spkn; adv bkg; quiet; red low ssn; ccard acc; CKE/CCI. "Busy
site; flats now built bet site & beach & new marina adj - now
no sea views; walks; gd facs; friendly staff; useful NH bef
leaving Spain." ♦ 1 Mar-1 Nov. € 43.00   2014*

ZEANURI *3A1* (3km SE Rural) *43.08444, -2.72333* **Camping
Zubizabala, Otxandio, 48144 Zeanuri [944-47 92 06
or 660-42 30 17 (mob); zubizabala@gmail.com; www.
zubizabala.com]** E fr Bilbao on A8, exit at Galdakao junc 19
onto N240 dir Vitoria/Gasteiz. 2.5km S of Barazar Pass, turn L
on minor rd B3542 to Otxandio. Site 300m on R. Sp. Sm, mkd
pitch, unshd; wc; chem disp; mv service pnt; baby facs; shwrs
inc; el pnts €3.55; lndtte; shop; bar; tradsmn; playgrnd; pool
4km; lake sw 20km; games area; no statics; phone; bus at site
ent; Eng spkn; adv bkg; quiet; CKE/CCI. "V pleasant, tranquil
site in woods; superb countryside; conv Bilbao & Vitoria/
Gasteiz." ♦ ltd 15 Jun-15 Sep. € 25.25   2012*

ZUBIA, LA see Granada *2G4*

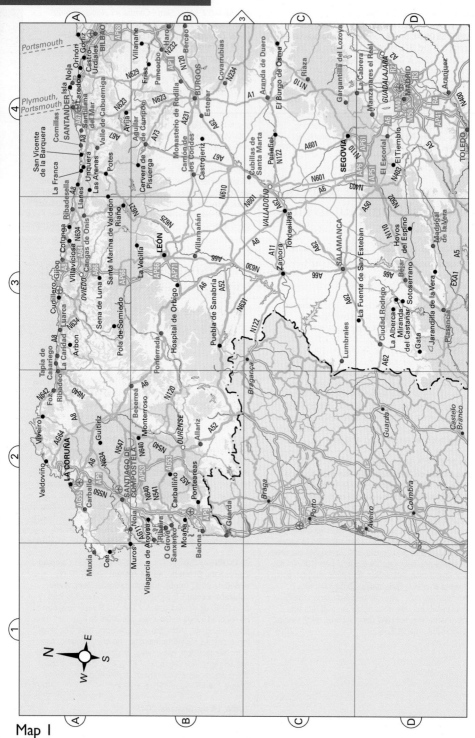

Map I

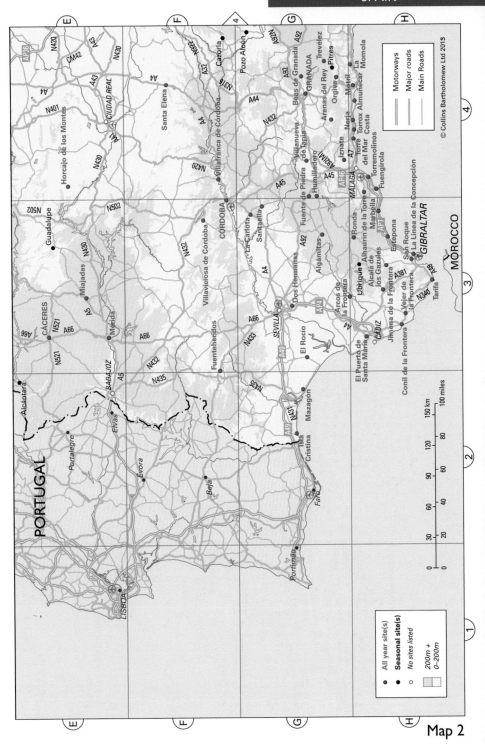

SPAIN

© Collins Bartholomew Ltd 2013

Motorways
Major roads
Main Roads

All year site(s)
Seasonal site(s)
No sites listed
200m +
0–200m

Map 2

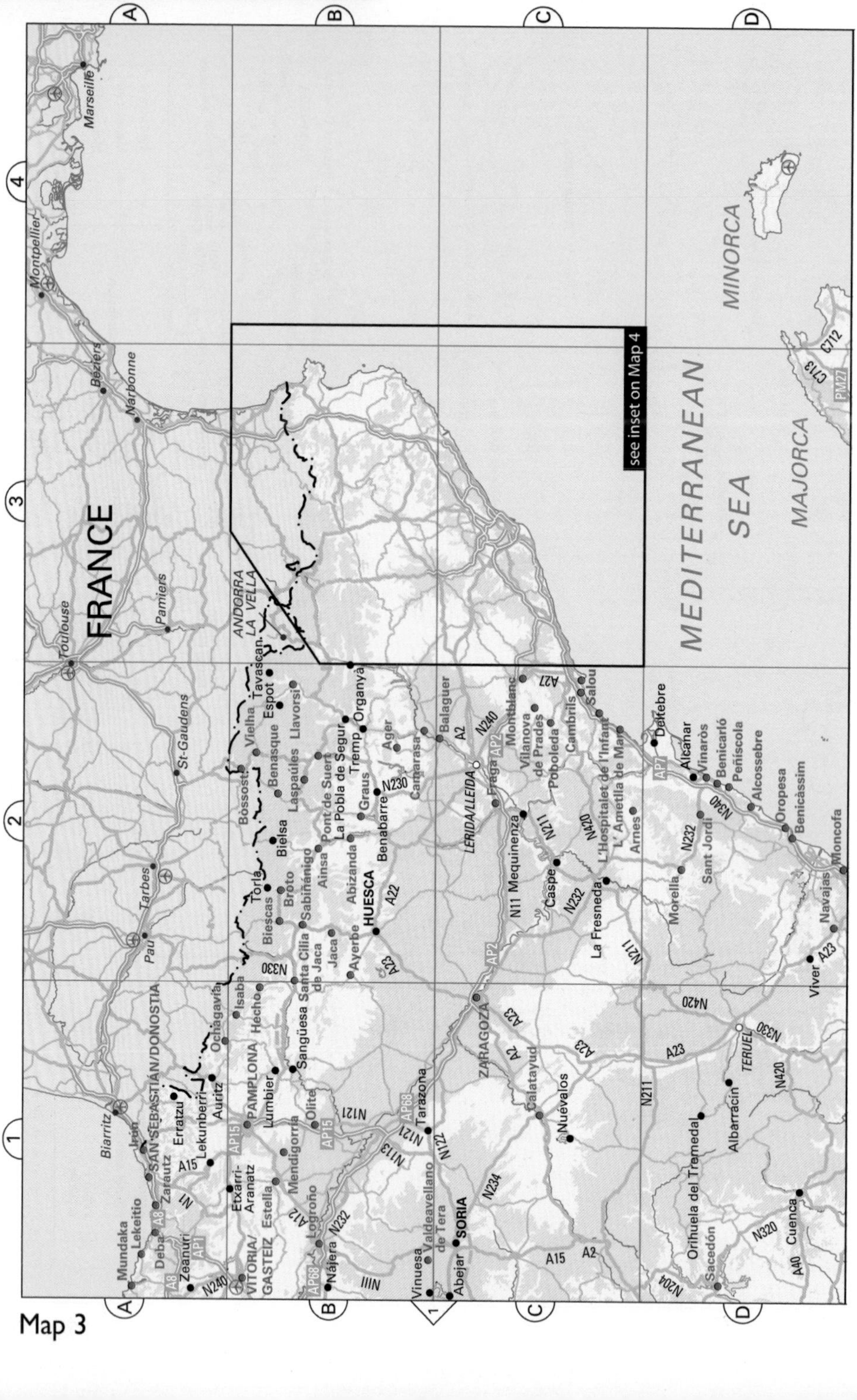

Map 3

FRANCE

Marseille
Montpellier
Béziers
Narbonne
Toulouse
Pamiers
St-Gaudens
Tarbes
Pau
Biarritz

MEDITERRANEAN SEA

MINORCA
MAJORCA

see inset on Map 4

ANDORRA LA VELLA

Mundaka
Lekeitio
Zafautz
Zeanuri
Debi
Iruñ
SAN SEBASTIAN/DONOSTIA
A15
Ekunberri
Erratzu
Auritz
Etxarri-Aranatz
VITORIA/GASTEIZ
Estella
Logroño
Nájera
PAMPLONA
Lumbier
Mendigorria
Olite
Sangüesa
Ochagavía
Isaba
Hecho
Santa Cilia de Jaca
Jaca
Sabiñánigo
Biescas
Torla
Broto
Bielsa
Benasque
Espot
Bossòst
Vielha
Tavascan
Llavorsí
Laspaúles
Ainsa
Abizanda
Ayerbe
HUESCA
Graus
La Pobla de Segur
Pont de Suert
Benabarre
Tremp
Organyà
Ager
Cambarasa
Balaguer
LERIDA/LLEIDA
Fraga
Mequinenza
Caspe
La Fresneda
Morella
Montblanc
Vilanova de Prades
Poboleda
L'Hospitalet de l'Infant
L'Ametlla de Mar
Arnes
Sant Jordi
Salou
Cambrils
Vinaròs
Benicarló
Peñíscola
Alcánar
Alcossebre
Oropesa
Benicàssim
Moncofa
Navajas
Viver
Deltebre

Vinuesa
de Tera
Valdeavellano
Abejar
SORIA
Tarazona
ZARAGOZA
Calatayud
Nuévalos
Orihuela del Tramedal
Sacedón
Albarracín
TERUEL
Viver
Cuenca

N240
AP1
A8
IN
AP1
A15
AP15
N121
AP68
A12
N232
NII
NIII
N122
N121
N113
AP68
A23
N330
A22
N230
A2
A27
A2
AP2
N240
N211
N420
N232
N232
N211
N340
A23
A23
A2
A15
N234
N211
N420
N330
N420
A40
N320
N204
C712
C713
PM721

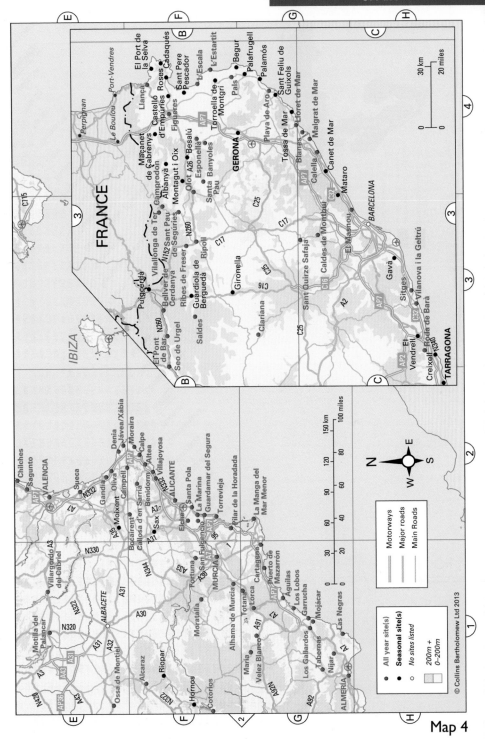

FRANCE

Perpignan
Port-Vendres
Le Boulou
El Port de la Selva
Cadaqués
Roses
Sant Pere Pescador
L'Escala
L'Estartit
Begur
Palafrugell
Palamós
Sant Feliu de Guíxols
Llançà
Castelló d'Empúries
Figueres
Torroella de Montgrí
Pals
Macanet de Cabrenys
Camprodon
Montagut i Oix
Albanyà
Besalú
Esponellà
Santa Banyoles Pau
GERONA
Playa de Aro
Tossa de Mar
Lloret de Mar
Olot A26
Vilallonga de Ter
Sant Pau de Seguries
N152
Ribes de Freser
Bellver de Cerdanya
N260
Ripoll
Guardiola de Berguedà
Gironella
Blanes
Malgrat de Mar
Canet de Mar
Mataró
AP7
Calella
Caldes de Montbui
El Masnou
C25
C17
C17
Sant Quirze Safaja
C16
C25
BARCELONA
Puigcerdà
El Pont de Bar
N260
Seo de Urgel
Saldes
Clariana
C25
Gavà
Sitges
Vilanova i la Geltrú
A2
AP7
El Vendrell
Creixell Roda de Barà
N340
TARRAGONA

IBIZA
C715

Chilches
Sagunto
VALENCIA
Denia
Jávea/Xàbia
Moraira
Calpe
Altea
AP7
Sueca
Gandia
Oliva
Benidorm
Villajoyosa
Moixent
Crímpell
Bocairent
Callosa d'en Sarrià
La Marina
ALICANTE
Santa Pola
Elche
Sax
N332
A7
Guardamar del Segura
Torrevieja
N332
A35
A31
Pilar de la Horadada
La Manga del Mar Menor
Villargordo del Cabriel
N330
A3
Motilla del Palancar
N322
N320
ALBACETE
A31
A32
A37
A43
N420
AP36
Ossa de Montiel
A3
Alcaraz
Riopar
N322
Hornos
Cotorios
Moratalla
Fortuna
San Fulgencio
MURCIA
A30
A30
Alhama de Murcia
Totana
Lorca
A7
AP7
Cartagena
Puerto de Mazarrón
Aguilas
Los Lobos
Mojácar
Garrucha
María
Velez Blanco
A91
Los Gallardos
Tabernas
Níjar
Las Negras
ALMERÍA
A92
A92N
A7

N
E
S
W

30 km
20 miles

150 km
120
90
60
30
0
100 miles
80
60
40
20
0

All year site(s)
Seasonal site(s)
No sites listed
200m +
0–200m

Motorways
Major roads
Main Roads

© Collins Bartholomew Ltd 2013

Map 4

France and Andorra

Central and South East Europe, Benelux and Scandinavia

Spain and Portugal

León to Valladolid = 134km

Distance table (km). Row/column labels read diagonally: Albacete, Alicante, Almería, Andorra-la-Vella, Badajoz, Barcelona, Bilbao, Burgos, Cáceres, Cádiz, Ciudad Real, Córdoba, La Coruña, Gibraltar, Gerona, Granada, Guadalajara, Huesca, León, Lérida (Lleida), Madrid, Málaga, Murcia, Ourense (Orense), Oviedo, Pamplona (Iruña), Salamanca, San Sebastián (Donostia), Santander, Santiago de Compostela, Segovia, Sevilla, Soria, Tarragona, Teruel, Toledo, Valencia, Valladolid, Vitoria (Gasteiz), Zaragoza.

Albacete	Alicante	Almería	Andorra-la-Vella	Badajoz	Barcelona	Bilbao	Burgos	Cáceres	Cádiz	Ciudad Real	Córdoba	La Coruña	Gibraltar	Gerona	Granada	Guadalajara	Huesca	León	Lérida (Lleida)	Madrid	Málaga	Murcia	Ourense (Orense)	Oviedo	Pamplona (Iruña)	Salamanca	San Sebastián (Donostia)	Santander	Santiago de Compostela	Segovia	Sevilla	Soria	Tarragona	Teruel	Toledo	Valencia	Valladolid	Vitoria (Gasteiz)	Zaragoza
172																																							
370	296																																						
711	686	998																																					
523	694	605	1062																																				
539	516	810	182	1025																																			
645	818	959	533	694	620																																		
489	657	799	578	537	584	157																																	
503	675	652	958	90	919	605	446																																
619	688	848	1312	342	1285	1049	900	389																															
208	379	408	851	318	812	586	424	325	462																														
355	524	333	1061	273	892	796	636	318	263	199																													
863	1029	1170	1168	774	1120	645	536	683	1070	799	997																												
603	612	349	1335	490	1127	1069	911	537	148	518	317	1220																												
642	615	908	206	1125	100	721	683	1020	1379	912	1009	1214	1227																											
362	354	167	1057	438	868	830	487	335	278	166	1043	259	968																										
308	483	619	603	460	563	395	240	352	719	248	458	668	732	663	492																								
494	570	828	259	799	275	323	358	694	1055	588	797	905	1071	374	830	338																							
583	756	898	824	495	785	360	202	409	796	511	733	334	1007	884	762	389	560																						
514	491	801	196	867	157	464	428	761	1122	655	865	974	1139	256	861	408	117	630																					
251	423	563	661	402	621	396	237	297	663	190	402	610	674	721	433	58	398	334	465																				
475	481	218	1205	437	998	940	782	505	264	387	187	1153	130	1097	129	602	940	877	1010	544																			
151	76	220	779	677	591	795	639	656	613	357	445	1010	537	690	280	460	611	734	583	314	441																		
773	944	1085	1062	645	1028	606	447	557	945	699	922	175	1195	1127	955	578	803	271	871	520	1066	920																	
700	873	1015	885	614	903	305	322	525	914	641	851	340	982	1004	885	508	118	703	452	997	850	338																	
601	675	971	384	754	438	160	204	653	1068	597	807	738	1081	537	841	349	162	403	280	409	952	712	650	462															
462	633	762	813	298	777	395	236	208	601	354	529	472	747	878	629	270	554	199	622	213	756	613	346	314	441														
692	767	1031	463	770	530	120	233	679	1132	659	869	764	1143	629	903	441	255	433	372	470	1014	807	679	423	93	469													
642	816	957	628	663	693	110	156	574	1056	583	793	546	1067	793	827	394	430	293	537	394	936	793	544	207	266	364	226												
871	1045	1184	1177	759	1131	658	550	670	1058	808	1012	62	1296	1232	1055	780	918	348	988	623	1165	1019	113	352	751	460	777	561												
339	511	651	685	384	652	355	197	298	749	277	497	560	761	750	519	144	426	245	494	87	630	487	466	363	370	164	429	360	575											
490	609	423	1199	217	1044	934	775	263	125	339	140	947	273	1151	256	596	935	672	1003	538	220	532	821	789	945	474	1012	837	922	561										
472	549	795	488	580	453	258	142	491	894	421	676	905	905	553	665	173	412	342	299	231	775	589	573	465	176	324	268	297	671	195	771									
442	417	710	280	934	99	556	519	832	1060	649	796	1061	1029	198	769	476	209	720	90	534	899	490	962	835	372	713	464	629	1185	585	953	390								
243	317	578	512	702	410	488	372	600	873	397	596	908	845	509	605	244	255	573	320	302	716	358	805	690	355	514	450	527	920	390	749	231	309							
241	411	526	727	369	694	405	309	264	583	120	321	675	637	792	398	130	467	393	536	71	508	390	580	511	477	235	541	464	609	159	457	303	605	339						
192	167	461	520	717	350	634	517	636	808	398	545	961	778	449	520	411	398	685	324	350	650	241	783	803	502	563	594	673	974	441	699	376	251	145	371					
445	614	757	698	415	664	281	123	325	713	377	578	435	867	761	630	251	440	134	508	195	737	593	355	252	327	115	354	249	468	112	589	211	598	257	544				
603	741	916	477	652	529	66	115	562	1016	540	751	649	1025	630	785	352	256	314	374	352	895	752	560	381	95	351	119	174	662	311	825	191	489	421	422	575	235		
424	500	758	292	726	297	321	287	620	989	515	725	834	999	396	758	267	73	488	141	325	867	541	731	604	174	480	269	399	847	354	864	157	229	180	397	328	369	261

Site Report Form

If campsite is already listed, complete only those sections of the form where changes apply or alternatively use the Abbreviated Site Report form on the following pages.

Sites not reported on for 5 years may be deleted from the guide

Year of guide used	20..........	Is site listed?	Listed on page no.	Unlisted	Date of visit	........./........./.........

A – CAMPSITE NAME AND LOCATION

Country		Name of town/village site listed under *(see Sites Location Maps)*					
Distance & direction from centre of town site is listed under *(in a straight line)*		....................km	eg N, NE, S, SW		Urban	Rural	Coastal
Site open all year?	Y / N	Period site is open *(if not all year)*	................/................	to	................/................		
Site name					Naturist site		Y / N
Site address							
Telephone				Fax			
E-mail				Website			

B – CAMPSITE CHARGES

Charge for outfit + 2 adults in local currency	PRICE		EL PNTS inc in this price?	Y / N	Amps ....

C – DIRECTIONS

Brief, specific directions to site (in km) *To convert miles to kilometres multiply by 8 and divide by 5 or use Conversion Table in guide*	
GPS	Latitude..*(eg 12.34567)* Longitude..*(eg 1.23456 or -1.23456)*

D – CAMPSITE DESCRIPTION

SITE size ie number of pitches	Small Max 50	SM	Medium 51-150	MED	Large 151-500	LGE	Very large 500+	V LGE	Unchanged
PITCH size	*eg small, medium, large, very large, various*								Unchanged
Pitch features if NOT open-plan/grassy		Hedged	HDG PITCH	Marked or numbered	MKD PITCH	Hardstanding or gravel		HDSTG	Unchanged
If site is NOT level, is it		Part sloping	PT SL	Sloping	SL	Terraced		TERR	Unchanged
Is site shaded?		Shaded	SHD	Part shaded	PT SHD	Unshaded		UNSHD	Unchanged

E – CAMPSITE FACILITIES

WC		Heated	HTD WC	Continental	CONT	Own San recommended		OWN SAN REC	
Chemical disposal point		CHEM DISP		Dedicated point			WC only		
Motorhome waste discharge and water refill point				MV SERVICE PNT					
Child / baby facilities (bathroom)		CHILD / BABY FACS		Family bathroom			FAM BTHRM		
Hot shower(s)		SHWR(S)		Inc in site fee?		Y / N	Price....................*(if not inc)*		
ELECTRIC HOOK UP *if not included in price above*		EL PNTS		Price...........................			Amps...........................		
Supplies of bottled gas		GAS		On site		Y / N	Or in .... Kms		
Launderette / Washing Machine		LNDTTE		Inc dryer Y / N			LNDRY RM *(if no washing machine)*		

You can also complete forms online: www.caravanclub.co.uk/europereport

F – FOOD & DRINK

Shop(s) / supermarket	SHOP(S) / SUPMKT	On site		or		.... kms	
Bread / milk delivered	TRADSMN						
Restaurant / cafeteria	REST	On site		or		.... kms	
Snack bar / take-away	SNACKS	On site		or		.... kms	
Bar	BAR	On site		or		.... kms	
Barbecue allowed	BBQ	Charcoal		Gas		Elec	Sep area
Cooking facilities	COOKING FACS						

G – LEISURE FACILITIES

Playground	PLAYGRND						
Swimming pool	POOL	On site		or ....km		Heated	Covered
Beach	BEACH	Adj		or ....km		Sand	Shingle
Alternative swimming (lake)	SW	Adj		or ....km		Sand	Shingle
Games /sports area / Games room	GAMES AREA	GAMES ROOM					
Entertainment in high season	ENTMNT						
Internet use by visitors	INTERNET	Wifi Internet		WIFI			
Television room	TV RM	Satellite / Cable to pitches		TV CAB / SAT			

H – OTHER INFORMATION

% Static caravans / mobile homes / chalets / cottages / fixed tents on site						.... % STATICS	
Dogs allowed	DOGS		Y / N	Price per night .... (if allowed)			
Phone	PHONE	On site		Adj			
Bus / tram / train	BUS / TRAM / TRAIN	Adj		or .... km			
Twin axles caravans allowed?	TWIN AXLES Y / N	Possibly crowded in high season				POSS CR	
English spoken	ENG SPKN						
Advance bookings accepted	ADV BKG	Y / N					
Noise levels on site in season	NOISY	QUIET	If noisy, why?				
Credit card accepted	CCARD ACC	Reduction low season				RED LOW SSN	
Camping Key Europe or Camping Card International accepted in lieu of passport	CKE/CCI	INF card required (If naturist site)				Y / N	
Facilities for disabled	Full wheelchair facilities	♦		Limited disabled facilities		♦ ltd	

I – ADDITIONAL REMARKS AND/OR ITEMS OF INTEREST

Tourist attractions, unusual features or other facilities, eg waterslide, tennis, cycle hire, watersports, horser-iding, separate car park, walking distance to shops etc	YOUR OPINION OF THE SITE:	
	EXCEL	
	VERY GOOD	
	GOOD	
	FAIR	POOR
	NIGHT HALT ONLY	

Your comments & opinions may be used in future editions of the guide, if you do not wish them to be used please tick ....

J – MEMBER DETAILS

ARE YOU A:	Caravanner			Motorhomer		Trailer-tenter?	
NAME:		MEMBERSHIP NO:					
		POST CODE:					
DO YOU NEED MORE BLANK SITE REPORT FORMS?			YES			NO	

Please use a separate form for each campsite and do not send receipts. Owing to the large number of site reports received, it is not possible to enter into correspondence. Please return completed form to:

The Editor, Overseas Touring Guides, The Caravan Club
FREEPOST, PO Box 386, (RRZG-SXKK-UCUJ)
East Grinstead RH19 1FH
(Please use this address only when mailing within the UK)

Site Report Form

If campsite is already listed, complete only those sections of the form where changes apply
or alternatively use the Abbreviated Site Report form on the following pages.

Sites not reported on for 5 years may be deleted from the guide

Year of guide used	20..........	Is site listed?	Listed on page no.	Unlisted	Date of visit	......../......../.........

A – CAMPSITE NAME AND LOCATION

Country		Name of town/village site listed under *(see Sites Location Maps)*				
Distance & direction from centre of town site is listed under *(in a straight line)*		....................km	eg N, NE, S, SW	Urban	Rural	Coastal

Site open all year?	Y / N	Period site is open *(if not all year)*	.................../................. to ..../.................

Site name			Naturist site	Y / N

Site address	

Telephone		Fax	
E-mail		Website	

B – CAMPSITE CHARGES

Charge for outfit + 2 adults in local currency	PRICE	EL PNTS inc in this price?	Y / N	Amps ....

C – DIRECTIONS

Brief, specific directions to site (in km) *To convert miles to kilometres multiply by 8 and divide by 5 or use Conversion Table in guide*	
GPS	Latitude...*(eg 12.34567)* Longitude.......................................*(eg 1.23456 or -1.23456)*

D – CAMPSITE DESCRIPTION

SITE size ie number of pitches	Small Max 50	SM	Medium 51-150	MED	Large 151-500	LGE	Very large 500+	V LGE	Unchanged

PITCH size	*eg small, medium, large, very large, various*								Unchanged

Pitch features if **NOT** open-plan/grassy	Hedged	HDG PITCH	Marked or numbered	MKD PITCH	Hardstanding or gravel	HDSTG	Unchanged

If site is **NOT** level, is it	Part sloping	PT SL	Sloping	SL	Terraced	TERR	Unchanged

Is site shaded?	Shaded	SHD	Part shaded	PT SHD	Unshaded	UNSHD	Unchanged

E – CAMPSITE FACILITIES

WC	Heated	HTD WC	Continental	CONT	Own San recommended		OWN SAN REC	
Chemical disposal point		CHEM DISP		Dedicated point		WC only		
Motorhome waste discharge and water refill point				MV SERVICE PNT				
Child / baby facilities (bathroom)		CHILD / BABY FACS		Family bathroom		FAM BTHRM		
Hot shower(s)		SHWR(S)		Inc in site fee?	Y / N	Price....................*(if not inc)*		
ELECTRIC HOOK UP *if not included in price above*		EL PNTS		Price............................		Amps.....................................		
Supplies of bottled gas		GAS		On site	Y / N	Or in .... Kms		
Launderette / Washing Machine	LNDTTE		Inc dryer Y / N		LNDRY RM *(if no washing machine)*			

You can also complete forms online: www.caravanclub.co.uk/europereport

CUT ALONG DOTTED LINE

F – FOOD & DRINK

Shop(s) / supermarket	SHOP(S) / SUPMKT	On site		or		.... kms	
Bread / milk delivered	TRADSMN						
Restaurant / cafeteria	REST	On site		or		.... kms	
Snack bar / take-away	SNACKS	On site		or		.... kms	
Bar	BAR	On site		or		.... kms	
Barbecue allowed	BBQ	Charcoal		Gas		Elec	Sep area
Cooking facilities	COOKING FACS						

G – LEISURE FACILITIES

Playground	PLAYGRND						
Swimming pool	POOL	On site		or ....km		Heated	Covered
Beach	BEACH	Adj		or ....km		Sand	Shingle
Alternative swimming (lake)	SW	Adj		or ....km		Sand	Shingle
Games /sports area / Games room	GAMES AREA	GAMES ROOM					
Entertainment in high season	ENTMNT						
Internet use by visitors	INTERNET	Wifi Internet		WIFI			
Television room	TV RM	Satellite / Cable to pitches		TV CAB / SAT			

H – OTHER INFORMATION

% Static caravans / mobile homes / chalets / cottages / fixed tents on site					..............% STATICS	
Dogs allowed	DOGS	Y / N	Price per night .... (if allowed)			
Phone	PHONE	On site	Adj			
Bus / tram / train	BUS / TRAM / TRAIN	Adj	or .... km			
Twin axles caravans allowed?	TWIN AXLES Y / N	Possibly crowded in high season		POSS CR		
English spoken	ENG SPKN					
Advance bookings accepted	ADV BKG	Y / N				
Noise levels on site in season	NOISY	QUIET	If noisy, why?			
Credit card accepted	CCARD ACC	Reduction low season		RED LOW SSN		
Camping Key Europe or Camping Card International accepted in lieu of passport	CKE/CCI	INF card required (If naturist site)		Y / N		
Facilities for disabled	Full wheelchair facilities	♦	Limited disabled facilities		♦ ltd	

I – ADDITIONAL REMARKS AND/OR ITEMS OF INTEREST

Tourist attractions, unusual features or other facilities, eg waterslide, tennis, cycle hire, watersports, horser-iding, separate car park, walking distance to shops etc	YOUR OPINION OF THE SITE:	
	EXCEL	
	VERY GOOD	
	GOOD	
	FAIR	POOR
	NIGHT HALT ONLY	
Your comments & opinions may be used in future editions of the guide, if you do not wish them to be used please tick		

J – MEMBER DETAILS

ARE YOU A:	Caravanner		Motorhomer		Trailer-tenter?	
NAME:		MEMBERSHIP NO:				
		POST CODE:				
DO YOU NEED MORE BLANK SITE REPORT FORMS?			YES		NO	

Please use a separate form for each campsite and do not send receipts. Owing to the large number of site reports received, it is not possible to enter into correspondence. Please return completed form to:

The Editor, Overseas Touring Guides, The Caravan Club
FREEPOST, PO Box 386, (RRZG-SXKK-UCUJ)
East Grinstead RH19 1FH
(Please use this address only when mailing within the UK)

Site Report Form

If campsite is already listed, complete only those sections of the form where changes apply
or alternatively use the Abbreviated Site Report form on the following pages.

Sites not reported on for 5 years may be deleted from the guide

Year of guide used	20..........	Is site listed?	Listed on page no.	Unlisted	Date of visit	......../......../.........

A – CAMPSITE NAME AND LOCATION

Country		Name of town/village site listed under *(see Sites Location Maps)*			

Distance & direction from centre of town site is listed under *(in a straight line)*	...................km	eg N, NE, S, SW	Urban	Rural	Coastal

Site open all year?	Y / N	Period site is open *(if not all year)*	................/................. to ..../.................

Site name		Naturist site	Y / N

Site address	

Telephone		Fax	
E-mail		Website	

B – CAMPSITE CHARGES

Charge for outfit + 2 adults in local currency	PRICE		EL PNTS inc in this price?	Y / N	Amps ....

C – DIRECTIONS

Brief, specific directions to site (in km) *To convert miles to kilometres multiply by 8 and divide by 5 or use Conversion Table in guide*	
GPS	Latitude...*(eg 12.34567)* Longitude...*(eg 1.23456 or -1.23456)*

D – CAMPSITE DESCRIPTION

SITE size ie number of pitches	Small Max 50	SM	Medium 51-150	MED	Large 151-500	LGE	Very large 500+	V LGE	Unchanged
PITCH size	eg small, medium, large, very large, various								Unchanged
Pitch features if NOT open-plan/grassy	Hedged	HDG PITCH	Marked or numbered	MKD PITCH	Hardstanding or gravel	HDSTG			Unchanged
If site is NOT level, is it	Part sloping	PT SL	Sloping	SL	Terraced	TERR			Unchanged
Is site shaded?	Shaded	SHD	Part shaded	PT SHD	Unshaded	UNSHD			Unchanged

E – CAMPSITE FACILITIES

WC		Heated	HTD WC	Continental	CONT	Own San recommended		OWN SAN REC	
Chemical disposal point			CHEM DISP		Dedicated point			WC only	
Motorhome waste discharge and water refill point				MV SERVICE PNT					
Child / baby facilities (bathroom)			CHILD / BABY FACS		Family bathroom		FAM BTHRM		
Hot shower(s)			SHWR(S)		Inc in site fee?	Y / N	Price....................*(if not inc)*		
ELECTRIC HOOK UP *if not included in price above*			EL PNTS		Price..........................		Amps.......................................		
Supplies of bottled gas			GAS		On site	Y / N	Or in .... Kms		
Launderette / Washing Machine			LNDTTE	Inc dryer Y / N		LNDRY RM *(if no washing machine)*			

You can also complete forms online: www.caravanclub.co.uk/europereport

CUT ALONG DOTTED LINE

F – FOOD & DRINK

Shop(s) / supermarket	SHOP(S) / SUPMKT	On site		or		.... kms		
Bread / milk delivered	TRADSMN							
Restaurant / cafeteria	REST	On site		or		.... kms		
Snack bar / take-away	SNACKS	On site		or		.... kms		
Bar	BAR	On site		or		.... kms		
Barbecue allowed	BBQ	Charcoal		Gas		Elec		Sep area
Cooking facilities	COOKING FACS							

G – LEISURE FACILITIES

Playground	PLAYGRND					
Swimming pool	POOL	On site		or ....km	Heated	Covered
Beach	BEACH	Adj		or ....km	Sand	Shingle
Alternative swimming *(lake)*	SW	Adj		or ....km	Sand	Shingle
Games /sports area / Games room	GAMES AREA	GAMES ROOM				
Entertainment in high season	ENTMNT					
Internet use by visitors	INTERNET	Wifi Internet		WIFI		
Television room	TV RM	Satellite / Cable to pitches		TV CAB / SAT		

H – OTHER INFORMATION

% Static caravans / mobile homes / chalets / cottages / fixed tents on site				...............% STATICS	
Dogs allowed	DOGS	Y / N	Price per night .... *(if allowed)*		
Phone	PHONE	On site	Adj		
Bus / tram / train	BUS / TRAM / TRAIN	Adj	or .... km		
Twin axles caravans allowed?	TWIN AXLES Y / N	Possibly crowded in high season		POSS CR	
English spoken	ENG SPKN				
Advance bookings accepted	ADV BKG	Y / N			
Noise levels on site in season	NOISY	QUIET	If noisy, why?		
Credit card accepted	CCARD ACC	Reduction low season		RED LOW SSN	
Camping Key Europe or Camping Card International accepted in lieu of passport	CKE/CCI	INF card required *(If naturist site)*		Y / N	
Facilities for disabled	Full wheelchair facilities	♦	Limited disabled facilities	♦ ltd	

I – ADDITIONAL REMARKS AND/OR ITEMS OF INTEREST

Tourist attractions, unusual features or other facilities, eg waterslide, tennis, cycle hire, watersports, horseriding, separate car park, walking distance to shops etc	YOUR OPINION OF THE SITE:
	EXCEL
	VERY GOOD
	GOOD
	FAIR POOR
	NIGHT HALT ONLY
Your comments & opinions may be used in future editions of the guide, if you do not wish them to be used please tick	

J – MEMBER DETAILS

ARE YOU A:	Caravanner		Motorhomer		Trailer-tenter?	
NAME:		MEMBERSHIP NO:				
		POST CODE:				
DO YOU NEED MORE BLANK SITE REPORT FORMS?			YES		NO	

Please use a separate form for each campsite and do not send receipts. Owing to the large number of site reports received, it is not possible to enter into correspondence. Please return completed form to:

The Editor, Overseas Touring Guides, The Caravan Club
FREEPOST, PO Box 386, (RRZG-SXKK-UCUJ)
East Grinstead RH19 1FH
(Please use this address only when mailing within the UK)

Abbreviated Site Report Form

Use this abbreviated Site Report Form if you have visited a number of sites and there are no changes (or only small changes) to their entries in the guide. If reporting on a new site, or reporting several changes, please use the full version of the report form. **If advising prices**, these should be for an outfit and 2 adults for one night's stay. **Please indicate high or low season prices and whether electricity is included.**

Remember, if you don't tell us about sites you have visited, they may eventually be deleted from the guide.

Year of guide used	20.........	Page No.	....	Name of town/village site listed under	
Site Name				Date of visit	.... /....... /.......
GPS	Latitude.......................................(eg 12.34567) Longitude...(eg 1.23456 or -1.23456)				

Site is in: Andorra / Austria / Belgium / Croatia / Czech Republic / Denmark / Finland / France / Germany / Greece / Hungary / Italy / Luxembourg / Netherlands / Norway / Poland / Portugal / Slovakia / Slovenia / Spain / Sweden / Switzerland

Comments:

Charge for outfit + 2 adults in local currency	High Season	Low Season	Elec inc in price?	Y / N	............amps
			Price of elec (if not inc)		............amps

Year of guide used	20.........	Page No.	....	Name of town/village site listed under	
Site Name				Date of visit	.... /....... /.......
GPS	Latitude.......................................(eg 12.34567) Longitude...(eg 1.23456 or -1.23456)				

Site is in: Andorra / Austria / Belgium / Croatia / Czech Republic / Denmark / Finland / France / Germany / Greece / Hungary / Italy / Luxembourg / Netherlands / Norway / Poland / Portugal / Slovakia / Slovenia / Spain / Sweden / Switzerland

Comments:

Charge for outfit + 2 adults in local currency	High Season	Low Season	Elec inc in price?	Y / N	............amps
			Price of elec (if not inc)		............amps

Year of guide used	20.........	Page No.	....	Name of town/village site listed under	
Site Name				Date of visit	.... /....... /.......
GPS	Latitude.......................................(eg 12.34567) Longitude...(eg 1.23456 or -1.23456)				

Site is in: Andorra / Austria / Belgium / Croatia / Czech Republic / Denmark / Finland / France / Germany / Greece / Hungary / Italy / Luxembourg / Netherlands / Norway / Poland / Portugal / Slovakia / Slovenia / Spain / Sweden / Switzerland

Comments:

Charge for outfit + 2 adults in local currency	High Season	Low Season	Elec inc in price?	Y / N	............amps
			Price of elec (if not inc)		............amps

Please fill in your details and send to the address on the reverse of this form

You can also complete forms online: www.caravanclub.co.uk/europereport

CUT ALONG DOTTED LINE

Year of guide used	20..........	Page No.	....	Name of town/village site listed under	

Site Name				Date of visit	.... /....... /........

GPS	Latitude..(eg 12.34567) Longitude...(eg 1.23456 or -1.23456)

Site is in: Andorra / Austria / Belgium / Croatia / Czech Republic / Denmark / Finland / France / Germany / Greece / Hungary / Italy / Luxembourg / Netherlands / Norway / Poland / Portugal / Slovakia / Slovenia / Spain / Sweden / Switzerland

Comments:

Charge for outfit + 2 adults in local currency	High Season	Low Season	Elec inc in price?	Y / N	............amps
			Price of elec (if not inc)		............amps

Year of guide used	20..........	Page No.	....	Name of town/village site listed under	

Site Name				Date of visit	.... /....... /........

GPS	Latitude..(eg 12.34567) Longitude...(eg 1.23456 or -1.23456)

Site is in:: Andorra / Austria / Belgium / Croatia / Czech Republic / Denmark / Finland / France / Germany / Greece / Hungary / Italy / Luxembourg / Netherlands / Norway / Poland / Portugal / Slovakia / Slovenia / Spain / Sweden / Switzerland

Comments:

Charge for outfit + 2 adults in local currency	High Season	Low Season	Elec inc in price?	Y / N	............amps
			Price of elec (if not inc)		............amps

Year of guide used	20..........	Page No.	....	Name of town/village site listed under	

Site Name				Date of visit	.... /....... /........

GPS	Latitude..(eg 12.34567) Longitude...(eg 1.23456 or -1.23456)

Site is in: Andorra / Austria / Belgium / Croatia / Czech Republic / Denmark / Finland / France / Germany / Greece / Hungary / Italy / Luxembourg / Netherlands / Norway / Poland / Portugal / Slovakia / Slovenia / Spain / Sweden / Switzerland

Comments:

Charge for outfit + 2 adults in local currency	High Season	Low Season	Elec inc in price?	Y / N	............amps
			Price of elec (if not inc)		............amps

Your comments & opinions may be used in future editions of the guide, if you do not wish them to be used please tick ....

Name ....

Membership No. ....

Post Code ....

Are you a Caravanner / Motorhomer / Trailer-Tenter?

Do you need more blank Site Report forms?   YES / NO

Please return completed forms to:
The Editor, Overseas Touring Guides
The Caravan Club
FREEPOST
PO Box 386 (RRZG-SXKK-UCUJ)
East Grinstead
RH19 1FH
(Please use this address only when mailing from within the UK)

You can also complete forms online: www.caravanclub.co.uk/europereport

Abbreviated Site Report Form

Use this abbreviated Site Report Form if you have visited a number of sites and there are no changes (or only small changes) to their entries in the guide. If reporting on a new site, or reporting several changes, please use the full version of the report form. **If advising prices**, these should be for an outfit and 2 adults for one night's stay. **Please indicate high or low season prices and whether electricity is included.**

Remember, if you don't tell us about sites you have visited, they may eventually be deleted from the guide.

Year of guide used	20.........	Page No.	....	Name of town/village site listed under		
Site Name					Date of visit	.... /....... /........
GPS	Latitude...(eg 12.34567) Longitude...(eg 1.23456 or -1.23456)					

Site is in: Andorra / Austria / Belgium / Croatia / Czech Republic / Denmark / Finland / France / Germany / Greece / Hungary / Italy / Luxembourg / Netherlands / Norway / Poland / Portugal / Slovakia / Slovenia / Spain / Sweden / Switzerland

Comments:

Charge for outfit + 2 adults in local currency	High Season	Low Season	Elec inc in price?		Y / N	.............amps
			Price of elec (if not inc)			.............amps

Year of guide used	20.........	Page No.	....	Name of town/village site listed under		
Site Name					Date of visit	.... /....... /........
GPS	Latitude...(eg 12.34567) Longitude...(eg 1.23456 or -1.23456)					

Site is in: Andorra / Austria / Belgium / Croatia / Czech Republic / Denmark / Finland / France / Germany / Greece / Hungary / Italy / Luxembourg / Netherlands / Norway / Poland / Portugal / Slovakia / Slovenia / Spain / Sweden / Switzerland

Comments:

Charge for outfit + 2 adults in local currency	High Season	Low Season	Elec inc in price?		Y / N	.............amps
			Price of elec (if not inc)			.............amps

Year of guide used	20.........	Page No.	....	Name of town/village site listed under		
Site Name					Date of visit	.... /....... /........
GPS	Latitude...(eg 12.34567) Longitude...(eg 1.23456 or -1.23456)					

Site is in: Andorra / Austria / Belgium / Croatia / Czech Republic / Denmark / Finland / France / Germany / Greece / Hungary / Italy / Luxembourg / Netherlands / Norway / Poland / Portugal / Slovakia / Slovenia / Spain / Sweden / Switzerland

Comments:

Charge for outfit + 2 adults in local currency	High Season	Low Season	Elec inc in price?		Y / N	.............amps
			Price of elec (if not inc)			.............amps

Please fill in your details and send to the address on the reverse of this form

You can also complete forms online: www.caravanclub.co.uk/europereport

CUT ALONG DOTTED LINE

Year of guide used	20..........	Page No.	....	Name of town/village site listed under	
Site Name				Date of visit	.... /....... /........
GPS	Latitude...(eg 12.34567) Longitude..(eg 1.23456 or -1.23456)				

Site is in: Andorra / Austria / Belgium / Croatia / Czech Republic / Denmark / Finland / France / Germany / Greece / Hungary / Italy / Luxembourg / Netherlands / Norway / Poland / Portugal / Slovakia / Slovenia / Spain / Sweden / Switzerland

Comments:

Charge for outfit + 2 adults in local currency	High Season	Low Season	Elec inc in price?	Y / N	............amps
			Price of elec (if not inc)		............amps

Year of guide used	20..........	Page No.	....	Name of town/village site listed under	
Site Name				Date of visit	.... /....... /........
GPS	Latitude...(eg 12.34567) Longitude..(eg 1.23456 or -1.23456)				

Site is in:: Andorra / Austria / Belgium / Croatia / Czech Republic / Denmark / Finland / France / Germany / Greece / Hungary / Italy / Luxembourg / Netherlands / Norway / Poland / Portugal / Slovakia / Slovenia / Spain / Sweden / Switzerland

Comments:

Charge for outfit + 2 adults in local currency	High Season	Low Season	Elec inc in price?	Y / N	............amps
			Price of elec (if not inc)		............amps

Year of guide used	20..........	Page No.	....	Name of town/village site listed under	
Site Name				Date of visit	.... /....... /........
GPS	Latitude...(eg 12.34567) Longitude..(eg 1.23456 or -1.23456)				

Site is in: Andorra / Austria / Belgium / Croatia / Czech Republic / Denmark / Finland / France / Germany / Greece / Hungary / Italy / Luxembourg / Netherlands / Norway / Poland / Portugal / Slovakia / Slovenia / Spain / Sweden / Switzerland

Comments:

Charge for outfit + 2 adults in local currency	High Season	Low Season	Elec inc in price?	Y / N	............amps
			Price of elec (if not inc)		............amps

Your comments & opinions may be used in future editions of the guide, if you do not wish them to be used please tick ....

Name ....

Membership No. ....

Post Code ....

Are you a Caravanner / Motorhomer / Trailer-Tenter?

Do you need more blank Site Report forms?   YES / NO

Please return completed forms to:
The Editor, Overseas Touring Guides
The Caravan Club
FREEPOST
PO Box 386 (RRZG-SXKK-UCUJ)
East Grinstead
RH19 1FH
(Please use this address only when mailing from within the UK)

You can also complete forms online: www.caravanclub.co.uk/europereport

Index

Index

PEFC Certified

This product is
from sustainably
managed forests and
controlled sources

PEFC/16-33-254   www.pefc.org